MIGHTY MARVEL MASTERWORKS

PRESENTS

the AMAZING SPIDER-MAN

V O L U M E   2

C O L L E C T I N G

THE AMAZING SPIDER-MAN Nos. 11-19
& ANNUAL No. 1

STAN LEE • STEVE DITKO

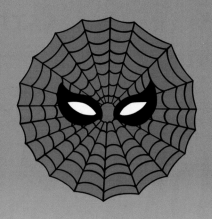

COLLECTION EDITOR
Cory Sedlmeier

BOOK DESIGN
Nickel DesignWorks

ART & COLOR RESTORATION
Michael Kelleher & Kellustration

COLLECTION COVER
Michael Cho

VARIANT CLASSIC COVER
Steve Ditko

VP PRODUCTION & SPECIAL PROJECTS
Jeff Youngquist

SVP PRINT, SALES & MARKETING
David Gabriel

EDITOR IN CHIEF
C.B. Cebulski

MIGHTY MARVEL MASTERWORKS: THE AMAZING SPIDER-MAN VOL. 2 — THE SINISTER SIX. Contains material originally published in magazine form as AMAZING SPIDER-MAN (1963) #11-19 and AMAZING SPIDER-MAN ANNUAL (1964) #1. Second printing 2022. ISBN 978-1-302-93195-7. Published by MARVEL WORLDWIDE, INC., a subsidiary of MARVEL ENTERTAINMENT, LLC. OFFICE OF PUBLICATION: 1290 Avenue of the Americas, New York, NY 10104. © 2021 MARVEL No similarity between any of the names, characters, persons, and/or institutions in this book with those of any living or dead person or institution is intended, and any such similarity which may exist is purely coincidental. **Printed in Canada.** KEVIN FEIGE, Chief Creative Officer; DAN BUCKLEY, President, Marvel Entertainment; JOE QUESADA, EVP & Creative Director; DAVID BOGART, Associate Publisher & SVP of Talent Affairs; TOM BREVOORT, VP, Executive Editor; NICK LOWE, Executive Editor, VP of Content, Digital Publishing; DAVID GABRIEL, VP of Print & Digital Publishing; SVEN LARSEN, VP of Licensed Publishing; MARK ANNUNZIATO, VP of Planning & Forecasting; JEFF YOUNGQUIST, VP of Production & Special Projects; ALEX MORALES, Director of Publishing Operations; DAN EDINGTON, Director of Editorial Operations; RICKEY PURDIN, Director of Talent Relations; JENNIFER GRÜNWALD, Director of Production & Special Projects; SUSAN CRESPI, Production Manager; STAN LEE, Chairman Emeritus. For information regarding advertising in Marvel Comics or on Marvel.com, please contact Vit DeBellis, Custom Solutions & Integrated Advertising Manager, at vdebellis@marvel.com. For Marvel subscription inquiries, please call 888-511-5480. **Manufactured between 4/8/2022 and 5/10/2022 by SOLISCO PRINTERS, SCOTT, QC, CANADA.**

10 9 8 7 6 5 4 3 2

THE
AMAZING SPIDER-MAN
Nos. 11-19 & Annual No. 1

WRITER:
Stan Lee

ARTIST:
Steve Ditko

LETTERERS:
Sam Rosen
Art Simek

EDITOR:
Stan Lee

SPECIAL THANKS:
Ralph Macchio
Tom Brevoort

SPIDER-MAN CREATED BY STAN LEE & STEVE DITKO

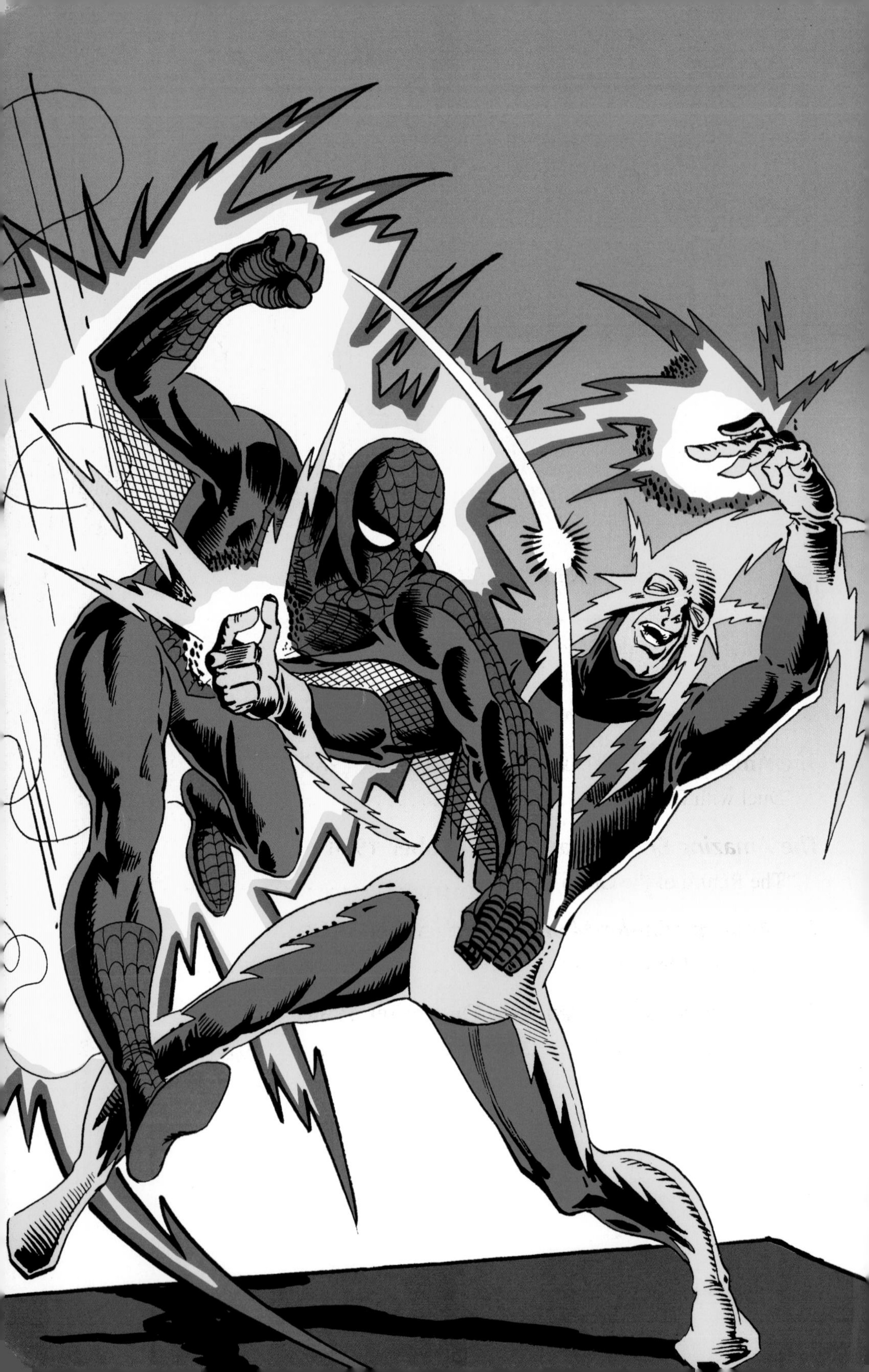

CONTENTS

The Amazing Spider-Man #11, April 1964
"Turning Point"   6

The Amazing Spider-Man #12, May 1964
"Umasked by Dr. Octopus!" 28

The Amazing Spider-Man #13, June 1964
"The Menace of Mysterio!" 51

The Amazing Spider-Man #14, July 1964
"The Grotesque Adventure of the Green Goblin" 74

The Amazing Spider-Man #15, August 1964
"Kraven the Hunter!" 97

The Amazing Spider-Man Annual #1, 1964
"The Sinister Six!" 120
"A Gallery of Spider-Man's Most Famous Foes!" 162
"The Secrets of Spider-Man!" 176
"How Stan Lee and Steve Ditko Create Spider-Man!" 190

The Amazing Spider-Man #16, September 1964
"Duel with Daredevil!" 193

The Amazing Spider-Man #17, October 1964
"The Return of the Green Goblin!" 216

The Amazing Spider-Man #18, November 1964
"The End of Spider-Man!" 239

The Amazing Spider-Man #19, December 1964
"Spidey Strikes Back!" 262

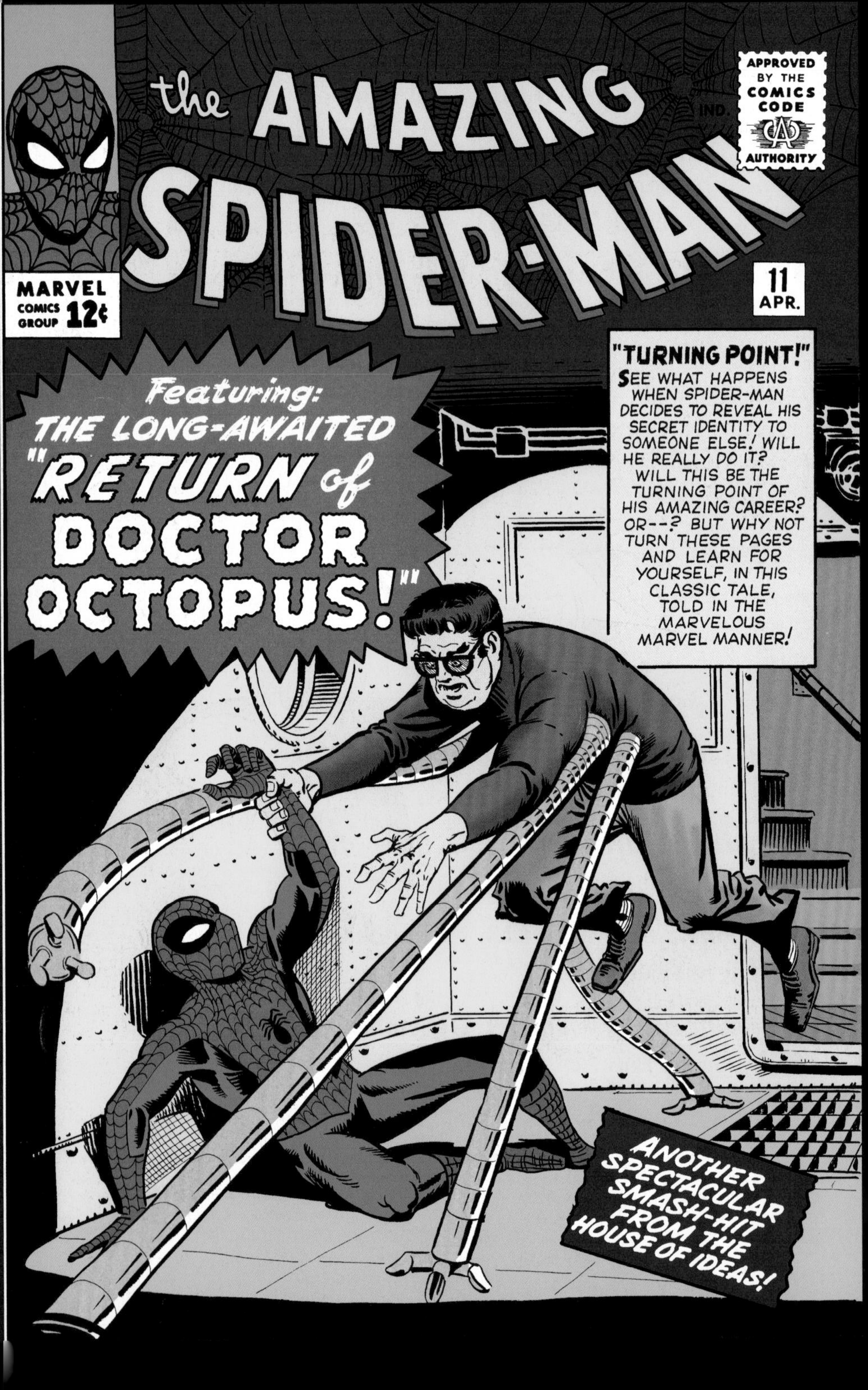

APPROVED BY THE COMICS CODE AUTHORITY
the AMAZING SPIDER-MAN
IND.
MARVEL COMICS GROUP 12¢
11 APR.
Featuring: THE LONG-AWAITED "RETURN of DOCTOR OCTOPUS!"
"TURNING POINT!" SEE WHAT HAPPENS WHEN SPIDER-MAN DECIDES TO REVEAL HIS SECRET IDENTITY TO SOMEONE ELSE! WILL HE REALLY DO IT? WILL THIS BE THE TURNING POINT OF HIS AMAZING CAREER? OR--? BUT WHY NOT TURN THESE PAGES AND LEARN FOR YOURSELF, IN THIS CLASSIC TALE, TOLD IN THE MARVELOUS MARVEL MANNER!
ANOTHER SPECTACULAR SMASH-HIT FROM THE HOUSE OF IDEAS!

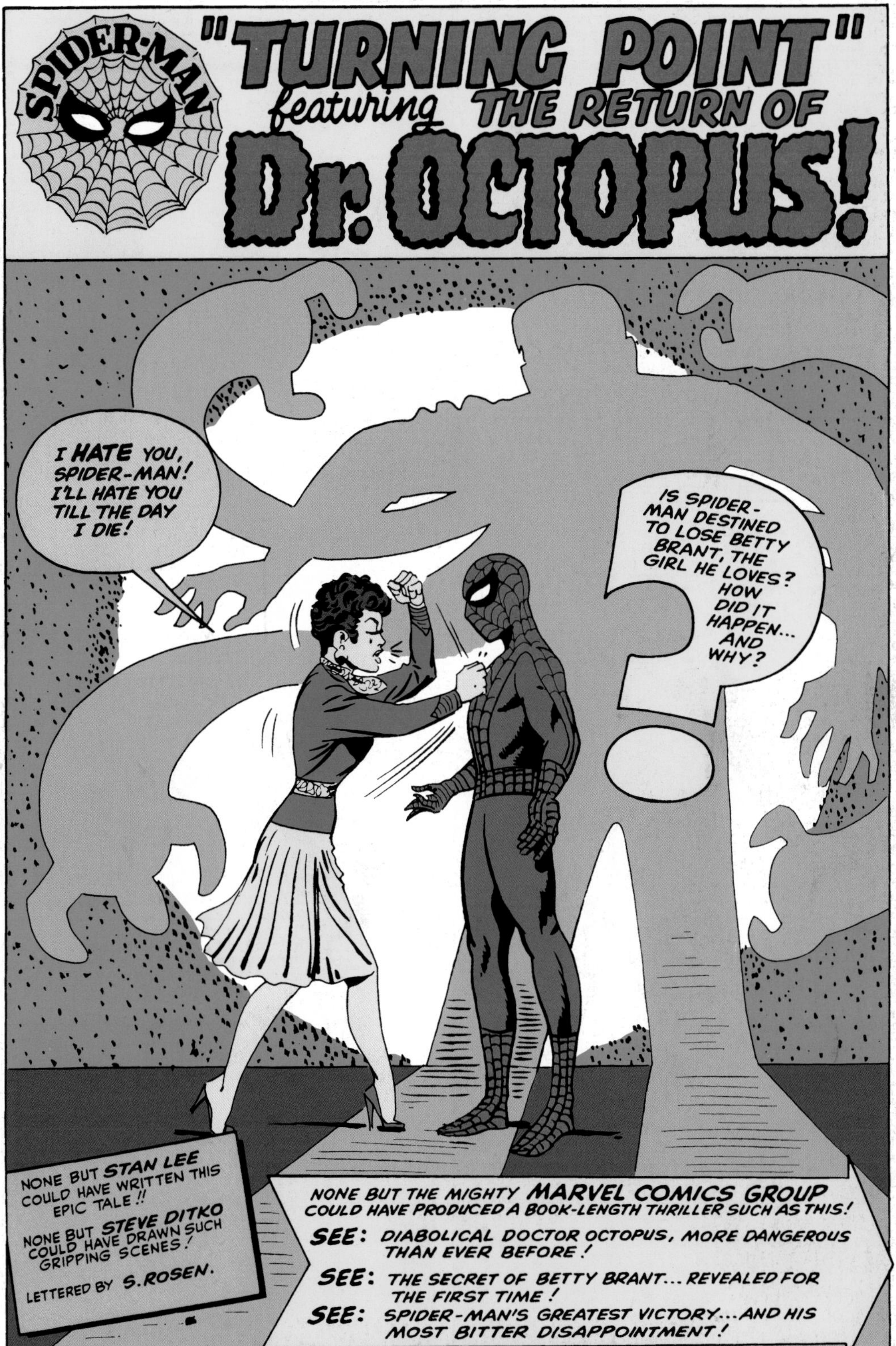
SPIDER-MAN
"TURNING POINT"
featuring THE RETURN OF
Dr. OCTOPUS!
I HATE YOU, SPIDER-MAN! I'LL HATE YOU TILL THE DAY I DIE!
IS SPIDER-MAN DESTINED TO LOSE BETTY BRANT, THE GIRL HE LOVES? HOW DID IT HAPPEN... AND WHY?
NONE BUT STAN LEE COULD HAVE WRITTEN THIS EPIC TALE!!
NONE BUT STEVE DITKO COULD HAVE DRAWN SUCH GRIPPING SCENES!
LETTERED BY S. ROSEN.
NONE BUT THE MIGHTY MARVEL COMICS GROUP COULD HAVE PRODUCED A BOOK-LENGTH THRILLER SUCH AS THIS!
SEE: DIABOLICAL DOCTOR OCTOPUS, MORE DANGEROUS THAN EVER BEFORE!
SEE: THE SECRET OF BETTY BRANT... REVEALED FOR THE FIRST TIME!
SEE: SPIDER-MAN'S GREATEST VICTORY... AND HIS MOST BITTER DISAPPOINTMENT!

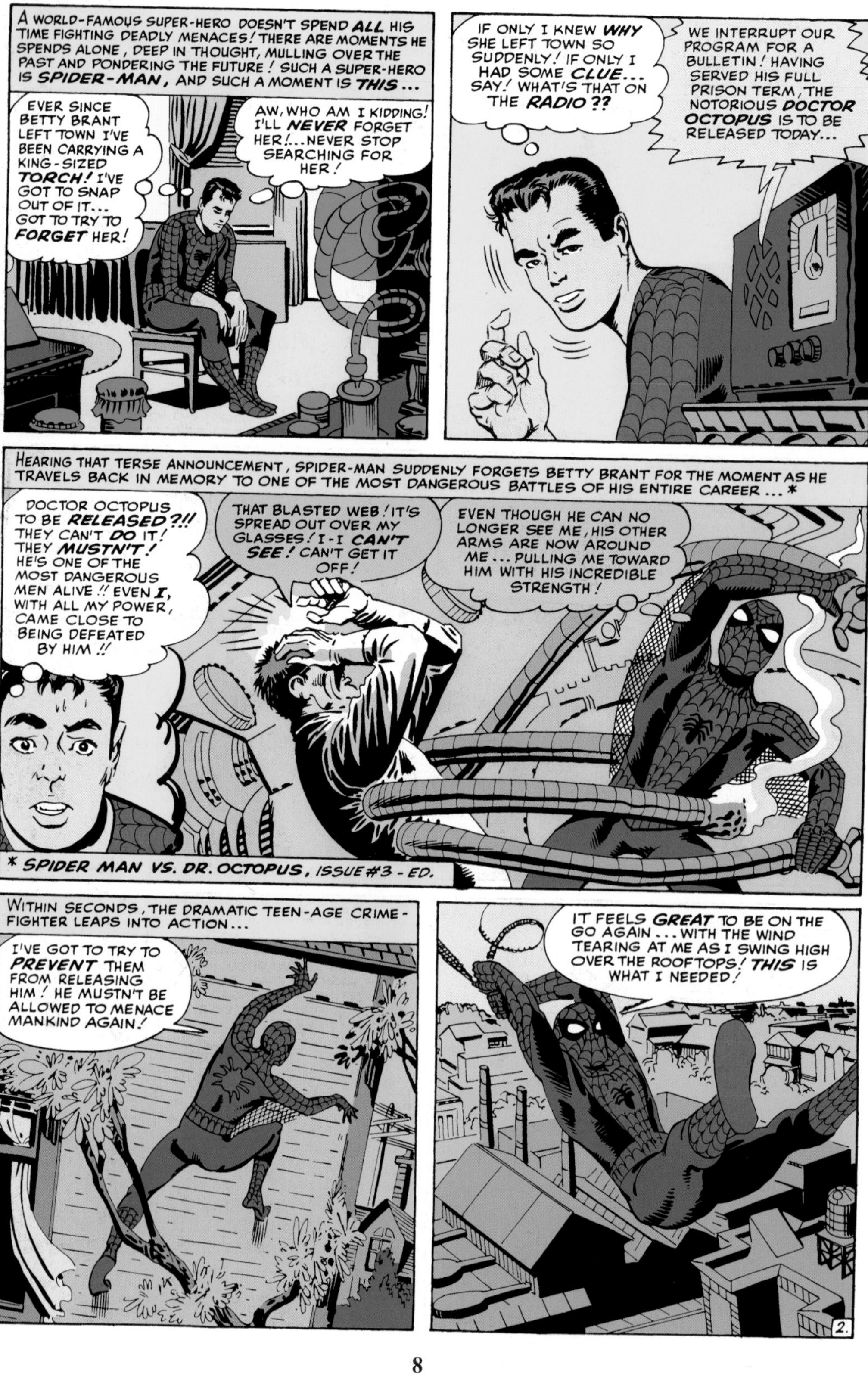
A WORLD-FAMOUS SUPER-HERO DOESN'T SPEND ALL HIS TIME FIGHTING DEADLY MENACES! THERE ARE MOMENTS HE SPENDS ALONE, DEEP IN THOUGHT, MULLING OVER THE PAST AND PONDERING THE FUTURE! SUCH A SUPER-HERO IS SPIDER-MAN, AND SUCH A MOMENT IS THIS...
EVER SINCE BETTY BRANT LEFT TOWN I'VE BEEN CARRYING A KING-SIZED TORCH! I'VE GOT TO SNAP OUT OF IT... GOT TO TRY TO FORGET HER!
AW, WHO AM I KIDDING! I'LL NEVER FORGET HER!...NEVER STOP SEARCHING FOR HER!
IF ONLY I KNEW WHY SHE LEFT TOWN SO SUDDENLY! IF ONLY I HAD SOME CLUE... SAY! WHAT'S THAT ON THE RADIO??
WE INTERRUPT OUR PROGRAM FOR A BULLETIN! HAVING SERVED HIS FULL PRISON TERM, THE NOTORIOUS DOCTOR OCTOPUS IS TO BE RELEASED TODAY...
HEARING THAT TERSE ANNOUNCEMENT, SPIDER-MAN SUDDENLY FORGETS BETTY BRANT FOR THE MOMENT AS HE TRAVELS BACK IN MEMORY TO ONE OF THE MOST DANGEROUS BATTLES OF HIS ENTIRE CAREER...*
DOCTOR OCTOPUS TO BE RELEASED?!! THEY CAN'T DO IT! THEY MUSTN'T! HE'S ONE OF THE MOST DANGEROUS MEN ALIVE!! EVEN I, WITH ALL MY POWER, CAME CLOSE TO BEING DEFEATED BY HIM!!
THAT BLASTED WEB! IT'S SPREAD OUT OVER MY GLASSES! I-I CAN'T SEE! CAN'T GET IT OFF!
EVEN THOUGH HE CAN NO LONGER SEE ME, HIS OTHER ARMS ARE NOW AROUND ME... PULLING ME TOWARD HIM WITH HIS INCREDIBLE STRENGTH!
* SPIDER MAN VS. DR. OCTOPUS, ISSUE #3 - ED.
WITHIN SECONDS, THE DRAMATIC TEEN-AGE CRIME-FIGHTER LEAPS INTO ACTION...
I'VE GOT TO TRY TO PREVENT THEM FROM RELEASING HIM! HE MUSTN'T BE ALLOWED TO MENACE MANKIND AGAIN!
IT FEELS GREAT TO BE ON THE GO AGAIN... WITH THE WIND TEARING AT ME AS I SWING HIGH OVER THE ROOFTOPS! THIS IS WHAT I NEEDED!
2.

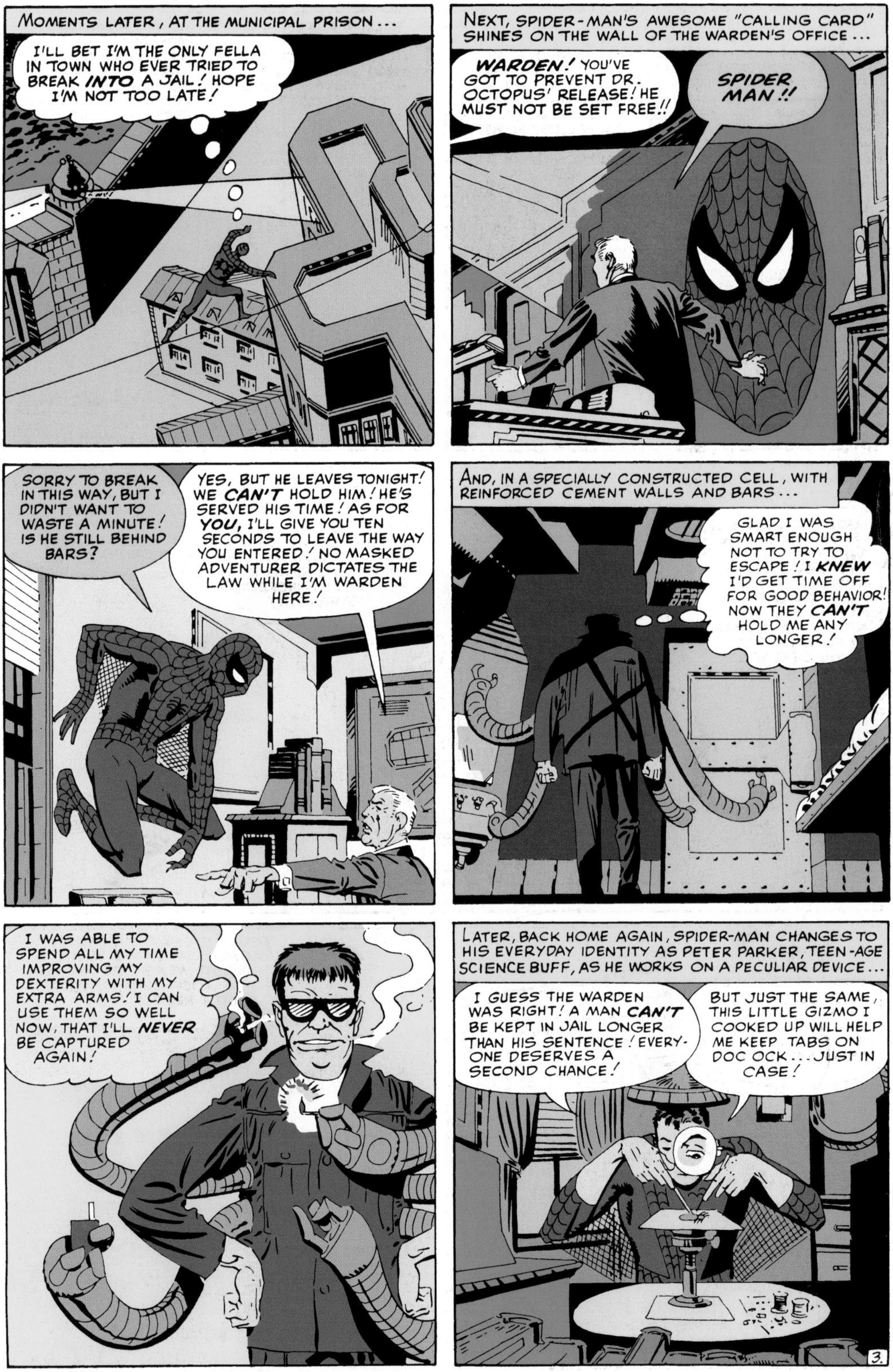
MOMENTS LATER, AT THE MUNICIPAL PRISON...
I'LL BET I'M THE ONLY FELLA IN TOWN WHO EVER TRIED TO BREAK INTO A JAIL! HOPE I'M NOT TOO LATE!
NEXT, SPIDER-MAN'S AWESOME "CALLING CARD" SHINES ON THE WALL OF THE WARDEN'S OFFICE...
WARDEN! YOU'VE GOT TO PREVENT DR. OCTOPUS' RELEASE! HE MUST NOT BE SET FREE!!
SPIDER MAN!!
SORRY TO BREAK IN THIS WAY, BUT I DIDN'T WANT TO WASTE A MINUTE! IS HE STILL BEHIND BARS?
YES, BUT HE LEAVES TONIGHT! WE CAN'T HOLD HIM! HE'S SERVED HIS TIME! AS FOR YOU, I'LL GIVE YOU TEN SECONDS TO LEAVE THE WAY YOU ENTERED! NO MASKED ADVENTURER DICTATES THE LAW WHILE I'M WARDEN HERE!
AND, IN A SPECIALLY CONSTRUCTED CELL, WITH REINFORCED CEMENT WALLS AND BARS...
GLAD I WAS SMART ENOUGH NOT TO TRY TO ESCAPE! I KNEW I'D GET TIME OFF FOR GOOD BEHAVIOR! NOW THEY CAN'T HOLD ME ANY LONGER!
I WAS ABLE TO SPEND ALL MY TIME IMPROVING MY DEXTERITY WITH MY EXTRA ARMS! I CAN USE THEM SO WELL NOW, THAT I'LL NEVER BE CAPTURED AGAIN!
LATER, BACK HOME AGAIN, SPIDER-MAN CHANGES TO HIS EVERYDAY IDENTITY AS PETER PARKER, TEEN-AGE SCIENCE BUFF, AS HE WORKS ON A PECULIAR DEVICE...
I GUESS THE WARDEN WAS RIGHT! A MAN CAN'T BE KEPT IN JAIL LONGER THAN HIS SENTENCE! EVERY-ONE DESERVES A SECOND CHANCE!
BUT JUST THE SAME, THIS LITTLE GIZMO I COOKED UP WILL HELP ME KEEP TABS ON DOC OCK... JUST IN CASE!
3.

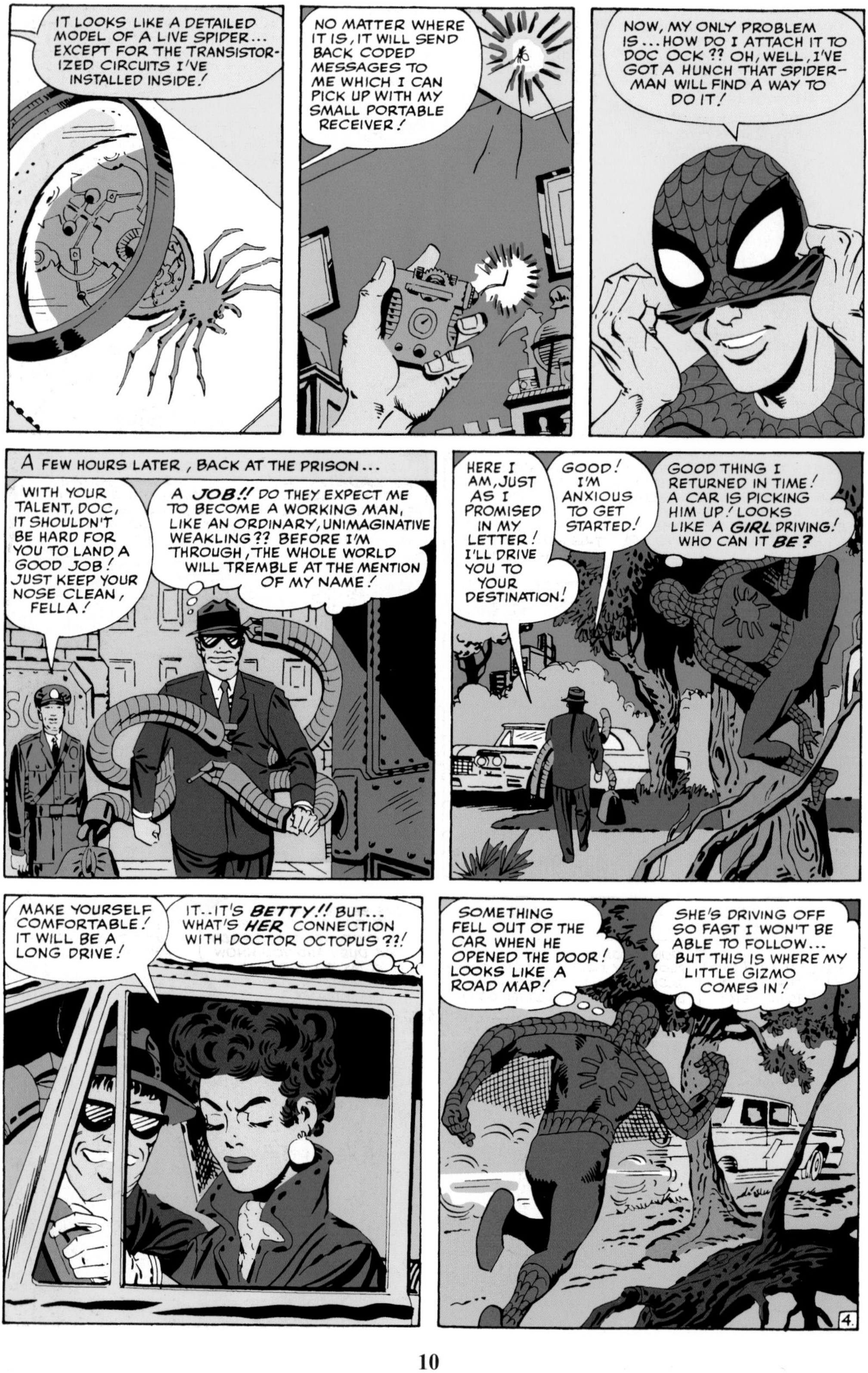
IT LOOKS LIKE A DETAILED MODEL OF A LIVE SPIDER... EXCEPT FOR THE TRANSISTORIZED CIRCUITS I'VE INSTALLED INSIDE!
NO MATTER WHERE IT IS, IT WILL SEND BACK CODED MESSAGES TO ME WHICH I CAN PICK UP WITH MY SMALL PORTABLE RECEIVER!
NOW, MY ONLY PROBLEM IS...HOW DO I ATTACH IT TO DOC OCK?? OH, WELL, I'VE GOT A HUNCH THAT SPIDER-MAN WILL FIND A WAY TO DO IT!
A FEW HOURS LATER, BACK AT THE PRISON...
WITH YOUR TALENT, DOC, IT SHOULDN'T BE HARD FOR YOU TO LAND A GOOD JOB! JUST KEEP YOUR NOSE CLEAN, FELLA!
A JOB!! DO THEY EXPECT ME TO BECOME A WORKING MAN, LIKE AN ORDINARY, UNIMAGINATIVE WEAKLING?? BEFORE I'M THROUGH, THE WHOLE WORLD WILL TREMBLE AT THE MENTION OF MY NAME!
HERE I AM, JUST AS I PROMISED IN MY LETTER! I'LL DRIVE YOU TO YOUR DESTINATION!
GOOD! I'M ANXIOUS TO GET STARTED!
GOOD THING I RETURNED IN TIME! A CAR IS PICKING HIM UP! LOOKS LIKE A GIRL DRIVING! WHO CAN IT BE?
MAKE YOURSELF COMFORTABLE! IT WILL BE A LONG DRIVE!
IT..IT'S BETTY!! BUT... WHAT'S HER CONNECTION WITH DOCTOR OCTOPUS??!
SOMETHING FELL OUT OF THE CAR WHEN HE OPENED THE DOOR! LOOKS LIKE A ROAD MAP!
SHE'S DRIVING OFF SO FAST I WON'T BE ABLE TO FOLLOW... BUT THIS IS WHERE MY LITTLE GIZMO COMES IN!
4.

IT'S NOT TOO HARD TO THROW SOMETHING AT A SPEEDING CAR AND MAKE SURE YOU HIT IT... NOT WHEN YOU'VE GOT THE HELP OF SPIDER-POWERED MUSCLES!

BULL'S-EYE! IT HIT THE CAR ROOF!...AND THE SPECIAL ADHESIVE I COATED IT WITH WILL KEEP IT STUCK THERE AS LONG AS I'LL NEED IT!

AND SO, UNAWARE OF THE STRANGE OBJECT ON TOP OF THE CAR, BETTY BRANT DRIVES OFF INTO THE NIGHT WITH HER SINISTER PASSENGER, AS OUR LITTLE CAST OF CHARACTERS COME CLOSER TO THEIR DATE WITH DESTINY!

MEANTIME... IT ALL HAPPENED SO FAST THAT I CAN HARDLY BELIEVE IT! HOW COULD THAT HAVE BEEN BETTY BRANT AT THE WHEEL?!

MAYBE SHE'S ON MY MIND SO MUCH THAT I'M IMAGINING I SEE HER! WELL, I'D BETTER PICK UP THIS MAP...IT MAY GIVE ME A CLUE!

IT'S A MAP OF PHILADELPHIA! AND THE CAR HAD PENNSY LICENSE PLATES! THAT MUST BE THEIR DESTINATION!

WELL, SPIDEY BOY, IT LOOKS LIKE YOU'RE GONNA TAKE A TRIP, TOO! I'VE GOT TO SEE THIS THROUGH TO THE END!

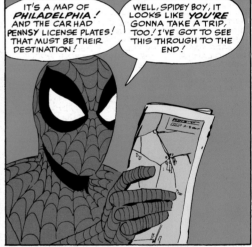

OUR SCENE NOW CHANGES TO THE CITY OF BROTHERLY LOVE, WHERE WE FIND AN ATTORNEY VISITING HIS CLIENT IN JAIL...

WELL, BRANT? DID YOUR SISTER DO AS I TOLD HER? I HOPE SO, MISTER, FOR YOUR SAKE!

DON'T WORRY, BLACKIE! SHE'S PROBABLY DRIVING DR. OCTOPUS BACK TO PHILLY RIGHT NOW! BETTY WOULDN'T LET ME DOWN!

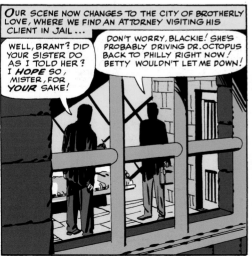

SHE BETTER NOT! THAT GAMBLING DEBT YOU OWE ME IS ALREADY PAST DUE! AND YOU KNOW WHAT MY BOYS DO TO WELCHERS...DON'T YOU, BRANT?

I KNOW, BLACKIE! I'VE BEEN YOUR LAWYER TOO LONG NOT TO KNOW!

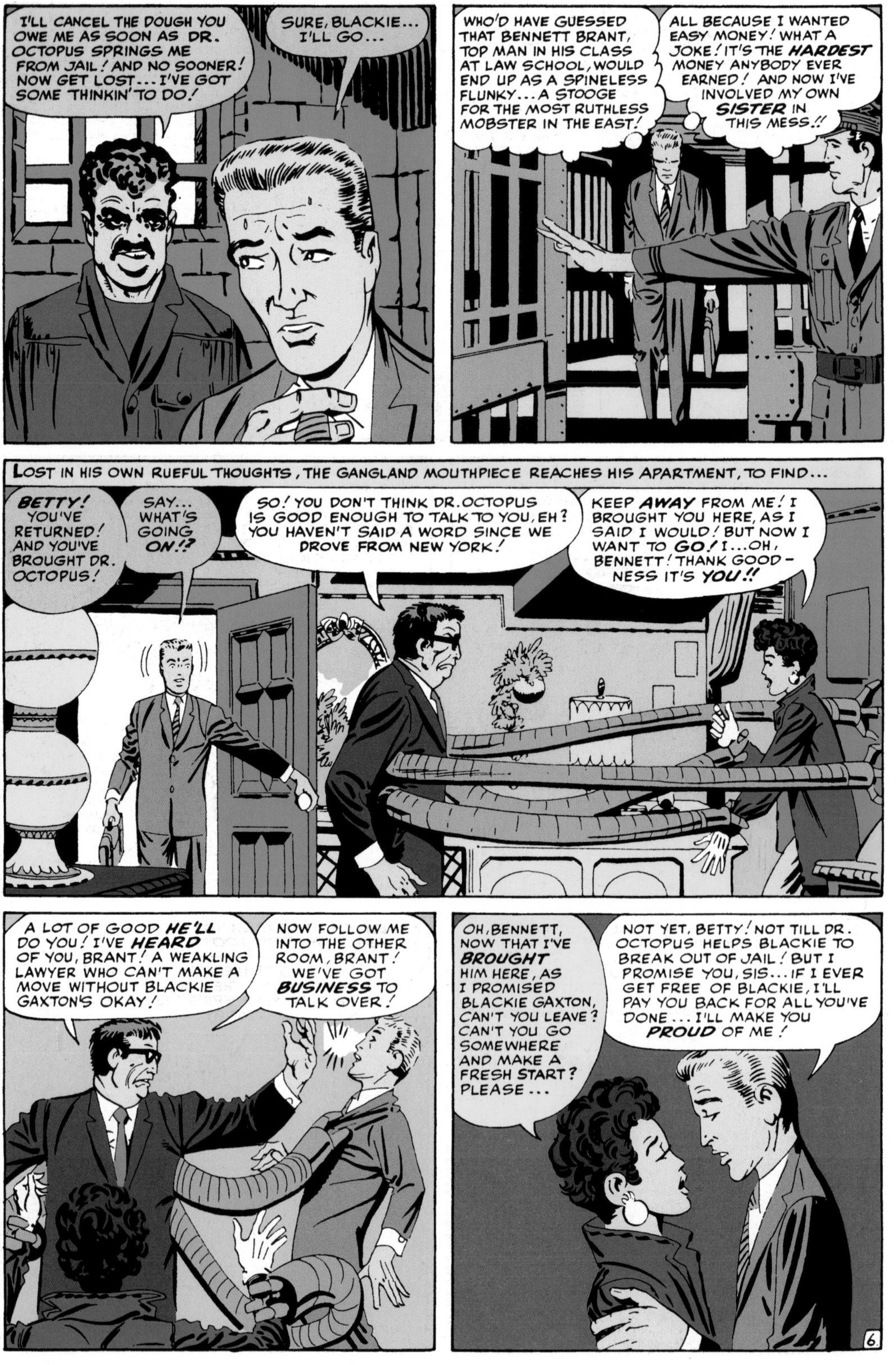
I'LL CANCEL THE DOUGH YOU OWE ME AS SOON AS DR. OCTOPUS SPRINGS ME FROM JAIL! AND NO SOONER! NOW GET LOST... I'VE GOT SOME THINKIN' TO DO!
SURE, BLACKIE... I'LL GO...
WHO'D HAVE GUESSED THAT BENNETT BRANT, TOP MAN IN HIS CLASS AT LAW SCHOOL, WOULD END UP AS A SPINELESS FLUNKY... A STOOGE FOR THE MOST RUTHLESS MOBSTER IN THE EAST!
ALL BECAUSE I WANTED EASY MONEY! WHAT A JOKE! IT'S THE HARDEST MONEY ANYBODY EVER EARNED! AND NOW I'VE INVOLVED MY OWN SISTER IN THIS MESS!!
LOST IN HIS OWN RUEFUL THOUGHTS, THE GANGLAND MOUTHPIECE REACHES HIS APARTMENT, TO FIND...
BETTY! YOU'VE RETURNED! AND YOU'VE BROUGHT DR. OCTOPUS!
SAY... WHAT'S GOING ON!?
SO! YOU DON'T THINK DR. OCTOPUS IS GOOD ENOUGH TO TALK TO YOU, EH? YOU HAVEN'T SAID A WORD SINCE WE DROVE FROM NEW YORK!
KEEP AWAY FROM ME! I BROUGHT YOU HERE, AS I SAID I WOULD! BUT NOW I WANT TO GO! I...OH, BENNETT! THANK GOOD-NESS IT'S YOU!!
A LOT OF GOOD HE'LL DO YOU! I'VE HEARD OF YOU, BRANT! A WEAKLING LAWYER WHO CAN'T MAKE A MOVE WITHOUT BLACKIE GAXTON'S OKAY!
NOW FOLLOW ME INTO THE OTHER ROOM, BRANT! WE'VE GOT BUSINESS TO TALK OVER!
OH, BENNETT, NOW THAT I'VE BROUGHT HIM HERE, AS I PROMISED BLACKIE GAXTON, CAN'T YOU LEAVE? CAN'T YOU GO SOMEWHERE AND MAKE A FRESH START? PLEASE...
NOT YET, BETTY! NOT TILL DR. OCTOPUS HELPS BLACKIE TO BREAK OUT OF JAIL! BUT I PROMISE YOU, SIS... IF I EVER GET FREE OF BLACKIE, I'LL PAY YOU BACK FOR ALL YOU'VE DONE... I'LL MAKE YOU PROUD OF ME!
6.

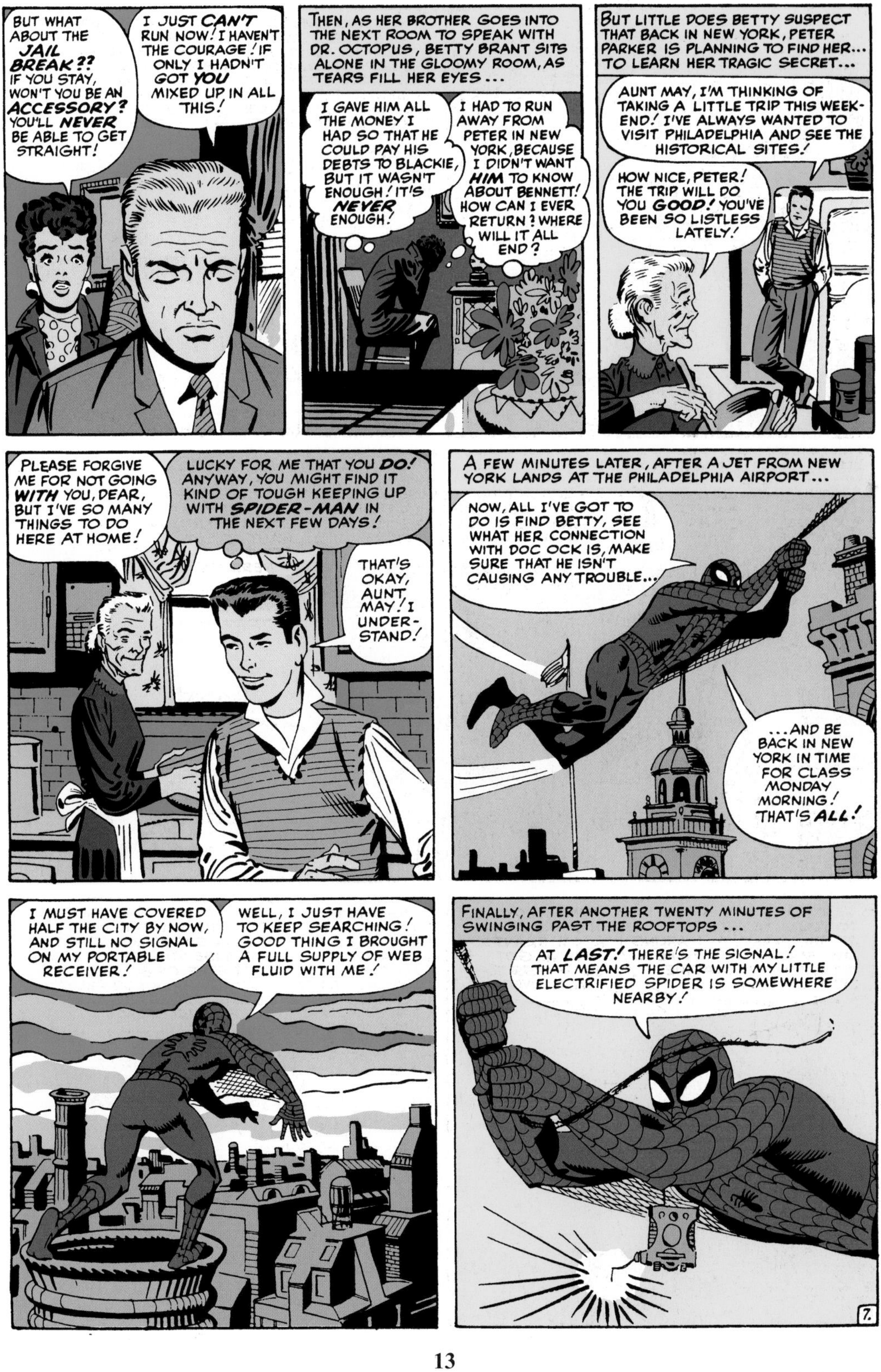
BUT WHAT ABOUT THE JAIL BREAK?? IF YOU STAY, WON'T YOU BE AN ACCESSORY? YOU'LL NEVER BE ABLE TO GET STRAIGHT!
I JUST CAN'T RUN NOW! I HAVEN'T THE COURAGE! IF ONLY I HADN'T GOT YOU MIXED UP IN ALL THIS!
THEN, AS HER BROTHER GOES INTO THE NEXT ROOM TO SPEAK WITH DR. OCTOPUS, BETTY BRANT SITS ALONE IN THE GLOOMY ROOM, AS TEARS FILL HER EYES...
I GAVE HIM ALL THE MONEY I HAD SO THAT HE COULD PAY HIS DEBTS TO BLACKIE, BUT IT WASN'T ENOUGH! IT'S NEVER ENOUGH!
I HAD TO RUN AWAY FROM PETER IN NEW YORK, BECAUSE I DIDN'T WANT HIM TO KNOW ABOUT BENNETT! HOW CAN I EVER RETURN? WHERE WILL IT ALL END?
BUT LITTLE DOES BETTY SUSPECT THAT BACK IN NEW YORK, PETER PARKER IS PLANNING TO FIND HER... TO LEARN HER TRAGIC SECRET...
AUNT MAY, I'M THINKING OF TAKING A LITTLE TRIP THIS WEEK-END! I'VE ALWAYS WANTED TO VISIT PHILADELPHIA AND SEE THE HISTORICAL SITES!
HOW NICE, PETER! THE TRIP WILL DO YOU GOOD! YOU'VE BEEN SO LISTLESS LATELY!
PLEASE FORGIVE ME FOR NOT GOING WITH YOU, DEAR, BUT I'VE SO MANY THINGS TO DO HERE AT HOME!
LUCKY FOR ME THAT YOU DO! ANYWAY, YOU MIGHT FIND IT KIND OF TOUGH KEEPING UP WITH SPIDER-MAN IN THE NEXT FEW DAYS!
THAT'S OKAY, AUNT MAY! I UNDER-STAND!
A FEW MINUTES LATER, AFTER A JET FROM NEW YORK LANDS AT THE PHILADELPHIA AIRPORT...
NOW, ALL I'VE GOT TO DO IS FIND BETTY, SEE WHAT HER CONNECTION WITH DOC OCK IS, MAKE SURE THAT HE ISN'T CAUSING ANY TROUBLE...
...AND BE BACK IN NEW YORK IN TIME FOR CLASS MONDAY MORNING! THAT'S ALL!
I MUST HAVE COVERED HALF THE CITY BY NOW, AND STILL NO SIGNAL ON MY PORTABLE RECEIVER!
WELL, I JUST HAVE TO KEEP SEARCHING! GOOD THING I BROUGHT A FULL SUPPLY OF WEB FLUID WITH ME!
FINALLY, AFTER ANOTHER TWENTY MINUTES OF SWINGING PAST THE ROOFTOPS...
AT LAST! THERE'S THE SIGNAL! THAT MEANS THE CAR WITH MY LITTLE ELECTRIFIED SPIDER IS SOMEWHERE NEARBY!
7.

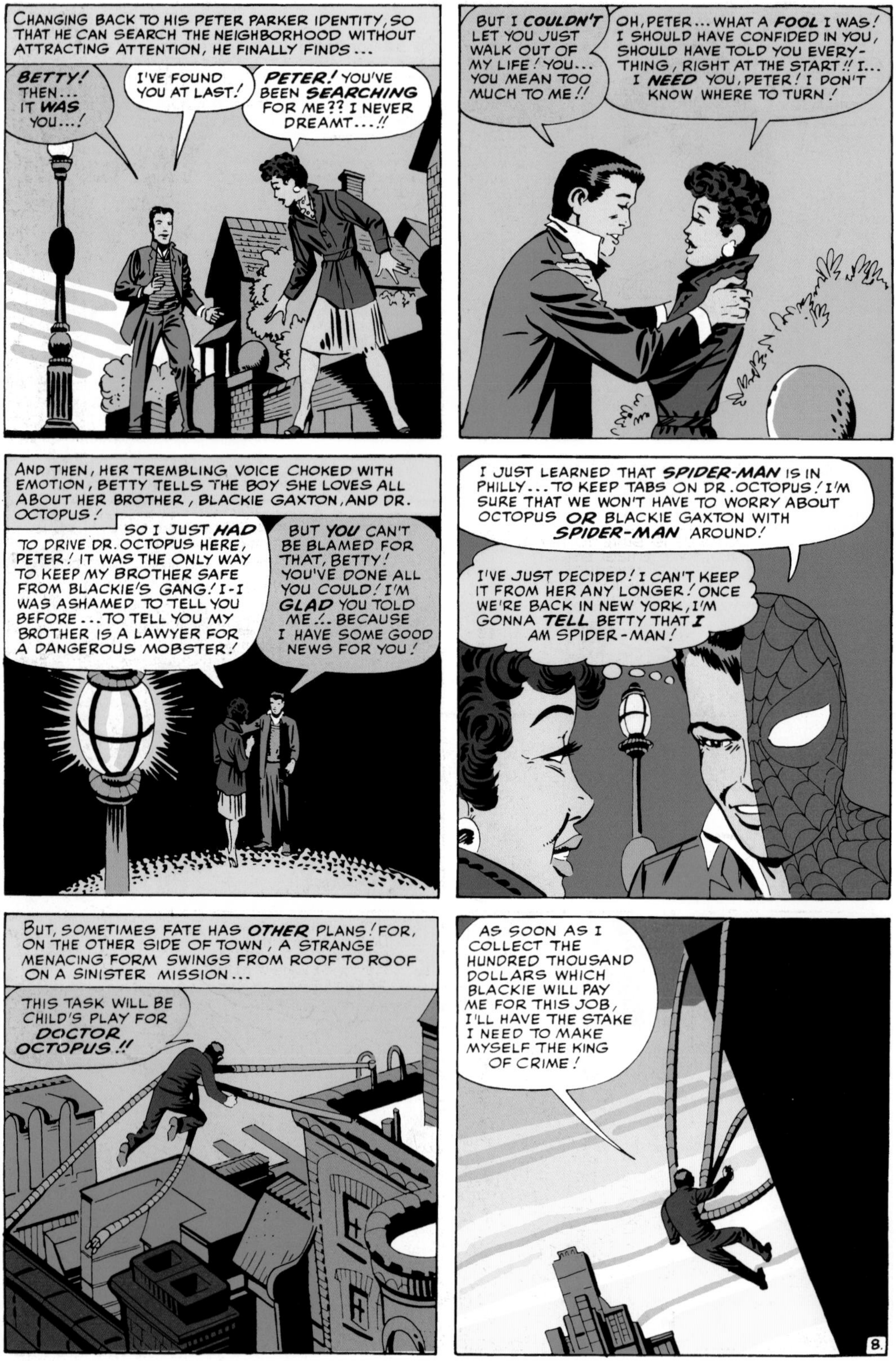
CHANGING BACK TO HIS PETER PARKER IDENTITY, SO THAT HE CAN SEARCH THE NEIGHBORHOOD WITHOUT ATTRACTING ATTENTION, HE FINALLY FINDS...
BETTY! THEN... IT WAS YOU...!
I'VE FOUND YOU AT LAST!
PETER! YOU'VE BEEN SEARCHING FOR ME?? I NEVER DREAMT...!!
BUT I COULDN'T LET YOU JUST WALK OUT OF MY LIFE! YOU... YOU MEAN TOO MUCH TO ME!!
OH, PETER... WHAT A FOOL I WAS! I SHOULD HAVE CONFIDED IN YOU, SHOULD HAVE TOLD YOU EVERYTHING, RIGHT AT THE START!! I... I NEED YOU, PETER! I DON'T KNOW WHERE TO TURN!
AND THEN, HER TREMBLING VOICE CHOKED WITH EMOTION, BETTY TELLS THE BOY SHE LOVES ALL ABOUT HER BROTHER, BLACKIE GAXTON, AND DR. OCTOPUS!
SO I JUST HAD TO DRIVE DR. OCTOPUS HERE, PETER! IT WAS THE ONLY WAY TO KEEP MY BROTHER SAFE FROM BLACKIE'S GANG! I-I WAS ASHAMED TO TELL YOU BEFORE... TO TELL YOU MY BROTHER IS A LAWYER FOR A DANGEROUS MOBSTER!
BUT YOU CAN'T BE BLAMED FOR THAT, BETTY! YOU'VE DONE ALL YOU COULD! I'M GLAD YOU TOLD ME...! BECAUSE I HAVE SOME GOOD NEWS FOR YOU!
I JUST LEARNED THAT SPIDER-MAN IS IN PHILLY... TO KEEP TABS ON DR. OCTOPUS! I'M SURE THAT WE WON'T HAVE TO WORRY ABOUT OCTOPUS OR BLACKIE GAXTON WITH SPIDER-MAN AROUND!
I'VE JUST DECIDED! I CAN'T KEEP IT FROM HER ANY LONGER! ONCE WE'RE BACK IN NEW YORK, I'M GONNA TELL BETTY THAT I AM SPIDER-MAN!
BUT, SOMETIMES FATE HAS OTHER PLANS! FOR, ON THE OTHER SIDE OF TOWN, A STRANGE MENACING FORM SWINGS FROM ROOF TO ROOF ON A SINISTER MISSION...
THIS TASK WILL BE CHILD'S PLAY FOR DOCTOR OCTOPUS!!
AS SOON AS I COLLECT THE HUNDRED THOUSAND DOLLARS WHICH BLACKIE WILL PAY ME FOR THIS JOB, I'LL HAVE THE STAKE I NEED TO MAKE MYSELF THE KING OF CRIME!
8.

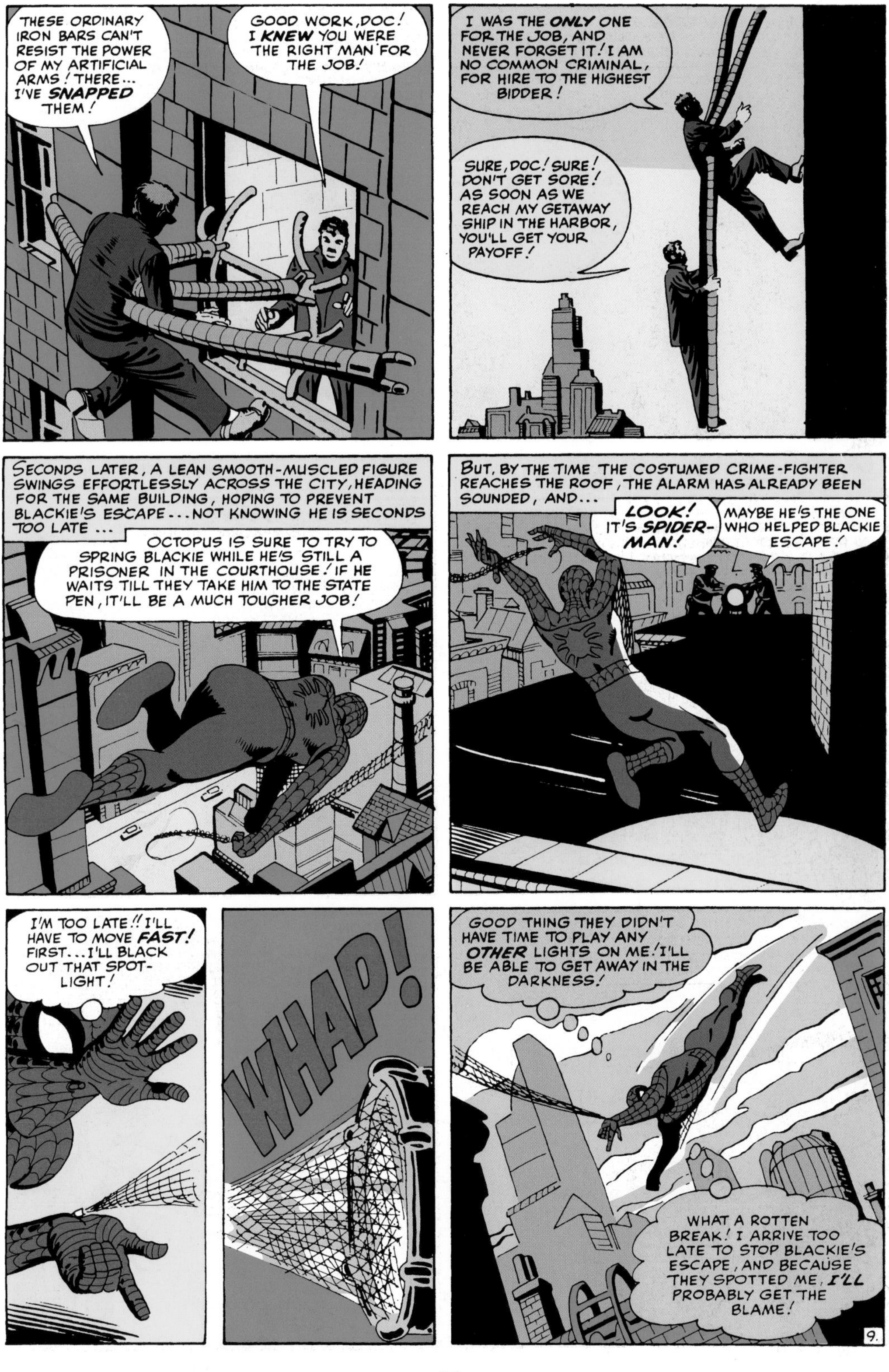
THESE ORDINARY IRON BARS CAN'T RESIST THE POWER OF MY ARTIFICIAL ARMS! THERE... I'VE SNAPPED THEM!
GOOD WORK, DOC! I KNEW YOU WERE THE RIGHT MAN FOR THE JOB!
I WAS THE ONLY ONE FOR THE JOB, AND NEVER FORGET IT! I AM NO COMMON CRIMINAL, FOR HIRE TO THE HIGHEST BIDDER!
SURE, DOC! SURE! DON'T GET SORE! AS SOON AS WE REACH MY GETAWAY SHIP IN THE HARBOR, YOU'LL GET YOUR PAYOFF!
SECONDS LATER, A LEAN SMOOTH-MUSCLED FIGURE SWINGS EFFORTLESSLY ACROSS THE CITY, HEADING FOR THE SAME BUILDING, HOPING TO PREVENT BLACKIE'S ESCAPE...NOT KNOWING HE IS SECONDS TOO LATE...
OCTOPUS IS SURE TO TRY TO SPRING BLACKIE WHILE HE'S STILL A PRISONER IN THE COURTHOUSE! IF HE WAITS TILL THEY TAKE HIM TO THE STATE PEN, IT'LL BE A MUCH TOUGHER JOB!
BUT, BY THE TIME THE COSTUMED CRIME-FIGHTER REACHES THE ROOF, THE ALARM HAS ALREADY BEEN SOUNDED, AND...
LOOK! IT'S SPIDER-MAN!
MAYBE HE'S THE ONE WHO HELPED BLACKIE ESCAPE!
I'M TOO LATE!! I'LL HAVE TO MOVE FAST! FIRST...I'LL BLACK OUT THAT SPOT-LIGHT!
WHAP!
GOOD THING THEY DIDN'T HAVE TIME TO PLAY ANY OTHER LIGHTS ON ME! I'LL BE ABLE TO GET AWAY IN THE DARKNESS!
WHAT A ROTTEN BREAK! I ARRIVE TOO LATE TO STOP BLACKIE'S ESCAPE, AND BECAUSE THEY SPOTTED ME, I'LL PROBABLY GET THE BLAME!
9.

SUFFERIN' SPIDER-WEBS.!! I JUST REMEMBERED.! WITH OCTOPUS AND BLACKIE ON THE LOOSE, I'D BETTER GET BACK TO BETTY! SHE MIGHT BE IN GREAT DANGER!

BUT ONCE AGAIN, A CAPRICIOUS FATE HAS MADE THE TEEN-AGE CRUSADER MINUTES TOO LATE! FOR, BEFORE SPIDER-MAN CAN REACH HIS GOAL...

C'MON, MOVE! BLACKIE WANTS US TO BRING YOU BOTH TO HIS GETAWAY SHIP!

BUT WHY?? WE'VE DONE WHAT HE WANTED! WHY DOESN'T HE LET US GO ???

I WAS A FOOL! I SHOULD HAVE KNOWN HE'D NEVER LET US GO!

YOU CAN SAY THAT AGAIN, MOUTH-PIECE!

LATER, THE HELPLESS GIRL AND HER BROTHER ARE TAKEN TO A DINGY TRAMP STEAMER...

WE'LL WAIT ON THIS OLD TUB UNTIL A LAUNCH COMES TO PICK US UP! BLACKIE HAS EVERYTHING ALL PLANNED!

YEAH! THEN WE'LL SKIP TO SOME FOREIGN COUNTRY WHERE NO ONE'LL EVER BE ABLE TO TOUCH US!

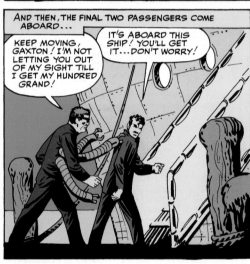

AND THEN, THE FINAL TWO PASSENGERS COME ABOARD...

KEEP MOVING, GAXTON! I'M NOT LETTING YOU OUT OF MY SIGHT TILL I GET MY HUNDRED GRAND!

IT'S ABOARD THIS SHIP! YOU'LL GET IT...DON'T WORRY!

BUT, UNSUSPECTED BY ANY OF THOSE ON BOARD, THERE IS STILL ANOTHER PASSENGER SWINGING ONTO THE SHIP!

GOOD THING THEY USED THE CAR WHICH HAD MY GIZMO ON IT! I WAS ABLE TO PICK UP THE SIGNAL AND FOLLOW THEM ALL THE WAY!

MEANTIME ...

YOU CAN'T DO THIS, BLACKIE! I'VE DONE EVERYTHING YOU ASKED! YOU'RE FREE NOW, JUST AS YOU WANTED TO BE, SO MY DEBT IS CANCELLED! YOU'VE GOT TO LET US GO!

I DO, HUH?

10.

16

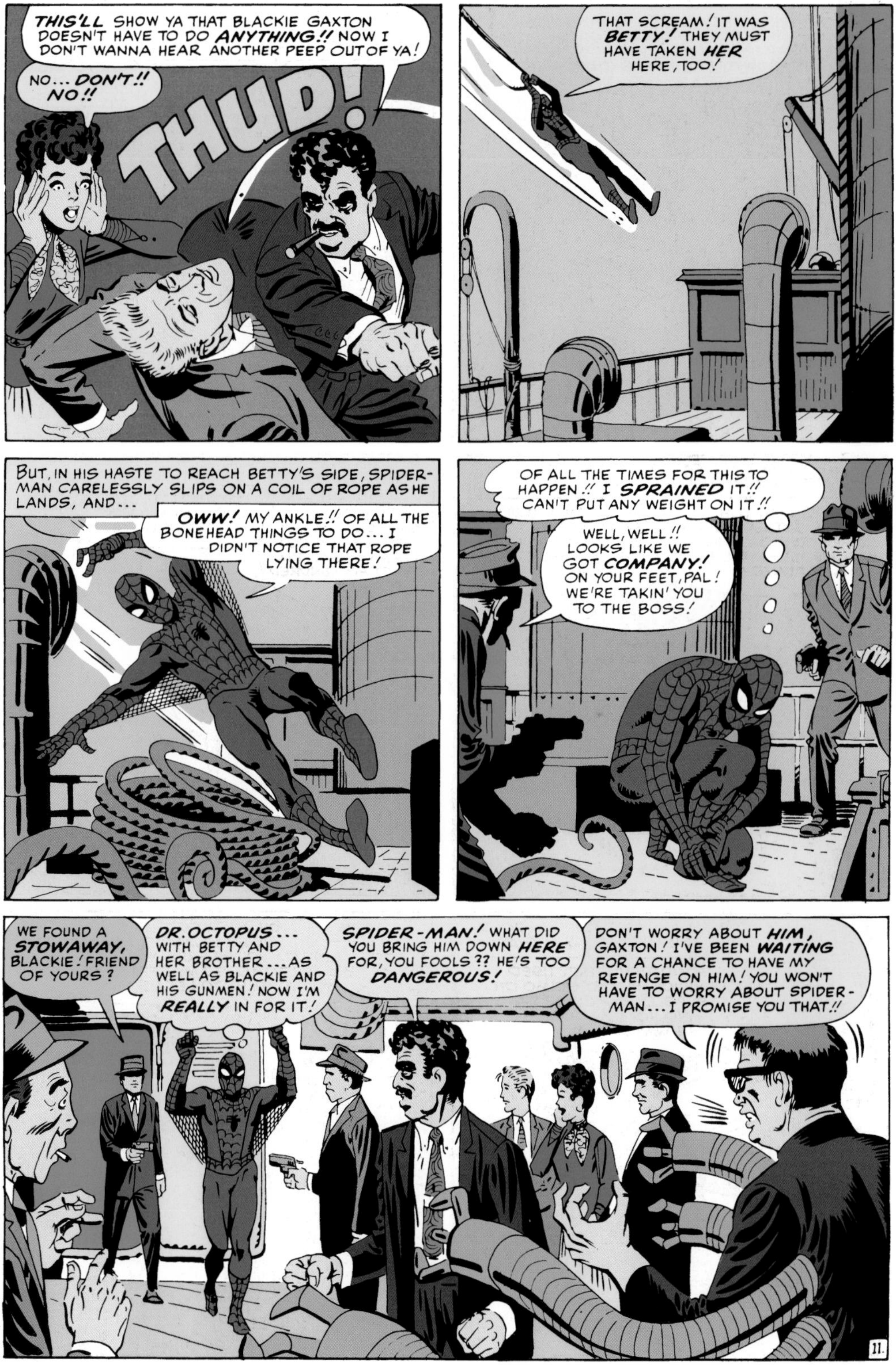
THIS'LL SHOW YA THAT BLACKIE GAXTON DOESN'T HAVE TO DO ANYTHING!! NOW I DON'T WANNA HEAR ANOTHER PEEP OUT OF YA!
NO... DON'T!! NO!!
THUD!
THAT SCREAM! IT WAS BETTY! THEY MUST HAVE TAKEN HER HERE, TOO!
BUT, IN HIS HASTE TO REACH BETTY'S SIDE, SPIDER-MAN CARELESSLY SLIPS ON A COIL OF ROPE AS HE LANDS, AND...
OWW! MY ANKLE!! OF ALL THE BONEHEAD THINGS TO DO... I DIDN'T NOTICE THAT ROPE LYING THERE!
OF ALL THE TIMES FOR THIS TO HAPPEN!! I SPRAINED IT!! CAN'T PUT ANY WEIGHT ON IT!!
WELL, WELL!! LOOKS LIKE WE GOT COMPANY! ON YOUR FEET, PAL! WE'RE TAKIN' YOU TO THE BOSS!
WE FOUND A STOWAWAY, BLACKIE! FRIEND OF YOURS?
DR. OCTOPUS... WITH BETTY AND HER BROTHER... AS WELL AS BLACKIE AND HIS GUNMEN! NOW I'M REALLY IN FOR IT!
SPIDER-MAN! WHAT DID YOU BRING HIM DOWN HERE FOR, YOU FOOLS?? HE'S TOO DANGEROUS!
DON'T WORRY ABOUT HIM, GAXTON! I'VE BEEN WAITING FOR A CHANCE TO HAVE MY REVENGE ON HIM! YOU WON'T HAVE TO WORRY ABOUT SPIDER-MAN... I PROMISE YOU THAT!!
11.

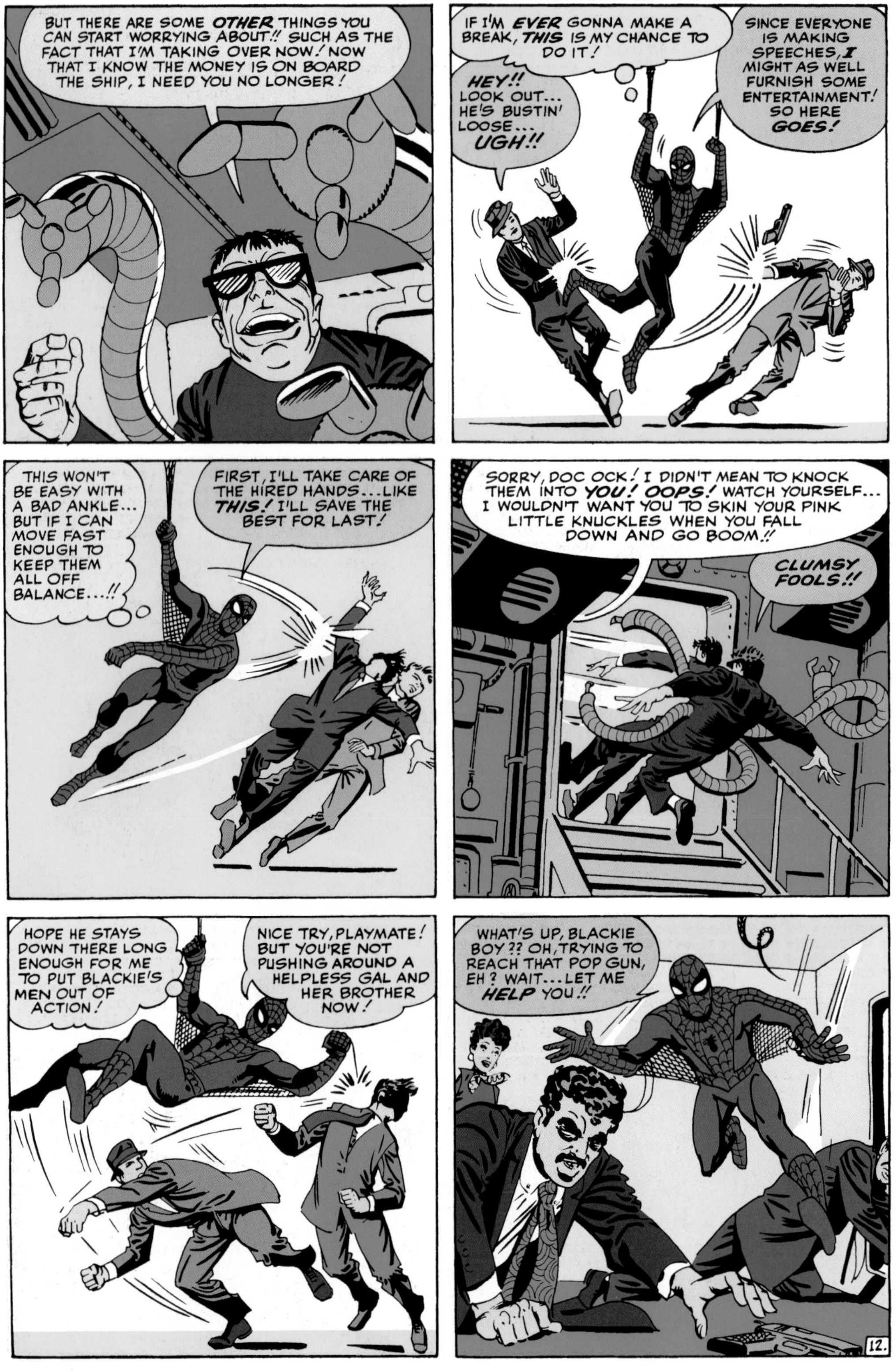
BUT THERE ARE SOME OTHER THINGS YOU CAN START WORRYING ABOUT!! SUCH AS THE FACT THAT I'M TAKING OVER NOW! NOW THAT I KNOW THE MONEY IS ON BOARD THE SHIP, I NEED YOU NO LONGER!
IF I'M EVER GONNA MAKE A BREAK, THIS IS MY CHANCE TO DO IT!
HEY!! LOOK OUT... HE'S BUSTIN' LOOSE... UGH!!
SINCE EVERYONE IS MAKING SPEECHES, I MIGHT AS WELL FURNISH SOME ENTERTAINMENT! SO HERE GOES!
THIS WON'T BE EASY WITH A BAD ANKLE... BUT IF I CAN MOVE FAST ENOUGH TO KEEP THEM ALL OFF BALANCE...!!
FIRST, I'LL TAKE CARE OF THE HIRED HANDS...LIKE THIS! I'LL SAVE THE BEST FOR LAST!
SORRY, DOC OCK! I DIDN'T MEAN TO KNOCK THEM INTO YOU! OOPS! WATCH YOURSELF... I WOULDN'T WANT YOU TO SKIN YOUR PINK LITTLE KNUCKLES WHEN YOU FALL DOWN AND GO BOOM!!
CLUMSY FOOLS!!
HOPE HE STAYS DOWN THERE LONG ENOUGH FOR ME TO PUT BLACKIE'S MEN OUT OF ACTION!
NICE TRY, PLAYMATE! BUT YOU'RE NOT PUSHING AROUND A HELPLESS GAL AND HER BROTHER NOW!
WHAT'S UP, BLACKIE BOY?? OH, TRYING TO REACH THAT POP GUN, EH? WAIT...LET ME HELP YOU!!
12.

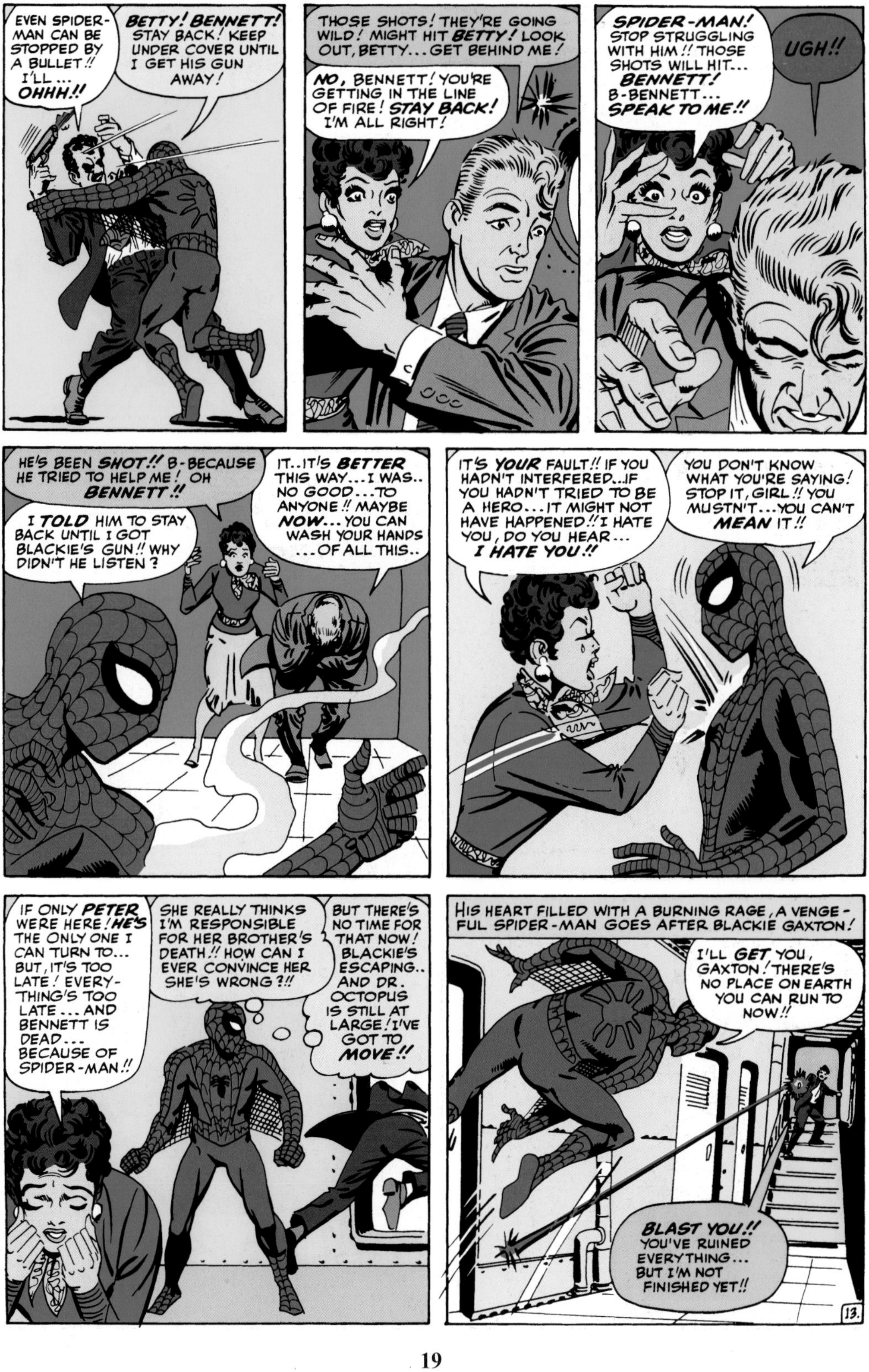
EVEN SPIDER-MAN CAN BE STOPPED BY A BULLET!! I'LL... OHHH!!
BETTY! BENNETT! STAY BACK! KEEP UNDER COVER UNTIL I GET HIS GUN AWAY!
THOSE SHOTS! THEY'RE GOING WILD! MIGHT HIT BETTY! LOOK OUT, BETTY... GET BEHIND ME!
NO, BENNETT! YOU'RE GETTING IN THE LINE OF FIRE! STAY BACK! I'M ALL RIGHT!
SPIDER-MAN! STOP STRUGGLING WITH HIM!! THOSE SHOTS WILL HIT... BENNETT! B-BENNETT... SPEAK TO ME!!
UGH!!
HE'S BEEN SHOT!! B-BECAUSE HE TRIED TO HELP ME! OH BENNETT!!
I TOLD HIM TO STAY BACK UNTIL I GOT BLACKIE'S GUN!! WHY DIDN'T HE LISTEN?
IT..IT'S BETTER THIS WAY...I WAS.. NO GOOD...TO ANYONE!! MAYBE NOW...YOU CAN WASH YOUR HANDS ...OF ALL THIS..
IT'S YOUR FAULT!! IF YOU HADN'T INTERFERED...IF YOU HADN'T TRIED TO BE A HERO...IT MIGHT NOT HAVE HAPPENED!! I HATE YOU, DO YOU HEAR... I HATE YOU!!
YOU DON'T KNOW WHAT YOU'RE SAYING! STOP IT, GIRL!! YOU MUSTN'T...YOU CAN'T MEAN IT!!
IF ONLY PETER WERE HERE! HE'S THE ONLY ONE I CAN TURN TO... BUT, IT'S TOO LATE! EVERYTHING'S TOO LATE... AND BENNETT IS DEAD... BECAUSE OF SPIDER-MAN!!
SHE REALLY THINKS I'M RESPONSIBLE FOR HER BROTHER'S DEATH!! HOW CAN I EVER CONVINCE HER SHE'S WRONG?!!
BUT THERE'S NO TIME FOR THAT NOW! BLACKIE'S ESCAPING.. AND DR. OCTOPUS IS STILL AT LARGE! I'VE GOT TO MOVE!!
HIS HEART FILLED WITH A BURNING RAGE, A VENGEFUL SPIDER-MAN GOES AFTER BLACKIE GAXTON!
I'LL GET YOU, GAXTON! THERE'S NO PLACE ON EARTH YOU CAN RUN TO NOW!!
BLAST YOU!! YOU'VE RUINED EVERYTHING... BUT I'M NOT FINISHED YET!!
13.

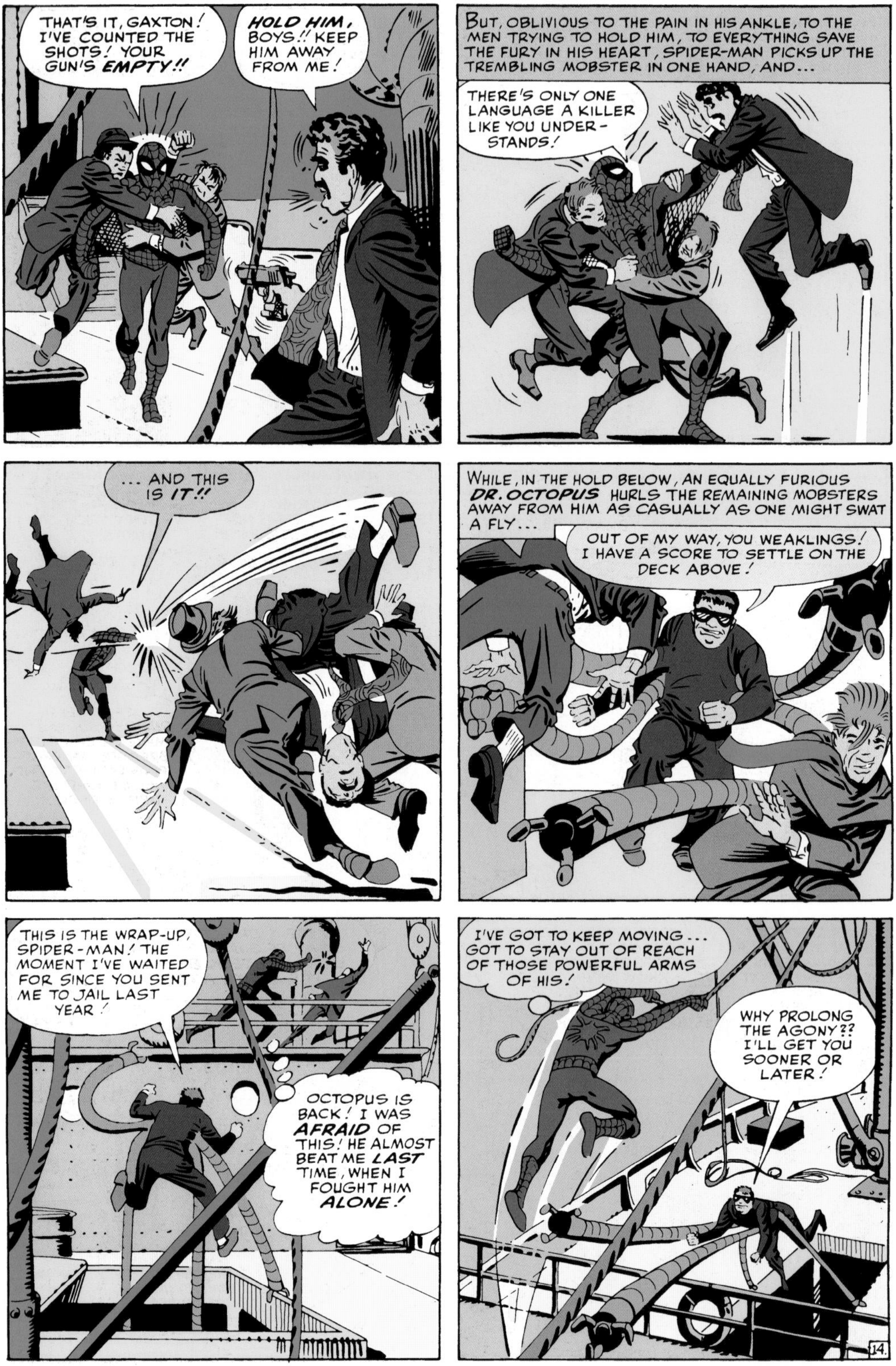
THAT'S IT, GAXTON! I'VE COUNTED THE SHOTS! YOUR GUN'S EMPTY!!
HOLD HIM, BOYS!! KEEP HIM AWAY FROM ME!
BUT, OBLIVIOUS TO THE PAIN IN HIS ANKLE, TO THE MEN TRYING TO HOLD HIM, TO EVERYTHING SAVE THE FURY IN HIS HEART, SPIDER-MAN PICKS UP THE TREMBLING MOBSTER IN ONE HAND, AND...
THERE'S ONLY ONE LANGUAGE A KILLER LIKE YOU UNDER-STANDS!
... AND THIS IS IT!!
WHILE, IN THE HOLD BELOW, AN EQUALLY FURIOUS DR. OCTOPUS HURLS THE REMAINING MOBSTERS AWAY FROM HIM AS CASUALLY AS ONE MIGHT SWAT A FLY...
OUT OF MY WAY, YOU WEAKLINGS! I HAVE A SCORE TO SETTLE ON THE DECK ABOVE!
THIS IS THE WRAP-UP, SPIDER-MAN! THE MOMENT I'VE WAITED FOR SINCE YOU SENT ME TO JAIL LAST YEAR!
OCTOPUS IS BACK! I WAS AFRAID OF THIS! HE ALMOST BEAT ME LAST TIME, WHEN I FOUGHT HIM ALONE!
I'VE GOT TO KEEP MOVING... GOT TO STAY OUT OF REACH OF THOSE POWERFUL ARMS OF HIS!
WHY PROLONG THE AGONY?? I'LL GET YOU SOONER OR LATER!
14

YOU CAN'T DO ANY MORE SWINGING IF I GRAB THE LINE YOU'RE SWINGING ON, CAN YOU?
JUST WATCH ME, DOC! I'LL GIVE YOU A LITTLE LESSON IN AERO-GYMNASTICS!!
I SURE WISH I FELT AS CONFIDENT AS I'M TRYING TO SOUND!
LUCKY I HAD ENOUGH MOMENTUM TO KEEP ME SWINGING OVER TO THIS SMOKESTACK!
BAH! KID STUFF! USING MY ARMS TO PROPEL ME, I CAN STILL MOVE FASTER THAN YOU!
'ZAT SO? HOW COME I'M ALWAYS 'WAY AHEAD OF YOU, BIG MOUTH??
CAN'T KEEP SWINGING FOREVER! MAYBE I CAN GET A BREATHER BY DROPPING DOWN TO THIS WALK UNDER THE UPPER DECK!
OHH! I FORGOT ABOUT MY ANKLE! GOT TO KEEP MY WEIGHT OFF IT! IT HURTS WORSE THAN EVER!!
SAY, I THOUGHT I GOT RID OF YOU GUYS BEFORE! DON'T YOU KNOW WHEN YOU'RE NOT WANTED??
MAYBE I CAN CATCH DOC OCK OFF GUARD BY SWINGING UP TO THE DECK BEHIND HIM! IT'S WORTH A TRY!!
15.

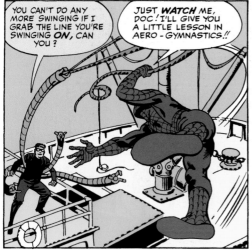

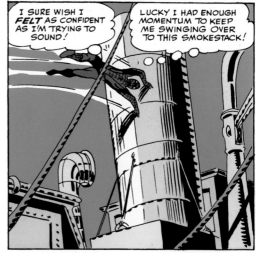

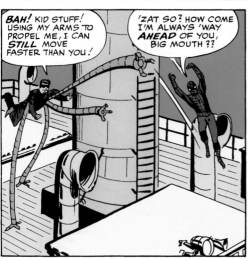

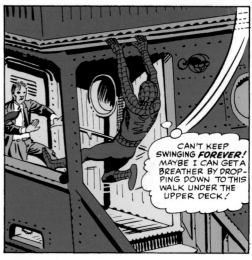

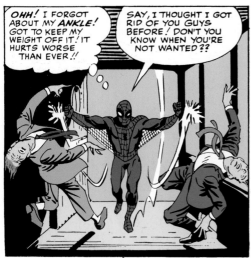

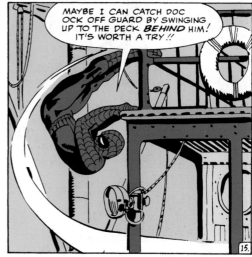

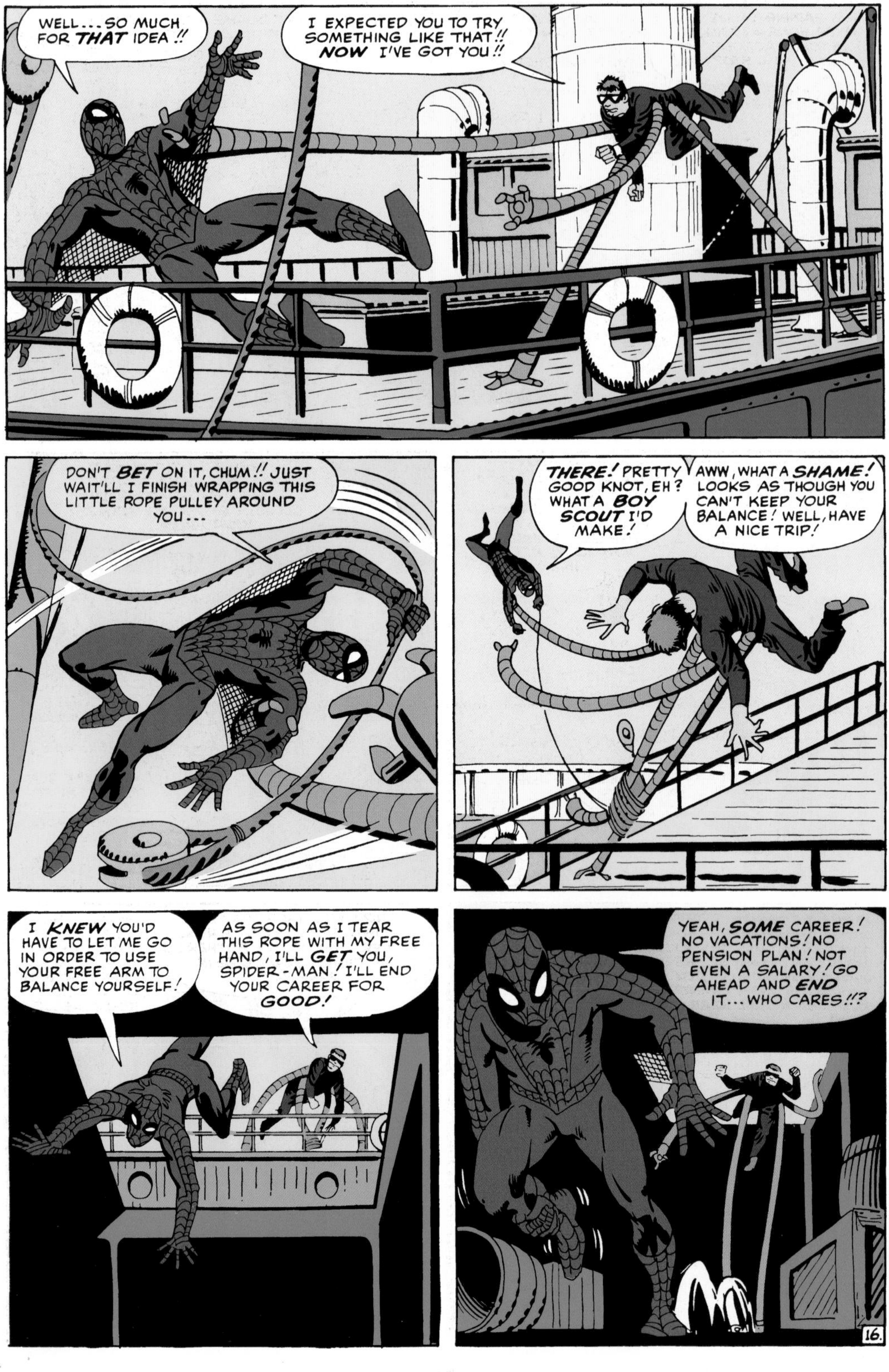
WELL... SO MUCH FOR THAT IDEA !!
I EXPECTED YOU TO TRY SOMETHING LIKE THAT!! NOW I'VE GOT YOU!!
DON'T BET ON IT, CHUM!! JUST WAIT'LL I FINISH WRAPPING THIS LITTLE ROPE PULLEY AROUND YOU...
THERE! PRETTY GOOD KNOT, EH? WHAT A BOY SCOUT I'D MAKE!
AWW, WHAT A SHAME! LOOKS AS THOUGH YOU CAN'T KEEP YOUR BALANCE! WELL, HAVE A NICE TRIP!
I KNEW YOU'D HAVE TO LET ME GO IN ORDER TO USE YOUR FREE ARM TO BALANCE YOURSELF!
AS SOON AS I TEAR THIS ROPE WITH MY FREE HAND, I'LL GET YOU, SPIDER-MAN! I'LL END YOUR CAREER FOR GOOD!
YEAH, SOME CAREER! NO VACATIONS! NO PENSION PLAN! NOT EVEN A SALARY! GO AHEAD AND END IT... WHO CARES!!?
16.

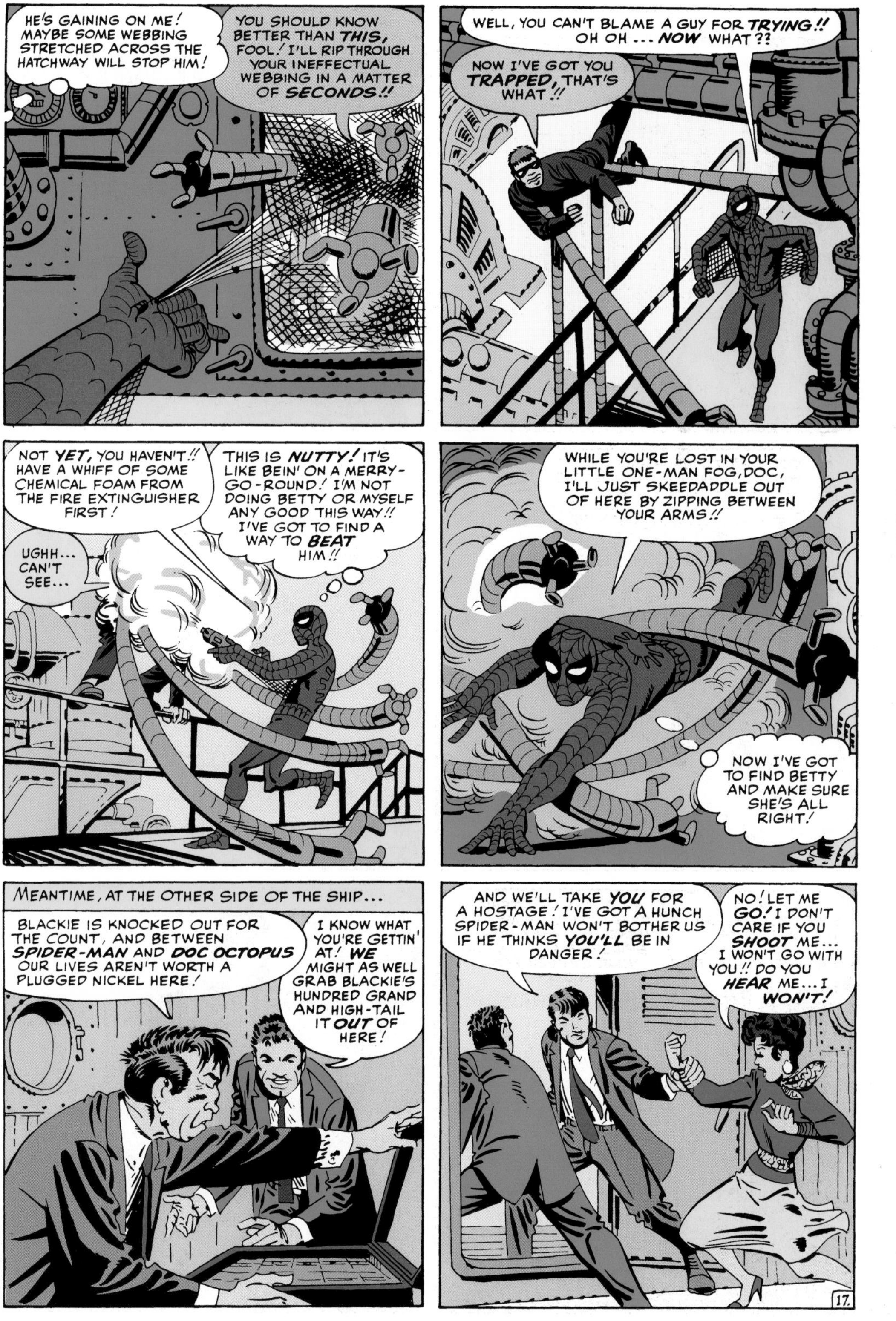
HE'S GAINING ON ME! MAYBE SOME WEBBING STRETCHED ACROSS THE HATCHWAY WILL STOP HIM!
YOU SHOULD KNOW BETTER THAN THIS, FOOL! I'LL RIP THROUGH YOUR INEFFECTUAL WEBBING IN A MATTER OF SECONDS!!
WELL, YOU CAN'T BLAME A GUY FOR TRYING!! OH OH ... NOW WHAT??
NOW I'VE GOT YOU TRAPPED, THAT'S WHAT!!
NOT YET, YOU HAVEN'T!! HAVE A WHIFF OF SOME CHEMICAL FOAM FROM THE FIRE EXTINGUISHER FIRST!
THIS IS NUTTY! IT'S LIKE BEIN' ON A MERRY-GO-ROUND! I'M NOT DOING BETTY OR MYSELF ANY GOOD THIS WAY!! I'VE GOT TO FIND A WAY TO BEAT HIM!!
UGHH... CAN'T SEE...
WHILE YOU'RE LOST IN YOUR LITTLE ONE-MAN FOG, DOC, I'LL JUST SKEEDADDLE OUT OF HERE BY ZIPPING BETWEEN YOUR ARMS!!
NOW I'VE GOT TO FIND BETTY AND MAKE SURE SHE'S ALL RIGHT!
MEANTIME, AT THE OTHER SIDE OF THE SHIP...
BLACKIE IS KNOCKED OUT FOR THE COUNT, AND BETWEEN SPIDER-MAN AND DOC OCTOPUS OUR LIVES AREN'T WORTH A PLUGGED NICKEL HERE!
I KNOW WHAT YOU'RE GETTIN' AT! WE MIGHT AS WELL GRAB BLACKIE'S HUNDRED GRAND AND HIGH-TAIL IT OUT OF HERE!
AND WE'LL TAKE YOU FOR A HOSTAGE! I'VE GOT A HUNCH SPIDER-MAN WON'T BOTHER US IF HE THINKS YOU'LL BE IN DANGER!
NO! LET ME GO! I DON'T CARE IF YOU SHOOT ME... I WON'T GO WITH YOU!! DO YOU HEAR ME... I WON'T!
17.

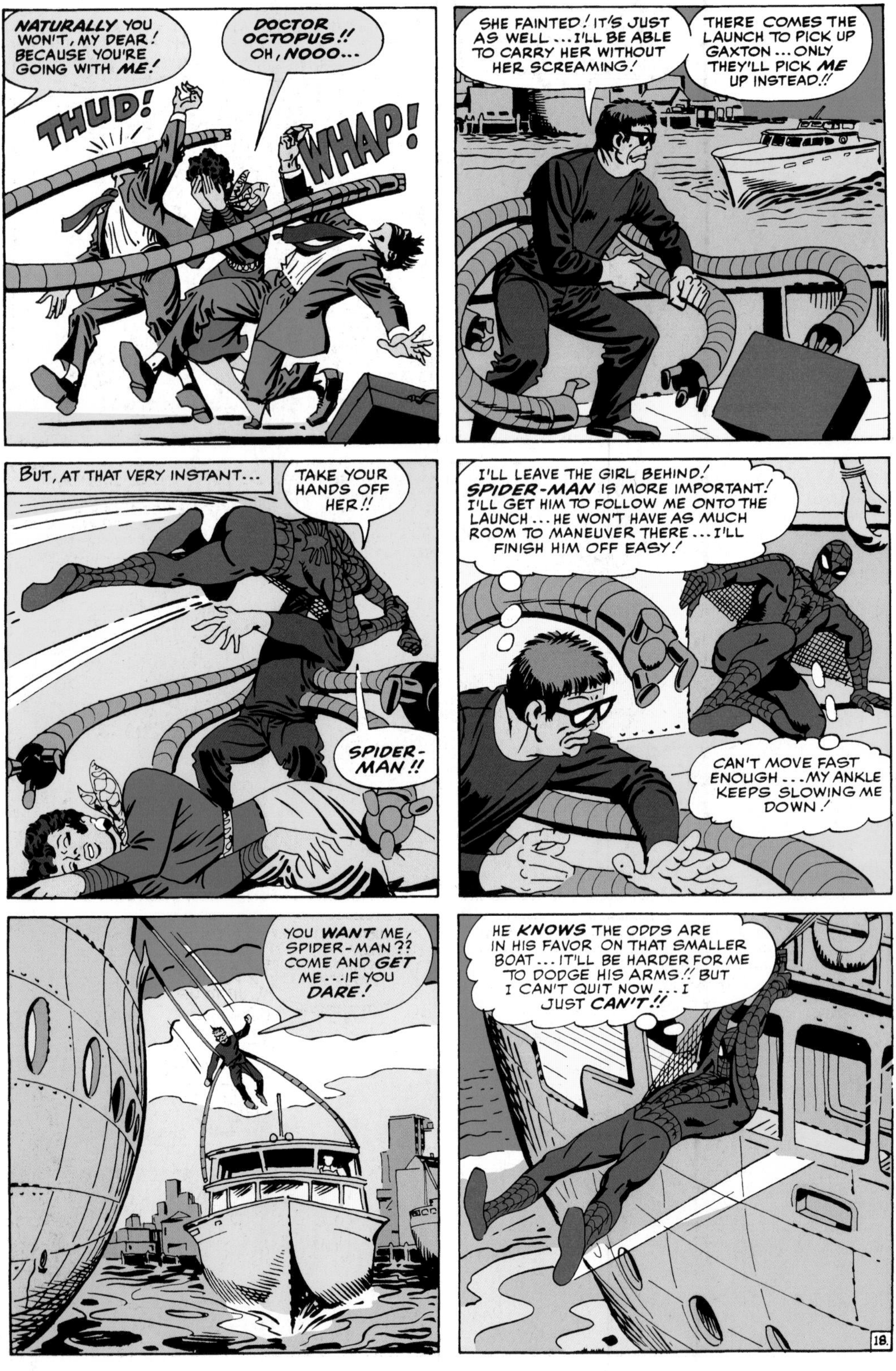
NATURALLY YOU WON'T, MY DEAR! BECAUSE YOU'RE GOING WITH ME!
DOCTOR OCTOPUS!! OH, NOOO...
THUD!
WHAP!
SHE FAINTED! IT'S JUST AS WELL... I'LL BE ABLE TO CARRY HER WITHOUT HER SCREAMING!
THERE COMES THE LAUNCH TO PICK UP GAXTON... ONLY THEY'LL PICK ME UP INSTEAD!!
BUT, AT THAT VERY INSTANT...
TAKE YOUR HANDS OFF HER!!
SPIDER-MAN!!
I'LL LEAVE THE GIRL BEHIND! SPIDER-MAN IS MORE IMPORTANT! I'LL GET HIM TO FOLLOW ME ONTO THE LAUNCH... HE WON'T HAVE AS MUCH ROOM TO MANEUVER THERE... I'LL FINISH HIM OFF EASY!
CAN'T MOVE FAST ENOUGH... MY ANKLE KEEPS SLOWING ME DOWN!
YOU WANT ME, SPIDER-MAN?? COME AND GET ME...IF YOU DARE!
HE KNOWS THE ODDS ARE IN HIS FAVOR ON THAT SMALLER BOAT... IT'LL BE HARDER FOR ME TO DODGE HIS ARMS!! BUT I CAN'T QUIT NOW... I JUST CAN'T!!
18.

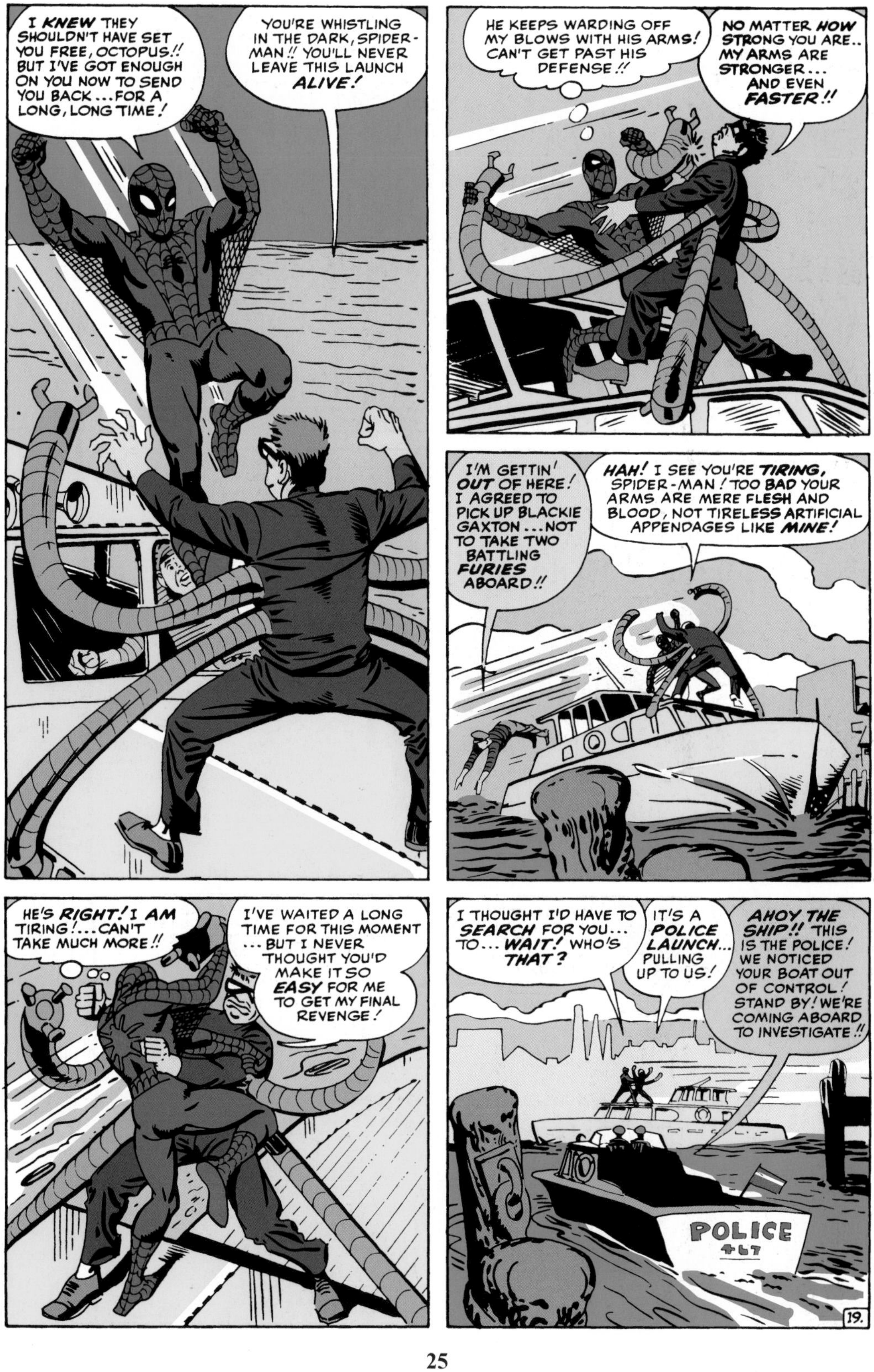
I KNEW THEY SHOULDN'T HAVE SET YOU FREE, OCTOPUS!! BUT I'VE GOT ENOUGH ON YOU NOW TO SEND YOU BACK...FOR A LONG, LONG TIME!
YOU'RE WHISTLING IN THE DARK, SPIDER-MAN!! YOU'LL NEVER LEAVE THIS LAUNCH ALIVE!
HE KEEPS WARDING OFF MY BLOWS WITH HIS ARMS! CAN'T GET PAST HIS DEFENSE!!
NO MATTER HOW STRONG YOU ARE.. MY ARMS ARE STRONGER... AND EVEN FASTER!!
I'M GETTIN' OUT OF HERE! I AGREED TO PICK UP BLACKIE GAXTON...NOT TO TAKE TWO BATTLING FURIES ABOARD!!
HAH! I SEE YOU'RE TIRING, SPIDER-MAN! TOO BAD YOUR ARMS ARE MERE FLESH AND BLOOD, NOT TIRELESS ARTIFICIAL APPENDAGES LIKE MINE!
HE'S RIGHT! I AM TIRING!...CAN'T TAKE MUCH MORE!!
I'VE WAITED A LONG TIME FOR THIS MOMENT ...BUT I NEVER THOUGHT YOU'D MAKE IT SO EASY FOR ME TO GET MY FINAL REVENGE!
I THOUGHT I'D HAVE TO SEARCH FOR YOU... TO...WAIT! WHO'S THAT?
IT'S A POLICE LAUNCH... PULLING UP TO US!
AHOY THE SHIP!! THIS IS THE POLICE! WE NOTICED YOUR BOAT OUT OF CONTROL! STAND BY! WE'RE COMING ABOARD TO INVESTIGATE!!
POLICE
467
19.

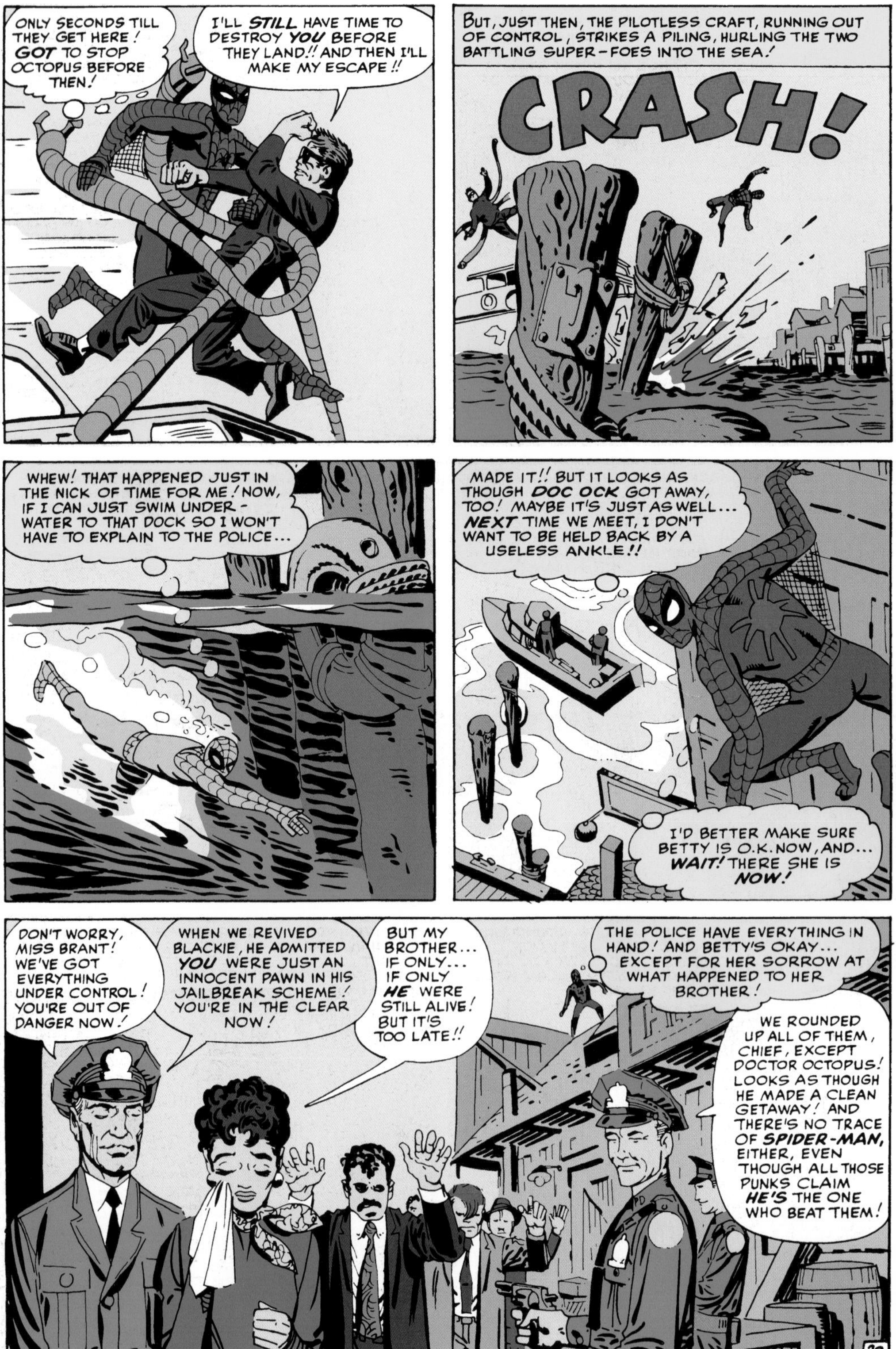

ONLY SECONDS TILL THEY GET HERE! GOT TO STOP OCTOPUS BEFORE THEN!
I'LL STILL HAVE TIME TO DESTROY YOU BEFORE THEY LAND!! AND THEN I'LL MAKE MY ESCAPE!!
BUT, JUST THEN, THE PILOTLESS CRAFT, RUNNING OUT OF CONTROL, STRIKES A PILING, HURLING THE TWO BATTLING SUPER-FOES INTO THE SEA!
CRASH!
WHEW! THAT HAPPENED JUST IN THE NICK OF TIME FOR ME! NOW, IF I CAN JUST SWIM UNDER-WATER TO THAT DOCK SO I WON'T HAVE TO EXPLAIN TO THE POLICE...
MADE IT!! BUT IT LOOKS AS THOUGH DOC OCK GOT AWAY, TOO! MAYBE IT'S JUST AS WELL... NEXT TIME WE MEET, I DON'T WANT TO BE HELD BACK BY A USELESS ANKLE!!
I'D BETTER MAKE SURE BETTY IS O.K. NOW, AND... WAIT! THERE SHE IS NOW!
DON'T WORRY, MISS BRANT! WE'VE GOT EVERYTHING UNDER CONTROL! YOU'RE OUT OF DANGER NOW!
WHEN WE REVIVED BLACKIE, HE ADMITTED YOU WERE JUST AN INNOCENT PAWN IN HIS JAILBREAK SCHEME! YOU'RE IN THE CLEAR NOW!
BUT MY BROTHER... IF ONLY... IF ONLY HE WERE STILL ALIVE! BUT IT'S TOO LATE!!
THE POLICE HAVE EVERYTHING IN HAND! AND BETTY'S OKAY... EXCEPT FOR HER SORROW AT WHAT HAPPENED TO HER BROTHER!
WE ROUNDED UP ALL OF THEM, CHIEF, EXCEPT DOCTOR OCTOPUS! LOOKS AS THOUGH HE MADE A CLEAN GETAWAY! AND THERE'S NO TRACE OF SPIDER-MAN, EITHER, EVEN THOUGH ALL THOSE PUNKS CLAIM HE'S THE ONE WHO BEAT THEM!
20.

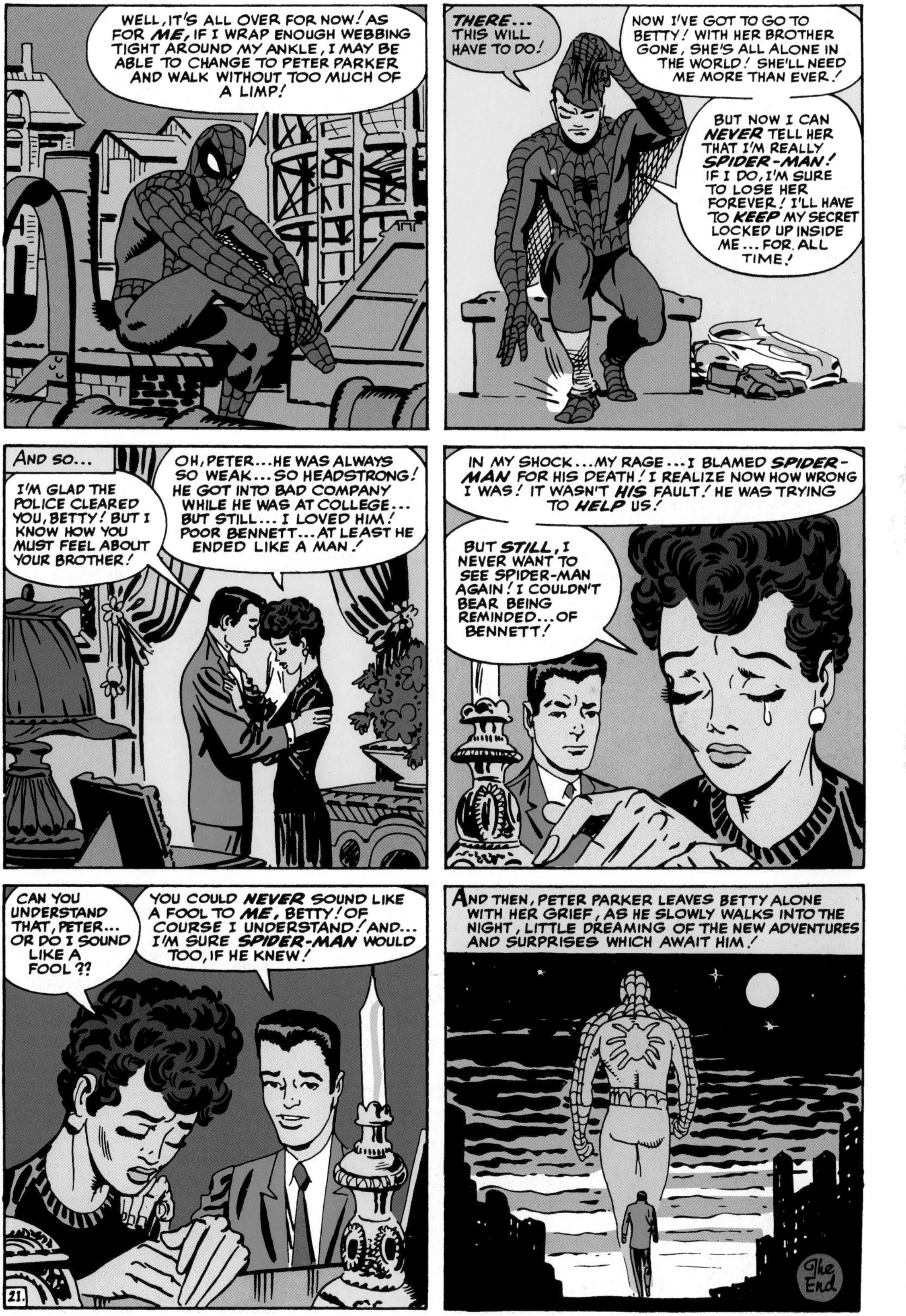
WELL, IT'S ALL OVER FOR NOW! AS FOR ME, IF I WRAP ENOUGH WEBBING TIGHT AROUND MY ANKLE, I MAY BE ABLE TO CHANGE TO PETER PARKER AND WALK WITHOUT TOO MUCH OF A LIMP!
THERE... THIS WILL HAVE TO DO!
NOW I'VE GOT TO GO TO BETTY! WITH HER BROTHER GONE, SHE'S ALL ALONE IN THE WORLD! SHE'LL NEED ME MORE THAN EVER!
BUT NOW I CAN NEVER TELL HER THAT I'M REALLY SPIDER-MAN! IF I DO, I'M SURE TO LOSE HER FOREVER! I'LL HAVE TO KEEP MY SECRET LOCKED UP INSIDE ME... FOR ALL TIME!
AND SO...
I'M GLAD THE POLICE CLEARED YOU, BETTY! BUT I KNOW HOW YOU MUST FEEL ABOUT YOUR BROTHER!
OH, PETER... HE WAS ALWAYS SO WEAK... SO HEADSTRONG! HE GOT INTO BAD COMPANY WHILE HE WAS AT COLLEGE... BUT STILL... I LOVED HIM! POOR BENNETT... AT LEAST HE ENDED LIKE A MAN!
IN MY SHOCK... MY RAGE... I BLAMED SPIDER-MAN FOR HIS DEATH! I REALIZE NOW HOW WRONG I WAS! IT WASN'T HIS FAULT! HE WAS TRYING TO HELP US!
BUT STILL, I NEVER WANT TO SEE SPIDER-MAN AGAIN! I COULDN'T BEAR BEING REMINDED... OF BENNETT!
CAN YOU UNDERSTAND THAT, PETER... OR DO I SOUND LIKE A FOOL??
YOU COULD NEVER SOUND LIKE A FOOL TO ME, BETTY! OF COURSE I UNDERSTAND! AND... I'M SURE SPIDER-MAN WOULD TOO, IF HE KNEW!
21.
AND THEN, PETER PARKER LEAVES BETTY ALONE WITH HER GRIEF, AS HE SLOWLY WALKS INTO THE NIGHT, LITTLE DREAMING OF THE NEW ADVENTURES AND SURPRISES WHICH AWAIT HIM!
The End

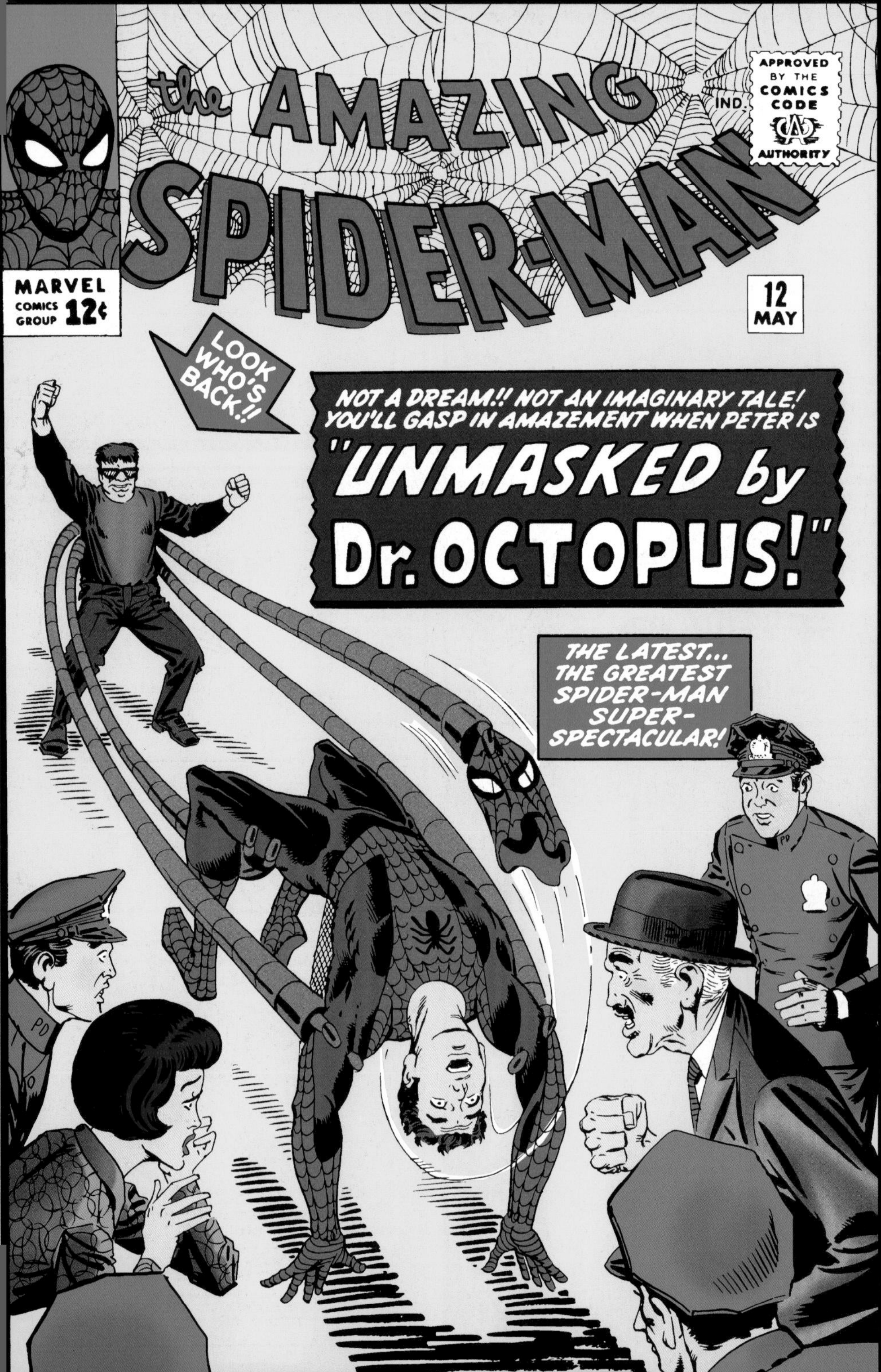
APPROVED BY THE COMICS CODE AUTHORITY
the AMAZING SPIDER-MAN
IND.
MARVEL COMICS GROUP 12¢
12 MAY
LOOK WHO'S BACK.!!
NOT A DREAM!! NOT AN IMAGINARY TALE! YOU'LL GASP IN AMAZEMENT WHEN PETER IS
"UNMASKED by Dr. OCTOPUS!"
THE LATEST... THE GREATEST SPIDER-MAN SUPER-SPECTACULAR!
PD
PD

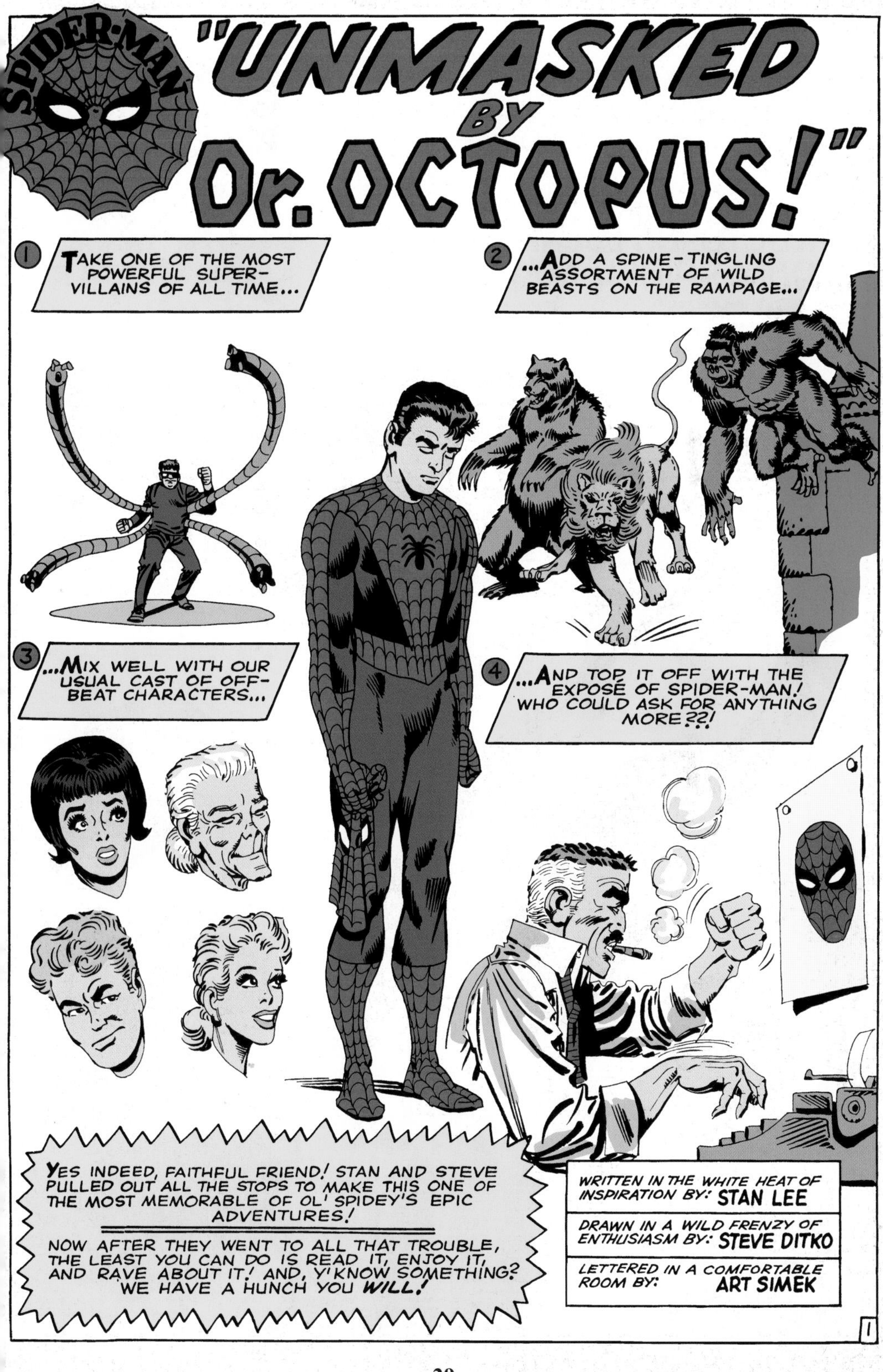

SPIDER-MAN
"UNMASKED BY Dr. OCTOPUS!"
1 TAKE ONE OF THE MOST POWERFUL SUPER-VILLAINS OF ALL TIME...
2 ...ADD A SPINE-TINGLING ASSORTMENT OF WILD BEASTS ON THE RAMPAGE...
3 ...MIX WELL WITH OUR USUAL CAST OF OFF-BEAT CHARACTERS...
4 ...AND TOP IT OFF WITH THE EXPOSÉ OF SPIDER-MAN! WHO COULD ASK FOR ANYTHING MORE??!
YES INDEED, FAITHFUL FRIEND! STAN AND STEVE PULLED OUT ALL THE STOPS TO MAKE THIS ONE OF THE MOST MEMORABLE OF OL' SPIDEY'S EPIC ADVENTURES!
NOW AFTER THEY WENT TO ALL THAT TROUBLE, THE LEAST YOU CAN DO IS READ IT, ENJOY IT, AND RAVE ABOUT IT! AND, Y'KNOW SOMETHING? WE HAVE A HUNCH YOU WILL!
WRITTEN IN THE WHITE HEAT OF INSPIRATION BY: STAN LEE
DRAWN IN A WILD FRENZY OF ENTHUSIASM BY: STEVE DITKO
LETTERED IN A COMFORTABLE ROOM BY: ART SIMEK
1

AS ALL OF OUR WELL-READ READERS KNOW, SPIDER-MAN BATTLED DR. OCTOPUS LAST ISSUE, AND WHILE THE AMAZING TEEN-AGER FOILED THE SUPER-VILLAIN'S PLANS, HE WAS UNABLE TO PREVENT HIS ESCAPE! HENCE THESE HEADLINES IN THE BUGLE...

DAILY BUGLE

WEATHER

FINAL EDITION

DR. OCTOPUS ESCAPES FROM SPIDER-MAN!

PHILADELPHIA, PA. (I.P.)

ONCE AGAIN, THE MYSTERIOUS SPIDER-MAN HAS INTERFERED WITH POLICE AND ALLOWED A DANGEROUS CRIMINAL TO GET AWAY SCOT FREE!

HOW MUCH LONGER IS THIS MASKED NUISANCE TO BE PERMITTED TO MAKE A COMPLETE MOCKERY OF JUSTICE AND TO USUAL FACE A SIGHT OUT OF ALL THE POLICE IM ALL IN THE ENTIRE DISTRICT OF TH...

SPIDER-MAN... OVERRATED CRIME-FIGHTER!

DR. OCTOPUS... STILL AT LARGE!

READING THE NEWS ITEM, WHICH WAS OBVIOUSLY WRITTEN BY ORDER OF PUBLISHER J. JONAH JAMESON WHO HATES SPIDER-MAN, THE ANGRY ADVENTURER DECIDES TO PAY JAMESON A VISIT...

IF I PUT OUT A FOREST FIRE SINGLE-HANDED, I'LL BET JONAH WOULD RAP ME FOR WASTING TOO MUCH WATER! SAY! WHAT'S GOING ON IN HIS OFFICE?

I QUIT! NOBODY COULD WORK FOR A TYRANT LIKE YOU!

THAT'S THE GAL HE HIRED TO FILL IN TILL BETTY RETURNED FROM PHILADELPHIA!

WAIT! YOU CAN'T DO THIS! I NEED A SECRETARY! COME BACK!

YOU DON'T NEED A SECRETARY--YOU NEED A PSYCHIATRIST!

HMMPH! BLAMED EMPLOYEES! THEY EXPECT TO BE TREATED WITH KID GLOVES! JUST BECAUSE I SHOUTED AT HER...

HELLO, MR. JAMESON! I'VE RETURNED--THAT IS, IF YOU STILL WANT ME?

BETTY BRANT! IF I WANT YOU?? DON'T JUST STAND THERE, GIRL-- GET TO WORK!

NOW THAT BETTY'S BACK, I'LL CHANGE TO PETER PARKER! I CAN'T WAIT TO SEE HER-- TO TALK TO HER...

MR. JAMESON, HAS PETER PARKER BEEN IN LATELY WITH ANY PHOTOS?

NO! I HAVEN'T SEEN HIM! HE'S PROBABLY TOO LAZY TO WORK... JUST LIKE EVERYONE ELSE I GET STUCK WITH!

MINUTES LATER...

BETTY! GOSH, I'M GLAD TO SEE YOU! I'VE BEEN WAITING TO HEAR FROM YOU...

OUT, PARKER! THIS IS AN OFFICE, NOT A SOCIAL CLUB! YOU CAN COME IN HERE WHENEVER YOU HAVE A SET OF EXCLUSIVE NEWS PHOTOS FOR ME, AND NOT BEFORE! NOW GET!

I'LL SEE YOU LATER, PETER! CALL ME AT HOME!

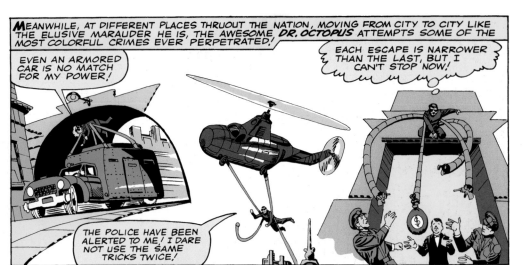

MEANWHILE, AT DIFFERENT PLACES THRUOUT THE NATION, MOVING FROM CITY TO CITY LIKE THE ELUSIVE MARAUDER HE IS, THE AWESOME *DR. OCTOPUS* ATTEMPTS SOME OF THE MOST COLORFUL CRIMES EVER PERPETRATED!

EVEN AN ARMORED CAR IS NO MATCH FOR MY POWER!

EACH ESCAPE IS NARROWER THAN THE LAST, BUT I CAN'T STOP NOW!

THE POLICE HAVE BEEN ALERTED TO ME! I DARE NOT USE THE SAME TRICKS TWICE!

I'VE GOT TO CONTINUE MY SPECTACULAR CAREER, SO THAT *SPIDER-MAN* WILL READ ABOUT MY EXPLOITS AND TRY TO ATTACK ME AGAIN!

I *KNOW* I'M STRONGER THAN HE IS! I KNOW THAT I'LL DESTROY HIM WHEN NEXT WE MEET! BUT, SO LONG AS HE LIVES, I'LL NEVER BE TRULY SAFE! I'VE *GOT* TO FORCE HIM TO FIGHT ME AGAIN!

BUT WHY HASN'T HE FOLLOWED ME? I'VE GIVEN HIM EVERY CHANCE-- ALL THE BAIT HE NEEDS! PERHAPS I'LL HAVE TO RETURN TO NEW YORK AND FIND *HIM!*

AND WHY *HASN'T* SPIDER-MAN FOLLOWED THE TRAIL OF HIS ARCH FOE AROUND THE COUNTRY?? THE ANSWER IS REALLY VERY SIMPLE, WHEN WE REALIZE WE'RE DEALING WITH A TRUE-TO-LIFE YOUNGSTER...

YOU FEEL A LITTLE WARM, PETER! YOU'D BETTER STAY IN TONIGHT, DEAR! YOU MAY BE GETTING A COLD!

IF ONLY I COULD HEAD OUT WEST WHERE DOC OCK WAS LAST RE-PORTED! BUT I HAVEN'T MONEY FOR THE FARE, AND MY END TERM EXAMS ARE COMING UP SOON, AND AUNT MAY WOULD NEVER LET ME GO *ANY-WAY!*

THE NEXT DAY...

OH WELL, MAYBE OCTOPUS WILL RETURN TO NEW YORK SOMEDAY, AND THEN--*SAY!* I WONDER WHAT THE KIDS ARE READING ABOUT?

HOW DO YOU LIKE *THIS?* THE DAILY BUGLE IS *STILL* WRIT-ING EDITORIALS CALLING SPIDER-MAN A FAKE AND A COWARD!

THAT'S EASY FOR JAMESON TO SAY! I'D LIKE TO SEE *HIM* TACKLE DR. OCTOPUS!

I WONDER IF WE'LL EVER FIND OUT WHO SPIDER-MAN REALLY *IS?*

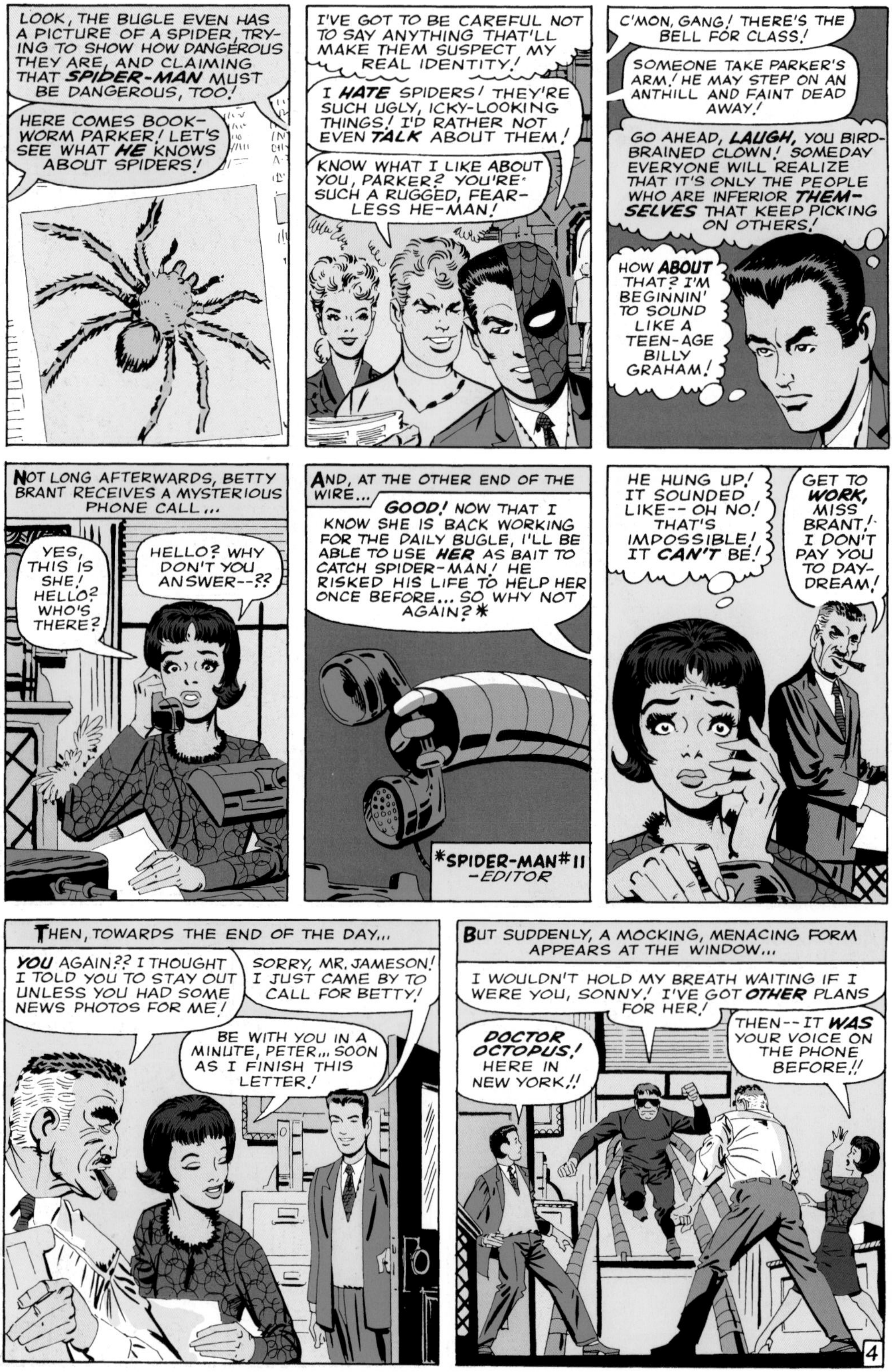
LOOK, THE BUGLE EVEN HAS A PICTURE OF A SPIDER, TRYING TO SHOW HOW DANGEROUS THEY ARE, AND CLAIMING THAT SPIDER-MAN MUST BE DANGEROUS, TOO!
HERE COMES BOOKWORM PARKER! LET'S SEE WHAT HE KNOWS ABOUT SPIDERS!
I'VE GOT TO BE CAREFUL NOT TO SAY ANYTHING THAT'LL MAKE THEM SUSPECT MY REAL IDENTITY!
I HATE SPIDERS! THEY'RE SUCH UGLY, ICKY-LOOKING THINGS! I'D RATHER NOT EVEN TALK ABOUT THEM!
KNOW WHAT I LIKE ABOUT YOU, PARKER? YOU'RE SUCH A RUGGED, FEARLESS HE-MAN!
C'MON, GANG! THERE'S THE BELL FOR CLASS!
SOMEONE TAKE PARKER'S ARM! HE MAY STEP ON AN ANTHILL AND FAINT DEAD AWAY!
GO AHEAD, LAUGH, YOU BIRD-BRAINED CLOWN! SOMEDAY EVERYONE WILL REALIZE THAT IT'S ONLY THE PEOPLE WHO ARE INFERIOR THEMSELVES THAT KEEP PICKING ON OTHERS!
HOW ABOUT THAT? I'M BEGINNIN' TO SOUND LIKE A TEEN-AGE BILLY GRAHAM!
NOT LONG AFTERWARDS, BETTY BRANT RECEIVES A MYSTERIOUS PHONE CALL...
YES, THIS IS SHE! HELLO? WHO'S THERE?
HELLO? WHY DON'T YOU ANSWER--??
AND, AT THE OTHER END OF THE WIRE...
GOOD! NOW THAT I KNOW SHE IS BACK WORKING FOR THE DAILY BUGLE, I'LL BE ABLE TO USE HER AS BAIT TO CATCH SPIDER-MAN! HE RISKED HIS LIFE TO HELP HER ONCE BEFORE... SO WHY NOT AGAIN?*
*SPIDER-MAN #11 -EDITOR
HE HUNG UP! IT SOUNDED LIKE-- OH NO! THAT'S IMPOSSIBLE! IT CAN'T BE!
GET TO WORK, MISS BRANT! I DON'T PAY YOU TO DAY-DREAM!
THEN, TOWARDS THE END OF THE DAY...
YOU AGAIN?? I THOUGHT I TOLD YOU TO STAY OUT UNLESS YOU HAD SOME NEWS PHOTOS FOR ME!
SORRY, MR. JAMESON! I JUST CAME BY TO CALL FOR BETTY!
BE WITH YOU IN A MINUTE, PETER... SOON AS I FINISH THIS LETTER!
BUT SUDDENLY, A MOCKING, MENACING FORM APPEARS AT THE WINDOW...
I WOULDN'T HOLD MY BREATH WAITING IF I WERE YOU, SONNY! I'VE GOT OTHER PLANS FOR HER!
DOCTOR OCTOPUS! HERE IN NEW YORK!!
THEN--IT WAS YOUR VOICE ON THE PHONE BEFORE!!
4

LIKE A POWERFUL OCTOPUS' TENTACLE, A LONG ARTIFICIAL ARM SNAKES OUT, AND...

DON'T BE ALARMED, YOUNG LADY! YOU WILL NOT BE HARMED!

NO-- NO! DON'T --YOU CAN'T! HELP!

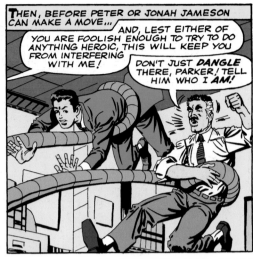

THEN, BEFORE PETER OR JONAH JAMESON CAN MAKE A MOVE...

AND, LEST EITHER OF YOU ARE FOOLISH ENOUGH TO TRY TO DO ANYTHING HEROIC, THIS WILL KEEP YOU FROM INTERFERING WITH ME!

DON'T JUST DANGLE THERE, PARKER! TELL HIM WHO I AM!

I CAN'T FIGHT BACK NOW-- NOT IN FRONT OF BETTY AND JAMESON! IT WOULD GIVE MY IDENTITY AWAY! I'VE GOT TO BIDE MY TIME!

NOW LISTEN-- NO ONE WILL BE HURT IF YOU DO AS I SAY! JAMESON, PUT A NOTE IN YOUR PAPER TELLING SPIDER-MAN TO CONTACT YOU! WHEN HE DOES, TELL HIM I HAVE THE GIRL PRISONER AT CONEY ISLAND! IF HE WANTS HER-- HE MUST COME FOR HER-- ALONE!

YOU MAY SEND ONE PHOTOGRAPHER ALSO-- TO TAKE PICTURES OF THE DEFEAT I SHALL HAND SPIDER-MAN! THAT IS ALL!

I'LL SEND YOU, PARKER! IT'LL BE THE SCOOP OF THE CENTURY!

HOW CAN I GO AS SPIDER-MAN AND AS PETER PARKER ???

REMEMBER-- SPIDER-MAN MUST SHOW UP IN ORDER TO SAVE THE GIRL! AND THE POLICE MUST NOT BE TOLD-- OR ELSE!

BETTY-- DON'T BE AFRAID! SPIDER-MAN WILL SAVE YOU!

I'VE GOT TO PRINT AN EXTRA RIGHT AWAY--TELLING SPIDER-MAN TO CON- TACT ME! I HOPE HE'LL SEE IT!

5

AND THEN, AS A SPECIAL, EXTRA EDITION OF THE BUGLE HITS THE NEWSSTANDS...

GET DOWN TO CONEY ISLAND, PARKER! WAIT FOR SPIDER-MAN TO SHOW UP! BRING PLENTY OF FILM! IF YOU BOTCH THIS ASSIGNMENT, I'LL HAVE YOUR HIDE!

DON'T WORRY-- NOTHING COULD KEEP ME AWAY!

STRANGE-- I FEEL KIND OF WOOSY-- MY HEAD IS WARM-- MAYBE I AM GETTING ILL, AS AUNT MAY SAID!

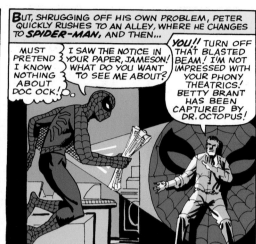

BUT, SHRUGGING OFF HIS OWN PROBLEM, PETER QUICKLY RUSHES TO AN ALLEY, WHERE HE CHANGES TO SPIDER-MAN, AND THEN...

MUST PRETEND I KNOW NOTHING ABOUT DOC OCK!

I SAW THE NOTICE IN YOUR PAPER, JAMESON! WHAT DO YOU WANT TO SEE ME ABOUT?

YOU!! TURN OFF THAT BLASTED BEAM! I'M NOT IMPRESSED WITH YOUR PHONY THEATRICS! BETTY BRANT HAS BEEN CAPTURED BY DR. OCTOPUS!

THEN, AFTER JAMESON HAS EXPLAINED...

NOW FOR CONEY ISLAND! HEY--I MUST BE SICK! I'M NOT CLINGING TO THE WALL AS WELL AS USUAL!

MEANWHILE... EVEN THOUGH PARKER IS MY BEST FREE-LANCE PHOTOGRAPHER, I CAN'T TAKE ANY CHANCE OF HIM MUFFING THIS JOB! MAYBE I'D BETTER GET TO CONEY ISLAND MYSELF!

IT'S MID-WINTER, SO THE AMUSEMENTS WILL ALL BE SHUT DOWN FOR THE SEASON! I'LL MAKE SURE THAT DR. OCTOPUS DOESN'T SEE ME, BUT I'LL HAVE A CHANCE TO OBSERVE WHATEVER HAPPENS, FIRST HAND!

AND, ATOP THE HIGHEST ROLLER COASTER AT THE AMUSEMENT PARK...

SPIDER-MAN SHOULD HAVE SEEN THE PAPER BY NOW! THAT MEANS HE'LL BE ARRIVING AT ANY MOMENT-- FOR HIS FINAL BATTLE!

B-BUT WHAT IF HE DOESN'T SHOW UP?

THAT WILL BE TOO BAD, MY DEAR! FOR YOU! AND NOW, I'LL LOWER YOU TO THE GROUND, SO THE PHOTOGRAPHER CAN EASILY GET GOOD PICTURES OF MY VICTORY OVER THAT MASKED FOOL! THOSE PICTURES, FOR THE WORLD TO SEE, WILL BE SPIDER-MAN'S GREATEST HUMILIATION!

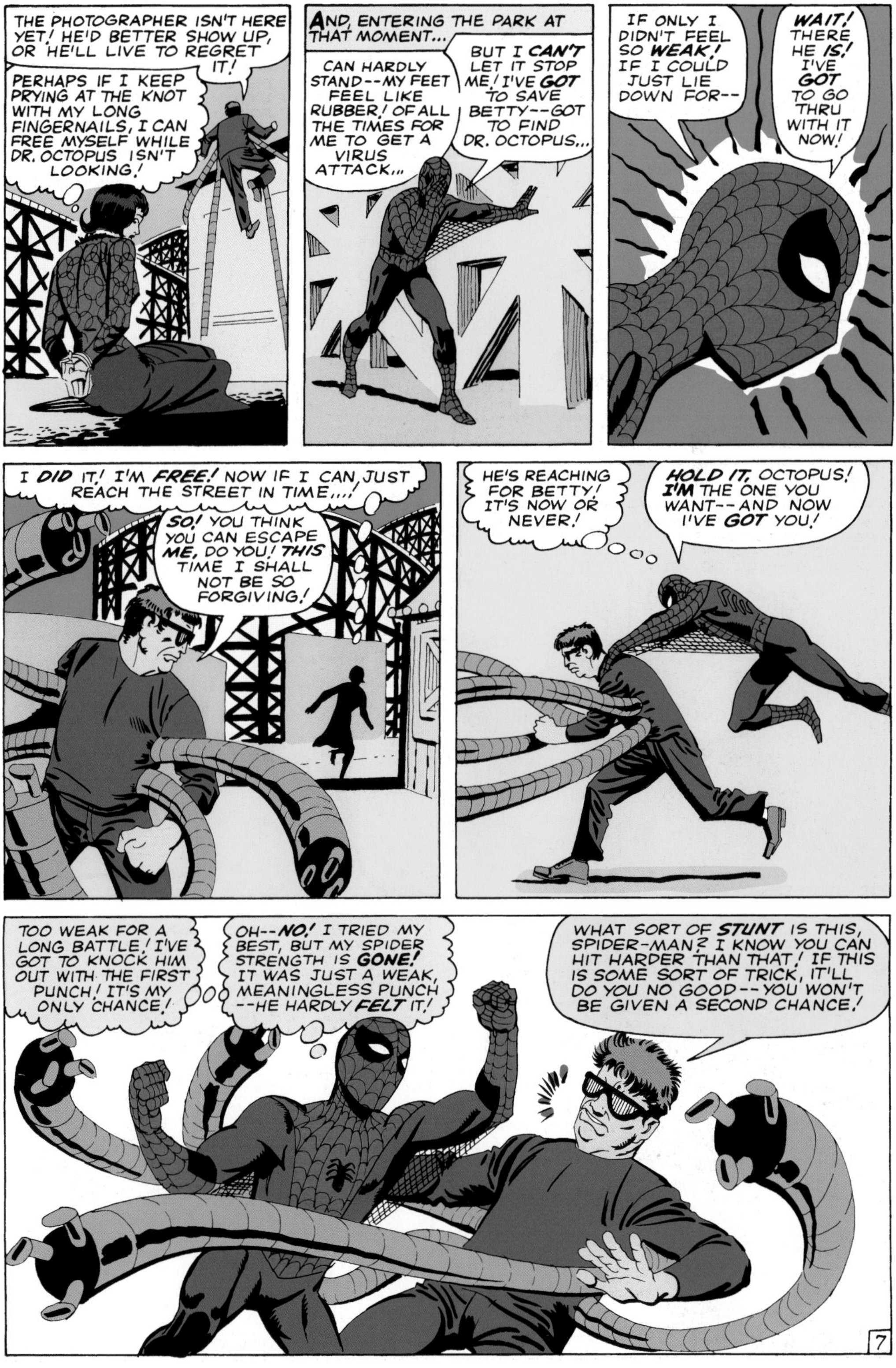
THE PHOTOGRAPHER ISN'T HERE YET! HE'D BETTER SHOW UP, OR HE'LL LIVE TO REGRET IT!
PERHAPS IF I KEEP PRYING AT THE KNOT WITH MY LONG FINGERNAILS, I CAN FREE MYSELF WHILE DR. OCTOPUS ISN'T LOOKING!
AND, ENTERING THE PARK AT THAT MOMENT...
CAN HARDLY STAND--MY FEET FEEL LIKE RUBBER! OF ALL THE TIMES FOR ME TO GET A VIRUS ATTACK...
BUT I CAN'T LET IT STOP ME! I'VE GOT TO SAVE BETTY--GOT TO FIND DR. OCTOPUS...
IF ONLY I DIDN'T FEEL SO WEAK! IF I COULD JUST LIE DOWN FOR--
WAIT! THERE HE IS! I'VE GOT TO GO THRU WITH IT NOW!
I DID IT! I'M FREE! NOW IF I CAN JUST REACH THE STREET IN TIME...!
SO! YOU THINK YOU CAN ESCAPE ME, DO YOU! THIS TIME I SHALL NOT BE SO FORGIVING!
HE'S REACHING FOR BETTY! IT'S NOW OR NEVER!
HOLD IT, OCTOPUS! I'M THE ONE YOU WANT--AND NOW I'VE GOT YOU!
TOO WEAK FOR A LONG BATTLE! I'VE GOT TO KNOCK HIM OUT WITH THE FIRST PUNCH! IT'S MY ONLY CHANCE!
OH--NO! I TRIED MY BEST, BUT MY SPIDER STRENGTH IS GONE! IT WAS JUST A WEAK, MEANINGLESS PUNCH --HE HARDLY FELT IT!
WHAT SORT OF STUNT IS THIS, SPIDER-MAN? I KNOW YOU CAN HIT HARDER THAN THAT! IF THIS IS SOME SORT OF TRICK, IT'LL DO YOU NO GOOD--YOU WON'T BE GIVEN A SECOND CHANCE!
7

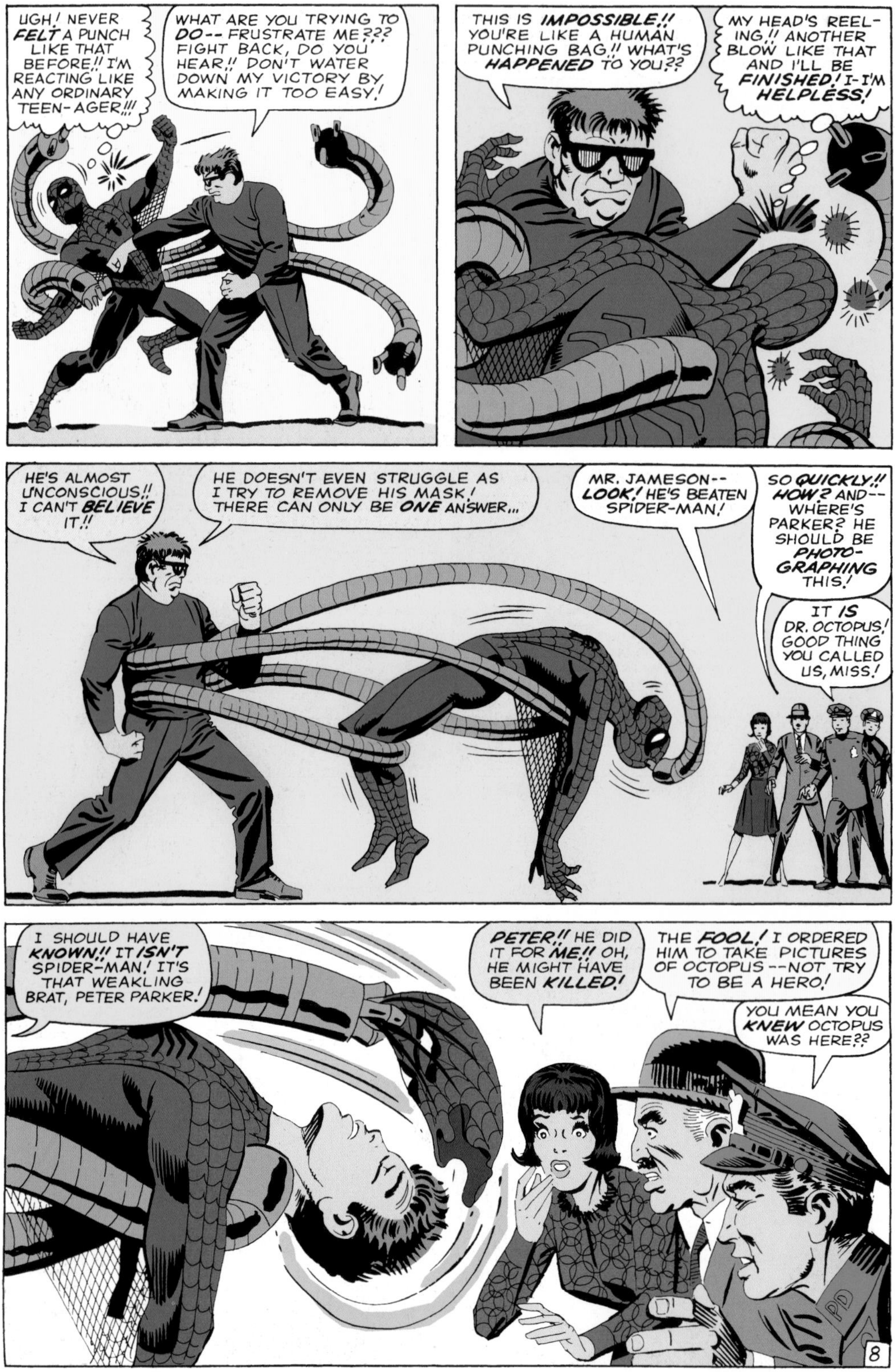
UGH! NEVER FELT A PUNCH LIKE THAT BEFORE!! I'M REACTING LIKE ANY ORDINARY TEEN-AGER!!!
WHAT ARE YOU TRYING TO DO-- FRUSTRATE ME??? FIGHT BACK, DO YOU HEAR!! DON'T WATER DOWN MY VICTORY BY MAKING IT TOO EASY!
THIS IS IMPOSSIBLE!! YOU'RE LIKE A HUMAN PUNCHING BAG!! WHAT'S HAPPENED TO YOU??
MY HEAD'S REEL-ING!! ANOTHER BLOW LIKE THAT AND I'LL BE FINISHED! I-I'M HELPLESS!
HE'S ALMOST UNCONSCIOUS!! I CAN'T BELIEVE IT!!
HE DOESN'T EVEN STRUGGLE AS I TRY TO REMOVE HIS MASK! THERE CAN ONLY BE ONE ANSWER...
MR. JAMESON-- LOOK! HE'S BEATEN SPIDER-MAN!
SO QUICKLY!! HOW? AND-- WHERE'S PARKER? HE SHOULD BE PHOTO-GRAPHING THIS!
IT IS DR. OCTOPUS! GOOD THING YOU CALLED US, MISS!
I SHOULD HAVE KNOWN!! IT ISN'T SPIDER-MAN! IT'S THAT WEAKLING BRAT, PETER PARKER!
PETER!! HE DID IT FOR ME!! OH, HE MIGHT HAVE BEEN KILLED!
THE FOOL! I ORDERED HIM TO TAKE PICTURES OF OCTOPUS --NOT TRY TO BE A HERO!
YOU MEAN YOU KNEW OCTOPUS WAS HERE??
PD
8

BAH!! *TAKE* YOUR PUNY HERO! HE'S OF NO INTEREST TO *ME!* IT'S THE *REAL* SPIDER-MAN I'M AFTER!!

BEFORE ANYONE CAN RECOVER THEIR BALANCE, THE SUPER-AGILE DR. OCTOPUS DISAPPEARS INTO THE NIGHT...

I WAS *SURE* SPIDER-MAN WOULD SHOW UP! PERHAPS THE *POLICE* SCARED HIM OFF!

BUT I'LL FIND HIM SOONER OR LATER! I'LL NEVER REST TILL I'VE SMASHED HIM!

JAMESON, NEXT TIME YOU WITHHOLD INFORMATION FROM US, IT'LL GO *HARD* WITH YOU! IF YOU HAD *TOLD* US ABOUT THIS, WE WOULD HAVE SET A *TRAP* FOR OCTOPUS AND CAUGHT HIM BY NOW!

BUT YOU THOUGHT MORE OF AN EXCLUSIVE *STORY* THAN ANYTHING ELSE!

OH, PETER-- PETER! YOU DEAR, FOOLISH, WONDERFUL BOY!! WHY DID YOU *DO* IT?? IF ANYTHING HAD *HAPPENED* TO YOU--!!

I BETTER NOT YELL AT PARKER NOW, IN FRONT OF THE POLICE! THEY'RE ANGRY ENOUGH AT ME NOW! THIS SURE WAS ONE BIG *FLOP!!*

HE'LL BE ALRIGHT, MISS! WE'LL SEE THAT HE GETS HOME SAFELY! HE'S A PRETTY BRAVE KID, IMPERSONATING SPIDER-MAN AND TACKLING DR. OCTOPUS LIKE THAT!

HOURS LATER, AT HOME...

POOR BOY! A NICE POLICEMAN BROUGHT HIM HOME! HE SAID HE HAD FAINTED IN THE STREET! I *KNEW* HE WAS COMING DOWN WITH SOMETHING!

NOTHING TO WORRY ABOUT, MRS. PARKER! IT'S JUST THE TWENTY-FOUR HOUR VIRUS! IT MAKES ONE WEAK AS A KITTEN FOR A DAY, BUT THEN IT PASSES! HE'LL BE FINE IN THE MORNING!

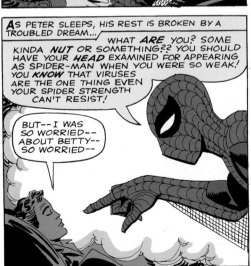

AS PETER SLEEPS, HIS REST IS BROKEN BY A TROUBLED DREAM...

WHAT *ARE* YOU? SOME KINDA *NUT* OR SOMETHING?? YOU SHOULD HAVE YOUR *HEAD* EXAMINED FOR APPEARING AS SPIDER-MAN WHEN YOU WERE SO WEAK! YOU *KNOW* THAT VIRUSES ARE THE ONE THING EVEN YOUR SPIDER STRENGTH CAN'T RESIST!

BUT-- I WAS SO WORRIED-- ABOUT BETTY-- SO WORRIED--

THEN, COMES THE NEXT MORNING-- MORE THAN TWENTY-FOUR HOURS AFTER THE VIRUS HAS STRUCK...

WHOOPEE! I FEEL LIKE A ZILLION BUCKS AGAIN!

I'VE GOT THE OL' *SPIDER STRENGTH* BACK! THE OL' *ZINGAROOO!*

9

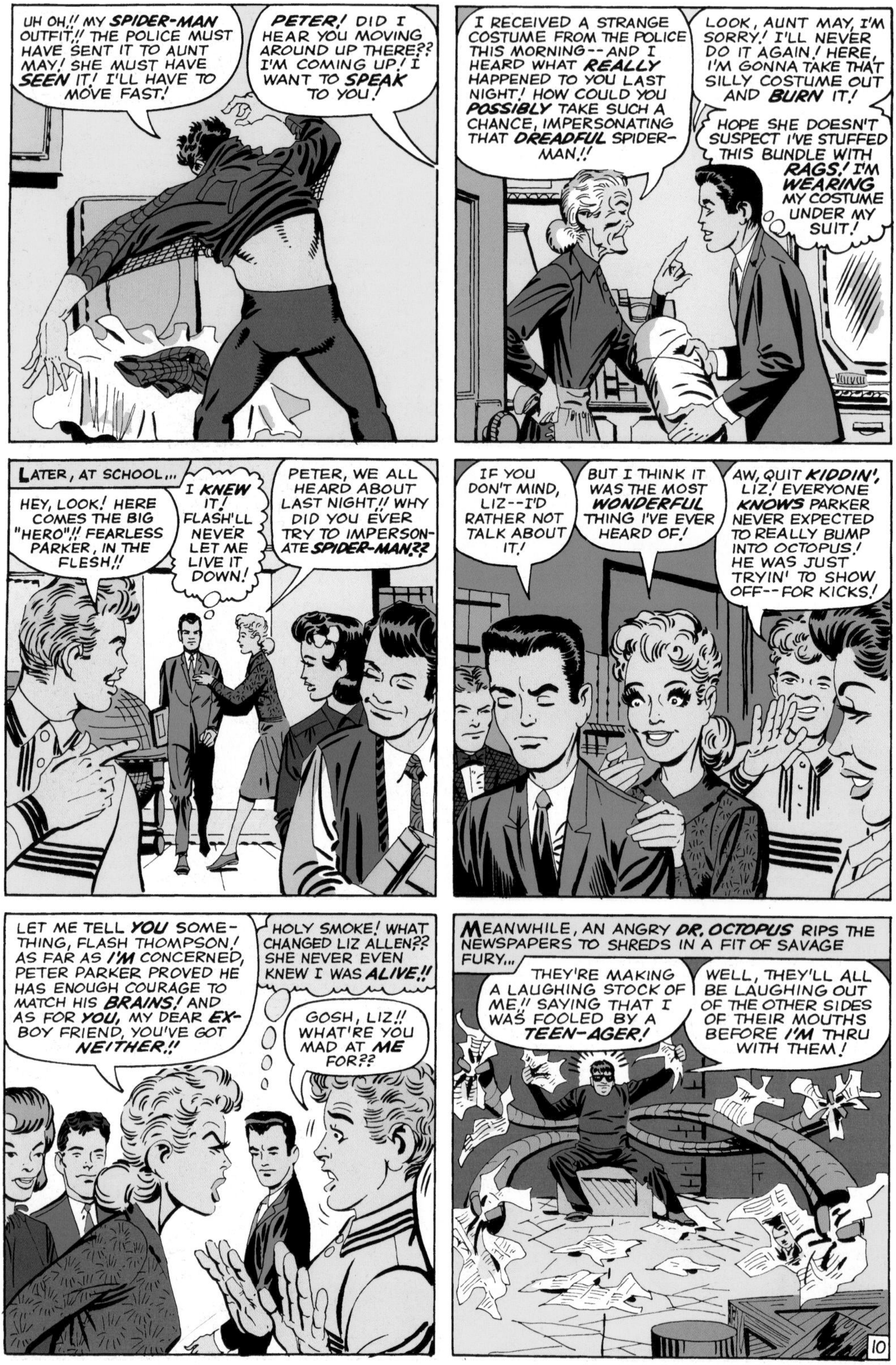
UH OH,!! MY SPIDER-MAN OUTFIT,!! THE POLICE MUST HAVE SENT IT TO AUNT MAY! SHE MUST HAVE SEEN IT! I'LL HAVE TO MOVE FAST!
PETER! DID I HEAR YOU MOVING AROUND UP THERE?? I'M COMING UP! I WANT TO SPEAK TO YOU!
I RECEIVED A STRANGE COSTUME FROM THE POLICE THIS MORNING-- AND I HEARD WHAT REALLY HAPPENED TO YOU LAST NIGHT! HOW COULD YOU POSSIBLY TAKE SUCH A CHANCE, IMPERSONATING THAT DREADFUL SPIDER-MAN!!
LOOK, AUNT MAY, I'M SORRY! I'LL NEVER DO IT AGAIN! HERE, I'M GONNA TAKE THAT SILLY COSTUME OUT AND BURN IT!
HOPE SHE DOESN'T SUSPECT I'VE STUFFED THIS BUNDLE WITH RAGS! I'M WEARING MY COSTUME UNDER MY SUIT!
LATER, AT SCHOOL...
HEY, LOOK! HERE COMES THE BIG "HERO"!! FEARLESS PARKER, IN THE FLESH!!
I KNEW IT! FLASH'LL NEVER LET ME LIVE IT DOWN!
PETER, WE ALL HEARD ABOUT LAST NIGHT!! WHY DID YOU EVER TRY TO IMPERSONATE SPIDER-MAN??
IF YOU DON'T MIND, LIZ--I'D RATHER NOT TALK ABOUT IT!
BUT I THINK IT WAS THE MOST WONDERFUL THING I'VE EVER HEARD OF!
AW, QUIT KIDDIN', LIZ! EVERYONE KNOWS PARKER NEVER EXPECTED TO REALLY BUMP INTO OCTOPUS! HE WAS JUST TRYIN' TO SHOW OFF--FOR KICKS!
LET ME TELL YOU SOMETHING, FLASH THOMPSON! AS FAR AS I'M CONCERNED, PETER PARKER PROVED HE HAS ENOUGH COURAGE TO MATCH HIS BRAINS! AND AS FOR YOU, MY DEAR EX-BOY FRIEND, YOU'VE GOT NEITHER!!
HOLY SMOKE! WHAT CHANGED LIZ ALLEN?? SHE NEVER EVEN KNEW I WAS ALIVE!!
GOSH, LIZ!! WHAT'RE YOU MAD AT ME FOR??
MEANWHILE, AN ANGRY DR. OCTOPUS RIPS THE NEWSPAPERS TO SHREDS IN A FIT OF SAVAGE FURY...
THEY'RE MAKING A LAUGHING STOCK OF ME!! SAYING THAT I WAS FOOLED BY A TEEN-AGER!
WELL, THEY'LL ALL BE LAUGHING OUT OF THE OTHER SIDES OF THEIR MOUTHS BEFORE I'M THRU WITH THEM!
10

SPIDER-MAN WILL BE ABLE TO HIDE FROM ME NO LONGER! I'LL **MAKE** HIM COME TO ME -- IF IT'S THE LAST THING I **DO!**

I'M THRU WITH HIDING OUT!! I FEAR **NOBODY!** I'M THE MOST POWERFUL ONE IN THE CITY!

I'LL LEAVE MY BASEMENT HIDEOUT AND MAKE SURE THAT NEW YORK NEVER -- NEVER FORGETS THIS DAY -- NEVER FORGETS THE POWER OF **DR. OCTOPUS!!**

NO PAR -ING

LATER, AT THE OUTSKIRTS OF THE ZOO...

RUN!! THE WILD BEASTS ARE LOOSE!!! **DR. OCTOPUS** SET THEM ALL FREE!!

HELP!! SOMEBODY **HELP!!**

WITHIN SECONDS, THE POLICE ARE ON THE SCENE, WORKING VALIANTLY TO TRAP THE RAMPAGING BEASTS BEFORE ANYONE CAN BE INJURED!!

CAREFUL, JOE! THIS BABY'S A **KILLER!!**

WE CAN'T **AFFORD** TO BE CAREFUL, BILL! TOO MANY LIVES MAY BE AT STAKE!!

MEANWHILE, A SHORT DISTANCE AWAY...

THIS IS **NUTS!** LIZ WOULDN'T GIVE ME A TUMBLE BEFORE -- BUT NOW SHE'S FOLLOWIN' ME AROUND LIKE A LOVESICK CALF!

PETER, WAIT FOR ME! I'LL WALK HOME WITH YOU! I WANT TO ASK YOU SOME-THING...

LIZ -- WAIT! I THOUGHT WE WERE GOIN' **BOWLING** THIS AFTERNOON! LIZ -- !!

11

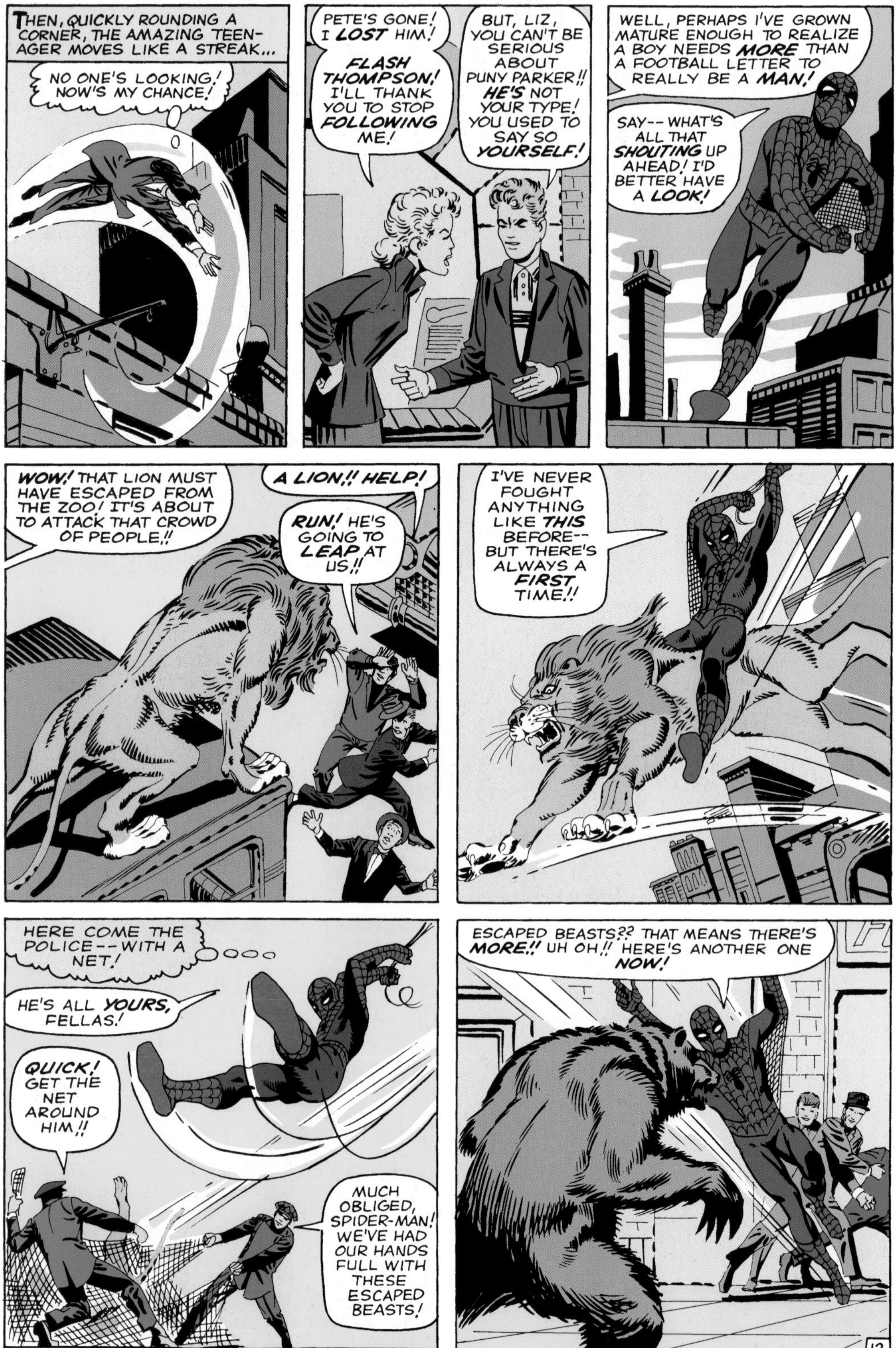
THEN, QUICKLY ROUNDING A CORNER, THE AMAZING TEEN-AGER MOVES LIKE A STREAK...
NO ONE'S LOOKING! NOW'S MY CHANCE!
PETE'S GONE! I LOST HIM!
FLASH THOMPSON! I'LL THANK YOU TO STOP FOLLOWING ME!
BUT, LIZ, YOU CAN'T BE SERIOUS ABOUT PUNY PARKER!! HE'S NOT YOUR TYPE! YOU USED TO SAY SO YOURSELF!
WELL, PERHAPS I'VE GROWN MATURE ENOUGH TO REALIZE A BOY NEEDS MORE THAN A FOOTBALL LETTER TO REALLY BE A MAN!
SAY-- WHAT'S ALL THAT SHOUTING UP AHEAD! I'D BETTER HAVE A LOOK!
WOW! THAT LION MUST HAVE ESCAPED FROM THE ZOO! IT'S ABOUT TO ATTACK THAT CROWD OF PEOPLE!!
A LION!! HELP!
RUN! HE'S GOING TO LEAP AT US!!
I'VE NEVER FOUGHT ANYTHING LIKE THIS BEFORE-- BUT THERE'S ALWAYS A FIRST TIME!!
HERE COME THE POLICE--WITH A NET!
HE'S ALL YOURS, FELLAS!
QUICK! GET THE NET AROUND HIM!!
MUCH OBLIGED, SPIDER-MAN! WE'VE HAD OUR HANDS FULL WITH THESE ESCAPED BEASTS!
ESCAPED BEASTS?? THAT MEANS THERE'S MORE!! UH OH!! HERE'S ANOTHER ONE NOW!
12

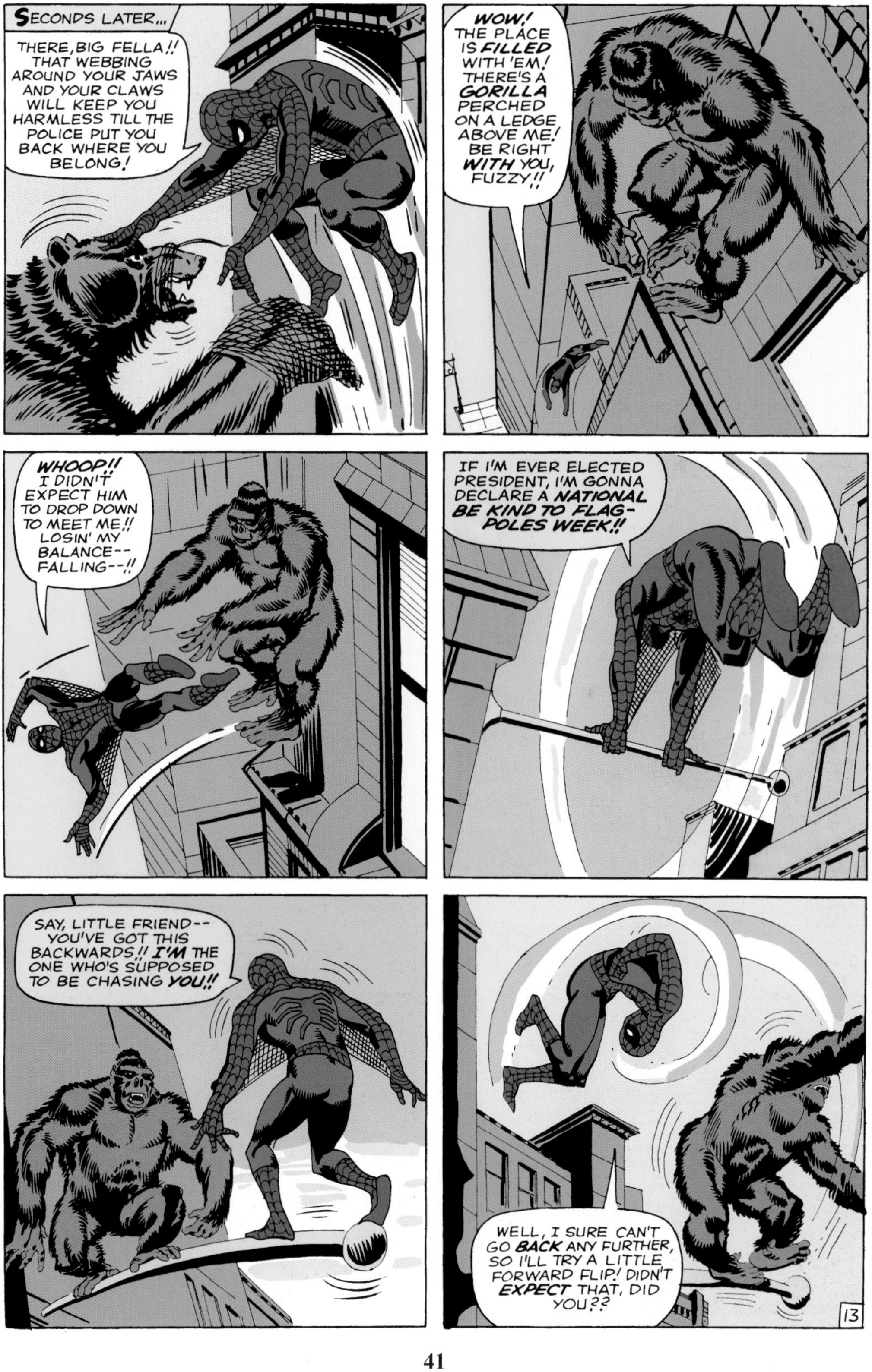
SECONDS LATER...
THERE, BIG FELLA!! THAT WEBBING AROUND YOUR JAWS AND YOUR CLAWS WILL KEEP YOU HARMLESS TILL THE POLICE PUT YOU BACK WHERE YOU BELONG!
WOW! THE PLACE IS FILLED WITH 'EM! THERE'S A GORILLA PERCHED ON A LEDGE ABOVE ME! BE RIGHT WITH YOU, FUZZY!!
WHOOP!! I DIDN'T EXPECT HIM TO DROP DOWN TO MEET ME!! LOSIN' MY BALANCE-- FALLING--!!
IF I'M EVER ELECTED PRESIDENT, I'M GONNA DECLARE A NATIONAL BE KIND TO FLAG-POLES WEEK!!
SAY, LITTLE FRIEND-- YOU'VE GOT THIS BACKWARDS!! I'M THE ONE WHO'S SUPPOSED TO BE CHASING YOU!!
WELL, I SURE CAN'T GO BACK ANY FURTHER, SO I'LL TRY A LITTLE FORWARD FLIP! DIDN'T EXPECT THAT, DID YOU??
13

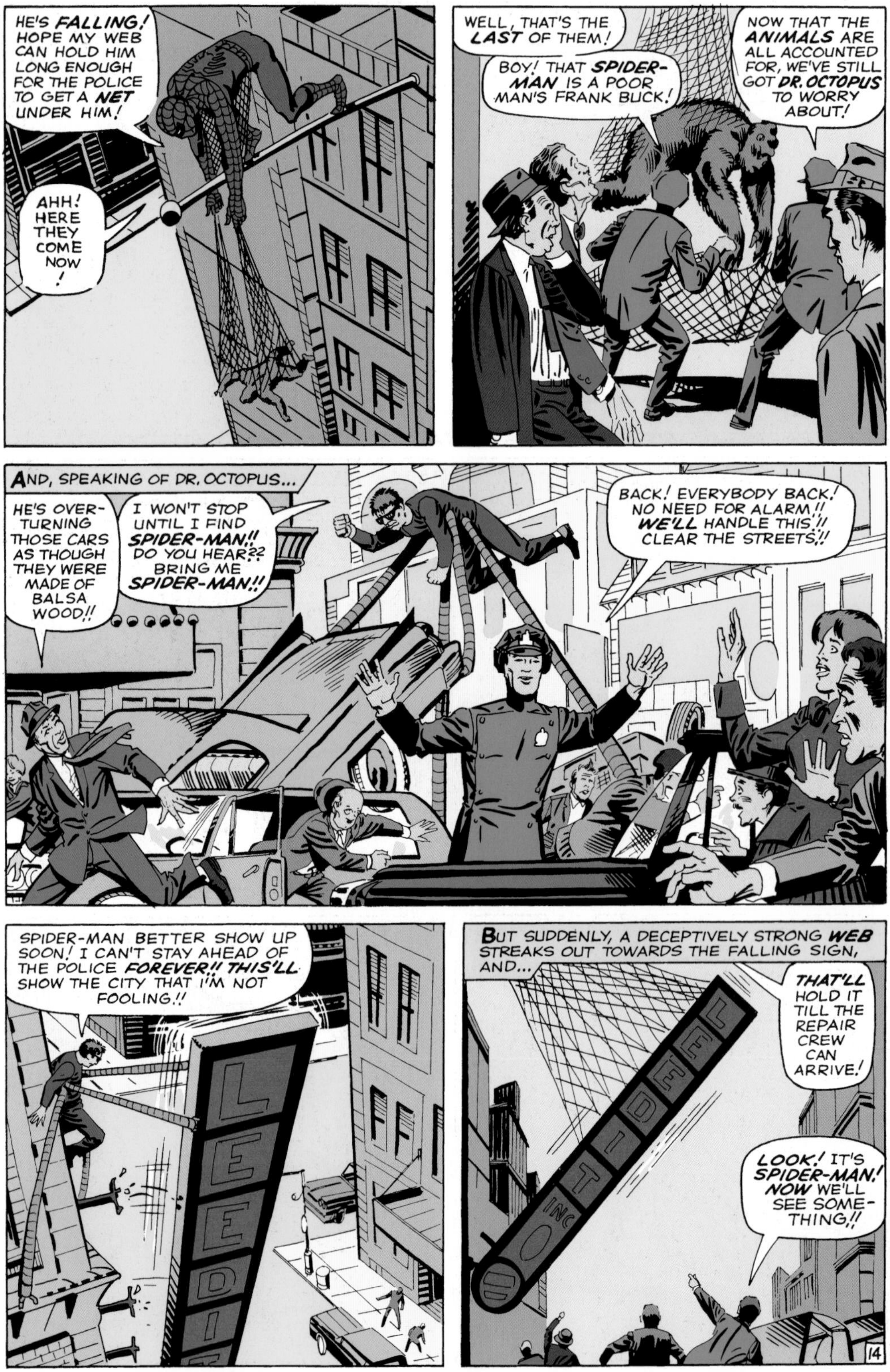
HE'S FALLING! HOPE MY WEB CAN HOLD HIM LONG ENOUGH FOR THE POLICE TO GET A NET UNDER HIM!
AHH! HERE THEY COME NOW!
WELL, THAT'S THE LAST OF THEM!
BOY! THAT SPIDER-MAN IS A POOR MAN'S FRANK BUCK!
NOW THAT THE ANIMALS ARE ALL ACCOUNTED FOR, WE'VE STILL GOT DR. OCTOPUS TO WORRY ABOUT!
AND, SPEAKING OF DR. OCTOPUS...
HE'S OVER-TURNING THOSE CARS AS THOUGH THEY WERE MADE OF BALSA WOOD!!
I WON'T STOP UNTIL I FIND SPIDER-MAN!! DO YOU HEAR?? BRING ME SPIDER-MAN!!
BACK! EVERYBODY BACK! NO NEED FOR ALARM!! WE'LL HANDLE THIS!! CLEAR THE STREETS!!
SPIDER-MAN BETTER SHOW UP SOON! I CAN'T STAY AHEAD OF THE POLICE FOREVER!! THIS'LL SHOW THE CITY THAT I'M NOT FOOLING!!
BUT SUDDENLY, A DECEPTIVELY STRONG WEB STREAKS OUT TOWARDS THE FALLING SIGN, AND...
THAT'LL HOLD IT TILL THE REPAIR CREW CAN ARRIVE!
LOOK! IT'S SPIDER-MAN! NOW WE'LL SEE SOME-THING!!
14

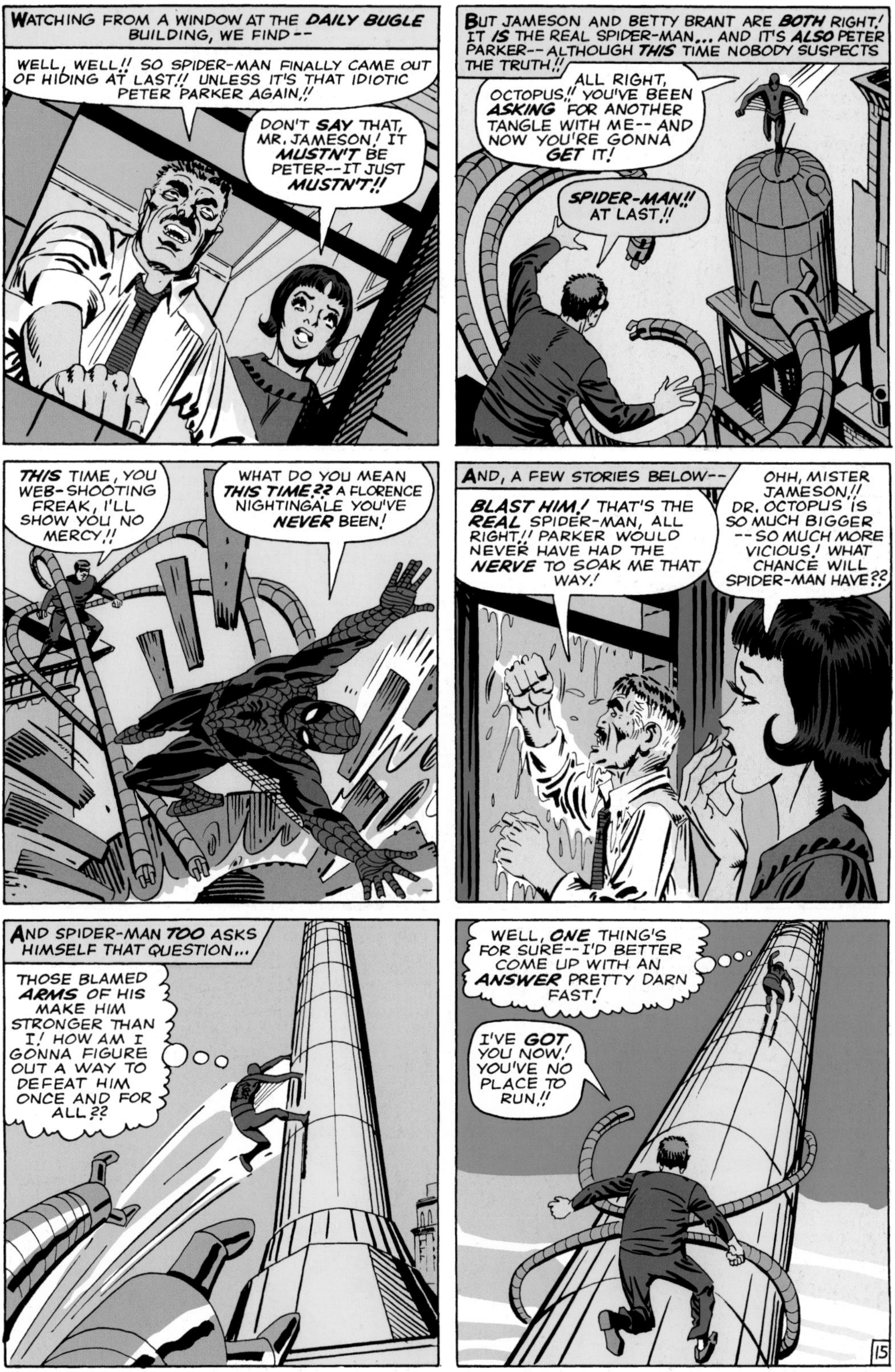
WATCHING FROM A WINDOW AT THE DAILY BUGLE BUILDING, WE FIND--
WELL, WELL!! SO SPIDER-MAN FINALLY CAME OUT OF HIDING AT LAST!! UNLESS IT'S THAT IDIOTIC PETER PARKER AGAIN!!
DON'T SAY THAT, MR. JAMESON! IT MUSTN'T BE PETER--IT JUST MUSTN'T!!
BUT JAMESON AND BETTY BRANT ARE BOTH RIGHT! IT IS THE REAL SPIDER-MAN... AND IT'S ALSO PETER PARKER-- ALTHOUGH THIS TIME NOBODY SUSPECTS THE TRUTH!!
ALL RIGHT, OCTOPUS!! YOU'VE BEEN ASKING FOR ANOTHER TANGLE WITH ME-- AND NOW YOU'RE GONNA GET IT!
SPIDER-MAN!! AT LAST!!
THIS TIME, YOU WEB-SHOOTING FREAK, I'LL SHOW YOU NO MERCY!!
WHAT DO YOU MEAN THIS TIME?? A FLORENCE NIGHTINGALE YOU'VE NEVER BEEN!
AND, A FEW STORIES BELOW--
BLAST HIM! THAT'S THE REAL SPIDER-MAN, ALL RIGHT!! PARKER WOULD NEVER HAVE HAD THE NERVE TO SOAK ME THAT WAY!
OHH, MISTER JAMESON!! DR. OCTOPUS IS SO MUCH BIGGER --SO MUCH MORE VICIOUS! WHAT CHANCE WILL SPIDER-MAN HAVE??
AND SPIDER-MAN TOO ASKS HIMSELF THAT QUESTION...
THOSE BLAMED ARMS OF HIS MAKE HIM STRONGER THAN I! HOW AM I GONNA FIGURE OUT A WAY TO DEFEAT HIM ONCE AND FOR ALL??
WELL, ONE THING'S FOR SURE--I'D BETTER COME UP WITH AN ANSWER PRETTY DARN FAST!
I'VE GOT YOU NOW! YOU'VE NO PLACE TO RUN!!
15

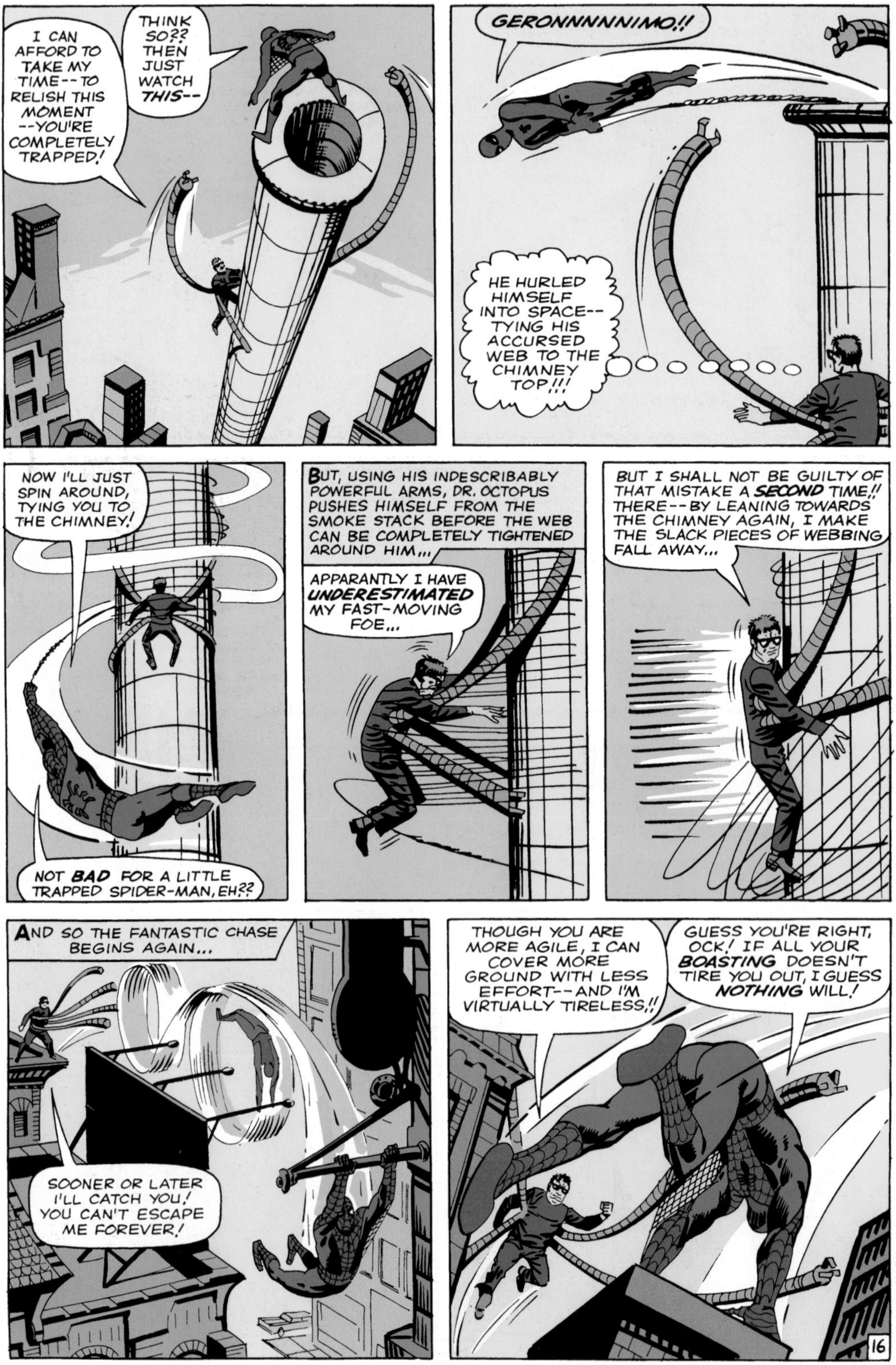
I CAN AFFORD TO TAKE MY TIME--TO RELISH THIS MOMENT --YOU'RE COMPLETELY TRAPPED!
THINK SO?? THEN JUST WATCH THIS--
GERONNNNNNIMO!!
HE HURLED HIMSELF INTO SPACE--TYING HIS ACCURSED WEB TO THE CHIMNEY TOP!!!
NOW I'LL JUST SPIN AROUND, TYING YOU TO THE CHIMNEY!
NOT BAD FOR A LITTLE TRAPPED SPIDER-MAN, EH??
BUT, USING HIS INDESCRIBABLY POWERFUL ARMS, DR. OCTOPUS PUSHES HIMSELF FROM THE SMOKE STACK BEFORE THE WEB CAN BE COMPLETELY TIGHTENED AROUND HIM...
APPARANTLY I HAVE UNDERESTIMATED MY FAST-MOVING FOE...
BUT I SHALL NOT BE GUILTY OF THAT MISTAKE A SECOND TIME!! THERE--BY LEANING TOWARDS THE CHIMNEY AGAIN, I MAKE THE SLACK PIECES OF WEBBING FALL AWAY...
AND SO THE FANTASTIC CHASE BEGINS AGAIN...
SOONER OR LATER I'LL CATCH YOU! YOU CAN'T ESCAPE ME FOREVER!
THOUGH YOU ARE MORE AGILE, I CAN COVER MORE GROUND WITH LESS EFFORT--AND I'M VIRTUALLY TIRELESS!!
GUESS YOU'RE RIGHT, OCK! IF ALL YOUR BOASTING DOESN'T TIRE YOU OUT, I GUESS NOTHING WILL!
16

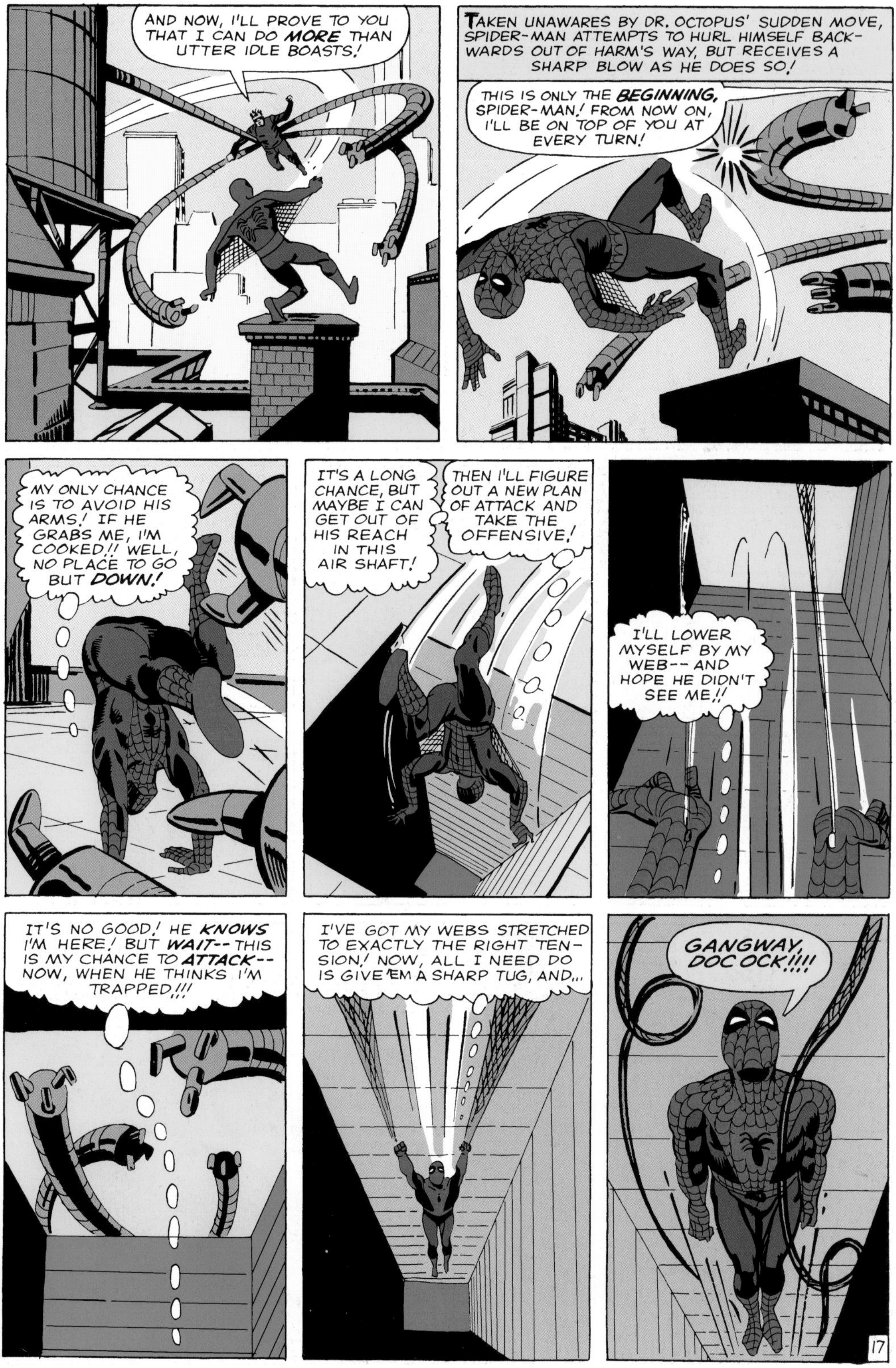
AND NOW, I'LL PROVE TO YOU THAT I CAN DO MORE THAN UTTER IDLE BOASTS!
TAKEN UNAWARES BY DR. OCTOPUS' SUDDEN MOVE, SPIDER-MAN ATTEMPTS TO HURL HIMSELF BACK-WARDS OUT OF HARM'S WAY, BUT RECEIVES A SHARP BLOW AS HE DOES SO!
THIS IS ONLY THE BEGINNING, SPIDER-MAN! FROM NOW ON, I'LL BE ON TOP OF YOU AT EVERY TURN!
MY ONLY CHANCE IS TO AVOID HIS ARMS! IF HE GRABS ME, I'M COOKED!! WELL, NO PLACE TO GO BUT DOWN!
IT'S A LONG CHANCE, BUT MAYBE I CAN GET OUT OF HIS REACH IN THIS AIR SHAFT!
THEN I'LL FIGURE OUT A NEW PLAN OF ATTACK AND TAKE THE OFFENSIVE!
I'LL LOWER MYSELF BY MY WEB-- AND HOPE HE DIDN'T SEE ME!!
IT'S NO GOOD! HE KNOWS I'M HERE! BUT WAIT-- THIS IS MY CHANCE TO ATTACK-- NOW, WHEN HE THINKS I'M TRAPPED!!!
I'VE GOT MY WEBS STRETCHED TO EXACTLY THE RIGHT TEN-SION! NOW, ALL I NEED DO IS GIVE 'EM A SHARP TUG, AND...
GANGWAY, DOC OCK!!!!
17

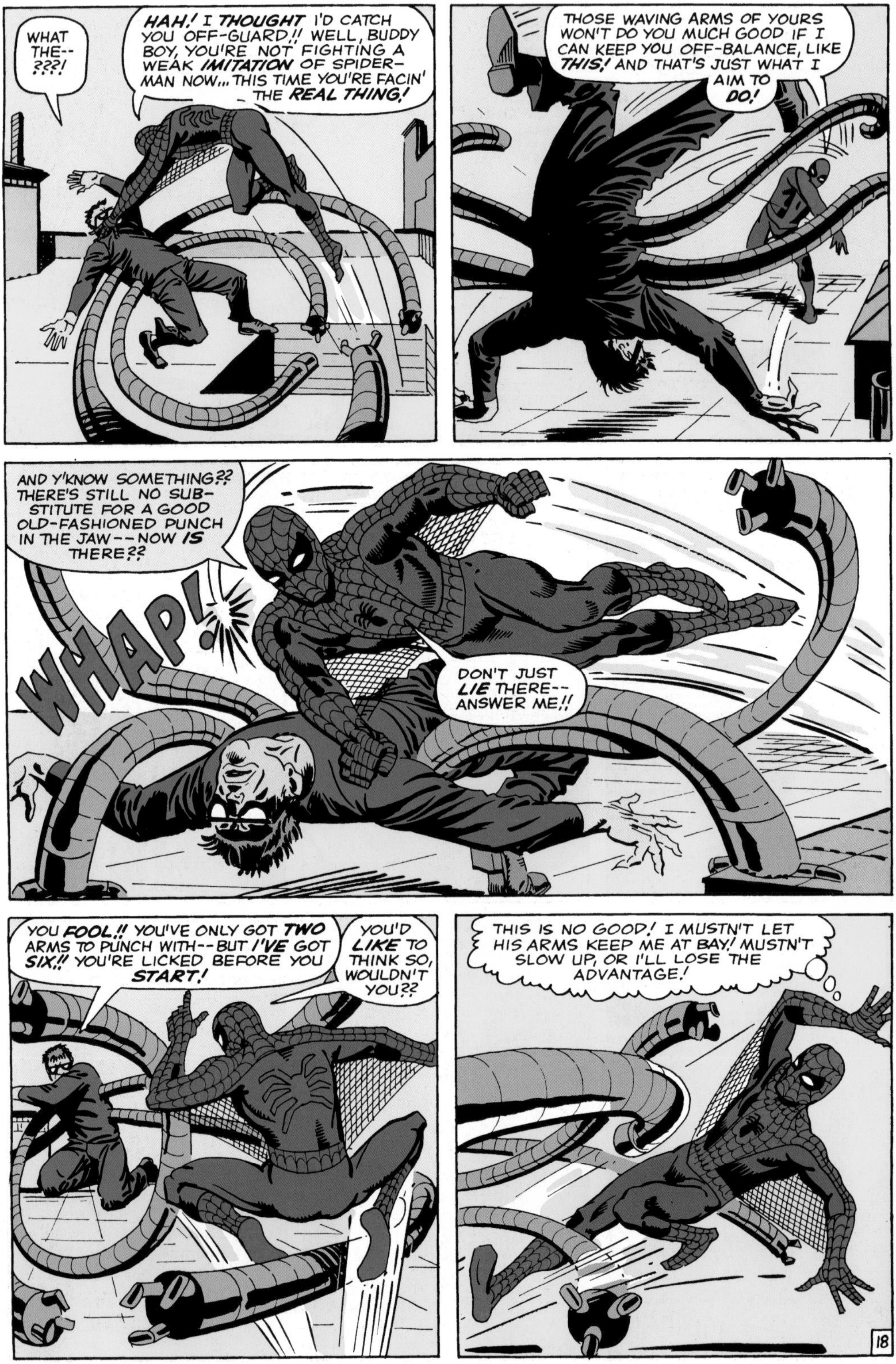
WHAT THE-- ???!
HAH! I THOUGHT I'D CATCH YOU OFF-GUARD!! WELL, BUDDY BOY, YOU'RE NOT FIGHTING A WEAK IMITATION OF SPIDER-MAN NOW... THIS TIME YOU'RE FACIN' THE REAL THING!
THOSE WAVING ARMS OF YOURS WON'T DO YOU MUCH GOOD IF I CAN KEEP YOU OFF-BALANCE, LIKE THIS! AND THAT'S JUST WHAT I AIM TO DO!
AND Y'KNOW SOMETHING?? THERE'S STILL NO SUB-STITUTE FOR A GOOD OLD-FASHIONED PUNCH IN THE JAW--NOW IS THERE??
WHAP!
DON'T JUST LIE THERE-- ANSWER ME!!
YOU FOOL!! YOU'VE ONLY GOT TWO ARMS TO PUNCH WITH--BUT I'VE GOT SIX!! YOU'RE LICKED BEFORE YOU START!
YOU'D LIKE TO THINK SO, WOULDN'T YOU??
THIS IS NO GOOD! I MUSTN'T LET HIS ARMS KEEP ME AT BAY! MUSTN'T SLOW UP, OR I'LL LOSE THE ADVANTAGE!
18

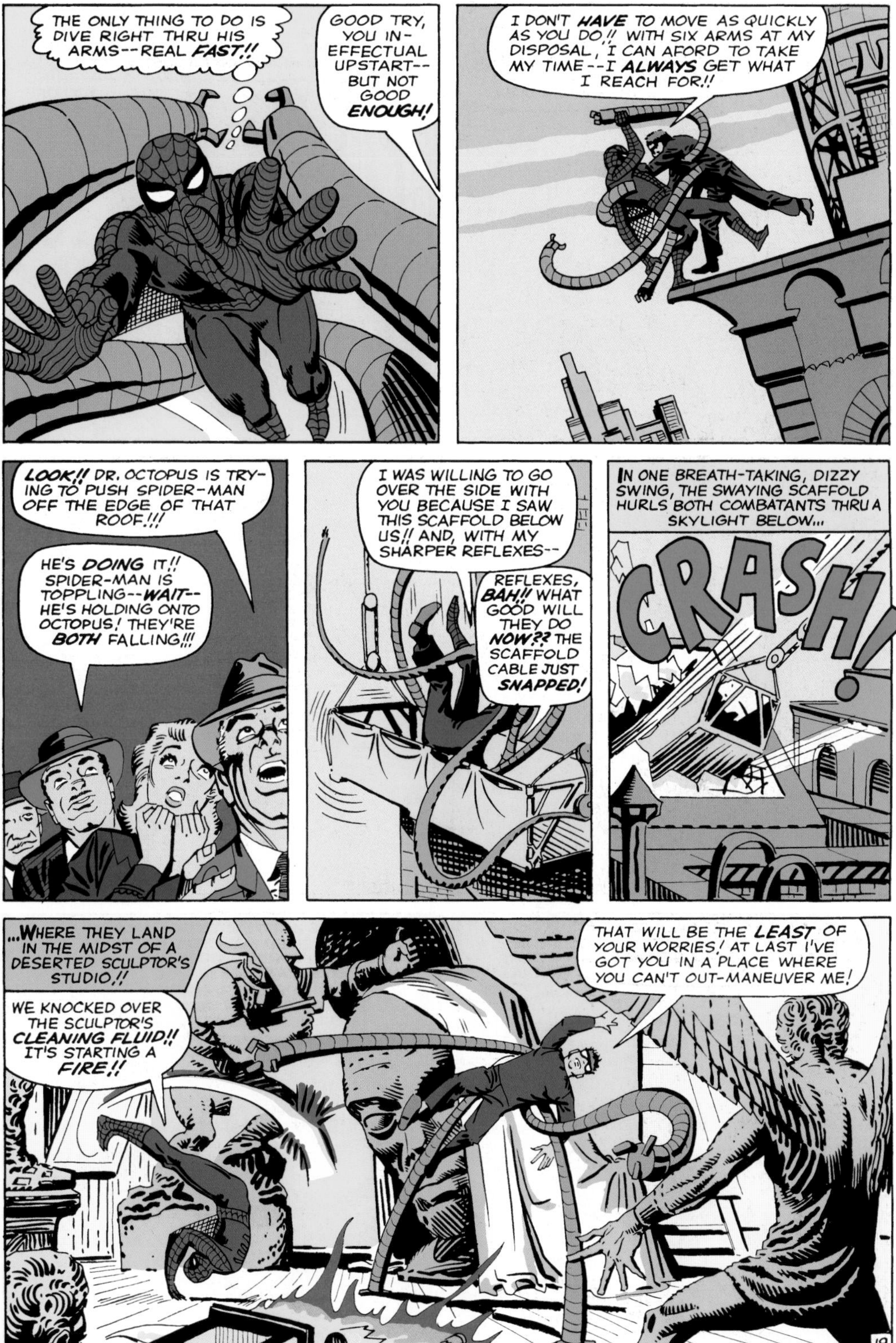
THE ONLY THING TO DO IS DIVE RIGHT THRU HIS ARMS--REAL FAST!!
GOOD TRY, YOU IN-EFFECTUAL UPSTART--BUT NOT GOOD ENOUGH!
I DON'T HAVE TO MOVE AS QUICKLY AS YOU DO!! WITH SIX ARMS AT MY DISPOSAL, I CAN AFORD TO TAKE MY TIME--I ALWAYS GET WHAT I REACH FOR!!
LOOK!! DR. OCTOPUS IS TRY-ING TO PUSH SPIDER-MAN OFF THE EDGE OF THAT ROOF!!!
HE'S DOING IT!! SPIDER-MAN IS TOPPLING--WAIT--HE'S HOLDING ONTO OCTOPUS! THEY'RE BOTH FALLING!!!
I WAS WILLING TO GO OVER THE SIDE WITH YOU BECAUSE I SAW THIS SCAFFOLD BELOW US!! AND, WITH MY SHARPER REFLEXES--
REFLEXES, BAH!! WHAT GOOD WILL THEY DO NOW?? THE SCAFFOLD CABLE JUST SNAPPED!
IN ONE BREATH-TAKING, DIZZY SWING, THE SWAYING SCAFFOLD HURLS BOTH COMBATANTS THRU A SKYLIGHT BELOW...
CRASH!
...WHERE THEY LAND IN THE MIDST OF A DESERTED SCULPTOR'S STUDIO!!
WE KNOCKED OVER THE SCULPTOR'S CLEANING FLUID!! IT'S STARTING A FIRE!!
THAT WILL BE THE LEAST OF YOUR WORRIES! AT LAST I'VE GOT YOU IN A PLACE WHERE YOU CAN'T OUT-MANEUVER ME!
19

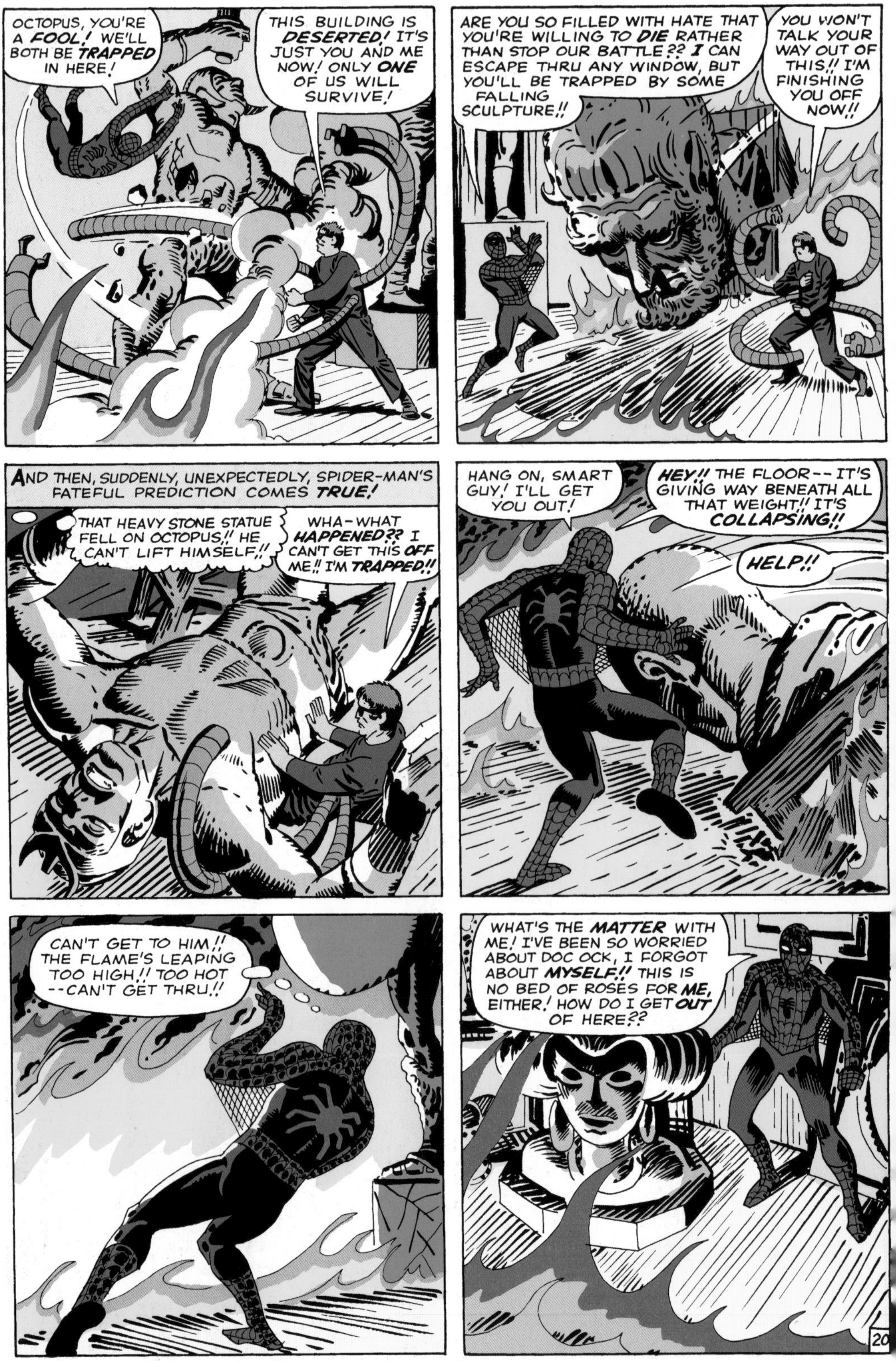

OCTOPUS, YOU'RE A FOOL! WE'LL BOTH BE TRAPPED IN HERE!
THIS BUILDING IS DESERTED! IT'S JUST YOU AND ME NOW! ONLY ONE OF US WILL SURVIVE!
ARE YOU SO FILLED WITH HATE THAT YOU'RE WILLING TO DIE RATHER THAN STOP OUR BATTLE?? I CAN ESCAPE THRU ANY WINDOW, BUT YOU'LL BE TRAPPED BY SOME FALLING SCULPTURE!!
YOU WON'T TALK YOUR WAY OUT OF THIS!! I'M FINISHING YOU OFF NOW!!
AND THEN, SUDDENLY, UNEXPECTEDLY, SPIDER-MAN'S FATEFUL PREDICTION COMES TRUE!
THAT HEAVY STONE STATUE FELL ON OCTOPUS!! HE CAN'T LIFT HIMSELF!!
WHA-WHAT HAPPENED?? I CAN'T GET THIS OFF ME!! I'M TRAPPED!!
HANG ON, SMART GUY! I'LL GET YOU OUT!
HEY!! THE FLOOR-- IT'S GIVING WAY BENEATH ALL THAT WEIGHT!! IT'S COLLAPSING!!
HELP!!
CAN'T GET TO HIM!! THE FLAME'S LEAPING TOO HIGH!! TOO HOT --CAN'T GET THRU!!
WHAT'S THE MATTER WITH ME! I'VE BEEN SO WORRIED ABOUT DOC OCK, I FORGOT ABOUT MYSELF!! THIS IS NO BED OF ROSES FOR ME, EITHER! HOW DO I GET OUT OF HERE??
20

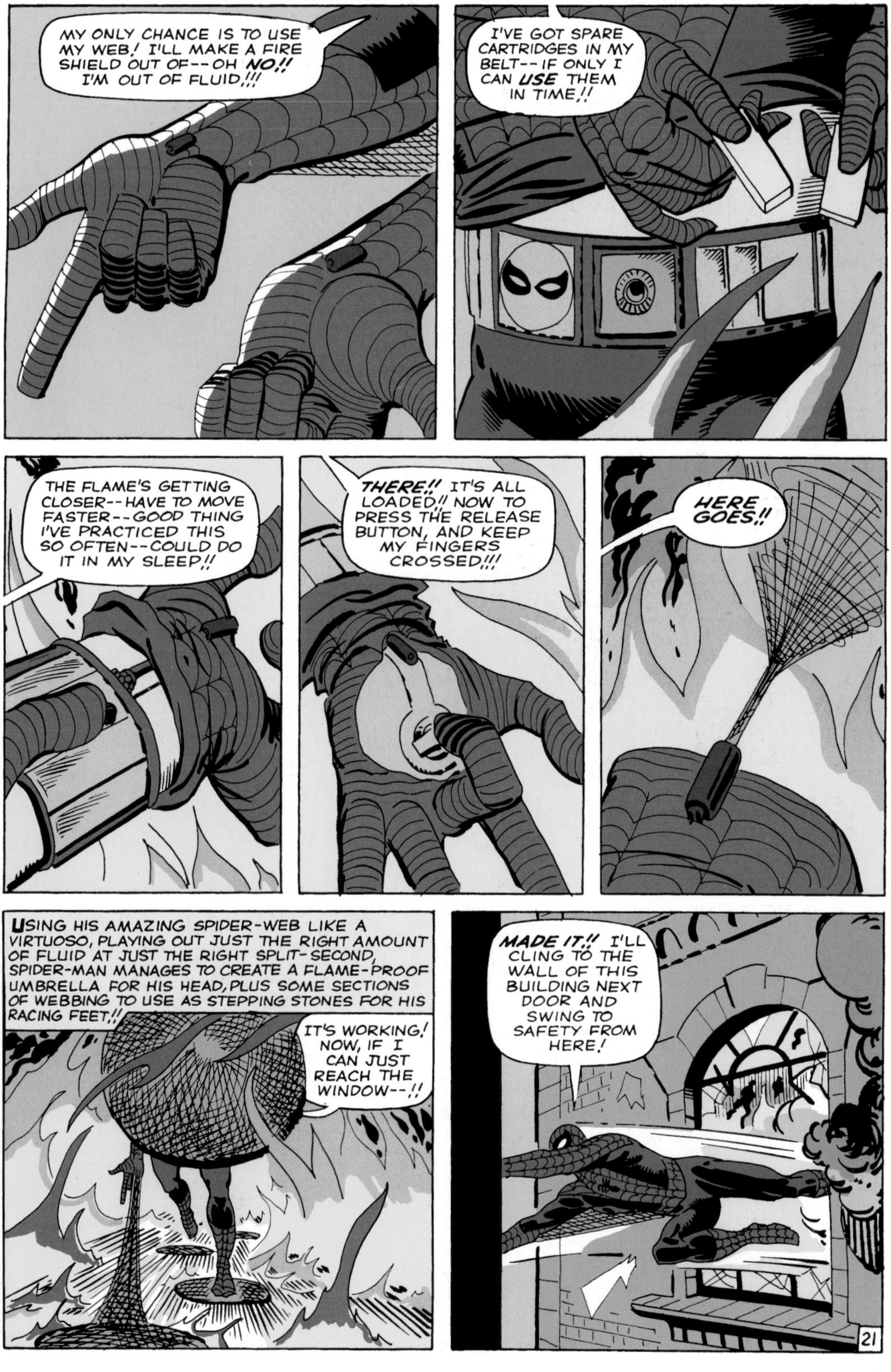
MY ONLY CHANCE IS TO USE MY WEB! I'LL MAKE A FIRE SHIELD OUT OF--OH NO!! I'M OUT OF FLUID!!!
I'VE GOT SPARE CARTRIDGES IN MY BELT--IF ONLY I CAN USE THEM IN TIME!!
THE FLAME'S GETTING CLOSER--HAVE TO MOVE FASTER--GOOD THING I'VE PRACTICED THIS SO OFTEN--COULD DO IT IN MY SLEEP!!
THERE!! IT'S ALL LOADED!! NOW TO PRESS THE RELEASE BUTTON, AND KEEP MY FINGERS CROSSED!!!
HERE GOES!!
USING HIS AMAZING SPIDER-WEB LIKE A VIRTUOSO, PLAYING OUT JUST THE RIGHT AMOUNT OF FLUID AT JUST THE RIGHT SPLIT-SECOND, SPIDER-MAN MANAGES TO CREATE A FLAME-PROOF UMBRELLA FOR HIS HEAD, PLUS SOME SECTIONS OF WEBBING TO USE AS STEPPING STONES FOR HIS RACING FEET!!
IT'S WORKING! NOW, IF I CAN JUST REACH THE WINDOW--!!
MADE IT!! I'LL CLING TO THE WALL OF THIS BUILDING NEXT DOOR AND SWING TO SAFETY FROM HERE!
21

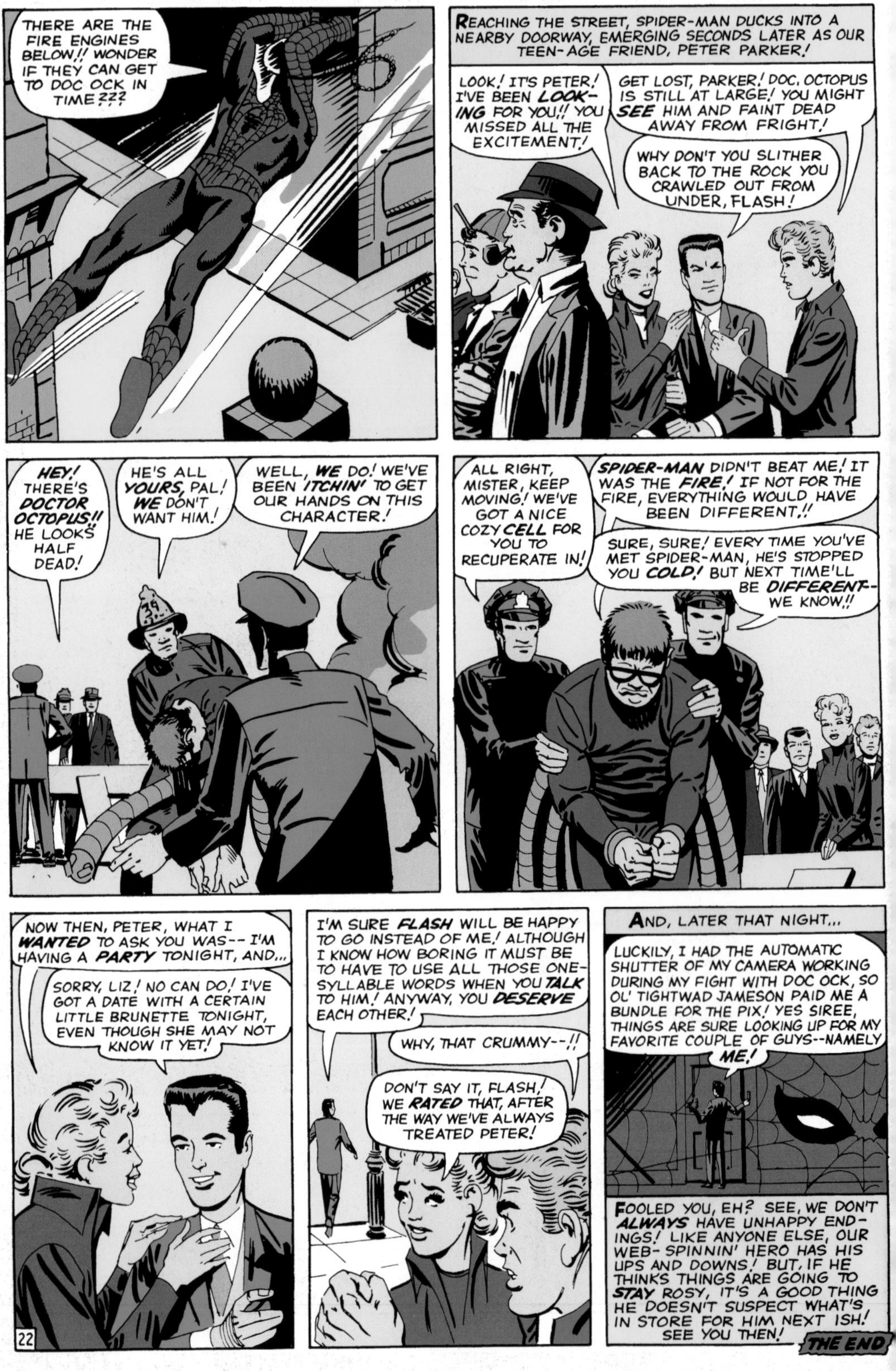
THERE ARE THE FIRE ENGINES BELOW!! WONDER IF THEY CAN GET TO DOC OCK IN TIME???
REACHING THE STREET, SPIDER-MAN DUCKS INTO A NEARBY DOORWAY, EMERGING SECONDS LATER AS OUR TEEN-AGE FRIEND, PETER PARKER!
LOOK! IT'S PETER! I'VE BEEN LOOKING FOR YOU!! YOU MISSED ALL THE EXCITEMENT!
GET LOST, PARKER! DOC. OCTOPUS IS STILL AT LARGE! YOU MIGHT SEE HIM AND FAINT DEAD AWAY FROM FRIGHT!
WHY DON'T YOU SLITHER BACK TO THE ROCK YOU CRAWLED OUT FROM UNDER, FLASH!
HEY! THERE'S DOCTOR OCTOPUS!! HE LOOKS HALF DEAD!
HE'S ALL YOURS, PAL! WE DON'T WANT HIM!
WELL, WE DO! WE'VE BEEN 'ITCHIN' TO GET OUR HANDS ON THIS CHARACTER!
39
ALL RIGHT, MISTER, KEEP MOVING! WE'VE GOT A NICE COZY CELL FOR YOU TO RECUPERATE IN!
SPIDER-MAN DIDN'T BEAT ME! IT WAS THE FIRE! IF NOT FOR THE FIRE, EVERYTHING WOULD HAVE BEEN DIFFERENT!!
SURE, SURE! EVERY TIME YOU'VE MET SPIDER-MAN, HE'S STOPPED YOU COLD! BUT NEXT TIME'LL BE DIFFERENT--WE KNOW!!
NOW THEN, PETER, WHAT I WANTED TO ASK YOU WAS-- I'M HAVING A PARTY TONIGHT, AND...
SORRY, LIZ! NO CAN DO! I'VE GOT A DATE WITH A CERTAIN LITTLE BRUNETTE TONIGHT, EVEN THOUGH SHE MAY NOT KNOW IT YET!
22
I'M SURE FLASH WILL BE HAPPY TO GO INSTEAD OF ME! ALTHOUGH I KNOW HOW BORING IT MUST BE TO HAVE TO USE ALL THOSE ONE-SYLLABLE WORDS WHEN YOU TALK TO HIM! ANYWAY, YOU DESERVE EACH OTHER!
WHY, THAT CRUMMY--!!
DON'T SAY IT, FLASH! WE RATED THAT, AFTER THE WAY WE'VE ALWAYS TREATED PETER!
AND, LATER THAT NIGHT...
LUCKILY, I HAD THE AUTOMATIC SHUTTER OF MY CAMERA WORKING DURING MY FIGHT WITH DOC OCK, SO OL' TIGHTWAD JAMESON PAID ME A BUNDLE FOR THE PIX! YES SIREE, THINGS ARE SURE LOOKING UP FOR MY FAVORITE COUPLE OF GUYS--NAMELY ME!
FOOLED YOU, EH? SEE, WE DON'T ALWAYS HAVE UNHAPPY ENDINGS! LIKE ANYONE ELSE, OUR WEB-SPINNIN' HERO HAS HIS UPS AND DOWNS! BUT, IF HE THINKS THINGS ARE GOING TO STAY ROSY, IT'S A GOOD THING HE DOESN'T SUSPECT WHAT'S IN STORE FOR HIM NEXT ISH! SEE YOU THEN!
THE END

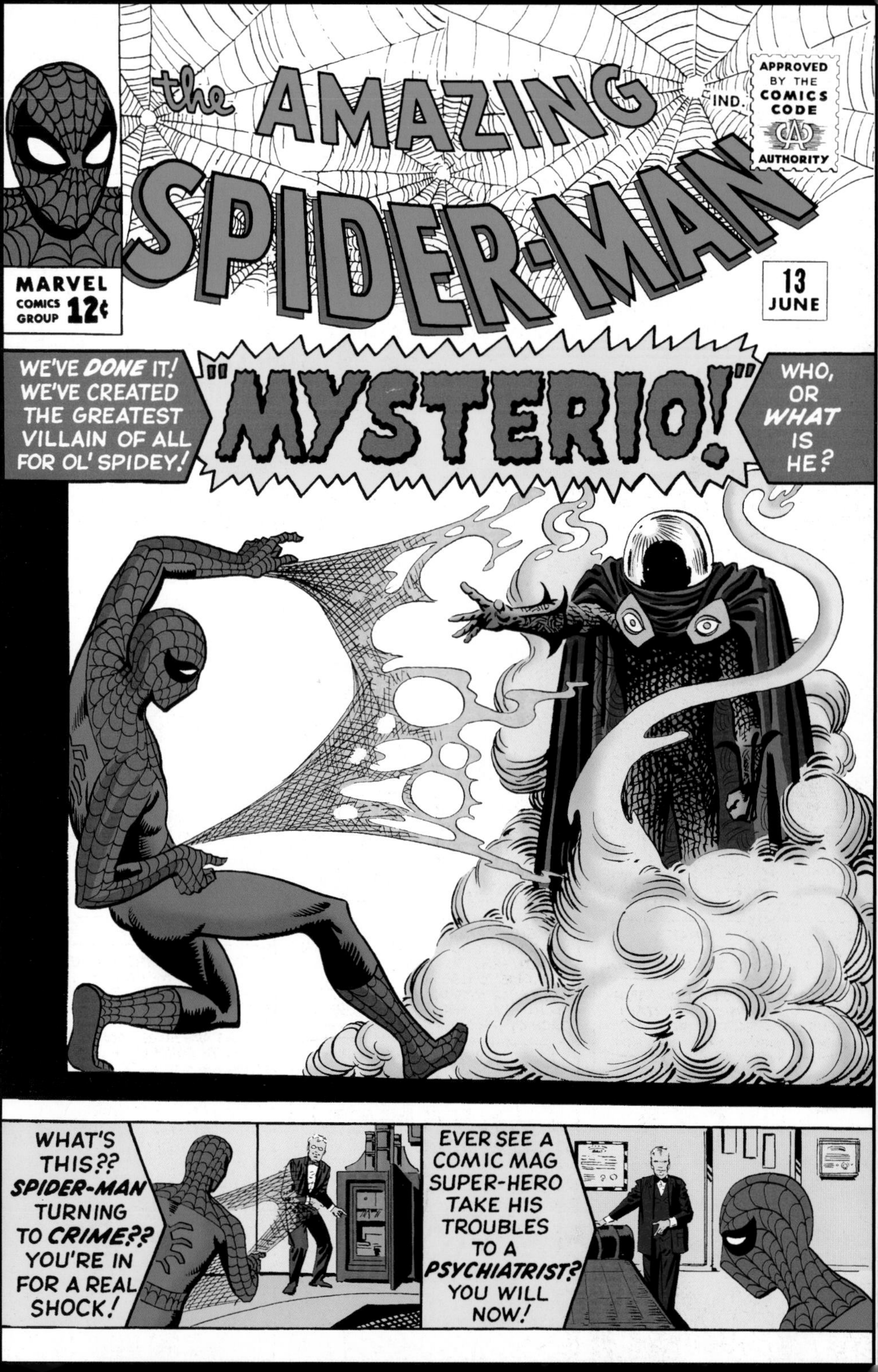

THE AMAZING SPIDER-MAN
APPROVED BY THE COMICS CODE AUTHORITY
IND.
MARVEL COMICS GROUP 12¢
13 JUNE
WE'VE DONE IT! WE'VE CREATED THE GREATEST VILLAIN OF ALL FOR OL' SPIDEY!
"MYSTERIO!"
WHO, OR WHAT IS HE?
WHAT'S THIS?? SPIDER-MAN TURNING TO CRIME?? YOU'RE IN FOR A REAL SHOCK!
EVER SEE A COMIC MAG SUPER-HERO TAKE HIS TROUBLES TO A PSYCHIATRIST? YOU WILL NOW!

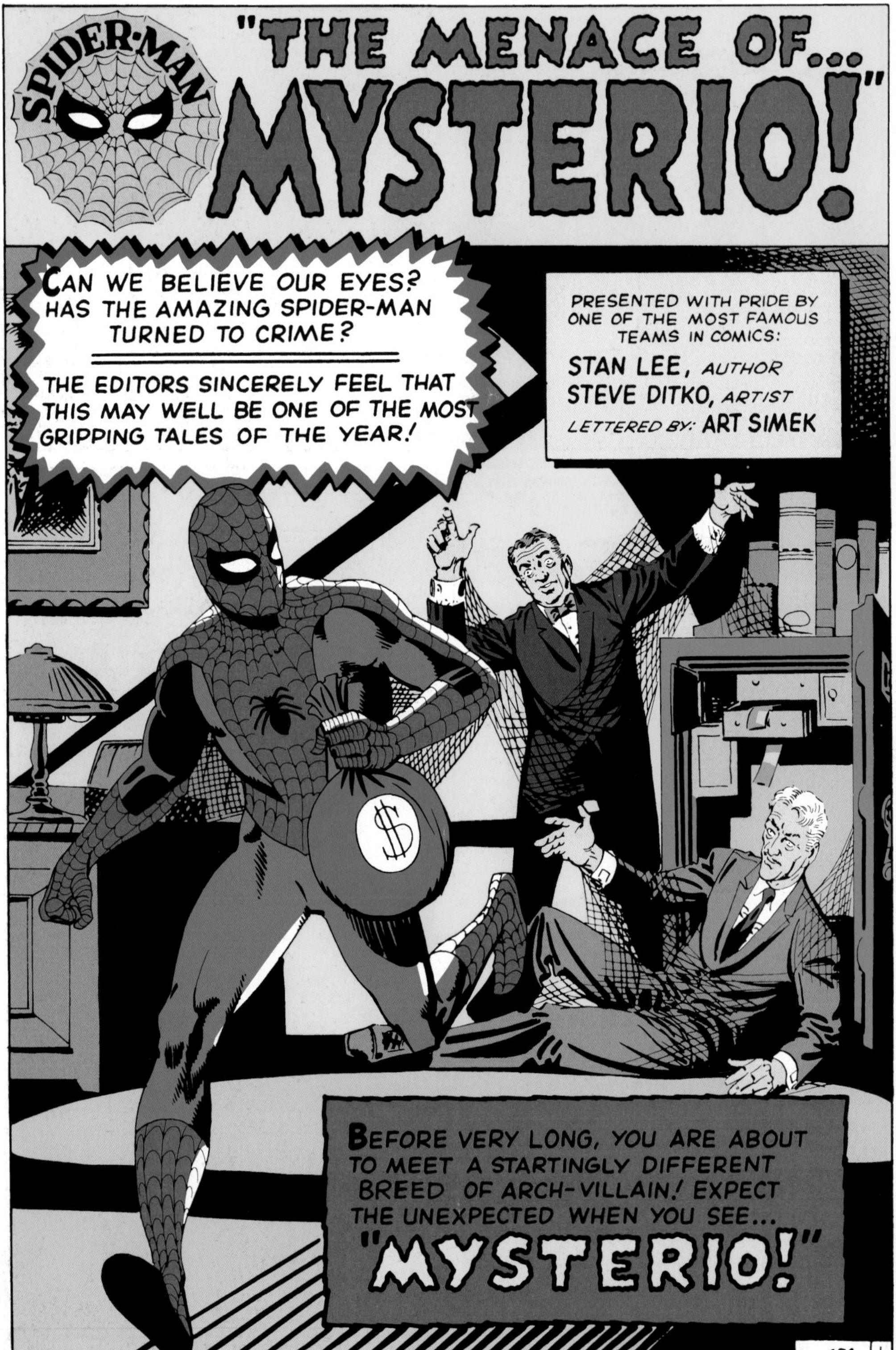
SPIDER-MAN
"THE MENACE OF... MYSTERIO!"
CAN WE BELIEVE OUR EYES? HAS THE AMAZING SPIDER-MAN TURNED TO CRIME?
THE EDITORS SINCERELY FEEL THAT THIS MAY WELL BE ONE OF THE MOST GRIPPING TALES OF THE YEAR!
PRESENTED WITH PRIDE BY ONE OF THE MOST FAMOUS TEAMS IN COMICS:
STAN LEE, AUTHOR
STEVE DITKO, ARTIST
LETTERED BY: ART SIMEK
BEFORE VERY LONG, YOU ARE ABOUT TO MEET A STARTINGLY DIFFERENT BREED OF ARCH-VILLAIN! EXPECT THE UNEXPECTED WHEN YOU SEE... "MYSTERIO!"
X-670 1

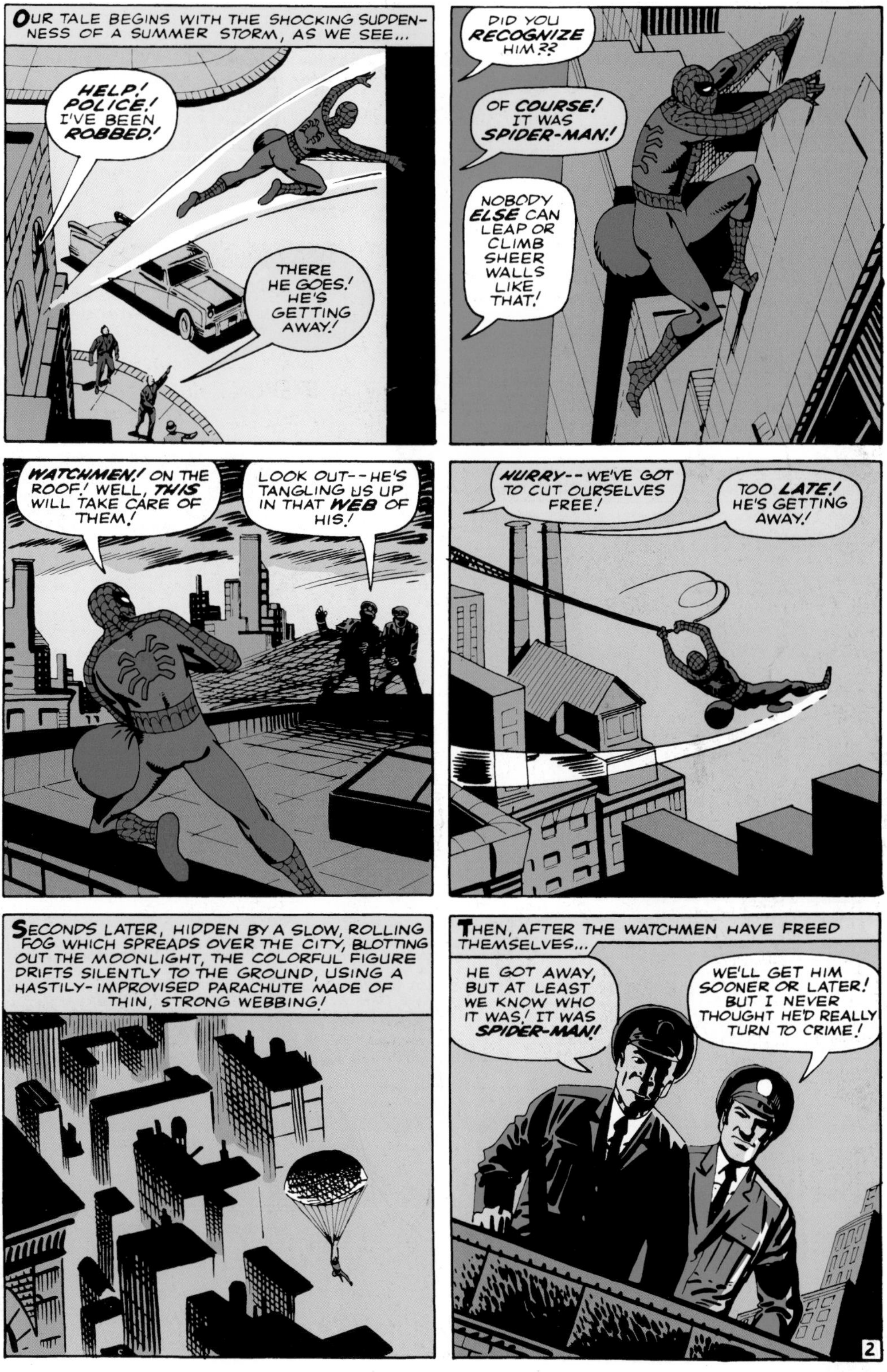
OUR TALE BEGINS WITH THE SHOCKING SUDDENNESS OF A SUMMER STORM, AS WE SEE...
HELP! POLICE! I'VE BEEN ROBBED!
THERE HE GOES! HE'S GETTING AWAY!
DID YOU RECOGNIZE HIM??
OF COURSE! IT WAS SPIDER-MAN!
NOBODY ELSE CAN LEAP OR CLIMB SHEER WALLS LIKE THAT!
WATCHMEN! ON THE ROOF! WELL, THIS WILL TAKE CARE OF THEM!
LOOK OUT--HE'S TANGLING US UP IN THAT WEB OF HIS!
HURRY--WE'VE GOT TO CUT OURSELVES FREE!
TOO LATE! HE'S GETTING AWAY!
SECONDS LATER, HIDDEN BY A SLOW, ROLLING FOG WHICH SPREADS OVER THE CITY, BLOTTING OUT THE MOONLIGHT, THE COLORFUL FIGURE DRIFTS SILENTLY TO THE GROUND, USING A HASTILY-IMPROVISED PARACHUTE MADE OF THIN, STRONG WEBBING!
THEN, AFTER THE WATCHMEN HAVE FREED THEMSELVES...
HE GOT AWAY, BUT AT LEAST WE KNOW WHO IT WAS! IT WAS SPIDER-MAN!
WE'LL GET HIM SOONER OR LATER! BUT I NEVER THOUGHT HE'D REALLY TURN TO CRIME!
2

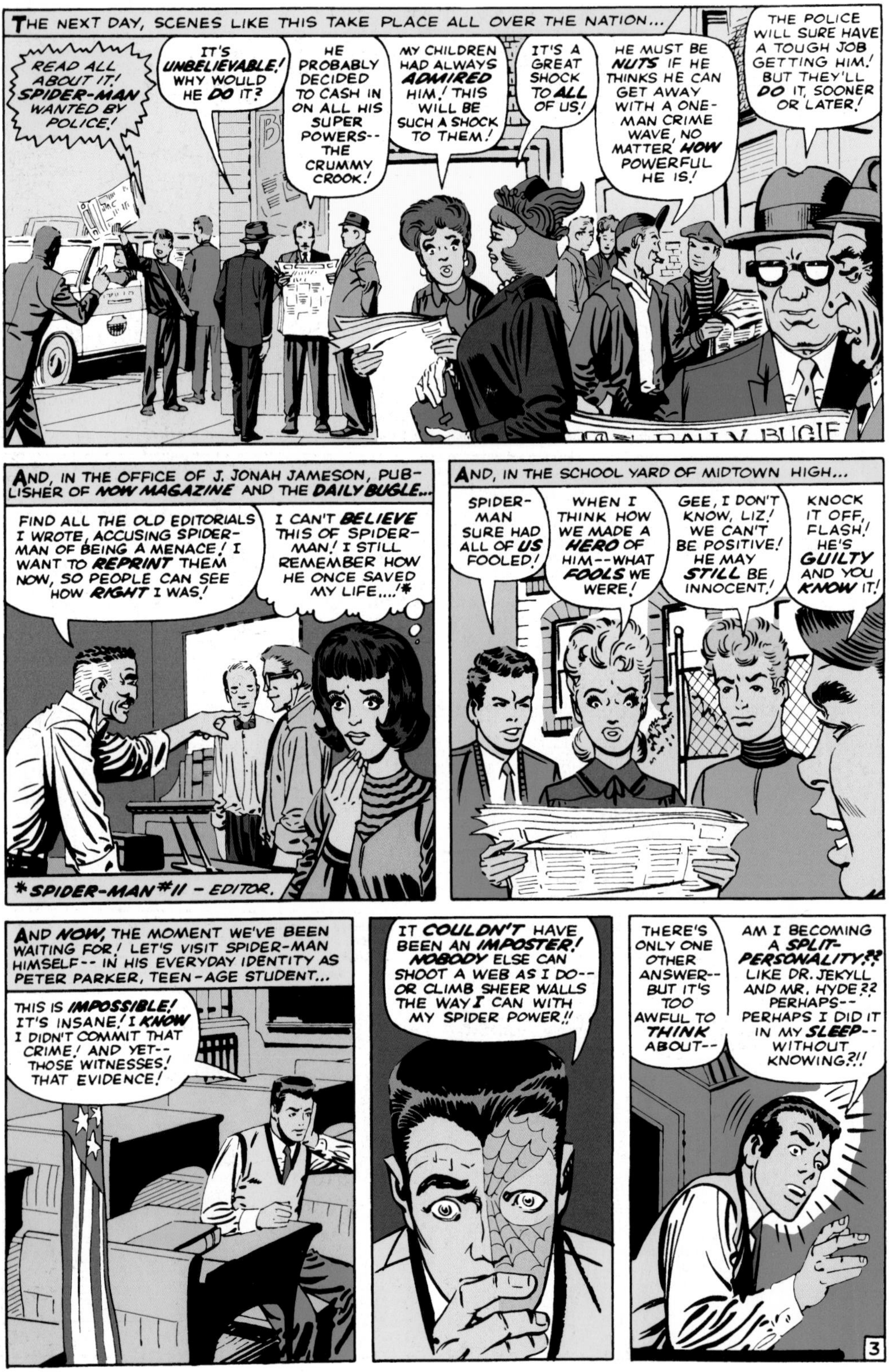
THE NEXT DAY, SCENES LIKE THIS TAKE PLACE ALL OVER THE NATION...
READ ALL ABOUT IT! SPIDER-MAN WANTED BY POLICE!
IT'S UNBELIEVABLE! WHY WOULD HE DO IT?
HE PROBABLY DECIDED TO CASH IN ON ALL HIS SUPER POWERS-- THE CRUMMY CROOK!
MY CHILDREN HAD ALWAYS ADMIRED HIM! THIS WILL BE SUCH A SHOCK TO THEM!
IT'S A GREAT SHOCK TO ALL OF US!
HE MUST BE NUTS IF HE THINKS HE CAN GET AWAY WITH A ONE-MAN CRIME WAVE, NO MATTER HOW POWERFUL HE IS!
THE POLICE WILL SURE HAVE A TOUGH JOB GETTING HIM! BUT THEY'LL DO IT, SOONER OR LATER!
AND, IN THE OFFICE OF J. JONAH JAMESON, PUBLISHER OF NOW MAGAZINE AND THE DAILY BUGLE...
FIND ALL THE OLD EDITORIALS I WROTE, ACCUSING SPIDER-MAN OF BEING A MENACE! I WANT TO REPRINT THEM NOW, SO PEOPLE CAN SEE HOW RIGHT I WAS!
I CAN'T BELIEVE THIS OF SPIDER-MAN! I STILL REMEMBER HOW HE ONCE SAVED MY LIFE...!*
*SPIDER-MAN #11 - EDITOR.
AND, IN THE SCHOOL YARD OF MIDTOWN HIGH...
SPIDER-MAN SURE HAD ALL OF US FOOLED!
WHEN I THINK HOW WE MADE A HERO OF HIM--WHAT FOOLS WE WERE!
GEE, I DON'T KNOW, LIZ! WE CAN'T BE POSITIVE! HE MAY STILL BE INNOCENT!
KNOCK IT OFF, FLASH! HE'S GUILTY AND YOU KNOW IT!
AND NOW, THE MOMENT WE'VE BEEN WAITING FOR! LET'S VISIT SPIDER-MAN HIMSELF-- IN HIS EVERYDAY IDENTITY AS PETER PARKER, TEEN-AGE STUDENT...
THIS IS IMPOSSIBLE! IT'S INSANE! I KNOW I DIDN'T COMMIT THAT CRIME! AND YET-- THOSE WITNESSES! THAT EVIDENCE!
IT COULDN'T HAVE BEEN AN IMPOSTER! NOBODY ELSE CAN SHOOT A WEB AS I DO-- OR CLIMB SHEER WALLS THE WAY I CAN WITH MY SPIDER POWER!!
THERE'S ONLY ONE OTHER ANSWER-- BUT IT'S TOO AWFUL TO THINK ABOUT--
AM I BECOMING A SPLIT-PERSONALITY?? LIKE DR. JEKYLL AND MR. HYDE?? PERHAPS-- PERHAPS I DID IT IN MY SLEEP-- WITHOUT KNOWING?!!
3

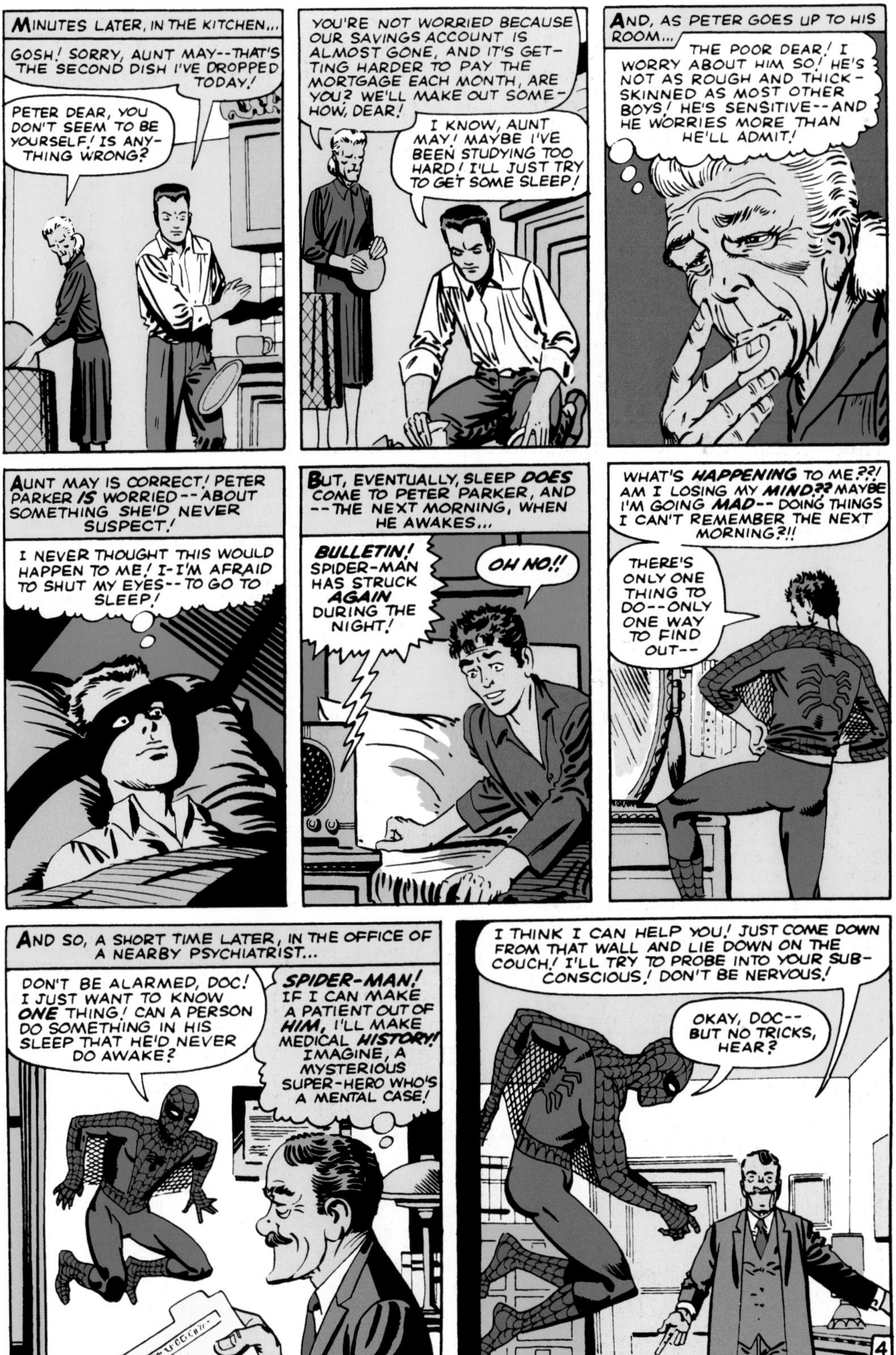
MINUTES LATER, IN THE KITCHEN...
GOSH! SORRY, AUNT MAY--THAT'S THE SECOND DISH I'VE DROPPED TODAY!
PETER DEAR, YOU DON'T SEEM TO BE YOURSELF! IS ANYTHING WRONG?
YOU'RE NOT WORRIED BECAUSE OUR SAVINGS ACCOUNT IS ALMOST GONE, AND IT'S GETTING HARDER TO PAY THE MORTGAGE EACH MONTH, ARE YOU? WE'LL MAKE OUT SOMEHOW, DEAR!
I KNOW, AUNT MAY! MAYBE I'VE BEEN STUDYING TOO HARD! I'LL JUST TRY TO GET SOME SLEEP!
AND, AS PETER GOES UP TO HIS ROOM...
THE POOR DEAR! I WORRY ABOUT HIM SO! HE'S NOT AS ROUGH AND THICK-SKINNED AS MOST OTHER BOYS! HE'S SENSITIVE--AND HE WORRIES MORE THAN HE'LL ADMIT!
AUNT MAY IS CORRECT! PETER PARKER IS WORRIED--ABOUT SOMETHING SHE'D NEVER SUSPECT!
I NEVER THOUGHT THIS WOULD HAPPEN TO ME! I-I'M AFRAID TO SHUT MY EYES--TO GO TO SLEEP!
BUT, EVENTUALLY, SLEEP DOES COME TO PETER PARKER, AND --THE NEXT MORNING, WHEN HE AWAKES...
BULLETIN! SPIDER-MAN HAS STRUCK AGAIN DURING THE NIGHT!
OH NO!!
WHAT'S HAPPENING TO ME??! AM I LOSING MY MIND?? MAYBE I'M GOING MAD-- DOING THINGS I CAN'T REMEMBER THE NEXT MORNING?!!
THERE'S ONLY ONE THING TO DO--ONLY ONE WAY TO FIND OUT--
AND SO, A SHORT TIME LATER, IN THE OFFICE OF A NEARBY PSYCHIATRIST...
DON'T BE ALARMED, DOC! I JUST WANT TO KNOW ONE THING! CAN A PERSON DO SOMETHING IN HIS SLEEP THAT HE'D NEVER DO AWAKE?
SPIDER-MAN! IF I CAN MAKE A PATIENT OUT OF HIM, I'LL MAKE MEDICAL HISTORY! IMAGINE, A MYSTERIOUS SUPER-HERO WHO'S A MENTAL CASE!
I THINK I CAN HELP YOU! JUST COME DOWN FROM THAT WALL AND LIE DOWN ON THE COUCH! I'LL TRY TO PROBE INTO YOUR SUB-CONSCIOUS! DON'T BE NERVOUS!
OKAY, DOC--BUT NO TRICKS, HEAR?
4

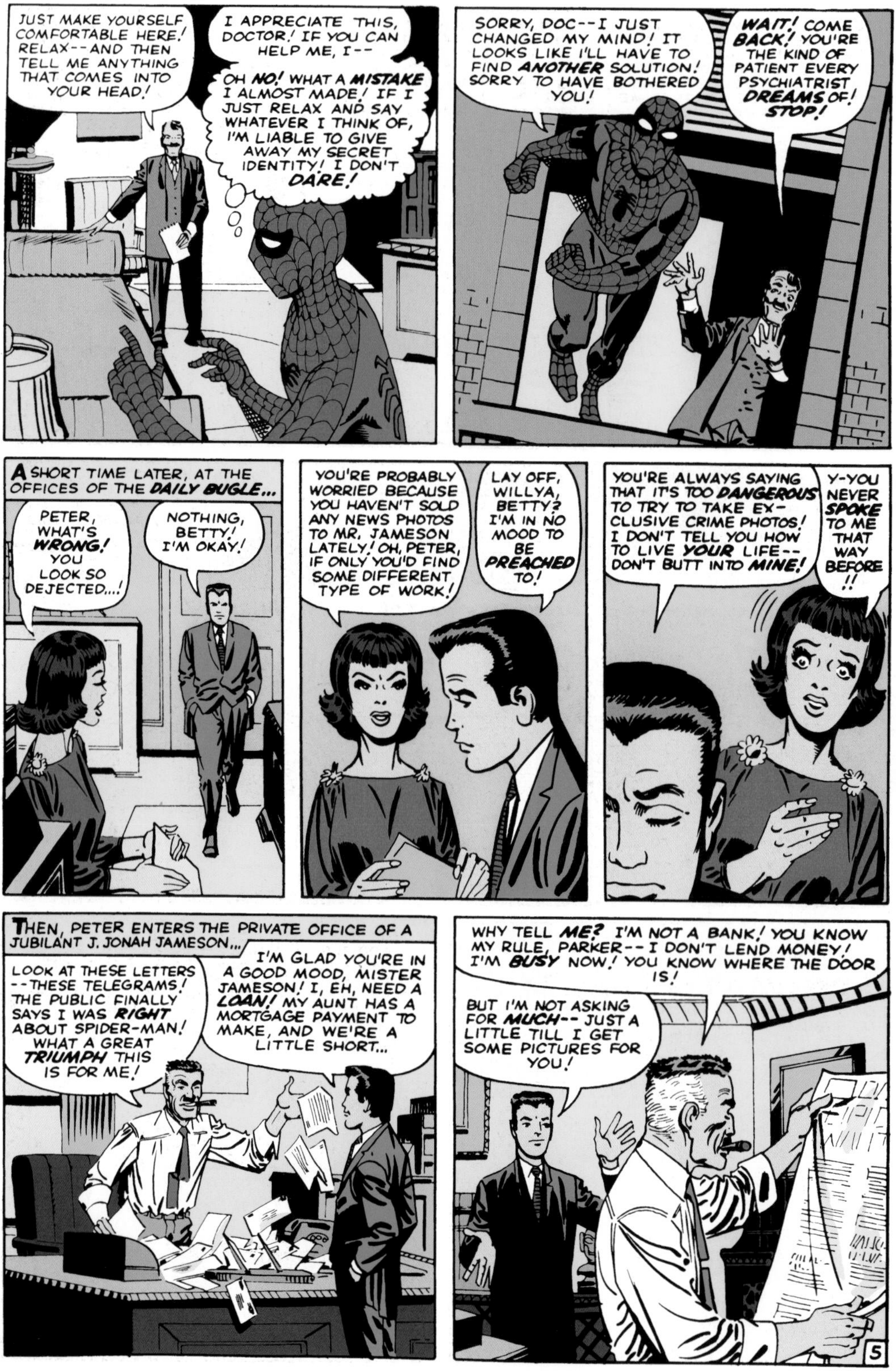
JUST MAKE YOURSELF COMFORTABLE HERE! RELAX--AND THEN TELL ME ANYTHING THAT COMES INTO YOUR HEAD!
I APPRECIATE THIS, DOCTOR! IF YOU CAN HELP ME, I--
OH NO! WHAT A MISTAKE I ALMOST MADE! IF I JUST RELAX AND SAY WHATEVER I THINK OF, I'M LIABLE TO GIVE AWAY MY SECRET IDENTITY! I DON'T DARE!
SORRY, DOC--I JUST CHANGED MY MIND! IT LOOKS LIKE I'LL HAVE TO FIND ANOTHER SOLUTION! SORRY TO HAVE BOTHERED YOU!
WAIT! COME BACK! YOU'RE THE KIND OF PATIENT EVERY PSYCHIATRIST DREAMS OF! STOP!
A SHORT TIME LATER, AT THE OFFICES OF THE DAILY BUGLE...
PETER, WHAT'S WRONG! YOU LOOK SO DEJECTED...!
NOTHING, BETTY! I'M OKAY!
YOU'RE PROBABLY WORRIED BECAUSE YOU HAVEN'T SOLD ANY NEWS PHOTOS TO MR. JAMESON LATELY! OH, PETER, IF ONLY YOU'D FIND SOME DIFFERENT TYPE OF WORK!
LAY OFF, WILLYA, BETTY? I'M IN NO MOOD TO BE PREACHED TO!
YOU'RE ALWAYS SAYING THAT IT'S TOO DANGEROUS TO TRY TO TAKE EX-CLUSIVE CRIME PHOTOS! I DON'T TELL YOU HOW TO LIVE YOUR LIFE--DON'T BUTT INTO MINE!
Y-YOU NEVER SPOKE TO ME THAT WAY BEFORE !!
THEN, PETER ENTERS THE PRIVATE OFFICE OF A JUBILANT J. JONAH JAMESON...
LOOK AT THESE LETTERS--THESE TELEGRAMS! THE PUBLIC FINALLY SAYS I WAS RIGHT ABOUT SPIDER-MAN! WHAT A GREAT TRIUMPH THIS IS FOR ME!
I'M GLAD YOU'RE IN A GOOD MOOD, MISTER JAMESON! I, EH, NEED A LOAN! MY AUNT HAS A MORTGAGE PAYMENT TO MAKE, AND WE'RE A LITTLE SHORT...
WHY TELL ME? I'M NOT A BANK! YOU KNOW MY RULE, PARKER--I DON'T LEND MONEY! I'M BUSY NOW! YOU KNOW WHERE THE DOOR IS!
BUT I'M NOT ASKING FOR MUCH--JUST A LITTLE TILL I GET SOME PICTURES FOR YOU!
5

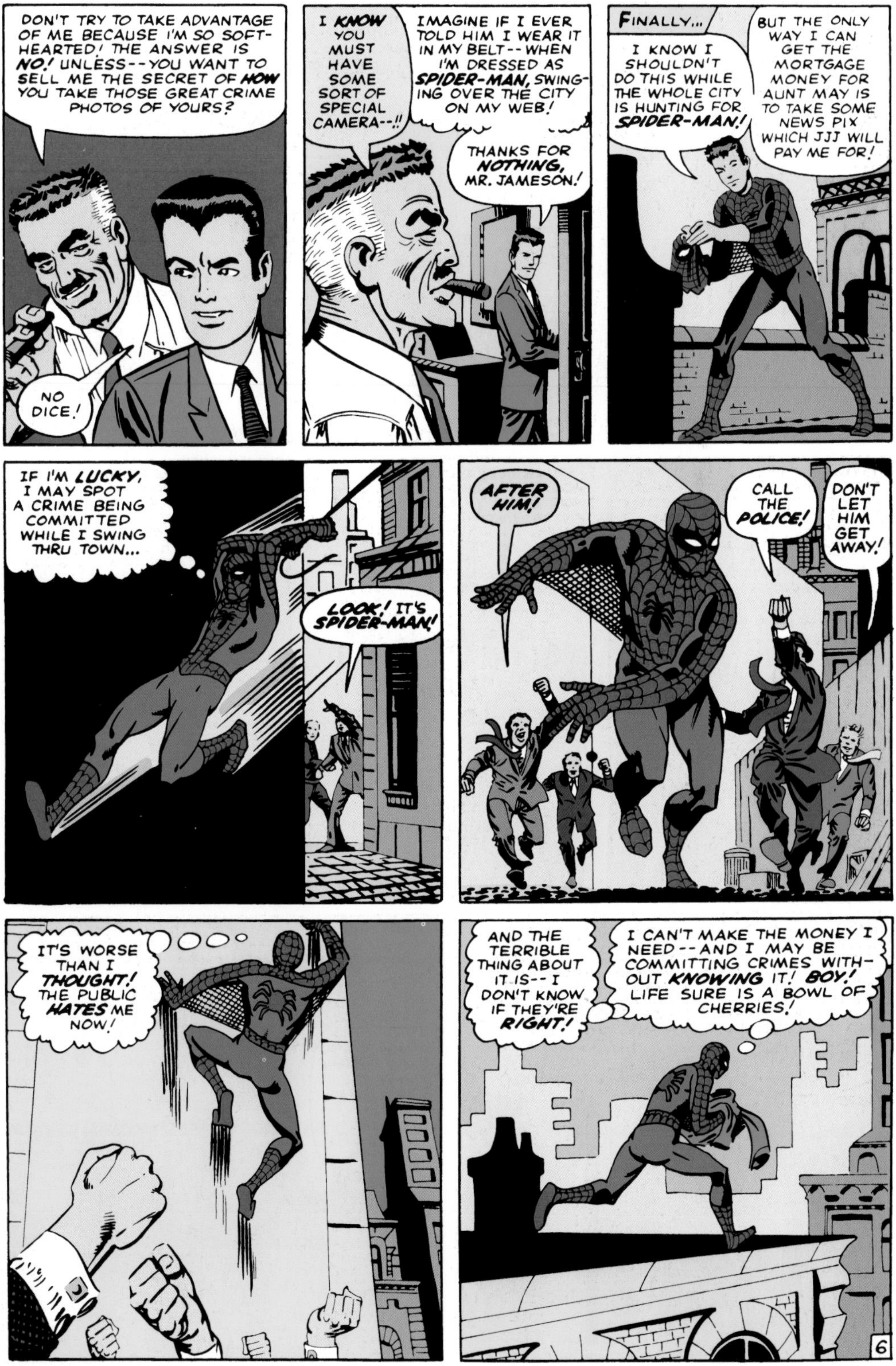
DON'T TRY TO TAKE ADVANTAGE OF ME BECAUSE I'M SO SOFT-HEARTED! THE ANSWER IS NO! UNLESS--YOU WANT TO SELL ME THE SECRET OF HOW YOU TAKE THOSE GREAT CRIME PHOTOS OF YOURS?
NO DICE!
I KNOW YOU MUST HAVE SOME SORT OF SPECIAL CAMERA--!!
IMAGINE IF I EVER TOLD HIM I WEAR IT IN MY BELT--WHEN I'M DRESSED AS SPIDER-MAN, SWINGING OVER THE CITY ON MY WEB!
THANKS FOR NOTHING, MR. JAMESON!
FINALLY...
I KNOW I SHOULDN'T DO THIS WHILE THE WHOLE CITY IS HUNTING FOR SPIDER-MAN!
BUT THE ONLY WAY I CAN GET THE MORTGAGE MONEY FOR AUNT MAY IS TO TAKE SOME NEWS PIX WHICH JJJ WILL PAY ME FOR!
IF I'M LUCKY, I MAY SPOT A CRIME BEING COMMITTED WHILE I SWING THRU TOWN...
LOOK! IT'S SPIDER-MAN!
AFTER HIM!
CALL THE POLICE!
DON'T LET HIM GET AWAY!
IT'S WORSE THAN I THOUGHT! THE PUBLIC HATES ME NOW!
AND THE TERRIBLE THING ABOUT IT IS--I DON'T KNOW IF THEY'RE RIGHT!
I CAN'T MAKE THE MONEY I NEED--AND I MAY BE COMMITTING CRIMES WITHOUT KNOWING IT! BOY! LIFE SURE IS A BOWL OF CHERRIES!
6

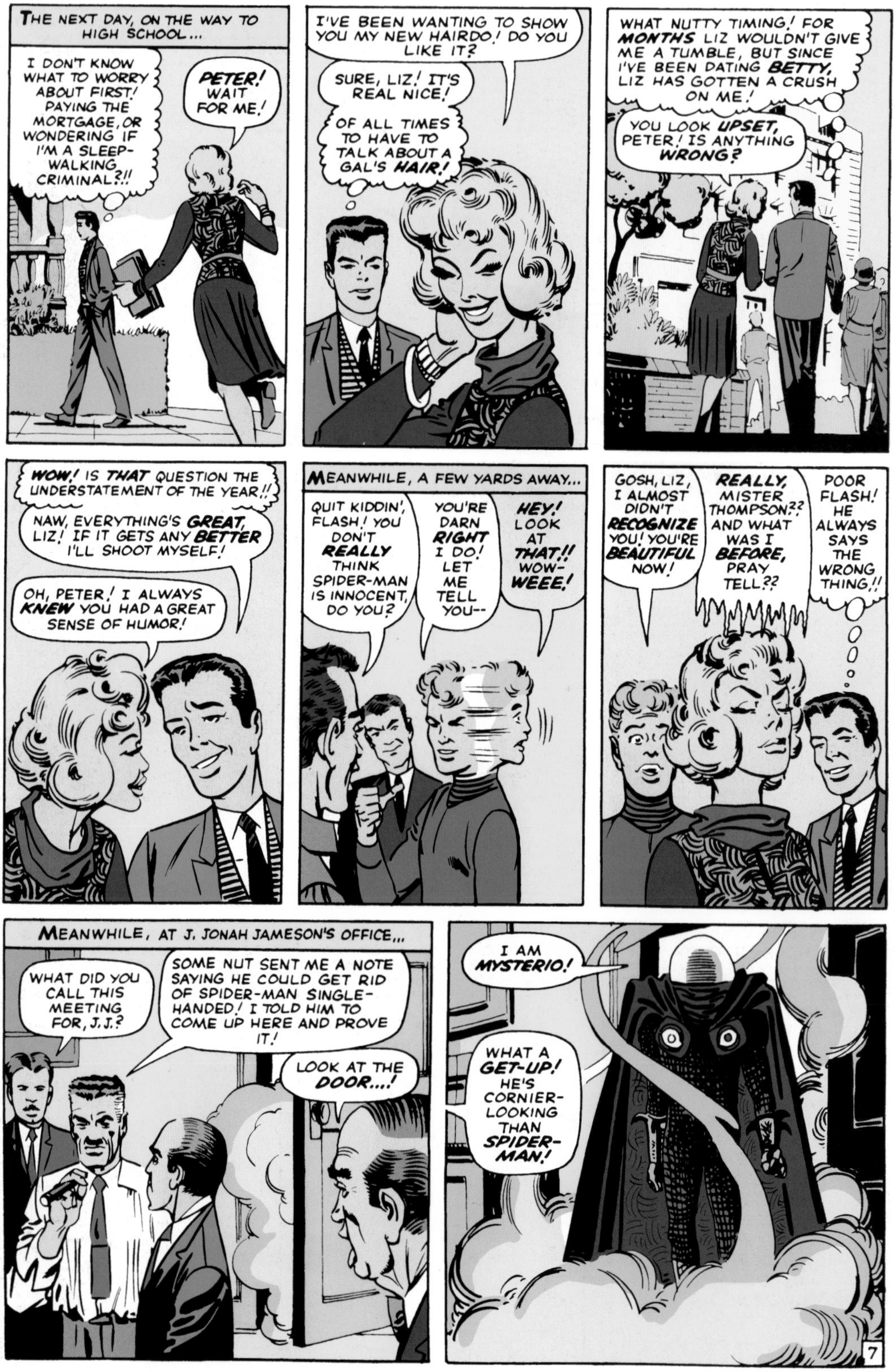
THE NEXT DAY, ON THE WAY TO HIGH SCHOOL...
I DON'T KNOW WHAT TO WORRY ABOUT FIRST! PAYING THE MORTGAGE, OR WONDERING IF I'M A SLEEP-WALKING CRIMINAL?!!
PETER! WAIT FOR ME!
I'VE BEEN WANTING TO SHOW YOU MY NEW HAIRDO! DO YOU LIKE IT?
SURE, LIZ! IT'S REAL NICE!
OF ALL TIMES TO HAVE TO TALK ABOUT A GAL'S HAIR!
WHAT NUTTY TIMING! FOR MONTHS LIZ WOULDN'T GIVE ME A TUMBLE, BUT SINCE I'VE BEEN DATING BETTY, LIZ HAS GOTTEN A CRUSH ON ME!
YOU LOOK UPSET, PETER! IS ANYTHING WRONG?
WOW! IS THAT QUESTION THE UNDERSTATEMENT OF THE YEAR!!
NAW, EVERYTHING'S GREAT, LIZ! IF IT GETS ANY BETTER I'LL SHOOT MYSELF!
OH, PETER! I ALWAYS KNEW YOU HAD A GREAT SENSE OF HUMOR!
MEANWHILE, A FEW YARDS AWAY...
QUIT KIDDIN', FLASH! YOU DON'T REALLY THINK SPIDER-MAN IS INNOCENT, DO YOU?
YOU'RE DARN RIGHT I DO! LET ME TELL YOU--
HEY! LOOK AT THAT!! WOW-WEEE!
GOSH, LIZ, I ALMOST DIDN'T RECOGNIZE YOU! YOU'RE BEAUTIFUL NOW!
REALLY, MISTER THOMPSON?? AND WHAT WAS I BEFORE, PRAY TELL??
POOR FLASH! HE ALWAYS SAYS THE WRONG THING!!
MEANWHILE, AT J. JONAH JAMESON'S OFFICE...
WHAT DID YOU CALL THIS MEETING FOR, J.J.?
SOME NUT SENT ME A NOTE SAYING HE COULD GET RID OF SPIDER-MAN SINGLE-HANDED! I TOLD HIM TO COME UP HERE AND PROVE IT!
LOOK AT THE DOOR...!
I AM MYSTERIO!
WHAT A GET-UP! HE'S CORNIER-LOOKING THAN SPIDER-MAN!
7

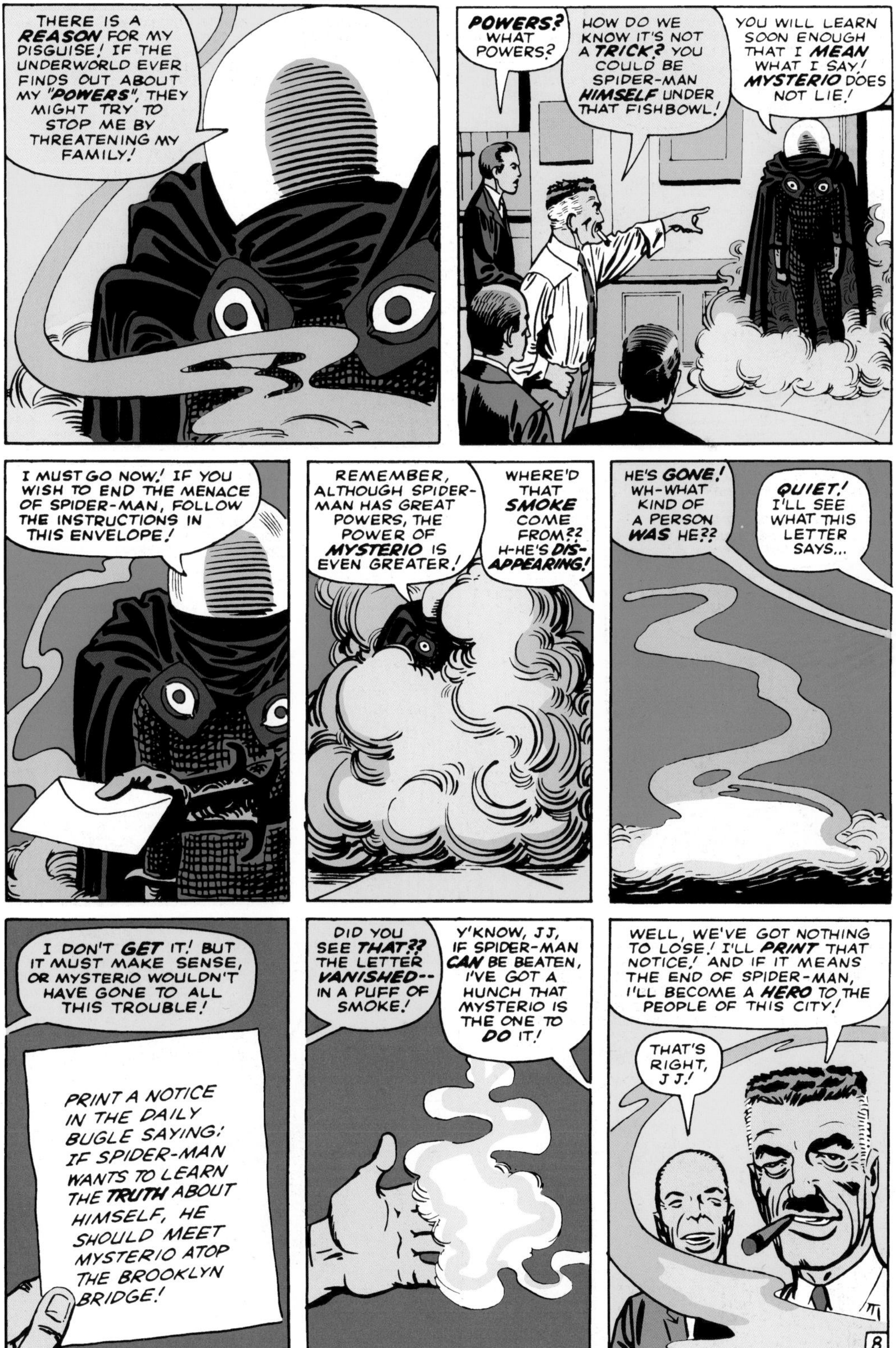
THERE IS A REASON FOR MY DISGUISE! IF THE UNDERWORLD EVER FINDS OUT ABOUT MY "POWERS", THEY MIGHT TRY TO STOP ME BY THREATENING MY FAMILY!
POWERS? WHAT POWERS?
HOW DO WE KNOW IT'S NOT A TRICK? YOU COULD BE SPIDER-MAN HIMSELF UNDER THAT FISHBOWL!
YOU WILL LEARN SOON ENOUGH THAT I MEAN WHAT I SAY! MYSTERIO DOES NOT LIE!
I MUST GO NOW! IF YOU WISH TO END THE MENACE OF SPIDER-MAN, FOLLOW THE INSTRUCTIONS IN THIS ENVELOPE!
REMEMBER, ALTHOUGH SPIDER-MAN HAS GREAT POWERS, THE POWER OF MYSTERIO IS EVEN GREATER!
WHERE'D THAT SMOKE COME FROM?? H-HE'S DIS-APPEARING!
HE'S GONE! WH-WHAT KIND OF A PERSON WAS HE??
QUIET! I'LL SEE WHAT THIS LETTER SAYS...
I DON'T GET IT! BUT IT MUST MAKE SENSE, OR MYSTERIO WOULDN'T HAVE GONE TO ALL THIS TROUBLE!
PRINT A NOTICE IN THE DAILY BUGLE SAYING: IF SPIDER-MAN WANTS TO LEARN THE TRUTH ABOUT HIMSELF, HE SHOULD MEET MYSTERIO ATOP THE BROOKLYN BRIDGE!
DID YOU SEE THAT?? THE LETTER VANISHED-- IN A PUFF OF SMOKE!
Y'KNOW, JJ, IF SPIDER-MAN CAN BE BEATEN, I'VE GOT A HUNCH THAT MYSTERIO IS THE ONE TO DO IT!
WELL, WE'VE GOT NOTHING TO LOSE! I'LL PRINT THAT NOTICE! AND IF IT MEANS THE END OF SPIDER-MAN, I'LL BECOME A HERO TO THE PEOPLE OF THIS CITY!
THAT'S RIGHT, J J!
8

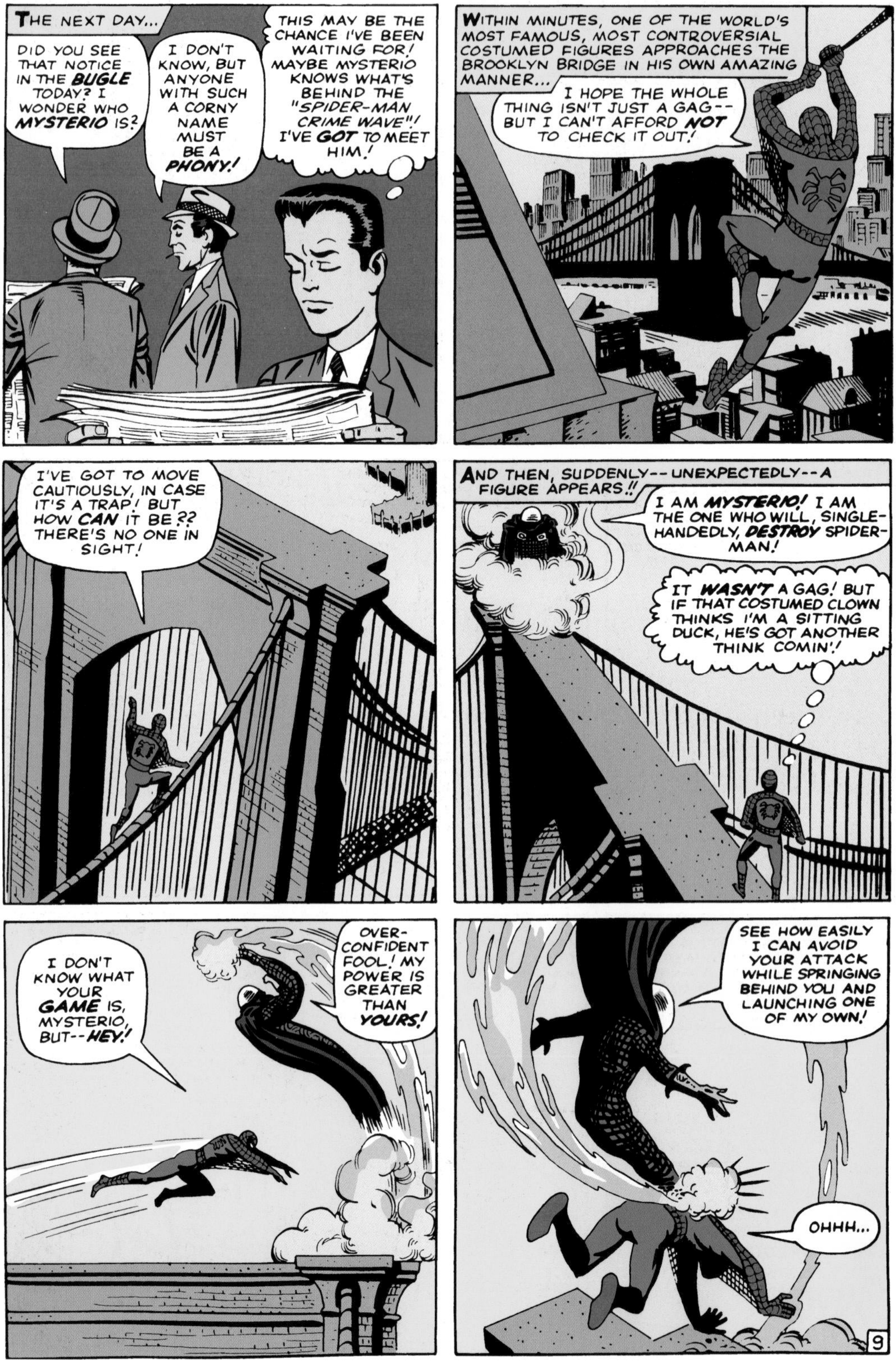
THE NEXT DAY...
DID YOU SEE THAT NOTICE IN THE BUGLE TODAY? I WONDER WHO MYSTERIO IS?
I DON'T KNOW, BUT ANYONE WITH SUCH A CORNY NAME MUST BE A PHONY!
THIS MAY BE THE CHANCE I'VE BEEN WAITING FOR! MAYBE MYSTERIO KNOWS WHAT'S BEHIND THE "SPIDER-MAN CRIME WAVE"! I'VE GOT TO MEET HIM!
WITHIN MINUTES, ONE OF THE WORLD'S MOST FAMOUS, MOST CONTROVERSIAL COSTUMED FIGURES APPROACHES THE BROOKLYN BRIDGE IN HIS OWN AMAZING MANNER...
I HOPE THE WHOLE THING ISN'T JUST A GAG-- BUT I CAN'T AFFORD NOT TO CHECK IT OUT!
I'VE GOT TO MOVE CAUTIOUSLY, IN CASE IT'S A TRAP! BUT HOW CAN IT BE?? THERE'S NO ONE IN SIGHT!
AND THEN, SUDDENLY--UNEXPECTEDLY--A FIGURE APPEARS!!
I AM MYSTERIO! I AM THE ONE WHO WILL, SINGLE-HANDEDLY, DESTROY SPIDER-MAN!
IT WASN'T A GAG! BUT IF THAT COSTUMED CLOWN THINKS I'M A SITTING DUCK, HE'S GOT ANOTHER THINK COMIN'!
I DON'T KNOW WHAT YOUR GAME IS, MYSTERIO, BUT--HEY!
OVER-CONFIDENT FOOL! MY POWER IS GREATER THAN YOURS!
SEE HOW EASILY I CAN AVOID YOUR ATTACK WHILE SPRINGING BEHIND YOU AND LAUNCHING ONE OF MY OWN!
OHHH...
9

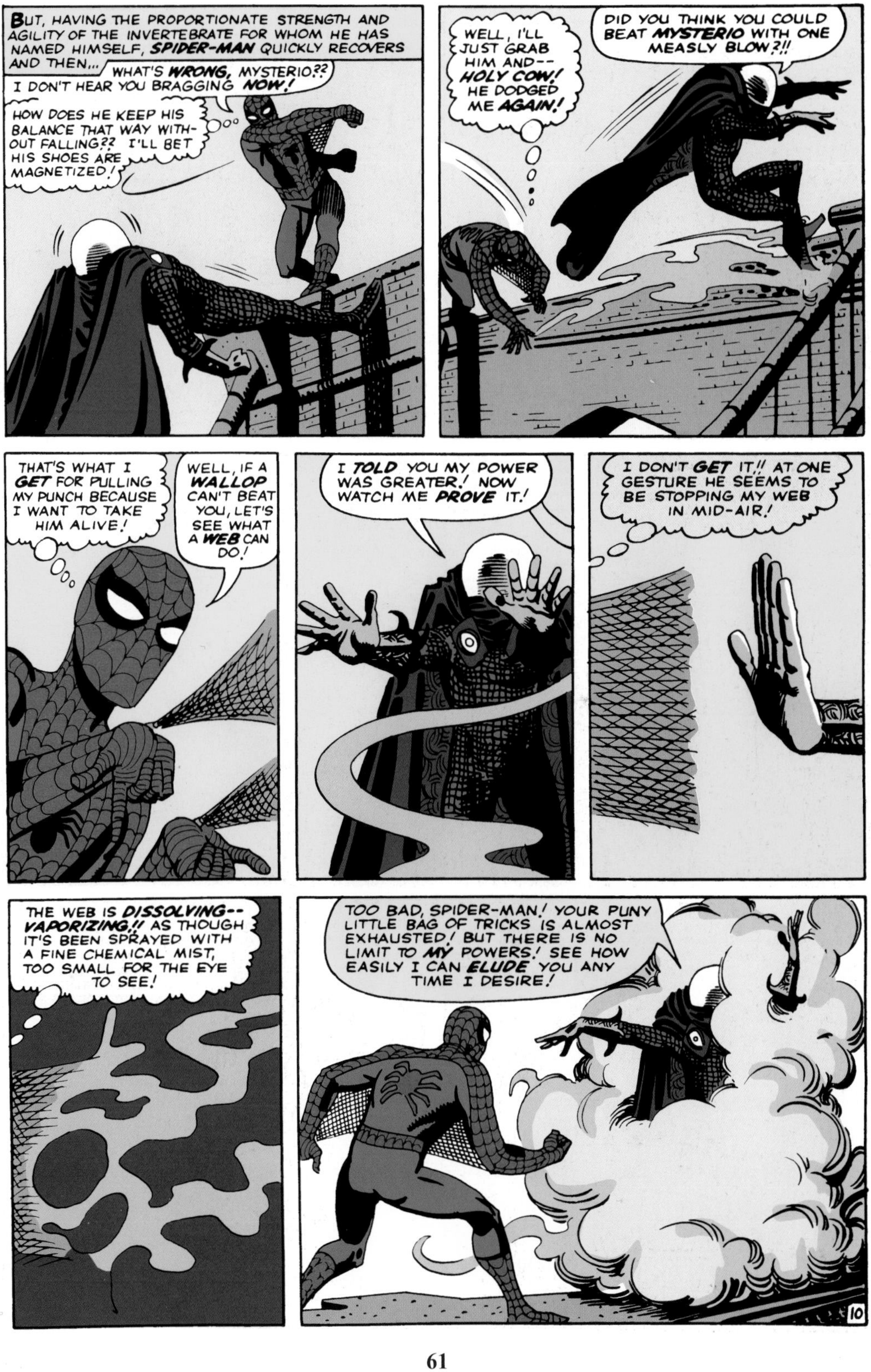
BUT, HAVING THE PROPORTIONATE STRENGTH AND AGILITY OF THE INVERTEBRATE FOR WHOM HE HAS NAMED HIMSELF, SPIDER-MAN QUICKLY RECOVERS AND THEN...
WHAT'S WRONG, MYSTERIO?? I DON'T HEAR YOU BRAGGING NOW!
HOW DOES HE KEEP HIS BALANCE THAT WAY WITHOUT FALLING?? I'LL BET HIS SHOES ARE MAGNETIZED!
WELL, I'LL JUST GRAB HIM AND-- HOLY COW! HE DODGED ME AGAIN!
DID YOU THINK YOU COULD BEAT MYSTERIO WITH ONE MEASLY BLOW?!!
THAT'S WHAT I GET FOR PULLING MY PUNCH BECAUSE I WANT TO TAKE HIM ALIVE!
WELL, IF A WALLOP CAN'T BEAT YOU, LET'S SEE WHAT A WEB CAN DO!
I TOLD YOU MY POWER WAS GREATER! NOW WATCH ME PROVE IT!
I DON'T GET IT!! AT ONE GESTURE HE SEEMS TO BE STOPPING MY WEB IN MID-AIR!
THE WEB IS DISSOLVING-- VAPORIZING!! AS THOUGH IT'S BEEN SPRAYED WITH A FINE CHEMICAL MIST, TOO SMALL FOR THE EYE TO SEE!
TOO BAD, SPIDER-MAN! YOUR PUNY LITTLE BAG OF TRICKS IS ALMOST EXHAUSTED! BUT THERE IS NO LIMIT TO MY POWERS! SEE HOW EASILY I CAN ELUDE YOU ANY TIME I DESIRE!
10

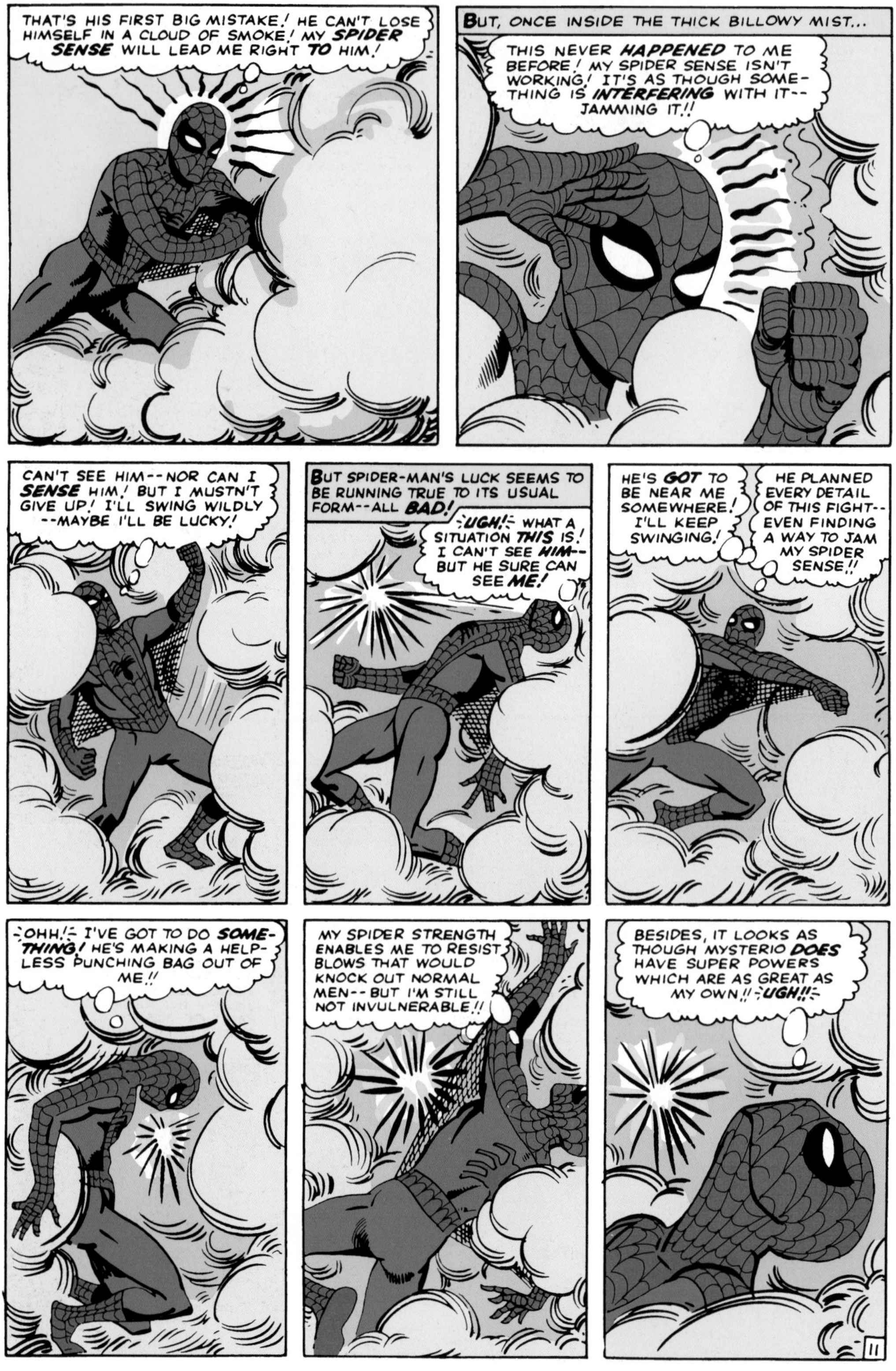
THAT'S HIS FIRST BIG MISTAKE! HE CAN'T LOSE HIMSELF IN A CLOUD OF SMOKE! MY SPIDER SENSE WILL LEAD ME RIGHT TO HIM!
BUT, ONCE INSIDE THE THICK BILLOWY MIST...
THIS NEVER HAPPENED TO ME BEFORE! MY SPIDER SENSE ISN'T WORKING! IT'S AS THOUGH SOMETHING IS INTERFERING WITH IT-- JAMMING IT!!
CAN'T SEE HIM--NOR CAN I SENSE HIM! BUT I MUSTN'T GIVE UP! I'LL SWING WILDLY --MAYBE I'LL BE LUCKY!
BUT SPIDER-MAN'S LUCK SEEMS TO BE RUNNING TRUE TO ITS USUAL FORM--ALL BAD!
UGH! WHAT A SITUATION THIS IS! I CAN'T SEE HIM-- BUT HE SURE CAN SEE ME!
HE'S GOT TO BE NEAR ME SOMEWHERE! I'LL KEEP SWINGING!
HE PLANNED EVERY DETAIL OF THIS FIGHT-- EVEN FINDING A WAY TO JAM MY SPIDER SENSE!!
OHH! I'VE GOT TO DO SOMETHING! HE'S MAKING A HELPLESS PUNCHING BAG OUT OF ME!!
MY SPIDER STRENGTH ENABLES ME TO RESIST BLOWS THAT WOULD KNOCK OUT NORMAL MEN-- BUT I'M STILL NOT INVULNERABLE!!
BESIDES, IT LOOKS AS THOUGH MYSTERIO DOES HAVE SUPER POWERS WHICH ARE AS GREAT AS MY OWN!! UGH!!
11

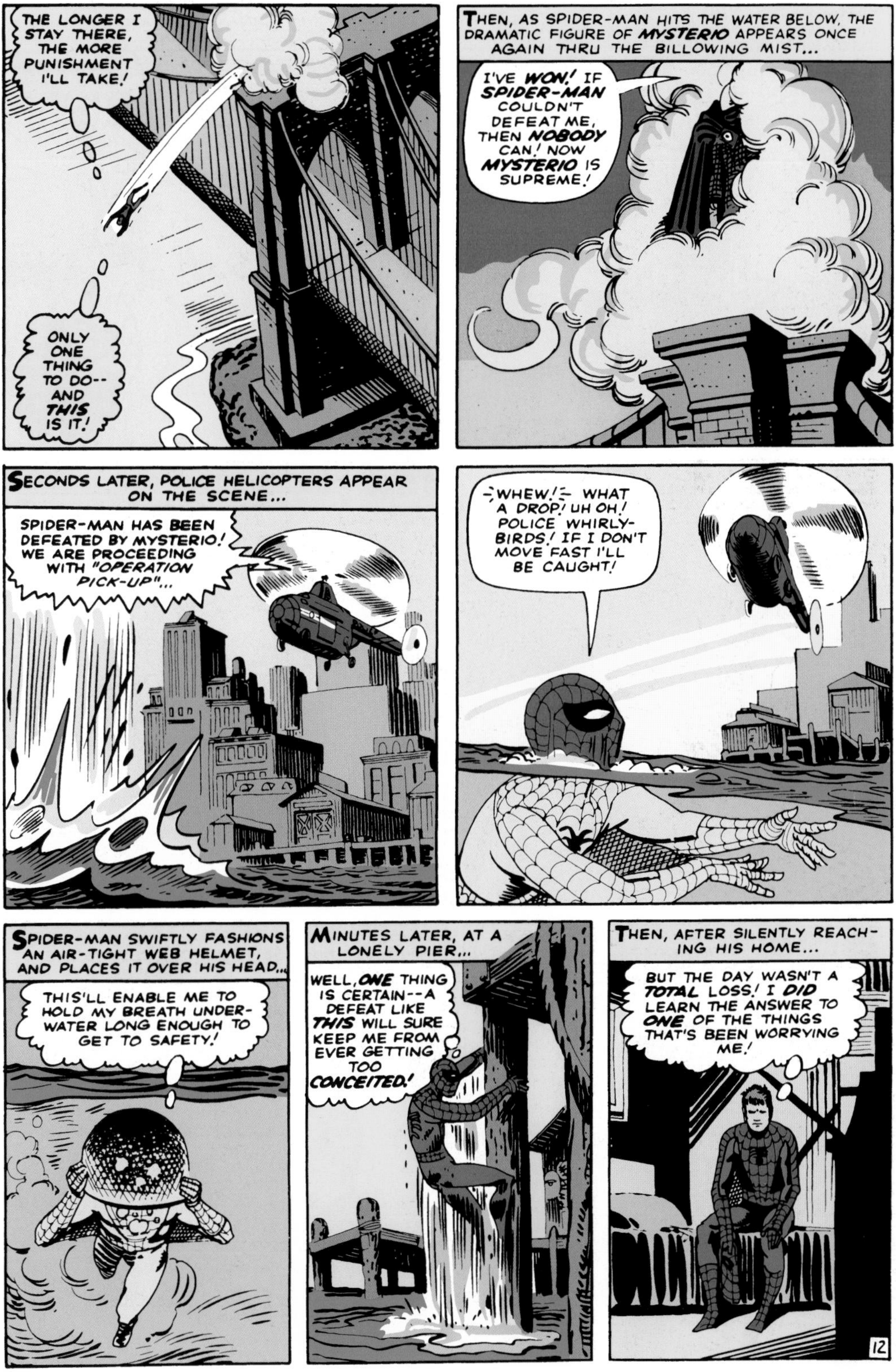
THE LONGER I STAY THERE, THE MORE PUNISHMENT I'LL TAKE!
ONLY ONE THING TO DO-- AND THIS IS IT!
THEN, AS SPIDER-MAN HITS THE WATER BELOW, THE DRAMATIC FIGURE OF MYSTERIO APPEARS ONCE AGAIN THRU THE BILLOWING MIST...
I'VE WON! IF SPIDER-MAN COULDN'T DEFEAT ME, THEN NOBODY CAN! NOW MYSTERIO IS SUPREME!
SECONDS LATER, POLICE HELICOPTERS APPEAR ON THE SCENE...
SPIDER-MAN HAS BEEN DEFEATED BY MYSTERIO! WE ARE PROCEEDING WITH "OPERATION PICK-UP"...
WHEW! WHAT A DROP! UH OH! POLICE WHIRLY-BIRDS! IF I DON'T MOVE FAST I'LL BE CAUGHT!
SPIDER-MAN SWIFTLY FASHIONS AN AIR-TIGHT WEB HELMET, AND PLACES IT OVER HIS HEAD...
THIS'LL ENABLE ME TO HOLD MY BREATH UNDER-WATER LONG ENOUGH TO GET TO SAFETY!
MINUTES LATER, AT A LONELY PIER...
WELL, ONE THING IS CERTAIN--A DEFEAT LIKE THIS WILL SURE KEEP ME FROM EVER GETTING TOO CONCEITED!
THEN, AFTER SILENTLY REACHING HIS HOME...
BUT THE DAY WASN'T A TOTAL LOSS! I DID LEARN THE ANSWER TO ONE OF THE THINGS THAT'S BEEN WORRYING ME!
12

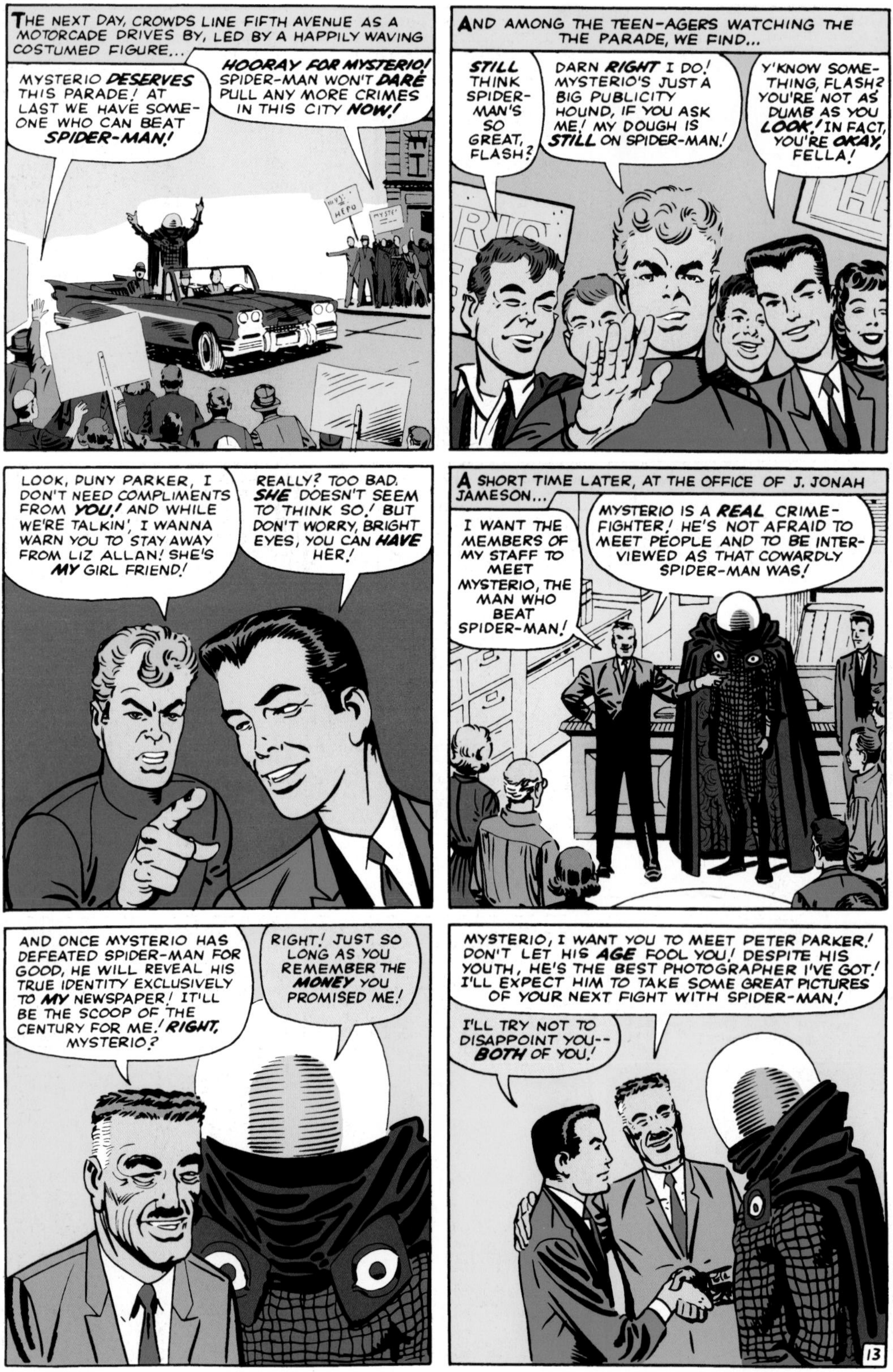
THE NEXT DAY, CROWDS LINE FIFTH AVENUE AS A MOTORCADE DRIVES BY, LED BY A HAPPILY WAVING COSTUMED FIGURE...
MYSTERIO DESERVES THIS PARADE! AT LAST WE HAVE SOMEONE WHO CAN BEAT SPIDER-MAN!
HOORAY FOR MYSTERIO! SPIDER-MAN WON'T DARE PULL ANY MORE CRIMES IN THIS CITY NOW!
AND AMONG THE TEEN-AGERS WATCHING THE THE PARADE, WE FIND...
STILL THINK SPIDER-MAN'S SO GREAT, FLASH?
DARN RIGHT I DO! MYSTERIO'S JUST A BIG PUBLICITY HOUND, IF YOU ASK ME! MY DOUGH IS STILL ON SPIDER-MAN!
Y'KNOW SOMETHING, FLASH? YOU'RE NOT AS DUMB AS YOU LOOK! IN FACT, YOU'RE OKAY, FELLA!
LOOK, PUNY PARKER, I DON'T NEED COMPLIMENTS FROM YOU! AND WHILE WE'RE TALKIN', I WANNA WARN YOU TO STAY AWAY FROM LIZ ALLAN! SHE'S MY GIRL FRIEND!
REALLY? TOO BAD. SHE DOESN'T SEEM TO THINK SO! BUT DON'T WORRY, BRIGHT EYES, YOU CAN HAVE HER!
A SHORT TIME LATER, AT THE OFFICE OF J. JONAH JAMESON...
I WANT THE MEMBERS OF MY STAFF TO MEET MYSTERIO, THE MAN WHO BEAT SPIDER-MAN!
MYSTERIO IS A REAL CRIME-FIGHTER! HE'S NOT AFRAID TO MEET PEOPLE AND TO BE INTERVIEWED AS THAT COWARDLY SPIDER-MAN WAS!
AND ONCE MYSTERIO HAS DEFEATED SPIDER-MAN FOR GOOD, HE WILL REVEAL HIS TRUE IDENTITY EXCLUSIVELY TO MY NEWSPAPER! IT'LL BE THE SCOOP OF THE CENTURY FOR ME! RIGHT, MYSTERIO?
RIGHT! JUST SO LONG AS YOU REMEMBER THE MONEY YOU PROMISED ME!
MYSTERIO, I WANT YOU TO MEET PETER PARKER! DON'T LET HIS AGE FOOL YOU! DESPITE HIS YOUTH, HE'S THE BEST PHOTOGRAPHER I'VE GOT! I'LL EXPECT HIM TO TAKE SOME GREAT PICTURES OF YOUR NEXT FIGHT WITH SPIDER-MAN!
I'LL TRY NOT TO DISAPPOINT YOU-- BOTH OF YOU!
13

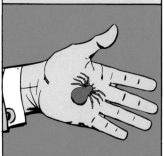

BUT, UNNOTICED BY ANYONE IN THE ROOM, PARKER'S LEFT HAND CONTAINS A SMALL ELECTRONIC-ALLY TREATED SPIDER PIN*...

* THE SAME TYPE OF DEVICE USED IN *SPIDER-MAN #11*, WHICH ENABLED HIM TO TRACK THE GETAWAY CAR OF *DR. OCTOPUS!* — EDITOR.

WHILE NO ONE IS PAYING ATTENTION, I'LL JUST SLIP MY *LITTLE* SPIDER DEVICE IN THE FOLDS OF MYSTERIO'S CLOAK...LIKE *THIS!*

NOW I'LL BE ABLE TO *TRACE* HIS MOVEMENTS! THERE'S *MORE* TO MYSTERIO THAN MEETS THE EYES-- AND I'M GONNA FIND OUT WHAT IT *IS!*

THEN, AS PETER LEAVES JAMESON'S OFFICE...

I'M GLAD TO SEE YOU *SMILING* AGAIN, PETER! ARE *YOU* CELEBRATING SPIDER-MAN'S DEFEAT, ALSO?

NOT EXACTLY, BETTY!

IN FACT, *I'M* NOT SO SURE THAT SPIDER-MAN HAS *BEEN* DEFEATED! WELL, I HAVE TO *RUSH* NOW! SEE YOU LATER...

YOU'RE *NOT* SURE--?? BUT...

HMM! HE'S NEVER BEEN SO ANXIOUS TO *LEAVE* ME BEFORE! CAN HE HAVE MET *ANOTHER* GIRL? I'VE NOTICED A PRETTY *BLONDE* WITH HIM OCCASIONALLY...

OH, *STOP* IT, BETTY BRANT! YOU'RE BECOMING *JEALOUS!*

WHILE BEHIND THE DOOR TO JAMESON'S OFFICE...

I SHALL *LEAVE* YOU, JAMESON! IN MY OWN MANNER! FAREWELL-- TILL NEXT TIME!

HE'S *GONE!* FOR HEAVEN'S SAKE, JJJ, HOW DOES HE *DO* IT?

WHO *CARES?* THE *IMPORTANT* THING IS THAT I'VE FINALLY FOUND SOMEONE WHO CAN BEAT SPIDER-MAN! I FEEL LIKE *CELEBRATING!*

BUT JAMESON MIGHT NOT FEEL SO TRIUMPHANT IF HE COULD SEE A DRAMATIC FIGURE ON A NEARBY ROOFTOP, WAITING TO RECEIVE THE ELECTRONIC SIGNAL FROM HIS HIDDEN SPIDER PIN!

AH, MY SPYING DEVICE IS BEGINNING TO REGISTER NOW!

14

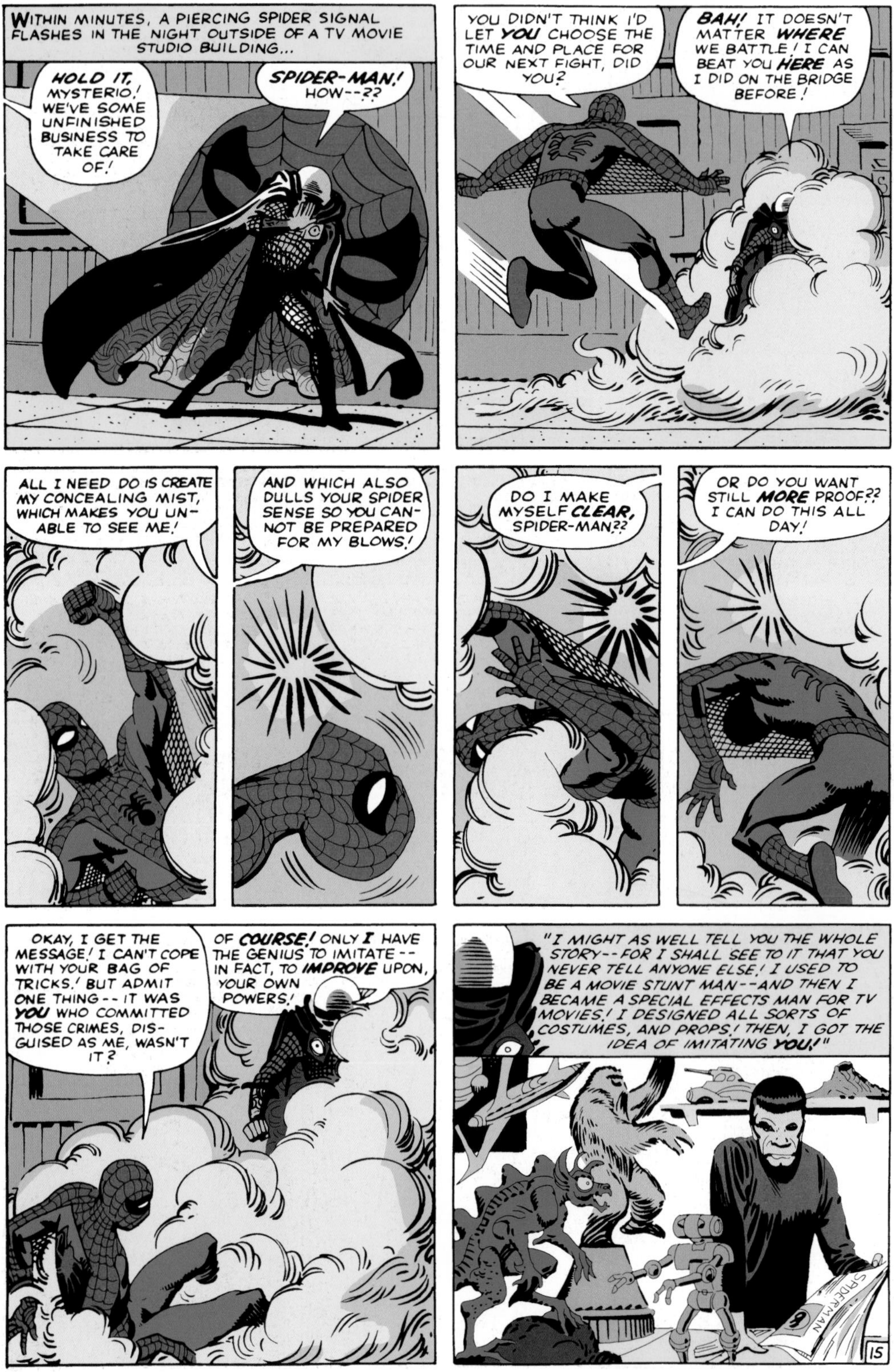

WITHIN MINUTES, A PIERCING SPIDER SIGNAL FLASHES IN THE NIGHT OUTSIDE OF A TV MOVIE STUDIO BUILDING...
HOLD IT, MYSTERIO! WE'VE SOME UNFINISHED BUSINESS TO TAKE CARE OF!
SPIDER-MAN! HOW--??
YOU DIDN'T THINK I'D LET YOU CHOOSE THE TIME AND PLACE FOR OUR NEXT FIGHT, DID YOU?
BAH! IT DOESN'T MATTER WHERE WE BATTLE! I CAN BEAT YOU HERE AS I DID ON THE BRIDGE BEFORE!
ALL I NEED DO IS CREATE MY CONCEALING MIST, WHICH MAKES YOU UNABLE TO SEE ME!
AND WHICH ALSO DULLS YOUR SPIDER SENSE SO YOU CANNOT BE PREPARED FOR MY BLOWS!
DO I MAKE MYSELF CLEAR, SPIDER-MAN??
OR DO YOU WANT STILL MORE PROOF?? I CAN DO THIS ALL DAY!
OKAY, I GET THE MESSAGE! I CAN'T COPE WITH YOUR BAG OF TRICKS! BUT ADMIT ONE THING--IT WAS YOU WHO COMMITTED THOSE CRIMES, DISGUISED AS ME, WASN'T IT?
OF COURSE! ONLY I HAVE THE GENIUS TO IMITATE--IN FACT, TO IMPROVE UPON, YOUR OWN POWERS!
"I MIGHT AS WELL TELL YOU THE WHOLE STORY--FOR I SHALL SEE TO IT THAT YOU NEVER TELL ANYONE ELSE! I USED TO BE A MOVIE STUNT MAN--AND THEN I BECAME A SPECIAL EFFECTS MAN FOR TV MOVIES! I DESIGNED ALL SORTS OF COSTUMES, AND PROPS! THEN, I GOT THE IDEA OF IMITATING YOU!"
SPIDERMAN
15

"I SPENT MANY LONG WEEKS STUDYING ALL YOUR POWERS, ALL YOUR ABILITIES -- EVERYTHING THAT WAS KNOWN ABOUT YOU! I WAS **SURE** I COULD DUPLICATE YOUR FEATS!"

WHATEVER SPIDER-MAN DOES *NATURALLY*, I'LL FIND A WAY TO DO *ARTIFICIALLY!*

"USING ALL THE SKILL I HAD AQUIRED DESIGNING MOVIE PROPS, I MADE A GUN WHICH FIRED A NYLON CORD RESEMBLING YOUR OWN WEB! I DESIGNED SHOES AND GLOVES WITH SPECIAL SUCTION CUPS, ENABLING ME TO CLING TO WALLS!"

MY SUCTION CUPS *WORK!* FROM A DISTANCE NO ONE WILL KNOW I'M NOT REALLY SPIDER-MAN!

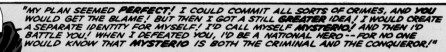

"MY PLAN SEEMED **PERFECT!** I COULD COMMIT ALL SORTS OF CRIMES, AND **YOU** WOULD GET THE BLAME! BUT THEN I GOT A STILL **GREATER** IDEA! I WOULD **CREATE** A SEPARATE IDENTITY FOR MYSELF! I'D CALL MYSELF **MYSTERIO!** AND THEN I'D BATTLE YOU! WHEN I DEFEATED YOU, I'D BE A NATIONAL HERO -- FOR NO ONE WOULD KNOW THAT **MYSTERIO** IS BOTH THE CRIMINAL AND THE CONQUEROR!"

"MY HELMET IS BASED ON THE PRINCIPLE OF YOUR EYE PIECES! I CAN SEE **OUT,** BUT NO ONE CAN SEE **IN!**"

"I CREATED A FINE SPRAY MADE OF SPECIALLY TREATED ACID WHICH WAS FOR THE SOLE PURPOSE OF DISSOLVING YOUR WEB IF YOU SHOULD EVER USE IT AGAINST ME!"

"THE BOTTOMS OF MY BOOTS CONTAIN CHEMICAL SMOKE EJECTORS AS WELL AS MAGNETIC PLATE SPRINGS WHICH ENABLE ME TO DUPLICATE YOUR OWN AMAZING LEAPS!"

EVEN MY NAME -- *MYSTERIO* -- WAS CREATED TO INSTIL AWE AND FEAR IN THE HEARTS OF MY ENEMIES!

I WAS ABLE TO SEE YOU WITHIN MY PROTECTIVE CLOUD BECAUSE I HAVE A BUILT IN **SONAR** DEVICE WHICH AIDS ME AT THE SAME TIME AS IT JAMS YOUR **OWN** SPIDER SENSE!

AND NOW, I SHALL DISPOSE OF YOU FOREVER!

DON'T **COUNT** ON IT, BIG MOUTH! I'VE GOT TO STAY AROUND LONG ENOUGH TO GIVE THIS **TAPE RECORDER** TO THE POLICE AND PROVE MY INNOCENCE!

A MINIATURE RECORDER!! **BAH!** IT WILL DO YOU NO **GOOD!** I'LL DESTROY IT -- **AFTER** I'VE DEFEATED YOU!

BUT, IN A SPLIT-SECOND, SPIDER-MAN FLIPS BACKWARDS, OUT OF THE SPREADING MIST!

NOT *THIS* TIME, MYSTERIO! REMEMBER ONE THING-- *YOUR* POWER IS ARTIFICIAL-- BUT *MINE* IS NATURAL!!

AND I'LL BET ON *MY* NATURAL SPIDER POWERS *ANY* TIME!

I'VE GOT TO CIRCLE AROUND-- TRY TO FIND HIM WITHIN THE MIST!

HAVE TO KEEP MOVING *FAST!* CAN'T LOSE THE ADVANTAGE!

HE'S NOT HERE--OR HERE! BUT HE'S GOT TO BE NEARBY!

IF I KEEP SWINGING, THEN SOONER OR LATER I'LL--*AHHH,* I WAS RIGHT! *THERE* HE IS!

WHAM!

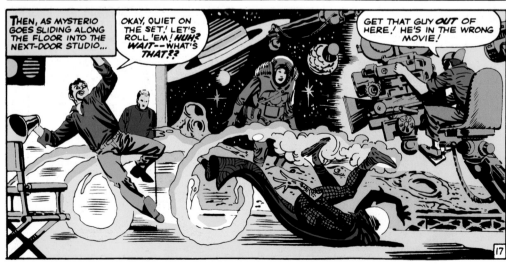

THEN, AS MYSTERIO GOES SLIDING ALONG THE FLOOR INTO THE NEXT-DOOR STUDIO...

OKAY, QUIET ON THE SET! LET'S ROLL 'EM! HUH? WAIT--WHAT'S *THAT??*

GET THAT GUY *OUT* OF HERE! HE'S IN THE WRONG MOVIE!

17

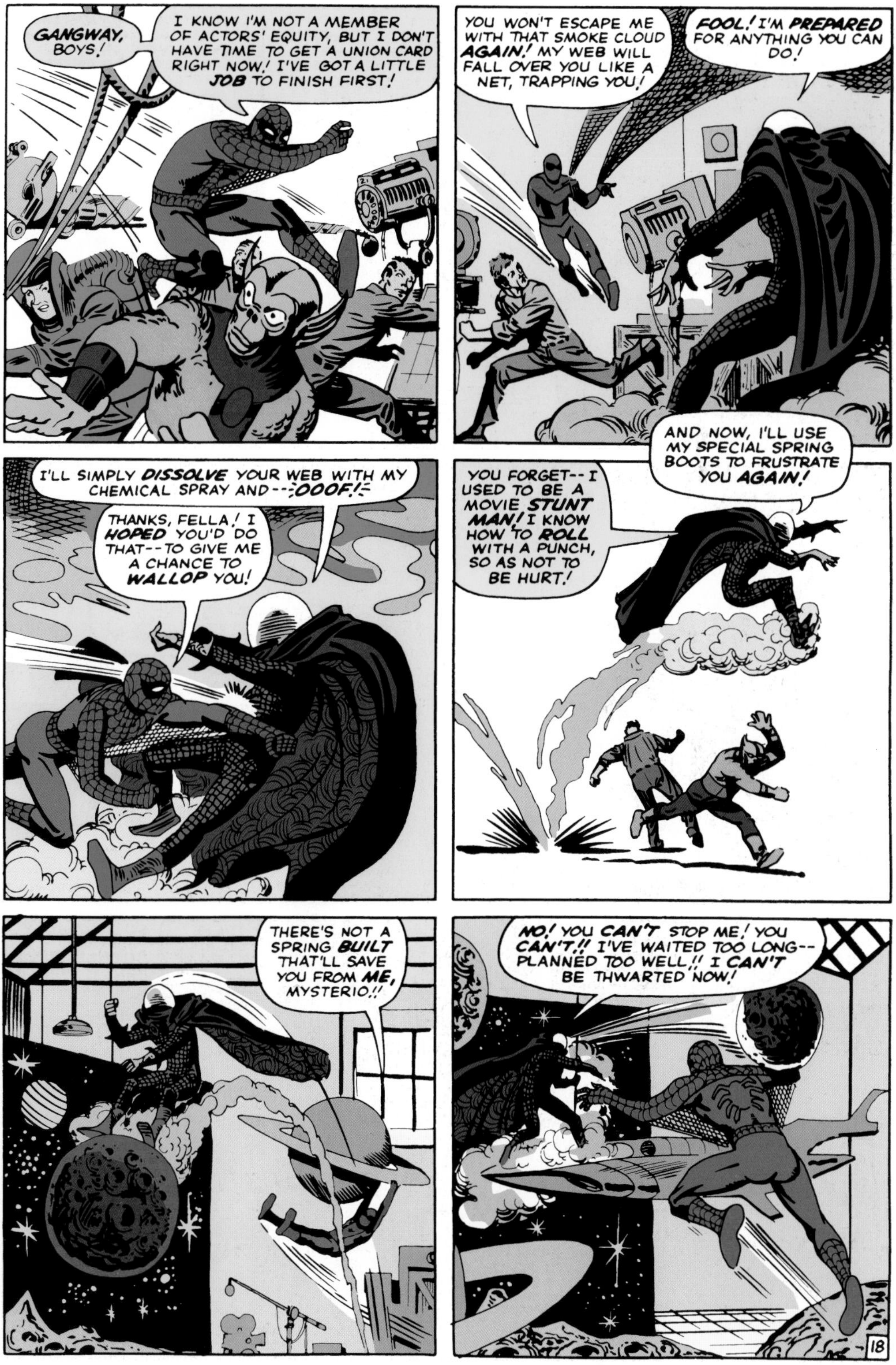

GANGWAY, BOYS!
I KNOW I'M NOT A MEMBER OF ACTORS' EQUITY, BUT I DON'T HAVE TIME TO GET A UNION CARD RIGHT NOW! I'VE GOT A LITTLE JOB TO FINISH FIRST!
YOU WON'T ESCAPE ME WITH THAT SMOKE CLOUD AGAIN! MY WEB WILL FALL OVER YOU LIKE A NET, TRAPPING YOU!
FOOL! I'M PREPARED FOR ANYTHING YOU CAN DO!
I'LL SIMPLY DISSOLVE YOUR WEB WITH MY CHEMICAL SPRAY AND--OOOF!
THANKS, FELLA! I HOPED YOU'D DO THAT--TO GIVE ME A CHANCE TO WALLOP YOU!
YOU FORGET-- I USED TO BE A MOVIE STUNT MAN! I KNOW HOW TO ROLL WITH A PUNCH, SO AS NOT TO BE HURT!
AND NOW, I'LL USE MY SPECIAL SPRING BOOTS TO FRUSTRATE YOU AGAIN!
THERE'S NOT A SPRING BUILT THAT'LL SAVE YOU FROM ME, MYSTERIO!!
NO! YOU CAN'T STOP ME! YOU CAN'T!! I'VE WAITED TOO LONG-- PLANNED TOO WELL!! I CAN'T BE THWARTED NOW!
18

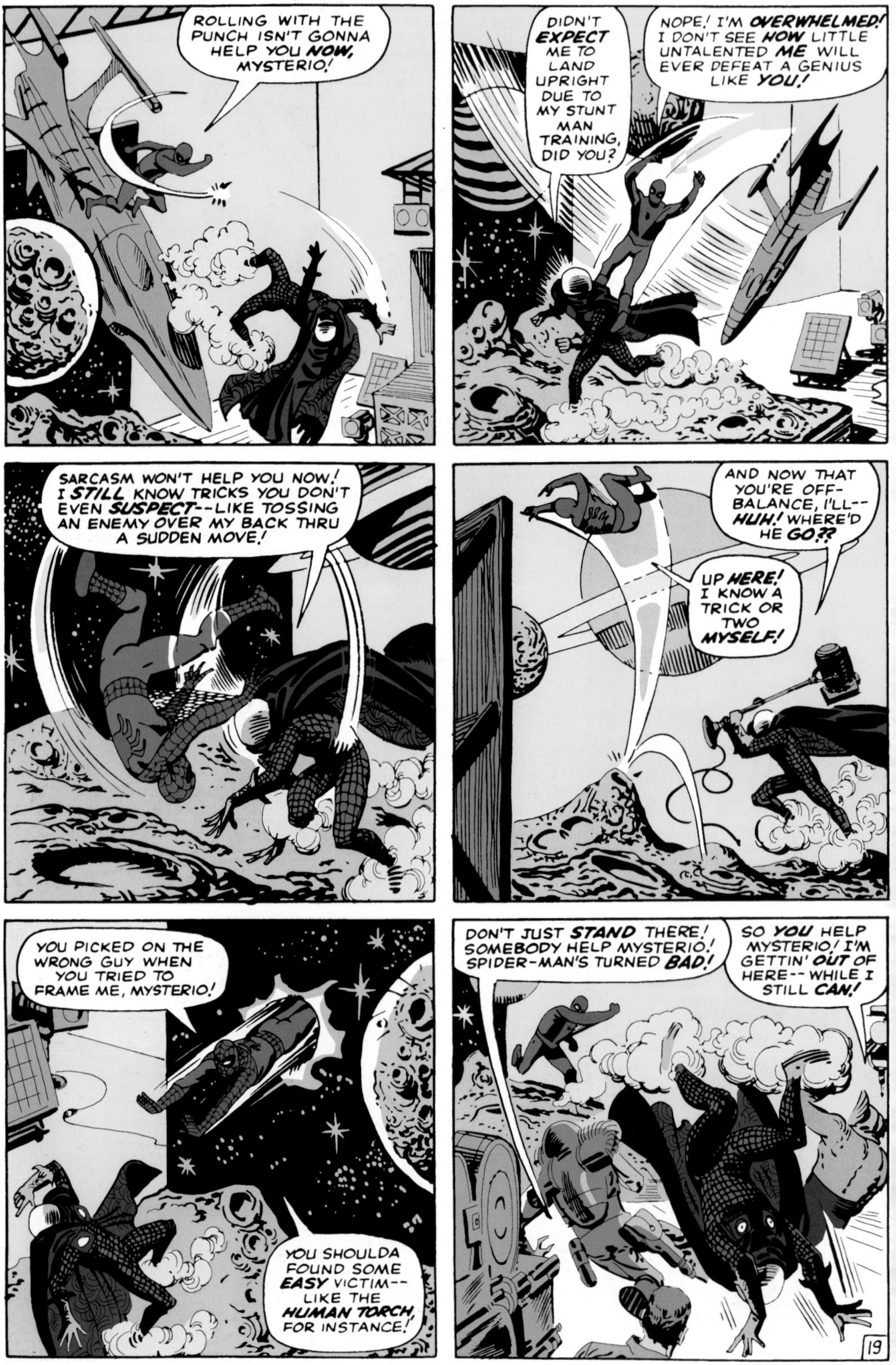
ROLLING WITH THE PUNCH ISN'T GONNA HELP YOU NOW, MYSTERIO!
DIDN'T EXPECT ME TO LAND UPRIGHT DUE TO MY STUNT MAN TRAINING, DID YOU?
NOPE! I'M OVERWHELMED! I DON'T SEE HOW LITTLE UNTALENTED ME WILL EVER DEFEAT A GENIUS LIKE YOU!
SARCASM WON'T HELP YOU NOW! I STILL KNOW TRICKS YOU DON'T EVEN SUSPECT--LIKE TOSSING AN ENEMY OVER MY BACK THRU A SUDDEN MOVE!
AND NOW THAT YOU'RE OFF-BALANCE, I'LL-- HUH! WHERE'D HE GO??
UP HERE! I KNOW A TRICK OR TWO MYSELF!
YOU PICKED ON THE WRONG GUY WHEN YOU TRIED TO FRAME ME, MYSTERIO!
YOU SHOULDA FOUND SOME EASY VICTIM-- LIKE THE HUMAN TORCH, FOR INSTANCE!
DON'T JUST STAND THERE! SOMEBODY HELP MYSTERIO! SPIDER-MAN'S TURNED BAD!
SO YOU HELP MYSTERIO! I'M GETTIN' OUT OF HERE-- WHILE I STILL CAN!
19

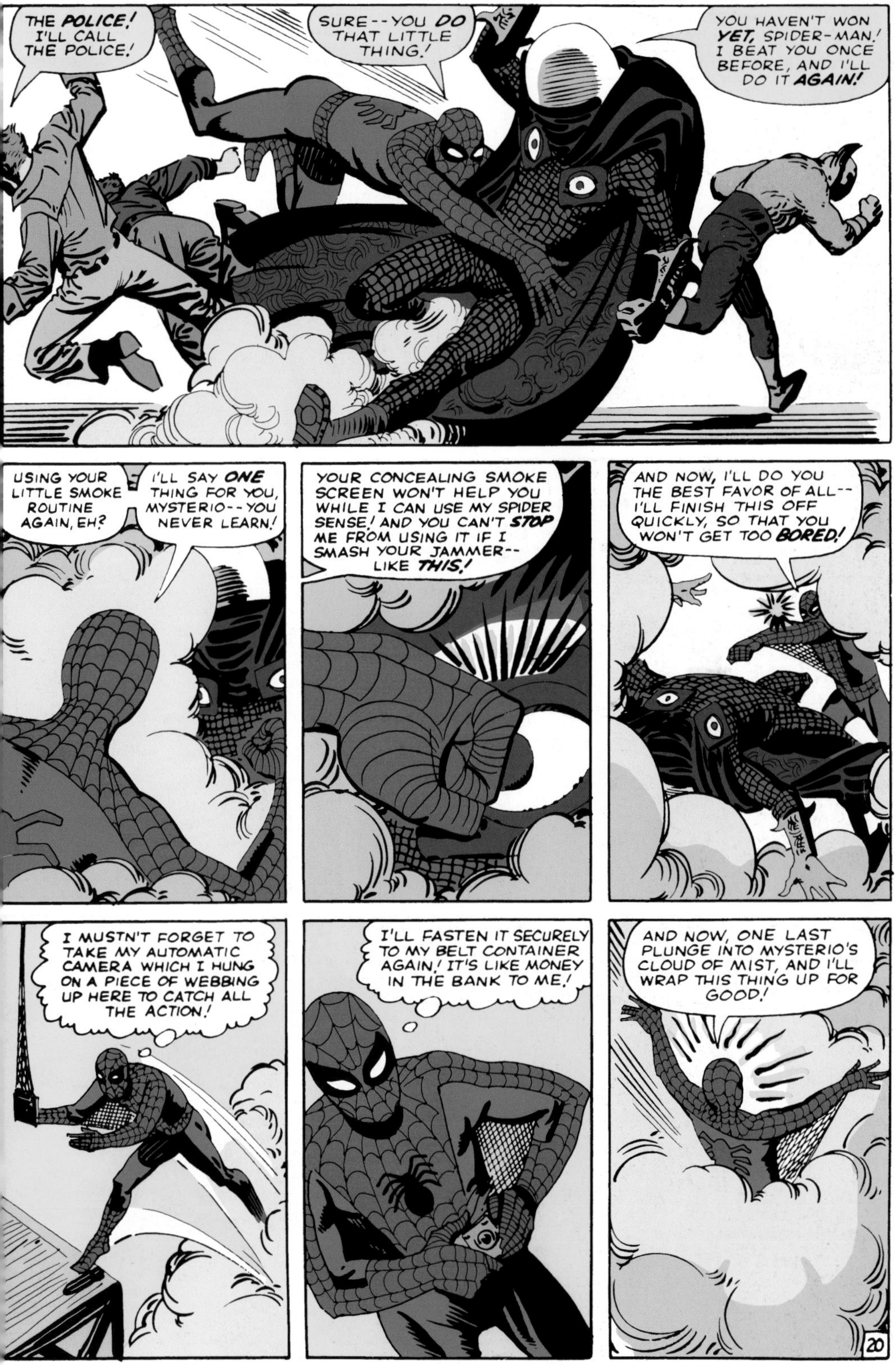
THE POLICE! I'LL CALL THE POLICE!
SURE--YOU DO THAT LITTLE THING!
YOU HAVEN'T WON YET, SPIDER-MAN! I BEAT YOU ONCE BEFORE, AND I'LL DO IT AGAIN!
USING YOUR LITTLE SMOKE ROUTINE AGAIN, EH?
I'LL SAY ONE THING FOR YOU, MYSTERIO--YOU NEVER LEARN!
YOUR CONCEALING SMOKE SCREEN WON'T HELP YOU WHILE I CAN USE MY SPIDER SENSE! AND YOU CAN'T STOP ME FROM USING IT IF I SMASH YOUR JAMMER--LIKE THIS!
AND NOW, I'LL DO YOU THE BEST FAVOR OF ALL--I'LL FINISH THIS OFF QUICKLY, SO THAT YOU WON'T GET TOO BORED!
I MUSTN'T FORGET TO TAKE MY AUTOMATIC CAMERA WHICH I HUNG ON A PIECE OF WEBBING UP HERE TO CATCH ALL THE ACTION!
I'LL FASTEN IT SECURELY TO MY BELT CONTAINER AGAIN! IT'S LIKE MONEY IN THE BANK TO ME!
AND NOW, ONE LAST PLUNGE INTO MYSTERIO'S CLOUD OF MIST, AND I'LL WRAP THIS THING UP FOR GOOD!
20

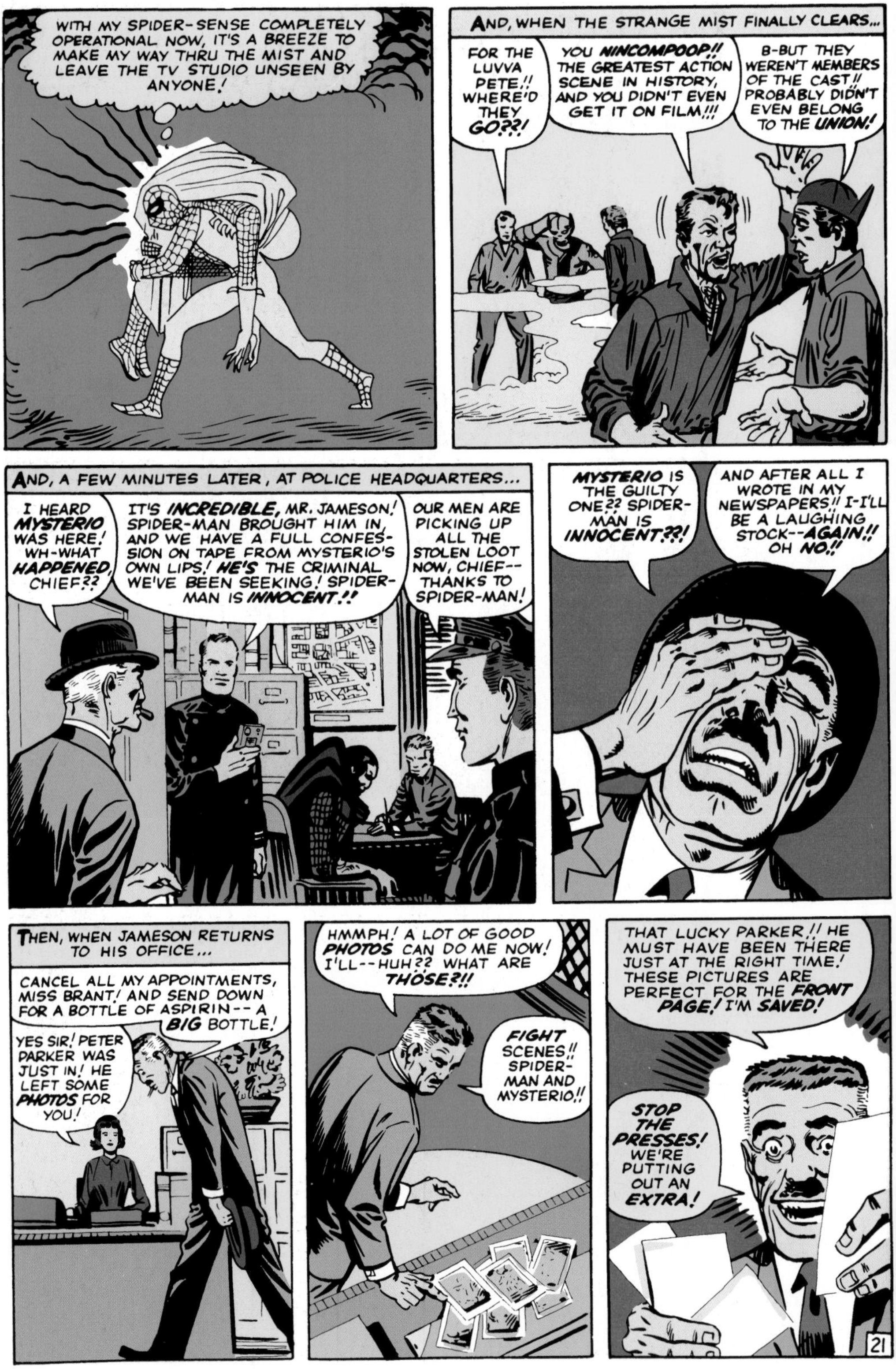
WITH MY SPIDER-SENSE COMPLETELY OPERATIONAL NOW, IT'S A BREEZE TO MAKE MY WAY THRU THE MIST AND LEAVE THE TV STUDIO UNSEEN BY ANYONE!
AND, WHEN THE STRANGE MIST FINALLY CLEARS...
FOR THE LUVVA PETE!! WHERE'D THEY GO??!
YOU NINCOMPOOP!! THE GREATEST ACTION SCENE IN HISTORY, AND YOU DIDN'T EVEN GET IT ON FILM!!!
B-BUT THEY WEREN'T MEMBERS OF THE CAST!! PROBABLY DIDN'T EVEN BELONG TO THE UNION!
AND, A FEW MINUTES LATER, AT POLICE HEADQUARTERS...
I HEARD MYSTERIO WAS HERE! WH-WHAT HAPPENED, CHIEF??
IT'S INCREDIBLE, MR. JAMESON! SPIDER-MAN BROUGHT HIM IN, AND WE HAVE A FULL CONFESSION ON TAPE FROM MYSTERIO'S OWN LIPS! HE'S THE CRIMINAL WE'VE BEEN SEEKING! SPIDER-MAN IS INNOCENT!!
OUR MEN ARE PICKING UP ALL THE STOLEN LOOT NOW, CHIEF-- THANKS TO SPIDER-MAN!
MYSTERIO IS THE GUILTY ONE?? SPIDER-MAN IS INNOCENT??!
AND AFTER ALL I WROTE IN MY NEWSPAPERS!! I-I'LL BE A LAUGHING STOCK--AGAIN!! OH NO!!
THEN, WHEN JAMESON RETURNS TO HIS OFFICE...
CANCEL ALL MY APPOINTMENTS, MISS BRANT! AND SEND DOWN FOR A BOTTLE OF ASPIRIN-- A BIG BOTTLE!
YES SIR! PETER PARKER WAS JUST IN! HE LEFT SOME PHOTOS FOR YOU!
HMMPH! A LOT OF GOOD PHOTOS CAN DO ME NOW! I'LL--HUH?? WHAT ARE THOSE?!!
FIGHT SCENES!! SPIDER-MAN AND MYSTERIO!!
THAT LUCKY PARKER!! HE MUST HAVE BEEN THERE JUST AT THE RIGHT TIME! THESE PICTURES ARE PERFECT FOR THE FRONT PAGE! I'M SAVED!
STOP THE PRESSES! WE'RE PUTTING OUT AN EXTRA!
21

I'LL WRITE OUT A CHECK FOR PARKER! HE WON'T HAVE TO WORRY ABOUT THAT MORTGAGE *NOW!* I'LL BE GENEROUS AND PAY HIM ALMOST *HALF* OF WHAT THESE PICTURES ARE WORTH!

GOT TIME FOR A *VISITOR,* JJJ?

YOU!!

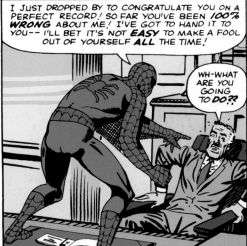

I JUST DROPPED BY TO CONGRATULATE YOU ON A PERFECT RECORD! SO FAR YOU'VE BEEN *100%* *WRONG* ABOUT ME! I'VE GOT TO HAND IT TO YOU-- I'LL BET IT'S NOT *EASY* TO MAKE A FOOL OUT OF YOURSELF *ALL* THE TIME!

WH-WHAT ARE YOU GOING TO *DO??*

I JUST DROPPED BY TO *HELP* YOU, OLD PAL!

I FIGURED YOU NEED A NEW OUTLOOK ON LIFE, SO I THOUGHT I'D *GIVE* YOU ONE-- *THERE!*

HELP! GET ME *DOWN* FROM HERE! I'LL *GET* YOU FOR THIS *YET,* YOU MASKED MENACE-- SEE IF I DON'T!!!

LOOK! IT'S *SPIDER-MAN* --THE ONE WHO CAUGHT MYSTERIO!!

AND SO, SPIDER-MAN IS VINDICATED BY THE PUBLIC! THEN, THE NEXT DAY...

LOOKS LIKE YOU WERE RIGHT ALL ALONG ABOUT SPIDER-MAN, FLASH!

I'M RIGHT ABOUT *EVERYTHING!* BUT WHAT ABOUT *YOU,* KNOTHEAD? ARE YOU SATISFIED NOW THAT SPIDER-MAN IS ONE OF THE GREAT-EST GUYS AROUND?

HECK NO, FLASH! PERSONALLY, I STILL WOULDN'T TRUST HIM ANY FURTHER THAN I CAN THROW HIM!

MINUTES LATER... POOR FLASH! IF HE ONLY KNEW THE REAL IDENTITY OF HIS FAVORITE HERO!

IT WOULD BE WORTH *ANYTHING* TO TELL HIM SOME DAY--JUST TO WATCH HIM EXPLODE!

The END

BUT, THAT DAY IS STILL IN THE FUTURE! AND, UNTIL THEN, FATE HAS MANY MORE SURPRISES IN STORE FOR SPIDEY! NEXT ISSUE WE PRESENT ANOTHER BOOK-LENGTH ADVENTURE WITH AN UNEXPECTED GUEST STAR! WE THINK YOU'LL LIKE IT, SO --WE'LL SEE YOU THEN!

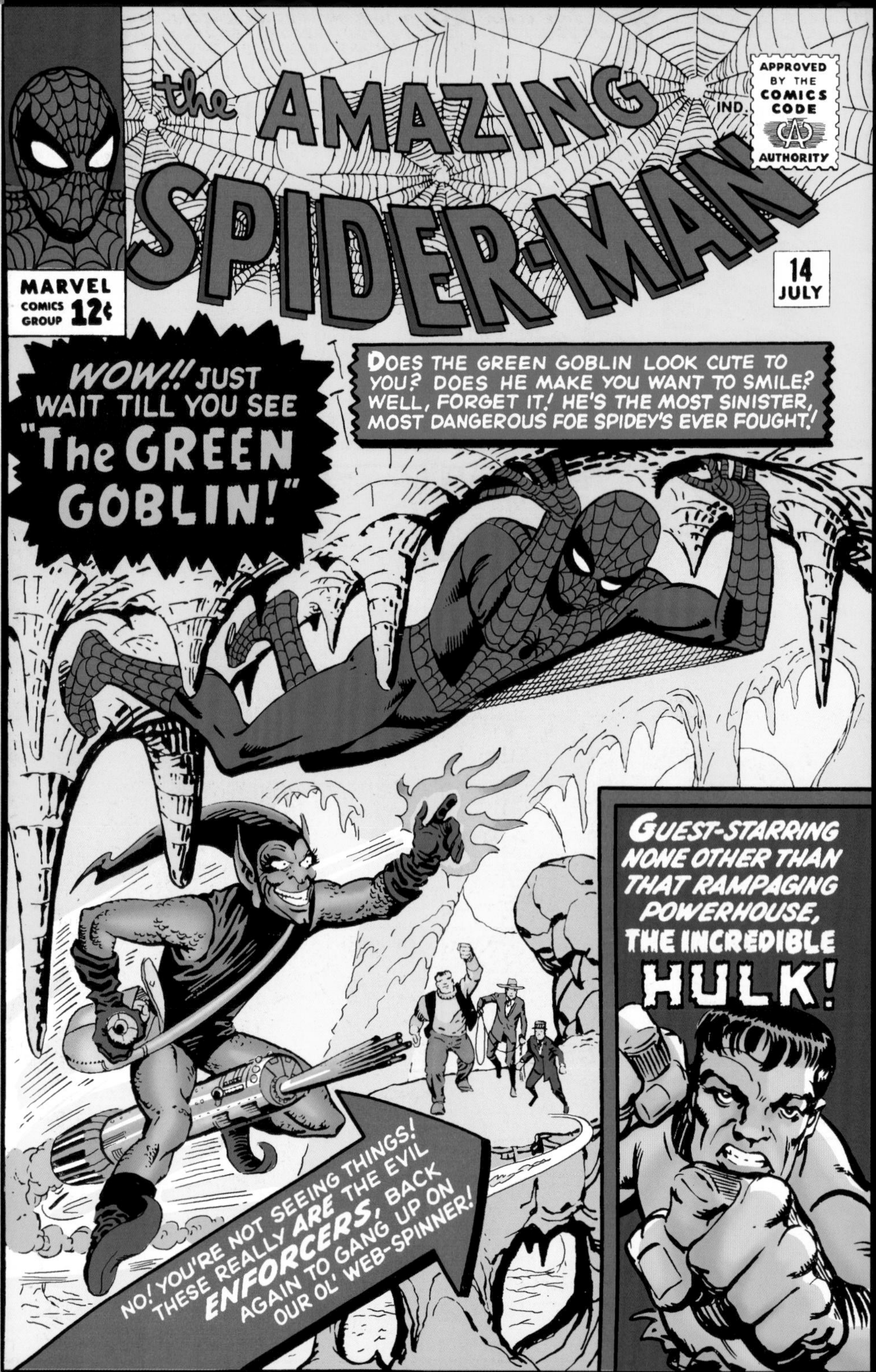

the AMAZING SPIDER-MAN
IND.
APPROVED BY THE COMICS CODE AUTHORITY
MARVEL COMICS GROUP 12¢
14 JULY
WOW!! JUST WAIT TILL YOU SEE "The GREEN GOBLIN!"
DOES THE GREEN GOBLIN LOOK CUTE TO YOU? DOES HE MAKE YOU WANT TO SMILE? WELL, FORGET IT! HE'S THE MOST SINISTER, MOST DANGEROUS FOE SPIDEY'S EVER FOUGHT!
GUEST-STARRING NONE OTHER THAN THAT RAMPAGING POWERHOUSE, THE INCREDIBLE HULK!
NO! YOU'RE NOT SEEING THINGS! THESE REALLY ARE THE EVIL ENFORCERS, BACK AGAIN TO GANG UP ON OUR OL' WEB-SPINNER!

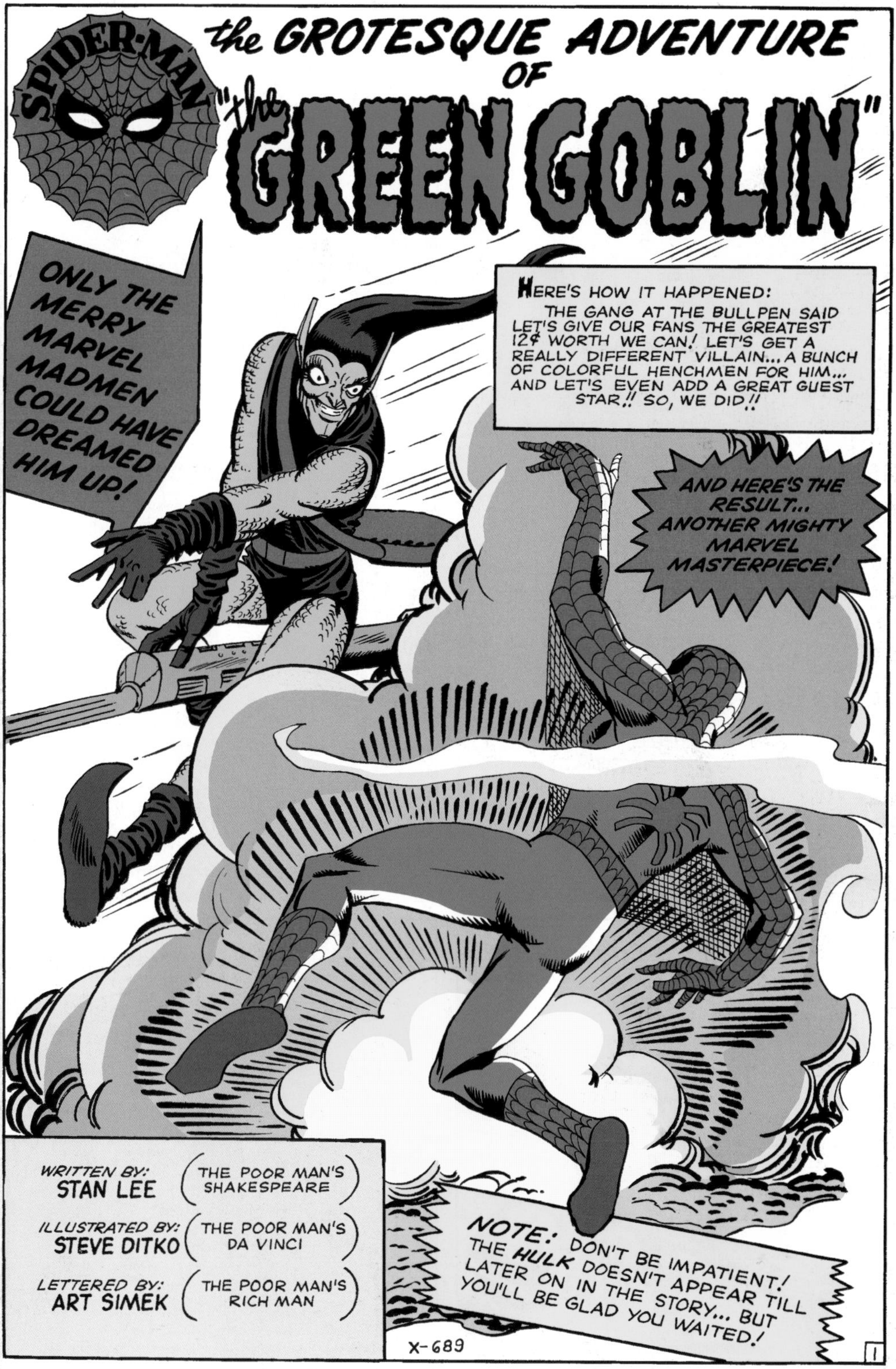
SPIDER-MAN
the GROTESQUE ADVENTURE OF "the GREEN GOBLIN"
ONLY THE MERRY MARVEL MADMEN COULD HAVE DREAMED HIM UP!
HERE'S HOW IT HAPPENED: THE GANG AT THE BULLPEN SAID LET'S GIVE OUR FANS THE GREATEST 12¢ WORTH WE CAN! LET'S GET A REALLY DIFFERENT VILLAIN... A BUNCH OF COLORFUL HENCHMEN FOR HIM... AND LET'S EVEN ADD A GREAT GUEST STAR!! SO, WE DID!!
AND HERE'S THE RESULT... ANOTHER MIGHTY MARVEL MASTERPIECE!
WRITTEN BY: STAN LEE (THE POOR MAN'S SHAKESPEARE)
ILLUSTRATED BY: STEVE DITKO (THE POOR MAN'S DA VINCI)
LETTERED BY: ART SIMEK (THE POOR MAN'S RICH MAN)
NOTE: DON'T BE IMPATIENT! THE HULK DOESN'T APPEAR TILL LATER ON IN THE STORY... BUT YOU'LL BE GLAD YOU WAITED!
X-689
1

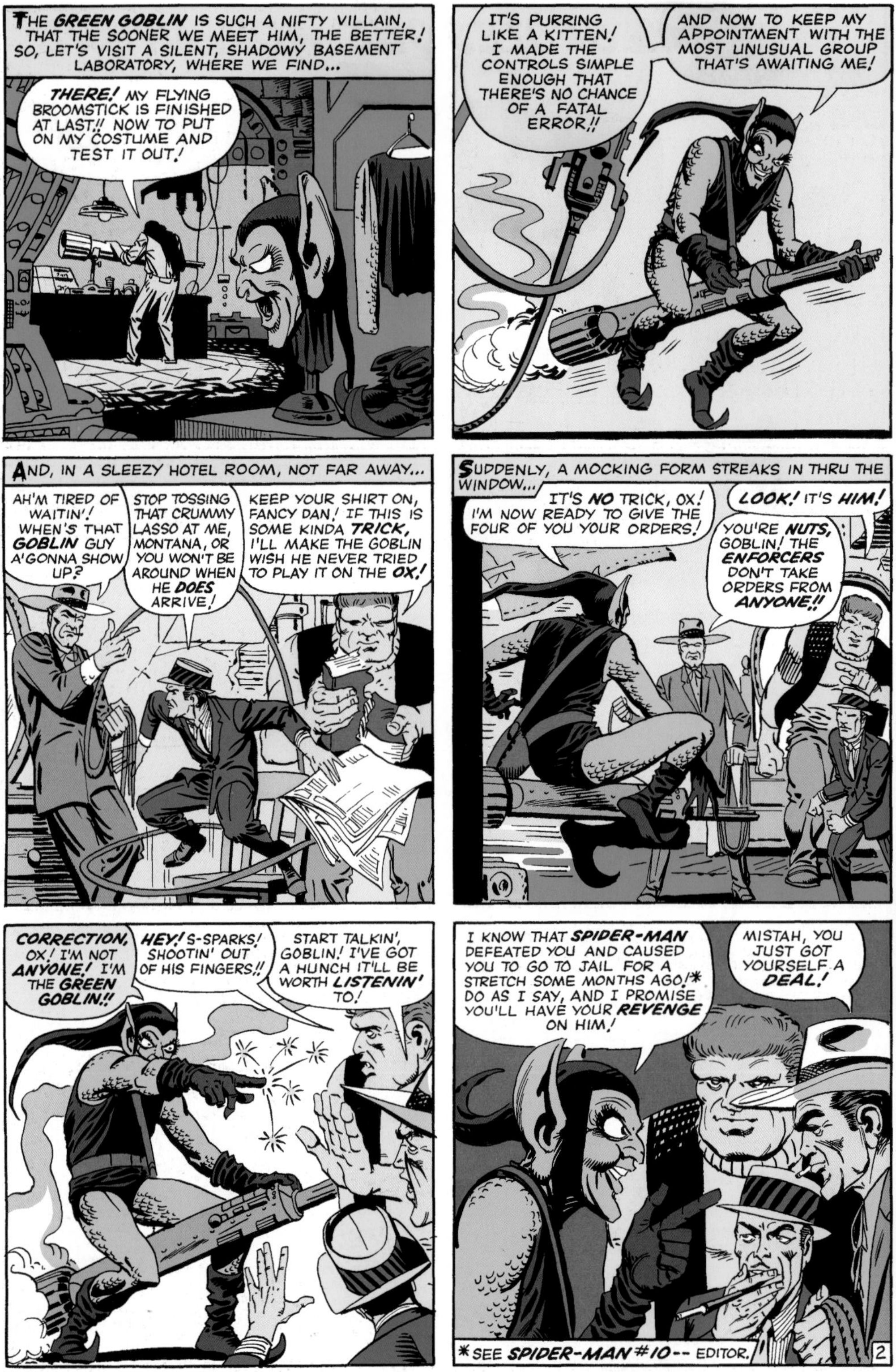
THE GREEN GOBLIN IS SUCH A NIFTY VILLAIN, THAT THE SOONER WE MEET HIM, THE BETTER! SO, LET'S VISIT A SILENT, SHADOWY BASEMENT LABORATORY, WHERE WE FIND...
THERE! MY FLYING BROOMSTICK IS FINISHED AT LAST!! NOW TO PUT ON MY COSTUME AND TEST IT OUT!
IT'S PURRING LIKE A KITTEN! I MADE THE CONTROLS SIMPLE ENOUGH THAT THERE'S NO CHANCE OF A FATAL ERROR!!
AND NOW TO KEEP MY APPOINTMENT WITH THE MOST UNUSUAL GROUP THAT'S AWAITING ME!
AND, IN A SLEEZY HOTEL ROOM, NOT FAR AWAY...
AH'M TIRED OF WAITIN'! WHEN'S THAT GOBLIN GUY A'GONNA SHOW UP?
STOP TOSSING THAT CRUMMY LASSO AT ME, MONTANA, OR YOU WON'T BE AROUND WHEN HE DOES ARRIVE!
KEEP YOUR SHIRT ON, FANCY DAN! IF THIS IS SOME KINDA TRICK, I'LL MAKE THE GOBLIN WISH HE NEVER TRIED TO PLAY IT ON THE OX!
SUDDENLY, A MOCKING FORM STREAKS IN THRU THE WINDOW...
IT'S NO TRICK, OX! I'M NOW READY TO GIVE THE FOUR OF YOU YOUR ORDERS!
LOOK! IT'S HIM!
YOU'RE NUTS, GOBLIN! THE ENFORCERS DON'T TAKE ORDERS FROM ANYONE!!
CORRECTION, OX! I'M NOT ANYONE! I'M THE GREEN GOBLIN!!
HEY! S-SPARKS! SHOOTIN' OUT OF HIS FINGERS!!
START TALKIN', GOBLIN! I'VE GOT A HUNCH IT'LL BE WORTH LISTENIN' TO!
I KNOW THAT SPIDER-MAN DEFEATED YOU AND CAUSED YOU TO GO TO JAIL FOR A STRETCH SOME MONTHS AGO!* DO AS I SAY, AND I PROMISE YOU'LL HAVE YOUR REVENGE ON HIM!
MISTAH, YOU JUST GOT YOURSELF A DEAL!
*SEE SPIDER-MAN #10-- EDITOR.
2

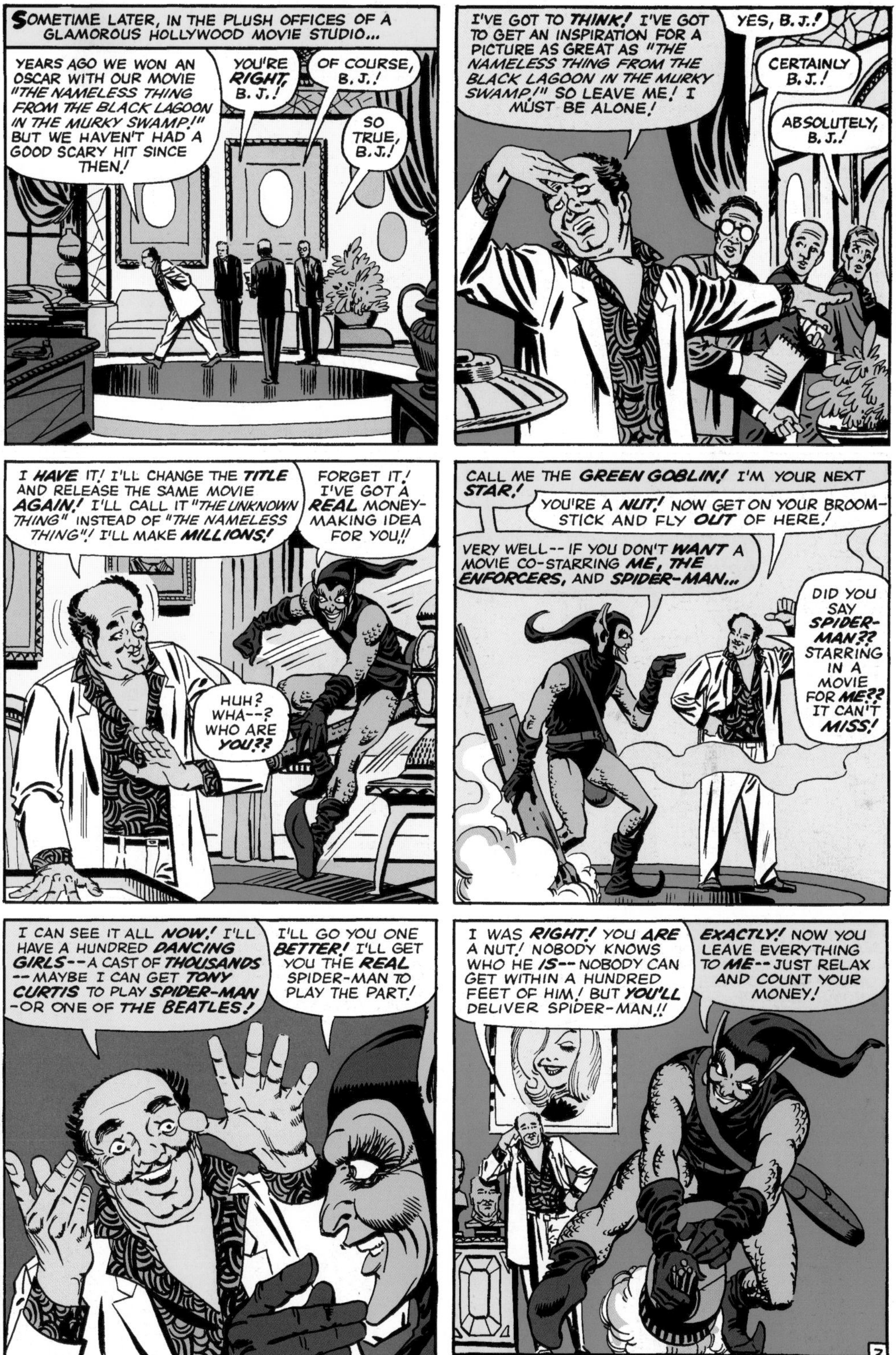
SOMETIME LATER, IN THE PLUSH OFFICES OF A GLAMOROUS HOLLYWOOD MOVIE STUDIO...
YEARS AGO WE WON AN OSCAR WITH OUR MOVIE "THE NAMELESS THING FROM THE BLACK LAGOON IN THE MURKY SWAMP!" BUT WE HAVEN'T HAD A GOOD SCARY HIT SINCE THEN!
YOU'RE RIGHT, B.J.!
OF COURSE, B.J.!
SO TRUE, B.J.!
I'VE GOT TO THINK! I'VE GOT TO GET AN INSPIRATION FOR A PICTURE AS GREAT AS "THE NAMELESS THING FROM THE BLACK LAGOON IN THE MURKY SWAMP!" SO LEAVE ME! I MUST BE ALONE!
YES, B.J.!
CERTAINLY B.J.!
ABSOLUTELY, B.J.!
I HAVE IT! I'LL CHANGE THE TITLE AND RELEASE THE SAME MOVIE AGAIN! I'LL CALL IT "THE UNKNOWN THING" INSTEAD OF "THE NAMELESS THING"! I'LL MAKE MILLIONS!
FORGET IT! I'VE GOT A REAL MONEY-MAKING IDEA FOR YOU!!
HUH? WHA--? WHO ARE YOU??
CALL ME THE GREEN GOBLIN! I'M YOUR NEXT STAR!
YOU'RE A NUT! NOW GET ON YOUR BROOM-STICK AND FLY OUT OF HERE!
VERY WELL-- IF YOU DON'T WANT A MOVIE CO-STARRING ME, THE ENFORCERS, AND SPIDER-MAN...
DID YOU SAY SPIDER-MAN?? STARRING IN A MOVIE FOR ME?? IT CAN'T MISS!
I CAN SEE IT ALL NOW! I'LL HAVE A HUNDRED DANCING GIRLS--A CAST OF THOUSANDS -- MAYBE I CAN GET TONY CURTIS TO PLAY SPIDER-MAN -OR ONE OF THE BEATLES!
I'LL GO YOU ONE BETTER! I'LL GET YOU THE REAL SPIDER-MAN TO PLAY THE PART!
I WAS RIGHT! YOU ARE A NUT! NOBODY KNOWS WHO HE IS-- NOBODY CAN GET WITHIN A HUNDRED FEET OF HIM! BUT YOU'LL DELIVER SPIDER-MAN!!
EXACTLY! NOW YOU LEAVE EVERYTHING TO ME-- JUST RELAX AND COUNT YOUR MONEY!
3

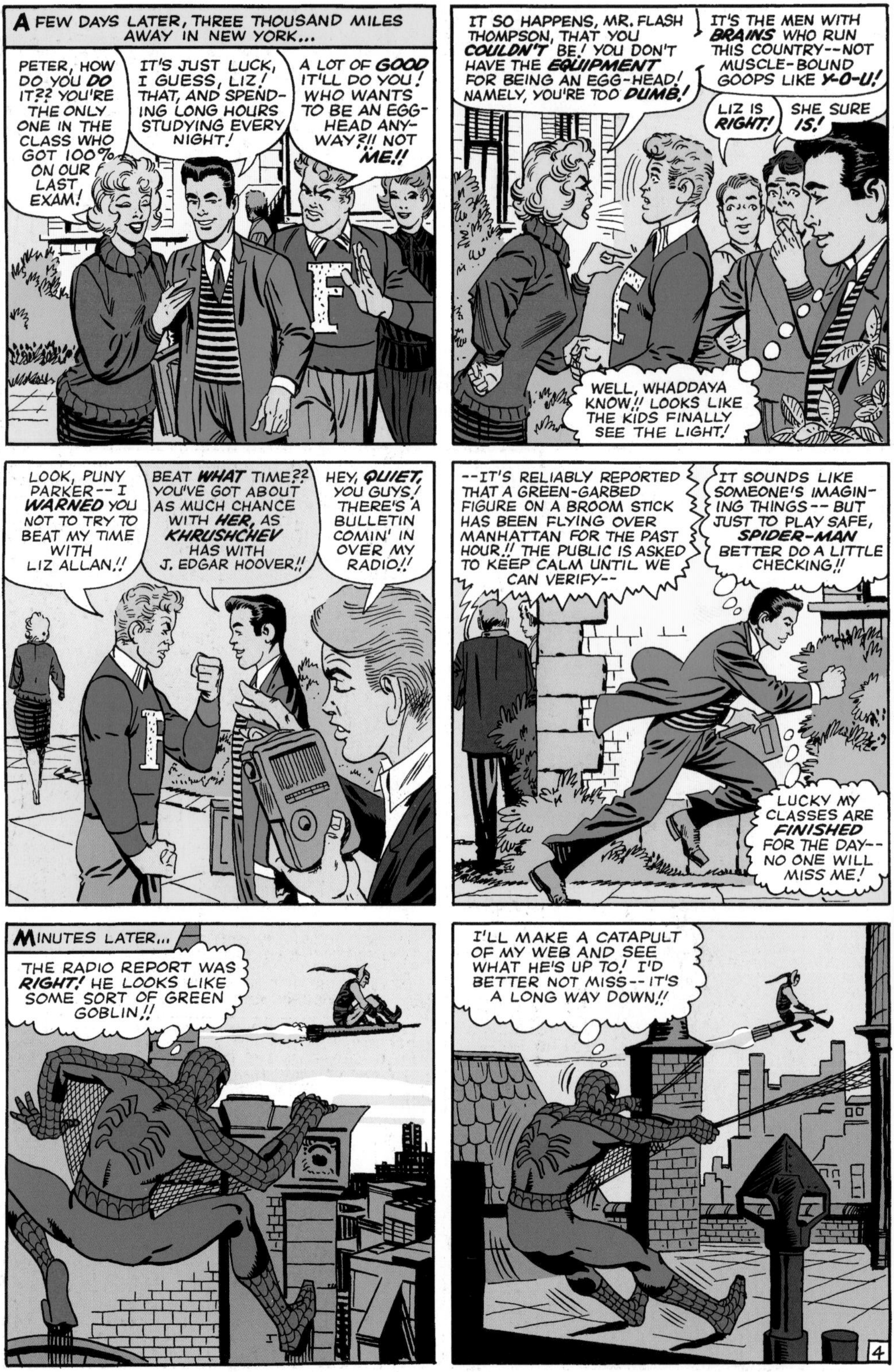

A FEW DAYS LATER, THREE THOUSAND MILES AWAY IN NEW YORK...
PETER, HOW DO YOU DO IT?? YOU'RE THE ONLY ONE IN THE CLASS WHO GOT 100% ON OUR LAST EXAM!
IT'S JUST LUCK, I GUESS, LIZ! THAT, AND SPENDING LONG HOURS STUDYING EVERY NIGHT!
A LOT OF GOOD IT'LL DO YOU! WHO WANTS TO BE AN EGG-HEAD ANYWAY?!! NOT ME!!
IT SO HAPPENS, MR. FLASH THOMPSON, THAT YOU COULDN'T BE! YOU DON'T HAVE THE EQUIPMENT FOR BEING AN EGG-HEAD! NAMELY, YOU'RE TOO DUMB!
IT'S THE MEN WITH BRAINS WHO RUN THIS COUNTRY--NOT MUSCLE-BOUND GOOPS LIKE Y-O-U!
LIZ IS RIGHT!
SHE SURE IS!
WELL, WHADDAYA KNOW!! LOOKS LIKE THE KIDS FINALLY SEE THE LIGHT!
LOOK, PUNY PARKER-- I WARNED YOU NOT TO TRY TO BEAT MY TIME WITH LIZ ALLAN!!
BEAT WHAT TIME?? YOU'VE GOT ABOUT AS MUCH CHANCE WITH HER, AS KHRUSHCHEV HAS WITH J. EDGAR HOOVER!!
HEY, QUIET, YOU GUYS! THERE'S A BULLETIN COMIN' IN OVER MY RADIO!!
--IT'S RELIABLY REPORTED THAT A GREEN-GARBED FIGURE ON A BROOM STICK HAS BEEN FLYING OVER MANHATTAN FOR THE PAST HOUR!! THE PUBLIC IS ASKED TO KEEP CALM UNTIL WE CAN VERIFY--
IT SOUNDS LIKE SOMEONE'S IMAGINING THINGS-- BUT JUST TO PLAY SAFE, SPIDER-MAN BETTER DO A LITTLE CHECKING!!
LUCKY MY CLASSES ARE FINISHED FOR THE DAY-- NO ONE WILL MISS ME!
MINUTES LATER...
THE RADIO REPORT WAS RIGHT! HE LOOKS LIKE SOME SORT OF GREEN GOBLIN!!
I'LL MAKE A CATAPULT OF MY WEB AND SEE WHAT HE'S UP TO! I'D BETTER NOT MISS-- IT'S A LONG WAY DOWN!!
4

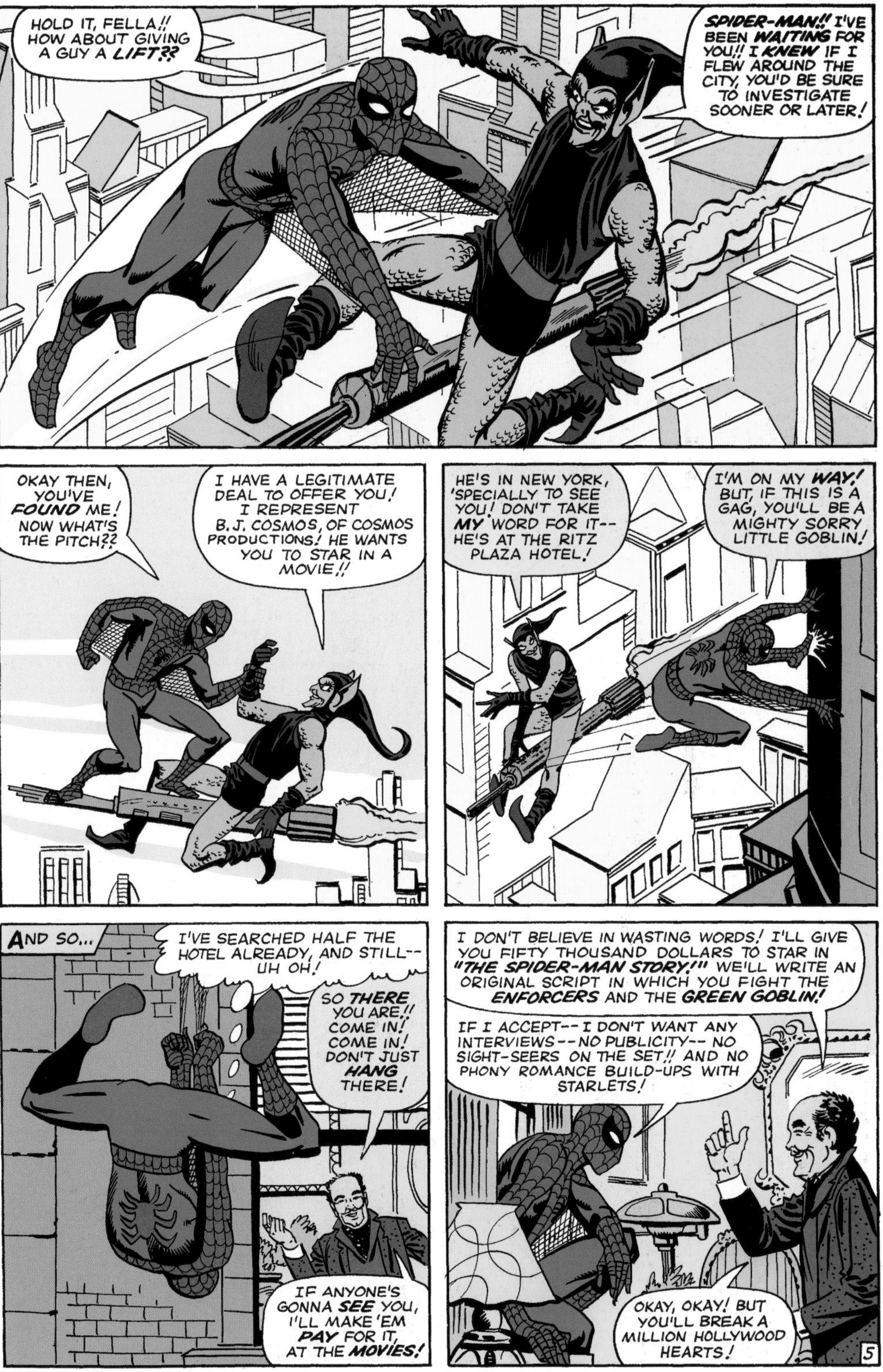
HOLD IT, FELLA!! HOW ABOUT GIVING A GUY A LIFT??
SPIDER-MAN!! I'VE BEEN WAITING FOR YOU!! I KNEW IF I FLEW AROUND THE CITY, YOU'D BE SURE TO INVESTIGATE SOONER OR LATER!
OKAY THEN, YOU'VE FOUND ME! NOW WHAT'S THE PITCH??
I HAVE A LEGITIMATE DEAL TO OFFER YOU! I REPRESENT B.J. COSMOS, OF COSMOS PRODUCTIONS! HE WANTS YOU TO STAR IN A MOVIE!!
HE'S IN NEW YORK, 'SPECIALLY TO SEE YOU! DON'T TAKE MY WORD FOR IT-- HE'S AT THE RITZ PLAZA HOTEL!
I'M ON MY WAY! BUT, IF THIS IS A GAG, YOU'LL BE A MIGHTY SORRY LITTLE GOBLIN!
AND SO...
I'VE SEARCHED HALF THE HOTEL ALREADY, AND STILL-- UH OH!
SO THERE YOU ARE!! COME IN! COME IN! DON'T JUST HANG THERE!
IF ANYONE'S GONNA SEE YOU, I'LL MAKE 'EM PAY FOR IT, AT THE MOVIES!
I DON'T BELIEVE IN WASTING WORDS! I'LL GIVE YOU FIFTY THOUSAND DOLLARS TO STAR IN "THE SPIDER-MAN STORY!" WE'LL WRITE AN ORIGINAL SCRIPT IN WHICH YOU FIGHT THE ENFORCERS AND THE GREEN GOBLIN!
IF I ACCEPT-- I DON'T WANT ANY INTERVIEWS--NO PUBLICITY-- NO SIGHT-SEERS ON THE SET!! AND NO PHONY ROMANCE BUILD-UPS WITH STARLETS!
OKAY, OKAY! BUT YOU'LL BREAK A MILLION HOLLYWOOD HEARTS!
5

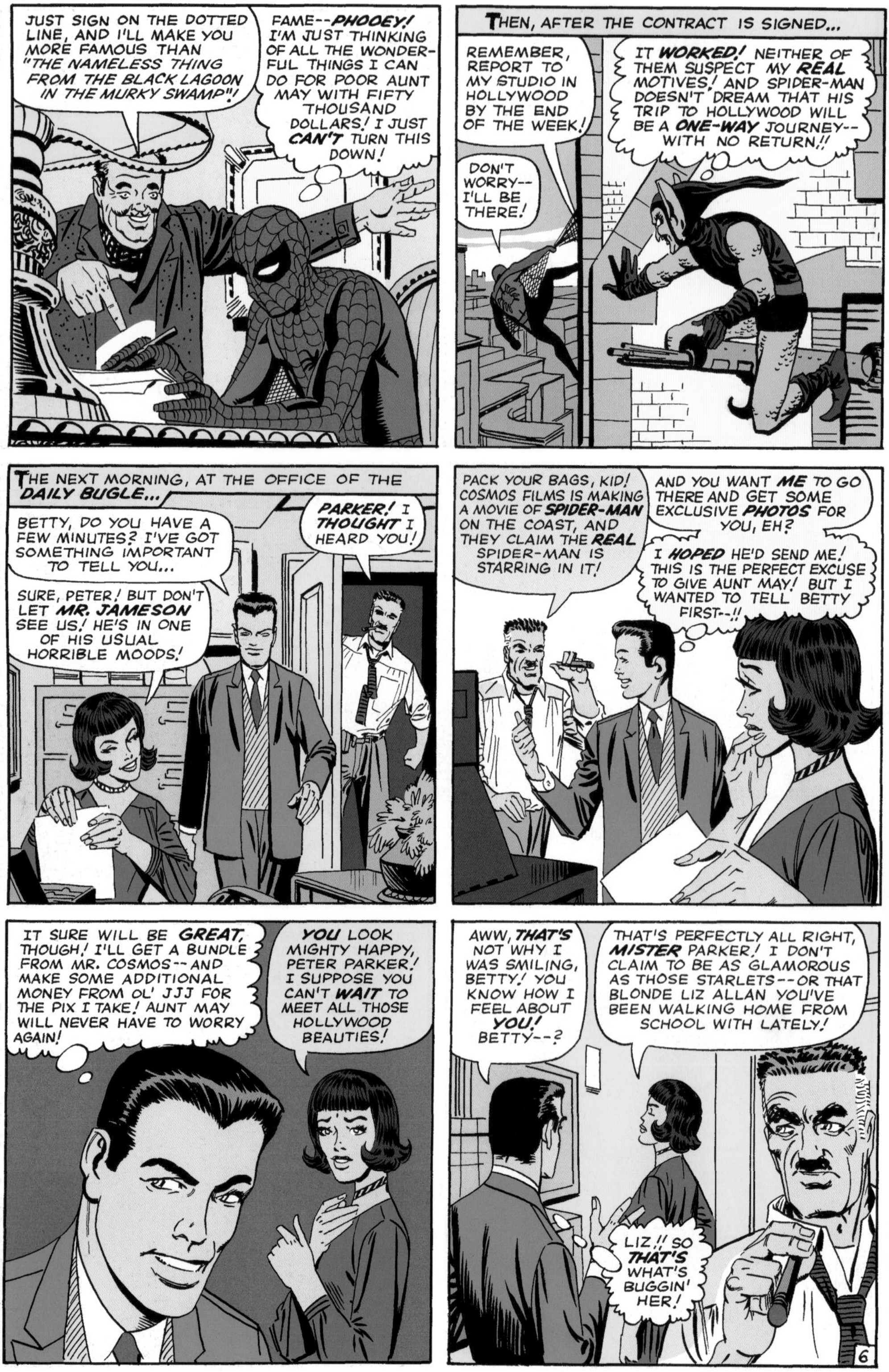
JUST SIGN ON THE DOTTED LINE, AND I'LL MAKE YOU MORE FAMOUS THAN "THE NAMELESS THING FROM THE BLACK LAGOON IN THE MURKY SWAMP"!
FAME--PHOOEY! I'M JUST THINKING OF ALL THE WONDERFUL THINGS I CAN DO FOR POOR AUNT MAY WITH FIFTY THOUSAND DOLLARS! I JUST CAN'T TURN THIS DOWN!
THEN, AFTER THE CONTRACT IS SIGNED...
REMEMBER, REPORT TO MY STUDIO IN HOLLYWOOD BY THE END OF THE WEEK!
DON'T WORRY-- I'LL BE THERE!
IT WORKED! NEITHER OF THEM SUSPECT MY REAL MOTIVES! AND SPIDER-MAN DOESN'T DREAM THAT HIS TRIP TO HOLLYWOOD WILL BE A ONE-WAY JOURNEY-- WITH NO RETURN!!
THE NEXT MORNING, AT THE OFFICE OF THE DAILY BUGLE...
BETTY, DO YOU HAVE A FEW MINUTES? I'VE GOT SOMETHING IMPORTANT TO TELL YOU...
PARKER! I THOUGHT I HEARD YOU!
SURE, PETER! BUT DON'T LET MR. JAMESON SEE US! HE'S IN ONE OF HIS USUAL HORRIBLE MOODS!
PACK YOUR BAGS, KID! COSMOS FILMS IS MAKING A MOVIE OF SPIDER-MAN ON THE COAST, AND THEY CLAIM THE REAL SPIDER-MAN IS STARRING IN IT!
AND YOU WANT ME TO GO THERE AND GET SOME EXCLUSIVE PHOTOS FOR YOU, EH?
I HOPED HE'D SEND ME! THIS IS THE PERFECT EXCUSE TO GIVE AUNT MAY! BUT I WANTED TO TELL BETTY FIRST--!!
IT SURE WILL BE GREAT, THOUGH! I'LL GET A BUNDLE FROM MR. COSMOS-- AND MAKE SOME ADDITIONAL MONEY FROM OL' JJJ FOR THE PIX I TAKE! AUNT MAY WILL NEVER HAVE TO WORRY AGAIN!
YOU LOOK MIGHTY HAPPY, PETER PARKER! I SUPPOSE YOU CAN'T WAIT TO MEET ALL THOSE HOLLYWOOD BEAUTIES!
AWW, THAT'S NOT WHY I WAS SMILING, BETTY! YOU KNOW HOW I FEEL ABOUT YOU! BETTY--?
THAT'S PERFECTLY ALL RIGHT, MISTER PARKER! I DON'T CLAIM TO BE AS GLAMOROUS AS THOSE STARLETS--OR THAT BLONDE LIZ ALLAN YOU'VE BEEN WALKING HOME FROM SCHOOL WITH LATELY!
LIZ!! SO THAT'S WHAT'S BUGGIN' HER!
6

LATER, DISCUSSING THE TRIP WITH AUNT MAY, PETE RUNS INTO STILL ANOTHER PROBLEM...

PETER DEAR, I THINK YOU'RE STILL TOO *YOUNG* TO GO TRAIPSING AROUND THE COUNTRY THAT WAY!

GOSH, AUNT MAY, I'M A HIGH SCHOOL SENIOR ALREADY! I'LL SOON BE READY FOR *COLLEGE!*

BUT I *WORRY* SO ABOUT YOU! YOU KNOW HOW *FRAGILE* YOU ARE!

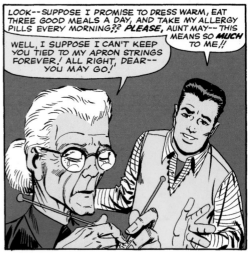

LOOK--SUPPOSE I PROMISE TO DRESS WARM, EAT THREE GOOD MEALS A DAY, AND TAKE MY ALLERGY PILLS EVERY MORNING?? *PLEASE,* AUNT MAY-- THIS MEANS SO *MUCH* TO ME!!

WELL, I SUPPOSE I CAN'T KEEP YOU TIED TO MY APRON STRINGS FOREVER! ALL RIGHT, DEAR-- YOU MAY GO!

AND SO, THE LITTLE CAST OF CHARACTERS IN OUR TRUE-TO-LIFE DRAMA ARE SOON ASSEMBLED ON THE COSMOS PRODUCTIONS MOVIE LOT, IN HOLLYWOOD...

REMEMBER, ALL OF YOU-- I WANT TO WIN ANOTHER *OSCAR* WITH THIS FILM! DON'T LET ME DOWN! I WANT ACTION! ACTION! ACTION!

B.J.'S MAKE-UP MAN MUST BE A *GENIUS!* THOSE ACTORS LOOK JUST LIKE THE *REAL* ENFORCERS!

I WISH WE COULD TACKLE HIM *NOW!*

NO! WAIT TILL WE GET ON LOCATION!

AFTER A DIFFICULT JOURNEY, THE CAMERA CREW AND THE STARS REACH A DESERTED AREA IN NEW MEXICO WHERE THE MOVIE IS TO BE FILMED...

LET'S GET STARTED! UNLOAD THAT EQUIPMENT AND HAVE THE CAMERAS READY TO ROLL IN THIRTY MINUTES! WE'LL SHOOT THE BIG FIGHT SCENE FIRST!

WHAT A LOCATION!! FEELS AS THOUGH WE'RE AT THE EDGE OF THE WORLD!!

SAY, SPIDER-MAN-- SUPPOSE WE GO OFF AND REHEARSE THAT FIGHT SCENE WHILE THEY'RE SETTING UP THE CAMERAS?

YEAH! WE WANNA MAKE SURE NOBODY GETS HURT WHEN WE PERFORM FOR THE CAMERAS!

IT'S OKAY WITH ME!

7

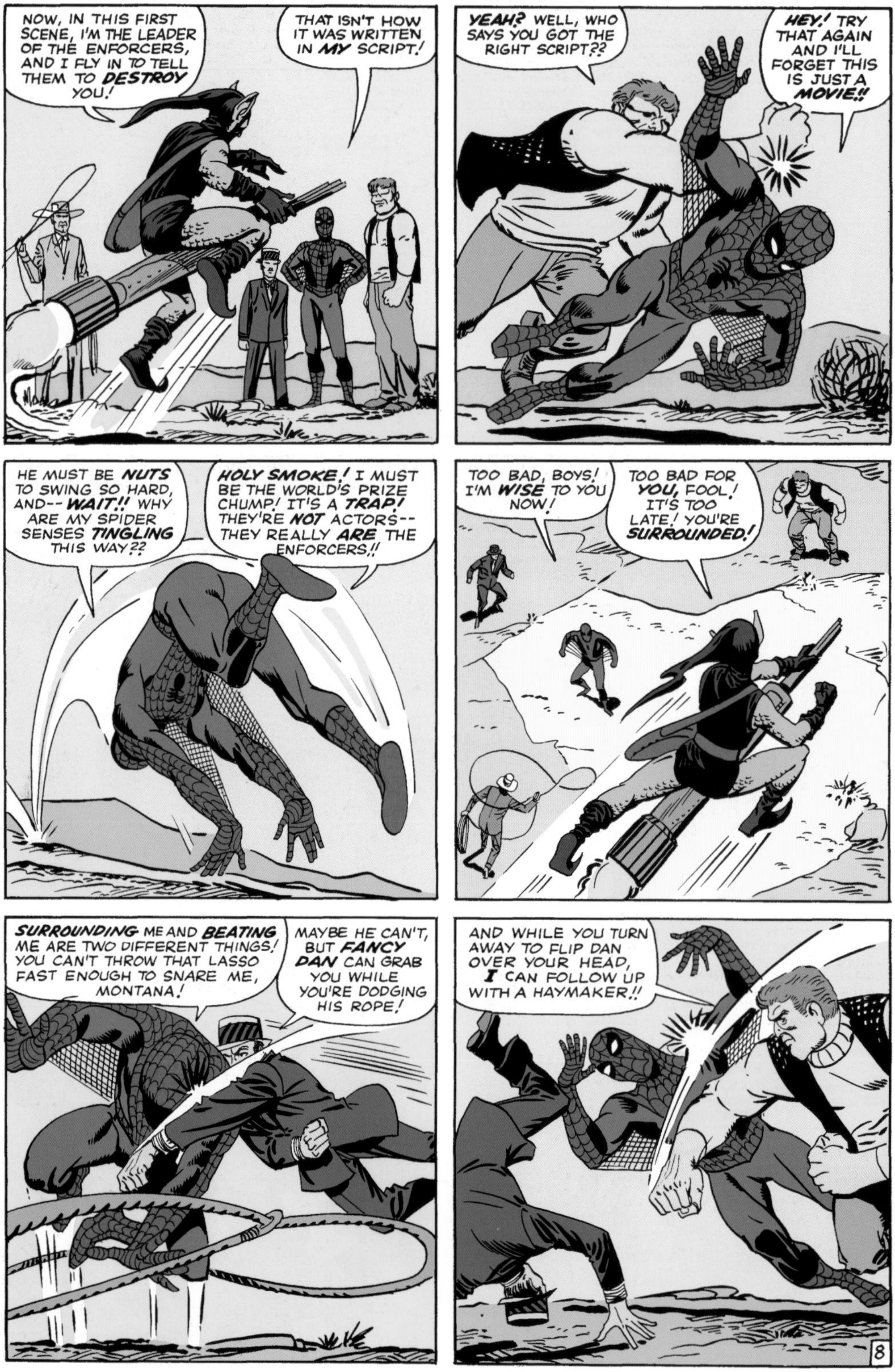
NOW, IN THIS FIRST SCENE, I'M THE LEADER OF THE ENFORCERS, AND I FLY IN TO TELL THEM TO DESTROY YOU!
THAT ISN'T HOW IT WAS WRITTEN IN MY SCRIPT!
YEAH? WELL, WHO SAYS YOU GOT THE RIGHT SCRIPT??
HEY! TRY THAT AGAIN AND I'LL FORGET THIS IS JUST A MOVIE!!
HE MUST BE NUTS TO SWING SO HARD, AND-- WAIT!! WHY ARE MY SPIDER SENSES TINGLING THIS WAY??
HOLY SMOKE! I MUST BE THE WORLD'S PRIZE CHUMP! IT'S A TRAP! THEY'RE NOT ACTORS-- THEY REALLY ARE THE ENFORCERS!!
TOO BAD, BOYS! I'M WISE TO YOU NOW!
TOO BAD FOR YOU, FOOL! IT'S TOO LATE! YOU'RE SURROUNDED!
SURROUNDING ME AND BEATING ME ARE TWO DIFFERENT THINGS! YOU CAN'T THROW THAT LASSO FAST ENOUGH TO SNARE ME, MONTANA!
MAYBE HE CAN'T, BUT FANCY DAN CAN GRAB YOU WHILE YOU'RE DODGING HIS ROPE!
AND WHILE YOU TURN AWAY TO FLIP DAN OVER YOUR HEAD, I CAN FOLLOW UP WITH A HAYMAKER!!
8

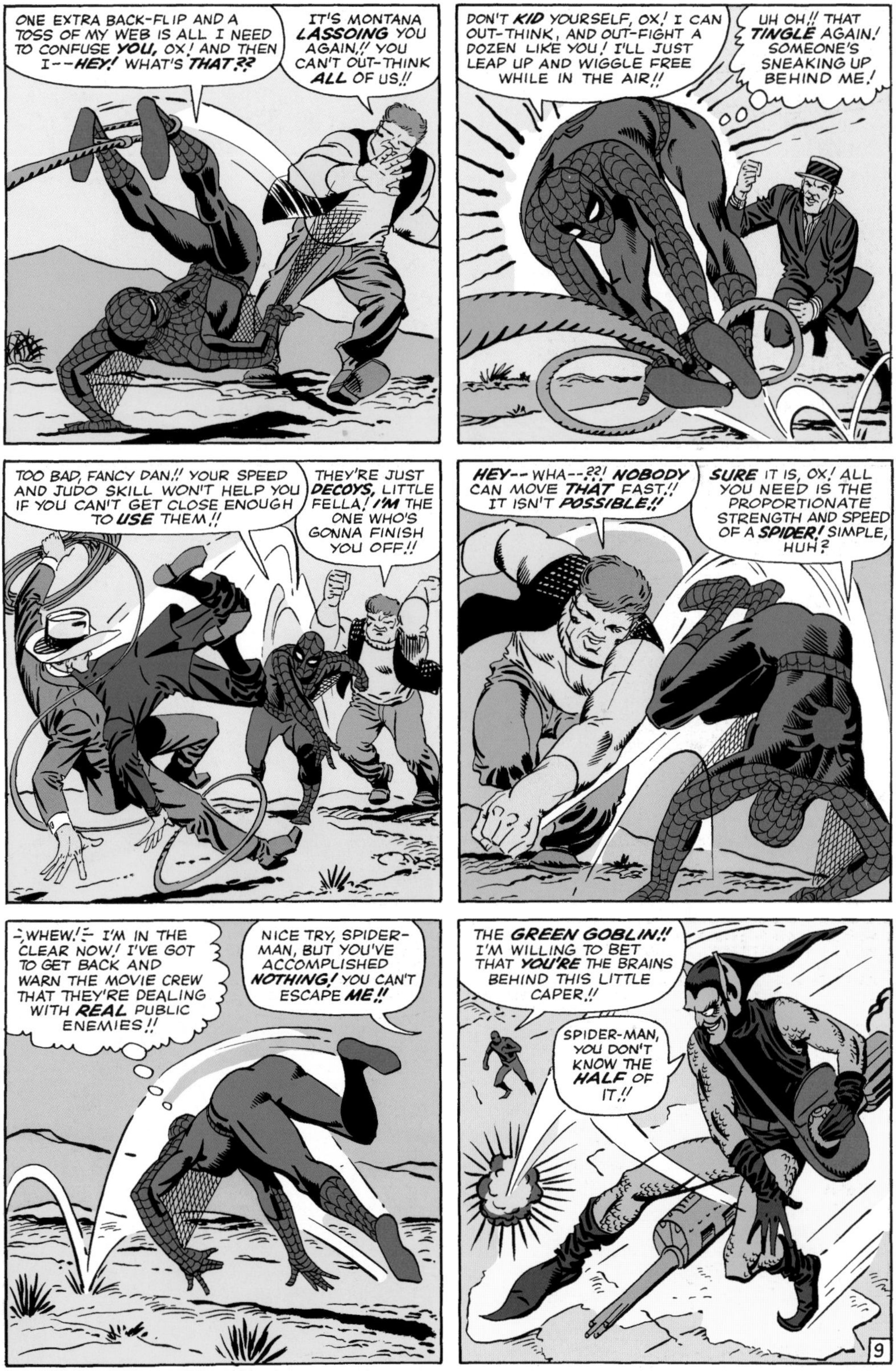
ONE EXTRA BACK-FLIP AND A TOSS OF MY WEB IS ALL I NEED TO CONFUSE YOU, OX! AND THEN I--HEY! WHAT'S THAT??
IT'S MONTANA LASSOING YOU AGAIN!! YOU CAN'T OUT-THINK ALL OF US!!
DON'T KID YOURSELF, OX! I CAN OUT-THINK, AND OUT-FIGHT A DOZEN LIKE YOU! I'LL JUST LEAP UP AND WIGGLE FREE WHILE IN THE AIR!!
UH OH!! THAT TINGLE AGAIN! SOMEONE'S SNEAKING UP BEHIND ME!
TOO BAD, FANCY DAN!! YOUR SPEED AND JUDO SKILL WON'T HELP YOU IF YOU CAN'T GET CLOSE ENOUGH TO USE THEM!!
THEY'RE JUST DECOYS, LITTLE FELLA! I'M THE ONE WHO'S GONNA FINISH YOU OFF!!
HEY-- WHA--??! NOBODY CAN MOVE THAT FAST!! IT ISN'T POSSIBLE!!
SURE IT IS, OX! ALL YOU NEED IS THE PROPORTIONATE STRENGTH AND SPEED OF A SPIDER! SIMPLE, HUH?
-WHEW!- I'M IN THE CLEAR NOW! I'VE GOT TO GET BACK AND WARN THE MOVIE CREW THAT THEY'RE DEALING WITH REAL PUBLIC ENEMIES!!
NICE TRY, SPIDER-MAN, BUT YOU'VE ACCOMPLISHED NOTHING! YOU CAN'T ESCAPE ME!!
THE GREEN GOBLIN!! I'M WILLING TO BET THAT YOU'RE THE BRAINS BEHIND THIS LITTLE CAPER!!
SPIDER-MAN, YOU DON'T KNOW THE HALF OF IT!!
9

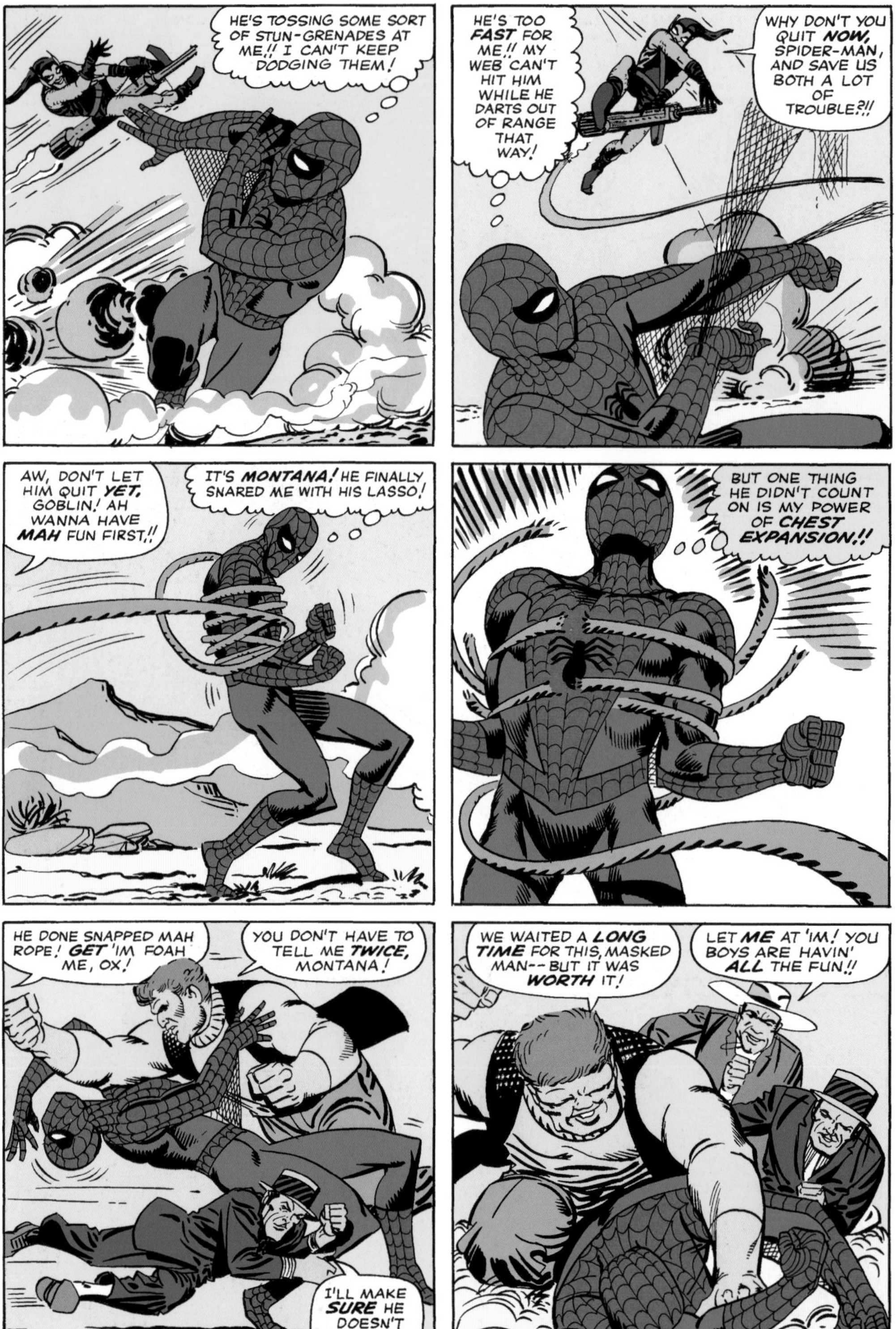
HE'S TOSSING SOME SORT OF STUN-GRENADES AT ME!! I CAN'T KEEP DODGING THEM!
HE'S TOO FAST FOR ME!! MY WEB CAN'T HIT HIM WHILE HE DARTS OUT OF RANGE THAT WAY!
WHY DON'T YOU QUIT NOW, SPIDER-MAN, AND SAVE US BOTH A LOT OF TROUBLE?!!
AW, DON'T LET HIM QUIT YET, GOBLIN! AH WANNA HAVE MAH FUN FIRST!!
IT'S MONTANA! HE FINALLY SNARED ME WITH HIS LASSO!
BUT ONE THING HE DIDN'T COUNT ON IS MY POWER OF CHEST EXPANSION!!
HE DONE SNAPPED MAH ROPE! GET 'IM FOAH ME, OX!
YOU DON'T HAVE TO TELL ME TWICE, MONTANA!
I'LL MAKE SURE HE DOESN'T SLIP AWAY AGAIN!
WE WAITED A LONG TIME FOR THIS, MASKED MAN-- BUT IT WAS WORTH IT!
LET ME AT 'IM! YOU BOYS ARE HAVIN' ALL THE FUN!!
10

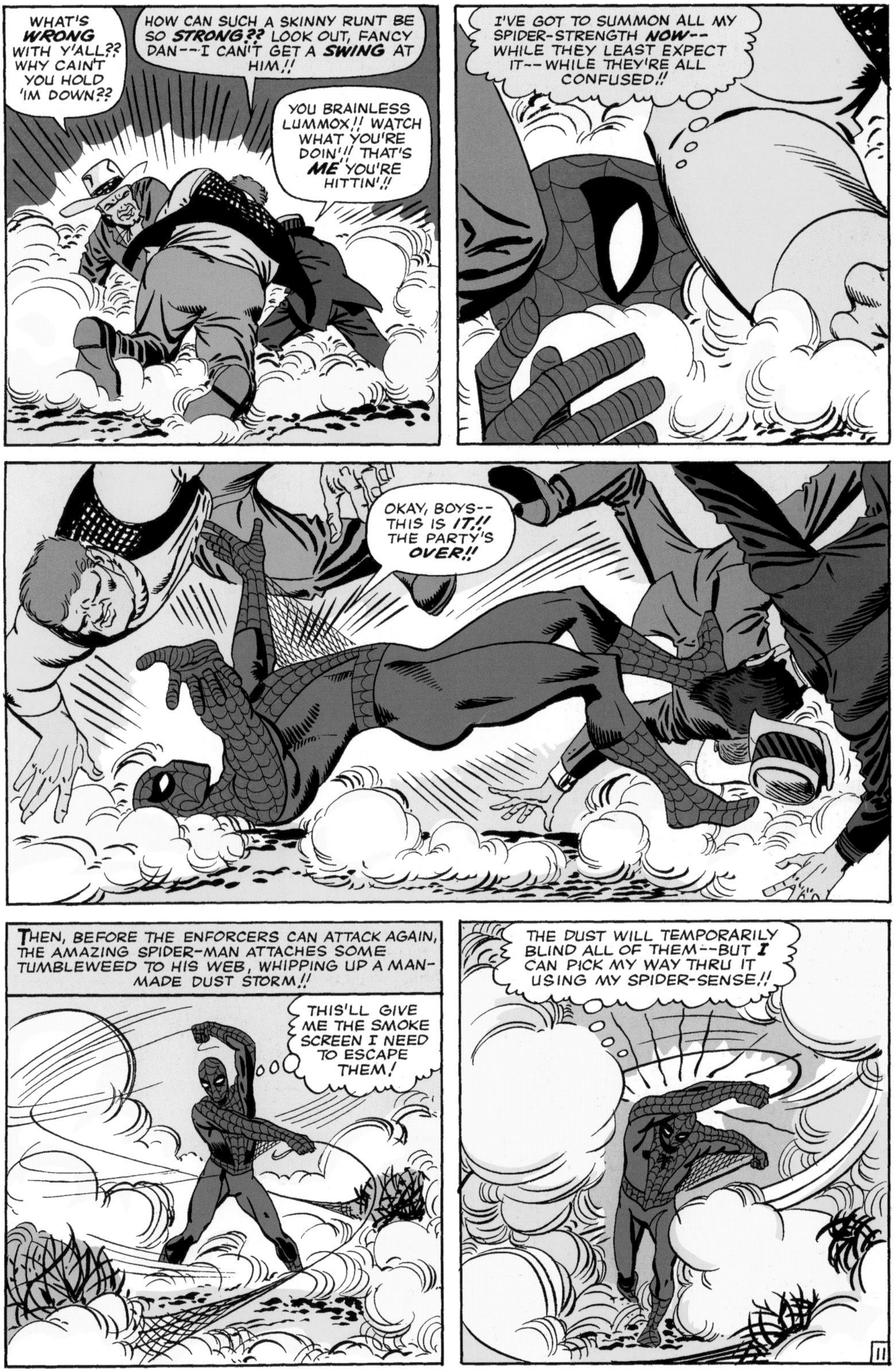
WHAT'S WRONG WITH Y'ALL?? WHY CAIN'T YOU HOLD 'IM DOWN??
HOW CAN SUCH A SKINNY RUNT BE SO STRONG?? LOOK OUT, FANCY DAN--I CAN'T GET A SWING AT HIM!!
YOU BRAINLESS LUMMOX!! WATCH WHAT YOU'RE DOIN'!! THAT'S ME YOU'RE HITTIN'!!
I'VE GOT TO SUMMON ALL MY SPIDER-STRENGTH NOW--WHILE THEY LEAST EXPECT IT--WHILE THEY'RE ALL CONFUSED!!
OKAY, BOYS--THIS IS IT!! THE PARTY'S OVER!!
THEN, BEFORE THE ENFORCERS CAN ATTACK AGAIN, THE AMAZING SPIDER-MAN ATTACHES SOME TUMBLEWEED TO HIS WEB, WHIPPING UP A MAN-MADE DUST STORM!!
THIS'LL GIVE ME THE SMOKE SCREEN I NEED TO ESCAPE THEM!
THE DUST WILL TEMPORARILY BLIND ALL OF THEM--BUT I CAN PICK MY WAY THRU IT USING MY SPIDER-SENSE!!
11

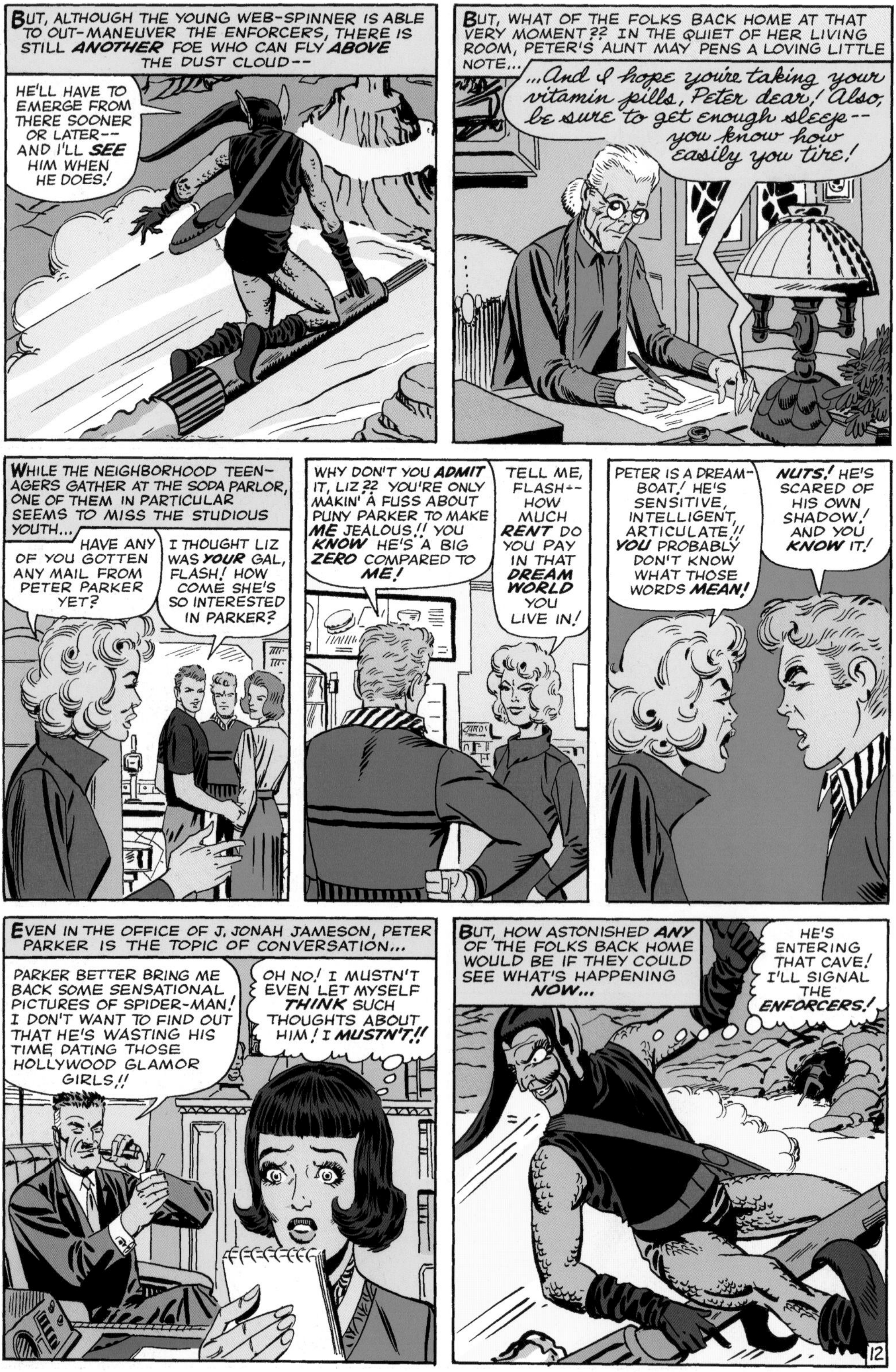
BUT, ALTHOUGH THE YOUNG WEB-SPINNER IS ABLE TO OUT-MANEUVER THE ENFORCERS, THERE IS STILL ANOTHER FOE WHO CAN FLY ABOVE THE DUST CLOUD--
HE'LL HAVE TO EMERGE FROM THERE SOONER OR LATER-- AND I'LL SEE HIM WHEN HE DOES!
BUT, WHAT OF THE FOLKS BACK HOME AT THAT VERY MOMENT?? IN THE QUIET OF HER LIVING ROOM, PETER'S AUNT MAY PENS A LOVING LITTLE NOTE...
...And I hope you're taking your vitamin pills, Peter dear! Also, be sure to get enough sleep-- you know how easily you tire!
WHILE THE NEIGHBORHOOD TEEN-AGERS GATHER AT THE SODA PARLOR, ONE OF THEM IN PARTICULAR SEEMS TO MISS THE STUDIOUS YOUTH...
HAVE ANY OF YOU GOTTEN ANY MAIL FROM PETER PARKER YET?
I THOUGHT LIZ WAS YOUR GAL, FLASH! HOW COME SHE'S SO INTERESTED IN PARKER?
WHY DON'T YOU ADMIT IT, LIZ?? YOU'RE ONLY MAKIN' A FUSS ABOUT PUNY PARKER TO MAKE ME JEALOUS!! YOU KNOW HE'S A BIG ZERO COMPARED TO ME!
TELL ME, FLASH-- HOW MUCH RENT DO YOU PAY IN THAT DREAM WORLD YOU LIVE IN!
PETER IS A DREAM-BOAT! HE'S SENSITIVE, INTELLIGENT, ARTICULATE!! YOU PROBABLY DON'T KNOW WHAT THOSE WORDS MEAN!
NUTS! HE'S SCARED OF HIS OWN SHADOW! AND YOU KNOW IT!
EVEN IN THE OFFICE OF J. JONAH JAMESON, PETER PARKER IS THE TOPIC OF CONVERSATION...
PARKER BETTER BRING ME BACK SOME SENSATIONAL PICTURES OF SPIDER-MAN! I DON'T WANT TO FIND OUT THAT HE'S WASTING HIS TIME DATING THOSE HOLLYWOOD GLAMOR GIRLS!!
OH NO! I MUSTN'T EVEN LET MYSELF THINK SUCH THOUGHTS ABOUT HIM! I MUSTN'T!!
BUT, HOW ASTONISHED ANY OF THE FOLKS BACK HOME WOULD BE IF THEY COULD SEE WHAT'S HAPPENING NOW...
HE'S ENTERING THAT CAVE! I'LL SIGNAL THE ENFORCERS!
12

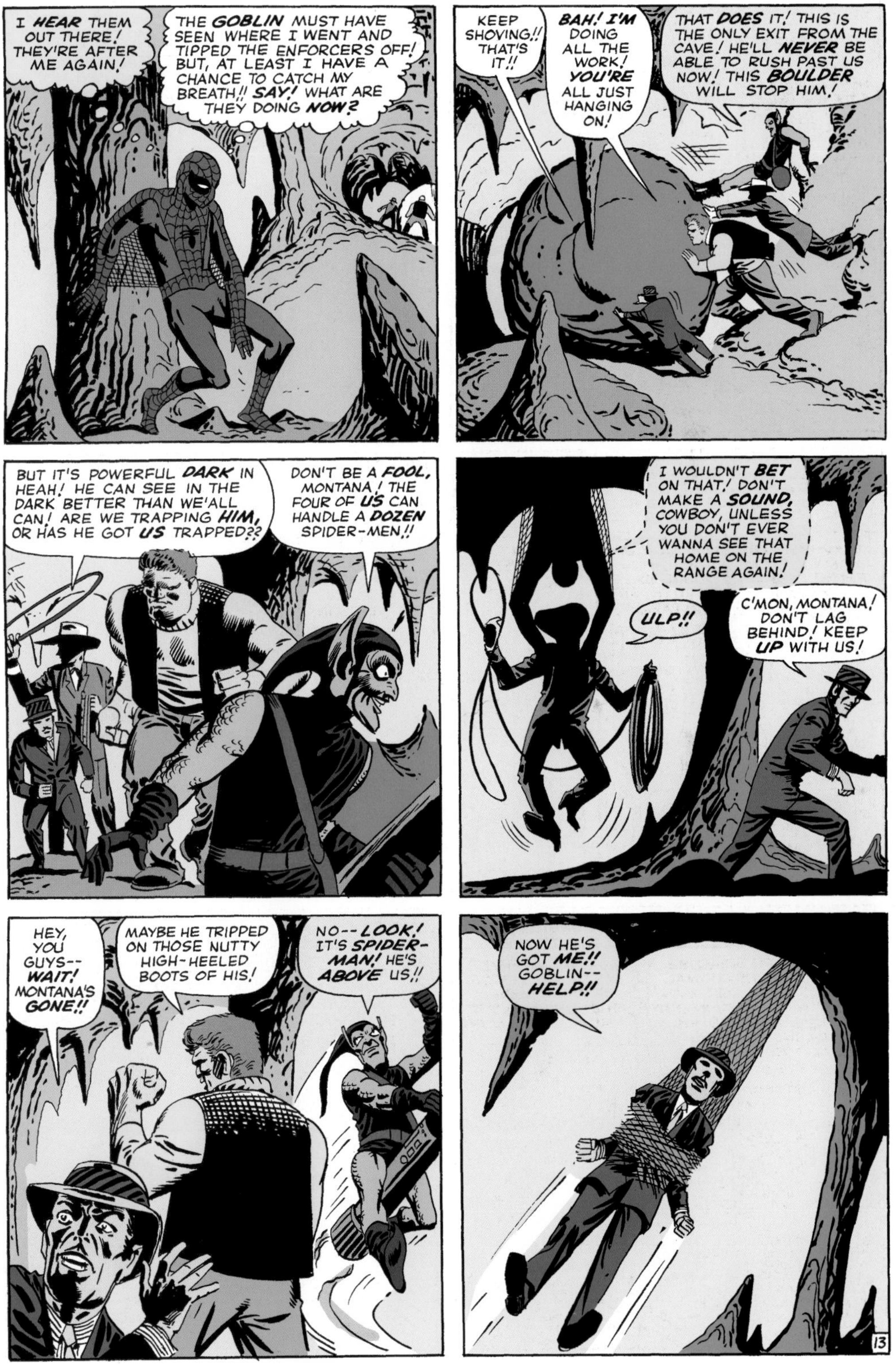
I HEAR THEM OUT THERE! THEY'RE AFTER ME AGAIN!
THE GOBLIN MUST HAVE SEEN WHERE I WENT AND TIPPED THE ENFORCERS OFF! BUT, AT LEAST I HAVE A CHANCE TO CATCH MY BREATH!! SAY! WHAT ARE THEY DOING NOW?
KEEP SHOVING!! THAT'S IT!!
BAH! I'M DOING ALL THE WORK! YOU'RE ALL JUST HANGING ON!
THAT DOES IT! THIS IS THE ONLY EXIT FROM THE CAVE! HE'LL NEVER BE ABLE TO RUSH PAST US NOW! THIS BOULDER WILL STOP HIM!
BUT IT'S POWERFUL DARK IN HEAH! HE CAN SEE IN THE DARK BETTER THAN WE'ALL CAN! ARE WE TRAPPING HIM, OR HAS HE GOT US TRAPPED??
DON'T BE A FOOL, MONTANA! THE FOUR OF US CAN HANDLE A DOZEN SPIDER-MEN!!
I WOULDN'T BET ON THAT! DON'T MAKE A SOUND, COWBOY, UNLESS YOU DON'T EVER WANNA SEE THAT HOME ON THE RANGE AGAIN!
ULP!!
C'MON, MONTANA! DON'T LAG BEHIND! KEEP UP WITH US!
HEY, YOU GUYS-- WAIT! MONTANA'S GONE!!
MAYBE HE TRIPPED ON THOSE NUTTY HIGH-HEELED BOOTS OF HIS!
NO--LOOK! IT'S SPIDER-MAN! HE'S ABOVE US!!
NOW HE'S GOT ME!! GOBLIN-- HELP!!
13

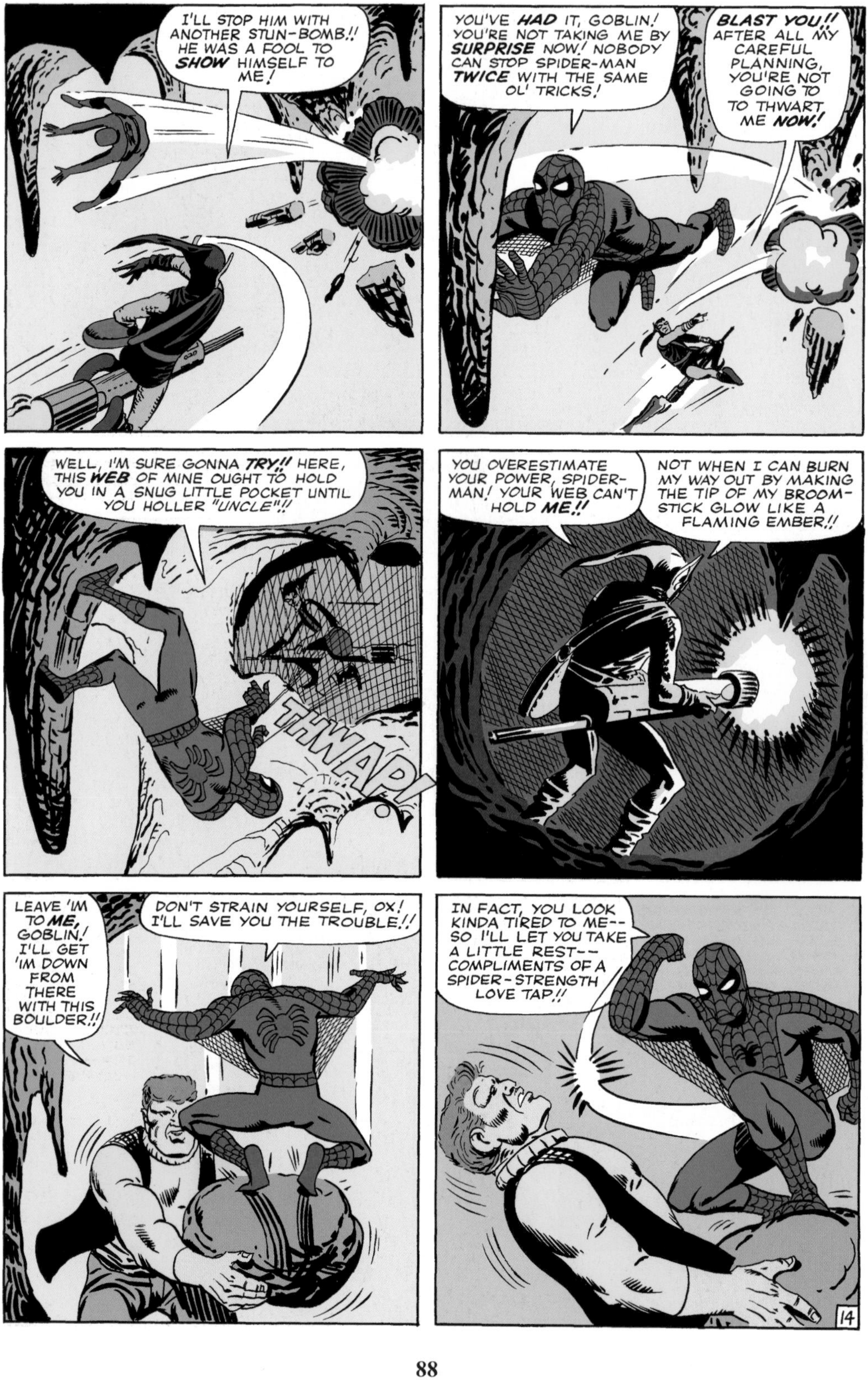
I'LL STOP HIM WITH ANOTHER STUN-BOMB!! HE WAS A FOOL TO SHOW HIMSELF TO ME!
YOU'VE HAD IT, GOBLIN! YOU'RE NOT TAKING ME BY SURPRISE NOW! NOBODY CAN STOP SPIDER-MAN TWICE WITH THE SAME OL' TRICKS!
BLAST YOU!! AFTER ALL MY CAREFUL PLANNING, YOU'RE NOT GOING TO TO THWART ME NOW!
WELL, I'M SURE GONNA TRY!! HERE, THIS WEB OF MINE OUGHT TO HOLD YOU IN A SNUG LITTLE POCKET UNTIL YOU HOLLER "UNCLE"!!
THWAP!
YOU OVERESTIMATE YOUR POWER, SPIDER-MAN! YOUR WEB CAN'T HOLD ME!!
NOT WHEN I CAN BURN MY WAY OUT BY MAKING THE TIP OF MY BROOM-STICK GLOW LIKE A FLAMING EMBER!!
LEAVE 'IM TO ME, GOBLIN! I'LL GET 'IM DOWN FROM THERE WITH THIS BOULDER!!
DON'T STRAIN YOURSELF, OX! I'LL SAVE YOU THE TROUBLE!!
IN FACT, YOU LOOK KINDA TIRED TO ME-- SO I'LL LET YOU TAKE A LITTLE REST-- COMPLIMENTS OF A SPIDER-STRENGTH LOVE TAP!!
14

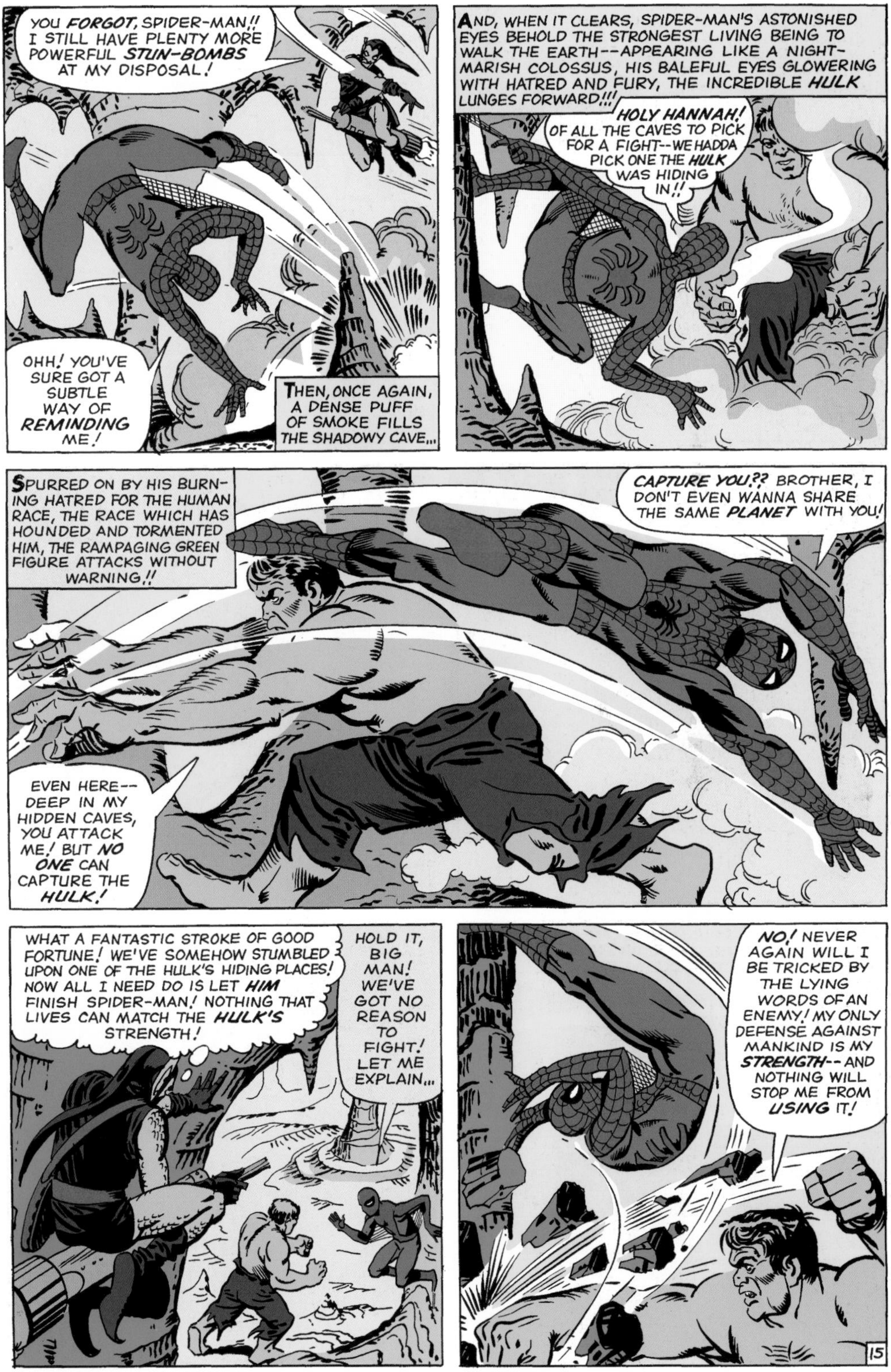
YOU FORGOT, SPIDER-MAN!! I STILL HAVE PLENTY MORE POWERFUL STUN-BOMBS AT MY DISPOSAL!
OHH! YOU'VE SURE GOT A SUBTLE WAY OF REMINDING ME!
THEN, ONCE AGAIN, A DENSE PUFF OF SMOKE FILLS THE SHADOWY CAVE...
AND, WHEN IT CLEARS, SPIDER-MAN'S ASTONISHED EYES BEHOLD THE STRONGEST LIVING BEING TO WALK THE EARTH--APPEARING LIKE A NIGHTMARISH COLOSSUS, HIS BALEFUL EYES GLOWERING WITH HATRED AND FURY, THE INCREDIBLE HULK LUNGES FORWARD!!!
HOLY HANNAH! OF ALL THE CAVES TO PICK FOR A FIGHT--WE HADDA PICK ONE THE HULK WAS HIDING IN!!
SPURRED ON BY HIS BURNING HATRED FOR THE HUMAN RACE, THE RACE WHICH HAS HOUNDED AND TORMENTED HIM, THE RAMPAGING GREEN FIGURE ATTACKS WITHOUT WARNING!!
EVEN HERE--DEEP IN MY HIDDEN CAVES, YOU ATTACK ME! BUT NO ONE CAN CAPTURE THE HULK!
CAPTURE YOU?? BROTHER, I DON'T EVEN WANNA SHARE THE SAME PLANET WITH YOU!
WHAT A FANTASTIC STROKE OF GOOD FORTUNE! WE'VE SOMEHOW STUMBLED UPON ONE OF THE HULK'S HIDING PLACES! NOW ALL I NEED DO IS LET HIM FINISH SPIDER-MAN! NOTHING THAT LIVES CAN MATCH THE HULK'S STRENGTH!
HOLD IT, BIG MAN! WE'VE GOT NO REASON TO FIGHT! LET ME EXPLAIN...
NO! NEVER AGAIN WILL I BE TRICKED BY THE LYING WORDS OF AN ENEMY! MY ONLY DEFENSE AGAINST MANKIND IS MY STRENGTH--AND NOTHING WILL STOP ME FROM USING IT!
15

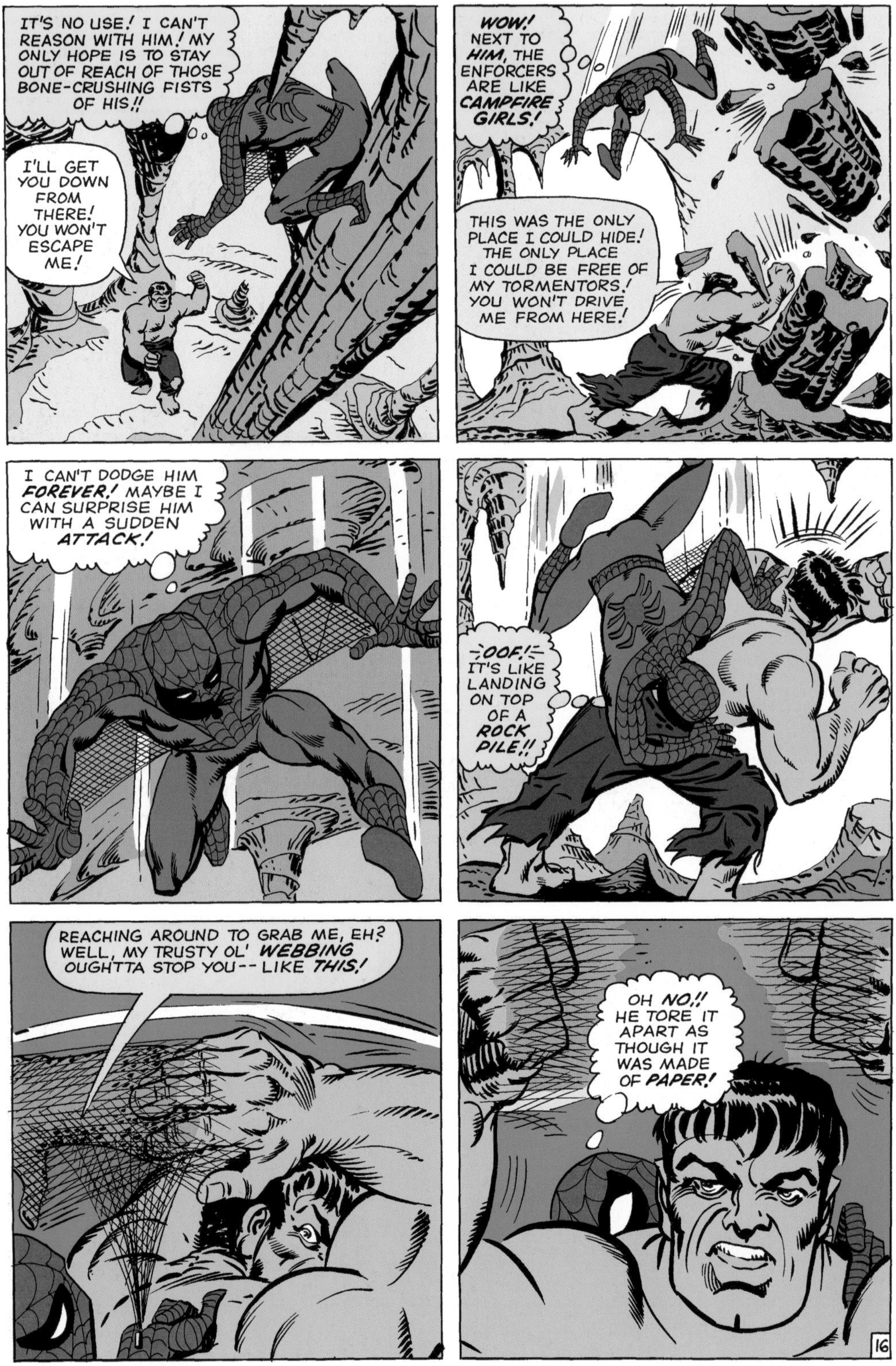
IT'S NO USE! I CAN'T REASON WITH HIM! MY ONLY HOPE IS TO STAY OUT OF REACH OF THOSE BONE-CRUSHING FISTS OF HIS!!
I'LL GET YOU DOWN FROM THERE! YOU WON'T ESCAPE ME!
WOW! NEXT TO HIM, THE ENFORCERS ARE LIKE CAMPFIRE GIRLS!
THIS WAS THE ONLY PLACE I COULD HIDE! THE ONLY PLACE I COULD BE FREE OF MY TORMENTORS! YOU WON'T DRIVE ME FROM HERE!
I CAN'T DODGE HIM FOREVER! MAYBE I CAN SURPRISE HIM WITH A SUDDEN ATTACK!
-OOF!- IT'S LIKE LANDING ON TOP OF A ROCK PILE!!
REACHING AROUND TO GRAB ME, EH? WELL, MY TRUSTY OL' WEBBING OUGHTTA STOP YOU-- LIKE THIS!
OH NO!! HE TORE IT APART AS THOUGH IT WAS MADE OF PAPER!
16

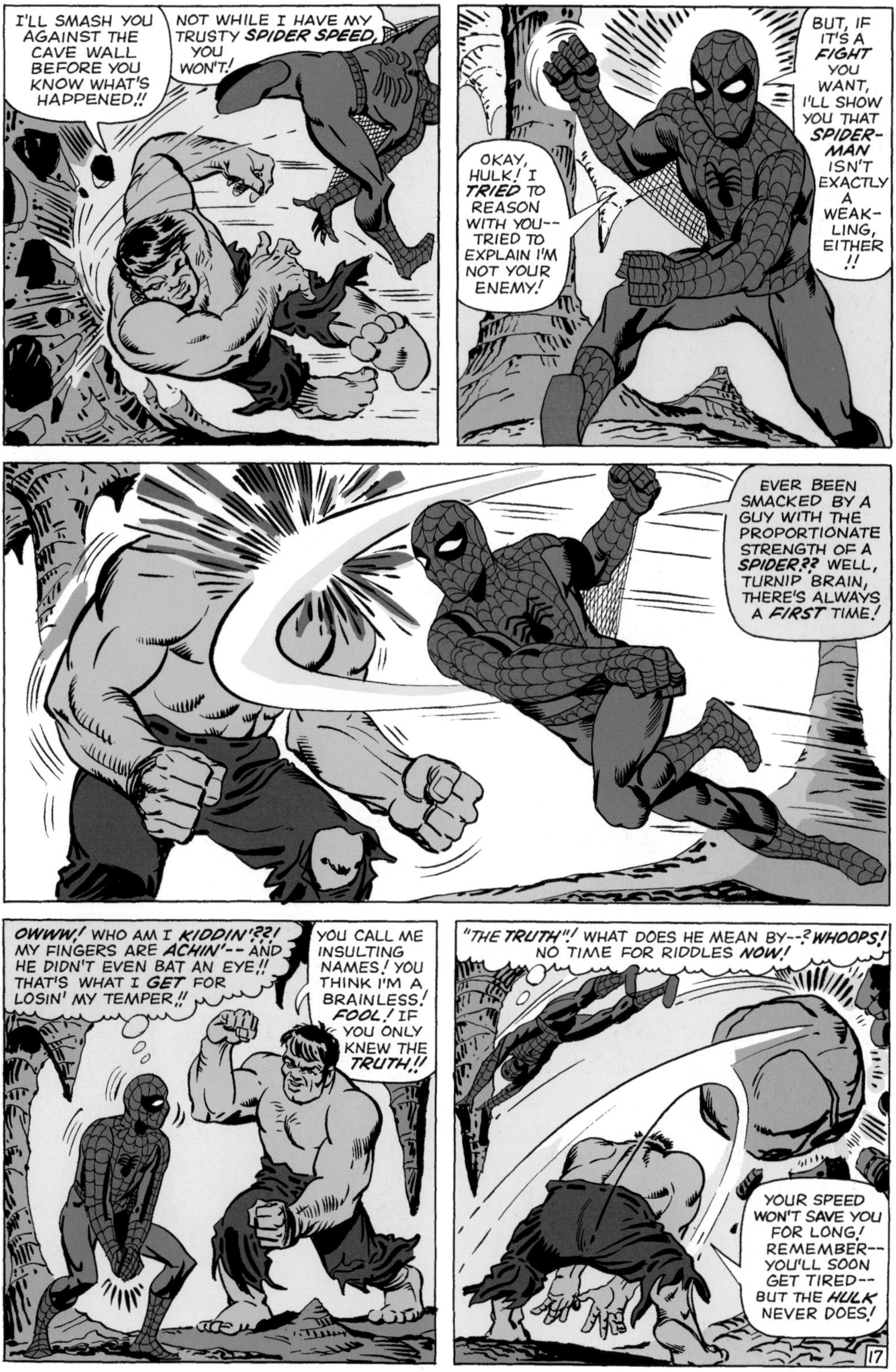

I'LL SMASH YOU AGAINST THE CAVE WALL BEFORE YOU KNOW WHAT'S HAPPENED!!
NOT WHILE I HAVE MY TRUSTY SPIDER SPEED, YOU WON'T!
OKAY, HULK! I TRIED TO REASON WITH YOU-- TRIED TO EXPLAIN I'M NOT YOUR ENEMY!
BUT, IF IT'S A FIGHT YOU WANT, I'LL SHOW YOU THAT SPIDER-MAN ISN'T EXACTLY A WEAK-LING, EITHER!!
EVER BEEN SMACKED BY A GUY WITH THE PROPORTIONATE STRENGTH OF A SPIDER?? WELL, TURNIP BRAIN, THERE'S ALWAYS A FIRST TIME!
OWWW! WHO AM I KIDDIN'??! MY FINGERS ARE ACHIN'-- AND HE DIDN'T EVEN BAT AN EYE!! THAT'S WHAT I GET FOR LOSIN' MY TEMPER!!
YOU CALL ME INSULTING NAMES! YOU THINK I'M A BRAINLESS! FOOL! IF YOU ONLY KNEW THE TRUTH!!
"THE TRUTH"! WHAT DOES HE MEAN BY--? WHOOPS! NO TIME FOR RIDDLES NOW!
YOUR SPEED WON'T SAVE YOU FOR LONG! REMEMBER-- YOU'LL SOON GET TIRED-- BUT THE HULK NEVER DOES!
17

HE'S RIGHT! I'VE GOTTA STOP KNOCKIN' MYSELF OUT AND START *THINKING! WAIT!* I'VE AN IDEA!

IF THIS DOESN'T WORK, IT'S *"GOOD-BYE SPIDER-MAN!"* BUT I'VE GOT TO CHANCE IT!

OKAY, HULK-- LET'S SETTLE THIS NOW-- MAN TO MAN!

YOU DON'T FOOL *ME!* YOU HAVE A *TRICK* IN MIND! BUT IT WON'T HELP YOU! *NOTHING* WILL!

HE WAS *RIGHT* BEFORE --HE *ISN'T* SO DUMB! BUT I CAN'T BACK DOWN NOW!

HE'S SWINGING! I'VE GOT TO TIME THIS *PERFECTLY* WITH MY SPIDER-SENSES! I CAN'T AFFORD TO MISS BY A SPLIT-SECOND!

NOW! I'LL MOVE JUST ENOUGH TO DEFLECT THE BLOW! BUT HE MUSTN'T SUSPECT--!

WHEW!-- EVEN THOUGH HE HARDLY *TOUCHED* ME, IT'S THE HARDEST PUNCH I EVER FELT!

THERE ARE *OTHERS* IN THE CAVE! ONCE I'VE FINISHED *YOU,* I'LL DO THE SAME TO *THEM!*

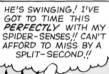

IF IT'S ALL THE SAME TO *YOU,* HULK-- I WISH YOU'D TACKLED THEM *FIRST!*

THIS IS *IT!* I'LL LEAN AGAINST THE BOULDER-- PRETEND TO BE STUNNED! HERE HE COMES--!

IT *WORKED!* I DODGED JUST IN TIME, AND THE FORCE OF HIS BLOW SHATTERED THE BOULDER LIKE A PANE OF GLASS!

18

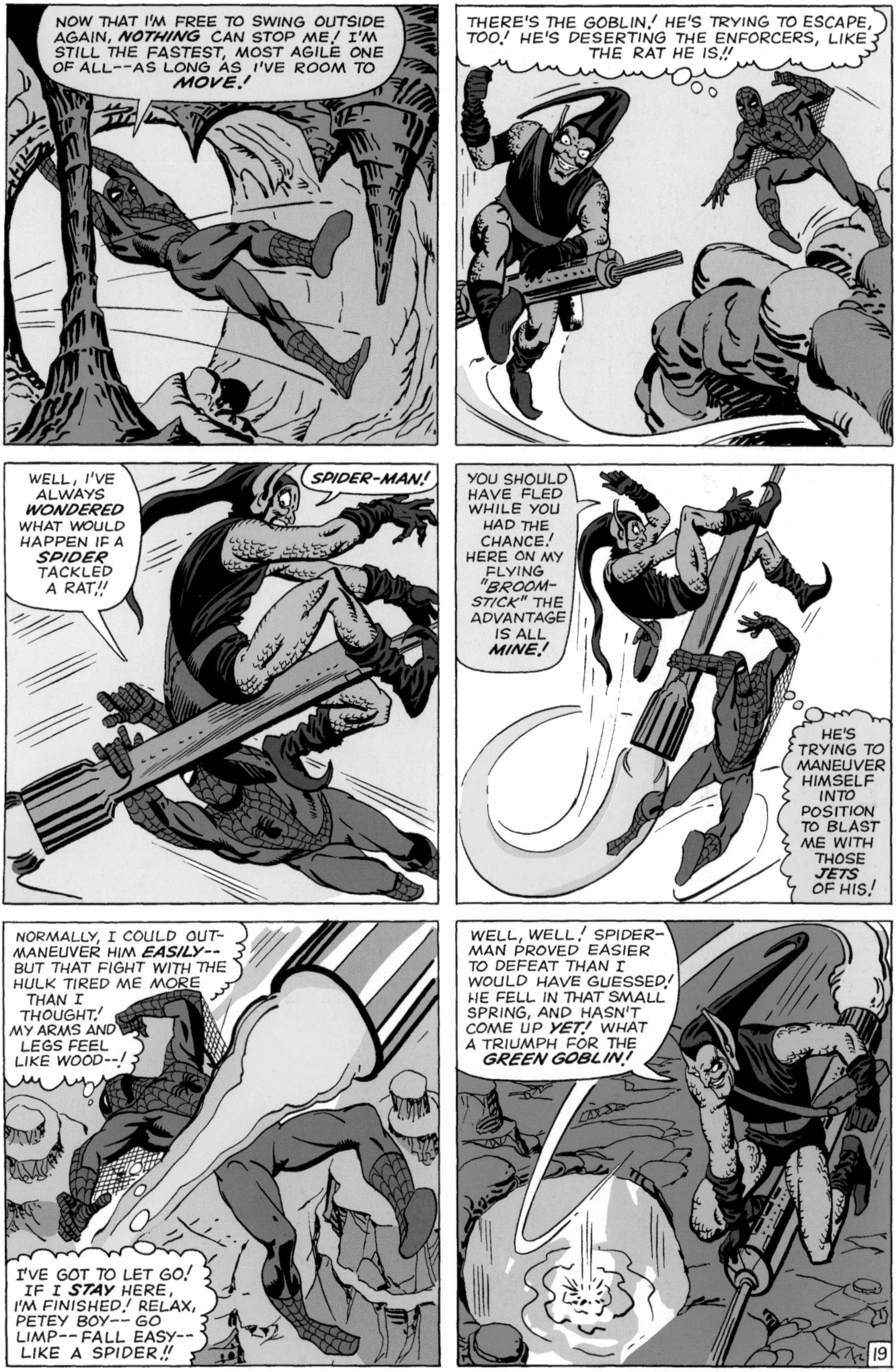
NOW THAT I'M FREE TO SWING OUTSIDE AGAIN, NOTHING CAN STOP ME! I'M STILL THE FASTEST, MOST AGILE ONE OF ALL--AS LONG AS I'VE ROOM TO MOVE!
THERE'S THE GOBLIN! HE'S TRYING TO ESCAPE, TOO! HE'S DESERTING THE ENFORCERS, LIKE THE RAT HE IS!!
SPIDER-MAN!
WELL, I'VE ALWAYS WONDERED WHAT WOULD HAPPEN IF A SPIDER TACKLED A RAT!!
YOU SHOULD HAVE FLED WHILE YOU HAD THE CHANCE! HERE ON MY FLYING "BROOM-STICK" THE ADVANTAGE IS ALL MINE!
HE'S TRYING TO MANEUVER HIMSELF INTO POSITION TO BLAST ME WITH THOSE JETS OF HIS!
NORMALLY, I COULD OUT-MANEUVER HIM EASILY-- BUT THAT FIGHT WITH THE HULK TIRED ME MORE THAN I THOUGHT! MY ARMS AND LEGS FEEL LIKE WOOD--!
I'VE GOT TO LET GO! IF I STAY HERE, I'M FINISHED! RELAX, PETEY BOY-- GO LIMP--FALL EASY-- LIKE A SPIDER!!
WELL, WELL! SPIDER-MAN PROVED EASIER TO DEFEAT THAN I WOULD HAVE GUESSED! HE FELL IN THAT SMALL SPRING, AND HASN'T COME UP YET! WHAT A TRIUMPH FOR THE GREEN GOBLIN!
19

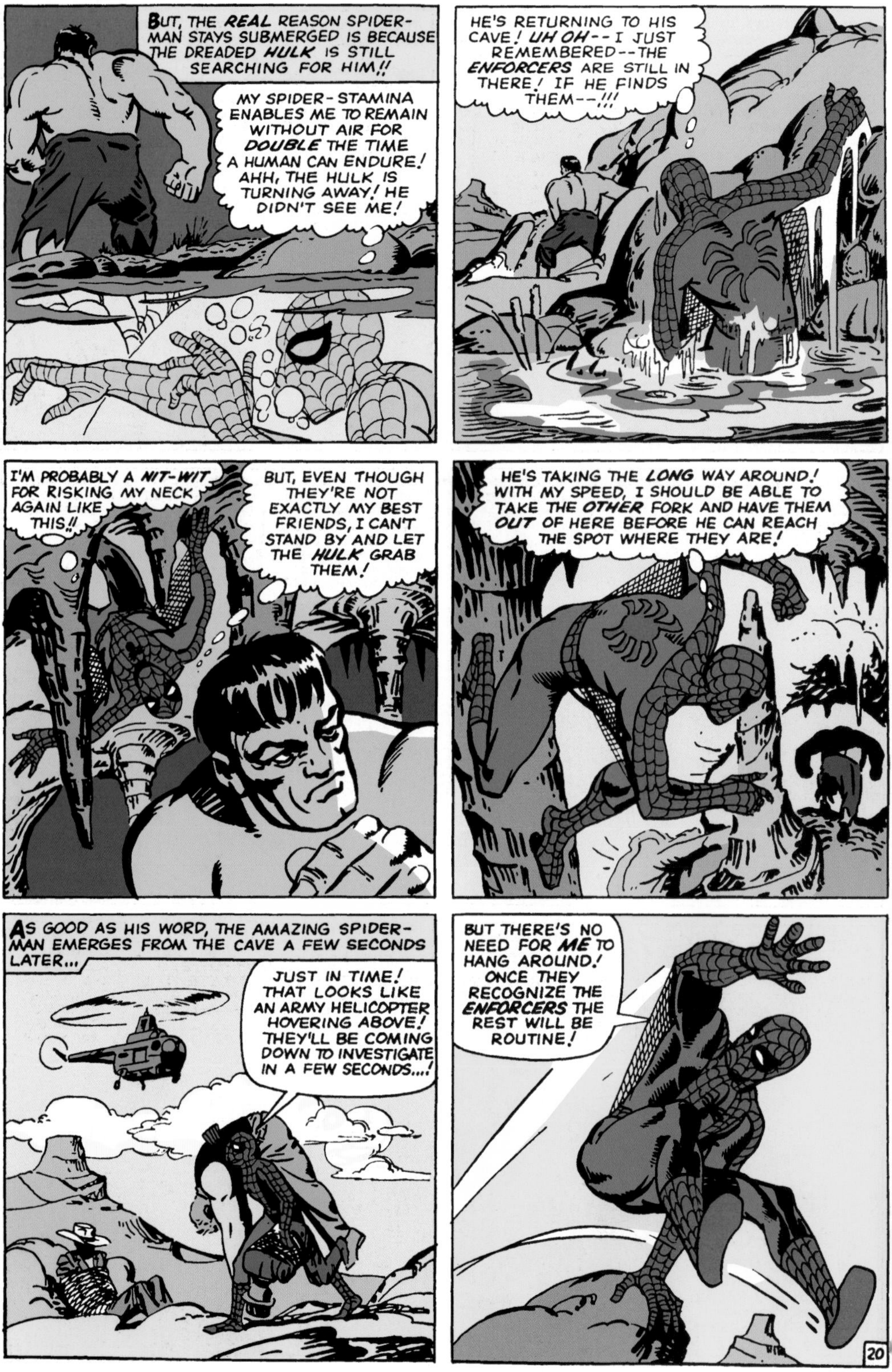
BUT, THE REAL REASON SPIDER-MAN STAYS SUBMERGED IS BECAUSE THE DREADED HULK IS STILL SEARCHING FOR HIM!!
MY SPIDER-STAMINA ENABLES ME TO REMAIN WITHOUT AIR FOR DOUBLE THE TIME A HUMAN CAN ENDURE! AHH, THE HULK IS TURNING AWAY! HE DIDN'T SEE ME!
HE'S RETURNING TO HIS CAVE! UH OH-- I JUST REMEMBERED--THE ENFORCERS ARE STILL IN THERE! IF HE FINDS THEM--!!!
I'M PROBABLY A NIT-WIT FOR RISKING MY NECK AGAIN LIKE THIS!!
BUT, EVEN THOUGH THEY'RE NOT EXACTLY MY BEST FRIENDS, I CAN'T STAND BY AND LET THE HULK GRAB THEM!
HE'S TAKING THE LONG WAY AROUND! WITH MY SPEED, I SHOULD BE ABLE TO TAKE THE OTHER FORK AND HAVE THEM OUT OF HERE BEFORE HE CAN REACH THE SPOT WHERE THEY ARE!
AS GOOD AS HIS WORD, THE AMAZING SPIDER-MAN EMERGES FROM THE CAVE A FEW SECONDS LATER...
JUST IN TIME! THAT LOOKS LIKE AN ARMY HELICOPTER HOVERING ABOVE! THEY'LL BE COMING DOWN TO INVESTIGATE IN A FEW SECONDS...!
BUT THERE'S NO NEED FOR ME TO HANG AROUND! ONCE THEY RECOGNIZE THE ENFORCERS THE REST WILL BE ROUTINE!
20

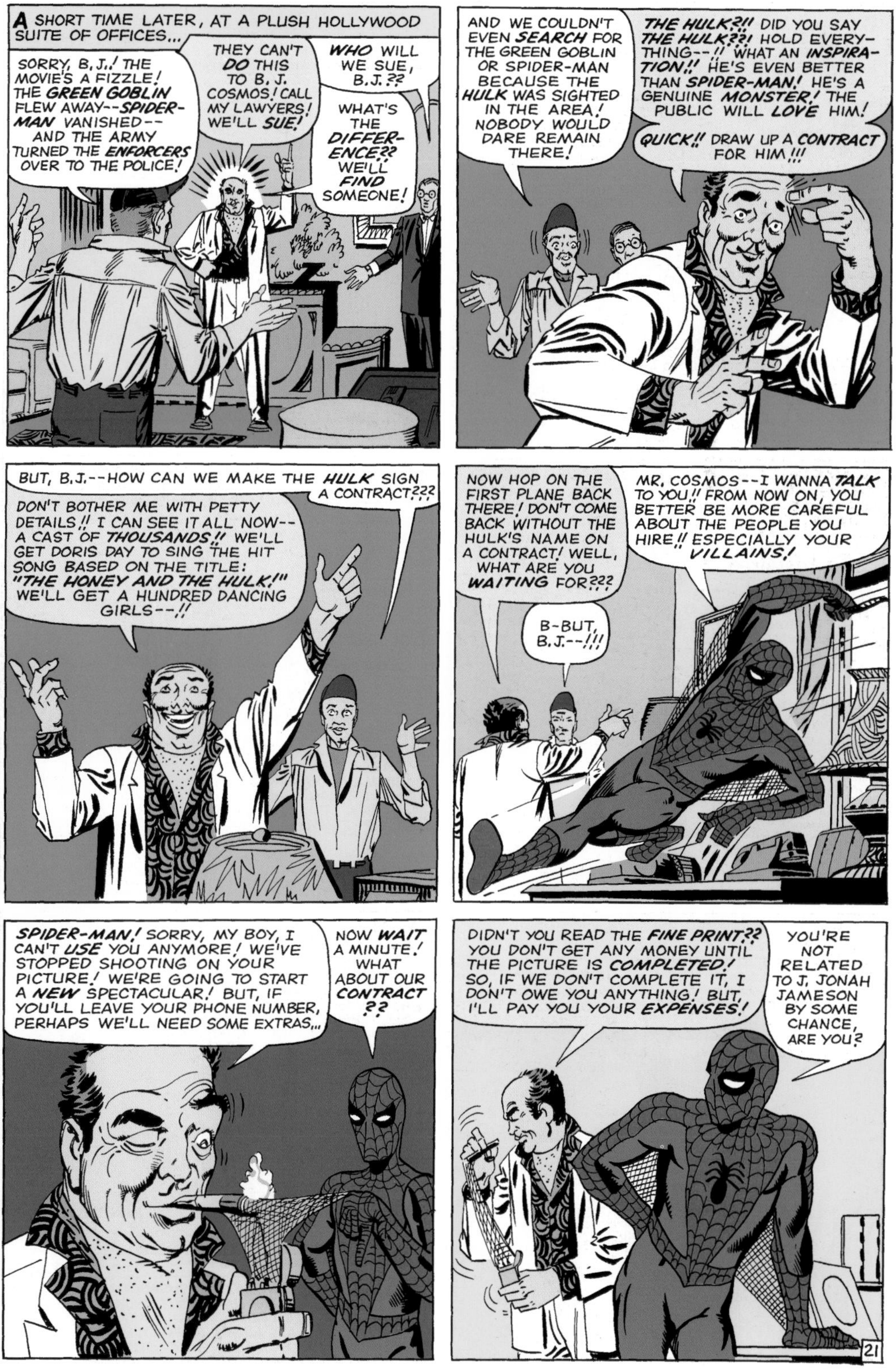
A SHORT TIME LATER, AT A PLUSH HOLLYWOOD SUITE OF OFFICES...
SORRY, B.J.! THE MOVIE'S A FIZZLE! THE GREEN GOBLIN FLEW AWAY--SPIDER-MAN VANISHED-- AND THE ARMY TURNED THE ENFORCERS OVER TO THE POLICE!
THEY CAN'T DO THIS TO B. J. COSMOS! CALL MY LAWYERS! WE'LL SUE!
WHO WILL WE SUE, B.J.??
WHAT'S THE DIFFERENCE?? WE'LL FIND SOMEONE!
AND WE COULDN'T EVEN SEARCH FOR THE GREEN GOBLIN OR SPIDER-MAN BECAUSE THE HULK WAS SIGHTED IN THE AREA! NOBODY WOULD DARE REMAIN THERE!
THE HULK?!! DID YOU SAY THE HULK??! HOLD EVERYTHING--!! WHAT AN INSPIRATION!! HE'S EVEN BETTER THAN SPIDER-MAN! HE'S A GENUINE MONSTER! THE PUBLIC WILL LOVE HIM!
QUICK!! DRAW UP A CONTRACT FOR HIM!!!
BUT, B.J.--HOW CAN WE MAKE THE HULK SIGN A CONTRACT???
DON'T BOTHER ME WITH PETTY DETAILS!! I CAN SEE IT ALL NOW-- A CAST OF THOUSANDS!! WE'LL GET DORIS DAY TO SING THE HIT SONG BASED ON THE TITLE: "THE HONEY AND THE HULK!" WE'LL GET A HUNDRED DANCING GIRLS--!!
NOW HOP ON THE FIRST PLANE BACK THERE! DON'T COME BACK WITHOUT THE HULK'S NAME ON A CONTRACT! WELL, WHAT ARE YOU WAITING FOR???
B-BUT, B.J.--!!!
MR. COSMOS--I WANNA TALK TO YOU!! FROM NOW ON, YOU BETTER BE MORE CAREFUL ABOUT THE PEOPLE YOU HIRE!! ESPECIALLY YOUR VILLAINS!
SPIDER-MAN! SORRY, MY BOY, I CAN'T USE YOU ANYMORE! WE'VE STOPPED SHOOTING ON YOUR PICTURE! WE'RE GOING TO START A NEW SPECTACULAR! BUT, IF YOU'LL LEAVE YOUR PHONE NUMBER, PERHAPS WE'LL NEED SOME EXTRAS...
NOW WAIT A MINUTE! WHAT ABOUT OUR CONTRACT??
DIDN'T YOU READ THE FINE PRINT?? YOU DON'T GET ANY MONEY UNTIL THE PICTURE IS COMPLETED! SO, IF WE DON'T COMPLETE IT, I DON'T OWE YOU ANYTHING! BUT, I'LL PAY YOU YOUR EXPENSES!
YOU'RE NOT RELATED TO J. JONAH JAMESON BY SOME CHANCE, ARE YOU?
21

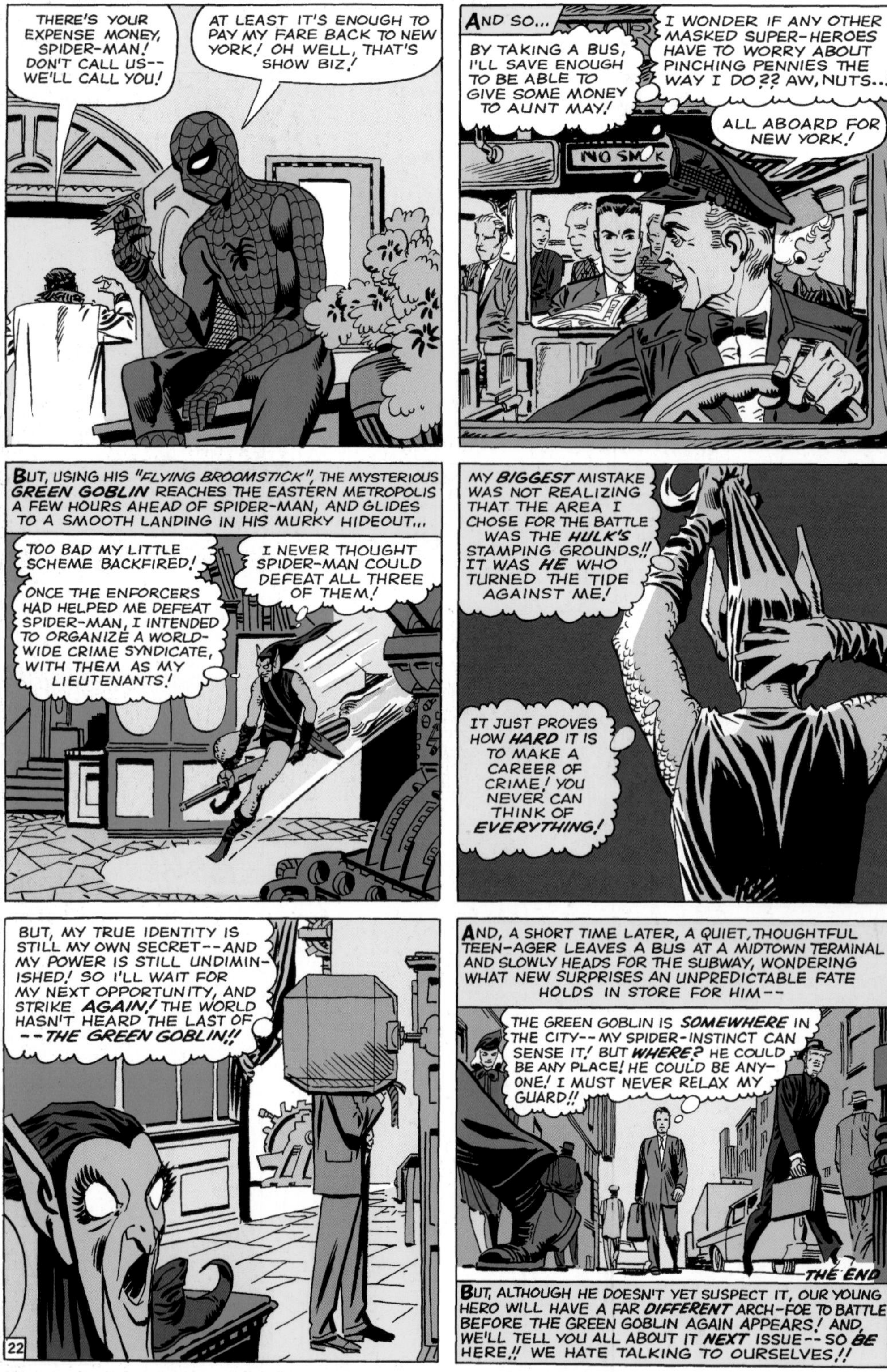
THERE'S YOUR EXPENSE MONEY, SPIDER-MAN! DON'T CALL US-- WE'LL CALL YOU!
AT LEAST IT'S ENOUGH TO PAY MY FARE BACK TO NEW YORK! OH WELL, THAT'S SHOW BIZ!
AND SO...
BY TAKING A BUS, I'LL SAVE ENOUGH TO BE ABLE TO GIVE SOME MONEY TO AUNT MAY!
I WONDER IF ANY OTHER MASKED SUPER-HEROES HAVE TO WORRY ABOUT PINCHING PENNIES THE WAY I DO?? AW, NUTS..!
ALL ABOARD FOR NEW YORK!
BUT, USING HIS "FLYING BROOMSTICK", THE MYSTERIOUS GREEN GOBLIN REACHES THE EASTERN METROPOLIS A FEW HOURS AHEAD OF SPIDER-MAN, AND GLIDES TO A SMOOTH LANDING IN HIS MURKY HIDEOUT...
TOO BAD MY LITTLE SCHEME BACKFIRED!
ONCE THE ENFORCERS HAD HELPED ME DEFEAT SPIDER-MAN, I INTENDED TO ORGANIZE A WORLD-WIDE CRIME SYNDICATE, WITH THEM AS MY LIEUTENANTS!
I NEVER THOUGHT SPIDER-MAN COULD DEFEAT ALL THREE OF THEM!
MY BIGGEST MISTAKE WAS NOT REALIZING THAT THE AREA I CHOSE FOR THE BATTLE WAS THE HULK'S STAMPING GROUNDS!! IT WAS HE WHO TURNED THE TIDE AGAINST ME!
IT JUST PROVES HOW HARD IT IS TO MAKE A CAREER OF CRIME! YOU NEVER CAN THINK OF EVERYTHING!
BUT, MY TRUE IDENTITY IS STILL MY OWN SECRET--AND MY POWER IS STILL UNDIMINISHED! SO I'LL WAIT FOR MY NEXT OPPORTUNITY, AND STRIKE AGAIN! THE WORLD HASN'T HEARD THE LAST OF --THE GREEN GOBLIN!!
22
AND, A SHORT TIME LATER, A QUIET, THOUGHTFUL TEEN-AGER LEAVES A BUS AT A MIDTOWN TERMINAL AND SLOWLY HEADS FOR THE SUBWAY, WONDERING WHAT NEW SURPRISES AN UNPREDICTABLE FATE HOLDS IN STORE FOR HIM--
THE GREEN GOBLIN IS SOMEWHERE IN THE CITY-- MY SPIDER-INSTINCT CAN SENSE IT! BUT WHERE? HE COULD BE ANY PLACE! HE COULD BE ANYONE! I MUST NEVER RELAX MY GUARD!!
THE END
BUT, ALTHOUGH HE DOESN'T YET SUSPECT IT, OUR YOUNG HERO WILL HAVE A FAR DIFFERENT ARCH-FOE TO BATTLE BEFORE THE GREEN GOBLIN AGAIN APPEARS! AND, WE'LL TELL YOU ALL ABOUT IT NEXT ISSUE-- SO BE HERE!! WE HATE TALKING TO OURSELVES!!

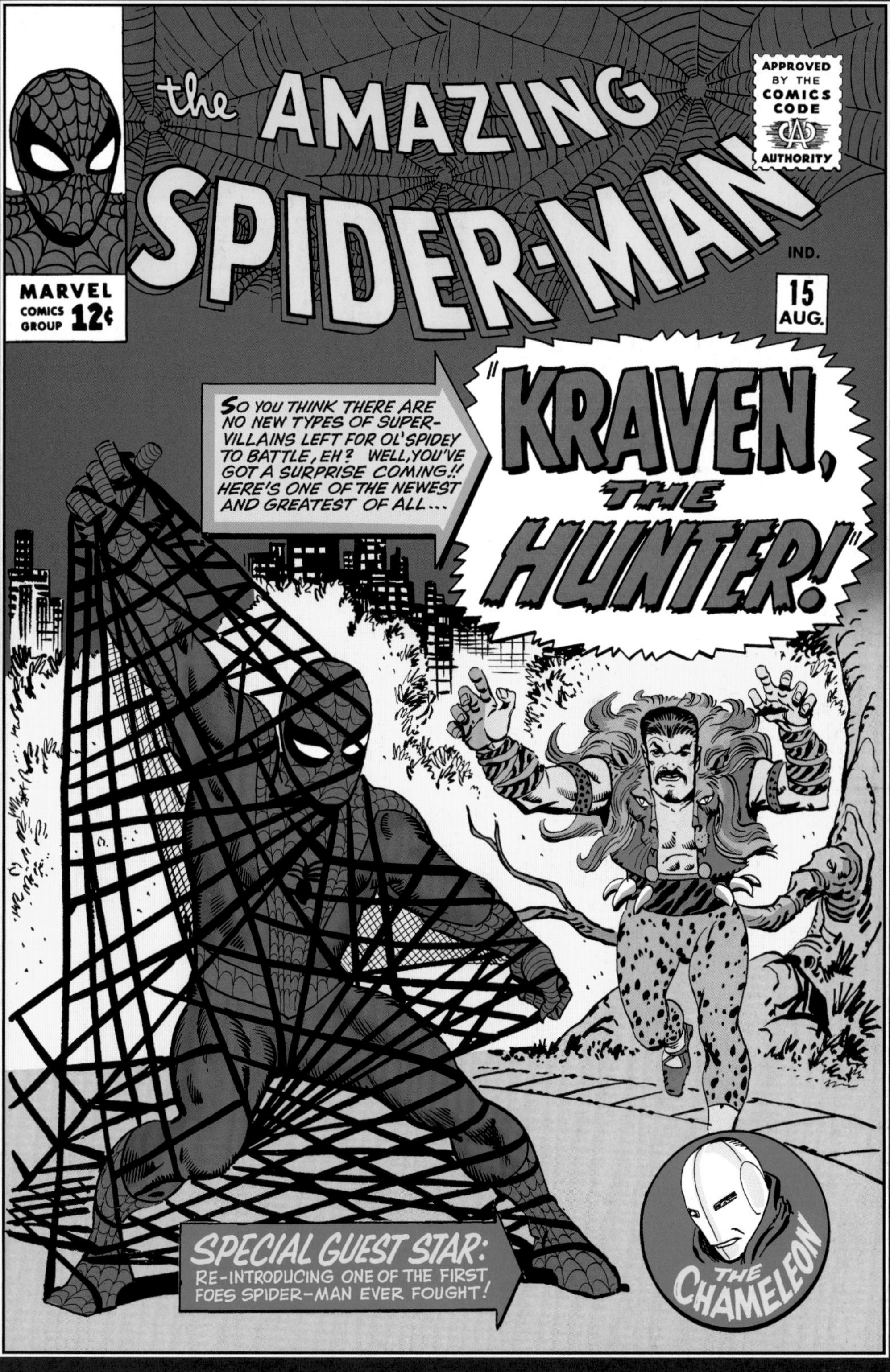
APPROVED BY THE COMICS CODE AUTHORITY
the AMAZING SPIDER-MAN
IND.
MARVEL COMICS GROUP 12¢
15 AUG.
SO YOU THINK THERE ARE NO NEW TYPES OF SUPER-VILLAINS LEFT FOR OL' SPIDEY TO BATTLE, EH? WELL, YOU'VE GOT A SURPRISE COMING!! HERE'S ONE OF THE NEWEST AND GREATEST OF ALL...
"KRAVEN, THE HUNTER!"
SPECIAL GUEST STAR:
RE-INTRODUCING ONE OF THE FIRST FOES SPIDER-MAN EVER FOUGHT!
THE CHAMELEON

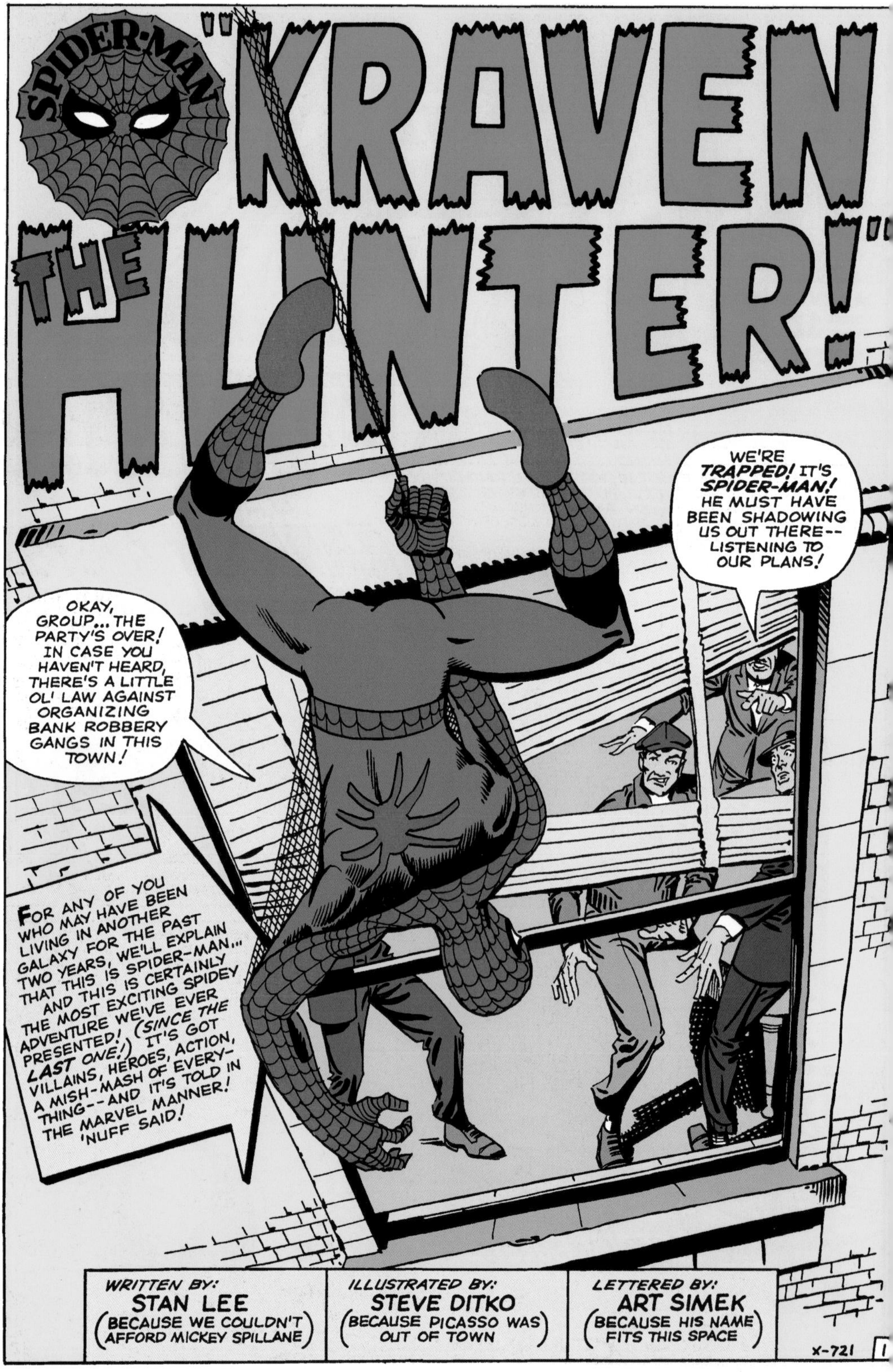
SPIDER-MAN
"KRAVEN THE HUNTER!"
OKAY, GROUP... THE PARTY'S OVER! IN CASE YOU HAVEN'T HEARD, THERE'S A LITTLE OL' LAW AGAINST ORGANIZING BANK ROBBERY GANGS IN THIS TOWN!
WE'RE TRAPPED! IT'S SPIDER-MAN! HE MUST HAVE BEEN SHADOWING US OUT THERE-- LISTENING TO OUR PLANS!
FOR ANY OF YOU WHO MAY HAVE BEEN LIVING IN ANOTHER GALAXY FOR THE PAST TWO YEARS, WE'LL EXPLAIN THAT THIS IS SPIDER-MAN... AND THIS IS CERTAINLY THE MOST EXCITING SPIDEY ADVENTURE WE'VE EVER PRESENTED! (SINCE THE LAST ONE!) IT'S GOT VILLAINS, HEROES, ACTION, A MISH-MASH OF EVERY-THING--AND IT'S TOLD IN THE MARVEL MANNER! 'NUFF SAID!
WRITTEN BY: STAN LEE (BECAUSE WE COULDN'T AFFORD MICKEY SPILLANE)
ILLUSTRATED BY: STEVE DITKO (BECAUSE PICASSO WAS OUT OF TOWN)
LETTERED BY: ART SIMEK (BECAUSE HIS NAME FITS THIS SPACE)
X-721
1

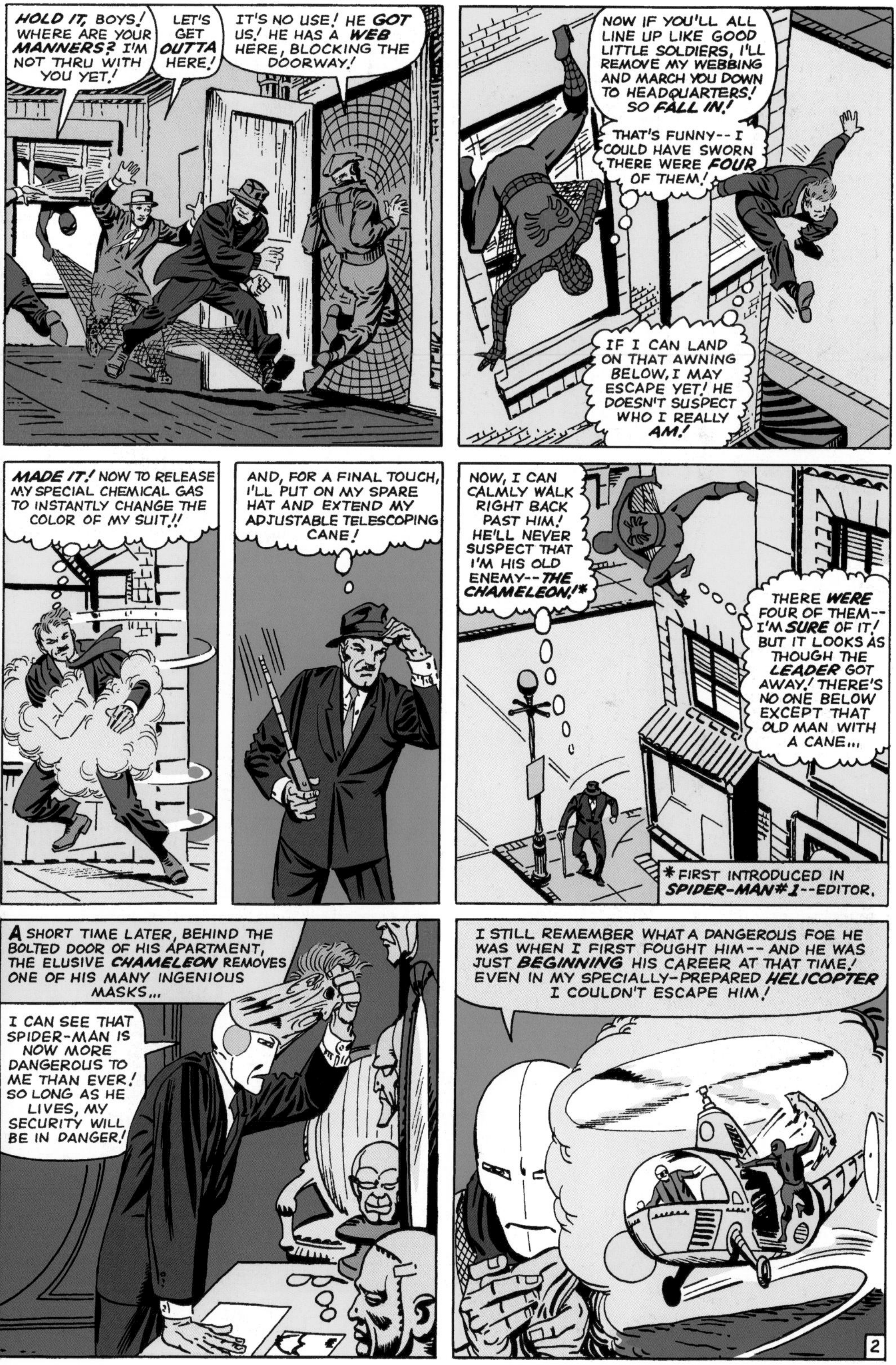
HOLD IT, BOYS! WHERE ARE YOUR MANNERS? I'M NOT THRU WITH YOU YET!
LET'S GET OUTTA HERE!
IT'S NO USE! HE GOT US! HE HAS A WEB HERE, BLOCKING THE DOORWAY!
NOW IF YOU'LL ALL LINE UP LIKE GOOD LITTLE SOLDIERS, I'LL REMOVE MY WEBBING AND MARCH YOU DOWN TO HEADQUARTERS! SO FALL IN!
THAT'S FUNNY-- I COULD HAVE SWORN THERE WERE FOUR OF THEM!
IF I CAN LAND ON THAT AWNING BELOW, I MAY ESCAPE YET! HE DOESN'T SUSPECT WHO I REALLY AM!
MADE IT! NOW TO RELEASE MY SPECIAL CHEMICAL GAS TO INSTANTLY CHANGE THE COLOR OF MY SUIT!!
AND, FOR A FINAL TOUCH, I'LL PUT ON MY SPARE HAT AND EXTEND MY ADJUSTABLE TELESCOPING CANE!
NOW, I CAN CALMLY WALK RIGHT BACK PAST HIM! HE'LL NEVER SUSPECT THAT I'M HIS OLD ENEMY--THE CHAMELEON!*
THERE WERE FOUR OF THEM-- I'M SURE OF IT! BUT IT LOOKS AS THOUGH THE LEADER GOT AWAY! THERE'S NO ONE BELOW EXCEPT THAT OLD MAN WITH A CANE...
* FIRST INTRODUCED IN SPIDER-MAN #1--EDITOR.
A SHORT TIME LATER, BEHIND THE BOLTED DOOR OF HIS APARTMENT, THE ELUSIVE CHAMELEON REMOVES ONE OF HIS MANY INGENIOUS MASKS...
I CAN SEE THAT SPIDER-MAN IS NOW MORE DANGEROUS TO ME THAN EVER! SO LONG AS HE LIVES, MY SECURITY WILL BE IN DANGER!
I STILL REMEMBER WHAT A DANGEROUS FOE HE WAS WHEN I FIRST FOUGHT HIM-- AND HE WAS JUST BEGINNING HIS CAREER AT THAT TIME! EVEN IN MY SPECIALLY-PREPARED HELICOPTER I COULDN'T ESCAPE HIM!
2

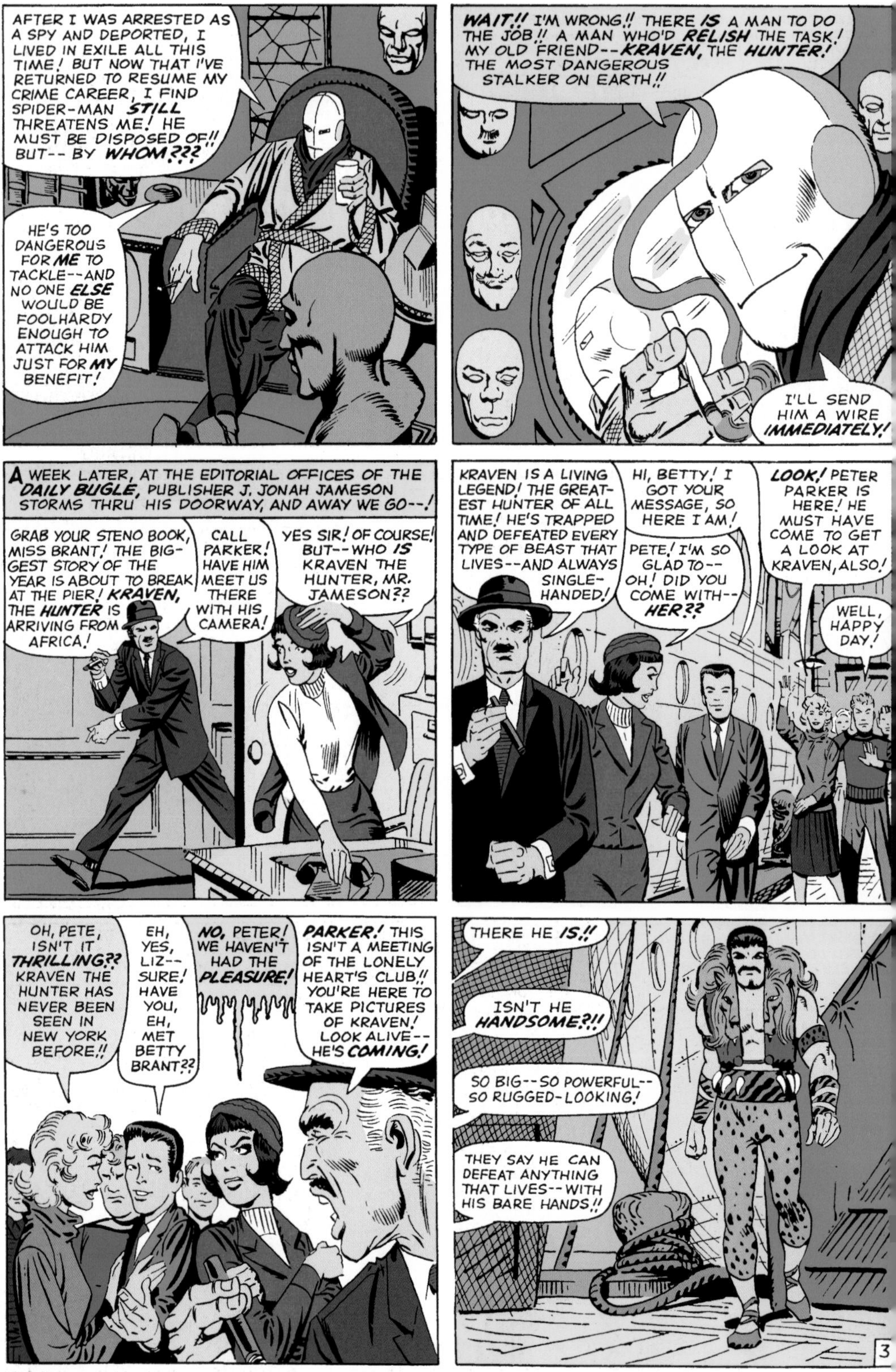
AFTER I WAS ARRESTED AS A SPY AND DEPORTED, I LIVED IN EXILE ALL THIS TIME! BUT NOW THAT I'VE RETURNED TO RESUME MY CRIME CAREER, I FIND SPIDER-MAN STILL THREATENS ME! HE MUST BE DISPOSED OF!! BUT-- BY WHOM???
HE'S TOO DANGEROUS FOR ME TO TACKLE--AND NO ONE ELSE WOULD BE FOOLHARDY ENOUGH TO ATTACK HIM JUST FOR MY BENEFIT!
WAIT!! I'M WRONG!! THERE IS A MAN TO DO THE JOB!! A MAN WHO'D RELISH THE TASK! MY OLD FRIEND--KRAVEN, THE HUNTER! THE MOST DANGEROUS STALKER ON EARTH!!
I'LL SEND HIM A WIRE IMMEDIATELY!
A WEEK LATER, AT THE EDITORIAL OFFICES OF THE DAILY BUGLE, PUBLISHER J. JONAH JAMESON STORMS THRU HIS DOORWAY, AND AWAY WE GO--!
GRAB YOUR STENO BOOK, MISS BRANT! THE BIGGEST STORY OF THE YEAR IS ABOUT TO BREAK AT THE PIER! KRAVEN, THE HUNTER IS ARRIVING FROM AFRICA!
CALL PARKER! HAVE HIM MEET US THERE WITH HIS CAMERA!
YES SIR! OF COURSE! BUT--WHO IS KRAVEN THE HUNTER, MR. JAMESON??
KRAVEN IS A LIVING LEGEND! THE GREATEST HUNTER OF ALL TIME! HE'S TRAPPED AND DEFEATED EVERY TYPE OF BEAST THAT LIVES--AND ALWAYS SINGLE-HANDED!
HI, BETTY! I GOT YOUR MESSAGE, SO HERE I AM!
PETE! I'M SO GLAD TO-- OH! DID YOU COME WITH-- HER??
LOOK! PETER PARKER IS HERE! HE MUST HAVE COME TO GET A LOOK AT KRAVEN, ALSO!
WELL, HAPPY DAY!
OH, PETE, ISN'T IT THRILLING?? KRAVEN THE HUNTER HAS NEVER BEEN SEEN IN NEW YORK BEFORE!!
EH, YES, LIZ-- SURE! HAVE YOU, EH, MET BETTY BRANT??
NO, PETER! WE HAVEN'T HAD THE PLEASURE!
PARKER! THIS ISN'T A MEETING OF THE LONELY HEART'S CLUB!! YOU'RE HERE TO TAKE PICTURES OF KRAVEN! LOOK ALIVE-- HE'S COMING!
THERE HE IS!!
ISN'T HE HANDSOME?!!
SO BIG--SO POWERFUL-- SO RUGGED-LOOKING!
THEY SAY HE CAN DEFEAT ANYTHING THAT LIVES--WITH HIS BARE HANDS!!
3

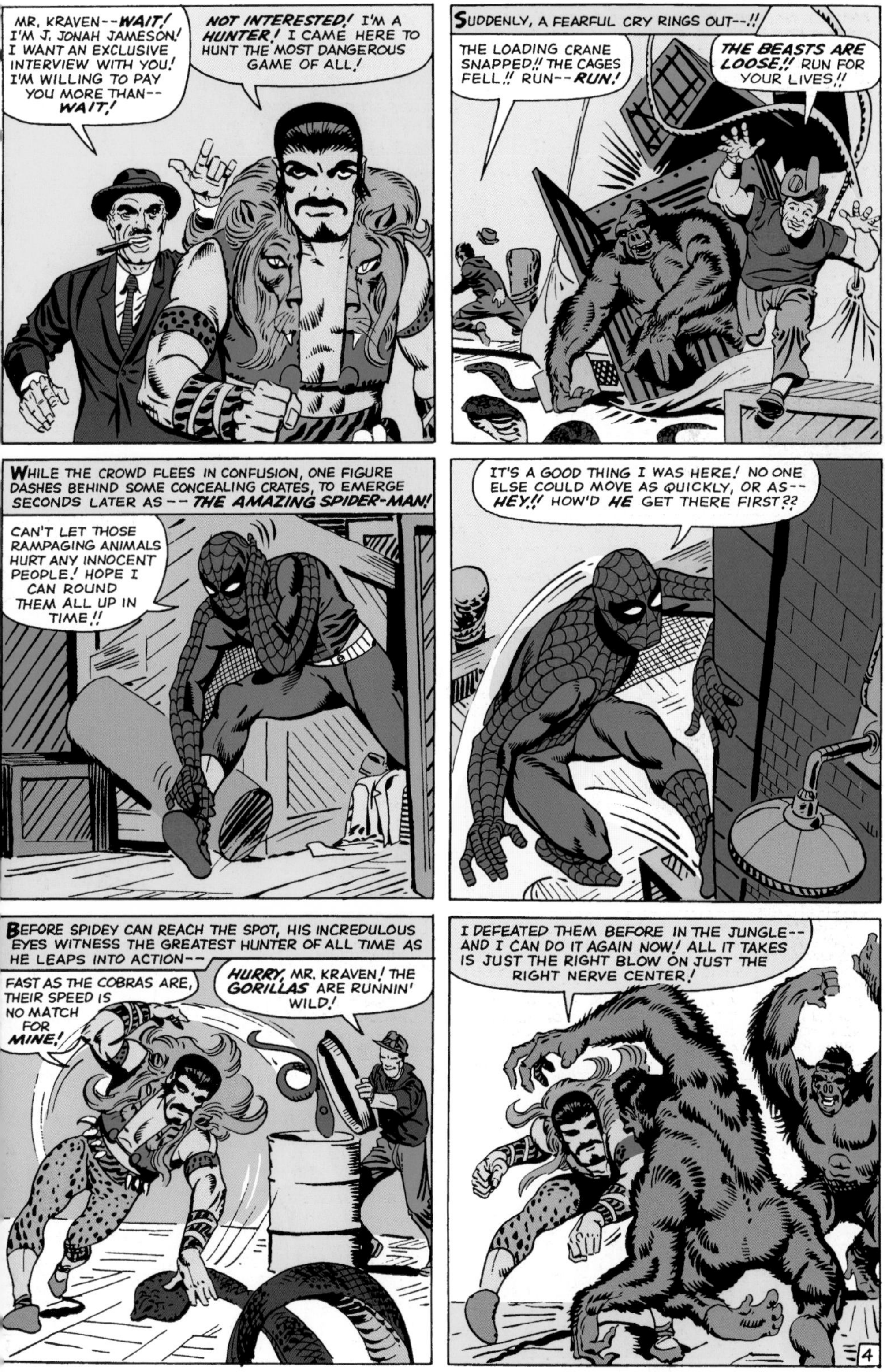

MR. KRAVEN--WAIT! I'M J. JONAH JAMESON! I WANT AN EXCLUSIVE INTERVIEW WITH YOU! I'M WILLING TO PAY YOU MORE THAN-- WAIT!
NOT INTERESTED! I'M A HUNTER! I CAME HERE TO HUNT THE MOST DANGEROUS GAME OF ALL!
SUDDENLY, A FEARFUL CRY RINGS OUT--!!
THE LOADING CRANE SNAPPED!! THE CAGES FELL!! RUN--RUN!
THE BEASTS ARE LOOSE!! RUN FOR YOUR LIVES!!
WHILE THE CROWD FLEES IN CONFUSION, ONE FIGURE DASHES BEHIND SOME CONCEALING CRATES, TO EMERGE SECONDS LATER AS --THE AMAZING SPIDER-MAN!
CAN'T LET THOSE RAMPAGING ANIMALS HURT ANY INNOCENT PEOPLE! HOPE I CAN ROUND THEM ALL UP IN TIME!!
IT'S A GOOD THING I WAS HERE! NO ONE ELSE COULD MOVE AS QUICKLY, OR AS-- HEY!! HOW'D HE GET THERE FIRST??
BEFORE SPIDEY CAN REACH THE SPOT, HIS INCREDULOUS EYES WITNESS THE GREATEST HUNTER OF ALL TIME AS HE LEAPS INTO ACTION--
FAST AS THE COBRAS ARE, THEIR SPEED IS NO MATCH FOR MINE!
HURRY, MR. KRAVEN! THE GORILLAS ARE RUNNIN' WILD!
I DEFEATED THEM BEFORE IN THE JUNGLE-- AND I CAN DO IT AGAIN NOW! ALL IT TAKES IS JUST THE RIGHT BLOW ON JUST THE RIGHT NERVE CENTER!
4

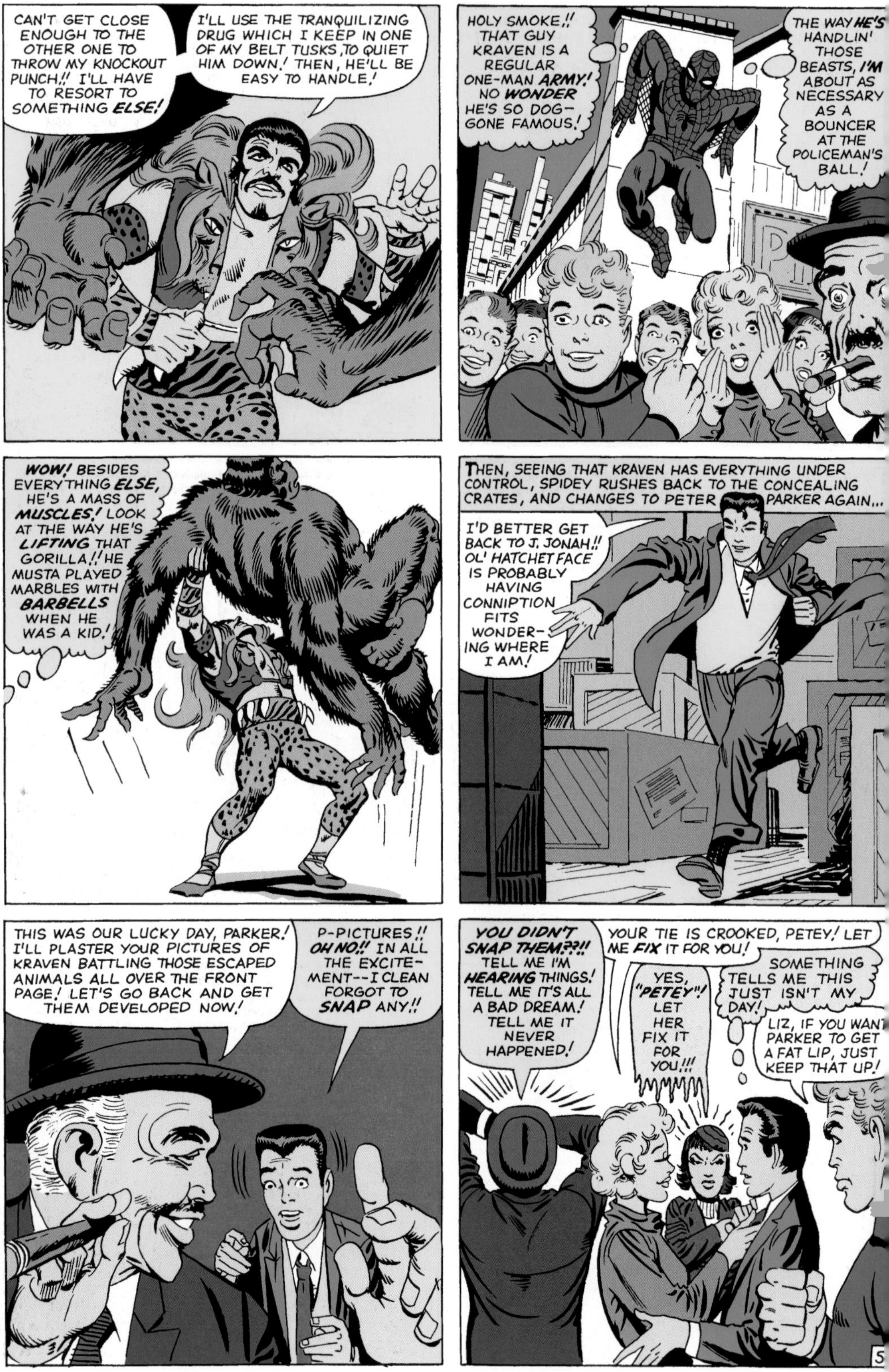

CAN'T GET CLOSE ENOUGH TO THE OTHER ONE TO THROW MY KNOCKOUT PUNCH!! I'LL HAVE TO RESORT TO SOMETHING ELSE!
I'LL USE THE TRANQUILIZING DRUG WHICH I KEEP IN ONE OF MY BELT TUSKS, TO QUIET HIM DOWN! THEN, HE'LL BE EASY TO HANDLE!
HOLY SMOKE!! THAT GUY KRAVEN IS A REGULAR ONE-MAN ARMY! NO WONDER HE'S SO DOG-GONE FAMOUS!
THE WAY HE'S HANDLIN' THOSE BEASTS, I'M ABOUT AS NECESSARY AS A BOUNCER AT THE POLICEMAN'S BALL!
WOW! BESIDES EVERYTHING ELSE, HE'S A MASS OF MUSCLES! LOOK AT THE WAY HE'S LIFTING THAT GORILLA!! HE MUSTA PLAYED MARBLES WITH BARBELLS WHEN HE WAS A KID!
THEN, SEEING THAT KRAVEN HAS EVERYTHING UNDER CONTROL, SPIDEY RUSHES BACK TO THE CONCEALING CRATES, AND CHANGES TO PETER PARKER AGAIN...
I'D BETTER GET BACK TO J. JONAH!! OL' HATCHET FACE IS PROBABLY HAVING CONNIPTION FITS WONDER-ING WHERE I AM!
THIS WAS OUR LUCKY DAY, PARKER! I'LL PLASTER YOUR PICTURES OF KRAVEN BATTLING THOSE ESCAPED ANIMALS ALL OVER THE FRONT PAGE! LET'S GO BACK AND GET THEM DEVELOPED NOW!
P-PICTURES!! OH NO!! IN ALL THE EXCITE-MENT--I CLEAN FORGOT TO SNAP ANY!!
YOU DIDN'T SNAP THEM??!! TELL ME I'M HEARING THINGS! TELL ME IT'S ALL A BAD DREAM! TELL ME IT NEVER HAPPENED!
YOUR TIE IS CROOKED, PETEY! LET ME FIX IT FOR YOU!
YES, "PETEY"! LET HER FIX IT FOR YOU!!!
SOMETHING TELLS ME THIS JUST ISN'T MY DAY!
LIZ, IF YOU WANT PARKER TO GET A FAT LIP, JUST KEEP THAT UP!
5

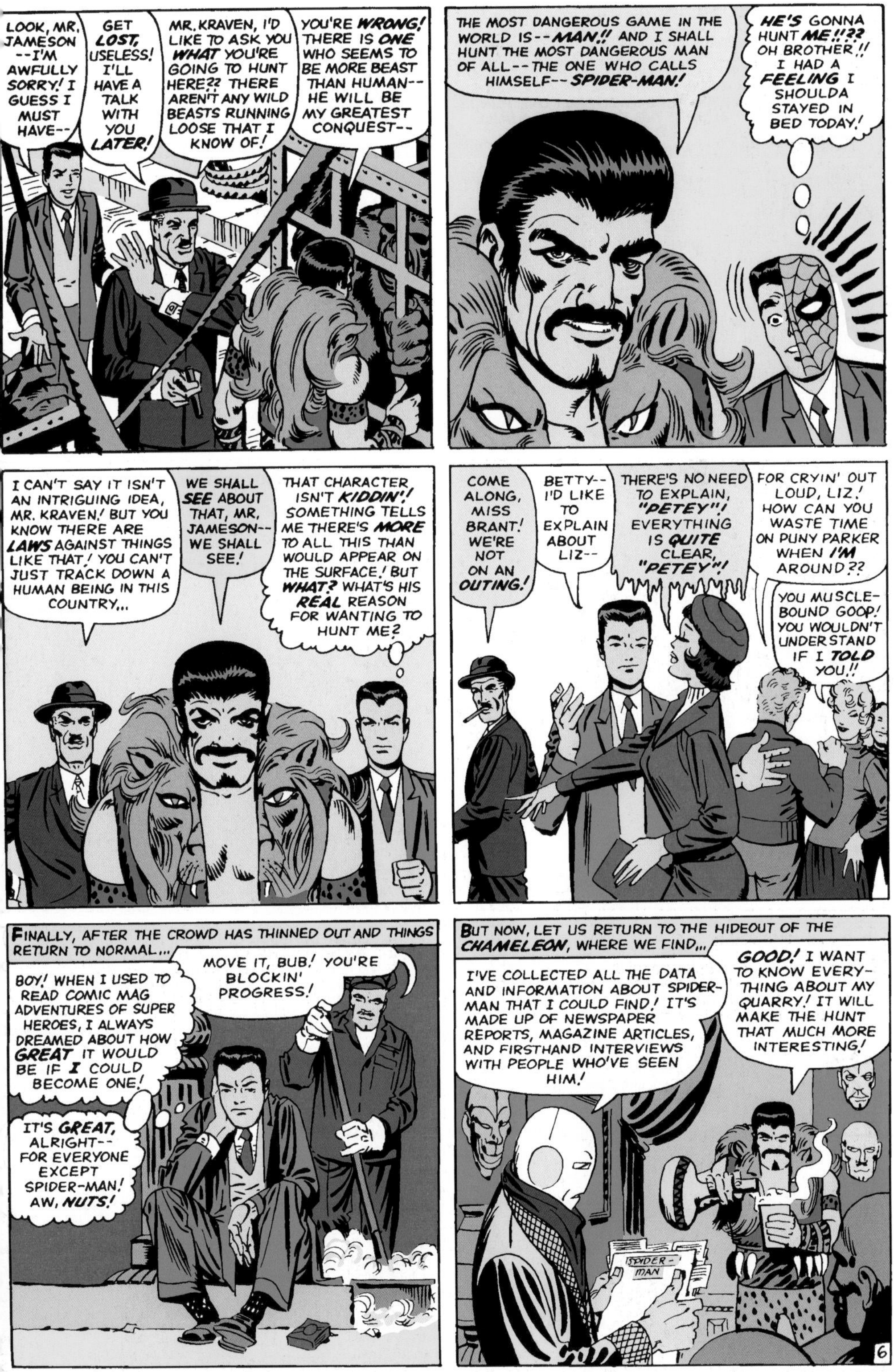
LOOK, MR. JAMESON --I'M AWFULLY SORRY! I GUESS I MUST HAVE--
GET LOST, USELESS! I'LL HAVE A TALK WITH YOU LATER!
MR. KRAVEN, I'D LIKE TO ASK YOU WHAT YOU'RE GOING TO HUNT HERE?? THERE AREN'T ANY WILD BEASTS RUNNING LOOSE THAT I KNOW OF!
YOU'RE WRONG! THERE IS ONE WHO SEEMS TO BE MORE BEAST THAN HUMAN-- HE WILL BE MY GREATEST CONQUEST--
THE MOST DANGEROUS GAME IN THE WORLD IS--MAN!! AND I SHALL HUNT THE MOST DANGEROUS MAN OF ALL--THE ONE WHO CALLS HIMSELF--SPIDER-MAN!
HE'S GONNA HUNT ME!!?? OH BROTHER!! I HAD A FEELING I SHOULDA STAYED IN BED TODAY!
I CAN'T SAY IT ISN'T AN INTRIGUING IDEA, MR. KRAVEN! BUT YOU KNOW THERE ARE LAWS AGAINST THINGS LIKE THAT! YOU CAN'T JUST TRACK DOWN A HUMAN BEING IN THIS COUNTRY...
WE SHALL SEE ABOUT THAT, MR. JAMESON-- WE SHALL SEE!
THAT CHARACTER ISN'T KIDDIN'! SOMETHING TELLS ME THERE'S MORE TO ALL THIS THAN WOULD APPEAR ON THE SURFACE! BUT WHAT? WHAT'S HIS REAL REASON FOR WANTING TO HUNT ME?
COME ALONG, MISS BRANT! WE'RE NOT ON AN OUTING!
BETTY-- I'D LIKE TO EXPLAIN ABOUT LIZ--
THERE'S NO NEED TO EXPLAIN, "PETEY"! EVERYTHING IS QUITE CLEAR, "PETEY"!
FOR CRYIN' OUT LOUD, LIZ! HOW CAN YOU WASTE TIME ON PUNY PARKER WHEN I'M AROUND??
YOU MUSCLE-BOUND GOOP! YOU WOULDN'T UNDERSTAND IF I TOLD YOU!!
FINALLY, AFTER THE CROWD HAS THINNED OUT AND THINGS RETURN TO NORMAL...
MOVE IT, BUB! YOU'RE BLOCKIN' PROGRESS!
BOY! WHEN I USED TO READ COMIC MAG ADVENTURES OF SUPER HEROES, I ALWAYS DREAMED ABOUT HOW GREAT IT WOULD BE IF I COULD BECOME ONE!
IT'S GREAT, ALRIGHT-- FOR EVERYONE EXCEPT SPIDER-MAN! AW, NUTS!
BUT NOW, LET US RETURN TO THE HIDEOUT OF THE CHAMELEON, WHERE WE FIND...
I'VE COLLECTED ALL THE DATA AND INFORMATION ABOUT SPIDER-MAN THAT I COULD FIND! IT'S MADE UP OF NEWSPAPER REPORTS, MAGAZINE ARTICLES, AND FIRSTHAND INTERVIEWS WITH PEOPLE WHO'VE SEEN HIM!
GOOD! I WANT TO KNOW EVERYTHING ABOUT MY QUARRY! IT WILL MAKE THE HUNT THAT MUCH MORE INTERESTING!
SPIDER-MAN
6

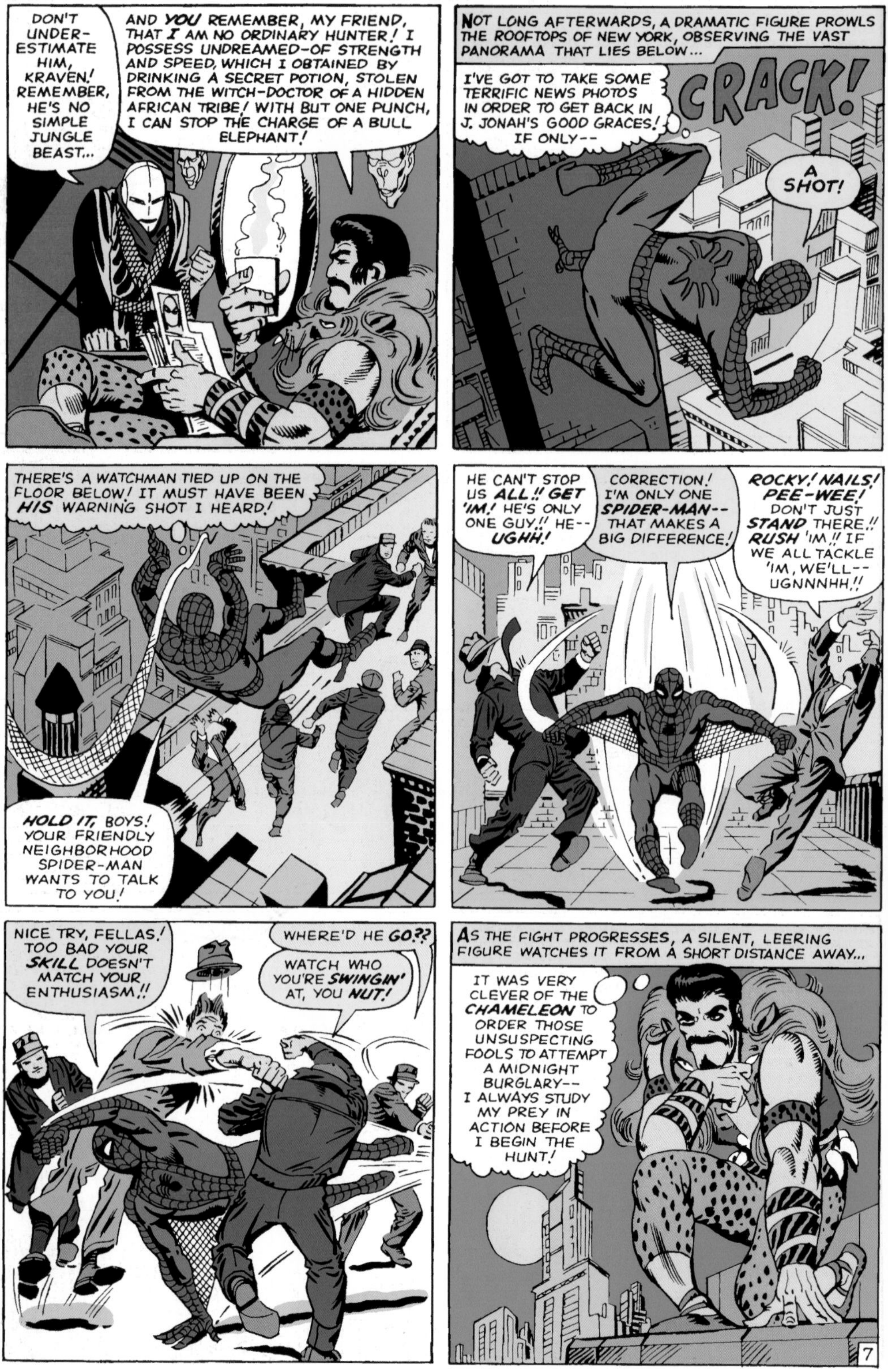
DON'T UNDER-ESTIMATE HIM, KRAVEN! REMEMBER, HE'S NO SIMPLE JUNGLE BEAST...
AND YOU REMEMBER, MY FRIEND, THAT I AM NO ORDINARY HUNTER! I POSSESS UNDREAMED-OF STRENGTH AND SPEED, WHICH I OBTAINED BY DRINKING A SECRET POTION, STOLEN FROM THE WITCH-DOCTOR OF A HIDDEN AFRICAN TRIBE! WITH BUT ONE PUNCH, I CAN STOP THE CHARGE OF A BULL ELEPHANT!
NOT LONG AFTERWARDS, A DRAMATIC FIGURE PROWLS THE ROOFTOPS OF NEW YORK, OBSERVING THE VAST PANORAMA THAT LIES BELOW...
I'VE GOT TO TAKE SOME TERRIFIC NEWS PHOTOS IN ORDER TO GET BACK IN J. JONAH'S GOOD GRACES! IF ONLY--
CRACK!
A SHOT!
THERE'S A WATCHMAN TIED UP ON THE FLOOR BELOW! IT MUST HAVE BEEN HIS WARNING SHOT I HEARD!
HOLD IT, BOYS! YOUR FRIENDLY NEIGHBORHOOD SPIDER-MAN WANTS TO TALK TO YOU!
HE CAN'T STOP US ALL!! GET 'IM! HE'S ONLY ONE GUY!! HE-- UGHH!
CORRECTION! I'M ONLY ONE SPIDER-MAN-- THAT MAKES A BIG DIFFERENCE!
ROCKY! NAILS! PEE-WEE! DON'T JUST STAND THERE!! RUSH 'IM!! IF WE ALL TACKLE 'IM, WE'LL-- UGNNNHH!!
NICE TRY, FELLAS! TOO BAD YOUR SKILL DOESN'T MATCH YOUR ENTHUSIASM!!
WHERE'D HE GO??
WATCH WHO YOU'RE SWINGIN' AT, YOU NUT!
AS THE FIGHT PROGRESSES, A SILENT, LEERING FIGURE WATCHES IT FROM A SHORT DISTANCE AWAY...
IT WAS VERY CLEVER OF THE CHAMELEON TO ORDER THOSE UNSUSPECTING FOOLS TO ATTEMPT A MIDNIGHT BURGLARY-- I ALWAYS STUDY MY PREY IN ACTION BEFORE I BEGIN THE HUNT!
7

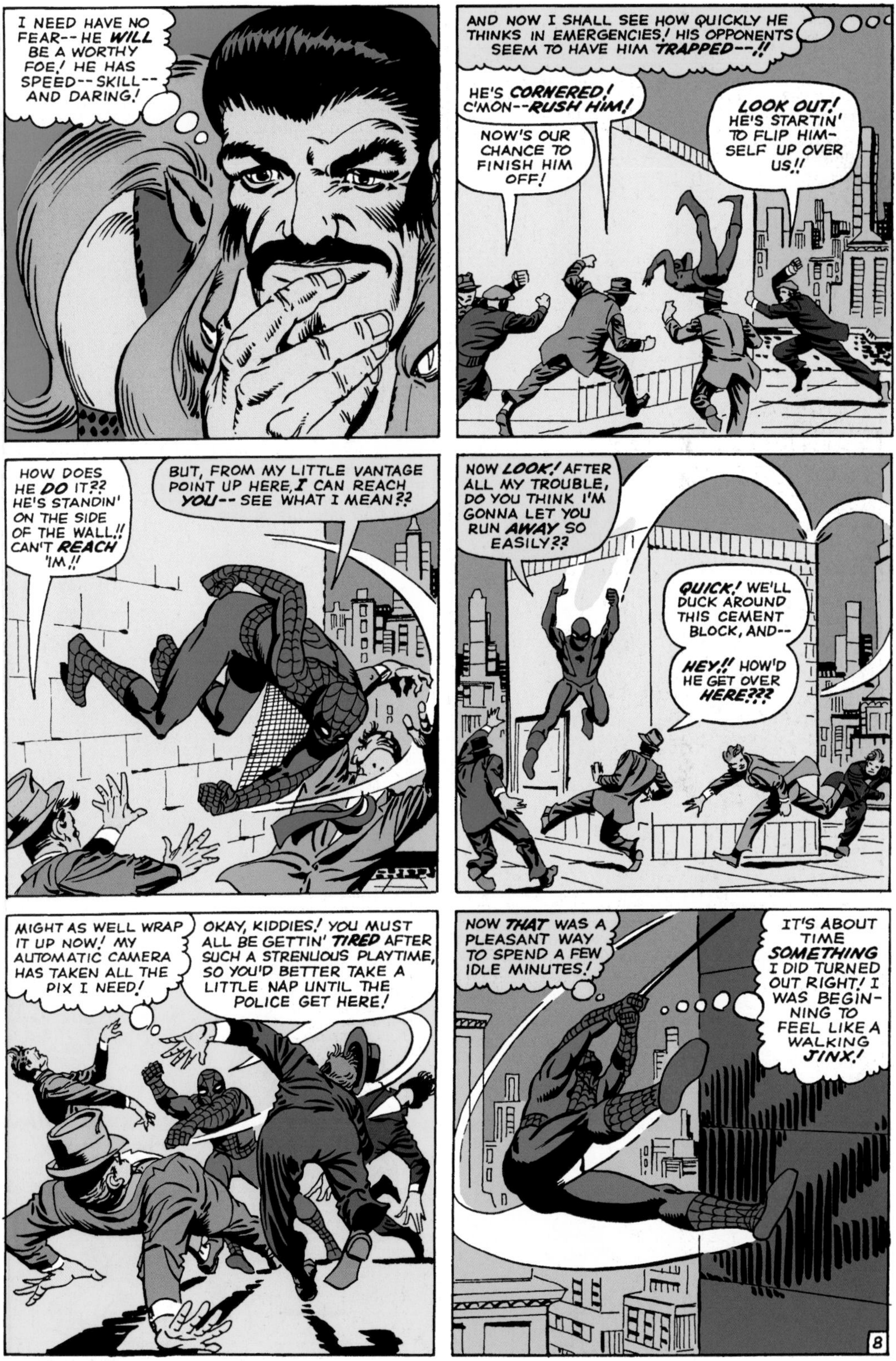

I NEED HAVE NO FEAR-- HE WILL BE A WORTHY FOE! HE HAS SPEED-- SKILL-- AND DARING!
AND NOW I SHALL SEE HOW QUICKLY HE THINKS IN EMERGENCIES! HIS OPPONENTS SEEM TO HAVE HIM TRAPPED--!!
HE'S CORNERED! C'MON--RUSH HIM!
NOW'S OUR CHANCE TO FINISH HIM OFF!
LOOK OUT! HE'S STARTIN' TO FLIP HIMSELF UP OVER US!!
HOW DOES HE DO IT?? HE'S STANDIN' ON THE SIDE OF THE WALL!! CAN'T REACH 'IM!!
BUT, FROM MY LITTLE VANTAGE POINT UP HERE, I CAN REACH YOU-- SEE WHAT I MEAN??
NOW LOOK! AFTER ALL MY TROUBLE, DO YOU THINK I'M GONNA LET YOU RUN AWAY SO EASILY??
QUICK! WE'LL DUCK AROUND THIS CEMENT BLOCK, AND--
HEY!! HOW'D HE GET OVER HERE???
MIGHT AS WELL WRAP IT UP NOW! MY AUTOMATIC CAMERA HAS TAKEN ALL THE PIX I NEED!
OKAY, KIDDIES! YOU MUST ALL BE GETTIN' TIRED AFTER SUCH A STRENUOUS PLAYTIME, SO YOU'D BETTER TAKE A LITTLE NAP UNTIL THE POLICE GET HERE!
NOW THAT WAS A PLEASANT WAY TO SPEND A FEW IDLE MINUTES!
IT'S ABOUT TIME SOMETHING I DID TURNED OUT RIGHT! I WAS BEGINNING TO FEEL LIKE A WALKING JINX!
8

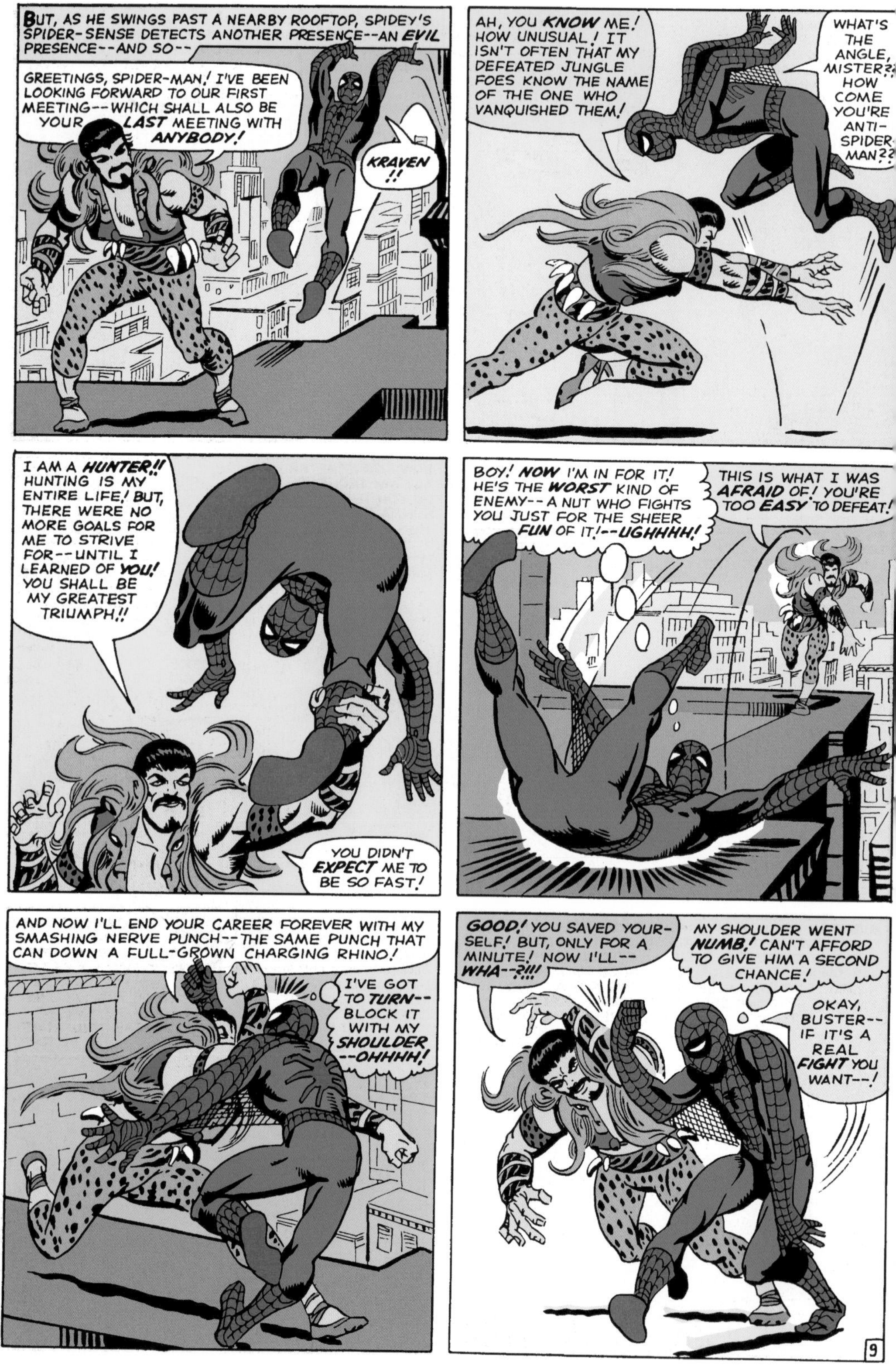

BUT, AS HE SWINGS PAST A NEARBY ROOFTOP, SPIDEY'S SPIDER-SENSE DETECTS ANOTHER PRESENCE--AN EVIL PRESENCE--AND SO--
GREETINGS, SPIDER-MAN! I'VE BEEN LOOKING FORWARD TO OUR FIRST MEETING--WHICH SHALL ALSO BE YOUR LAST MEETING WITH ANYBODY!
KRAVEN!!
AH, YOU KNOW ME! HOW UNUSUAL! IT ISN'T OFTEN THAT MY DEFEATED JUNGLE FOES KNOW THE NAME OF THE ONE WHO VANQUISHED THEM!
WHAT'S THE ANGLE, MISTER?? HOW COME YOU'RE ANTI-SPIDER-MAN??
I AM A HUNTER!! HUNTING IS MY ENTIRE LIFE! BUT, THERE WERE NO MORE GOALS FOR ME TO STRIVE FOR--UNTIL I LEARNED OF YOU! YOU SHALL BE MY GREATEST TRIUMPH!!
YOU DIDN'T EXPECT ME TO BE SO FAST!
BOY! NOW I'M IN FOR IT! HE'S THE WORST KIND OF ENEMY--A NUT WHO FIGHTS YOU JUST FOR THE SHEER FUN OF IT!--UGHHHH!
THIS IS WHAT I WAS AFRAID OF! YOU'RE TOO EASY TO DEFEAT!
AND NOW I'LL END YOUR CAREER FOREVER WITH MY SMASHING NERVE PUNCH--THE SAME PUNCH THAT CAN DOWN A FULL-GROWN CHARGING RHINO!
I'VE GOT TO TURN--BLOCK IT WITH MY SHOULDER--OHHHH!
GOOD! YOU SAVED YOURSELF! BUT, ONLY FOR A MINUTE! NOW I'LL--WHA--?!!!
MY SHOULDER WENT NUMB! CAN'T AFFORD TO GIVE HIM A SECOND CHANCE!
OKAY, BUSTER--IF IT'S A REAL FIGHT YOU WANT--!
9

HE'S STRONGER THAN I *THOUGHT!* EVEN WITH *ONE* HAND HE'S BEATING ME! I CAN'T DEFEAT HIM *FAIRLY,* BUT--

IF I CAN MANAGE TO NICK HIM WITH ONE OF MY SPECIAL POTION WEAPONS-- *AHH--* I *DID* IT!

HEY! SOMETHING *SCRATCHED* ME! YOU'RE NOT GONNA BEAT ME LIKE *THAT,* KRAVEN!

I-I FEEL KINDA *WOOZY!* THAT WAS *MORE* THAN A SIMPLE SCRATCH! HE GOT SOME SORT OF *POTION* IN MY BLOODSTREAM!! BUT WHAT *WAS* IT??

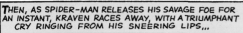

THEN, AS SPIDER-MAN RELEASES HIS SAVAGE FOE FOR AN INSTANT, KRAVEN RACES AWAY, WITH A TRIUMPHANT CRY RINGING FROM HIS SNEERING LIPS...

I'VE *WON,* SPIDER-MAN! MY POTION WILL WEAKEN YOU ENOUGH FOR ME TO BEAT YOU ANY TIME I DESIRE! BUT, I'LL *PROLONG* MY ENJOYMENT! I'LL FINISH YOU OFF *ANOTHER* TIME!

I'LL *LET* HIM GO FOR NOW! I'VE GOT TO CLEAR MY HEAD--!!

I'M GETTING DIZZIER BY THE MINUTE! I'LL JUST GRAB MY CAMERA FROM WHERE I LEFT IT, AND TRY TO MAKE IT HOME!

FOR THE NEXT FEW MINUTES, THE AMAZING TEEN-AGER SLOWLY AND CAUTIOUSLY HUGS THE ROOF-TOPS ON HIS JOURNEY HOME, AND THEN FINALLY...

-=WHEW!=- MY *SHOULDER* IS GETTING BACK TO NORMAL NOW, BUT I CAN'T LOSE THIS DIZZINESS!

AND NOW MY *HANDS* HAVE STARTED TO TWITCH!! I CAN'T MAKE THEM STOP! NO *WONDER* KRAVEN IS SUCH A SUCCESSFUL HUNTER IF HE USES POTIONS SUCH AS THOSE!!

WELL, MAYBE I'LL BE OKAY AGAIN IN THE MORNING, AFTER A GOOD NIGHT'S SLEEP! I'VE GOT A HUNCH I'M GONNA *NEED* ALL THE STRENGTH AND POWERS I'VE GOT!

AND, IN ANOTHER PART OF TOWN...

I DON'T *GET* IT, KRAVEN! YOU SAY HE'S FAR STRONGER, FAR MORE DANGEROUS THAN YOU THOUGHT--AND YET YOU'RE *HAPPY* ABOUT IT!

OF *COURSE* I AM! HE'S THE KIND OF FOE I'VE ALWAYS *WANTED* --ONE TO TEST MY METTLE TO ITS FULLEST! WHAT A *TRIUMPH* THIS WILL BE FOR ME! HOW *SWEET* WILL BE THE FRUITS OF MY VICTORY!

10

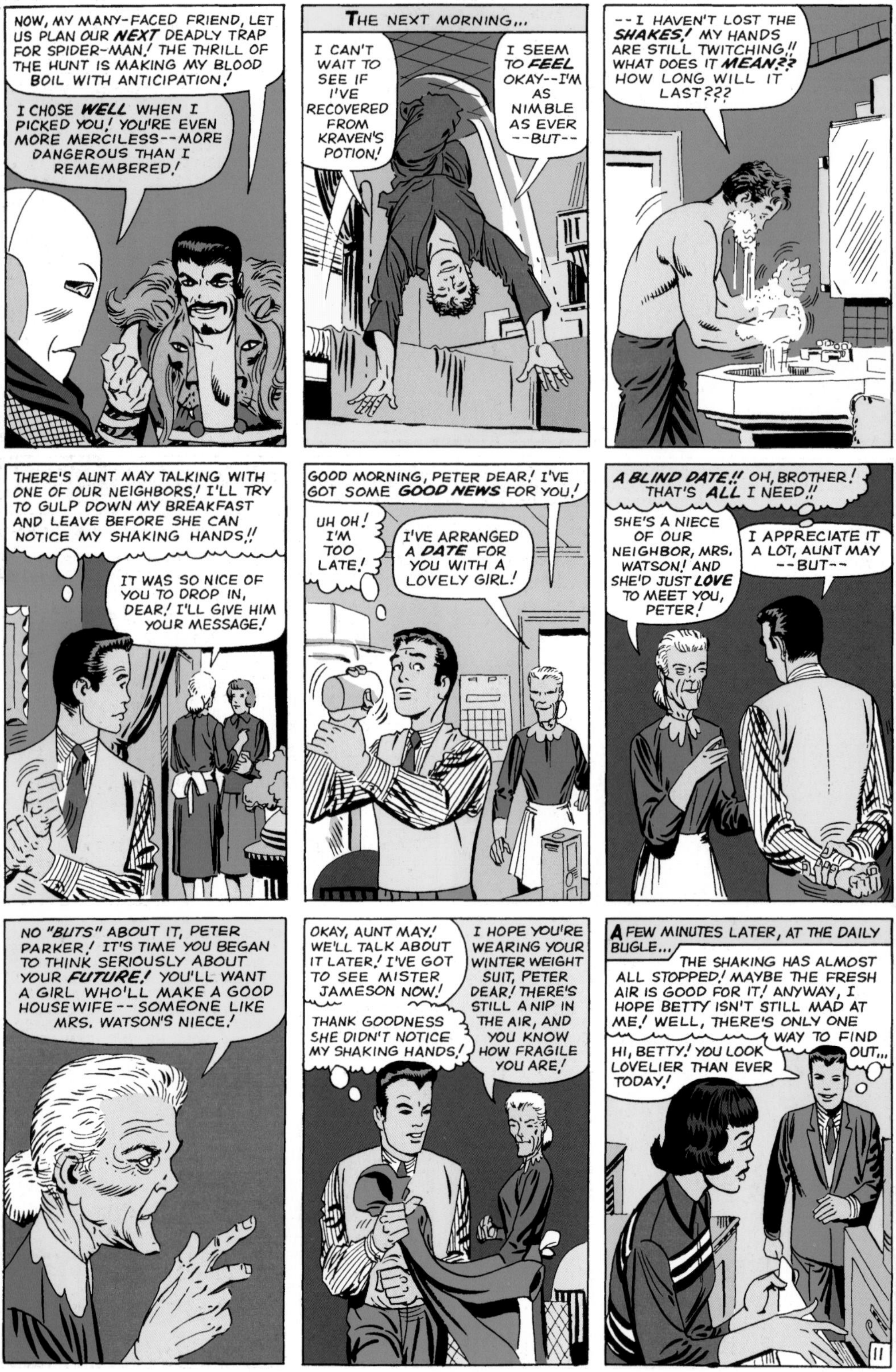
NOW, MY MANY-FACED FRIEND, LET US PLAN OUR NEXT DEADLY TRAP FOR SPIDER-MAN! THE THRILL OF THE HUNT IS MAKING MY BLOOD BOIL WITH ANTICIPATION!
I CHOSE WELL WHEN I PICKED YOU! YOU'RE EVEN MORE MERCILESS--MORE DANGEROUS THAN I REMEMBERED!
THE NEXT MORNING...
I CAN'T WAIT TO SEE IF I'VE RECOVERED FROM KRAVEN'S POTION!
I SEEM TO FEEL OKAY--I'M AS NIMBLE AS EVER --BUT--
--I HAVEN'T LOST THE SHAKES! MY HANDS ARE STILL TWITCHING!! WHAT DOES IT MEAN?? HOW LONG WILL IT LAST???
THERE'S AUNT MAY TALKING WITH ONE OF OUR NEIGHBORS! I'LL TRY TO GULP DOWN MY BREAKFAST AND LEAVE BEFORE SHE CAN NOTICE MY SHAKING HANDS!!
IT WAS SO NICE OF YOU TO DROP IN, DEAR! I'LL GIVE HIM YOUR MESSAGE!
GOOD MORNING, PETER DEAR! I'VE GOT SOME GOOD NEWS FOR YOU!
UH OH! I'M TOO LATE!
I'VE ARRANGED A DATE FOR YOU WITH A LOVELY GIRL!
A BLIND DATE!! OH, BROTHER! THAT'S ALL I NEED!!
SHE'S A NIECE OF OUR NEIGHBOR, MRS. WATSON! AND SHE'D JUST LOVE TO MEET YOU, PETER!
I APPRECIATE IT A LOT, AUNT MAY --BUT--
NO "BUTS" ABOUT IT, PETER PARKER! IT'S TIME YOU BEGAN TO THINK SERIOUSLY ABOUT YOUR FUTURE! YOU'LL WANT A GIRL WHO'LL MAKE A GOOD HOUSEWIFE -- SOMEONE LIKE MRS. WATSON'S NIECE!
OKAY, AUNT MAY! WE'LL TALK ABOUT IT LATER! I'VE GOT TO SEE MISTER JAMESON NOW!
THANK GOODNESS SHE DIDN'T NOTICE MY SHAKING HANDS!
I HOPE YOU'RE WEARING YOUR WINTER WEIGHT SUIT, PETER DEAR! THERE'S STILL A NIP IN THE AIR, AND YOU KNOW HOW FRAGILE YOU ARE!
A FEW MINUTES LATER, AT THE DAILY BUGLE...
THE SHAKING HAS ALMOST ALL STOPPED! MAYBE THE FRESH AIR IS GOOD FOR IT! ANYWAY, I HOPE BETTY ISN'T STILL MAD AT ME! WELL, THERE'S ONLY ONE WAY TO FIND OUT...
HI, BETTY! YOU LOOK LOVELIER THAN EVER TODAY!
11

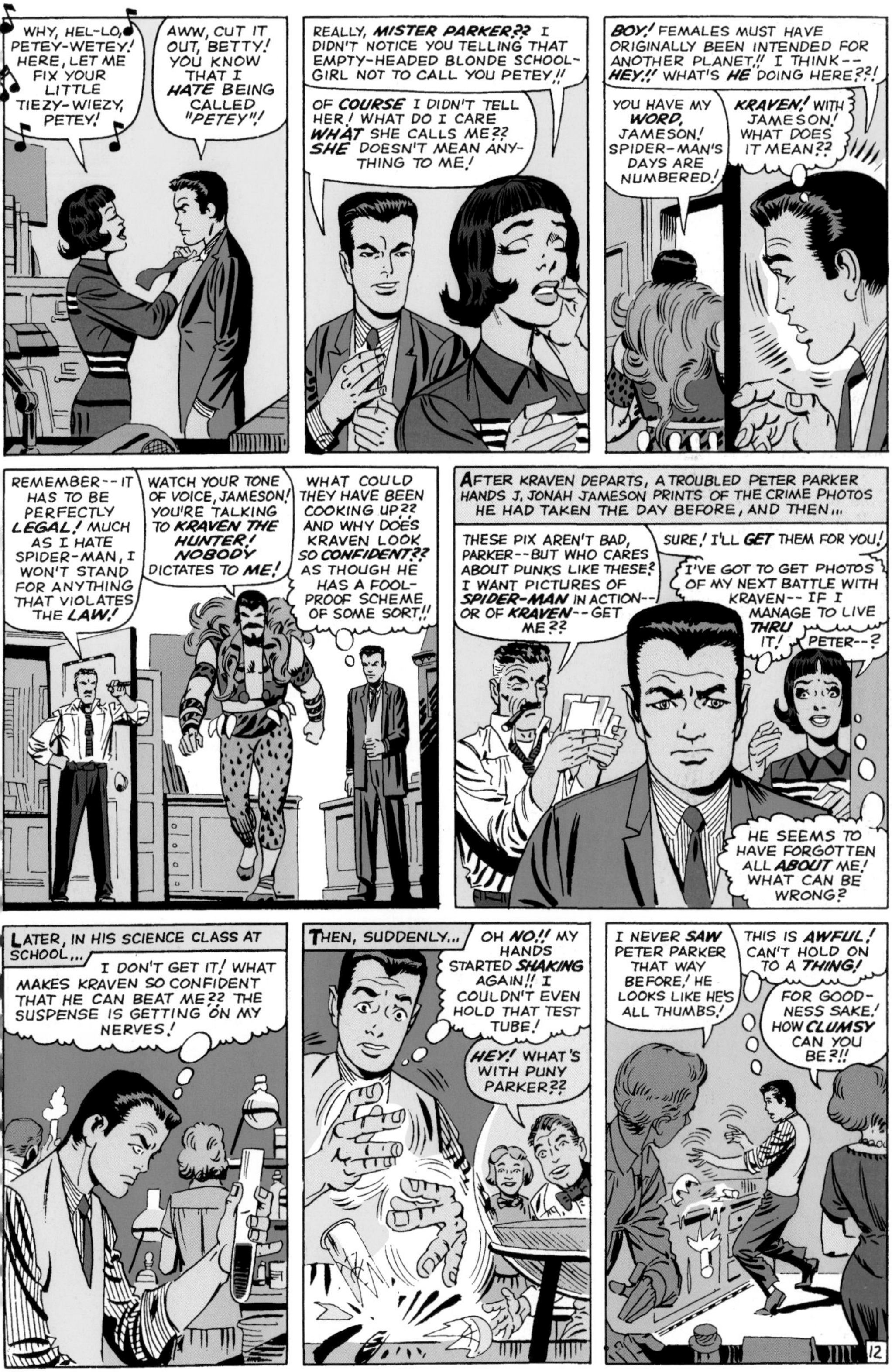
WHY, HEL-LO, PETEY-WETEY! HERE, LET ME FIX YOUR LITTLE TIEZY-WIEZY, PETEY!
AWW, CUT IT OUT, BETTY! YOU KNOW THAT I HATE BEING CALLED "PETEY"!
REALLY, MISTER PARKER?? I DIDN'T NOTICE YOU TELLING THAT EMPTY-HEADED BLONDE SCHOOL-GIRL NOT TO CALL YOU PETEY!!
OF COURSE I DIDN'T TELL HER! WHAT DO I CARE WHAT SHE CALLS ME?? SHE DOESN'T MEAN ANY-THING TO ME!
BOY! FEMALES MUST HAVE ORIGINALLY BEEN INTENDED FOR ANOTHER PLANET!! I THINK-- HEY!! WHAT'S HE DOING HERE??!
YOU HAVE MY WORD, JAMESON! SPIDER-MAN'S DAYS ARE NUMBERED!
KRAVEN! WITH JAMESON! WHAT DOES IT MEAN??
REMEMBER-- IT HAS TO BE PERFECTLY LEGAL! MUCH AS I HATE SPIDER-MAN, I WON'T STAND FOR ANYTHING THAT VIOLATES THE LAW!
WATCH YOUR TONE OF VOICE, JAMESON! YOU'RE TALKING TO KRAVEN THE HUNTER! NOBODY DICTATES TO ME!
WHAT COULD THEY HAVE BEEN COOKING UP?? AND WHY DOES KRAVEN LOOK SO CONFIDENT?? AS THOUGH HE HAS A FOOL-PROOF SCHEME OF SOME SORT!!
AFTER KRAVEN DEPARTS, A TROUBLED PETER PARKER HANDS J. JONAH JAMESON PRINTS OF THE CRIME PHOTOS HE HAD TAKEN THE DAY BEFORE, AND THEN...
THESE PIX AREN'T BAD, PARKER--BUT WHO CARES ABOUT PUNKS LIKE THESE? I WANT PICTURES OF SPIDER-MAN IN ACTION-- OR OF KRAVEN--GET ME??
SURE! I'LL GET THEM FOR YOU!
I'VE GOT TO GET PHOTOS OF MY NEXT BATTLE WITH KRAVEN-- IF I MANAGE TO LIVE THRU IT!
PETER--?
HE SEEMS TO HAVE FORGOTTEN ALL ABOUT ME! WHAT CAN BE WRONG?
LATER, IN HIS SCIENCE CLASS AT SCHOOL...
I DON'T GET IT! WHAT MAKES KRAVEN SO CONFIDENT THAT HE CAN BEAT ME?? THE SUSPENSE IS GETTING ON MY NERVES!
THEN, SUDDENLY...
OH NO!! MY HANDS STARTED SHAKING AGAIN!! I COULDN'T EVEN HOLD THAT TEST TUBE!
HEY! WHAT'S WITH PUNY PARKER??
I NEVER SAW PETER PARKER THAT WAY BEFORE! HE LOOKS LIKE HE'S ALL THUMBS!
THIS IS AWFUL! CAN'T HOLD ON TO A THING!
FOR GOOD-NESS SAKE! HOW CLUMSY CAN YOU BE?!!
12

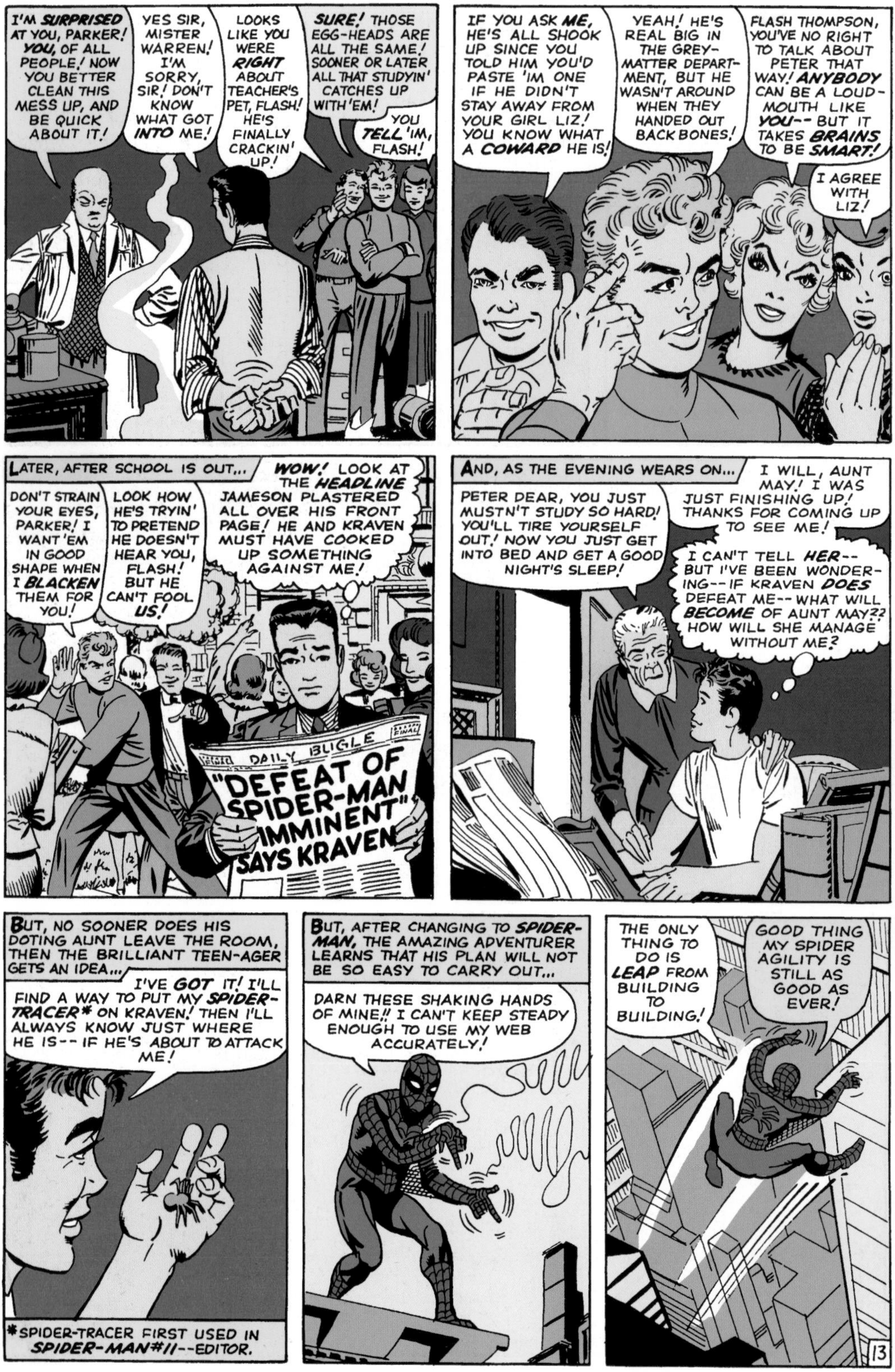
I'M SURPRISED AT YOU, PARKER! YOU, OF ALL PEOPLE! NOW YOU BETTER CLEAN THIS MESS UP, AND BE QUICK ABOUT IT!
YES SIR, MISTER WARREN! I'M SORRY, SIR! DON'T KNOW WHAT GOT INTO ME!
LOOKS LIKE YOU WERE RIGHT ABOUT TEACHER'S PET, FLASH! HE'S FINALLY CRACKIN' UP!
SURE! THOSE EGG-HEADS ARE ALL THE SAME! SOONER OR LATER ALL THAT STUDYIN' CATCHES UP WITH 'EM!
YOU TELL 'IM, FLASH!
IF YOU ASK ME, HE'S ALL SHOOK UP SINCE YOU TOLD HIM YOU'D PASTE 'IM ONE IF HE DIDN'T STAY AWAY FROM YOUR GIRL LIZ! YOU KNOW WHAT A COWARD HE IS!
YEAH! HE'S REAL BIG IN THE GREY-MATTER DEPARTMENT, BUT HE WASN'T AROUND WHEN THEY HANDED OUT BACK BONES!
FLASH THOMPSON, YOU'VE NO RIGHT TO TALK ABOUT PETER THAT WAY! ANYBODY CAN BE A LOUD-MOUTH LIKE YOU-- BUT IT TAKES BRAINS TO BE SMART!
I AGREE WITH LIZ!
LATER, AFTER SCHOOL IS OUT...
DON'T STRAIN YOUR EYES, PARKER! I WANT 'EM IN GOOD SHAPE WHEN I BLACKEN THEM FOR YOU!
LOOK HOW HE'S TRYIN' TO PRETEND HE DOESN'T HEAR YOU, FLASH! BUT HE CAN'T FOOL US!
WOW! LOOK AT THE HEADLINE JAMESON PLASTERED ALL OVER HIS FRONT PAGE! HE AND KRAVEN MUST HAVE COOKED UP SOMETHING AGAINST ME!
DAILY BUGLE
FINAL
"DEFEAT OF SPIDER-MAN IMMINENT" SAYS KRAVEN
AND, AS THE EVENING WEARS ON...
PETER DEAR, YOU JUST MUSTN'T STUDY SO HARD! YOU'LL TIRE YOURSELF OUT! NOW YOU JUST GET INTO BED AND GET A GOOD NIGHT'S SLEEP!
I WILL, AUNT MAY! I WAS JUST FINISHING UP! THANKS FOR COMING UP TO SEE ME!
I CAN'T TELL HER-- BUT I'VE BEEN WONDERING-- IF KRAVEN DOES DEFEAT ME-- WHAT WILL BECOME OF AUNT MAY?? HOW WILL SHE MANAGE WITHOUT ME?
BUT, NO SOONER DOES HIS DOTING AUNT LEAVE THE ROOM, THEN THE BRILLIANT TEEN-AGER GETS AN IDEA...
I'VE GOT IT! I'LL FIND A WAY TO PUT MY SPIDER-TRACER* ON KRAVEN! THEN I'LL ALWAYS KNOW JUST WHERE HE IS-- IF HE'S ABOUT TO ATTACK ME!
*SPIDER-TRACER FIRST USED IN SPIDER-MAN #11--EDITOR.
BUT, AFTER CHANGING TO SPIDER-MAN, THE AMAZING ADVENTURER LEARNS THAT HIS PLAN WILL NOT BE SO EASY TO CARRY OUT...
DARN THESE SHAKING HANDS OF MINE!! I CAN'T KEEP STEADY ENOUGH TO USE MY WEB ACCURATELY!
THE ONLY THING TO DO IS LEAP FROM BUILDING TO BUILDING!
GOOD THING MY SPIDER AGILITY IS STILL AS GOOD AS EVER!
13

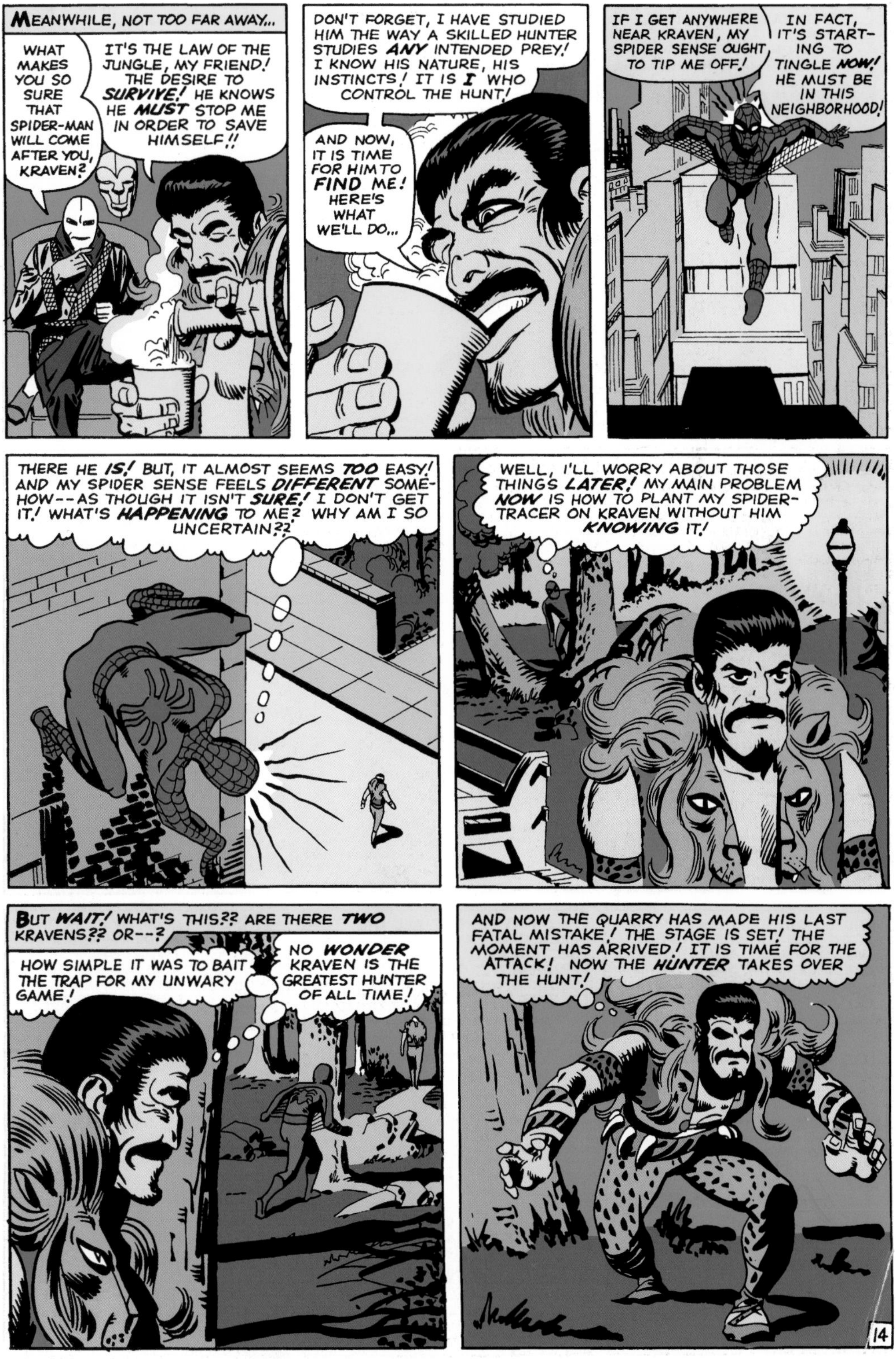
MEANWHILE, NOT TOO FAR AWAY...
WHAT MAKES YOU SO SURE THAT SPIDER-MAN WILL COME AFTER YOU, KRAVEN?
IT'S THE LAW OF THE JUNGLE, MY FRIEND! THE DESIRE TO SURVIVE! HE KNOWS HE MUST STOP ME IN ORDER TO SAVE HIMSELF!!
DON'T FORGET, I HAVE STUDIED HIM THE WAY A SKILLED HUNTER STUDIES ANY INTENDED PREY! I KNOW HIS NATURE, HIS INSTINCTS! IT IS I WHO CONTROL THE HUNT!
AND NOW, IT IS TIME FOR HIM TO FIND ME! HERE'S WHAT WE'LL DO...
IF I GET ANYWHERE NEAR KRAVEN, MY SPIDER SENSE OUGHT TO TIP ME OFF!
IN FACT, IT'S STARTING TO TINGLE NOW! HE MUST BE IN THIS NEIGHBORHOOD!
THERE HE IS! BUT, IT ALMOST SEEMS TOO EASY! AND MY SPIDER SENSE FEELS DIFFERENT SOMEHOW--AS THOUGH IT ISN'T SURE! I DON'T GET IT! WHAT'S HAPPENING TO ME? WHY AM I SO UNCERTAIN??
WELL, I'LL WORRY ABOUT THOSE THINGS LATER! MY MAIN PROBLEM NOW IS HOW TO PLANT MY SPIDER-TRACER ON KRAVEN WITHOUT HIM KNOWING IT!
BUT WAIT! WHAT'S THIS?? ARE THERE TWO KRAVENS?? OR--?
HOW SIMPLE IT WAS TO BAIT THE TRAP FOR MY UNWARY GAME!
NO WONDER KRAVEN IS THE GREATEST HUNTER OF ALL TIME!
AND NOW THE QUARRY HAS MADE HIS LAST FATAL MISTAKE! THE STAGE IS SET! THE MOMENT HAS ARRIVED! IT IS TIME FOR THE ATTACK! NOW THE HUNTER TAKES OVER THE HUNT!
14

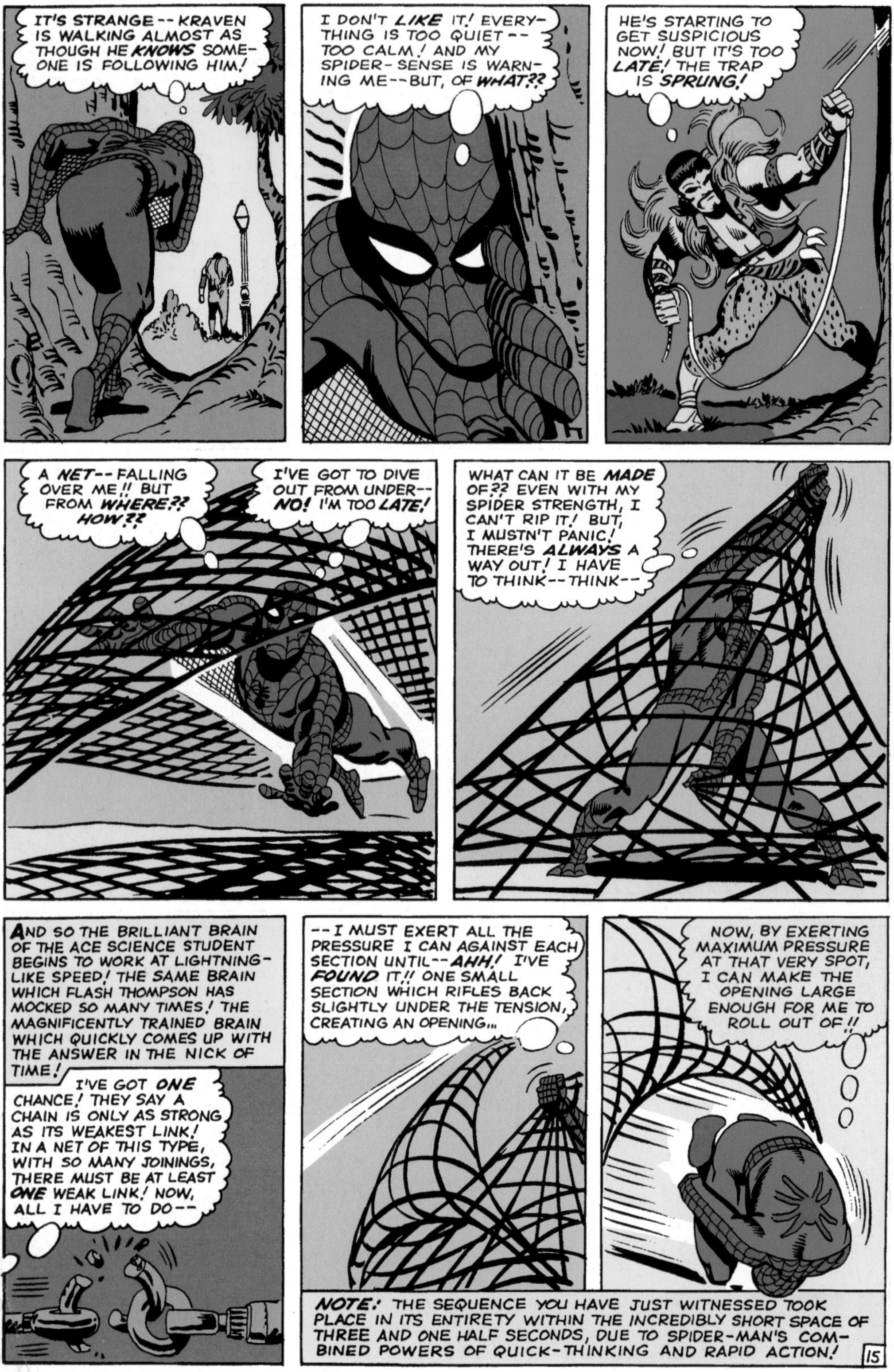
IT'S STRANGE -- KRAVEN IS WALKING ALMOST AS THOUGH HE KNOWS SOMEONE IS FOLLOWING HIM!
I DON'T LIKE IT! EVERYTHING IS TOO QUIET -- TOO CALM! AND MY SPIDER-SENSE IS WARNING ME -- BUT, OF WHAT??
HE'S STARTING TO GET SUSPICIOUS NOW! BUT IT'S TOO LATE! THE TRAP IS SPRUNG!
A NET -- FALLING OVER ME!! BUT FROM WHERE?? HOW??
I'VE GOT TO DIVE OUT FROM UNDER -- NO! I'M TOO LATE!
WHAT CAN IT BE MADE OF?? EVEN WITH MY SPIDER STRENGTH, I CAN'T RIP IT! BUT, I MUSTN'T PANIC! THERE'S ALWAYS A WAY OUT! I HAVE TO THINK -- THINK --
AND SO THE BRILLIANT BRAIN OF THE ACE SCIENCE STUDENT BEGINS TO WORK AT LIGHTNING-LIKE SPEED! THE SAME BRAIN WHICH FLASH THOMPSON HAS MOCKED SO MANY TIMES! THE MAGNIFICENTLY TRAINED BRAIN WHICH QUICKLY COMES UP WITH THE ANSWER IN THE NICK OF TIME!
I'VE GOT ONE CHANCE! THEY SAY A CHAIN IS ONLY AS STRONG AS ITS WEAKEST LINK! IN A NET OF THIS TYPE, WITH SO MANY JOININGS, THERE MUST BE AT LEAST ONE WEAK LINK! NOW, ALL I HAVE TO DO --
-- I MUST EXERT ALL THE PRESSURE I CAN AGAINST EACH SECTION UNTIL -- AHH! I'VE FOUND IT!! ONE SMALL SECTION WHICH RIFLES BACK SLIGHTLY UNDER THE TENSION, CREATING AN OPENING...
NOW, BY EXERTING MAXIMUM PRESSURE AT THAT VERY SPOT, I CAN MAKE THE OPENING LARGE ENOUGH FOR ME TO ROLL OUT OF!!
NOTE: THE SEQUENCE YOU HAVE JUST WITNESSED TOOK PLACE IN ITS ENTIRETY WITHIN THE INCREDIBLY SHORT SPACE OF THREE AND ONE HALF SECONDS, DUE TO SPIDER-MAN'S COMBINED POWERS OF QUICK-THINKING AND RAPID ACTION!
15

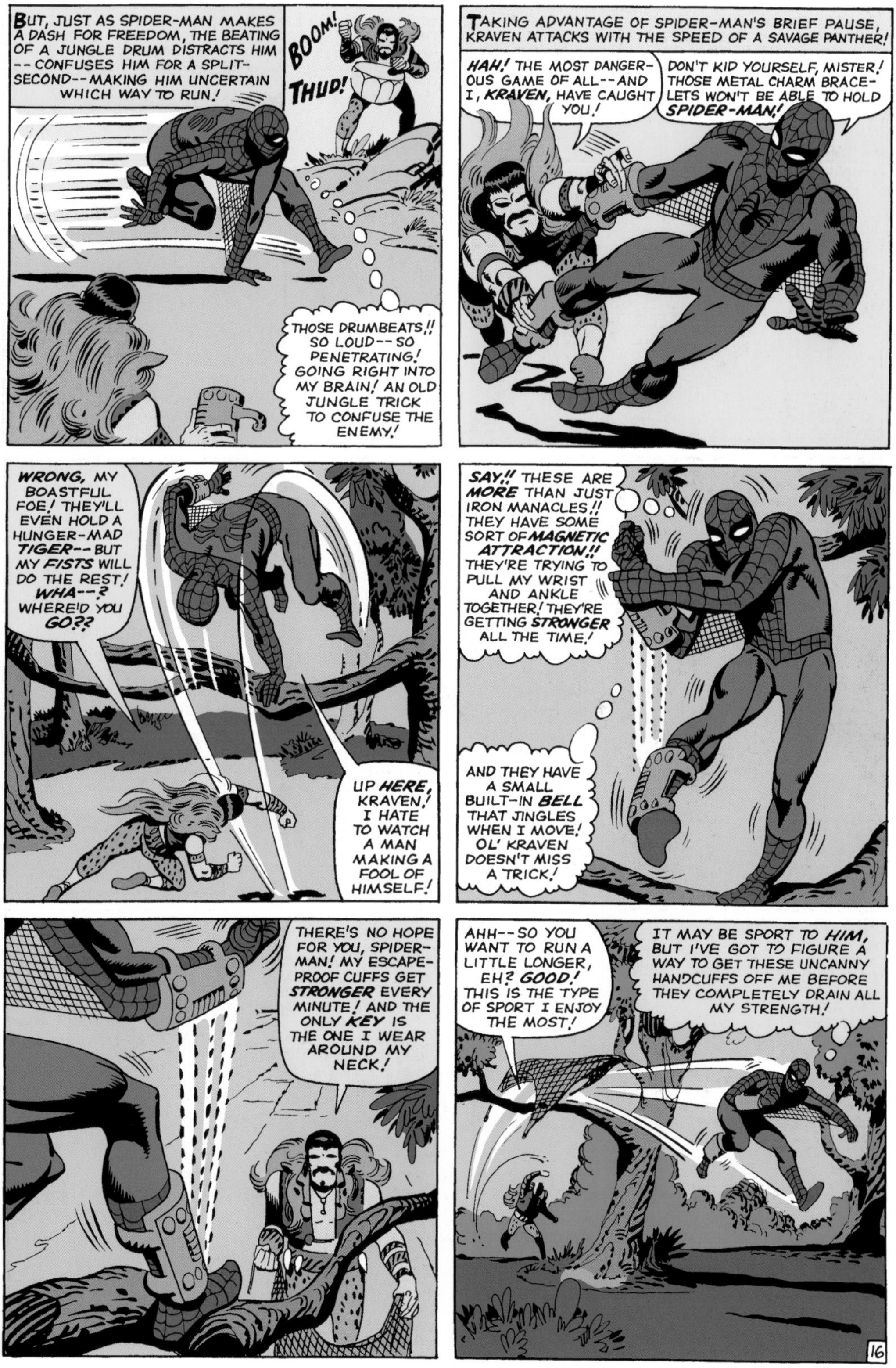
BUT, JUST AS SPIDER-MAN MAKES A DASH FOR FREEDOM, THE BEATING OF A JUNGLE DRUM DISTRACTS HIM -- CONFUSES HIM FOR A SPLIT-SECOND--MAKING HIM UNCERTAIN WHICH WAY TO RUN!
BOOM!
THUD!
THOSE DRUMBEATS!! SO LOUD-- SO PENETRATING! GOING RIGHT INTO MY BRAIN! AN OLD JUNGLE TRICK TO CONFUSE THE ENEMY!
TAKING ADVANTAGE OF SPIDER-MAN'S BRIEF PAUSE, KRAVEN ATTACKS WITH THE SPEED OF A SAVAGE PANTHER!
HAH! THE MOST DANGER-OUS GAME OF ALL--AND I, KRAVEN, HAVE CAUGHT YOU!
DON'T KID YOURSELF, MISTER! THOSE METAL CHARM BRACE-LETS WON'T BE ABLE TO HOLD SPIDER-MAN!
WRONG, MY BOASTFUL FOE! THEY'LL EVEN HOLD A HUNGER-MAD TIGER-- BUT MY FISTS WILL DO THE REST! WHA--? WHERE'D YOU GO??
UP HERE, KRAVEN! I HATE TO WATCH A MAN MAKING A FOOL OF HIMSELF!
SAY!! THESE ARE MORE THAN JUST IRON MANACLES!! THEY HAVE SOME SORT OF MAGNETIC ATTRACTION!! THEY'RE TRYING TO PULL MY WRIST AND ANKLE TOGETHER! THEY'RE GETTING STRONGER ALL THE TIME!
AND THEY HAVE A SMALL BUILT-IN BELL THAT JINGLES WHEN I MOVE! OL' KRAVEN DOESN'T MISS A TRICK!
THERE'S NO HOPE FOR YOU, SPIDER-MAN! MY ESCAPE-PROOF CUFFS GET STRONGER EVERY MINUTE! AND THE ONLY KEY IS THE ONE I WEAR AROUND MY NECK!
AHH--SO YOU WANT TO RUN A LITTLE LONGER, EH? GOOD! THIS IS THE TYPE OF SPORT I ENJOY THE MOST!
IT MAY BE SPORT TO HIM, BUT I'VE GOT TO FIGURE A WAY TO GET THESE UNCANNY HANDCUFFS OFF ME BEFORE THEY COMPLETELY DRAIN ALL MY STRENGTH!
16

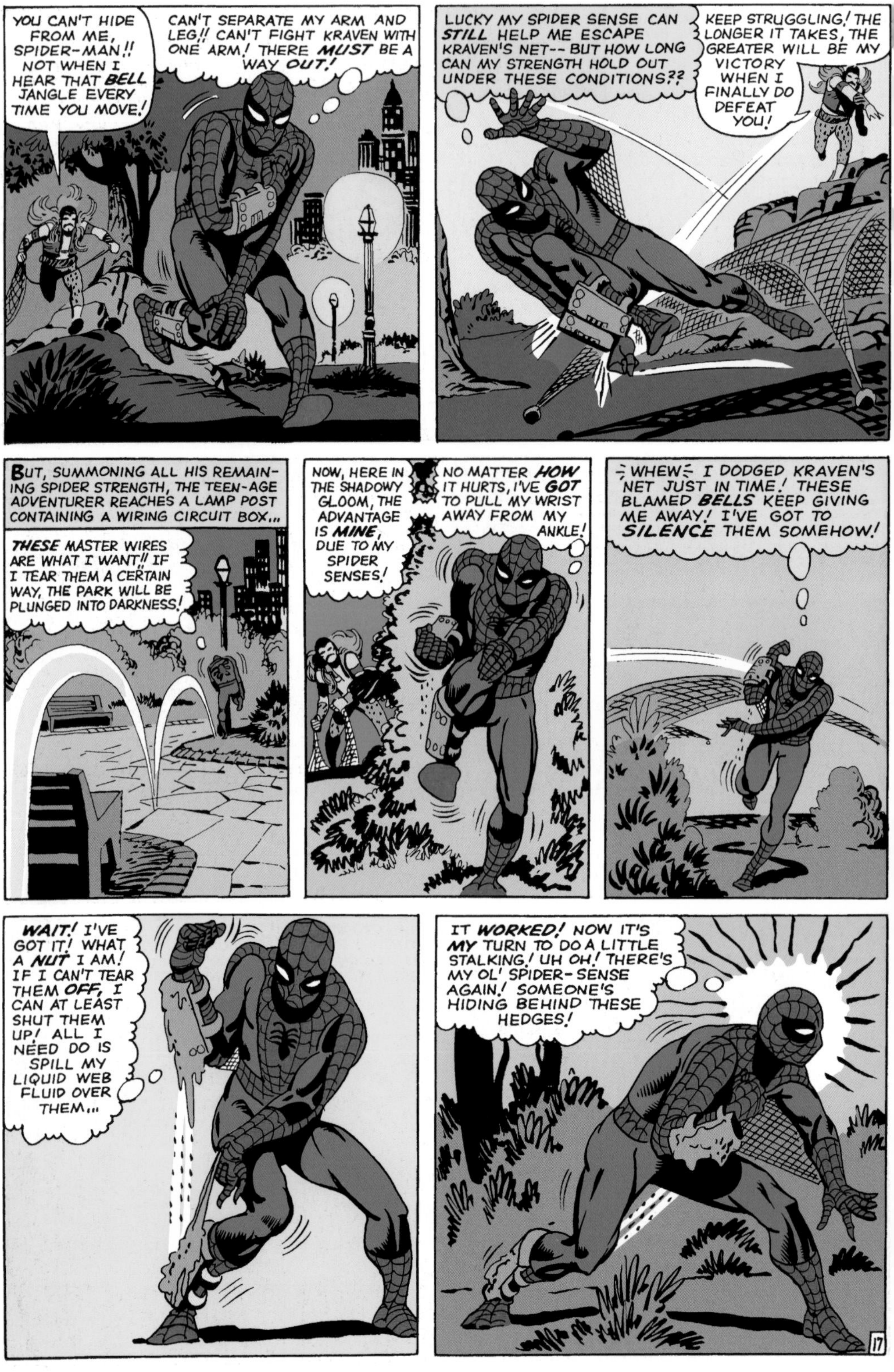

YOU CAN'T HIDE FROM ME, SPIDER-MAN!! NOT WHEN I HEAR THAT BELL JANGLE EVERY TIME YOU MOVE!
CAN'T SEPARATE MY ARM AND LEG!! CAN'T FIGHT KRAVEN WITH ONE ARM! THERE MUST BE A WAY OUT!
LUCKY MY SPIDER SENSE CAN STILL HELP ME ESCAPE KRAVEN'S NET-- BUT HOW LONG CAN MY STRENGTH HOLD OUT UNDER THESE CONDITIONS??
KEEP STRUGGLING! THE LONGER IT TAKES, THE GREATER WILL BE MY VICTORY WHEN I FINALLY DO DEFEAT YOU!
BUT, SUMMONING ALL HIS REMAINING SPIDER STRENGTH, THE TEEN-AGE ADVENTURER REACHES A LAMP POST CONTAINING A WIRING CIRCUIT BOX...
THESE MASTER WIRES ARE WHAT I WANT!! IF I TEAR THEM A CERTAIN WAY, THE PARK WILL BE PLUNGED INTO DARKNESS!
NOW, HERE IN THE SHADOWY GLOOM, THE ADVANTAGE IS MINE, DUE TO MY SPIDER SENSES!
NO MATTER HOW IT HURTS, I'VE GOT TO PULL MY WRIST AWAY FROM MY ANKLE!
WHEW! I DODGED KRAVEN'S NET JUST IN TIME! THESE BLAMED BELLS KEEP GIVING ME AWAY! I'VE GOT TO SILENCE THEM SOMEHOW!
WAIT! I'VE GOT IT! WHAT A NUT I AM! IF I CAN'T TEAR THEM OFF, I CAN AT LEAST SHUT THEM UP! ALL I NEED DO IS SPILL MY LIQUID WEB FLUID OVER THEM...
IT WORKED! NOW IT'S MY TURN TO DO A LITTLE STALKING! UH OH! THERE'S MY OL' SPIDER-SENSE AGAIN! SOMEONE'S HIDING BEHIND THESE HEDGES!
17

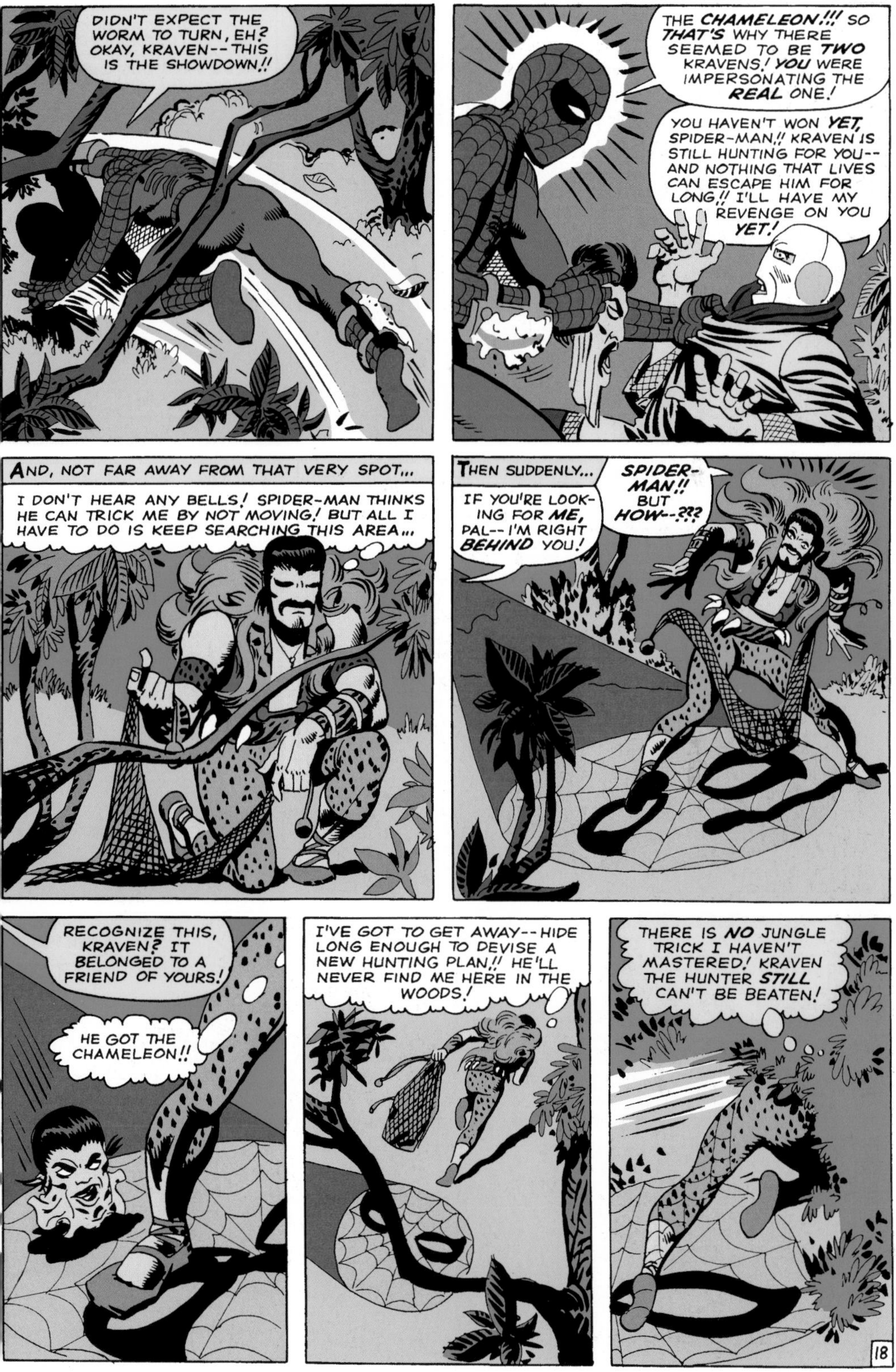
DIDN'T EXPECT THE WORM TO TURN, EH? OKAY, KRAVEN-- THIS IS THE SHOWDOWN!!
THE CHAMELEON!!! SO THAT'S WHY THERE SEEMED TO BE TWO KRAVENS! YOU WERE IMPERSONATING THE REAL ONE!
YOU HAVEN'T WON YET, SPIDER-MAN!! KRAVEN IS STILL HUNTING FOR YOU-- AND NOTHING THAT LIVES CAN ESCAPE HIM FOR LONG!! I'LL HAVE MY REVENGE ON YOU YET!
AND, NOT FAR AWAY FROM THAT VERY SPOT...
I DON'T HEAR ANY BELLS! SPIDER-MAN THINKS HE CAN TRICK ME BY NOT MOVING! BUT ALL I HAVE TO DO IS KEEP SEARCHING THIS AREA...
THEN SUDDENLY...
IF YOU'RE LOOKING FOR ME, PAL-- I'M RIGHT BEHIND YOU!
SPIDER-MAN!! BUT HOW--???
RECOGNIZE THIS, KRAVEN? IT BELONGED TO A FRIEND OF YOURS!
HE GOT THE CHAMELEON!!
I'VE GOT TO GET AWAY-- HIDE LONG ENOUGH TO DEVISE A NEW HUNTING PLAN!! HE'LL NEVER FIND ME HERE IN THE WOODS!
THERE IS NO JUNGLE TRICK I HAVEN'T MASTERED! KRAVEN THE HUNTER STILL CAN'T BE BEATEN!
18

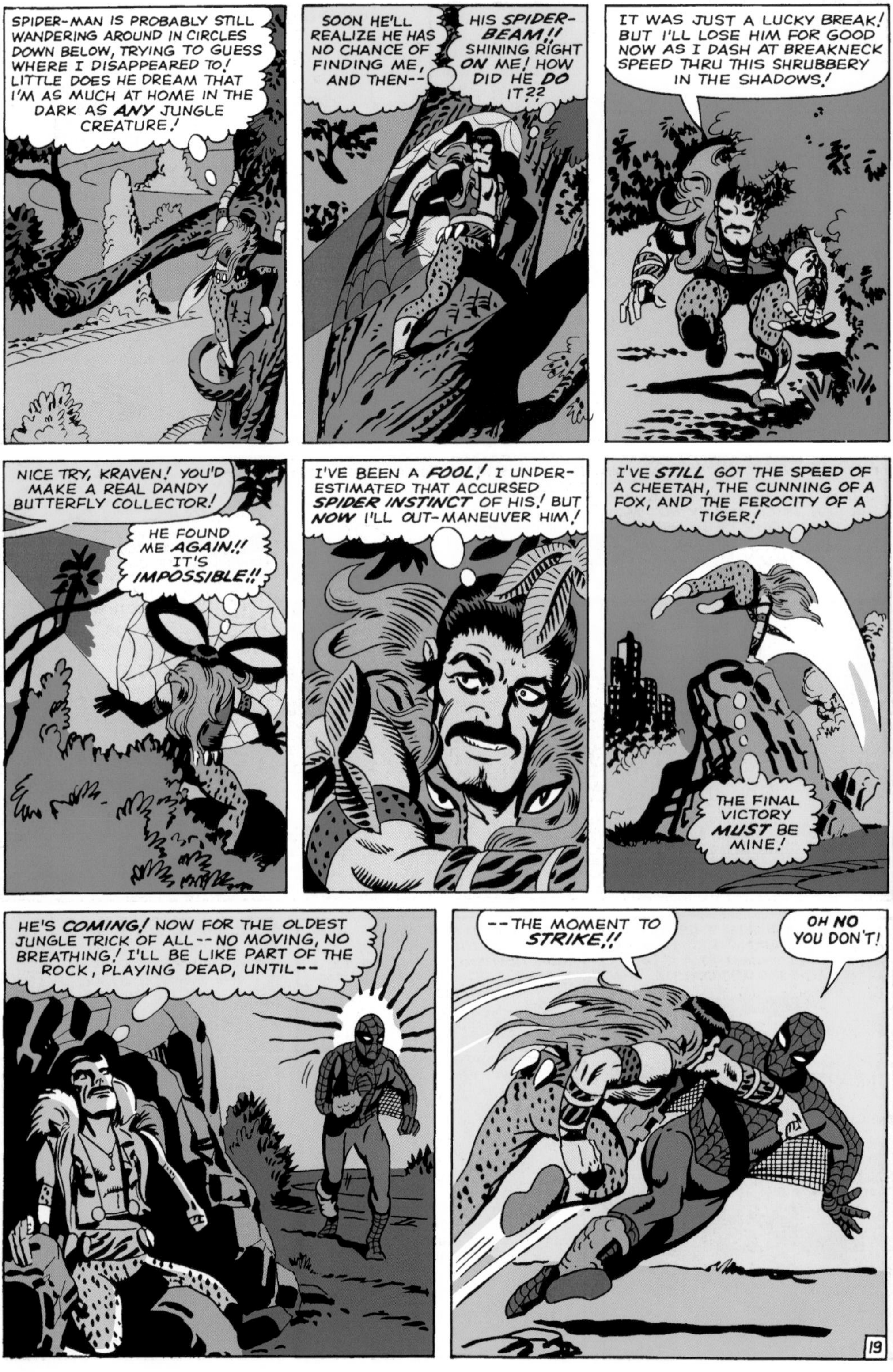
SPIDER-MAN IS PROBABLY STILL WANDERING AROUND IN CIRCLES DOWN BELOW, TRYING TO GUESS WHERE I DISAPPEARED TO! LITTLE DOES HE DREAM THAT I'M AS MUCH AT HOME IN THE DARK AS ANY JUNGLE CREATURE!
SOON HE'LL REALIZE HE HAS NO CHANCE OF FINDING ME, AND THEN--
HIS SPIDER-BEAM!! SHINING RIGHT ON ME! HOW DID HE DO IT??
IT WAS JUST A LUCKY BREAK! BUT I'LL LOSE HIM FOR GOOD NOW AS I DASH AT BREAKNECK SPEED THRU THIS SHRUBBERY IN THE SHADOWS!
NICE TRY, KRAVEN! YOU'D MAKE A REAL DANDY BUTTERFLY COLLECTOR!
HE FOUND ME AGAIN!! IT'S IMPOSSIBLE!!
I'VE BEEN A FOOL! I UNDER-ESTIMATED THAT ACCURSED SPIDER INSTINCT OF HIS! BUT NOW I'LL OUT-MANEUVER HIM!
I'VE STILL GOT THE SPEED OF A CHEETAH, THE CUNNING OF A FOX, AND THE FEROCITY OF A TIGER!
THE FINAL VICTORY MUST BE MINE!
HE'S COMING! NOW FOR THE OLDEST JUNGLE TRICK OF ALL-- NO MOVING, NO BREATHING! I'LL BE LIKE PART OF THE ROCK, PLAYING DEAD, UNTIL--
--THE MOMENT TO STRIKE!!
OH NO YOU DON'T!
19

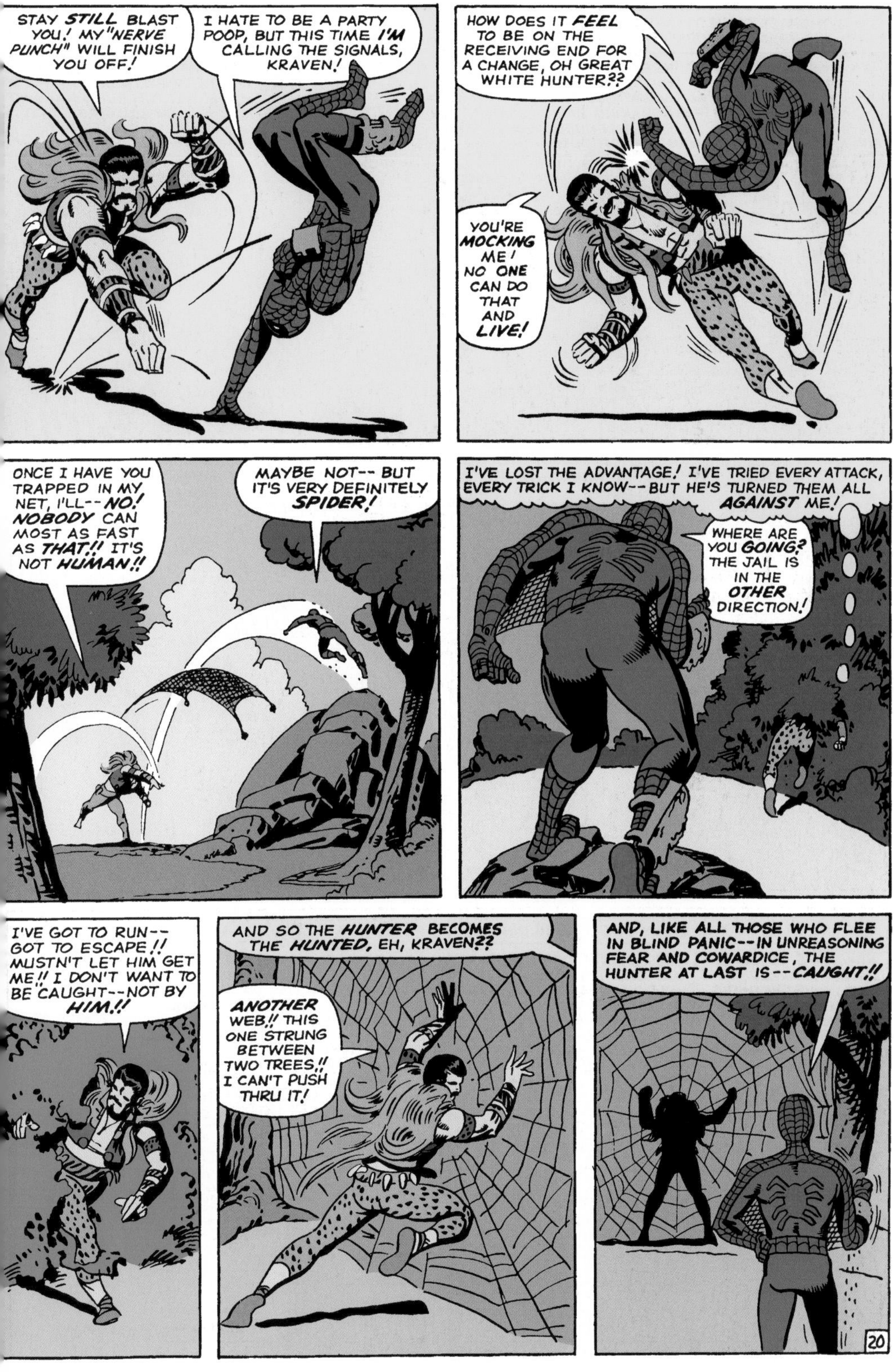

STAY STILL BLAST YOU! MY "NERVE PUNCH" WILL FINISH YOU OFF!
I HATE TO BE A PARTY POOP, BUT THIS TIME I'M CALLING THE SIGNALS, KRAVEN!
HOW DOES IT FEEL TO BE ON THE RECEIVING END FOR A CHANGE, OH GREAT WHITE HUNTER??
YOU'RE MOCKING ME! NO ONE CAN DO THAT AND LIVE!
ONCE I HAVE YOU TRAPPED IN MY NET, I'LL-- NO! NOBODY CAN MOST AS FAST AS THAT!! IT'S NOT HUMAN!!
MAYBE NOT-- BUT IT'S VERY DEFINITELY SPIDER!
I'VE LOST THE ADVANTAGE! I'VE TRIED EVERY ATTACK, EVERY TRICK I KNOW-- BUT HE'S TURNED THEM ALL AGAINST ME!
WHERE ARE YOU GOING? THE JAIL IS IN THE OTHER DIRECTION!
I'VE GOT TO RUN-- GOT TO ESCAPE!! MUSTN'T LET HIM GET ME!! I DON'T WANT TO BE CAUGHT--NOT BY HIM!!
AND SO THE HUNTER BECOMES THE HUNTED, EH, KRAVEN??
ANOTHER WEB!! THIS ONE STRUNG BETWEEN TWO TREES!! I CAN'T PUSH THRU IT!
AND, LIKE ALL THOSE WHO FLEE IN BLIND PANIC--IN UNREASONING FEAR AND COWARDICE, THE HUNTER AT LAST IS--CAUGHT!!
20

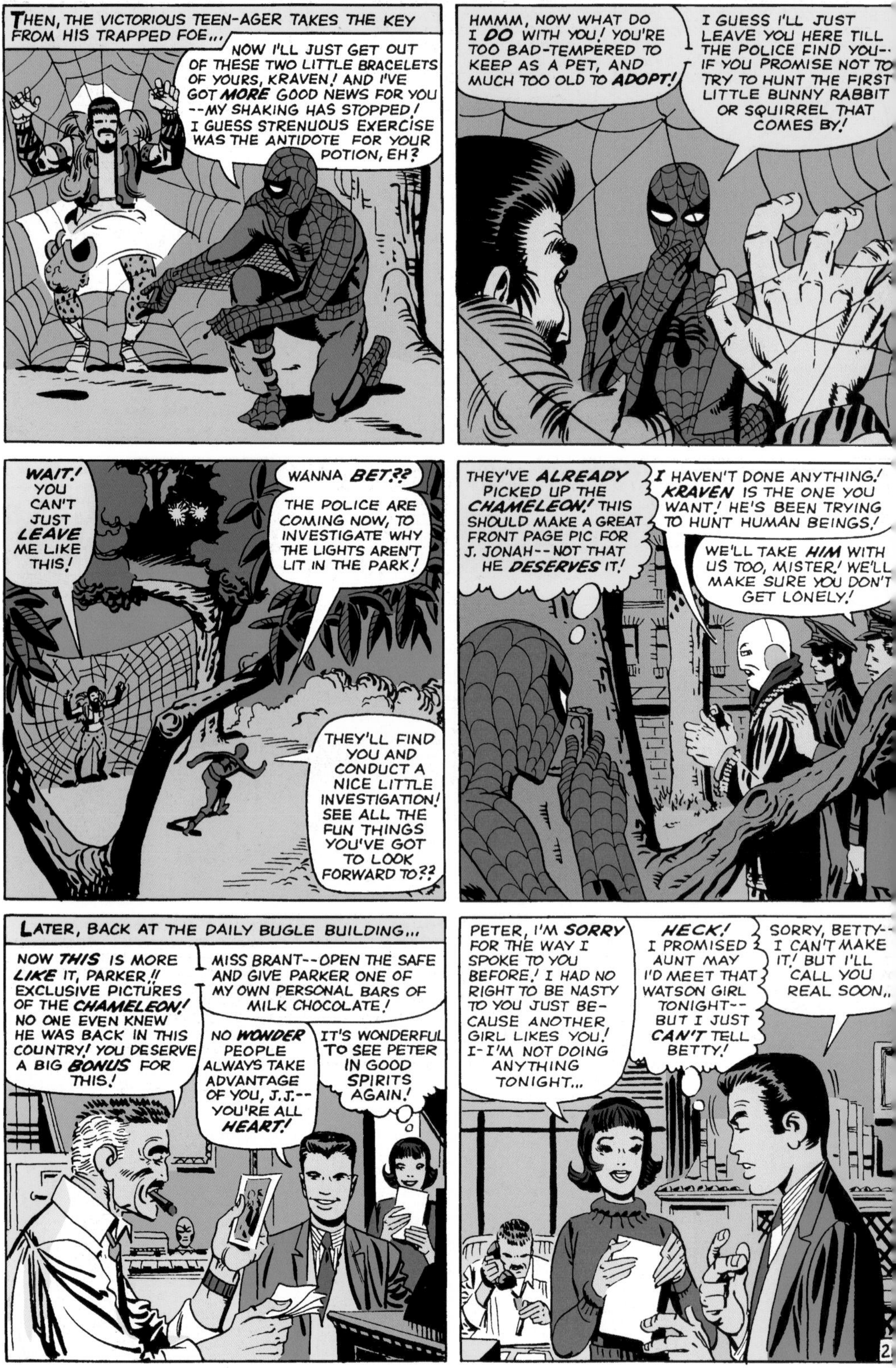

THEN, THE VICTORIOUS TEEN-AGER TAKES THE KEY FROM HIS TRAPPED FOE...
NOW I'LL JUST GET OUT OF THESE TWO LITTLE BRACELETS OF YOURS, KRAVEN! AND I'VE GOT MORE GOOD NEWS FOR YOU --MY SHAKING HAS STOPPED! I GUESS STRENUOUS EXERCISE WAS THE ANTIDOTE FOR YOUR POTION, EH?
HMMM, NOW WHAT DO I DO WITH YOU! YOU'RE TOO BAD-TEMPERED TO KEEP AS A PET, AND MUCH TOO OLD TO ADOPT!
I GUESS I'LL JUST LEAVE YOU HERE TILL THE POLICE FIND YOU-- IF YOU PROMISE NOT TO TRY TO HUNT THE FIRST LITTLE BUNNY RABBIT OR SQUIRREL THAT COMES BY!
WAIT! YOU CAN'T JUST LEAVE ME LIKE THIS!
WANNA BET??
THE POLICE ARE COMING NOW, TO INVESTIGATE WHY THE LIGHTS AREN'T LIT IN THE PARK!
THEY'LL FIND YOU AND CONDUCT A NICE LITTLE INVESTIGATION! SEE ALL THE FUN THINGS YOU'VE GOT TO LOOK FORWARD TO??
THEY'VE ALREADY PICKED UP THE CHAMELEON! THIS SHOULD MAKE A GREAT FRONT PAGE PIC FOR J. JONAH-- NOT THAT HE DESERVES IT!
I HAVEN'T DONE ANYTHING! KRAVEN IS THE ONE YOU WANT! HE'S BEEN TRYING TO HUNT HUMAN BEINGS!
WE'LL TAKE HIM WITH US TOO, MISTER! WE'LL MAKE SURE YOU DON'T GET LONELY!
LATER, BACK AT THE DAILY BUGLE BUILDING...
NOW THIS IS MORE LIKE IT, PARKER!! EXCLUSIVE PICTURES OF THE CHAMELEON! NO ONE EVEN KNEW HE WAS BACK IN THIS COUNTRY! YOU DESERVE A BIG BONUS FOR THIS!
MISS BRANT--OPEN THE SAFE AND GIVE PARKER ONE OF MY OWN PERSONAL BARS OF MILK CHOCOLATE!
NO WONDER PEOPLE ALWAYS TAKE ADVANTAGE OF YOU, J.J.-- YOU'RE ALL HEART!
IT'S WONDERFUL TO SEE PETER IN GOOD SPIRITS AGAIN!
PETER, I'M SORRY FOR THE WAY I SPOKE TO YOU BEFORE! I HAD NO RIGHT TO BE NASTY TO YOU JUST BECAUSE ANOTHER GIRL LIKES YOU! I-I'M NOT DOING ANYTHING TONIGHT...
HECK! I PROMISED AUNT MAY I'D MEET THAT WATSON GIRL TONIGHT-- BUT I JUST CAN'T TELL BETTY!
SORRY, BETTY-- I CAN'T MAKE IT! BUT I'LL CALL YOU REAL SOON...

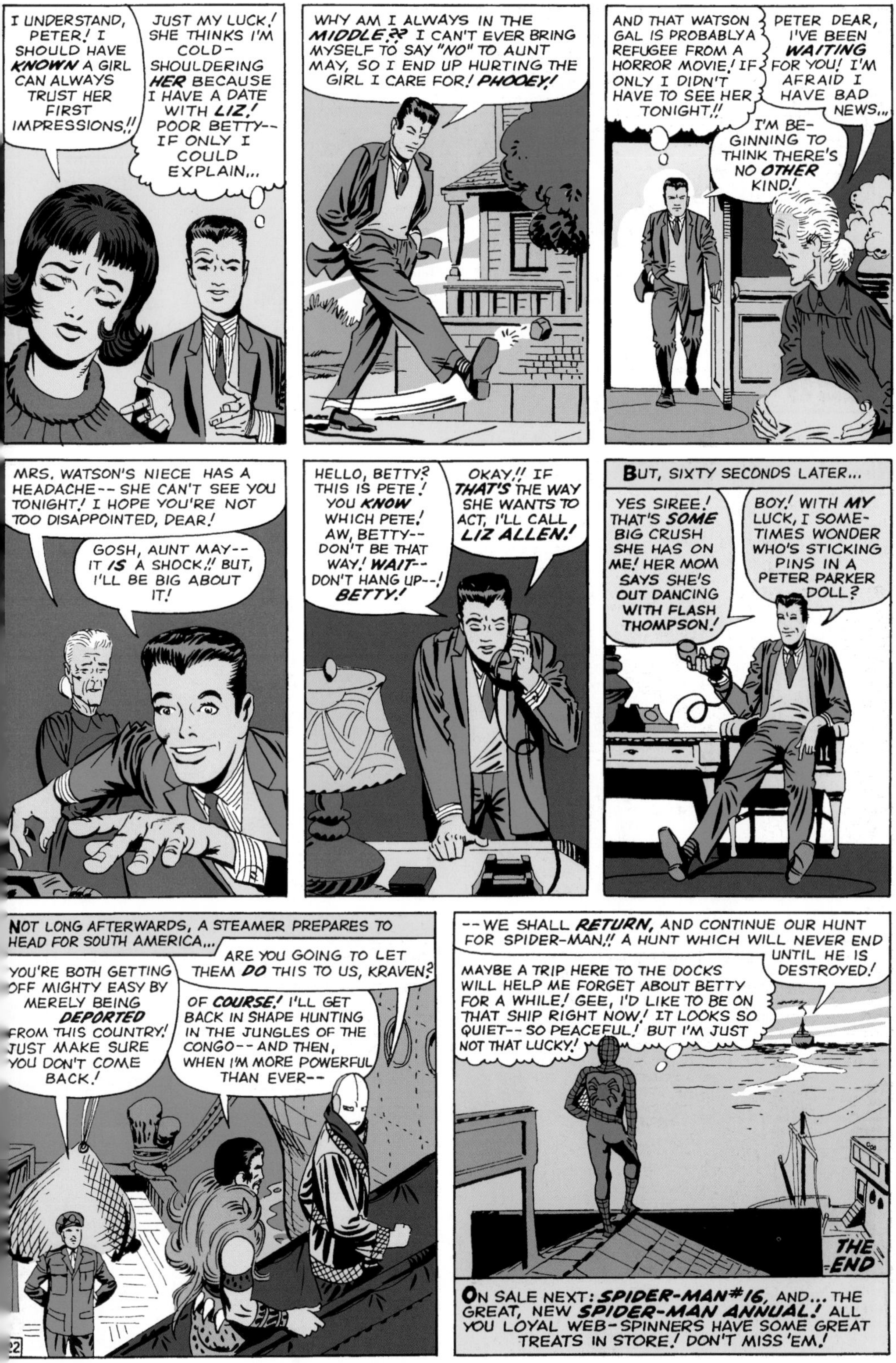
I UNDERSTAND, PETER! I SHOULD HAVE KNOWN A GIRL CAN ALWAYS TRUST HER FIRST IMPRESSIONS!!
JUST MY LUCK! SHE THINKS I'M COLD-SHOULDERING HER BECAUSE I HAVE A DATE WITH LIZ! POOR BETTY-- IF ONLY I COULD EXPLAIN...
WHY AM I ALWAYS IN THE MIDDLE?? I CAN'T EVER BRING MYSELF TO SAY "NO" TO AUNT MAY, SO I END UP HURTING THE GIRL I CARE FOR! PHOOEY!
AND THAT WATSON GAL IS PROBABLY A REFUGEE FROM A HORROR MOVIE! IF ONLY I DIDN'T HAVE TO SEE HER TONIGHT!!
PETER DEAR, I'VE BEEN WAITING FOR YOU! I'M AFRAID I HAVE BAD NEWS...
I'M BE-GINNING TO THINK THERE'S NO OTHER KIND!
MRS. WATSON'S NIECE HAS A HEADACHE-- SHE CAN'T SEE YOU TONIGHT! I HOPE YOU'RE NOT TOO DISAPPOINTED, DEAR!
GOSH, AUNT MAY-- IT IS A SHOCK!! BUT, I'LL BE BIG ABOUT IT!
HELLO, BETTY? THIS IS PETE! YOU KNOW WHICH PETE! AW, BETTY-- DON'T BE THAT WAY! WAIT-- DON'T HANG UP--! BETTY!
OKAY!! IF THAT'S THE WAY SHE WANTS TO ACT, I'LL CALL LIZ ALLEN!
BUT, SIXTY SECONDS LATER...
YES SIREE! THAT'S SOME BIG CRUSH SHE HAS ON ME! HER MOM SAYS SHE'S OUT DANCING WITH FLASH THOMPSON!
BOY! WITH MY LUCK, I SOME-TIMES WONDER WHO'S STICKING PINS IN A PETER PARKER DOLL?
NOT LONG AFTERWARDS, A STEAMER PREPARES TO HEAD FOR SOUTH AMERICA...
YOU'RE BOTH GETTING OFF MIGHTY EASY BY MERELY BEING DEPORTED FROM THIS COUNTRY! JUST MAKE SURE YOU DON'T COME BACK!
ARE YOU GOING TO LET THEM DO THIS TO US, KRAVEN?
OF COURSE! I'LL GET BACK IN SHAPE HUNTING IN THE JUNGLES OF THE CONGO-- AND THEN, WHEN I'M MORE POWERFUL THAN EVER--
22
--WE SHALL RETURN, AND CONTINUE OUR HUNT FOR SPIDER-MAN!! A HUNT WHICH WILL NEVER END UNTIL HE IS DESTROYED!
MAYBE A TRIP HERE TO THE DOCKS WILL HELP ME FORGET ABOUT BETTY FOR A WHILE! GEE, I'D LIKE TO BE ON THAT SHIP RIGHT NOW! IT LOOKS SO QUIET-- SO PEACEFUL! BUT I'M JUST NOT THAT LUCKY!
THE END
ON SALE NEXT: SPIDER-MAN #16, AND... THE GREAT, NEW SPIDER-MAN ANNUAL! ALL YOU LOYAL WEB-SPINNERS HAVE SOME GREAT TREATS IN STORE! DON'T MISS 'EM!

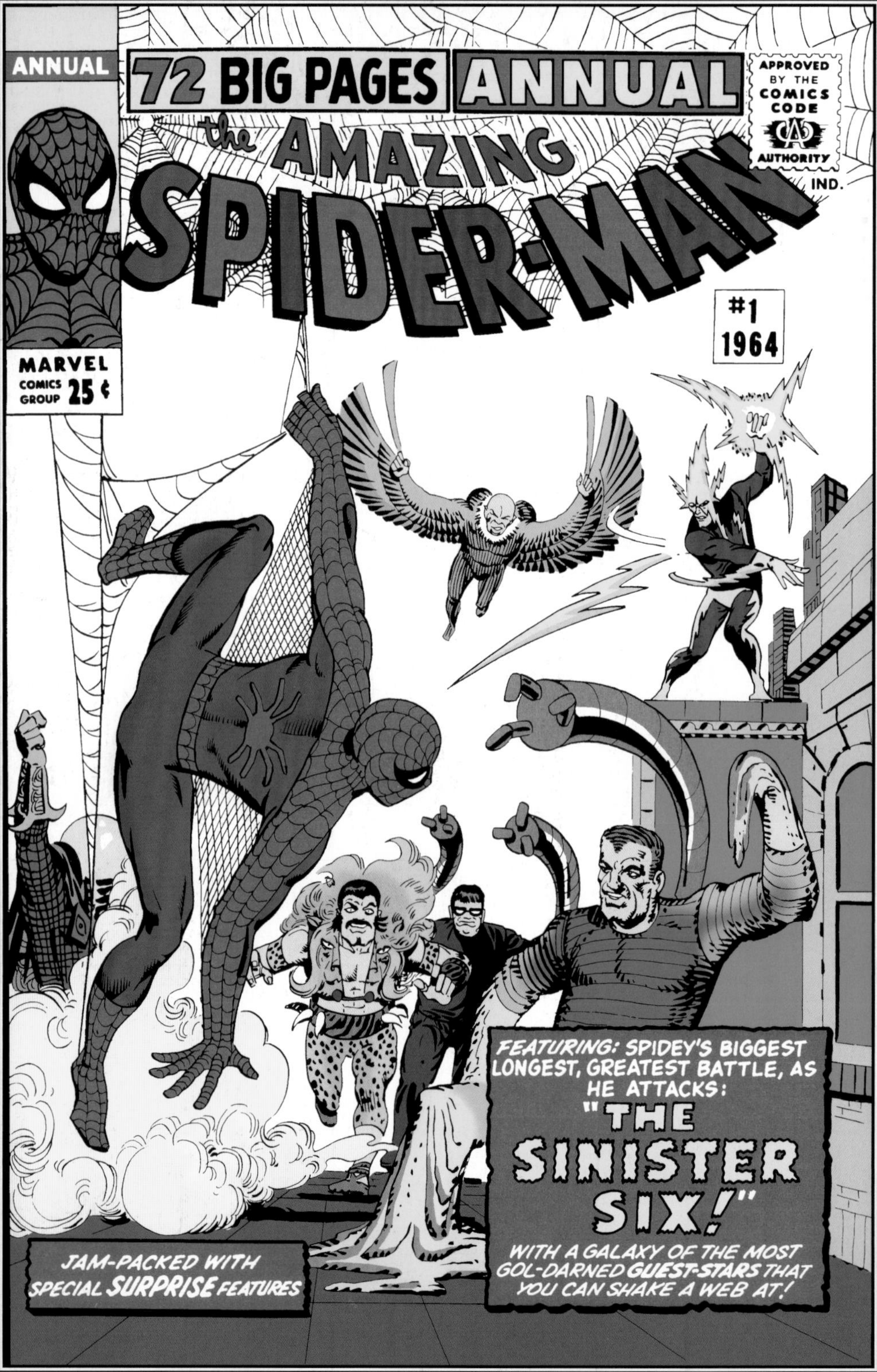
ANNUAL
72 BIG PAGES
ANNUAL
APPROVED BY THE COMICS CODE AUTHORITY
the AMAZING
SPIDER-MAN
IND.
MARVEL COMICS GROUP 25¢
#1 1964
FEATURING: SPIDEY'S BIGGEST LONGEST, GREATEST BATTLE, AS HE ATTACKS:
"THE SINISTER SIX!"
WITH A GALAXY OF THE MOST GOL-DARNED GUEST-STARS THAT YOU CAN SHAKE A WEB AT!
JAM-PACKED WITH SPECIAL SURPRISE FEATURES

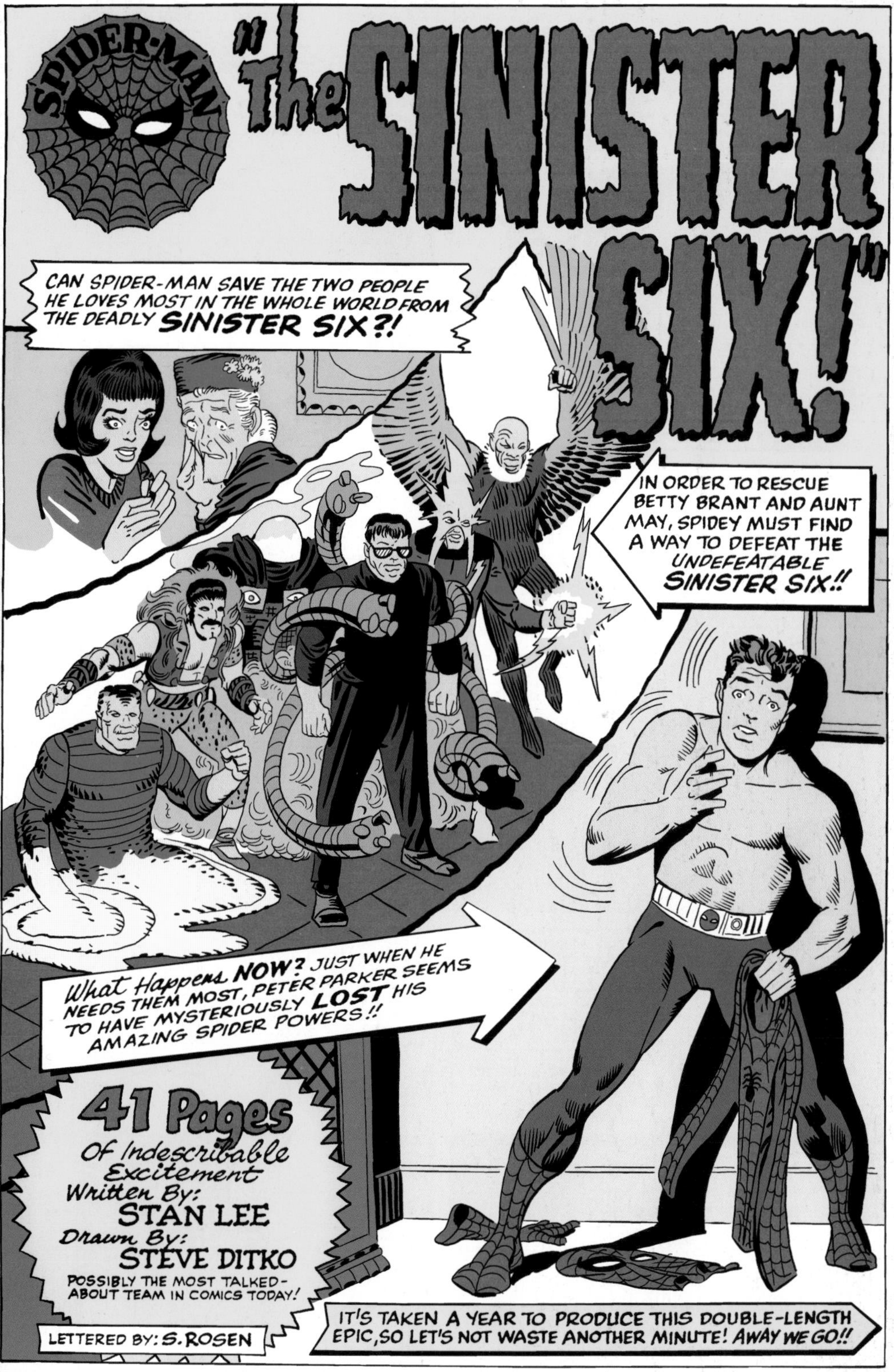

SPIDER-MAN
"The SINISTER SIX!"
CAN SPIDER-MAN SAVE THE TWO PEOPLE HE LOVES MOST IN THE WHOLE WORLD FROM THE DEADLY SINISTER SIX?!
IN ORDER TO RESCUE BETTY BRANT AND AUNT MAY, SPIDEY MUST FIND A WAY TO DEFEAT THE UNDEFEATABLE SINISTER SIX!!
What Happens NOW? JUST WHEN HE NEEDS THEM MOST, PETER PARKER SEEMS TO HAVE MYSTERIOUSLY LOST HIS AMAZING SPIDER POWERS!!
41 Pages Of Indescribable Excitement
Written By: STAN LEE
Drawn By: STEVE DITKO
POSSIBLY THE MOST TALKED-ABOUT TEAM IN COMICS TODAY!
LETTERED BY: S. ROSEN
IT'S TAKEN A YEAR TO PRODUCE THIS DOUBLE-LENGTH EPIC, SO LET'S NOT WASTE ANOTHER MINUTE! AWAY WE GO!!

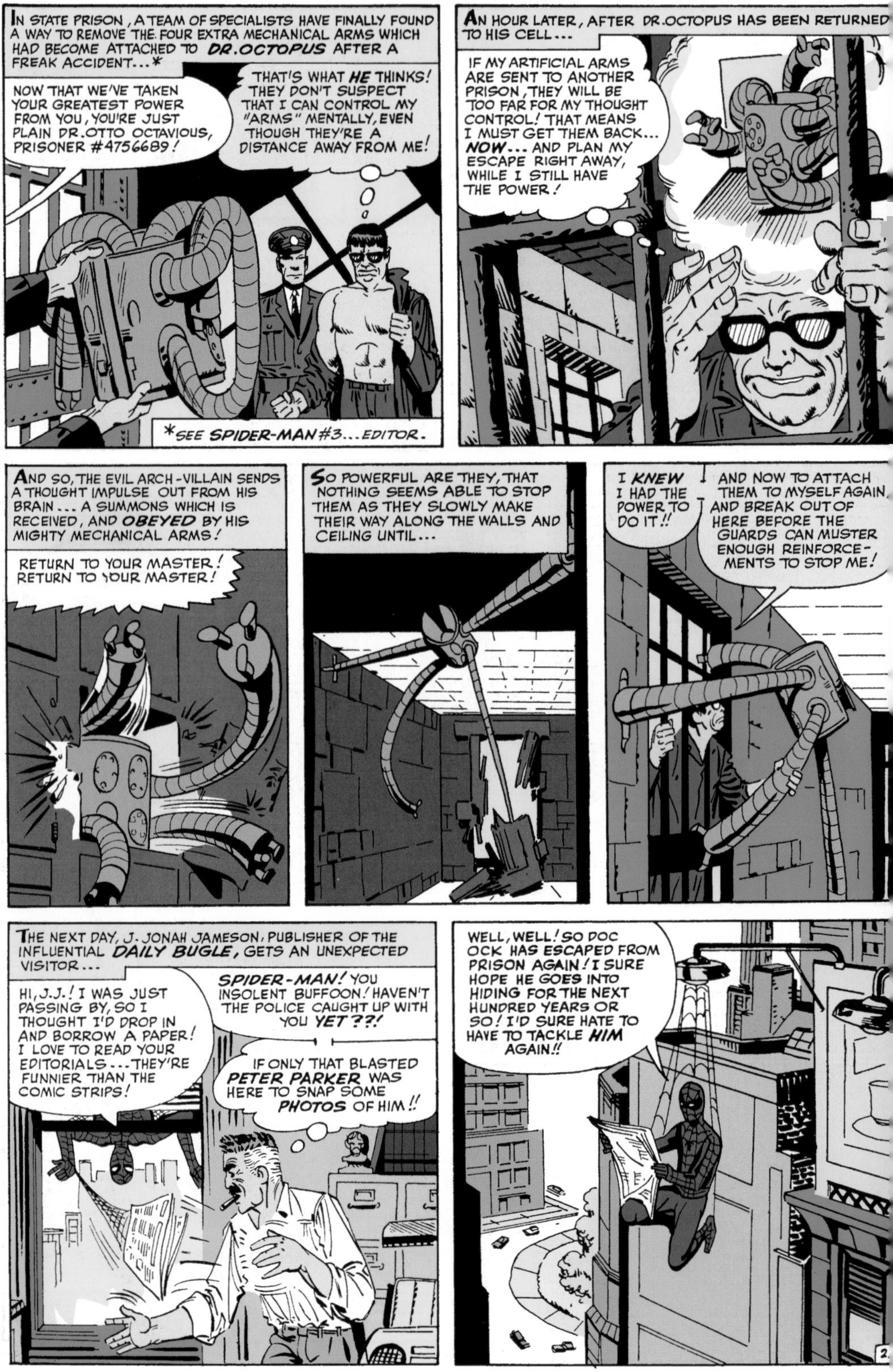
IN STATE PRISON, A TEAM OF SPECIALISTS HAVE FINALLY FOUND A WAY TO REMOVE THE FOUR EXTRA MECHANICAL ARMS WHICH HAD BECOME ATTACHED TO DR. OCTOPUS AFTER A FREAK ACCIDENT...*
NOW THAT WE'VE TAKEN YOUR GREATEST POWER FROM YOU, YOU'RE JUST PLAIN DR. OTTO OCTAVIOUS, PRISONER #4756689!
THAT'S WHAT HE THINKS! THEY DON'T SUSPECT THAT I CAN CONTROL MY "ARMS" MENTALLY, EVEN THOUGH THEY'RE A DISTANCE AWAY FROM ME!
*SEE SPIDER-MAN #3... EDITOR.
AN HOUR LATER, AFTER DR. OCTOPUS HAS BEEN RETURNED TO HIS CELL...
IF MY ARTIFICIAL ARMS ARE SENT TO ANOTHER PRISON, THEY WILL BE TOO FAR FOR MY THOUGHT CONTROL! THAT MEANS I MUST GET THEM BACK... NOW... AND PLAN MY ESCAPE RIGHT AWAY, WHILE I STILL HAVE THE POWER!
AND SO, THE EVIL ARCH-VILLAIN SENDS A THOUGHT IMPULSE OUT FROM HIS BRAIN... A SUMMONS WHICH IS RECEIVED, AND OBEYED BY HIS MIGHTY MECHANICAL ARMS!
RETURN TO YOUR MASTER! RETURN TO YOUR MASTER!
SO POWERFUL ARE THEY, THAT NOTHING SEEMS ABLE TO STOP THEM AS THEY SLOWLY MAKE THEIR WAY ALONG THE WALLS AND CEILING UNTIL...
I KNEW I HAD THE POWER TO DO IT!!
AND NOW TO ATTACH THEM TO MYSELF AGAIN, AND BREAK OUT OF HERE BEFORE THE GUARDS CAN MUSTER ENOUGH REINFORCEMENTS TO STOP ME!
THE NEXT DAY, J. JONAH JAMESON, PUBLISHER OF THE INFLUENTIAL DAILY BUGLE, GETS AN UNEXPECTED VISITOR...
HI, J.J.! I WAS JUST PASSING BY, SO I THOUGHT I'D DROP IN AND BORROW A PAPER! I LOVE TO READ YOUR EDITORIALS... THEY'RE FUNNIER THAN THE COMIC STRIPS!
SPIDER-MAN! YOU INSOLENT BUFFOON! HAVEN'T THE POLICE CAUGHT UP WITH YOU YET??!
IF ONLY THAT BLASTED PETER PARKER WAS HERE TO SNAP SOME PHOTOS OF HIM!!
WELL, WELL! SO DOC OCK HAS ESCAPED FROM PRISON AGAIN! I SURE HOPE HE GOES INTO HIDING FOR THE NEXT HUNDRED YEARS OR SO! I'D SURE HATE TO HAVE TO TACKLE HIM AGAIN!!

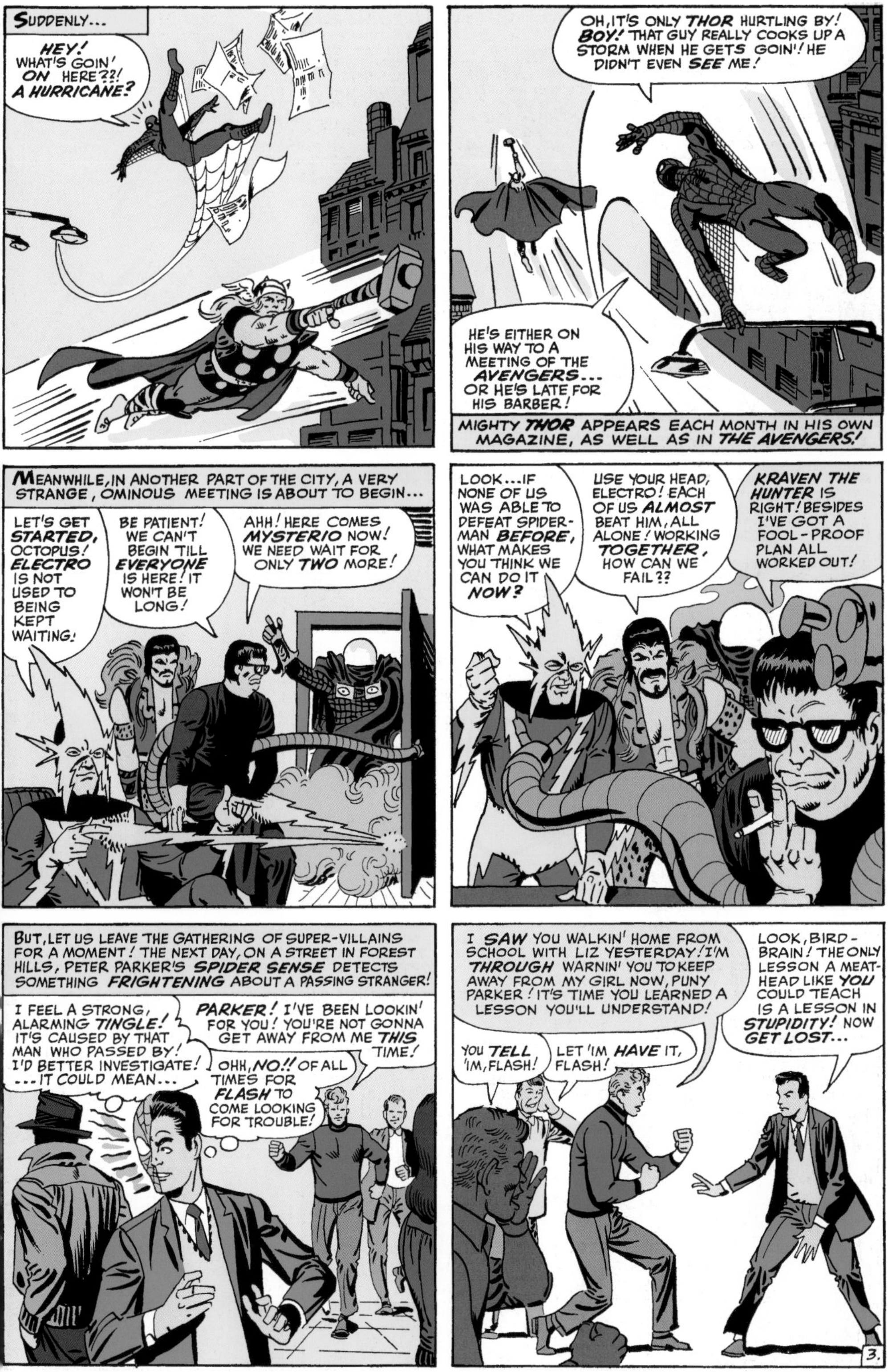
SUDDENLY...
HEY! WHAT'S GOIN' ON HERE??! A HURRICANE?
OH, IT'S ONLY THOR HURTLING BY! BOY! THAT GUY REALLY COOKS UP A STORM WHEN HE GETS GOIN'! HE DIDN'T EVEN SEE ME!
HE'S EITHER ON HIS WAY TO A MEETING OF THE AVENGERS... OR HE'S LATE FOR HIS BARBER!
MIGHTY THOR APPEARS EACH MONTH IN HIS OWN MAGAZINE, AS WELL AS IN THE AVENGERS!
MEANWHILE, IN ANOTHER PART OF THE CITY, A VERY STRANGE, OMINOUS MEETING IS ABOUT TO BEGIN...
LET'S GET STARTED, OCTOPUS! ELECTRO IS NOT USED TO BEING KEPT WAITING!
BE PATIENT! WE CAN'T BEGIN TILL EVERYONE IS HERE! IT WON'T BE LONG!
AHH! HERE COMES MYSTERIO NOW! WE NEED WAIT FOR ONLY TWO MORE!
LOOK...IF NONE OF US WAS ABLE TO DEFEAT SPIDER-MAN BEFORE, WHAT MAKES YOU THINK WE CAN DO IT NOW?
USE YOUR HEAD, ELECTRO! EACH OF US ALMOST BEAT HIM, ALL ALONE! WORKING TOGETHER, HOW CAN WE FAIL??
KRAVEN THE HUNTER IS RIGHT! BESIDES I'VE GOT A FOOL-PROOF PLAN ALL WORKED OUT!
BUT, LET US LEAVE THE GATHERING OF SUPER-VILLAINS FOR A MOMENT! THE NEXT DAY, ON A STREET IN FOREST HILLS, PETER PARKER'S SPIDER SENSE DETECTS SOMETHING FRIGHTENING ABOUT A PASSING STRANGER!
I FEEL A STRONG, ALARMING TINGLE! IT'S CAUSED BY THAT MAN WHO PASSED BY! I'D BETTER INVESTIGATE! ---IT COULD MEAN...
PARKER! I'VE BEEN LOOKIN' FOR YOU! YOU'RE NOT GONNA GET AWAY FROM ME THIS TIME!
OHH, NO!! OF ALL TIMES FOR FLASH TO COME LOOKING FOR TROUBLE!
I SAW YOU WALKIN' HOME FROM SCHOOL WITH LIZ YESTERDAY! I'M THROUGH WARNIN' YOU TO KEEP AWAY FROM MY GIRL NOW, PUNY PARKER! IT'S TIME YOU LEARNED A LESSON YOU'LL UNDERSTAND!
YOU TELL 'IM, FLASH!
LET 'IM HAVE IT, FLASH!
LOOK, BIRD-BRAIN! THE ONLY LESSON A MEAT-HEAD LIKE YOU COULD TEACH IS A LESSON IN STUPIDITY! NOW GET LOST...
3.

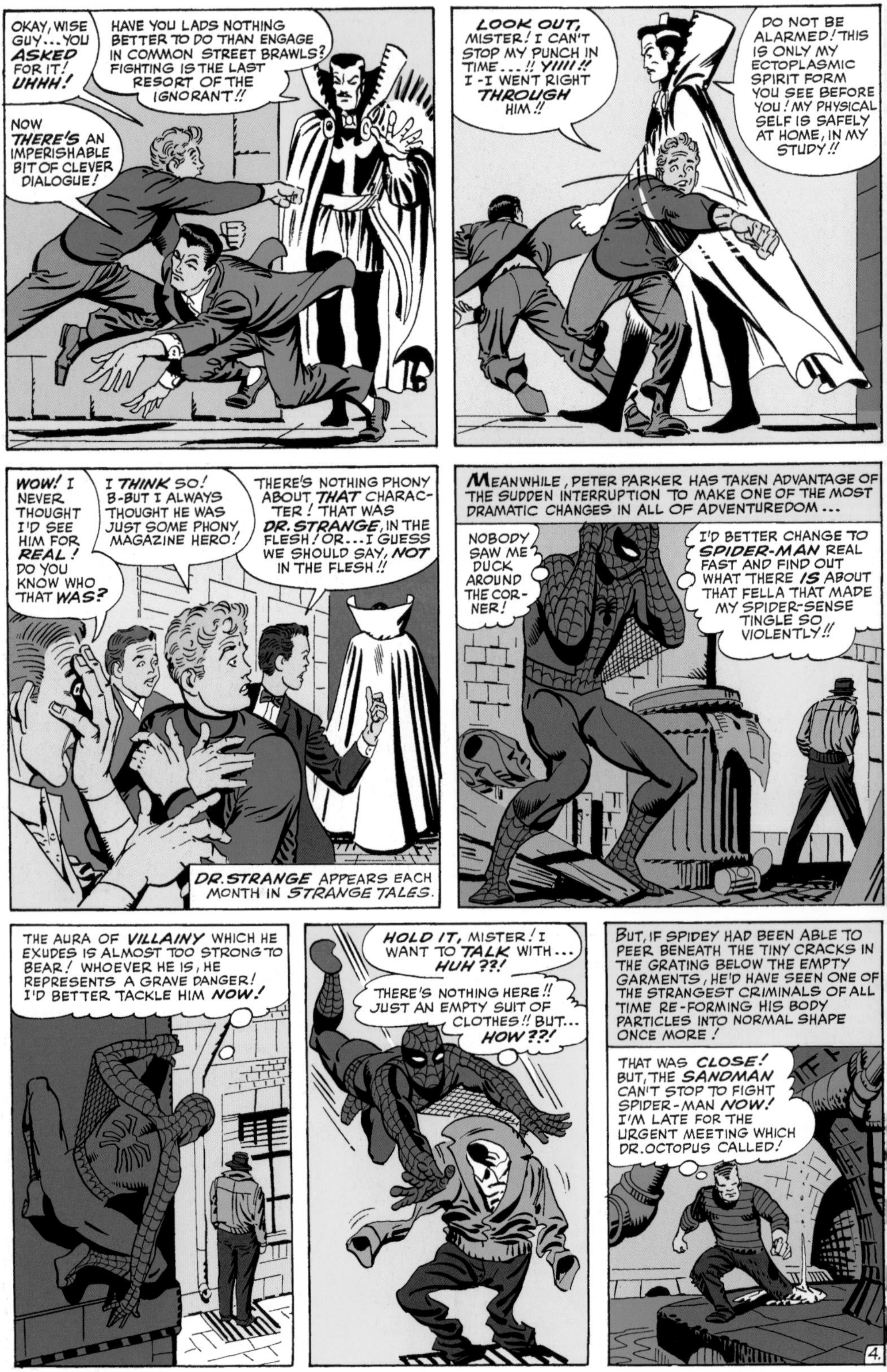
OKAY, WISE GUY... YOU ASKED FOR IT! UHHH!
HAVE YOU LADS NOTHING BETTER TO DO THAN ENGAGE IN COMMON STREET BRAWLS? FIGHTING IS THE LAST RESORT OF THE IGNORANT!!
NOW THERE'S AN IMPERISHABLE BIT OF CLEVER DIALOGUE!
LOOK OUT, MISTER! I CAN'T STOP MY PUNCH IN TIME...!! YIIII!! I -I WENT RIGHT THROUGH HIM!!
DO NOT BE ALARMED! THIS IS ONLY MY ECTOPLASMIC SPIRIT FORM YOU SEE BEFORE YOU! MY PHYSICAL SELF IS SAFELY AT HOME, IN MY STUDY!!
WOW! I NEVER THOUGHT I'D SEE HIM FOR REAL! DO YOU KNOW WHO THAT WAS?
I THINK SO! B-BUT I ALWAYS THOUGHT HE WAS JUST SOME PHONY MAGAZINE HERO!
THERE'S NOTHING PHONY ABOUT THAT CHARACTER! THAT WAS DR. STRANGE, IN THE FLESH! OR... I GUESS WE SHOULD SAY, NOT IN THE FLESH!!
DR. STRANGE APPEARS EACH MONTH IN STRANGE TALES.
MEANWHILE, PETER PARKER HAS TAKEN ADVANTAGE OF THE SUDDEN INTERRUPTION TO MAKE ONE OF THE MOST DRAMATIC CHANGES IN ALL OF ADVENTUREDOM...
NOBODY SAW ME DUCK AROUND THE CORNER!
I'D BETTER CHANGE TO SPIDER-MAN REAL FAST AND FIND OUT WHAT THERE IS ABOUT THAT FELLA THAT MADE MY SPIDER-SENSE TINGLE SO VIOLENTLY!!
THE AURA OF VILLAINY WHICH HE EXUDES IS ALMOST TOO STRONG TO BEAR! WHOEVER HE IS, HE REPRESENTS A GRAVE DANGER! I'D BETTER TACKLE HIM NOW!
HOLD IT, MISTER! I WANT TO TALK WITH... HUH??!
THERE'S NOTHING HERE!! JUST AN EMPTY SUIT OF CLOTHES!! BUT... HOW??!
BUT, IF SPIDEY HAD BEEN ABLE TO PEER BENEATH THE TINY CRACKS IN THE GRATING BELOW THE EMPTY GARMENTS, HE'D HAVE SEEN ONE OF THE STRANGEST CRIMINALS OF ALL TIME RE-FORMING HIS BODY PARTICLES INTO NORMAL SHAPE ONCE MORE!
THAT WAS CLOSE! BUT, THE SANDMAN CAN'T STOP TO FIGHT SPIDER-MAN NOW! I'M LATE FOR THE URGENT MEETING WHICH DR. OCTOPUS CALLED!
4.

MOMENTS LATER...

MY SPIDER SENSE INDICATES THAT THE ONE I'M AFTER IS DOWN *HERE* SOMEWHERE! BUT HE HAS TOO MUCH OF A HEAD START...TOO MANY TUNNELS! I WONDER WHO HE COULD HAVE BEEN ??

I'D BETTER GET *HOME* NOW! IT'S ALMOST DINNER TIME, AND I DON'T WANT TO WORRY AUNT MAY!

SAY, *THAT'S* STRANGE! THERE'S A LIGHT ON IN THE ATTIC! WHY WOULD SHE BE UP *THERE* ?

SHE OPENED UNCLE BEN'S TRUNK!... LOOKING AT HIS OLD LETTERS, AND PHOTOS! GOSH!

I *HATE* TO SEE HER WEEP THAT WAY! I GUESS SHE NEVER REALLY GOT OVER UNCLE BEN'S DEATH AT THE HANDS OF THAT BURGLAR MONTHS AGO!

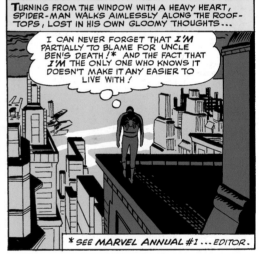

TURNING FROM THE WINDOW WITH A HEAVY HEART, SPIDER-MAN WALKS AIMLESSLY ALONG THE ROOF-TOPS, LOST IN HIS OWN GLOOMY THOUGHTS...

I CAN NEVER FORGET THAT *I'M* PARTIALLY TO BLAME FOR UNCLE BEN'S DEATH!* AND THE FACT THAT *I'M* THE ONLY ONE WHO KNOWS IT DOESN'T MAKE IT ANY EASIER TO LIVE WITH!

* SEE *MARVEL ANNUAL #1*...EDITOR.

HE WAS ALWAYS SO GOOD TO ME... SUCH A REAL PAL! WE WENT EVERYWHERE! HE LOVED ME LIKE HIS OWN SON! HE WANTED ME TO *BE* SOMEONE!

"I STILL REMEMBER THAT TERRIBLE DAY! I HADN'T BEEN *SPIDER-MAN* FOR VERY LONG, AND I DIDN'T WANT TO *WASTE* MY POWERS! I REMEMBER HOW I STOOD CALMLY BY WHEN I MIGHT HAVE HELPED TO CATCH AN ESCAPING CRIMINAL!"

STOP HIM! IF HE MAKES IT TO THE ELEVATOR, HE'LL GET AWAY!

WHY SHOULD *I* BUTT IN?

5.

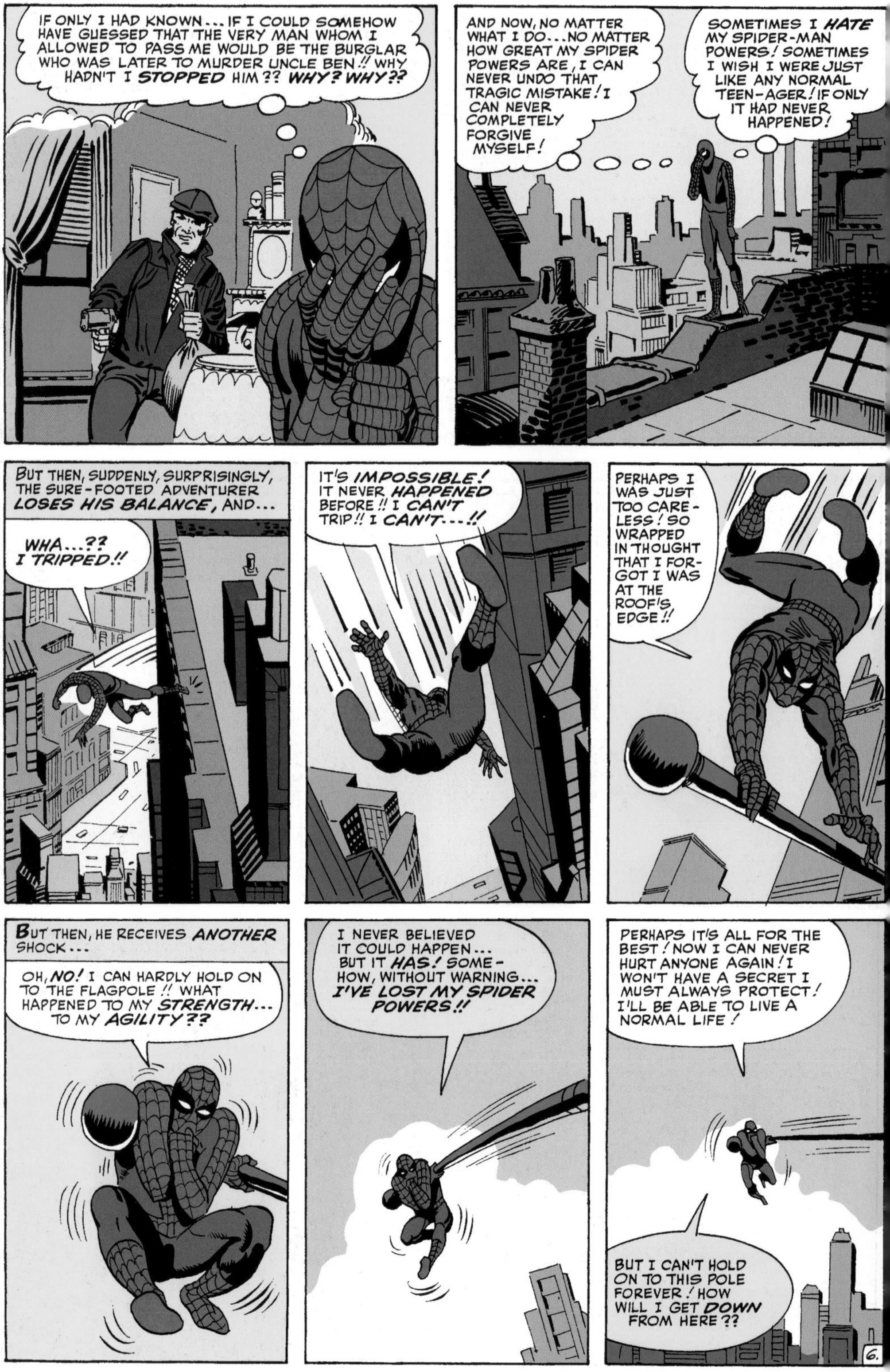
IF ONLY I HAD KNOWN... IF I COULD SOMEHOW HAVE GUESSED THAT THE VERY MAN WHOM I ALLOWED TO PASS ME WOULD BE THE BURGLAR WHO WAS LATER TO MURDER UNCLE BEN!! WHY HADN'T I STOPPED HIM?? WHY? WHY??
AND NOW, NO MATTER WHAT I DO... NO MATTER HOW GREAT MY SPIDER POWERS ARE, I CAN NEVER UNDO THAT TRAGIC MISTAKE! I CAN NEVER COMPLETELY FORGIVE MYSELF!
SOMETIMES I HATE MY SPIDER-MAN POWERS! SOMETIMES I WISH I WERE JUST LIKE ANY NORMAL TEEN-AGER! IF ONLY IT HAD NEVER HAPPENED!
BUT THEN, SUDDENLY, SURPRISINGLY, THE SURE-FOOTED ADVENTURER LOSES HIS BALANCE, AND...
WHA...?? I TRIPPED!!
IT'S IMPOSSIBLE! IT NEVER HAPPENED BEFORE!! I CAN'T TRIP!! I CAN'T...!!
PERHAPS I WAS JUST TOO CARE-LESS! SO WRAPPED IN THOUGHT THAT I FOR-GOT I WAS AT THE ROOF'S EDGE!!
BUT THEN, HE RECEIVES ANOTHER SHOCK...
OH, NO! I CAN HARDLY HOLD ON TO THE FLAGPOLE!! WHAT HAPPENED TO MY STRENGTH... TO MY AGILITY??
I NEVER BELIEVED IT COULD HAPPEN... BUT IT HAS! SOME-HOW, WITHOUT WARNING... I'VE LOST MY SPIDER POWERS!!
PERHAPS IT'S ALL FOR THE BEST! NOW I CAN NEVER HURT ANYONE AGAIN! I WON'T HAVE A SECRET I MUST ALWAYS PROTECT! I'LL BE ABLE TO LIVE A NORMAL LIFE!
BUT I CAN'T HOLD ON TO THIS POLE FOREVER! HOW WILL I GET DOWN FROM HERE??
6.

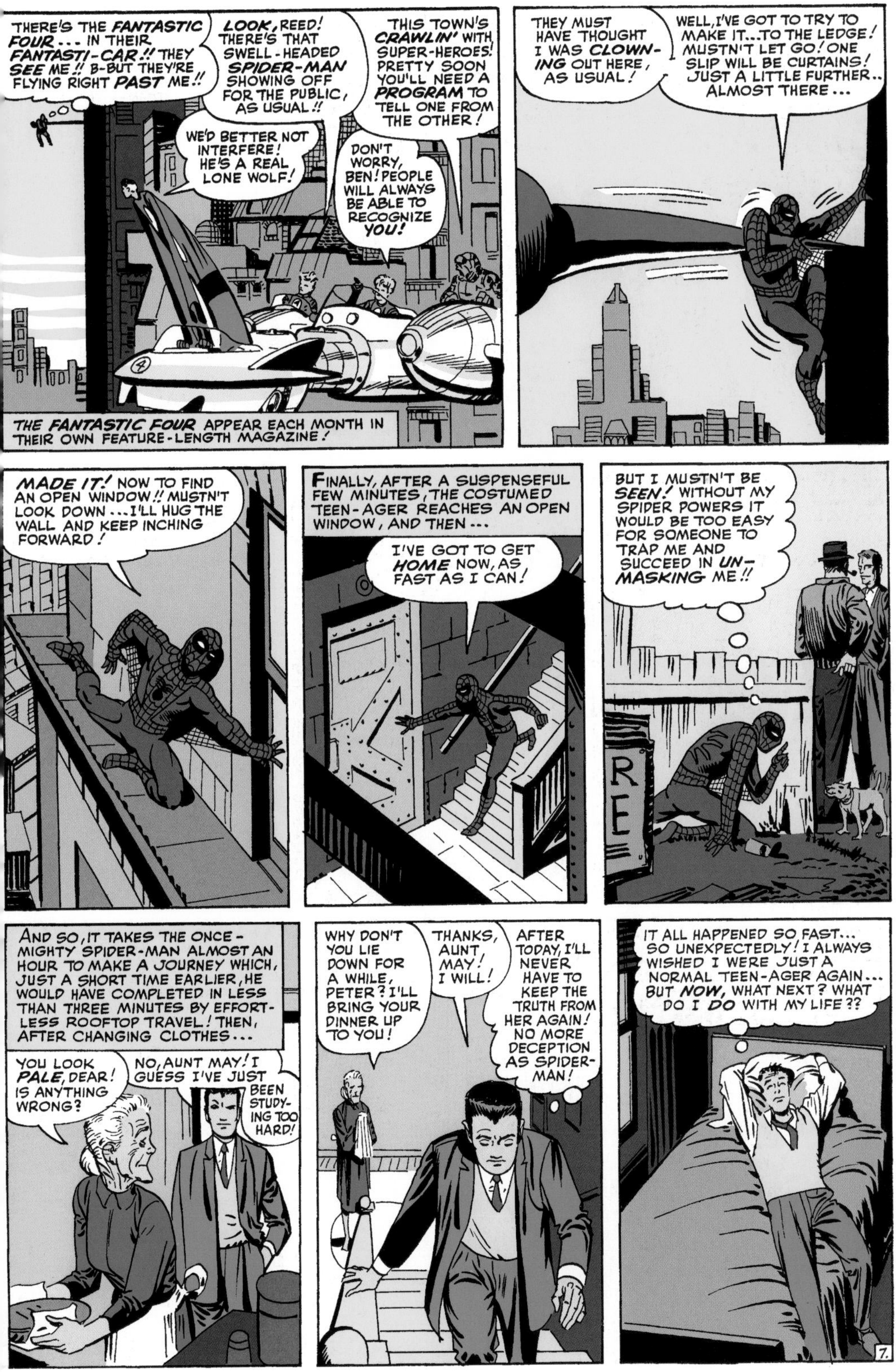
THERE'S THE FANTASTIC FOUR... IN THEIR FANTASTI-CAR!! THEY SEE ME!! B-BUT THEY'RE FLYING RIGHT PAST ME!!
LOOK, REED! THERE'S THAT SWELL-HEADED SPIDER-MAN SHOWING OFF FOR THE PUBLIC, AS USUAL!!
THIS TOWN'S CRAWLIN' WITH SUPER-HEROES! PRETTY SOON YOU'LL NEED A PROGRAM TO TELL ONE FROM THE OTHER!
WE'D BETTER NOT INTERFERE! HE'S A REAL LONE WOLF!
DON'T WORRY, BEN! PEOPLE WILL ALWAYS BE ABLE TO RECOGNIZE YOU!
THE FANTASTIC FOUR APPEAR EACH MONTH IN THEIR OWN FEATURE-LENGTH MAGAZINE!
THEY MUST HAVE THOUGHT I WAS CLOWNING OUT HERE, AS USUAL!
WELL, I'VE GOT TO TRY TO MAKE IT...TO THE LEDGE! MUSTN'T LET GO! ONE SLIP WILL BE CURTAINS! JUST A LITTLE FURTHER.. ALMOST THERE...
MADE IT! NOW TO FIND AN OPEN WINDOW!! MUSTN'T LOOK DOWN...I'LL HUG THE WALL AND KEEP INCHING FORWARD!
FINALLY, AFTER A SUSPENSEFUL FEW MINUTES, THE COSTUMED TEEN-AGER REACHES AN OPEN WINDOW, AND THEN...
I'VE GOT TO GET HOME NOW, AS FAST AS I CAN!
BUT I MUSTN'T BE SEEN! WITHOUT MY SPIDER POWERS IT WOULD BE TOO EASY FOR SOMEONE TO TRAP ME AND SUCCEED IN UN-MASKING ME!!
RE
AND SO, IT TAKES THE ONCE-MIGHTY SPIDER-MAN ALMOST AN HOUR TO MAKE A JOURNEY WHICH, JUST A SHORT TIME EARLIER, HE WOULD HAVE COMPLETED IN LESS THAN THREE MINUTES BY EFFORTLESS ROOFTOP TRAVEL! THEN, AFTER CHANGING CLOTHES...
YOU LOOK PALE, DEAR! IS ANYTHING WRONG?
NO, AUNT MAY! I GUESS I'VE JUST BEEN STUDYING TOO HARD!
WHY DON'T YOU LIE DOWN FOR A WHILE, PETER? I'LL BRING YOUR DINNER UP TO YOU!
THANKS, AUNT MAY! I WILL!
AFTER TODAY, I'LL NEVER HAVE TO KEEP THE TRUTH FROM HER AGAIN! NO MORE DECEPTION AS SPIDER-MAN!
IT ALL HAPPENED SO FAST... SO UNEXPECTEDLY! I ALWAYS WISHED I WERE JUST A NORMAL TEEN-AGER AGAIN... BUT NOW, WHAT NEXT? WHAT DO I DO WITH MY LIFE??
7.

MEANWHILE, AT THE HIDEOUT OF **DR. OCTOPUS**, THE "GUEST LIST" IS COMPLETED WITH THE ARRIVAL OF THE WINGED **VULTURE!**

NOW THAT WE'RE ALL HERE, WE'LL GET DOWN TO BUSINESS IMMEDIATELY! THIS MEETING WILL BE A TURNING POINT OF OUR CAREERS!

SKIP THE DRAMATIC SPEECHES, OCTOPUS! JUST STATE THE PLAN!

WHATEVER THE PLAN IS, **SAND-MAN** IS **FOR** IT! I CAN'T WAIT TO PAY SPIDER-MAN BACK!

WE **ALL** HAVE A SCORE TO SETTLE WITH THE ELUSIVE **SPIDER-MAN!**

HE DEFEATED ME **TWICE!** BUT THIS WILL BE **DIFFERENT!** THE **THIRD** VICTORY WILL BE **MINE!**

WE CAN'T BEAT HIM WITH **WORDS!** LET'S BAND TOGETHER AND **ATTACK** HIM! NOW!

HE'S TOO **FAST!** HE'D FIND **SOME** WAY TO ESCAPE US!

PERHAPS YOU'RE RIGHT! BUT THERE MUST BE A WAY TO **FORCE** HIM TO BATTLE US!

OF **COURSE** THERE IS! THAT'S THE PURPOSE OF THIS MEETING! NOW BE QUIET, ALL OF YOU! I HAVE IT ALL FIGURED OUT!

I SAY WE MUST ATTACK ALL AT **ONCE!** HIS POWER IS NOT GREAT ENOUGH TO DEFEAT ALL **SIX** OF US!

BAH! I'M WISE TO HIS TRICKS BY NOW! I CAN LICK HIM **ALONE** NEXT TIME WE MEET!

KRAVEN DOES NOT HUNT IN A PACK! ONLY BY A **SOLO** VICTORY WILL I ACHIEVE THE REVENGE I SEEK!

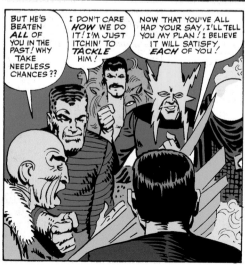

BUT HE'S BEATEN **ALL** OF YOU IN THE PAST! WHY TAKE NEEDLESS CHANCES??

I DON'T CARE **HOW** WE DO IT! I'M JUST ITCHIN' TO **TACKLE** HIM!

NOW THAT YOU'VE ALL HAD YOUR SAY, I'LL TELL YOU MY PLAN! I BELIEVE IT WILL SATISFY **EACH** OF YOU!

WE WILL EACH DRAW A NUMBER, AND WE WILL FIGHT HIM, ONE AT A TIME, IN THE ORDER OF THE DRAWING! I HAVE WORKED OUT A DETAILED SCHEME WHICH WILL **FORCE** HIM TO BATTLE US! NOW **DRAW!**

GOOD! ACTION AT **LAST!**

8

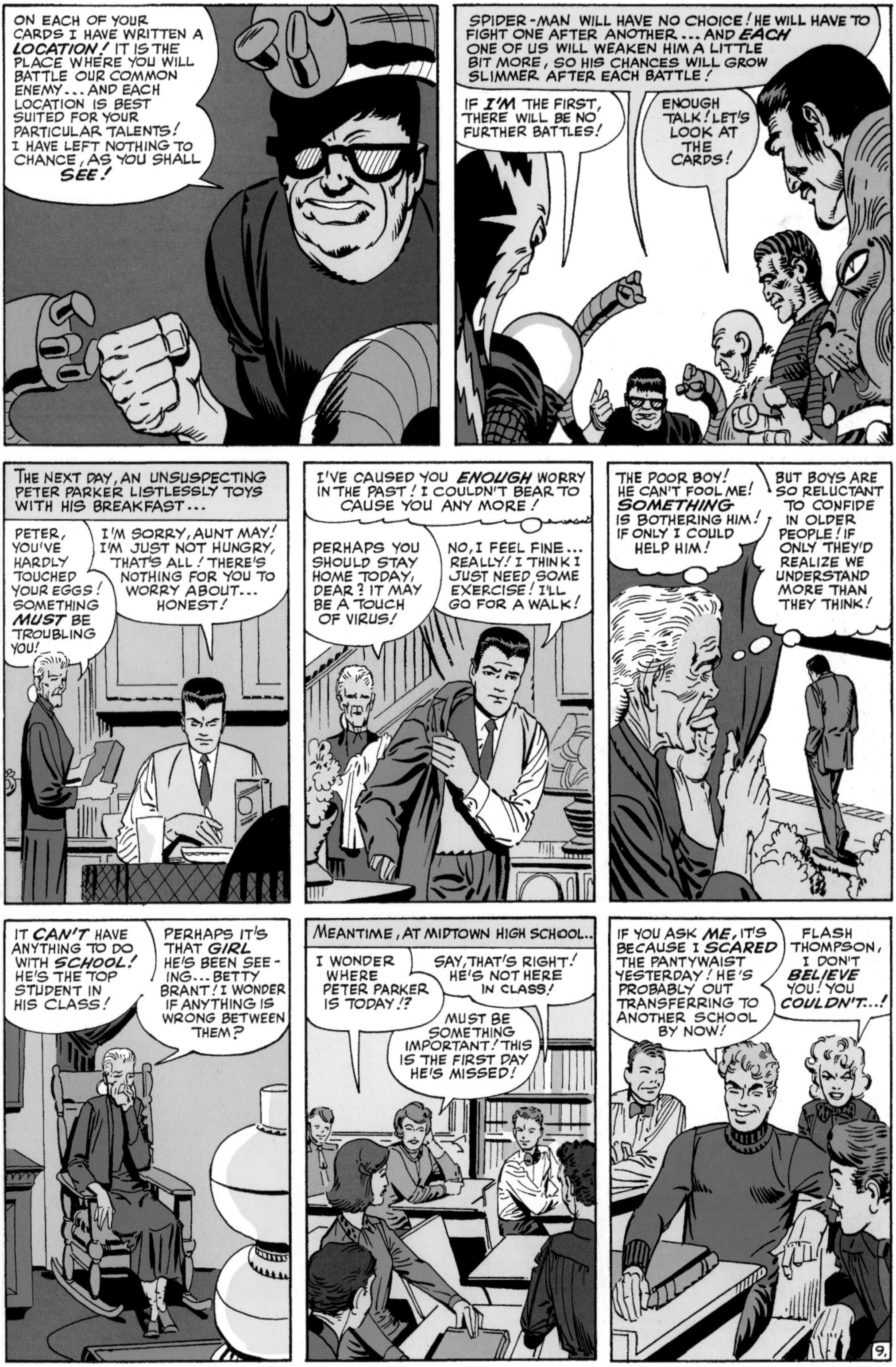
ON EACH OF YOUR CARDS I HAVE WRITTEN A LOCATION! IT IS THE PLACE WHERE YOU WILL BATTLE OUR COMMON ENEMY... AND EACH LOCATION IS BEST SUITED FOR YOUR PARTICULAR TALENTS! I HAVE LEFT NOTHING TO CHANCE, AS YOU SHALL SEE!
SPIDER-MAN WILL HAVE NO CHOICE! HE WILL HAVE TO FIGHT ONE AFTER ANOTHER... AND EACH ONE OF US WILL WEAKEN HIM A LITTLE BIT MORE, SO HIS CHANCES WILL GROW SLIMMER AFTER EACH BATTLE!
IF I'M THE FIRST, THERE WILL BE NO FURTHER BATTLES!
ENOUGH TALK! LET'S LOOK AT THE CARDS!
THE NEXT DAY, AN UNSUSPECTING PETER PARKER LISTLESSLY TOYS WITH HIS BREAKFAST...
PETER, YOU'VE HARDLY TOUCHED YOUR EGGS! SOMETHING MUST BE TROUBLING YOU!
I'M SORRY, AUNT MAY! I'M JUST NOT HUNGRY, THAT'S ALL! THERE'S NOTHING FOR YOU TO WORRY ABOUT... HONEST!
I'VE CAUSED YOU ENOUGH WORRY IN THE PAST! I COULDN'T BEAR TO CAUSE YOU ANY MORE!
PERHAPS YOU SHOULD STAY HOME TODAY, DEAR? IT MAY BE A TOUCH OF VIRUS!
NO, I FEEL FINE... REALLY! I THINK I JUST NEED SOME EXERCISE! I'LL GO FOR A WALK!
THE POOR BOY! HE CAN'T FOOL ME! SOMETHING IS BOTHERING HIM! IF ONLY I COULD HELP HIM!
BUT BOYS ARE SO RELUCTANT TO CONFIDE IN OLDER PEOPLE! IF ONLY THEY'D REALIZE WE UNDERSTAND MORE THAN THEY THINK!
IT CAN'T HAVE ANYTHING TO DO WITH SCHOOL! HE'S THE TOP STUDENT IN HIS CLASS!
PERHAPS IT'S THAT GIRL HE'S BEEN SEE-ING... BETTY BRANT! I WONDER IF ANYTHING IS WRONG BETWEEN THEM?
MEANTIME, AT MIDTOWN HIGH SCHOOL...
I WONDER WHERE PETER PARKER IS TODAY!?
SAY, THAT'S RIGHT! HE'S NOT HERE IN CLASS!
MUST BE SOMETHING IMPORTANT! THIS IS THE FIRST DAY HE'S MISSED!
IF YOU ASK ME, IT'S BECAUSE I SCARED THE PANTYWAIST YESTERDAY! HE'S PROBABLY OUT TRANSFERRING TO ANOTHER SCHOOL BY NOW!
FLASH THOMPSON, I DON'T BELIEVE YOU! YOU COULDN'T...!
9.

SURE I COULD, DOLLFACE! I KNEW YOU REALLY DIDN'T WANT PUNY PARKER BOTHERING YOU, BUT YOU WERE TOO SOFT-HEARTED TO **TELL** HIM SO!

OHH! OF ALL THE BRAINLESS, BRASH, CONCEITED BOYS I'VE EVER MET...

AND BACK AT PETER'S HOUSE ...

WHY, **NO**, MRS. PARKER! PETER DIDN'T COME TO SCHOOL TODAY! WE THOUGHT HE WAS HOME... WITH YOU!

OH, **DEAR!** NOW I JUST **KNOW** SOMETHING IS WRONG! HE'S NEVER PLAYED HOOKEY BEFORE! IT **MUST** HAVE SOMETHING TO DO WITH THAT BETTY BRANT!

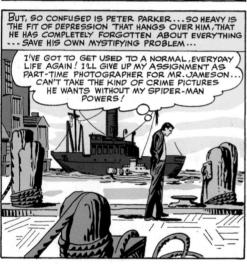

BUT, SO CONFUSED IS PETER PARKER...SO HEAVY IS THE FIT OF DEPRESSION THAT HANGS OVER HIM, THAT HE HAS *COMPLETELY* FORGOTTEN ABOUT EVERYTHING ... SAVE HIS OWN MYSTIFYING PROBLEM ...

I'VE GOT TO GET USED TO A NORMAL, EVERYDAY LIFE AGAIN! I'LL GIVE UP MY ASSIGNMENT AS PART-TIME PHOTOGRAPHER FOR MR. JAMESON... CAN'T TAKE THE KIND OF CRIME PICTURES HE WANTS WITHOUT MY SPIDER-MAN POWERS!

MAYBE I CAN EVEN FIND THE COURAGE TO TELL BETTY THE TRUTH ABOUT MYSELF! AFTER ALL, WHAT HARM CAN IT DO NOW?

HEY, **LOOK!** DO YOU SEE WHAT **I** SEE?

WOW! I NEVER EXPECTED TO SEE **THEM** IN REAL LIFE!

HURRY! LET'S GET A BETTER LOOK AT THEM!

IT'S **GIANT-MAN**... AND THE **WASP!** THEY'VE TRAPPED A GANG OF CRIMINALS!

ALL RIGHT, BOYS...THE PARTY'S OVER! BETTER PHONE FOR THE POLICE, WASP!

OKAY, BLUE EYES, BUT THIS TIME LET'S USE **YOUR** DIME! YOU ALWAYS FORGET TO PAY ME BACK FOR THOSE PHONE CALLS!

BUT, AS THE CROWD GATHERS AROUND THE TOWERING CRIME-FIGHTER ...

A FEW DAYS AGO I'D HAVE BEEN RIGHT IN THE CENTER OF THINGS! BUT NOW, I DON'T EVEN WANT TO BE **NEAR** ANY CRIMINALS!

GIANT-MAN AND THE *WASP* APPEAR MONTHLY IN *TALES TO ASTONISH*.

10.

AT THAT MOMENT, WAITING AT THE ENTRANCE OF THE *DAILY BUGLE* BUILDING, WE FIND...

MISS BETTY! MAY I SPEAK WITH YOU FOR A MOMENT?

WHY, MRS. PARKER, OF *COURSE* YOU MAY! I WAS JUST GOING FOR A CUP OF COFFEE!

WHILE TWO SINISTER FIGURES WATCH NEARBY...

THERE'S THAT BRANT GIRL NOW! BUT WHO'S THAT *WITH* HER?

WHAT'S THE DIFFERENCE?! WE'LL TAKE THEM *BOTH* IF WE HAVE TO! LET'S GO!

AND, AT THE WINDOW OF JONAH JAMESON'S PRIVATE OFFICE...

I FORGOT TO ASK BETTY BRANT FOR THE FRISBY FILE! MAYBE I CAN CALL TO HER FROM HERE!

SAY! WHAT'S GOING *ON* THERE ??!

SHE'S WITH PETER PARKER'S AUNT... BUT WHOSE *CAR* IS SHE GETTING INTO ?? I'D SWEAR THAT'S THE *SANDMAN*... WITH *ELECTRO* INSIDE!

WAIT! COME *BACK! STOP!!*

NO USE! THEY'VE *GONE!* BUT... *WHERE?!*

MINUTES LATER...

THEY'RE *HERE!* ALL RIGHT, VULTURE... GET GOING! YOU KNOW WHAT TO DO!

AH, MISS BRANT! COME IN! I'VE BEEN *EXPECTING* YOU! AND WHO IS THAT CHARMING LADY *WITH* YOU?

SHE SAYS SHE'S THE AUNT OF SOME KID NAMED PETER PARKER, DOC!

IT'S... *DOCTOR OCTOPUS!* WHY DID YOU HAVE US BROUGHT HERE?

A DOCTOR! HOW NICE! SUCH A CHARMING, SOFT-SPOKEN GENTLE-MAN!

YOU MEAN YOU HAVEN'T *HEARD* OF HIM?! DON'T LET HIS LOOKS *DECEIVE* YOU, MRS. PARKER!

NOW, NOW, DEAR... WE MUSTN'T BE PREJUDICED AGAINST THE POOR MAN JUST BECAUSE HE SEEMS TO HAVE SOME TROUBLE WITH HIS ARMS!

SIT DOWN, PLEASE ... MAKE YOUR-SELVES COMFORT-ABLE! I'LL HAVE MY ASSOCIATES BRING YOU SOME REFRESHMENTS!

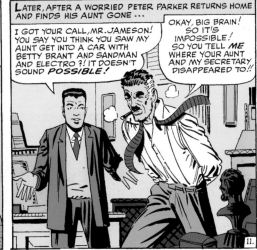

LATER, AFTER A WORRIED PETER PARKER RETURNS HOME AND FINDS HIS AUNT GONE...

I GOT YOUR CALL, MR. JAMESON! YOU SAY YOU THINK YOU SAW MY AUNT GET INTO A CAR WITH BETTY BRANT AND SANDMAN AND ELECTRO ?! IT DOESN'T SOUND *POSSIBLE!*

OKAY, BIG BRAIN! SO IT'S *IMPOSSIBLE!* SO YOU TELL *ME* WHERE YOUR AUNT AND MY SECRETARY DISAPPEARED TO!!

11.

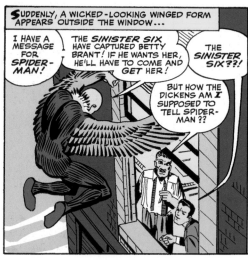

SUDDENLY, A WICKED-LOOKING WINGED FORM APPEARS OUTSIDE THE WINDOW...

I HAVE A MESSAGE FOR SPIDER-MAN!

THE SINISTER SIX HAVE CAPTURED BETTY BRANT! IF HE WANTS HER, HE'LL HAVE TO COME AND GET HER!

THE SINISTER SIX??!

BUT HOW THE DICKENS AM I SUPPOSED TO TELL SPIDER-MAN??

PUT A NOTICE IN YOUR PAPER! HE'S SURE TO READ IT! TELL HIM HE MUST GO TO THE STARK ELECTRIC PLANT... BUILDING #4!

ALL RIGHT, I'LL DO IT! BUT TAKE GOOD CARE OF MISS BRANT! GOOD SECRETARIES ARE HARD TO FIND NOWADAYS!

EVERYTHING'S FALLING IN PLACE! SIX OF MY OLD ENEMIES HAVE BANDED TOGETHER TO TRAP ME! THEY KNOW I WAS WILLING TO FIGHT FOR BETTY BRANT TWICE BEFORE!*

* SPIDER-MAN #11 AND #12...ED.

BUT WHAT CAN I DO NOW?? WHAT GOOD AM I WITHOUT MY SPIDER-POWERS?? HOW CAN I SAVE HER THIS TIME??

REMEMBER! SEE THAT SPIDER-MAN GETS OUR MESSAGE! ...OR WE'LL HOLD YOU ACCOUNTABLE!

I'LL PRINT IT IN MY PAPER, LIKE YOU ASK! BUT I CAN'T EVEN SWEAR THAT HE KNOWS HOW TO READ!

MY NEXT EDITION WON'T BE OUT FOR HOURS! MAYBE I CAN NOTIFY SPIDER-MAN FASTER BY CONTACTING SOME OF THE OTHER COSTUMED CLOWNS IN TOWN! THEY PROBABLY ALL BELONG TO THE SAME CLUB!

BUT IF THE SINISTER SIX ARE HOLDING AUNT MAY ALSO, WHAT WILL THE SHOCK DO TO HER! SHE'S JUST A FRAIL OLD WOMAN! I'VE GOT TO DO SOMETHING...BUT WHAT?!

OPERATOR! GET ME THE FANTASTIC FOUR! HOW SHOULD I KNOW? LOOK IN THE PHONE BOOK!

THEN, ACROSS TOWN, IN THE WORLD'S MOST FAMOUS SKYSCRAPER HEADQUARTERS...

SPIDER-MAN? NO, WE HAVEN'T SEEN HIM SINCE YESTERDAY WHEN HE WAS SITTING ON A FLAGPOLE OVER ON MADISON AVENUE! HOW DO I KNOW WHAT HE WAS DOING ON A FLAGPOLE?!

IF SOMEONE'S LOOKIN' FOR SPIDER-MAN, TRY THE AVENGERS! THOSE CORNBALLS ARE ALWAYS KEEPIN' TABS ON EVERYBODY!

WHAT'S WITH OL' WEB-HEAD LATELY? ALL OF A SUDDEN HE'S BECOME MR. POPULAR!

NEXT, AN ELECTRONIC CIRCUIT IS ACTIVATED AT AVENGERS HEADQUARTERS, AND...

I DON'T KNOW WHAT IT'S ALL ABOUT, BUT IT MIGHT BE IMPORTANT, CAP!

SORRY, I NEVER EVEN MET SPIDER-MAN! AND NONE OF MY TEAMMATES ARE HERE AT THE MOMENT!

CAPTAIN AMERICA APPEARS EACH MONTH IN THE AVENGERS.

12.

132

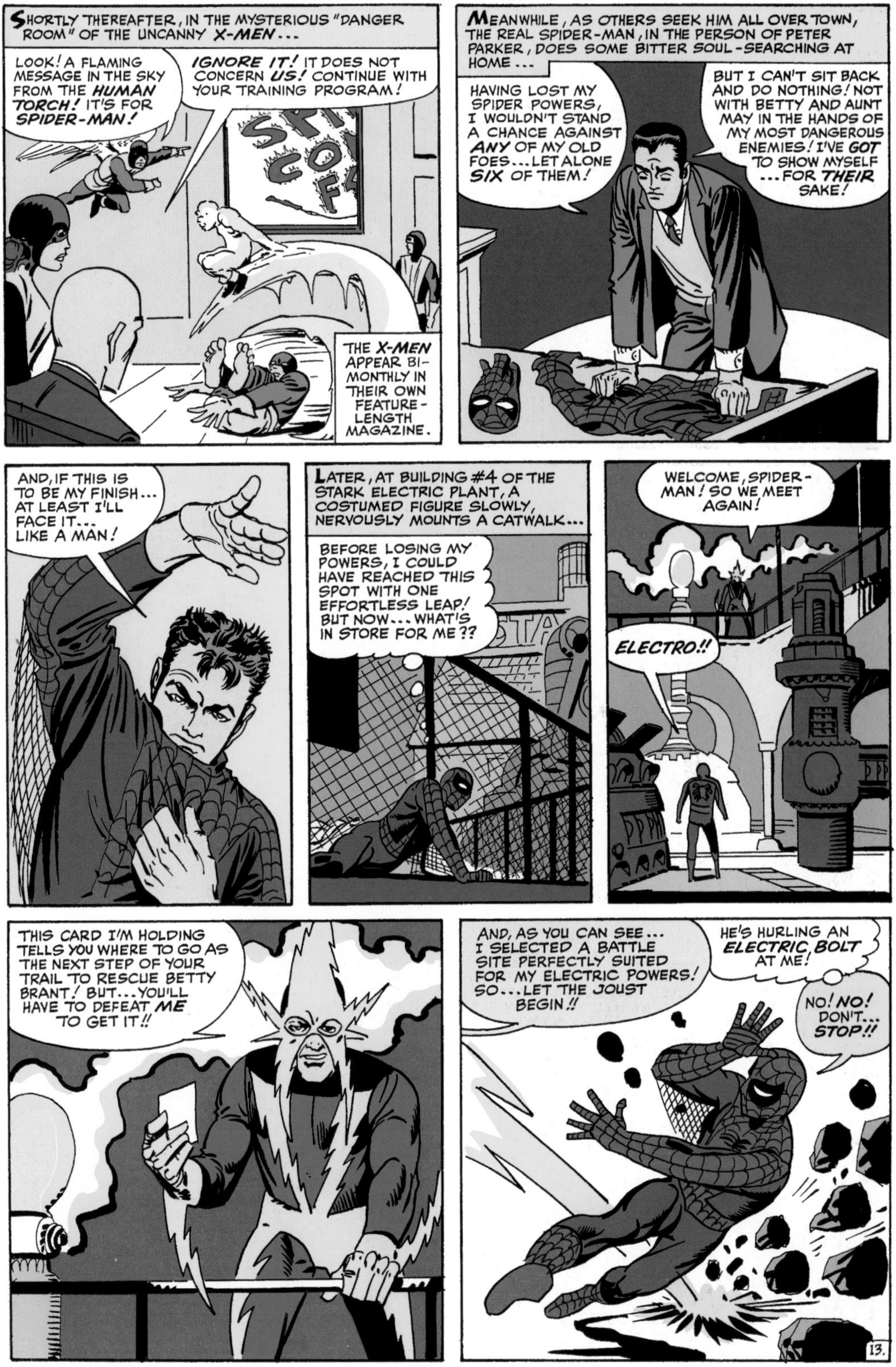
SHORTLY THEREAFTER, IN THE MYSTERIOUS "DANGER ROOM" OF THE UNCANNY X-MEN...
LOOK! A FLAMING MESSAGE IN THE SKY FROM THE HUMAN TORCH! IT'S FOR SPIDER-MAN!
IGNORE IT! IT DOES NOT CONCERN US! CONTINUE WITH YOUR TRAINING PROGRAM!
THE X-MEN APPEAR BI-MONTHLY IN THEIR OWN FEATURE-LENGTH MAGAZINE.
MEANWHILE, AS OTHERS SEEK HIM ALL OVER TOWN, THE REAL SPIDER-MAN, IN THE PERSON OF PETER PARKER, DOES SOME BITTER SOUL-SEARCHING AT HOME...
HAVING LOST MY SPIDER POWERS, I WOULDN'T STAND A CHANCE AGAINST ANY OF MY OLD FOES... LET ALONE SIX OF THEM!
BUT I CAN'T SIT BACK AND DO NOTHING! NOT WITH BETTY AND AUNT MAY IN THE HANDS OF MY MOST DANGEROUS ENEMIES! I'VE GOT TO SHOW MYSELF ...FOR THEIR SAKE!
AND, IF THIS IS TO BE MY FINISH... AT LEAST I'LL FACE IT... LIKE A MAN!
LATER, AT BUILDING #4 OF THE STARK ELECTRIC PLANT, A COSTUMED FIGURE SLOWLY, NERVOUSLY MOUNTS A CATWALK...
BEFORE LOSING MY POWERS, I COULD HAVE REACHED THIS SPOT WITH ONE EFFORTLESS LEAP! BUT NOW... WHAT'S IN STORE FOR ME??
WELCOME, SPIDER-MAN! SO WE MEET AGAIN!
ELECTRO!!
THIS CARD I'M HOLDING TELLS YOU WHERE TO GO AS THE NEXT STEP OF YOUR TRAIL TO RESCUE BETTY BRANT! BUT... YOU'LL HAVE TO DEFEAT ME TO GET IT!!
AND, AS YOU CAN SEE... I SELECTED A BATTLE SITE PERFECTLY SUITED FOR MY ELECTRIC POWERS! SO... LET THE JOUST BEGIN!!
HE'S HURLING AN ELECTRIC BOLT AT ME!
NO! NO! DON'T... STOP!!
13.

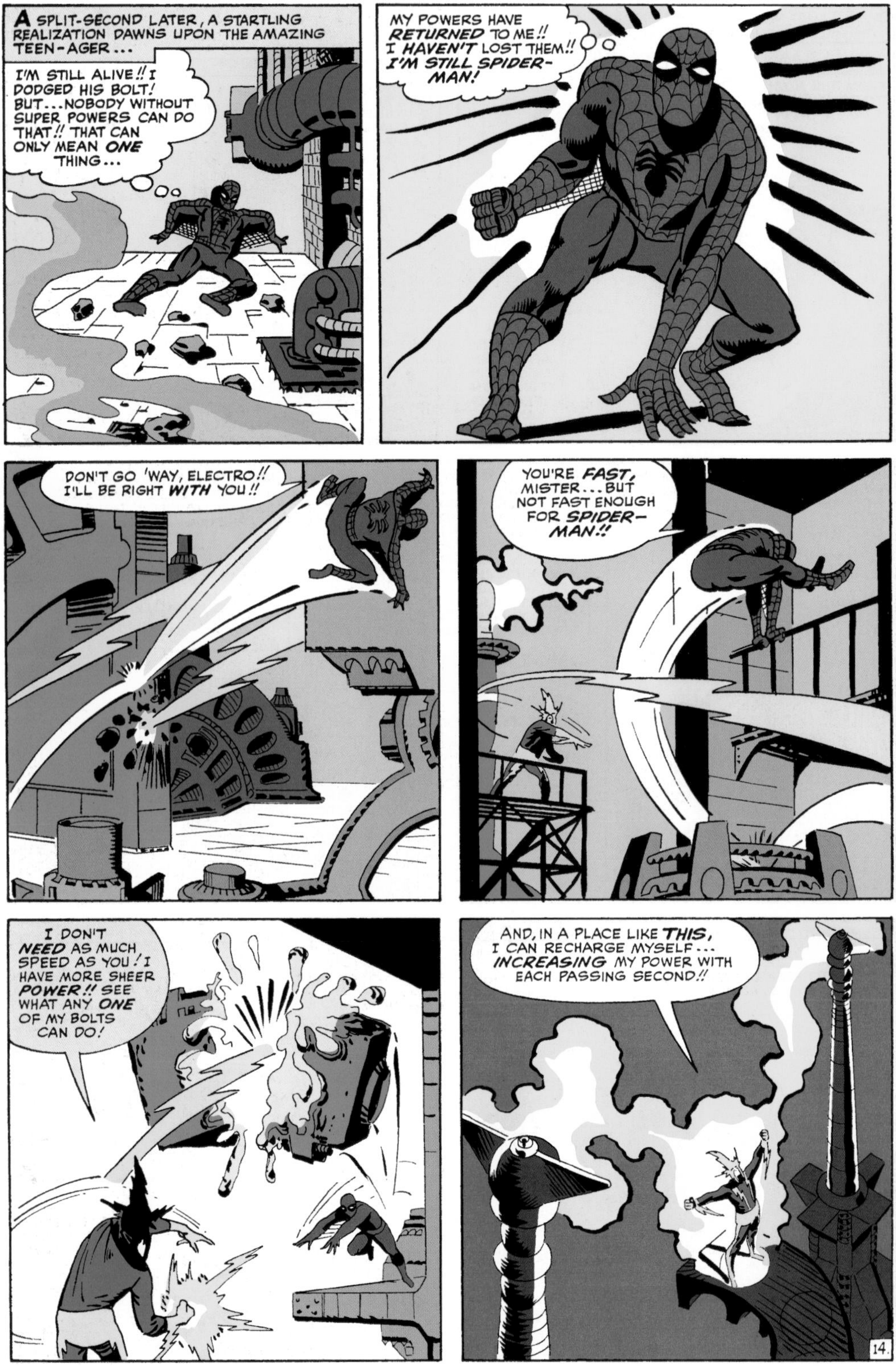
A SPLIT-SECOND LATER, A STARTLING REALIZATION DAWNS UPON THE AMAZING TEEN-AGER...
I'M STILL ALIVE!! I DODGED HIS BOLT! BUT...NOBODY WITHOUT SUPER POWERS CAN DO THAT!! THAT CAN ONLY MEAN ONE THING...
MY POWERS HAVE RETURNED TO ME!! I HAVEN'T LOST THEM!! I'M STILL SPIDER-MAN!
DON'T GO 'WAY, ELECTRO!! I'LL BE RIGHT WITH YOU!!
YOU'RE FAST, MISTER...BUT NOT FAST ENOUGH FOR SPIDER-MAN!!
I DON'T NEED AS MUCH SPEED AS YOU! I HAVE MORE SHEER POWER!! SEE WHAT ANY ONE OF MY BOLTS CAN DO!
AND, IN A PLACE LIKE THIS, I CAN RECHARGE MYSELF... INCREASING MY POWER WITH EACH PASSING SECOND!!
14.

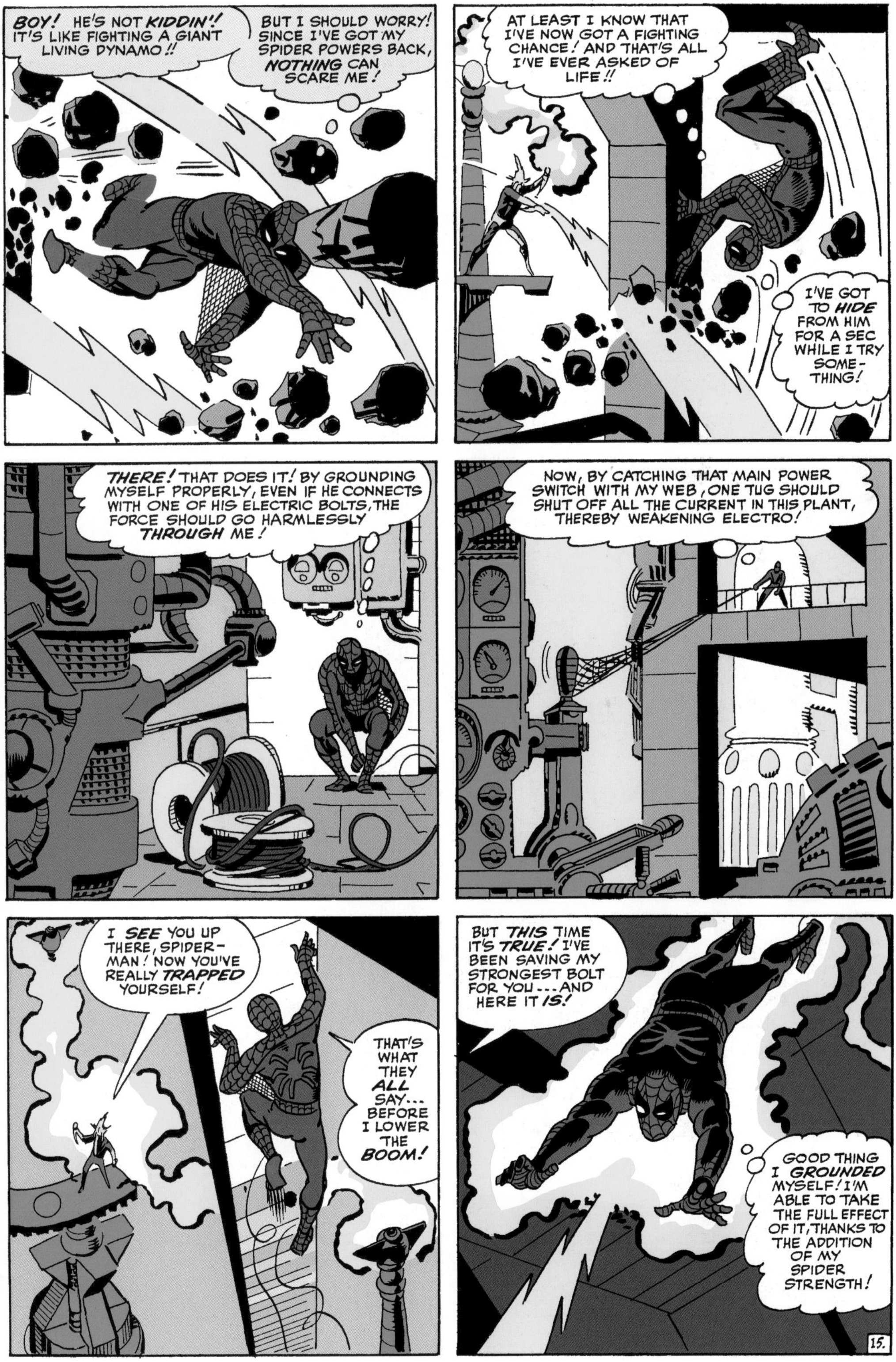
BOY! HE'S NOT KIDDIN'! IT'S LIKE FIGHTING A GIANT LIVING DYNAMO!!
BUT I SHOULD WORRY! SINCE I'VE GOT MY SPIDER POWERS BACK, NOTHING CAN SCARE ME!
AT LEAST I KNOW THAT I'VE NOW GOT A FIGHTING CHANCE! AND THAT'S ALL I'VE EVER ASKED OF LIFE!!
I'VE GOT TO HIDE FROM HIM FOR A SEC WHILE I TRY SOME-THING!
THERE! THAT DOES IT! BY GROUNDING MYSELF PROPERLY, EVEN IF HE CONNECTS WITH ONE OF HIS ELECTRIC BOLTS, THE FORCE SHOULD GO HARMLESSLY THROUGH ME!
NOW, BY CATCHING THAT MAIN POWER SWITCH WITH MY WEB, ONE TUG SHOULD SHUT OFF ALL THE CURRENT IN THIS PLANT, THEREBY WEAKENING ELECTRO!
I SEE YOU UP THERE, SPIDER-MAN! NOW YOU'VE REALLY TRAPPED YOURSELF!
THAT'S WHAT THEY ALL SAY... BEFORE I LOWER THE BOOM!
BUT THIS TIME IT'S TRUE! I'VE BEEN SAVING MY STRONGEST BOLT FOR YOU... AND HERE IT IS!
GOOD THING I GROUNDED MYSELF! I'M ABLE TO TAKE THE FULL EFFECT OF IT, THANKS TO THE ADDITION OF MY SPIDER STRENGTH!
15.

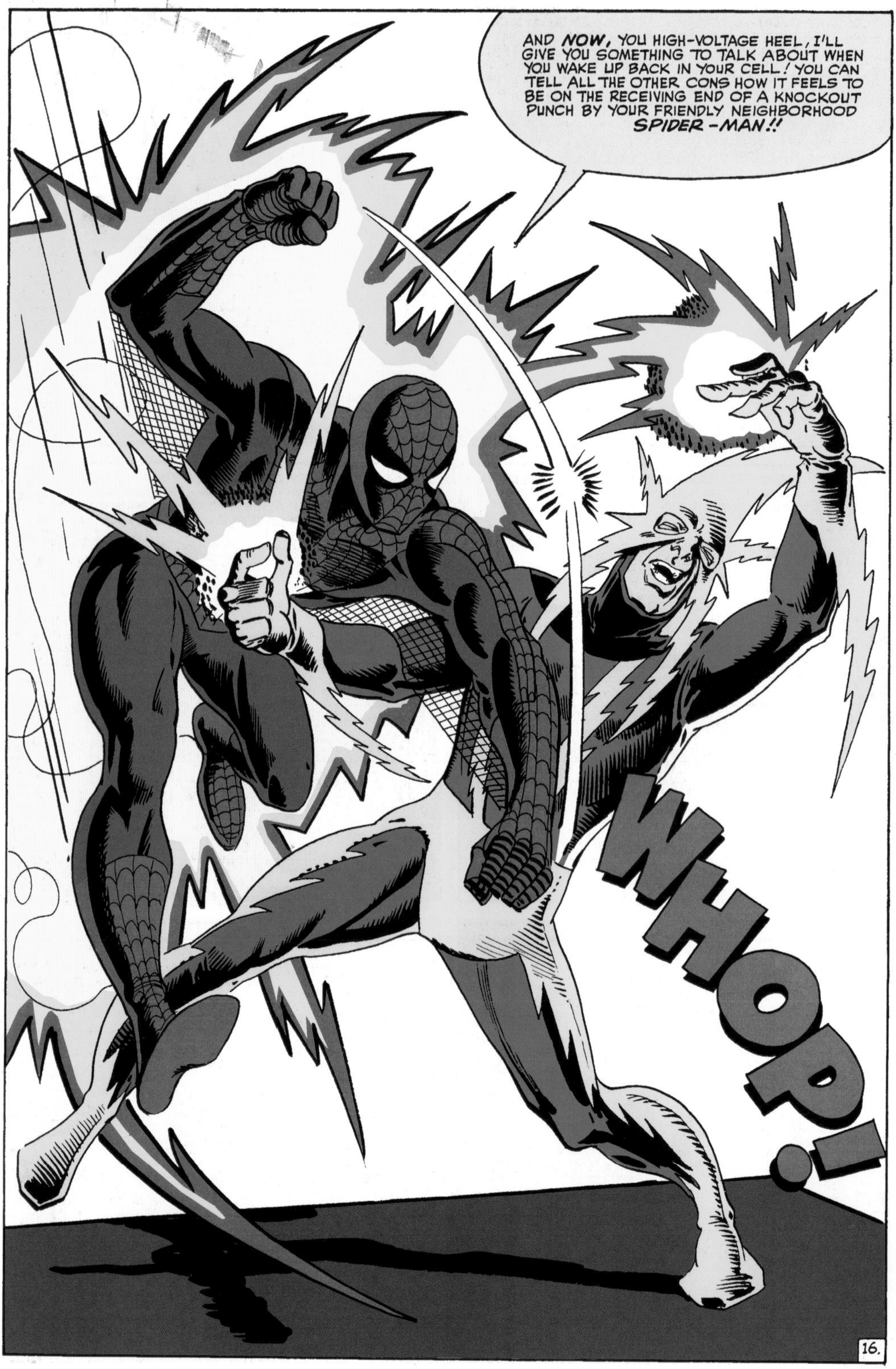
AND NOW, YOU HIGH-VOLTAGE HEEL, I'LL GIVE YOU SOMETHING TO TALK ABOUT WHEN YOU WAKE UP BACK IN YOUR CELL! YOU CAN TELL ALL THE OTHER CONS HOW IT FEELS TO BE ON THE RECEIVING END OF A KNOCKOUT PUNCH BY YOUR FRIENDLY NEIGHBORHOOD SPIDER-MAN!!
WHOP!
16.

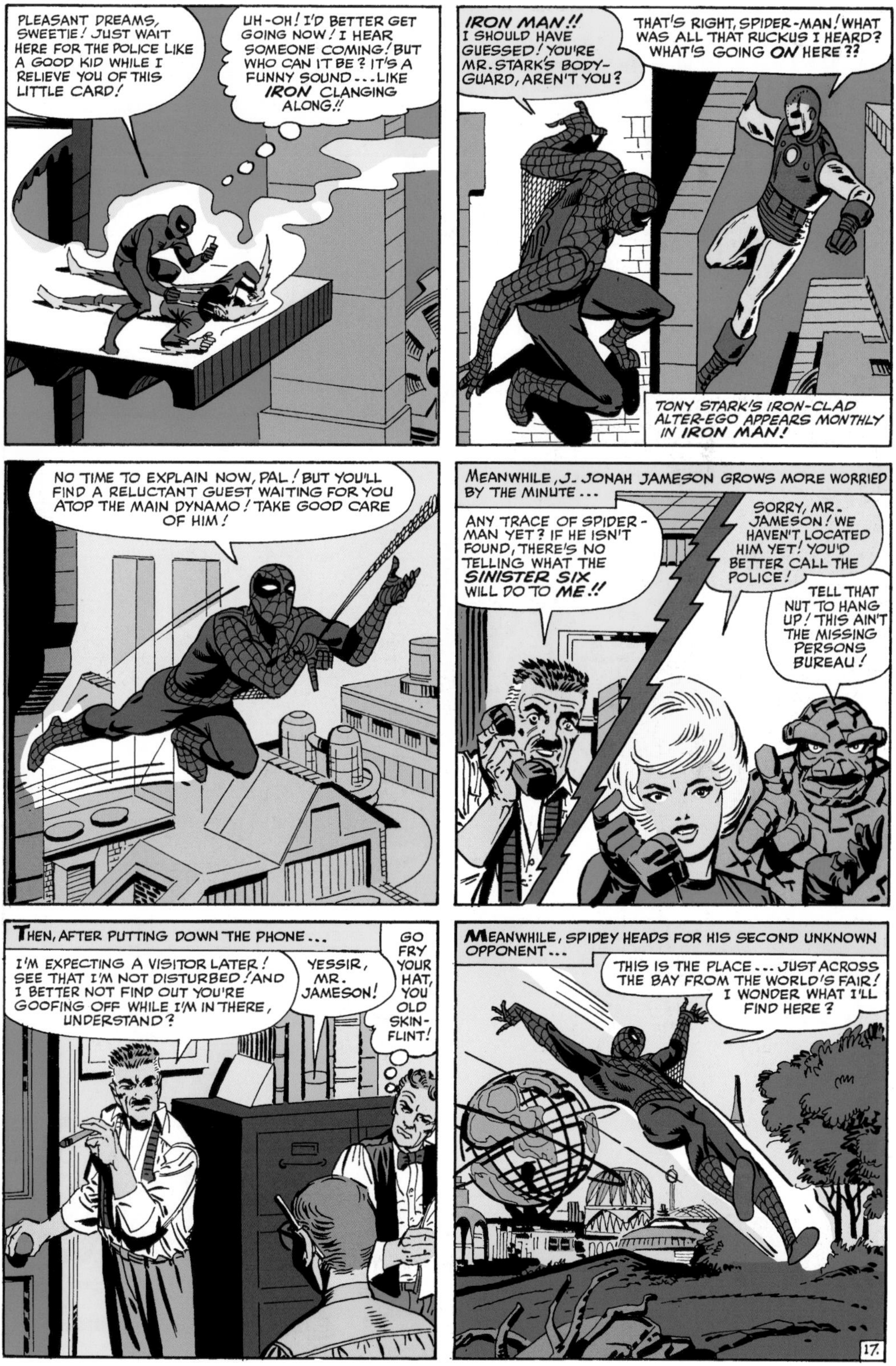
PLEASANT DREAMS, SWEETIE! JUST WAIT HERE FOR THE POLICE LIKE A GOOD KID WHILE I RELIEVE YOU OF THIS LITTLE CARD!
UH-OH! I'D BETTER GET GOING NOW! I HEAR SOMEONE COMING! BUT WHO CAN IT BE? IT'S A FUNNY SOUND...LIKE IRON CLANGING ALONG!!
IRON MAN!! I SHOULD HAVE GUESSED! YOU'RE MR. STARK'S BODY-GUARD, AREN'T YOU?
THAT'S RIGHT, SPIDER-MAN! WHAT WAS ALL THAT RUCKUS I HEARD? WHAT'S GOING ON HERE??
TONY STARK'S IRON-CLAD ALTER-EGO APPEARS MONTHLY IN IRON MAN!
NO TIME TO EXPLAIN NOW, PAL! BUT YOU'LL FIND A RELUCTANT GUEST WAITING FOR YOU ATOP THE MAIN DYNAMO! TAKE GOOD CARE OF HIM!
MEANWHILE, J. JONAH JAMESON GROWS MORE WORRIED BY THE MINUTE...
ANY TRACE OF SPIDER-MAN YET? IF HE ISN'T FOUND, THERE'S NO TELLING WHAT THE SINISTER SIX WILL DO TO ME!!
SORRY, MR. JAMESON! WE HAVEN'T LOCATED HIM YET! YOU'D BETTER CALL THE POLICE!
TELL THAT NUT TO HANG UP! THIS AIN'T THE MISSING PERSONS BUREAU!
THEN, AFTER PUTTING DOWN THE PHONE...
I'M EXPECTING A VISITOR LATER! SEE THAT I'M NOT DISTURBED! AND I BETTER NOT FIND OUT YOU'RE GOOFING OFF WHILE I'M IN THERE, UNDERSTAND?
YESSIR, MR. JAMESON!
GO FRY YOUR HAT, YOU OLD SKIN-FLINT!
MEANWHILE, SPIDEY HEADS FOR HIS SECOND UNKNOWN OPPONENT...
THIS IS THE PLACE...JUST ACROSS THE BAY FROM THE WORLD'S FAIR! I WONDER WHAT I'LL FIND HERE?
17.

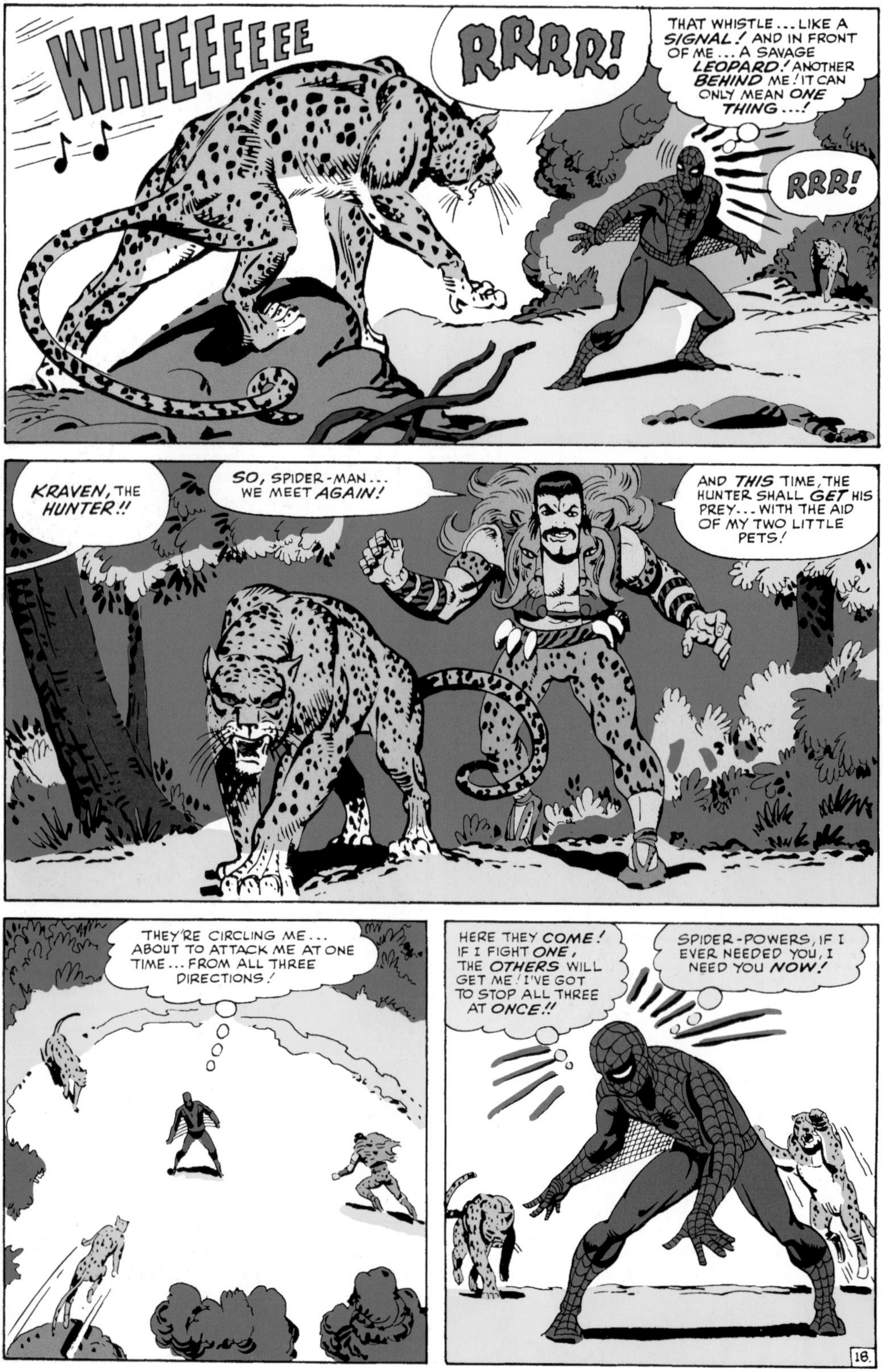

WHEEEEEEE
RRRR!
THAT WHISTLE... LIKE A SIGNAL! AND IN FRONT OF ME... A SAVAGE LEOPARD! ANOTHER BEHIND ME! IT CAN ONLY MEAN ONE THING...!
RRR!
KRAVEN, THE HUNTER!!
SO, SPIDER-MAN... WE MEET AGAIN!
AND THIS TIME, THE HUNTER SHALL GET HIS PREY... WITH THE AID OF MY TWO LITTLE PETS!
THEY'RE CIRCLING ME... ABOUT TO ATTACK ME AT ONE TIME... FROM ALL THREE DIRECTIONS!
HERE THEY COME! IF I FIGHT ONE, THE OTHERS WILL GET ME! I'VE GOT TO STOP ALL THREE AT ONCE!!
SPIDER-POWERS, IF I EVER NEEDED YOU, I NEED YOU NOW!
18.

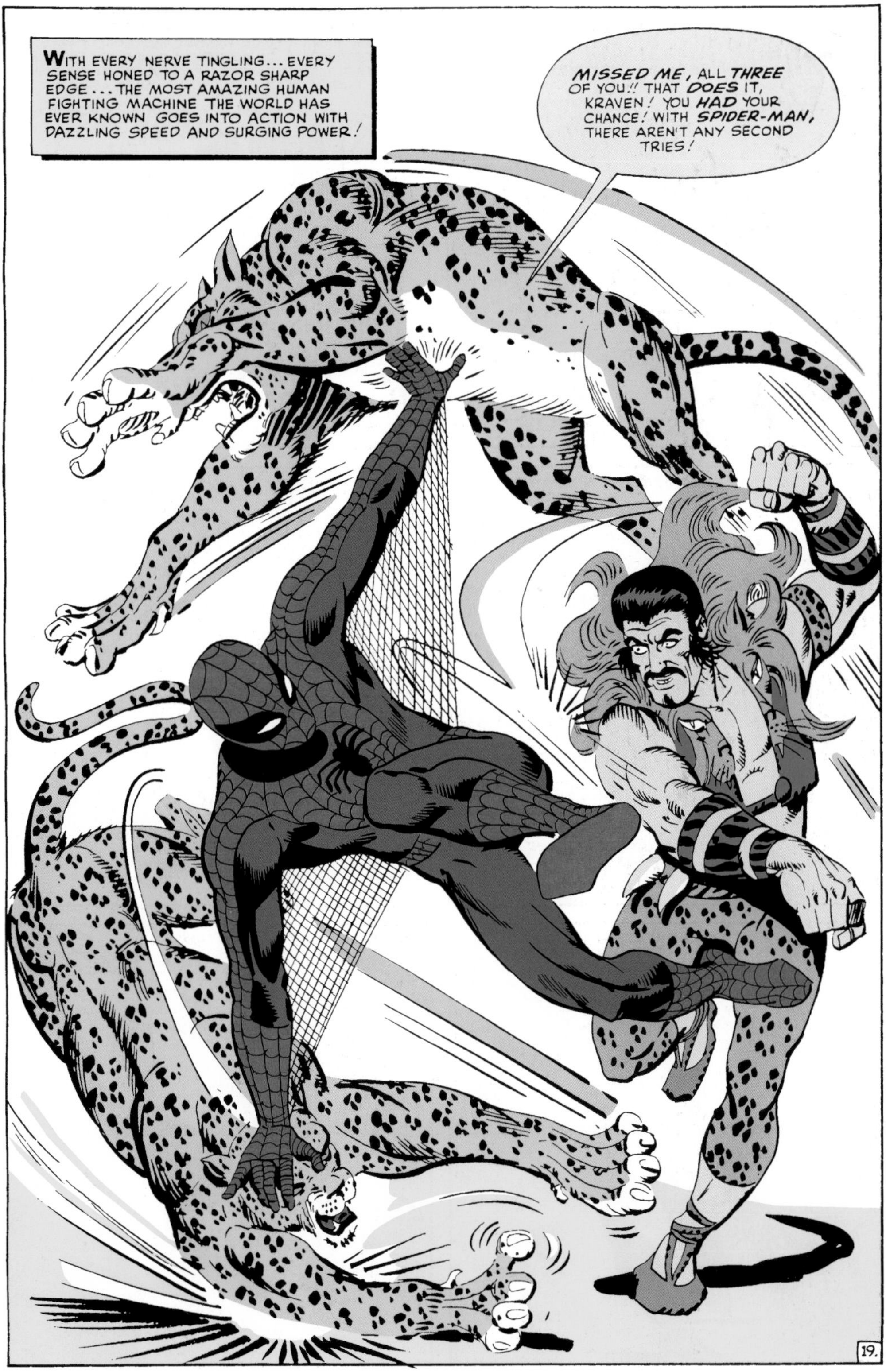
WITH EVERY NERVE TINGLING... EVERY SENSE HONED TO A RAZOR SHARP EDGE... THE MOST AMAZING HUMAN FIGHTING MACHINE THE WORLD HAS EVER KNOWN GOES INTO ACTION WITH DAZZLING SPEED AND SURGING POWER!
MISSED ME, ALL THREE OF YOU!! THAT DOES IT, KRAVEN! YOU HAD YOUR CHANCE! WITH SPIDER-MAN, THERE AREN'T ANY SECOND TRIES!
19.

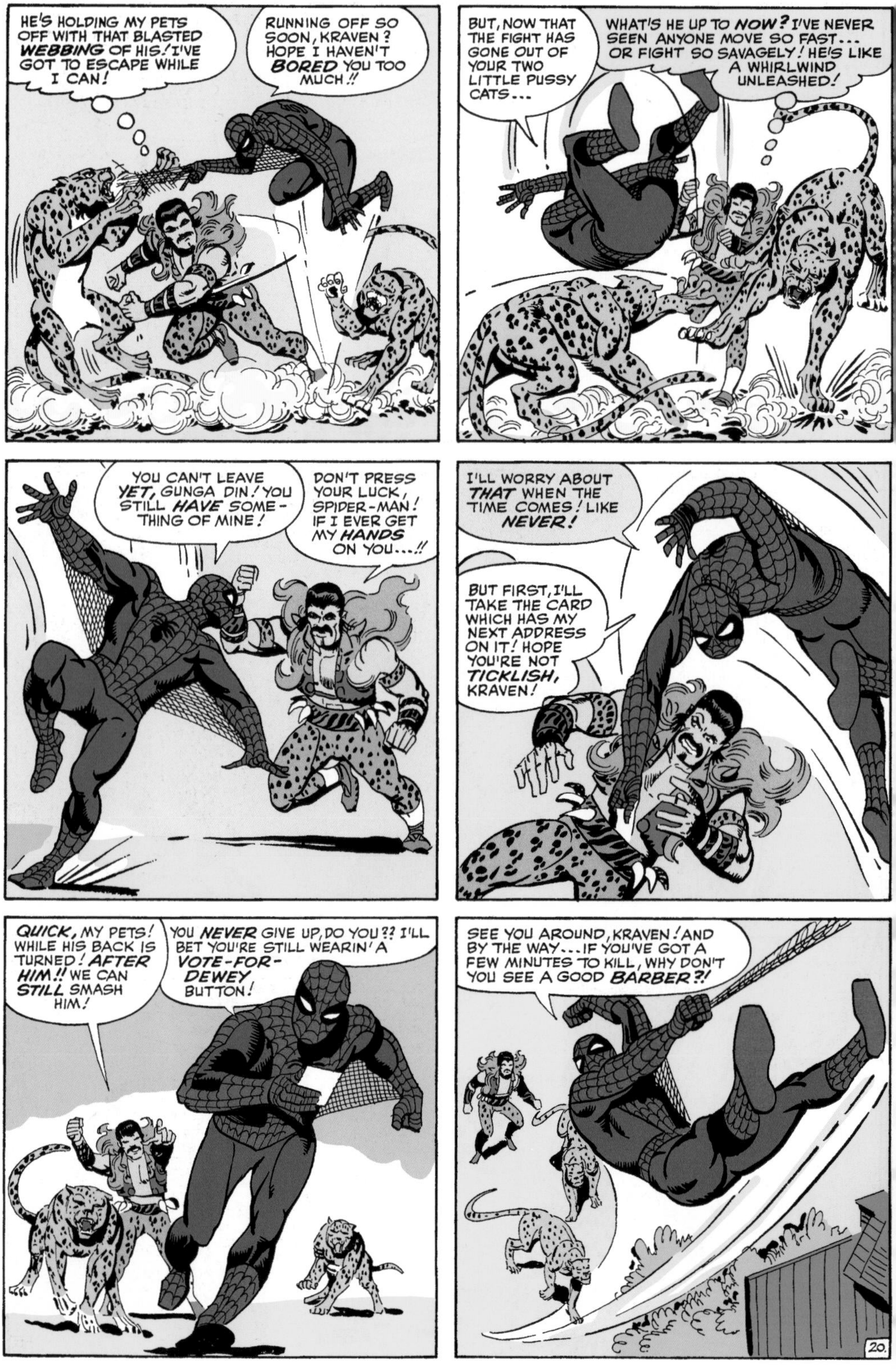
HE'S HOLDING MY PETS OFF WITH THAT BLASTED WEBBING OF HIS! I'VE GOT TO ESCAPE WHILE I CAN!
RUNNING OFF SO SOON, KRAVEN? HOPE I HAVEN'T BORED YOU TOO MUCH!!
BUT, NOW THAT THE FIGHT HAS GONE OUT OF YOUR TWO LITTLE PUSSY CATS...
WHAT'S HE UP TO NOW? I'VE NEVER SEEN ANYONE MOVE SO FAST... OR FIGHT SO SAVAGELY! HE'S LIKE A WHIRLWIND UNLEASHED!
YOU CAN'T LEAVE YET, GUNGA DIN! YOU STILL HAVE SOME-THING OF MINE!
DON'T PRESS YOUR LUCK, SPIDER-MAN! IF I EVER GET MY HANDS ON YOU...!!
I'LL WORRY ABOUT THAT WHEN THE TIME COMES! LIKE NEVER!
BUT FIRST, I'LL TAKE THE CARD WHICH HAS MY NEXT ADDRESS ON IT! HOPE YOU'RE NOT TICKLISH, KRAVEN!
QUICK, MY PETS! WHILE HIS BACK IS TURNED! AFTER HIM!! WE CAN STILL SMASH HIM!
YOU NEVER GIVE UP, DO YOU?? I'LL BET YOU'RE STILL WEARIN' A VOTE-FOR-DEWEY BUTTON!
SEE YOU AROUND, KRAVEN! AND BY THE WAY... IF YOU'VE GOT A FEW MINUTES TO KILL, WHY DON'T YOU SEE A GOOD BARBER?!
20.

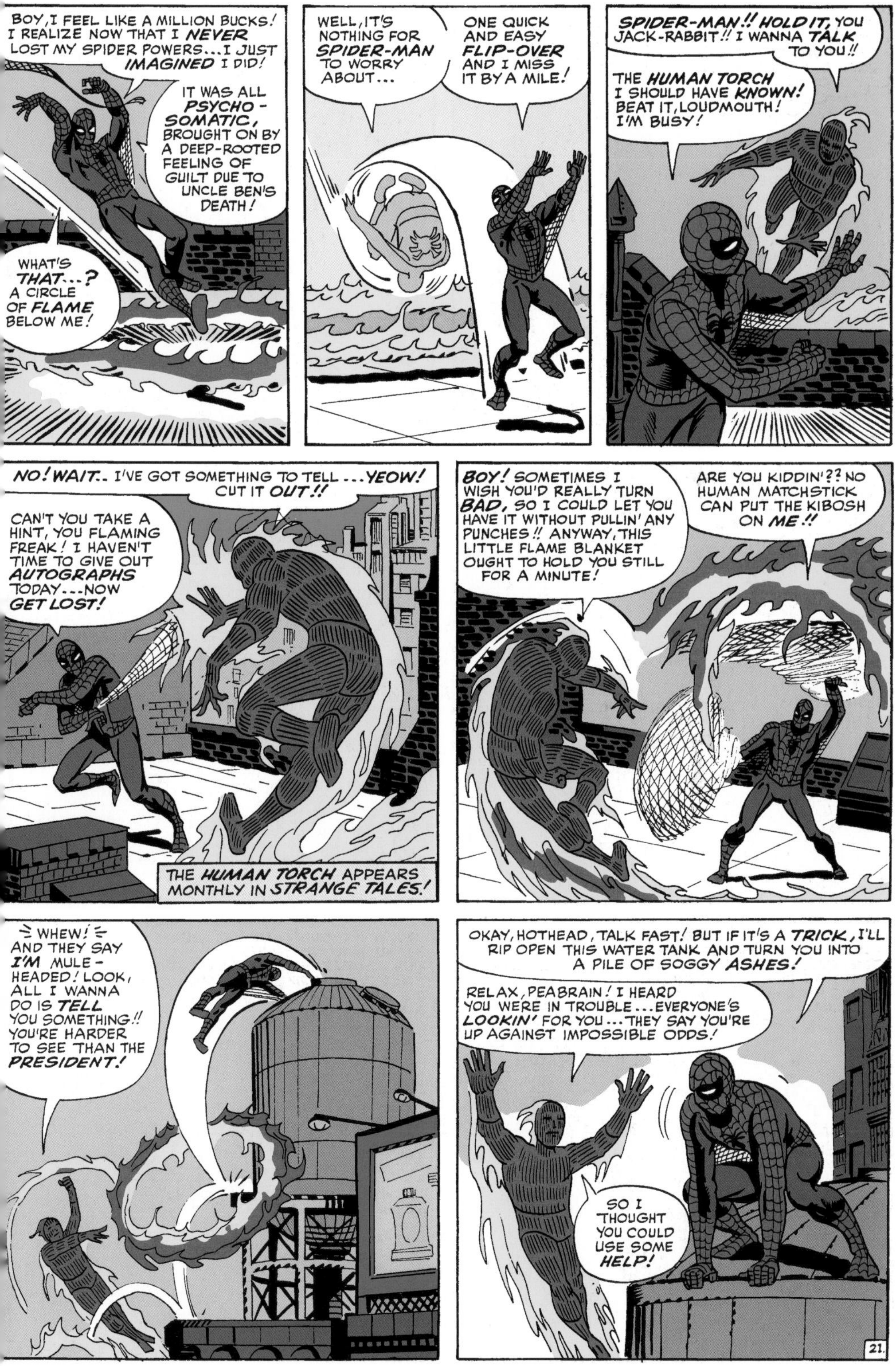
BOY, I FEEL LIKE A MILLION BUCKS! I REALIZE NOW THAT I NEVER LOST MY SPIDER POWERS... I JUST IMAGINED I DID!
IT WAS ALL PSYCHO-SOMATIC, BROUGHT ON BY A DEEP-ROOTED FEELING OF GUILT DUE TO UNCLE BEN'S DEATH!
WHAT'S THAT...? A CIRCLE OF FLAME BELOW ME!
WELL, IT'S NOTHING FOR SPIDER-MAN TO WORRY ABOUT...
ONE QUICK AND EASY FLIP-OVER AND I MISS IT BY A MILE!
SPIDER-MAN!! HOLD IT, YOU JACK-RABBIT!! I WANNA TALK TO YOU!!
THE HUMAN TORCH I SHOULD HAVE KNOWN! BEAT IT, LOUDMOUTH! I'M BUSY!
NO! WAIT.. I'VE GOT SOMETHING TO TELL ...YEOW! CUT IT OUT!!
CAN'T YOU TAKE A HINT, YOU FLAMING FREAK! I HAVEN'T TIME TO GIVE OUT AUTOGRAPHS TODAY---NOW GET LOST!
THE HUMAN TORCH APPEARS MONTHLY IN STRANGE TALES!
BOY! SOMETIMES I WISH YOU'D REALLY TURN BAD, SO I COULD LET YOU HAVE IT WITHOUT PULLIN' ANY PUNCHES!! ANYWAY, THIS LITTLE FLAME BLANKET OUGHT TO HOLD YOU STILL FOR A MINUTE!
ARE YOU KIDDIN'?? NO HUMAN MATCHSTICK CAN PUT THE KIBOSH ON ME!!
WHEW! AND THEY SAY I'M MULE-HEADED! LOOK, ALL I WANNA DO IS TELL YOU SOMETHING!! YOU'RE HARDER TO SEE THAN THE PRESIDENT!
OKAY, HOTHEAD, TALK FAST! BUT IF IT'S A TRICK, I'LL RIP OPEN THIS WATER TANK AND TURN YOU INTO A PILE OF SOGGY ASHES!
RELAX, PEABRAIN! I HEARD YOU WERE IN TROUBLE... EVERYONE'S LOOKIN' FOR YOU... THEY SAY YOU'RE UP AGAINST IMPOSSIBLE ODDS!
SO I THOUGHT YOU COULD USE SOME HELP!
21.

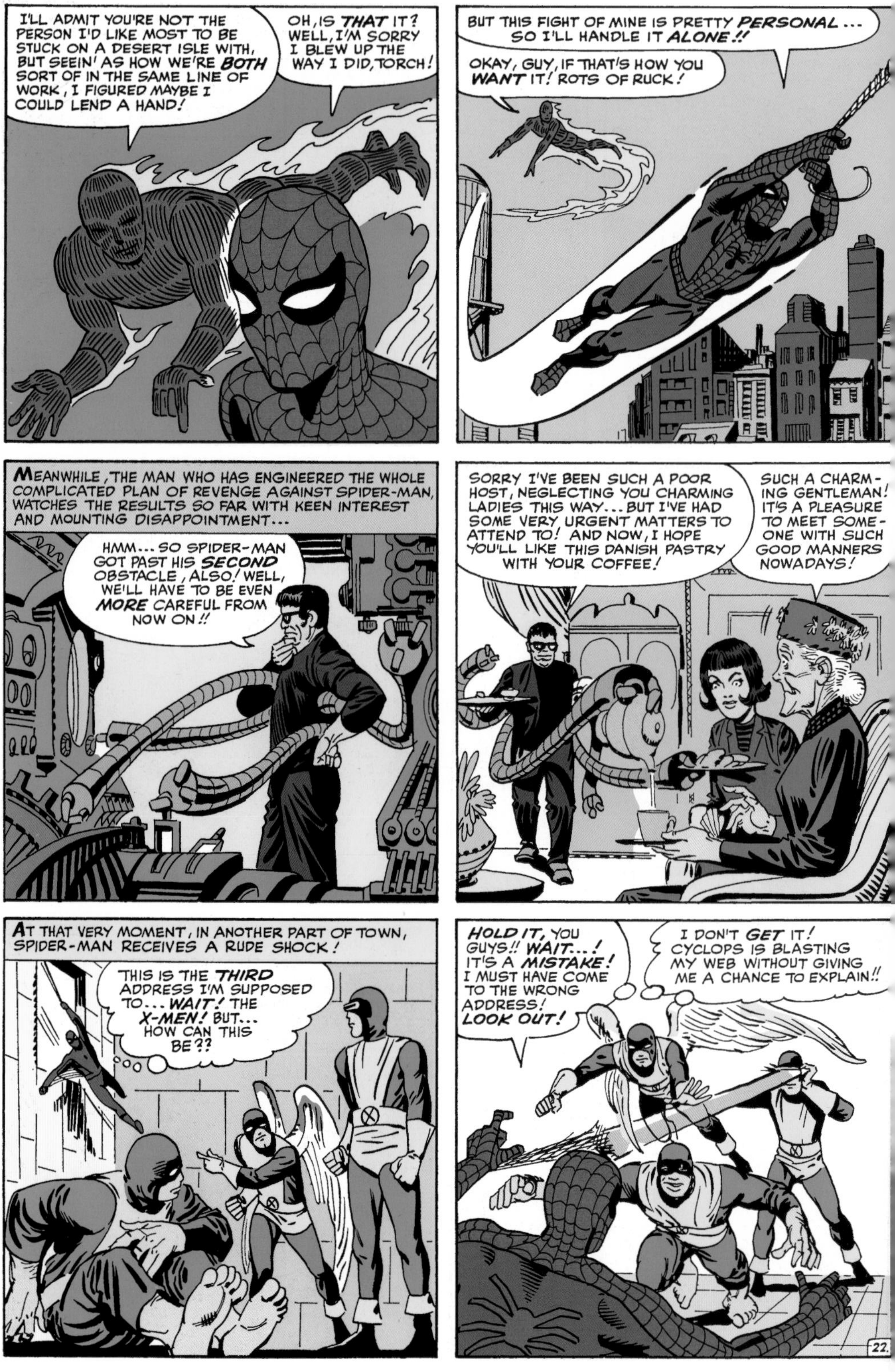
I'LL ADMIT YOU'RE NOT THE PERSON I'D LIKE MOST TO BE STUCK ON A DESERT ISLE WITH, BUT SEEIN' AS HOW WE'RE BOTH SORT OF IN THE SAME LINE OF WORK, I FIGURED MAYBE I COULD LEND A HAND!
OH, IS THAT IT? WELL, I'M SORRY I BLEW UP THE WAY I DID, TORCH!
BUT THIS FIGHT OF MINE IS PRETTY PERSONAL... SO I'LL HANDLE IT ALONE!!
OKAY, GUY, IF THAT'S HOW YOU WANT IT! ROTS OF RUCK!
MEANWHILE, THE MAN WHO HAS ENGINEERED THE WHOLE COMPLICATED PLAN OF REVENGE AGAINST SPIDER-MAN, WATCHES THE RESULTS SO FAR WITH KEEN INTEREST AND MOUNTING DISAPPOINTMENT...
HMM... SO SPIDER-MAN GOT PAST HIS SECOND OBSTACLE, ALSO! WELL, WE'LL HAVE TO BE EVEN MORE CAREFUL FROM NOW ON!!
SORRY I'VE BEEN SUCH A POOR HOST, NEGLECTING YOU CHARMING LADIES THIS WAY... BUT I'VE HAD SOME VERY URGENT MATTERS TO ATTEND TO! AND NOW, I HOPE YOU'LL LIKE THIS DANISH PASTRY WITH YOUR COFFEE!
SUCH A CHARMING GENTLEMAN! IT'S A PLEASURE TO MEET SOMEONE WITH SUCH GOOD MANNERS NOWADAYS!
AT THAT VERY MOMENT, IN ANOTHER PART OF TOWN, SPIDER-MAN RECEIVES A RUDE SHOCK!
THIS IS THE THIRD ADDRESS I'M SUPPOSED TO... WAIT! THE X-MEN! BUT... HOW CAN THIS BE??
HOLD IT, YOU GUYS!! WAIT...! IT'S A MISTAKE! I MUST HAVE COME TO THE WRONG ADDRESS! LOOK OUT!
I DON'T GET IT! CYCLOPS IS BLASTING MY WEB WITHOUT GIVING ME A CHANCE TO EXPLAIN!!
22

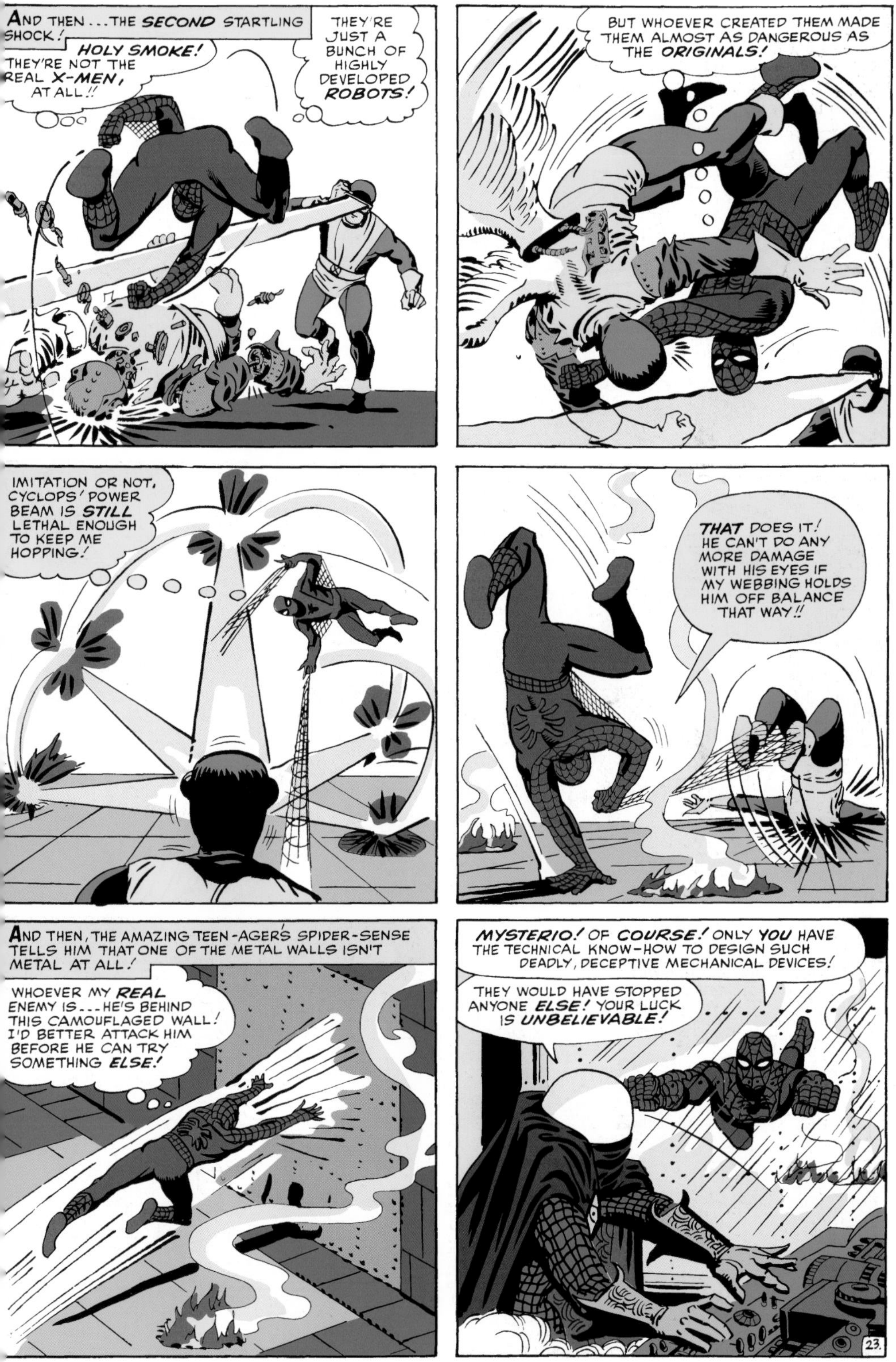
AND THEN... THE SECOND STARTLING SHOCK!
HOLY SMOKE! THEY'RE NOT THE REAL X-MEN, AT ALL!!
THEY'RE JUST A BUNCH OF HIGHLY DEVELOPED ROBOTS!
BUT WHOEVER CREATED THEM MADE THEM ALMOST AS DANGEROUS AS THE ORIGINALS!
IMITATION OR NOT, CYCLOPS' POWER BEAM IS STILL LETHAL ENOUGH TO KEEP ME HOPPING!
THAT DOES IT! HE CAN'T DO ANY MORE DAMAGE WITH HIS EYES IF MY WEBBING HOLDS HIM OFF BALANCE THAT WAY!!
AND THEN, THE AMAZING TEEN-AGER'S SPIDER-SENSE TELLS HIM THAT ONE OF THE METAL WALLS ISN'T METAL AT ALL!
WHOEVER MY REAL ENEMY IS... HE'S BEHIND THIS CAMOUFLAGED WALL! I'D BETTER ATTACK HIM BEFORE HE CAN TRY SOMETHING ELSE!
MYSTERIO! OF COURSE! ONLY YOU HAVE THE TECHNICAL KNOW-HOW TO DESIGN SUCH DEADLY, DECEPTIVE MECHANICAL DEVICES!
THEY WOULD HAVE STOPPED ANYONE ELSE! YOUR LUCK IS UNBELIEVABLE!
23.

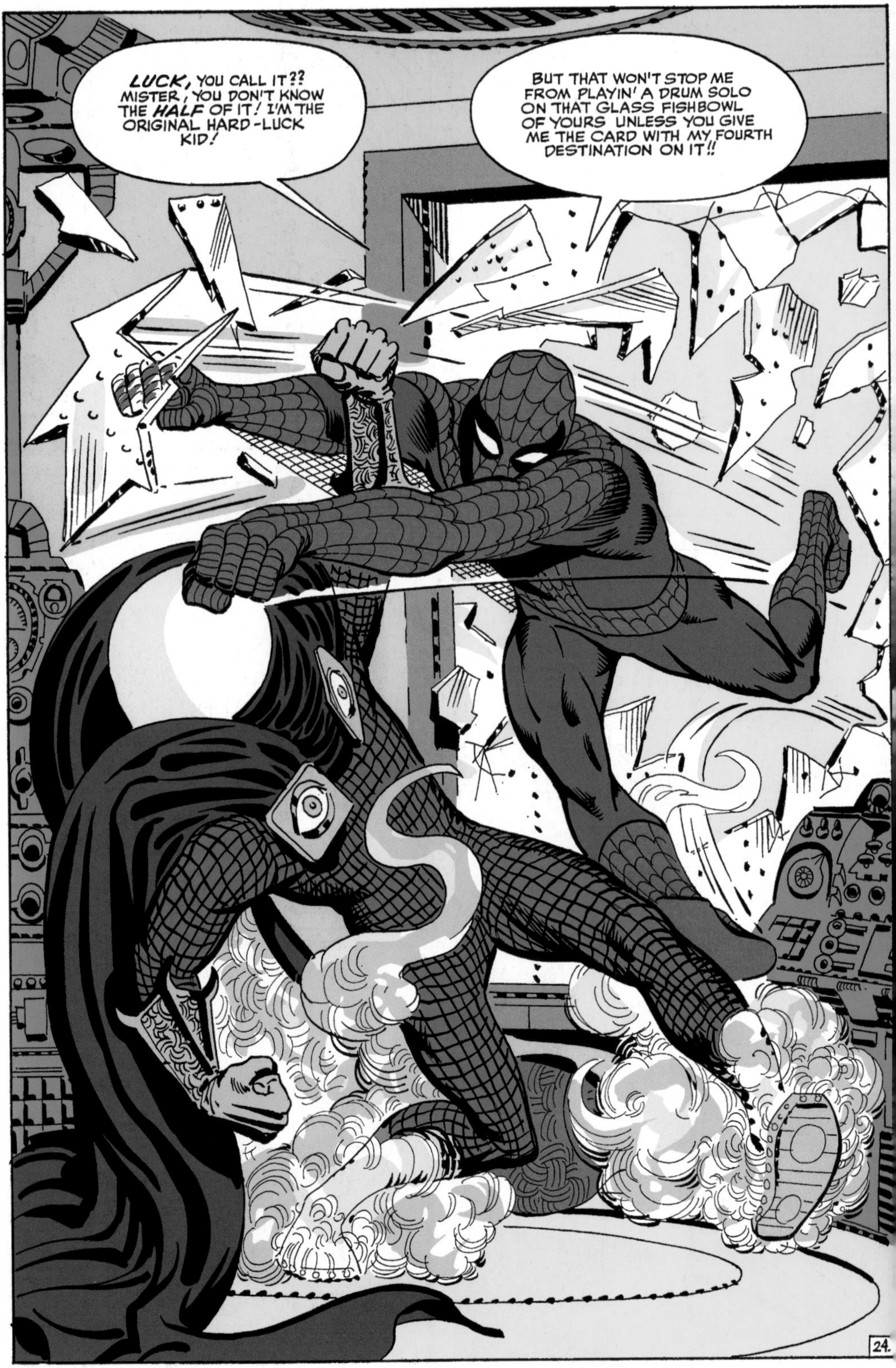
LUCK, YOU CALL IT?? MISTER, YOU DON'T KNOW THE HALF OF IT! I'M THE ORIGINAL HARD-LUCK KID!
BUT THAT WON'T STOP ME FROM PLAYIN' A DRUM SOLO ON THAT GLASS FISHBOWL OF YOURS UNLESS YOU GIVE ME THE CARD WITH MY FOURTH DESTINATION ON IT!!
24.

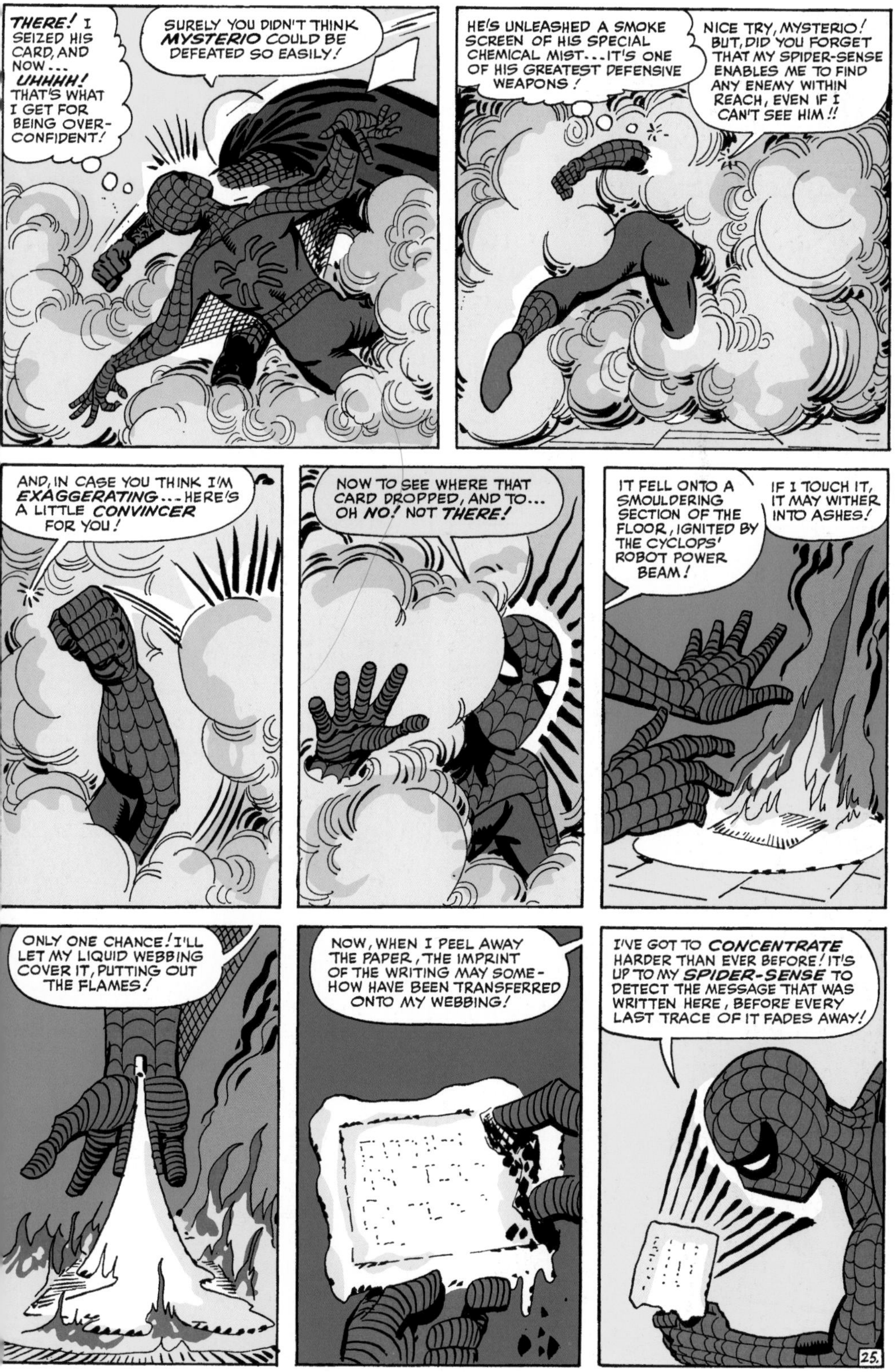
THERE! I SEIZED HIS CARD, AND NOW... UHHHH! THAT'S WHAT I GET FOR BEING OVER-CONFIDENT!
SURELY YOU DIDN'T THINK MYSTERIO COULD BE DEFEATED SO EASILY!
HE'S UNLEASHED A SMOKE SCREEN OF HIS SPECIAL CHEMICAL MIST... IT'S ONE OF HIS GREATEST DEFENSIVE WEAPONS!
NICE TRY, MYSTERIO! BUT, DID YOU FORGET THAT MY SPIDER-SENSE ENABLES ME TO FIND ANY ENEMY WITHIN REACH, EVEN IF I CAN'T SEE HIM!!
AND, IN CASE YOU THINK I'M EXAGGERATING... HERE'S A LITTLE CONVINCER FOR YOU!
NOW TO SEE WHERE THAT CARD DROPPED, AND TO... OH NO! NOT THERE!
IT FELL ONTO A SMOULDERING SECTION OF THE FLOOR, IGNITED BY THE CYCLOPS' ROBOT POWER BEAM!
IF I TOUCH IT, IT MAY WITHER INTO ASHES!
ONLY ONE CHANCE! I'LL LET MY LIQUID WEBBING COVER IT, PUTTING OUT THE FLAMES!
NOW, WHEN I PEEL AWAY THE PAPER, THE IMPRINT OF THE WRITING MAY SOME-HOW HAVE BEEN TRANSFERRED ONTO MY WEBBING!
I'VE GOT TO CONCENTRATE HARDER THAN EVER BEFORE! IT'S UP TO MY SPIDER-SENSE TO DETECT THE MESSAGE THAT WAS WRITTEN HERE, BEFORE EVERY LAST TRACE OF IT FADES AWAY!
25.

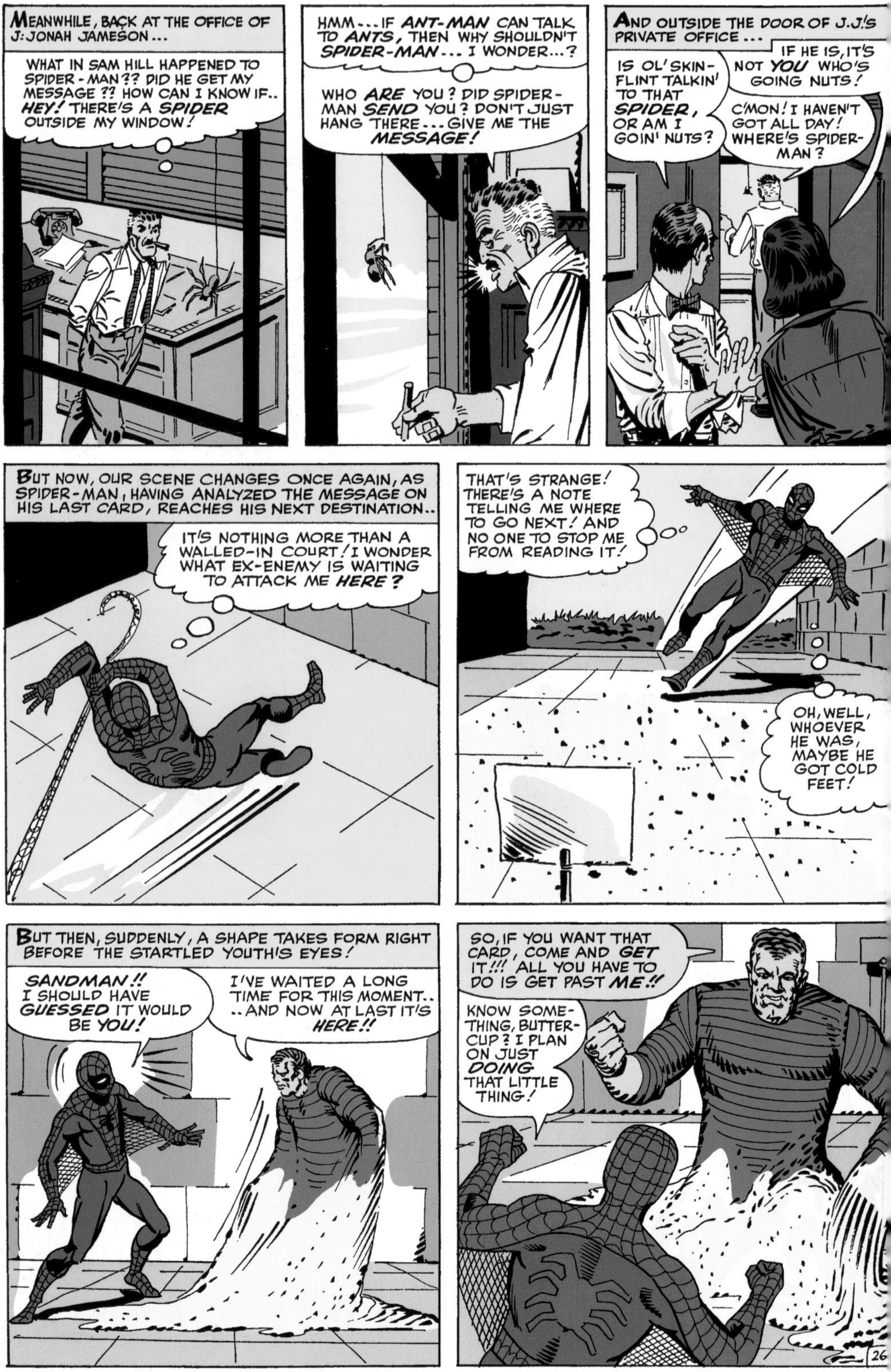
MEANWHILE, BACK AT THE OFFICE OF J. JONAH JAMESON...
WHAT IN SAM HILL HAPPENED TO SPIDER-MAN?? DID HE GET MY MESSAGE?? HOW CAN I KNOW IF.. HEY! THERE'S A SPIDER OUTSIDE MY WINDOW!
HMM... IF ANT-MAN CAN TALK TO ANTS, THEN WHY SHOULDN'T SPIDER-MAN... I WONDER...?
WHO ARE YOU? DID SPIDER-MAN SEND YOU? DON'T JUST HANG THERE... GIVE ME THE MESSAGE!
AND OUTSIDE THE DOOR OF J.J.'S PRIVATE OFFICE...
IS OL' SKIN-FLINT TALKIN' TO THAT SPIDER, OR AM I GOIN' NUTS?
IF HE IS, IT'S NOT YOU WHO'S GOING NUTS!
C'MON! I HAVEN'T GOT ALL DAY! WHERE'S SPIDER-MAN?
BUT NOW, OUR SCENE CHANGES ONCE AGAIN, AS SPIDER-MAN, HAVING ANALYZED THE MESSAGE ON HIS LAST CARD, REACHES HIS NEXT DESTINATION..
IT'S NOTHING MORE THAN A WALLED-IN COURT! I WONDER WHAT EX-ENEMY IS WAITING TO ATTACK ME HERE?
THAT'S STRANGE! THERE'S A NOTE TELLING ME WHERE TO GO NEXT! AND NO ONE TO STOP ME FROM READING IT!
OH, WELL, WHOEVER HE WAS, MAYBE HE GOT COLD FEET!
BUT THEN, SUDDENLY, A SHAPE TAKES FORM RIGHT BEFORE THE STARTLED YOUTH'S EYES!
SANDMAN!! I SHOULD HAVE GUESSED IT WOULD BE YOU!
I'VE WAITED A LONG TIME FOR THIS MOMENT.. ..AND NOW AT LAST IT'S HERE!!
SO, IF YOU WANT THAT CARD, COME AND GET IT!!! ALL YOU HAVE TO DO IS GET PAST ME!!
KNOW SOME-THING, BUTTER-CUP? I PLAN ON JUST DOING THAT LITTLE THING!
26

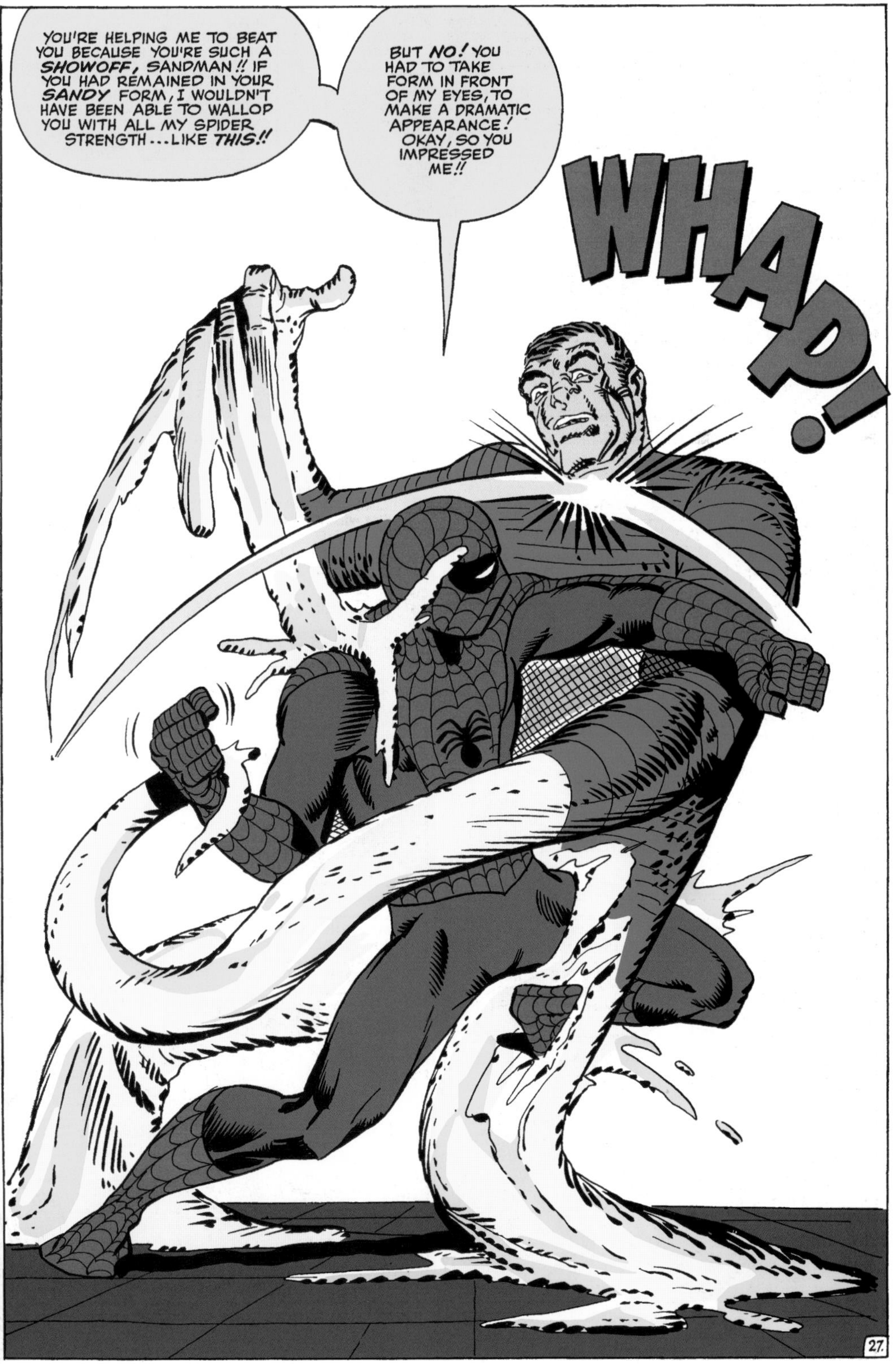
YOU'RE HELPING ME TO BEAT YOU BECAUSE YOU'RE SUCH A SHOWOFF, SANDMAN!! IF YOU HAD REMAINED IN YOUR SANDY FORM, I WOULDN'T HAVE BEEN ABLE TO WALLOP YOU WITH ALL MY SPIDER STRENGTH...LIKE THIS!!
BUT NO! YOU HAD TO TAKE FORM IN FRONT OF MY EYES, TO MAKE A DRAMATIC APPEARANCE! OKAY, SO YOU IMPRESSED ME!!
WHAP!
27.

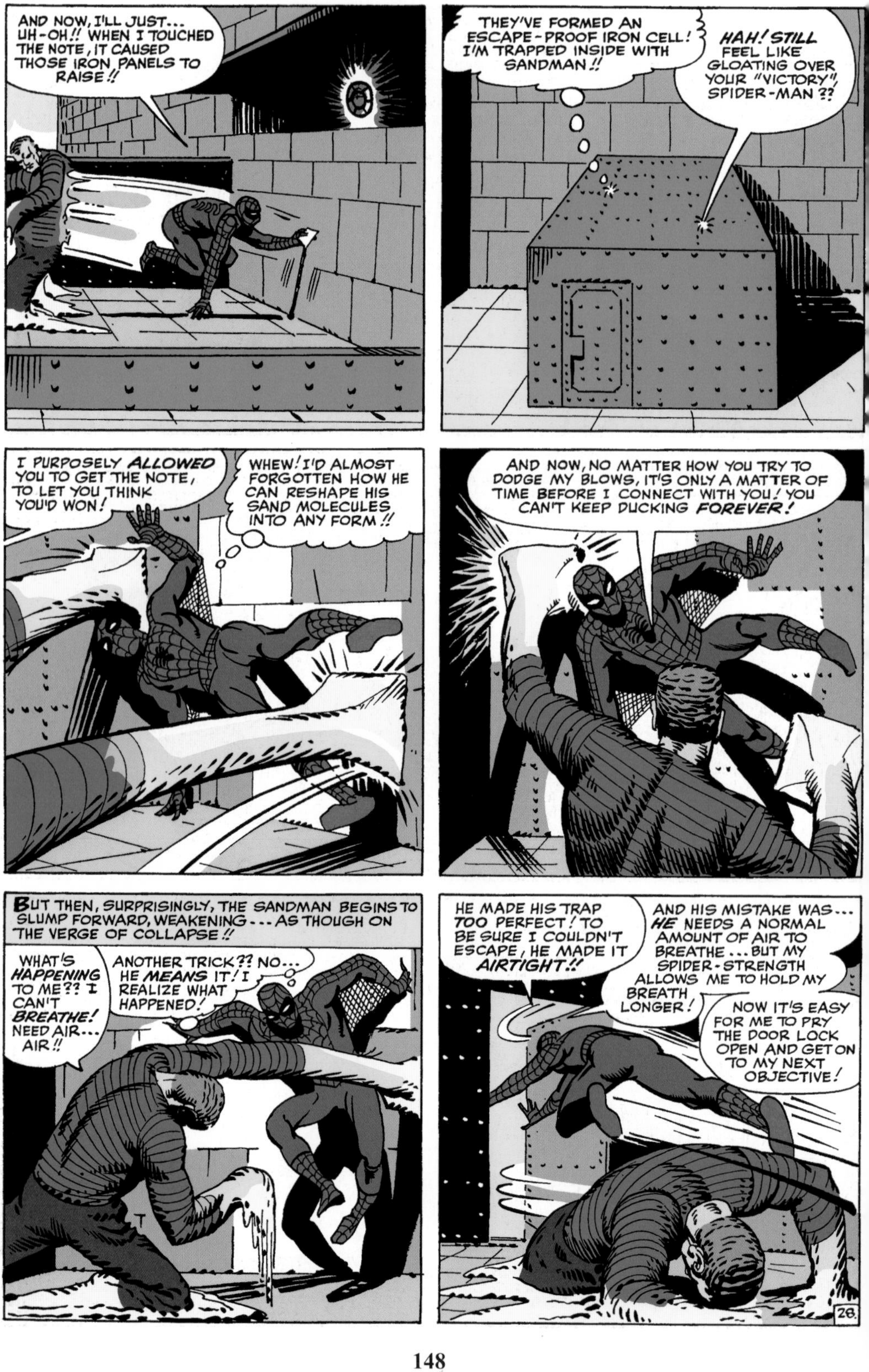
AND NOW, I'LL JUST... UH-OH!! WHEN I TOUCHED THE NOTE, IT CAUSED THOSE IRON PANELS TO RAISE!!
THEY'VE FORMED AN ESCAPE-PROOF IRON CELL! I'M TRAPPED INSIDE WITH SANDMAN!!
HAH! STILL FEEL LIKE GLOATING OVER YOUR "VICTORY", SPIDER-MAN??
I PURPOSELY ALLOWED YOU TO GET THE NOTE, TO LET YOU THINK YOU'D WON!
WHEW! I'D ALMOST FORGOTTEN HOW HE CAN RESHAPE HIS SAND MOLECULES INTO ANY FORM!!
AND NOW, NO MATTER HOW YOU TRY TO DODGE MY BLOWS, IT'S ONLY A MATTER OF TIME BEFORE I CONNECT WITH YOU! YOU CAN'T KEEP DUCKING FOREVER!
BUT THEN, SURPRISINGLY, THE SANDMAN BEGINS TO SLUMP FORWARD, WEAKENING... AS THOUGH ON THE VERGE OF COLLAPSE!!
WHAT'S HAPPENING TO ME?? I CAN'T BREATHE! NEED AIR... AIR!!
ANOTHER TRICK?? NO... HE MEANS IT! I REALIZE WHAT HAPPENED!
HE MADE HIS TRAP TOO PERFECT! TO BE SURE I COULDN'T ESCAPE, HE MADE IT AIRTIGHT!!
AND HIS MISTAKE WAS... HE NEEDS A NORMAL AMOUNT OF AIR TO BREATHE... BUT MY SPIDER-STRENGTH ALLOWS ME TO HOLD MY BREATH LONGER!
NOW IT'S EASY FOR ME TO PRY THE DOOR LOCK OPEN AND GET ON TO MY NEXT OBJECTIVE!
28.

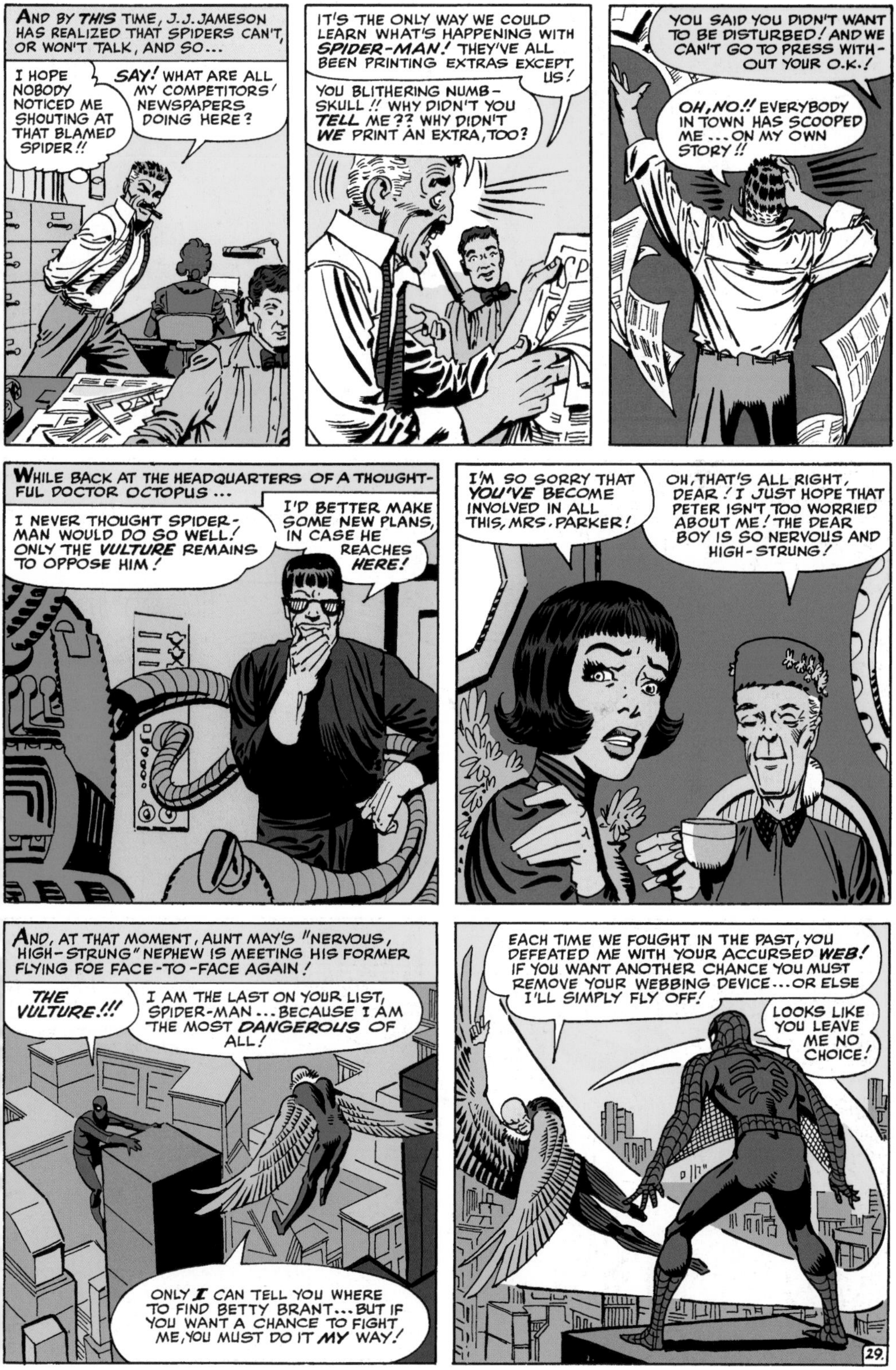

AND BY THIS TIME, J.J. JAMESON HAS REALIZED THAT SPIDERS CAN'T, OR WON'T TALK, AND SO...
I HOPE NOBODY NOTICED ME SHOUTING AT THAT BLAMED SPIDER!!
SAY! WHAT ARE ALL MY COMPETITORS' NEWSPAPERS DOING HERE?
IT'S THE ONLY WAY WE COULD LEARN WHAT'S HAPPENING WITH SPIDER-MAN! THEY'VE ALL BEEN PRINTING EXTRAS EXCEPT US!
YOU BLITHERING NUMB-SKULL!! WHY DIDN'T YOU TELL ME?? WHY DIDN'T WE PRINT AN EXTRA, TOO?
YOU SAID YOU DIDN'T WANT TO BE DISTURBED! AND WE CAN'T GO TO PRESS WITH-OUT YOUR O.K.!
OH, NO!! EVERYBODY IN TOWN HAS SCOOPED ME...ON MY OWN STORY!!
WHILE BACK AT THE HEADQUARTERS OF A THOUGHT-FUL DOCTOR OCTOPUS...
I NEVER THOUGHT SPIDER-MAN WOULD DO SO WELL! ONLY THE VULTURE REMAINS TO OPPOSE HIM!
I'D BETTER MAKE SOME NEW PLANS, IN CASE HE REACHES HERE!
I'M SO SORRY THAT YOU'VE BECOME INVOLVED IN ALL THIS, MRS. PARKER!
OH, THAT'S ALL RIGHT, DEAR! I JUST HOPE THAT PETER ISN'T TOO WORRIED ABOUT ME! THE DEAR BOY IS SO NERVOUS AND HIGH-STRUNG!
AND, AT THAT MOMENT, AUNT MAY'S "NERVOUS, HIGH-STRUNG" NEPHEW IS MEETING HIS FORMER FLYING FOE FACE-TO-FACE AGAIN!
THE VULTURE!!!
I AM THE LAST ON YOUR LIST, SPIDER-MAN... BECAUSE I AM THE MOST DANGEROUS OF ALL!
ONLY I CAN TELL YOU WHERE TO FIND BETTY BRANT... BUT IF YOU WANT A CHANCE TO FIGHT ME, YOU MUST DO IT MY WAY!
EACH TIME WE FOUGHT IN THE PAST, YOU DEFEATED ME WITH YOUR ACCURSED WEB! IF YOU WANT ANOTHER CHANCE YOU MUST REMOVE YOUR WEBBING DEVICE...OR ELSE I'LL SIMPLY FLY OFF!
LOOKS LIKE YOU LEAVE ME NO CHOICE!
29.

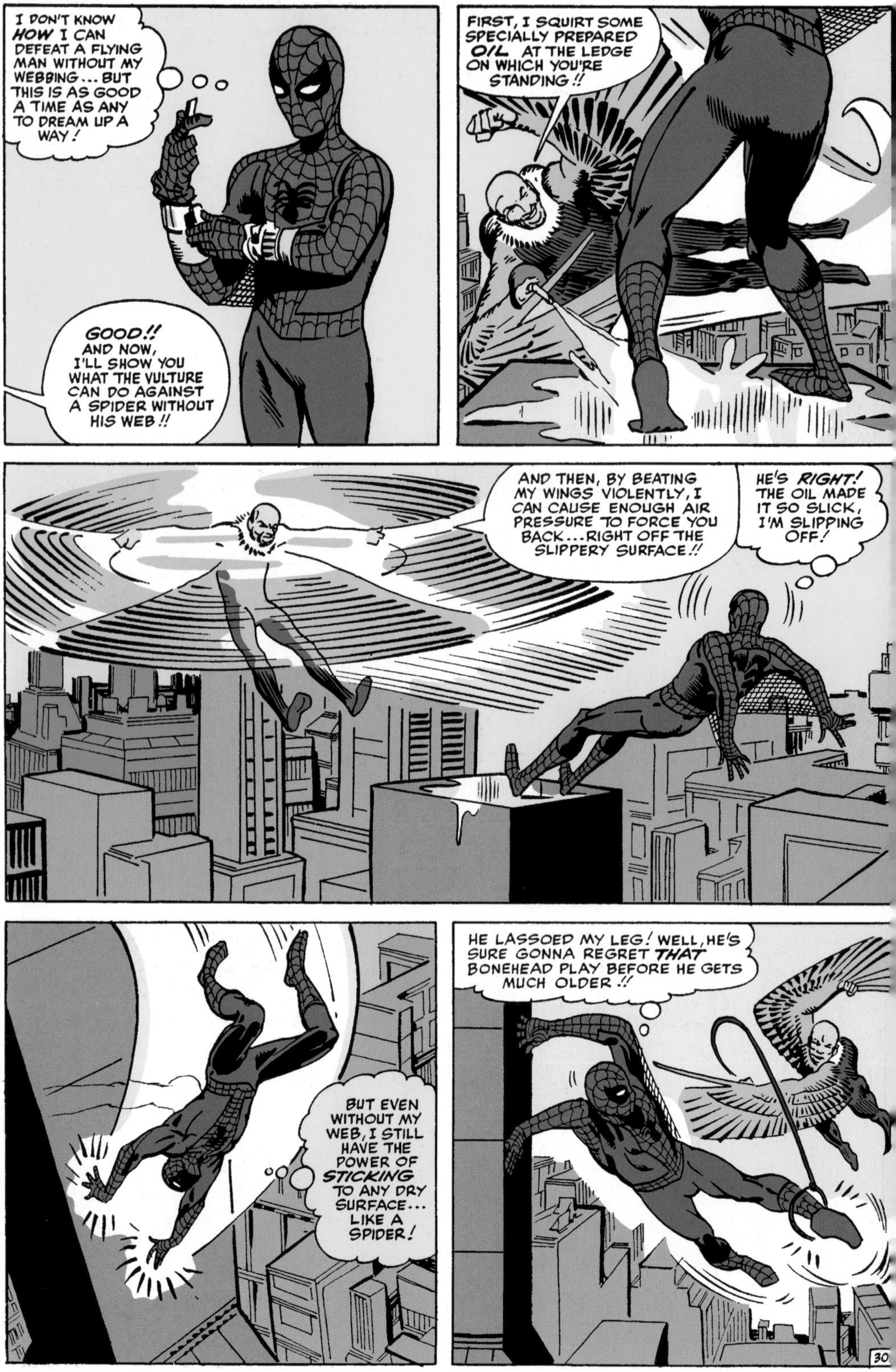
I DON'T KNOW HOW I CAN DEFEAT A FLYING MAN WITHOUT MY WEBBING... BUT THIS IS AS GOOD A TIME AS ANY TO DREAM UP A WAY!
GOOD!! AND NOW, I'LL SHOW YOU WHAT THE VULTURE CAN DO AGAINST A SPIDER WITHOUT HIS WEB!!
FIRST, I SQUIRT SOME SPECIALLY PREPARED OIL AT THE LEDGE ON WHICH YOU'RE STANDING!!
AND THEN, BY BEATING MY WINGS VIOLENTLY, I CAN CAUSE ENOUGH AIR PRESSURE TO FORCE YOU BACK...RIGHT OFF THE SLIPPERY SURFACE!!
HE'S RIGHT! THE OIL MADE IT SO SLICK, I'M SLIPPING OFF!
BUT EVEN WITHOUT MY WEB, I STILL HAVE THE POWER OF STICKING TO ANY DRY SURFACE... LIKE A SPIDER!
HE LASSOED MY LEG! WELL, HE'S SURE GONNA REGRET THAT BONEHEAD PLAY BEFORE HE GETS MUCH OLDER!!
30

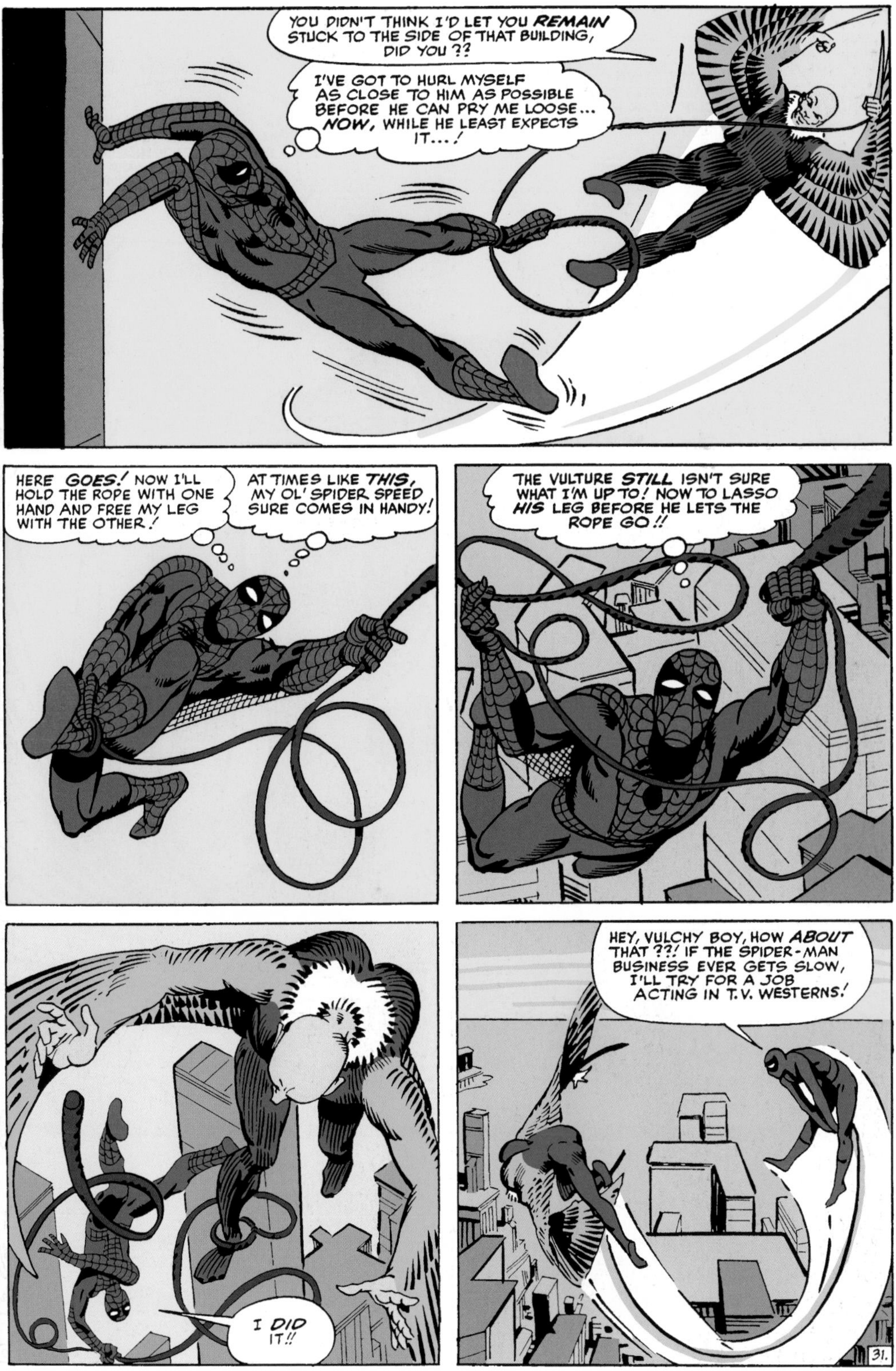
YOU DIDN'T THINK I'D LET YOU REMAIN STUCK TO THE SIDE OF THAT BUILDING, DID YOU??
I'VE GOT TO HURL MYSELF AS CLOSE TO HIM AS POSSIBLE BEFORE HE CAN PRY ME LOOSE... NOW, WHILE HE LEAST EXPECTS IT...!
HERE GOES! NOW I'LL HOLD THE ROPE WITH ONE HAND AND FREE MY LEG WITH THE OTHER!
AT TIMES LIKE THIS, MY OL' SPIDER SPEED SURE COMES IN HANDY!
THE VULTURE STILL ISN'T SURE WHAT I'M UP TO! NOW TO LASSO HIS LEG BEFORE HE LETS THE ROPE GO!!
I DID IT!!
HEY, VULCHY BOY, HOW ABOUT THAT??! IF THE SPIDER-MAN BUSINESS EVER GETS SLOW, I'LL TRY FOR A JOB ACTING IN T.V. WESTERNS!
31.

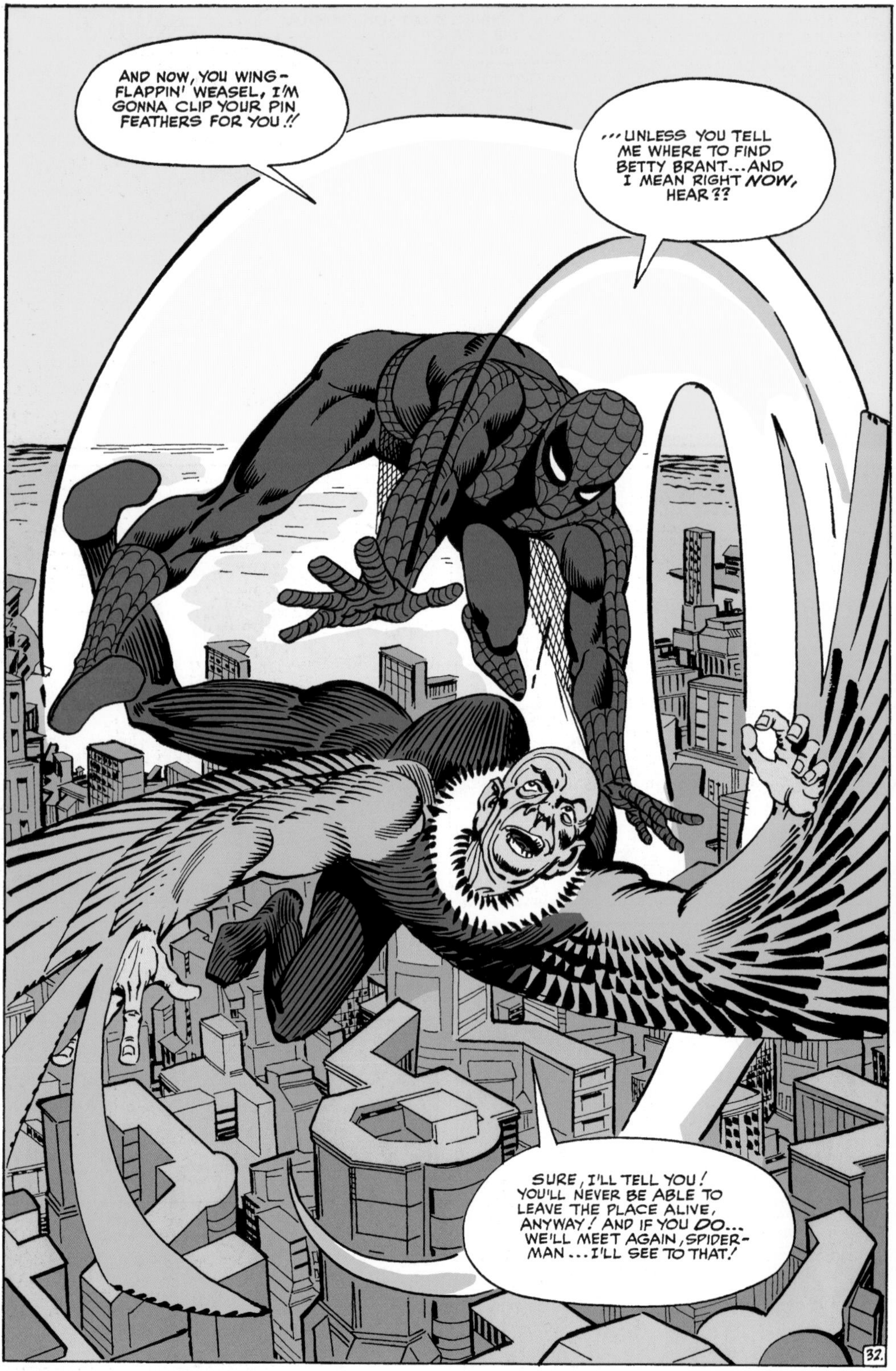
AND NOW, YOU WING-FLAPPIN' WEASEL, I'M GONNA CLIP YOUR PIN FEATHERS FOR YOU!!
...UNLESS YOU TELL ME WHERE TO FIND BETTY BRANT...AND I MEAN RIGHT NOW, HEAR??
SURE, I'LL TELL YOU! YOU'LL NEVER BE ABLE TO LEAVE THE PLACE ALIVE, ANYWAY! AND IF YOU DO... WE'LL MEET AGAIN, SPIDER-MAN...I'LL SEE TO THAT!
32.

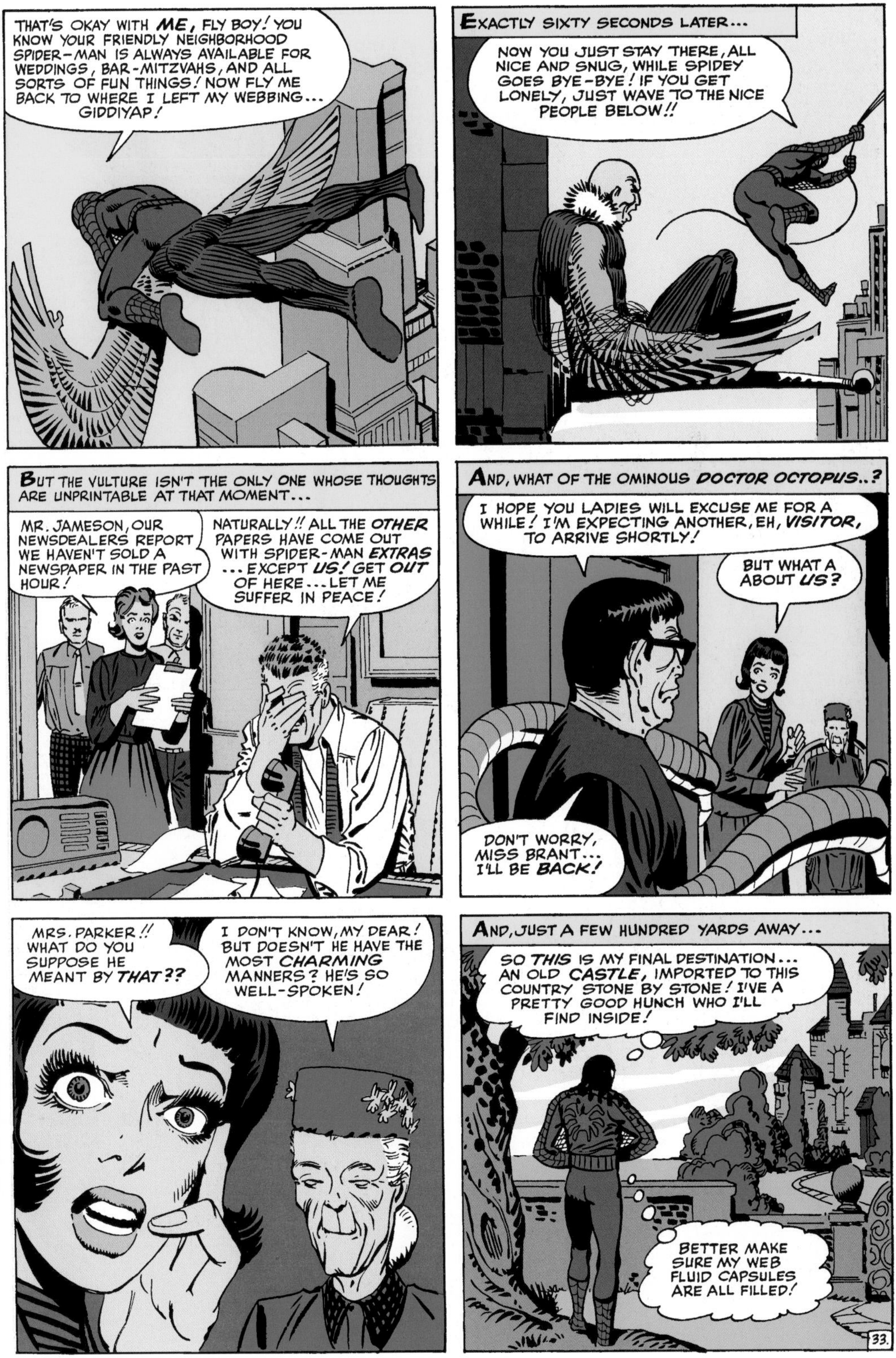
THAT'S OKAY WITH ME, FLY BOY! YOU KNOW YOUR FRIENDLY NEIGHBORHOOD SPIDER-MAN IS ALWAYS AVAILABLE FOR WEDDINGS, BAR-MITZVAHS, AND ALL SORTS OF FUN THINGS! NOW FLY ME BACK TO WHERE I LEFT MY WEBBING... GIDDIYAP!
EXACTLY SIXTY SECONDS LATER...
NOW YOU JUST STAY THERE, ALL NICE AND SNUG, WHILE SPIDEY GOES BYE-BYE! IF YOU GET LONELY, JUST WAVE TO THE NICE PEOPLE BELOW!!
BUT THE VULTURE ISN'T THE ONLY ONE WHOSE THOUGHTS ARE UNPRINTABLE AT THAT MOMENT...
MR. JAMESON, OUR NEWSDEALERS REPORT WE HAVEN'T SOLD A NEWSPAPER IN THE PAST HOUR!
NATURALLY!! ALL THE OTHER PAPERS HAVE COME OUT WITH SPIDER-MAN EXTRAS ... EXCEPT US! GET OUT OF HERE...LET ME SUFFER IN PEACE!
AND, WHAT OF THE OMINOUS DOCTOR OCTOPUS..?
I HOPE YOU LADIES WILL EXCUSE ME FOR A WHILE! I'M EXPECTING ANOTHER, EH, VISITOR, TO ARRIVE SHORTLY!
BUT WHAT A ABOUT US?
DON'T WORRY, MISS BRANT... I'LL BE BACK!
MRS. PARKER!! WHAT DO YOU SUPPOSE HE MEANT BY THAT??
I DON'T KNOW, MY DEAR! BUT DOESN'T HE HAVE THE MOST CHARMING MANNERS? HE'S SO WELL-SPOKEN!
AND, JUST A FEW HUNDRED YARDS AWAY...
SO THIS IS MY FINAL DESTINATION... AN OLD CASTLE, IMPORTED TO THIS COUNTRY STONE BY STONE! I'VE A PRETTY GOOD HUNCH WHO I'LL FIND INSIDE!
BETTER MAKE SURE MY WEB FLUID CAPSULES ARE ALL FILLED!
33.

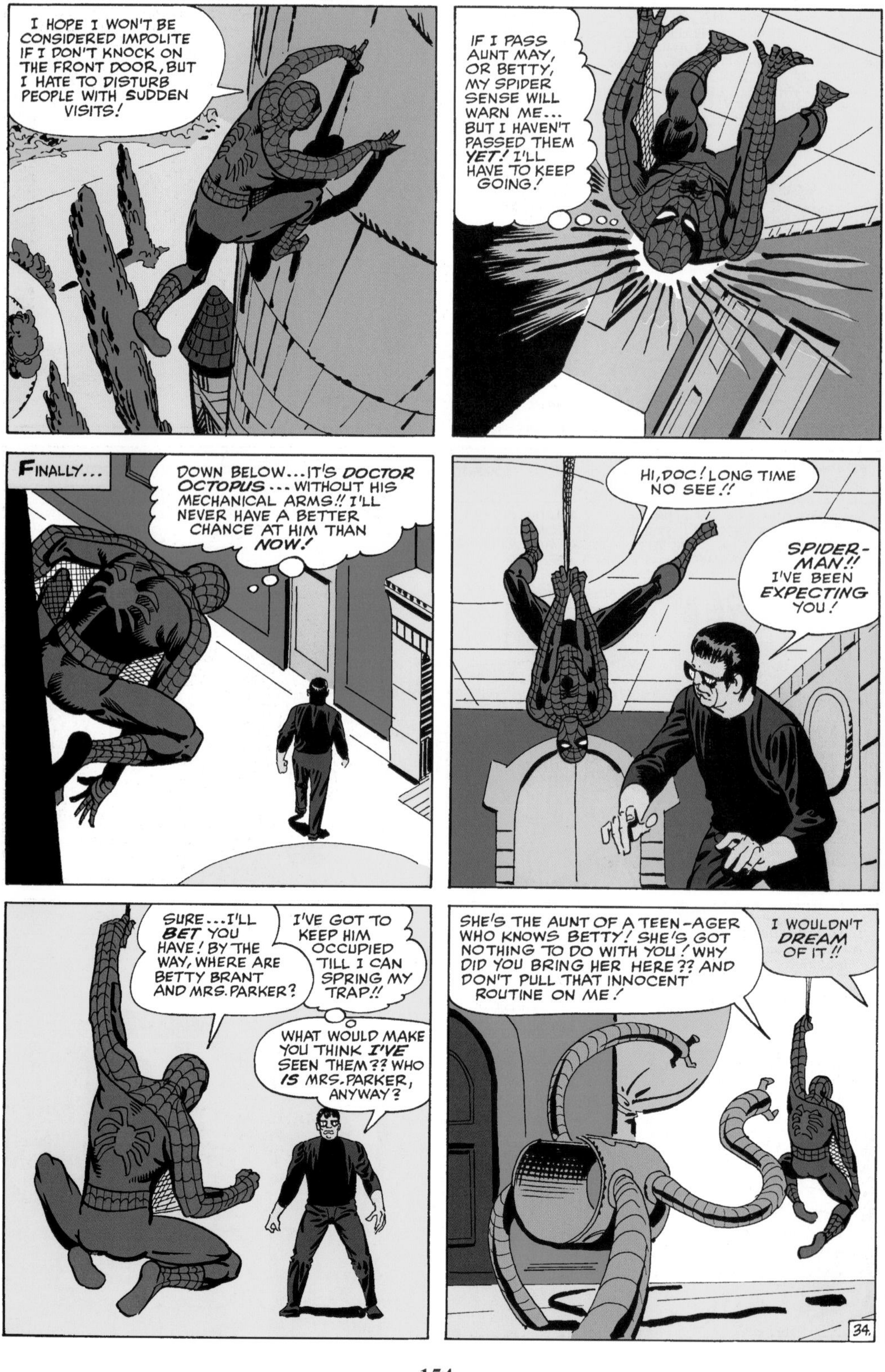
I HOPE I WON'T BE CONSIDERED IMPOLITE IF I DON'T KNOCK ON THE FRONT DOOR, BUT I HATE TO DISTURB PEOPLE WITH SUDDEN VISITS!
IF I PASS AUNT MAY, OR BETTY, MY SPIDER SENSE WILL WARN ME... BUT I HAVEN'T PASSED THEM YET! I'LL HAVE TO KEEP GOING!
FINALLY...
DOWN BELOW...IT'S DOCTOR OCTOPUS... WITHOUT HIS MECHANICAL ARMS!! I'LL NEVER HAVE A BETTER CHANCE AT HIM THAN NOW!
HI, DOC! LONG TIME NO SEE!!
SPIDER-MAN!! I'VE BEEN EXPECTING YOU!
SURE...I'LL BET YOU HAVE! BY THE WAY, WHERE ARE BETTY BRANT AND MRS. PARKER?
I'VE GOT TO KEEP HIM OCCUPIED TILL I CAN SPRING MY TRAP!!
WHAT WOULD MAKE YOU THINK I'VE SEEN THEM?? WHO IS MRS. PARKER, ANYWAY?
SHE'S THE AUNT OF A TEEN-AGER WHO KNOWS BETTY! SHE'S GOT NOTHING TO DO WITH YOU! WHY DID YOU BRING HER HERE?? AND DON'T PULL THAT INNOCENT ROUTINE ON ME!
I WOULDN'T DREAM OF IT!!
34.

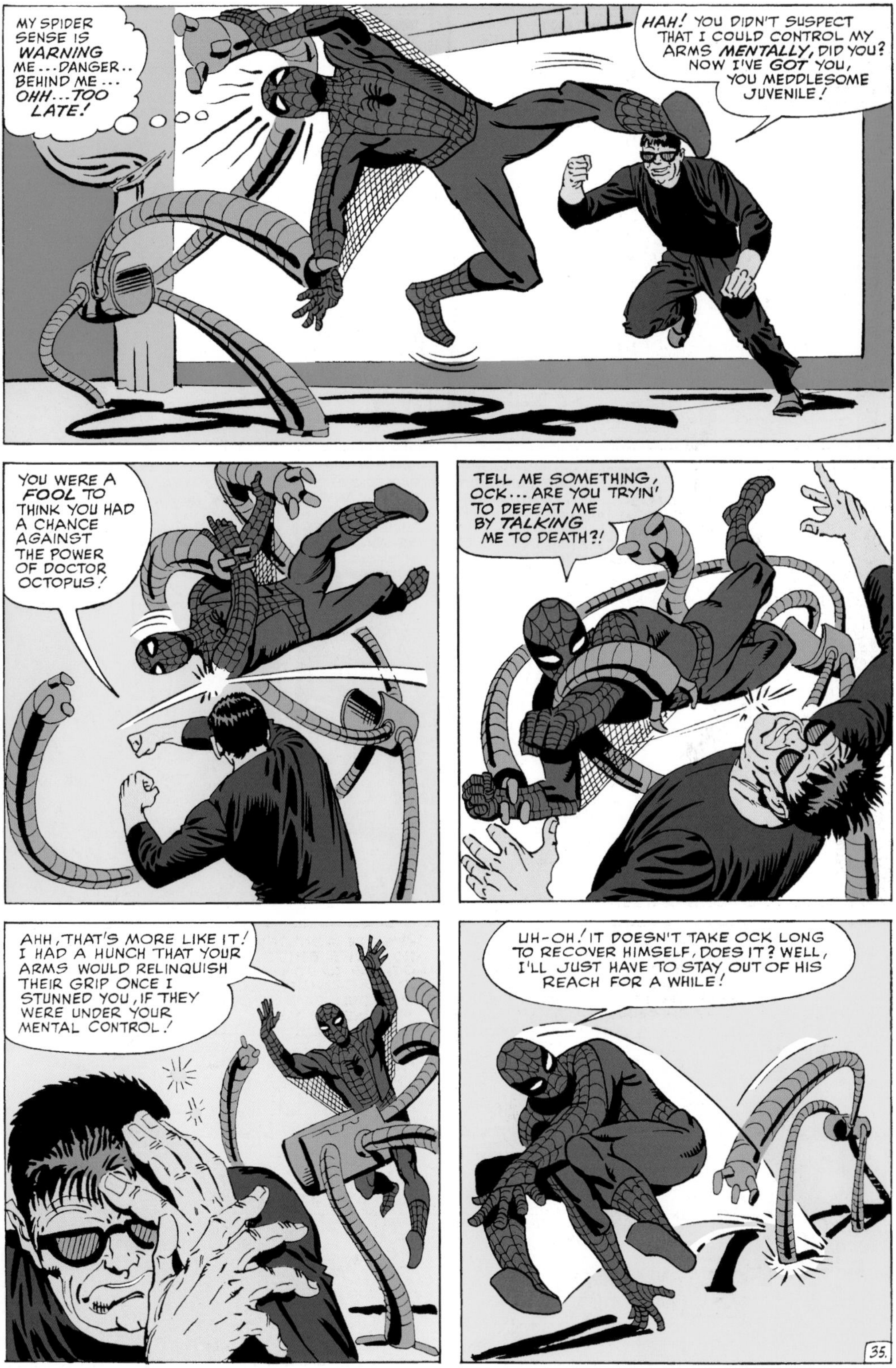
MY SPIDER SENSE IS WARNING ME... DANGER.. BEHIND ME... OHH...TOO LATE!
HAH! YOU DIDN'T SUSPECT THAT I COULD CONTROL MY ARMS MENTALLY, DID YOU? NOW I'VE GOT YOU, YOU MEDDLESOME JUVENILE!
YOU WERE A FOOL TO THINK YOU HAD A CHANCE AGAINST THE POWER OF DOCTOR OCTOPUS!
TELL ME SOMETHING, OCK... ARE YOU TRYIN' TO DEFEAT ME BY TALKING ME TO DEATH?!
AHH, THAT'S MORE LIKE IT! I HAD A HUNCH THAT YOUR ARMS WOULD RELINQUISH THEIR GRIP ONCE I STUNNED YOU, IF THEY WERE UNDER YOUR MENTAL CONTROL!
UH-OH! IT DOESN'T TAKE OCK LONG TO RECOVER HIMSELF, DOES IT? WELL, I'LL JUST HAVE TO STAY OUT OF HIS REACH FOR A WHILE!
35.

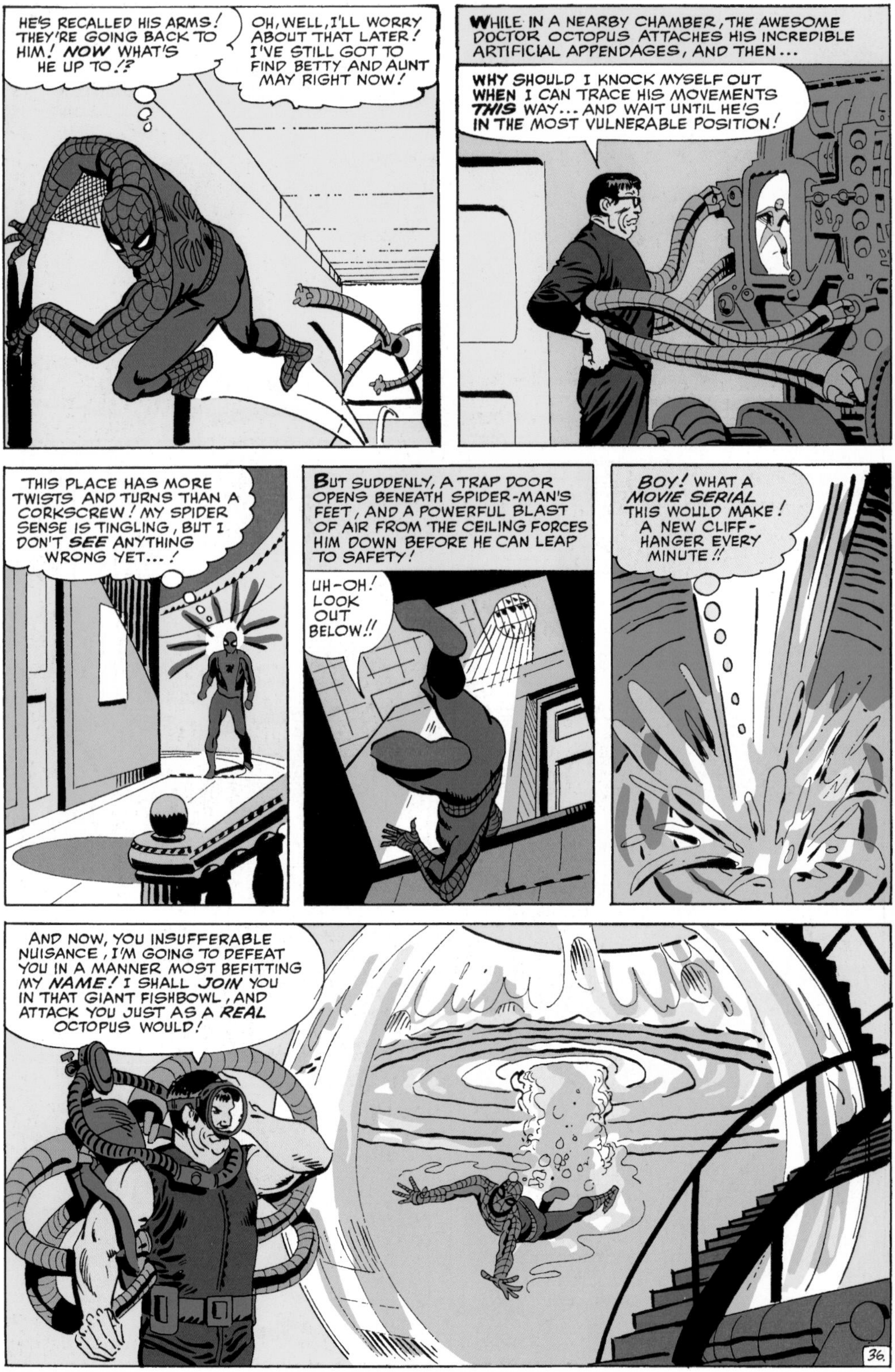
HE'S RECALLED HIS ARMS! THEY'RE GOING BACK TO HIM! NOW WHAT'S HE UP TO!?
OH, WELL, I'LL WORRY ABOUT THAT LATER! I'VE STILL GOT TO FIND BETTY AND AUNT MAY RIGHT NOW!
WHILE IN A NEARBY CHAMBER, THE AWESOME DOCTOR OCTOPUS ATTACHES HIS INCREDIBLE ARTIFICIAL APPENDAGES, AND THEN...
WHY SHOULD I KNOCK MYSELF OUT WHEN I CAN TRACE HIS MOVEMENTS THIS WAY... AND WAIT UNTIL HE'S IN THE MOST VULNERABLE POSITION!
THIS PLACE HAS MORE TWISTS AND TURNS THAN A CORKSCREW! MY SPIDER SENSE IS TINGLING, BUT I DON'T SEE ANYTHING WRONG YET...!
BUT SUDDENLY, A TRAP DOOR OPENS BENEATH SPIDER-MAN'S FEET, AND A POWERFUL BLAST OF AIR FROM THE CEILING FORCES HIM DOWN BEFORE HE CAN LEAP TO SAFETY!
UH-OH! LOOK OUT BELOW!!
BOY! WHAT A MOVIE SERIAL THIS WOULD MAKE! A NEW CLIFF-HANGER EVERY MINUTE!!
AND NOW, YOU INSUFFERABLE NUISANCE, I'M GOING TO DEFEAT YOU IN A MANNER MOST BEFITTING MY NAME! I SHALL JOIN YOU IN THAT GIANT FISHBOWL, AND ATTACK YOU JUST AS A REAL OCTOPUS WOULD!
36.

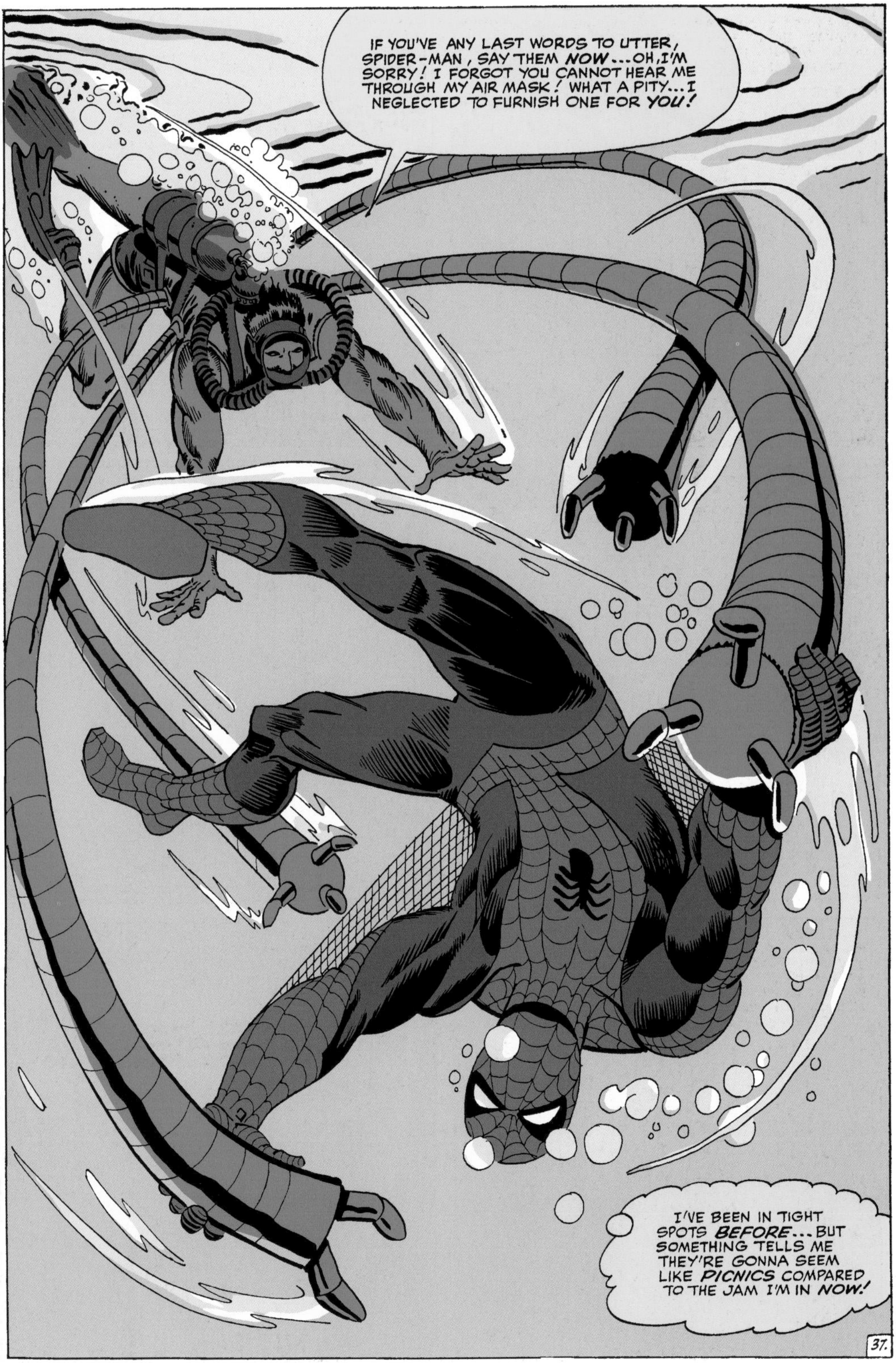
IF YOU'VE ANY LAST WORDS TO UTTER, SPIDER-MAN, SAY THEM NOW...OH, I'M SORRY! I FORGOT YOU CANNOT HEAR ME THROUGH MY AIR MASK! WHAT A PITY...I NEGLECTED TO FURNISH ONE FOR YOU!
I'VE BEEN IN TIGHT SPOTS BEFORE...BUT SOMETHING TELLS ME THEY'RE GONNA SEEM LIKE PICNICS COMPARED TO THE JAM I'M IN NOW!
37.

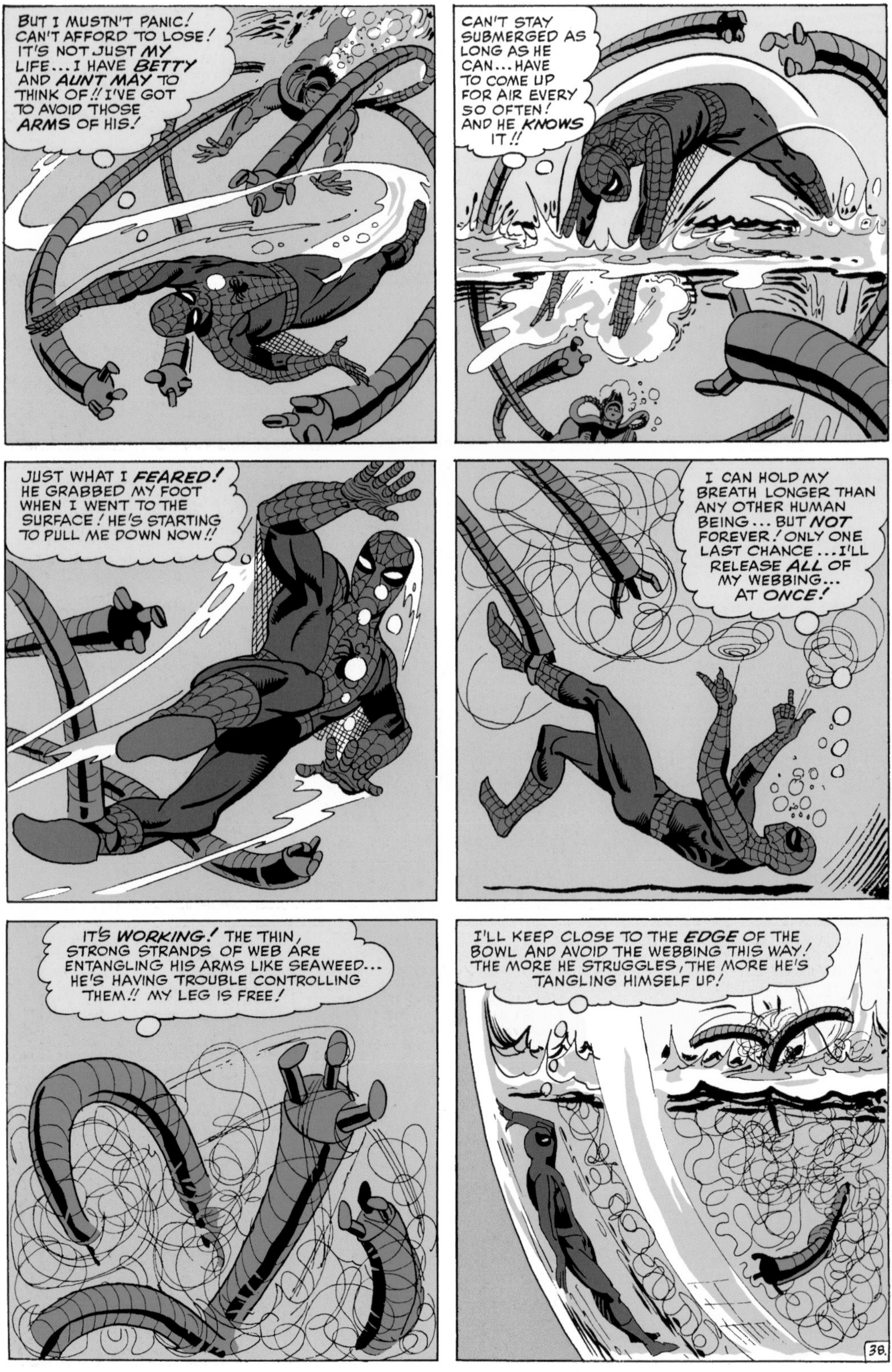
BUT I MUSTN'T PANIC! CAN'T AFFORD TO LOSE! IT'S NOT JUST MY LIFE... I HAVE BETTY AND AUNT MAY TO THINK OF!! I'VE GOT TO AVOID THOSE ARMS OF HIS!
CAN'T STAY SUBMERGED AS LONG AS HE CAN... HAVE TO COME UP FOR AIR EVERY SO OFTEN! AND HE KNOWS IT!!
JUST WHAT I FEARED! HE GRABBED MY FOOT WHEN I WENT TO THE SURFACE! HE'S STARTING TO PULL ME DOWN NOW!!
I CAN HOLD MY BREATH LONGER THAN ANY OTHER HUMAN BEING... BUT NOT FOREVER! ONLY ONE LAST CHANCE... I'LL RELEASE ALL OF MY WEBBING... AT ONCE!
IT'S WORKING! THE THIN, STRONG STRANDS OF WEB ARE ENTANGLING HIS ARMS LIKE SEAWEED... HE'S HAVING TROUBLE CONTROLLING THEM!! MY LEG IS FREE!
I'LL KEEP CLOSE TO THE EDGE OF THE BOWL AND AVOID THE WEBBING THIS WAY! THE MORE HE STRUGGLES, THE MORE HE'S TANGLING HIMSELF UP!
38.

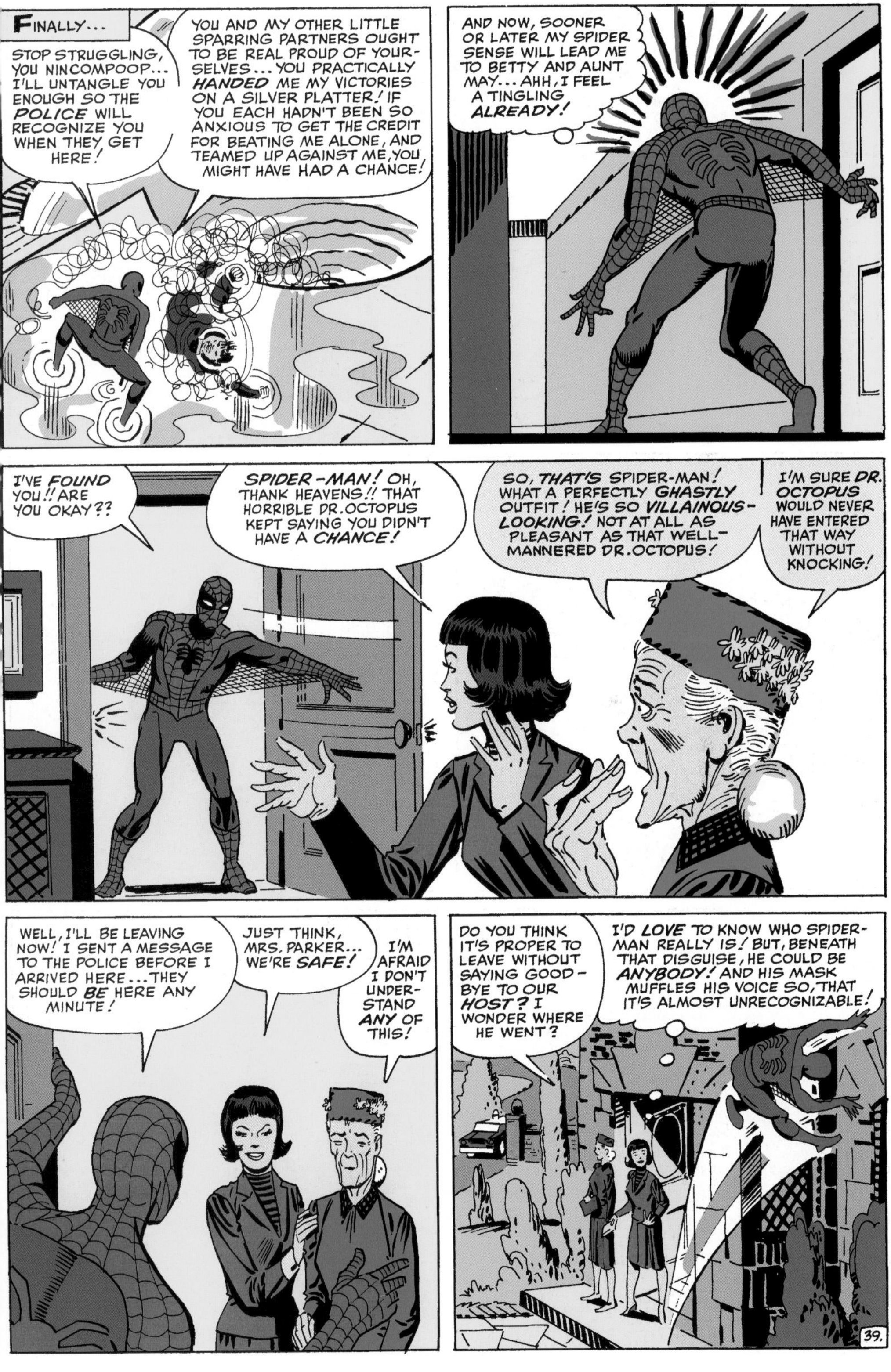
FINALLY...
STOP STRUGGLING, YOU NINCOMPOOP... I'LL UNTANGLE YOU ENOUGH SO THE POLICE WILL RECOGNIZE YOU WHEN THEY GET HERE!
YOU AND MY OTHER LITTLE SPARRING PARTNERS OUGHT TO BE REAL PROUD OF YOURSELVES... YOU PRACTICALLY HANDED ME MY VICTORIES ON A SILVER PLATTER! IF YOU EACH HADN'T BEEN SO ANXIOUS TO GET THE CREDIT FOR BEATING ME ALONE, AND TEAMED UP AGAINST ME, YOU MIGHT HAVE HAD A CHANCE!
AND NOW, SOONER OR LATER MY SPIDER SENSE WILL LEAD ME TO BETTY AND AUNT MAY... AHH, I FEEL A TINGLING ALREADY!
I'VE FOUND YOU!! ARE YOU OKAY??
SPIDER-MAN! OH, THANK HEAVENS!! THAT HORRIBLE DR. OCTOPUS KEPT SAYING YOU DIDN'T HAVE A CHANCE!
SO, THAT'S SPIDER-MAN! WHAT A PERFECTLY GHASTLY OUTFIT! HE'S SO VILLAINOUS-LOOKING! NOT AT ALL AS PLEASANT AS THAT WELL-MANNERED DR. OCTOPUS!
I'M SURE DR. OCTOPUS WOULD NEVER HAVE ENTERED THAT WAY WITHOUT KNOCKING!
WELL, I'LL BE LEAVING NOW! I SENT A MESSAGE TO THE POLICE BEFORE I ARRIVED HERE... THEY SHOULD BE HERE ANY MINUTE!
JUST THINK, MRS. PARKER... WE'RE SAFE!
I'M AFRAID I DON'T UNDERSTAND ANY OF THIS!
DO YOU THINK IT'S PROPER TO LEAVE WITHOUT SAYING GOOD-BYE TO OUR HOST? I WONDER WHERE HE WENT?
I'D LOVE TO KNOW WHO SPIDER-MAN REALLY IS! BUT, BENEATH THAT DISGUISE, HE COULD BE ANYBODY! AND HIS MASK MUFFLES HIS VOICE SO, THAT IT'S ALMOST UNRECOGNIZABLE!
39.

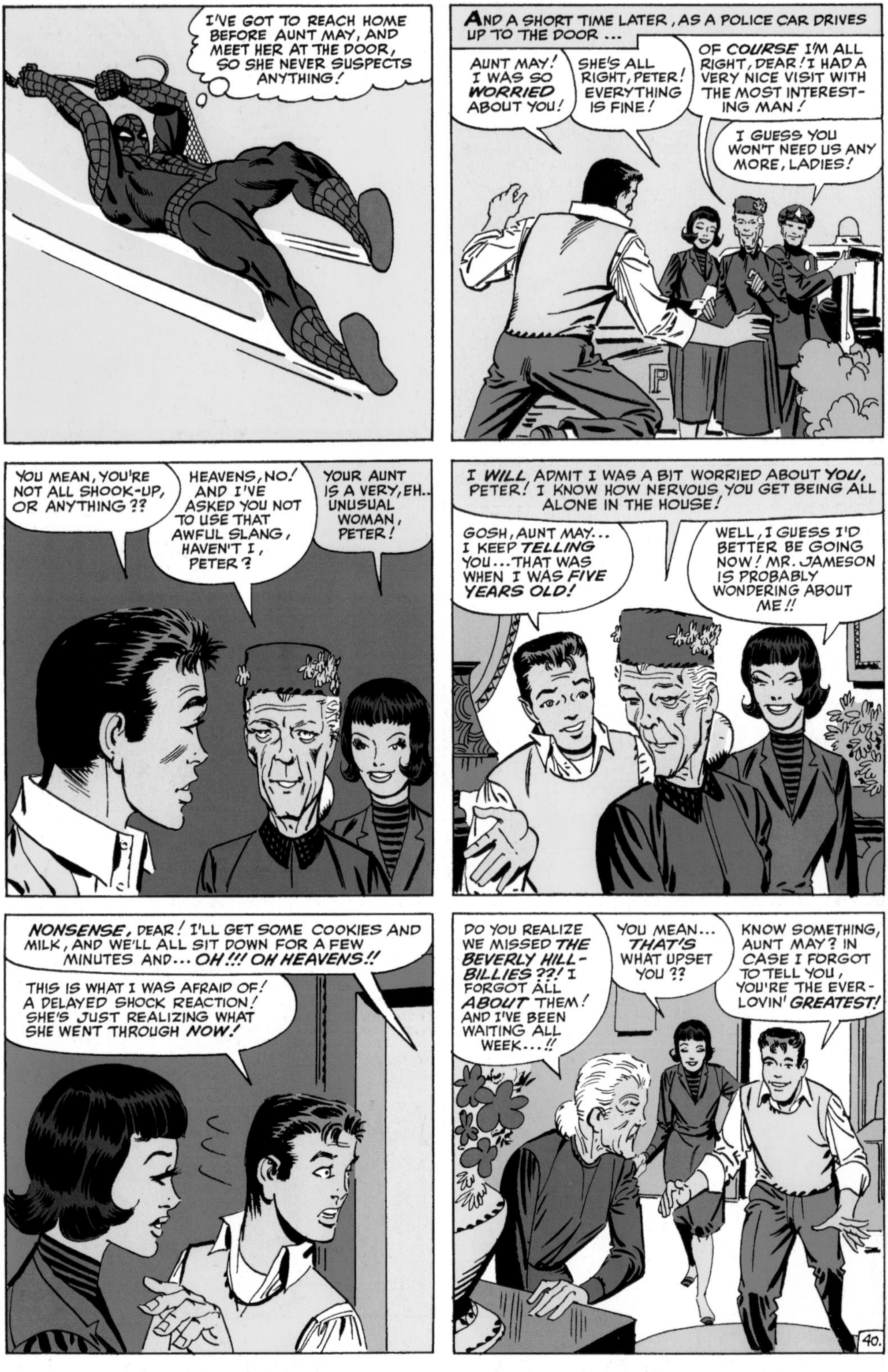
I'VE GOT TO REACH HOME BEFORE AUNT MAY, AND MEET HER AT THE DOOR, SO SHE NEVER SUSPECTS ANYTHING!
AND A SHORT TIME LATER, AS A POLICE CAR DRIVES UP TO THE DOOR ...
AUNT MAY! I WAS SO WORRIED ABOUT YOU!
SHE'S ALL RIGHT, PETER! EVERYTHING IS FINE!
OF COURSE I'M ALL RIGHT, DEAR! I HAD A VERY NICE VISIT WITH THE MOST INTERESTING MAN!
I GUESS YOU WON'T NEED US ANY MORE, LADIES!
YOU MEAN, YOU'RE NOT ALL SHOOK-UP, OR ANYTHING??
HEAVENS, NO! AND I'VE ASKED YOU NOT TO USE THAT AWFUL SLANG, HAVEN'T I, PETER?
YOUR AUNT IS A VERY, EH.. UNUSUAL WOMAN, PETER!
I WILL ADMIT I WAS A BIT WORRIED ABOUT YOU, PETER! I KNOW HOW NERVOUS YOU GET BEING ALL ALONE IN THE HOUSE!
GOSH, AUNT MAY... I KEEP TELLING YOU... THAT WAS WHEN I WAS FIVE YEARS OLD!
WELL, I GUESS I'D BETTER BE GOING NOW! MR. JAMESON IS PROBABLY WONDERING ABOUT ME!!
NONSENSE, DEAR! I'LL GET SOME COOKIES AND MILK, AND WE'LL ALL SIT DOWN FOR A FEW MINUTES AND... OH!!! OH HEAVENS!!
THIS IS WHAT I WAS AFRAID OF! A DELAYED SHOCK REACTION! SHE'S JUST REALIZING WHAT SHE WENT THROUGH NOW!
DO YOU REALIZE WE MISSED THE BEVERLY HILL-BILLIES??! I FORGOT ALL ABOUT THEM! AND I'VE BEEN WAITING ALL WEEK...!!
YOU MEAN... THAT'S WHAT UPSET YOU??
KNOW SOMETHING, AUNT MAY? IN CASE I FORGOT TO TELL YOU, YOU'RE THE EVER-LOVIN' GREATEST!
40.

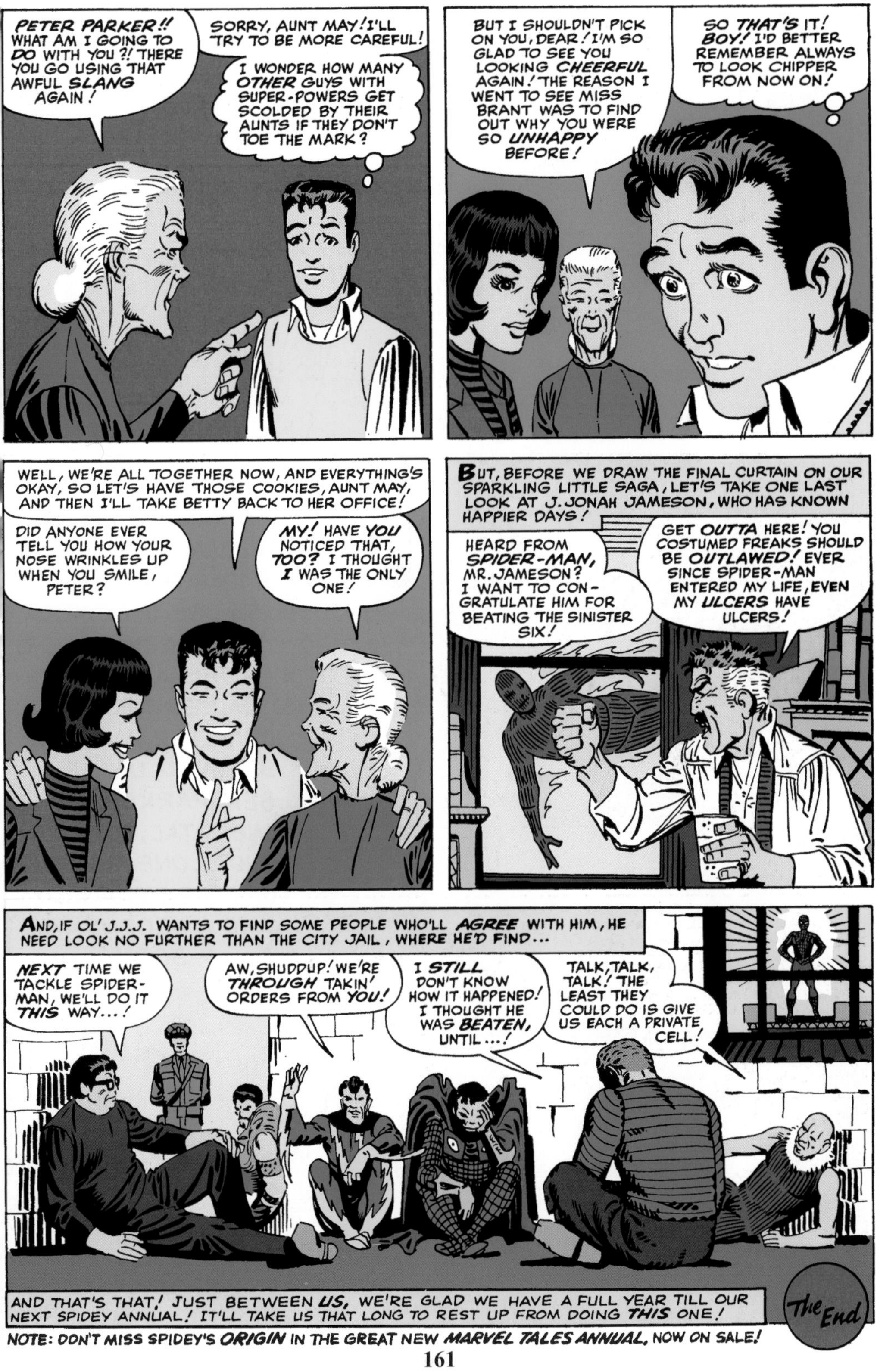
PETER PARKER!! WHAT AM I GOING TO DO WITH YOU?! THERE YOU GO USING THAT AWFUL SLANG AGAIN!
SORRY, AUNT MAY! I'LL TRY TO BE MORE CAREFUL!
I WONDER HOW MANY OTHER GUYS WITH SUPER-POWERS GET SCOLDED BY THEIR AUNTS IF THEY DON'T TOE THE MARK?
BUT I SHOULDN'T PICK ON YOU, DEAR! I'M SO GLAD TO SEE YOU LOOKING CHEERFUL AGAIN! THE REASON I WENT TO SEE MISS BRANT WAS TO FIND OUT WHY YOU WERE SO UNHAPPY BEFORE!
SO THAT'S IT! BOY! I'D BETTER REMEMBER ALWAYS TO LOOK CHIPPER FROM NOW ON!
WELL, WE'RE ALL TOGETHER NOW, AND EVERYTHING'S OKAY, SO LET'S HAVE THOSE COOKIES, AUNT MAY, AND THEN I'LL TAKE BETTY BACK TO HER OFFICE!
DID ANYONE EVER TELL YOU HOW YOUR NOSE WRINKLES UP WHEN YOU SMILE, PETER?
MY! HAVE YOU NOTICED THAT, TOO? I THOUGHT I WAS THE ONLY ONE!
BUT, BEFORE WE DRAW THE FINAL CURTAIN ON OUR SPARKLING LITTLE SAGA, LET'S TAKE ONE LAST LOOK AT J. JONAH JAMESON, WHO HAS KNOWN HAPPIER DAYS!
HEARD FROM SPIDER-MAN, MR. JAMESON? I WANT TO CON-GRATULATE HIM FOR BEATING THE SINISTER SIX!
GET OUTTA HERE! YOU COSTUMED FREAKS SHOULD BE OUTLAWED! EVER SINCE SPIDER-MAN ENTERED MY LIFE, EVEN MY ULCERS HAVE ULCERS!
AND, IF OL' J.J.J. WANTS TO FIND SOME PEOPLE WHO'LL AGREE WITH HIM, HE NEED LOOK NO FURTHER THAN THE CITY JAIL, WHERE HE'D FIND...
NEXT TIME WE TACKLE SPIDER-MAN, WE'LL DO IT THIS WAY...!
AW, SHUDDUP! WE'RE THROUGH TAKIN' ORDERS FROM YOU!
I STILL DON'T KNOW HOW IT HAPPENED! I THOUGHT HE WAS BEATEN, UNTIL...!
TALK, TALK, TALK! THE LEAST THEY COULD DO IS GIVE US EACH A PRIVATE CELL!
AND THAT'S THAT! JUST BETWEEN US, WE'RE GLAD WE HAVE A FULL YEAR TILL OUR NEXT SPIDEY ANNUAL! IT'LL TAKE US THAT LONG TO REST UP FROM DOING THIS ONE!
The End
NOTE: DON'T MISS SPIDEY'S ORIGIN IN THE GREAT NEW MARVEL TALES ANNUAL, NOW ON SALE!

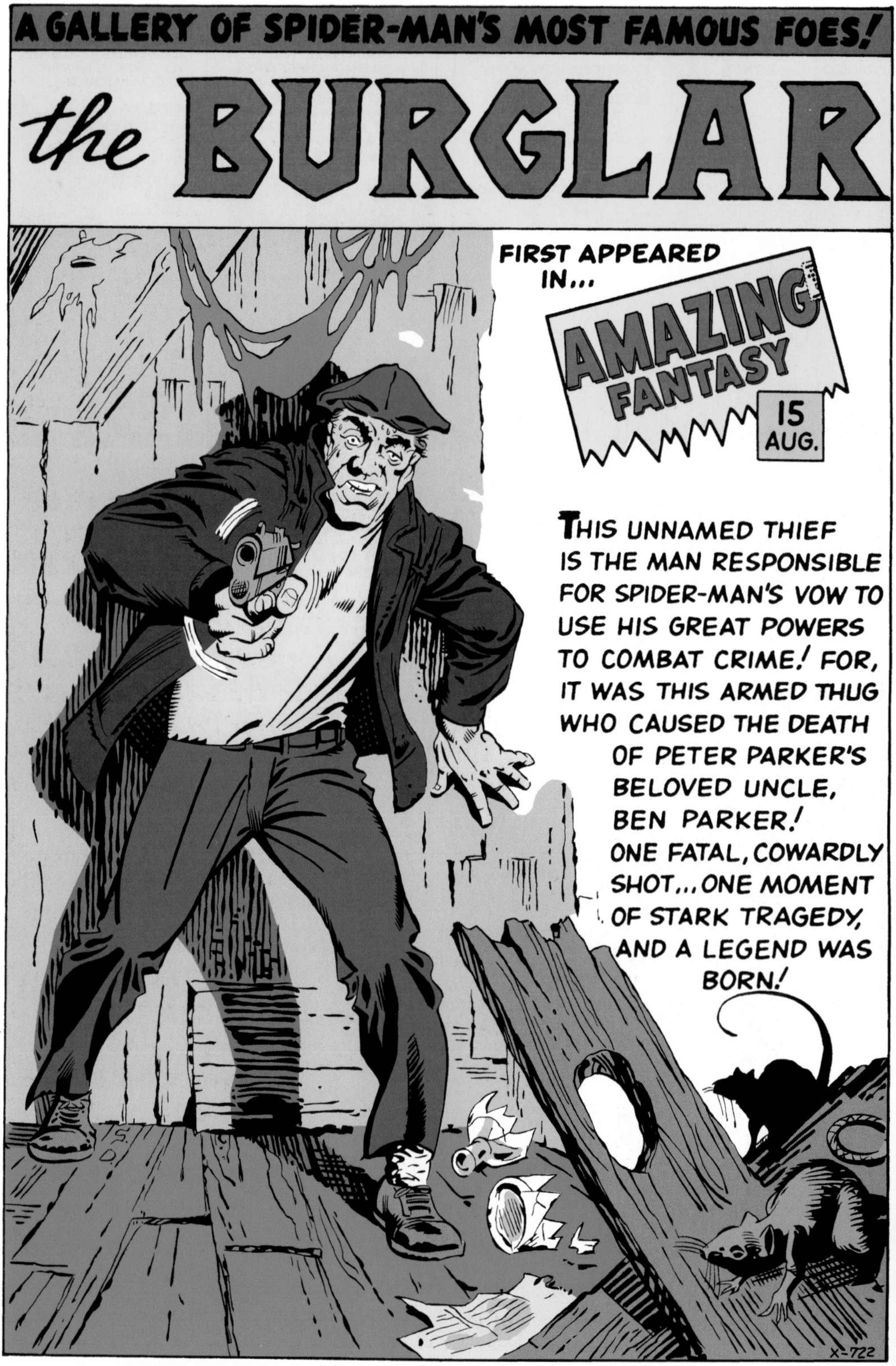
A GALLERY OF SPIDER-MAN'S MOST FAMOUS FOES!
the BURGLAR
FIRST APPEARED IN...
AMAZING FANTASY 15 AUG.
THIS UNNAMED THIEF IS THE MAN RESPONSIBLE FOR SPIDER-MAN'S VOW TO USE HIS GREAT POWERS TO COMBAT CRIME! FOR, IT WAS THIS ARMED THUG WHO CAUSED THE DEATH OF PETER PARKER'S BELOVED UNCLE, BEN PARKER! ONE FATAL, COWARDLY SHOT... ONE MOMENT OF STARK TRAGEDY, AND A LEGEND WAS BORN!
X-722

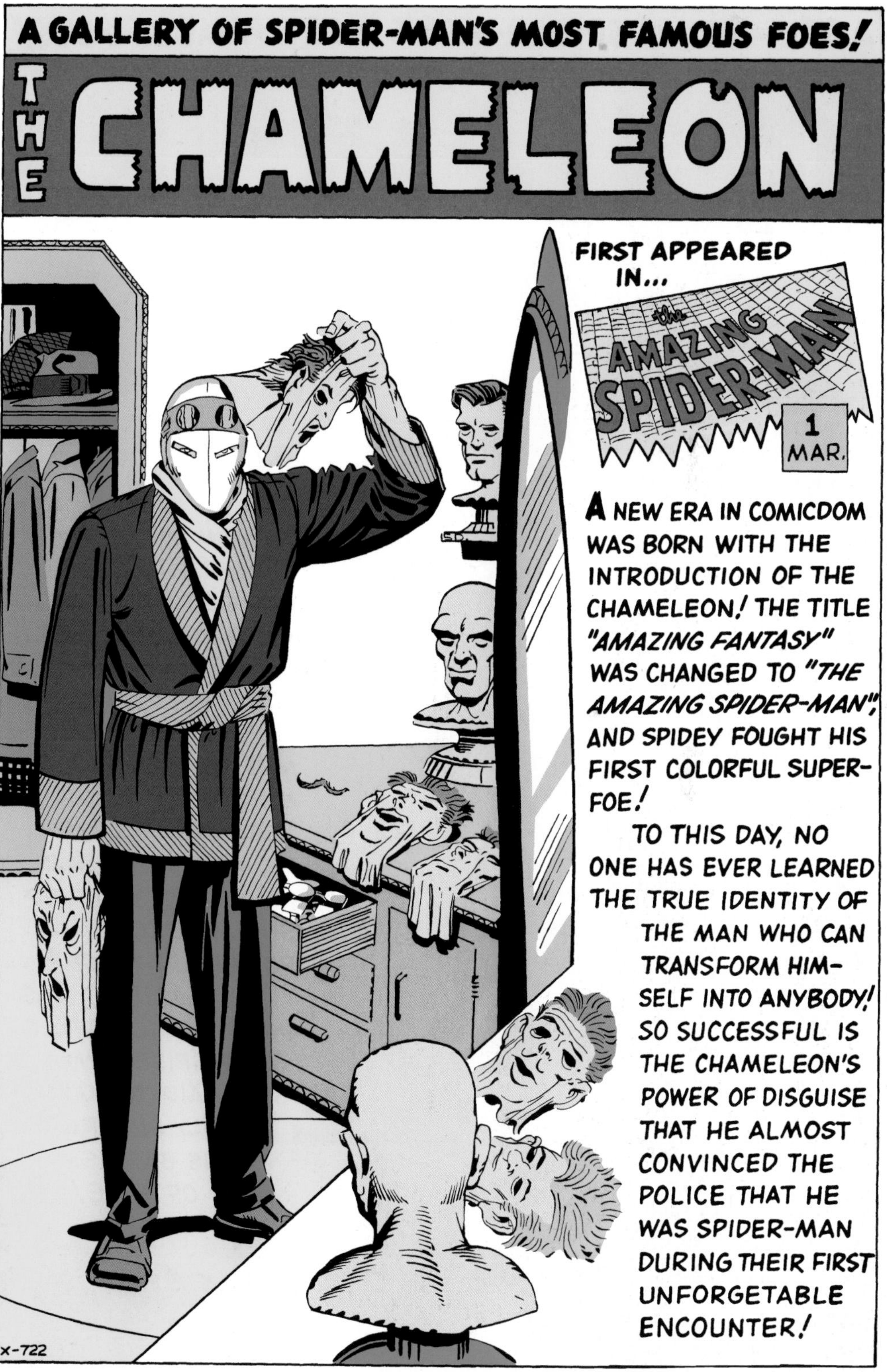
A GALLERY OF SPIDER-MAN'S MOST FAMOUS FOES!
THE CHAMELEON
FIRST APPEARED IN...
THE AMAZING SPIDER-MAN 1 MAR.
A NEW ERA IN COMICDOM WAS BORN WITH THE INTRODUCTION OF THE CHAMELEON! THE TITLE "AMAZING FANTASY" WAS CHANGED TO "THE AMAZING SPIDER-MAN", AND SPIDEY FOUGHT HIS FIRST COLORFUL SUPER-FOE!
TO THIS DAY, NO ONE HAS EVER LEARNED THE TRUE IDENTITY OF THE MAN WHO CAN TRANSFORM HIMSELF INTO ANYBODY! SO SUCCESSFUL IS THE CHAMELEON'S POWER OF DISGUISE THAT HE ALMOST CONVINCED THE POLICE THAT HE WAS SPIDER-MAN DURING THEIR FIRST UNFORGETABLE ENCOUNTER!
X-722

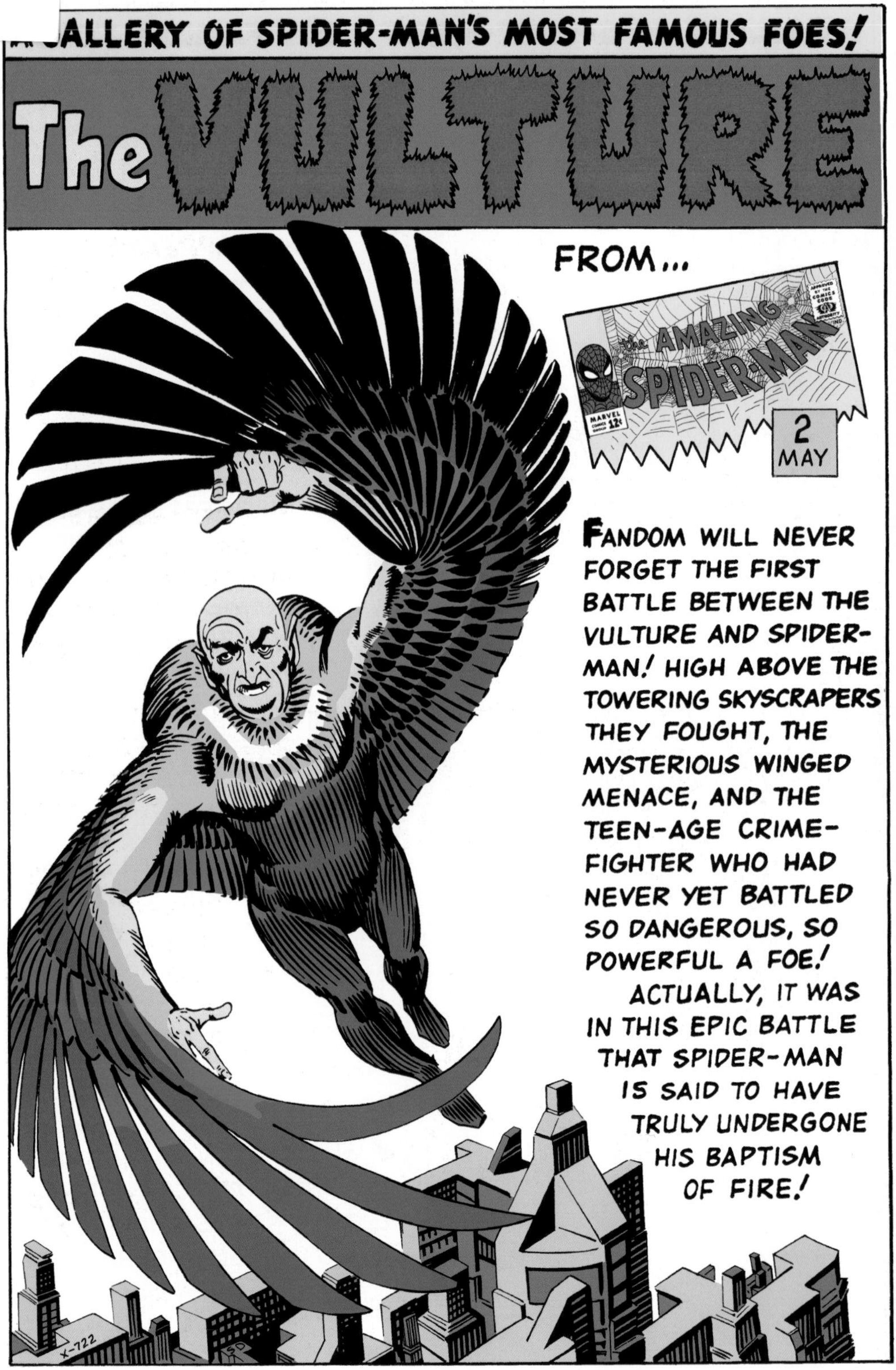
ALLERY OF SPIDER-MAN'S MOST FAMOUS FOES!
The VULTURE
FROM...
THE AMAZING SPIDER-MAN
MARVEL COMICS GROUP 12¢
2 MAY
FANDOM WILL NEVER FORGET THE FIRST BATTLE BETWEEN THE VULTURE AND SPIDER-MAN! HIGH ABOVE THE TOWERING SKYSCRAPERS THEY FOUGHT, THE MYSTERIOUS WINGED MENACE, AND THE TEEN-AGE CRIME-FIGHTER WHO HAD NEVER YET BATTLED SO DANGEROUS, SO POWERFUL A FOE!
ACTUALLY, IT WAS IN THIS EPIC BATTLE THAT SPIDER-MAN IS SAID TO HAVE TRULY UNDERGONE HIS BAPTISM OF FIRE!
X-722

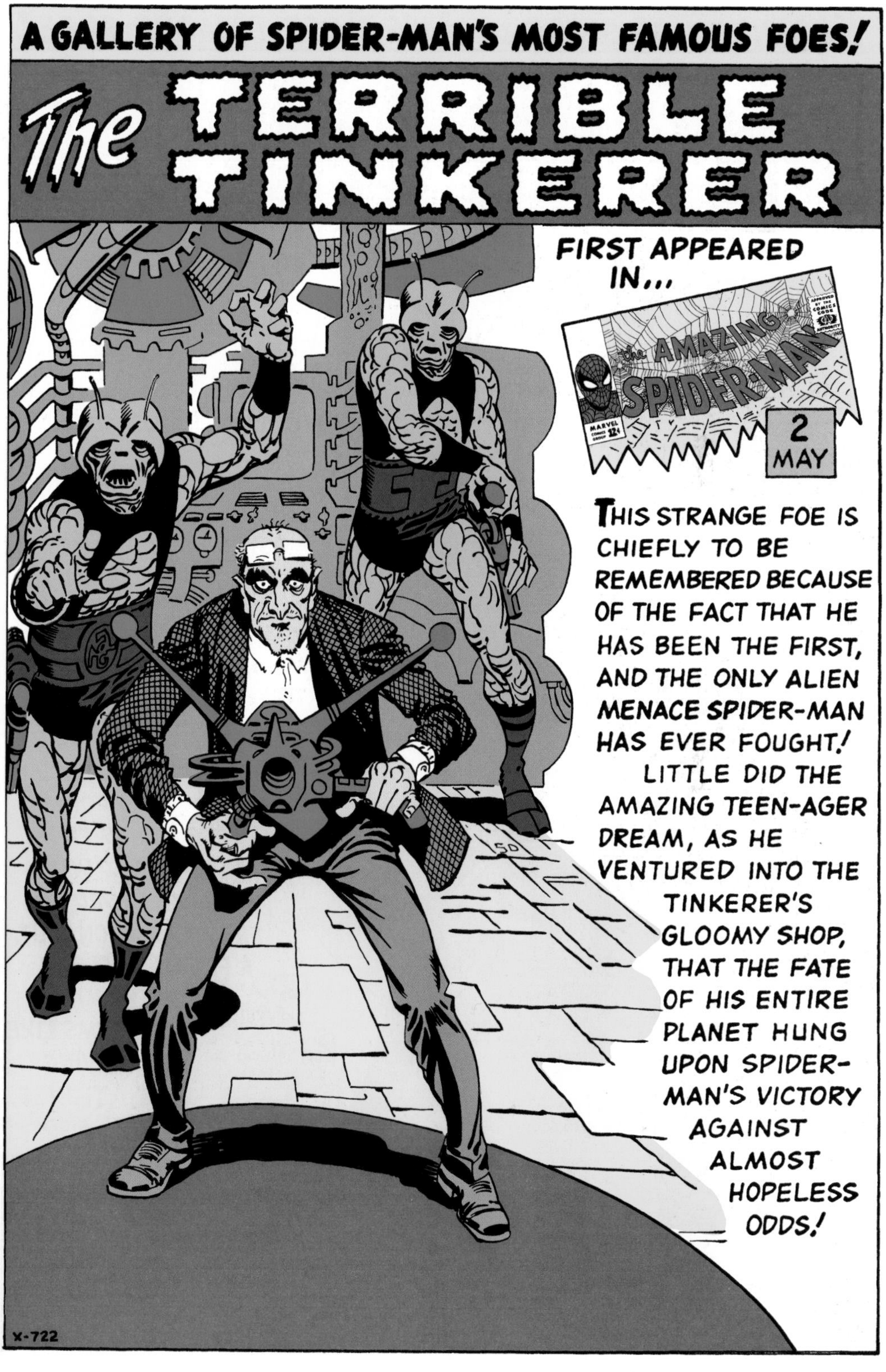
A GALLERY OF SPIDER-MAN'S MOST FAMOUS FOES!
The TERRIBLE TINKERER
FIRST APPEARED IN...
THE AMAZING SPIDER-MAN
MARVEL COMICS GROUP 12¢
APPROVED BY THE COMICS CODE AUTHORITY
2 MAY
THIS STRANGE FOE IS CHIEFLY TO BE REMEMBERED BECAUSE OF THE FACT THAT HE HAS BEEN THE FIRST, AND THE ONLY ALIEN MENACE SPIDER-MAN HAS EVER FOUGHT!
LITTLE DID THE AMAZING TEEN-AGER DREAM, AS HE VENTURED INTO THE TINKERER'S GLOOMY SHOP, THAT THE FATE OF HIS ENTIRE PLANET HUNG UPON SPIDER-MAN'S VICTORY AGAINST ALMOST HOPELESS ODDS!
X-722

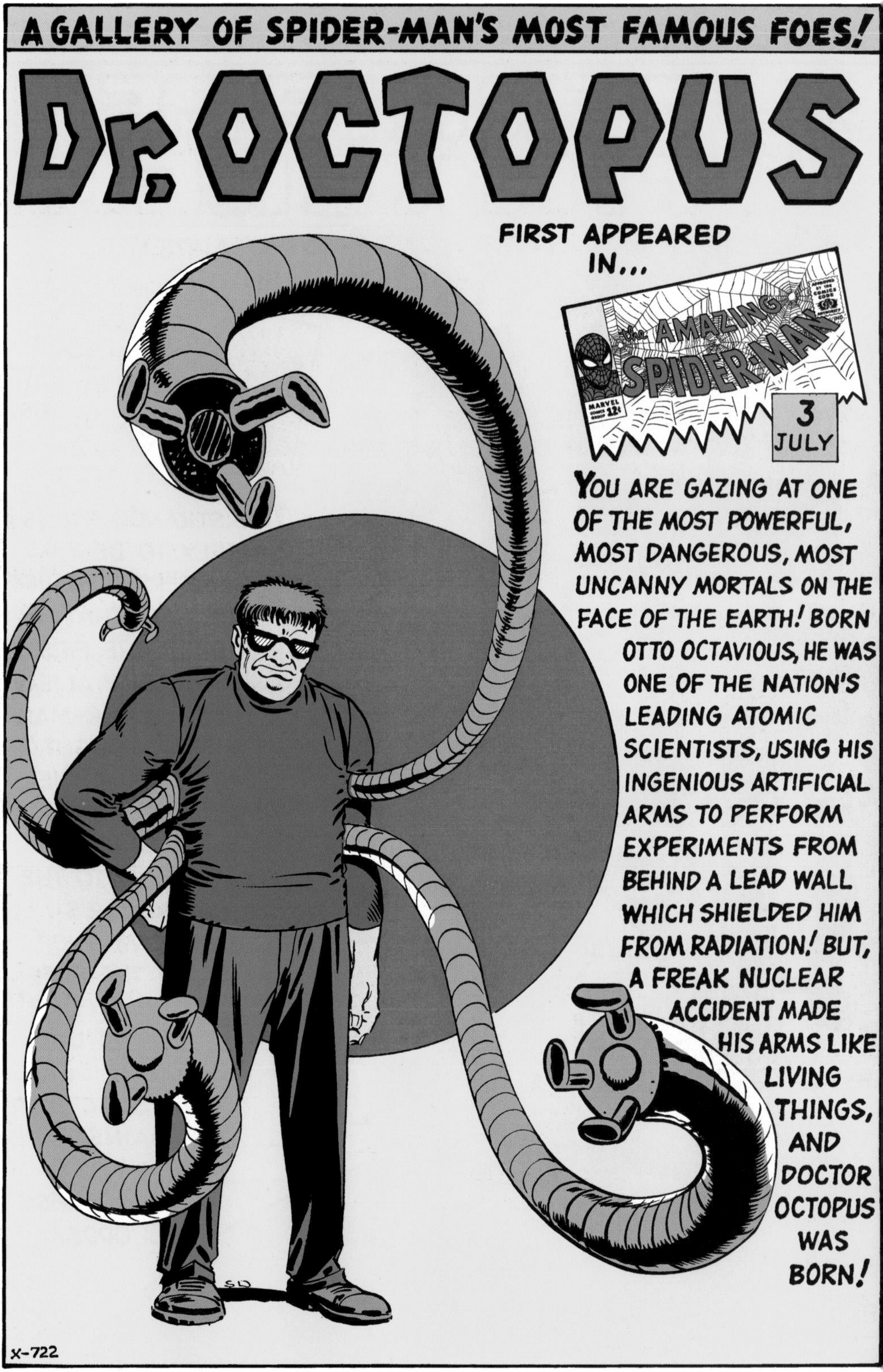
A GALLERY OF SPIDER-MAN'S MOST FAMOUS FOES!
Dr. OCTOPUS
FIRST APPEARED IN...
THE AMAZING SPIDER-MAN
MARVEL COMICS GROUP 12¢
3 JULY
YOU ARE GAZING AT ONE OF THE MOST POWERFUL, MOST DANGEROUS, MOST UNCANNY MORTALS ON THE FACE OF THE EARTH! BORN OTTO OCTAVIOUS, HE WAS ONE OF THE NATION'S LEADING ATOMIC SCIENTISTS, USING HIS INGENIOUS ARTIFICIAL ARMS TO PERFORM EXPERIMENTS FROM BEHIND A LEAD WALL WHICH SHIELDED HIM FROM RADIATION! BUT, A FREAK NUCLEAR ACCIDENT MADE HIS ARMS LIKE LIVING THINGS, AND DOCTOR OCTOPUS WAS BORN!
X-722

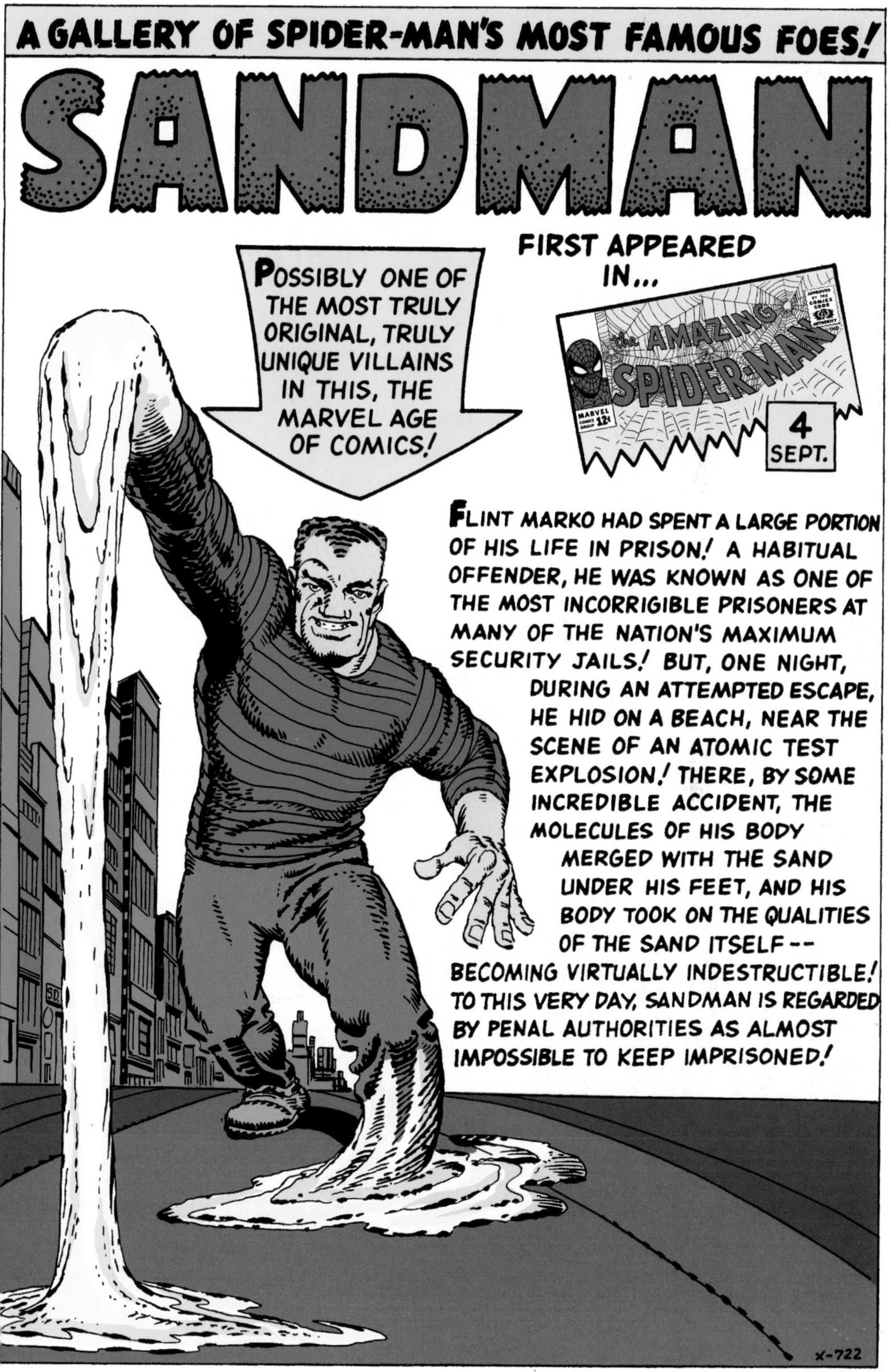
A GALLERY OF SPIDER-MAN'S MOST FAMOUS FOES!
SANDMAN
FIRST APPEARED IN...
the AMAZING SPIDER-MAN
MARVEL COMICS GROUP 12¢
4 SEPT.
POSSIBLY ONE OF THE MOST TRULY ORIGINAL, TRULY UNIQUE VILLAINS IN THIS, THE MARVEL AGE OF COMICS!
FLINT MARKO HAD SPENT A LARGE PORTION OF HIS LIFE IN PRISON! A HABITUAL OFFENDER, HE WAS KNOWN AS ONE OF THE MOST INCORRIGIBLE PRISONERS AT MANY OF THE NATION'S MAXIMUM SECURITY JAILS! BUT, ONE NIGHT, DURING AN ATTEMPTED ESCAPE, HE HID ON A BEACH, NEAR THE SCENE OF AN ATOMIC TEST EXPLOSION! THERE, BY SOME INCREDIBLE ACCIDENT, THE MOLECULES OF HIS BODY MERGED WITH THE SAND UNDER HIS FEET, AND HIS BODY TOOK ON THE QUALITIES OF THE SAND ITSELF -- BECOMING VIRTUALLY INDESTRUCTIBLE! TO THIS VERY DAY, SANDMAN IS REGARDED BY PENAL AUTHORITIES AS ALMOST IMPOSSIBLE TO KEEP IMPRISONED!
X-722

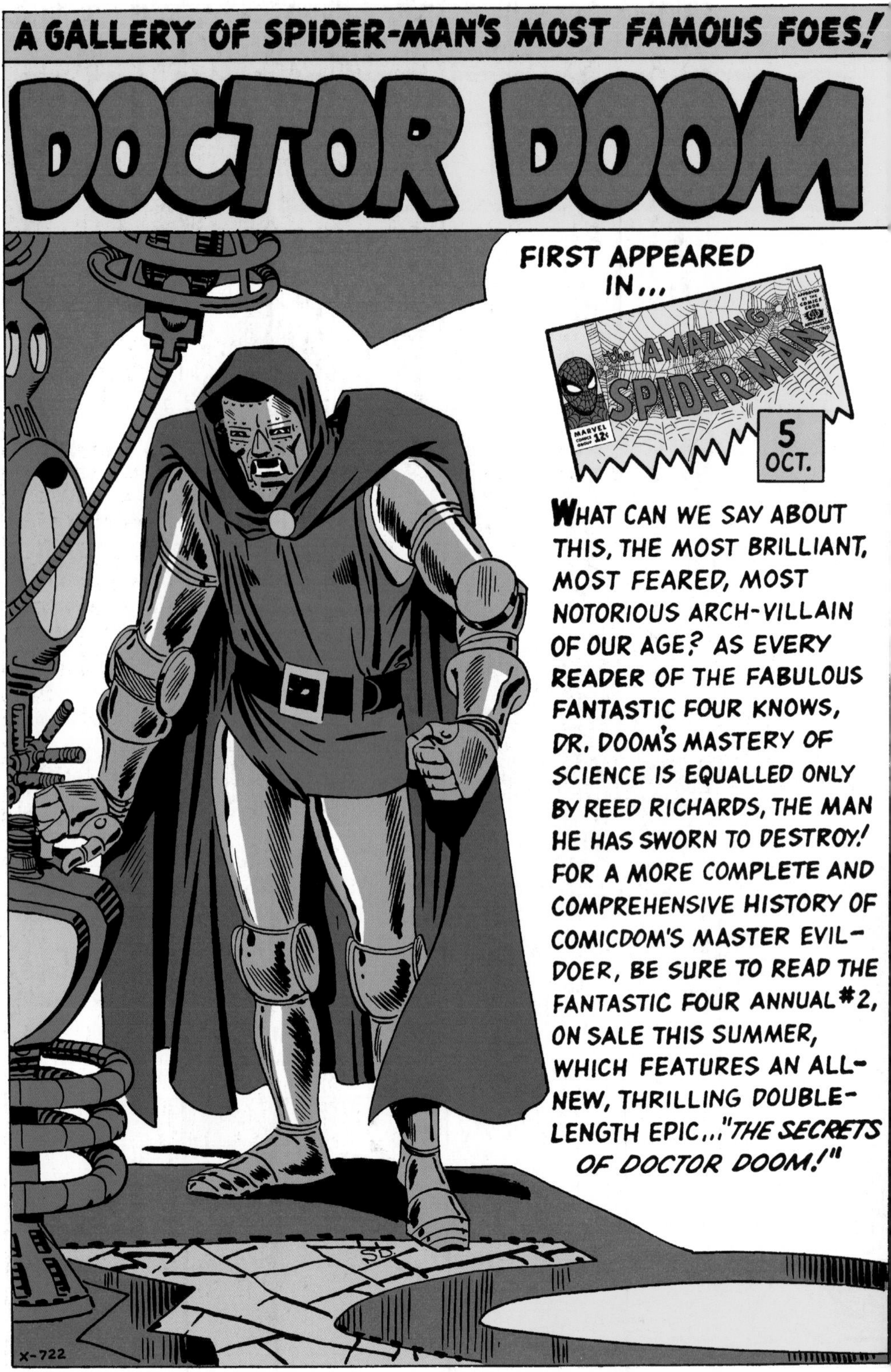
A GALLERY OF SPIDER-MAN'S MOST FAMOUS FOES!
DOCTOR DOOM
FIRST APPEARED IN...
THE AMAZING SPIDER-MAN
MARVEL COMICS GROUP 12¢
5 OCT.
WHAT CAN WE SAY ABOUT THIS, THE MOST BRILLIANT, MOST FEARED, MOST NOTORIOUS ARCH-VILLAIN OF OUR AGE? AS EVERY READER OF THE FABULOUS FANTASTIC FOUR KNOWS, DR. DOOM'S MASTERY OF SCIENCE IS EQUALLED ONLY BY REED RICHARDS, THE MAN HE HAS SWORN TO DESTROY! FOR A MORE COMPLETE AND COMPREHENSIVE HISTORY OF COMICDOM'S MASTER EVIL-DOER, BE SURE TO READ THE FANTASTIC FOUR ANNUAL #2, ON SALE THIS SUMMER, WHICH FEATURES AN ALL-NEW, THRILLING DOUBLE-LENGTH EPIC..."THE SECRETS OF DOCTOR DOOM!"
X-722

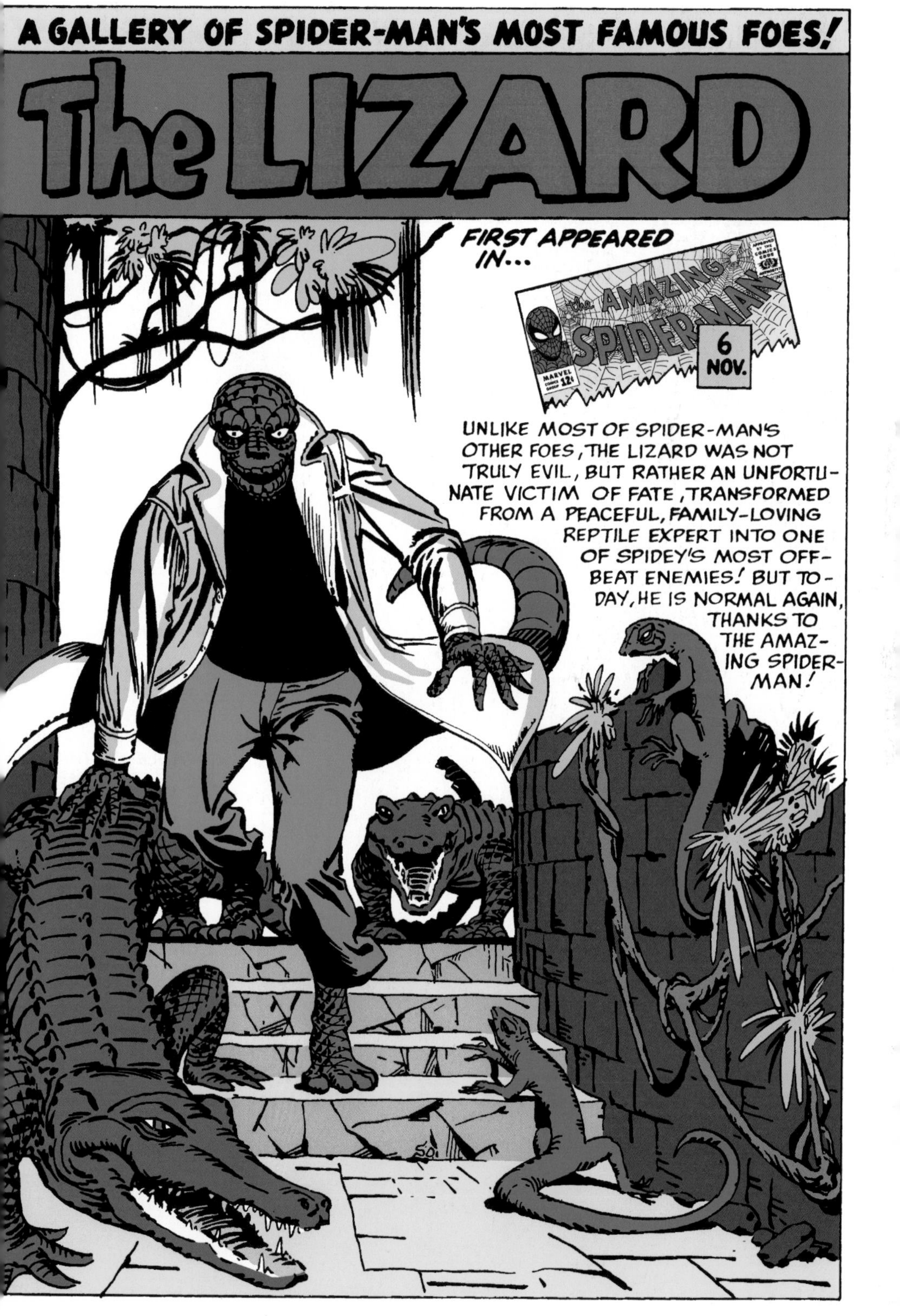
A GALLERY OF SPIDER-MAN'S MOST FAMOUS FOES!
The LIZARD
FIRST APPEARED IN...
THE AMAZING SPIDER-MAN
6 NOV.
UNLIKE MOST OF SPIDER-MAN'S OTHER FOES, THE LIZARD WAS NOT TRULY EVIL, BUT RATHER AN UNFORTUNATE VICTIM OF FATE, TRANSFORMED FROM A PEACEFUL, FAMILY-LOVING REPTILE EXPERT INTO ONE OF SPIDEY'S MOST OFF-BEAT ENEMIES! BUT TODAY, HE IS NORMAL AGAIN, THANKS TO THE AMAZING SPIDER-MAN!

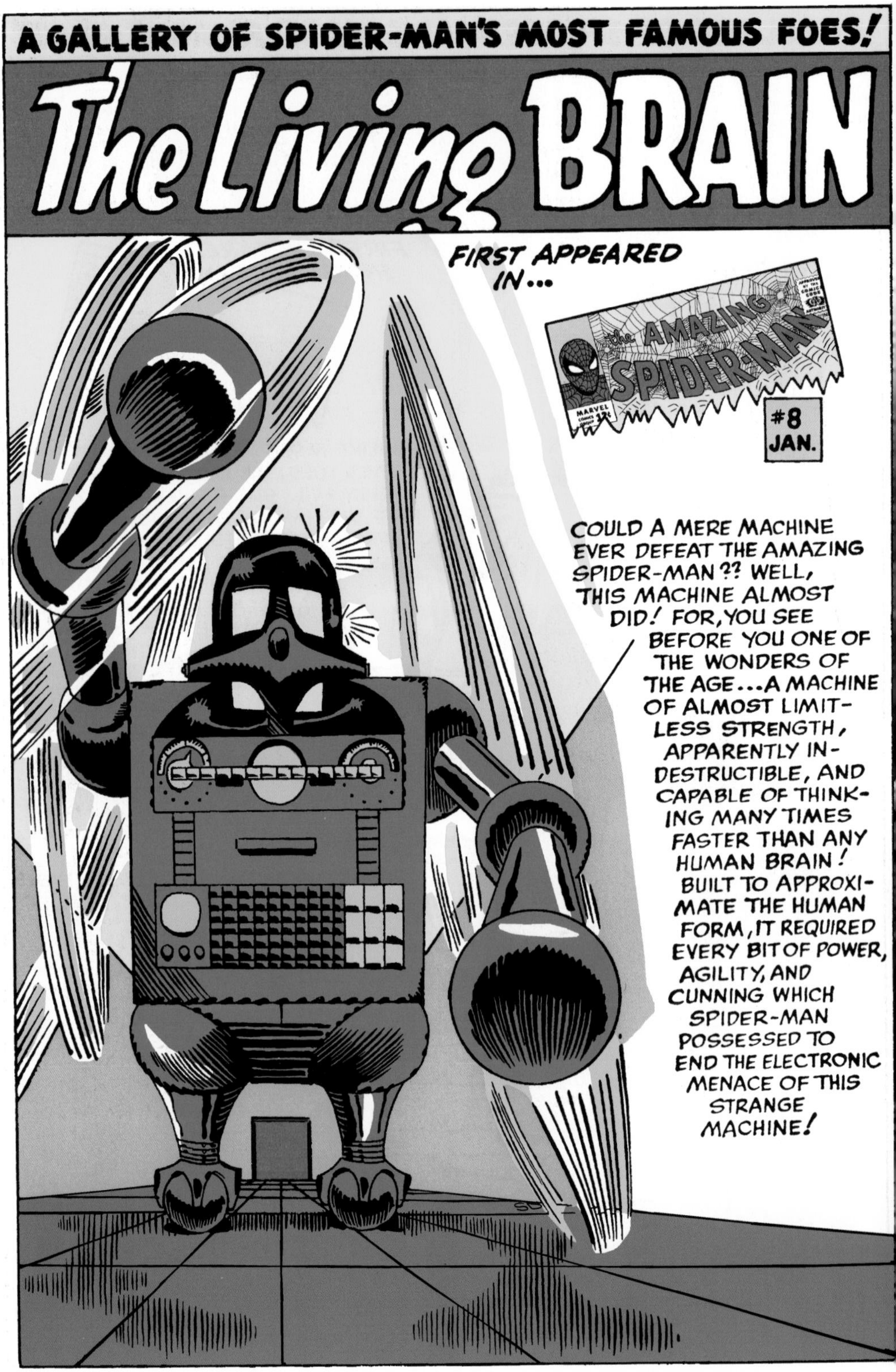
A GALLERY OF SPIDER-MAN'S MOST FAMOUS FOES!
The Living BRAIN
FIRST APPEARED IN...
the AMAZING SPIDER-MAN
MARVEL COMICS GROUP 12¢
#8 JAN.
COULD A MERE MACHINE EVER DEFEAT THE AMAZING SPIDER-MAN ?? WELL, THIS MACHINE ALMOST DID! FOR, YOU SEE BEFORE YOU ONE OF THE WONDERS OF THE AGE...A MACHINE OF ALMOST LIMIT-LESS STRENGTH, APPARENTLY IN-DESTRUCTIBLE, AND CAPABLE OF THINK-ING MANY TIMES FASTER THAN ANY HUMAN BRAIN! BUILT TO APPROXI-MATE THE HUMAN FORM, IT REQUIRED EVERY BIT OF POWER, AGILITY, AND CUNNING WHICH SPIDER-MAN POSSESSED TO END THE ELECTRONIC MENACE OF THIS STRANGE MACHINE!

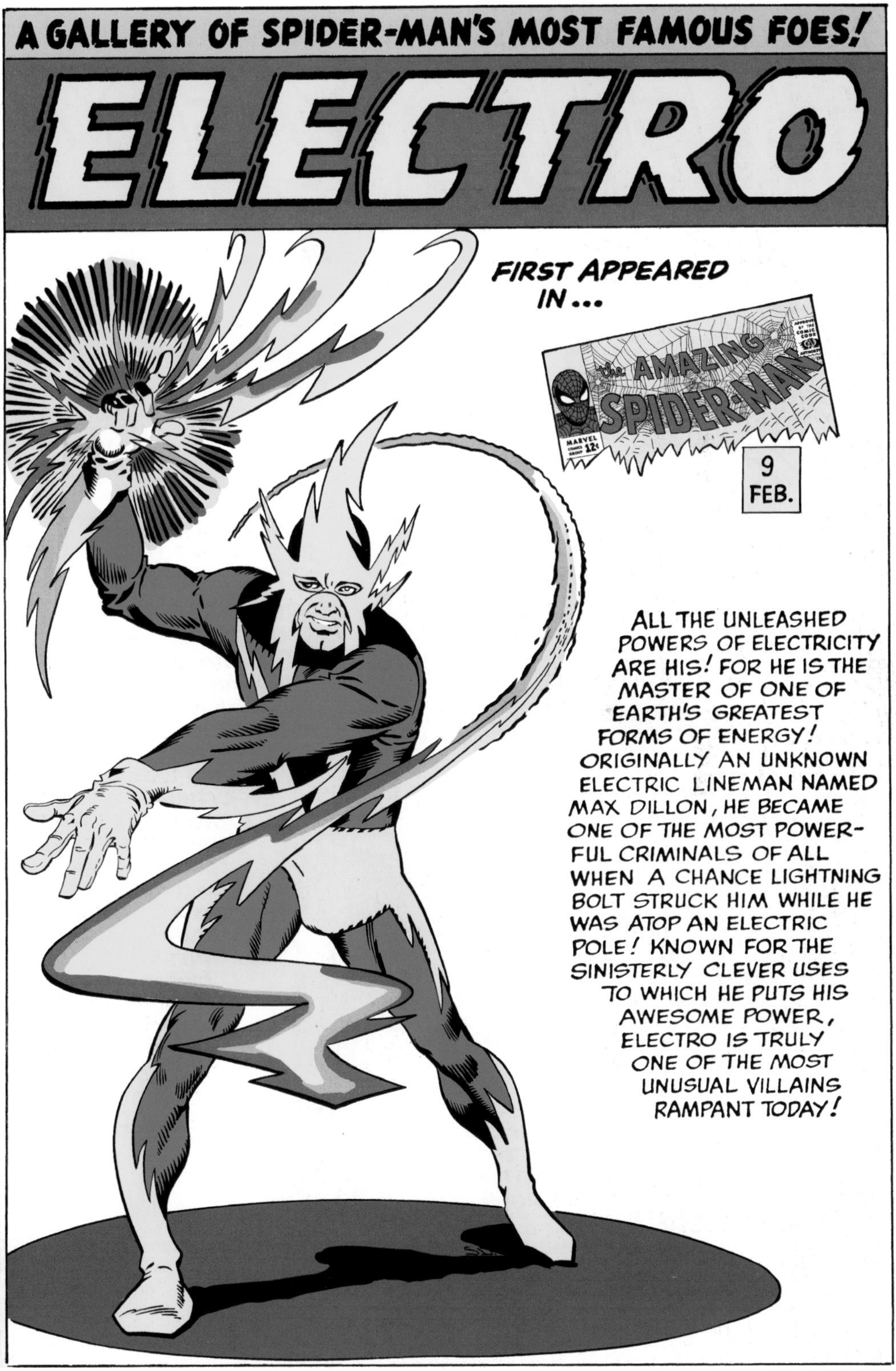
A GALLERY OF SPIDER-MAN'S MOST FAMOUS FOES!
ELECTRO
FIRST APPEARED IN...
the AMAZING SPIDER-MAN
MARVEL COMICS GROUP 12¢
9 FEB.
ALL THE UNLEASHED POWERS OF ELECTRICITY ARE HIS! FOR HE IS THE MASTER OF ONE OF EARTH'S GREATEST FORMS OF ENERGY! ORIGINALLY AN UNKNOWN ELECTRIC LINEMAN NAMED MAX DILLON, HE BECAME ONE OF THE MOST POWER-FUL CRIMINALS OF ALL WHEN A CHANCE LIGHTNING BOLT STRUCK HIM WHILE HE WAS ATOP AN ELECTRIC POLE! KNOWN FOR THE SINISTERLY CLEVER USES TO WHICH HE PUTS HIS AWESOME POWER, ELECTRO IS TRULY ONE OF THE MOST UNUSUAL VILLAINS RAMPANT TODAY!

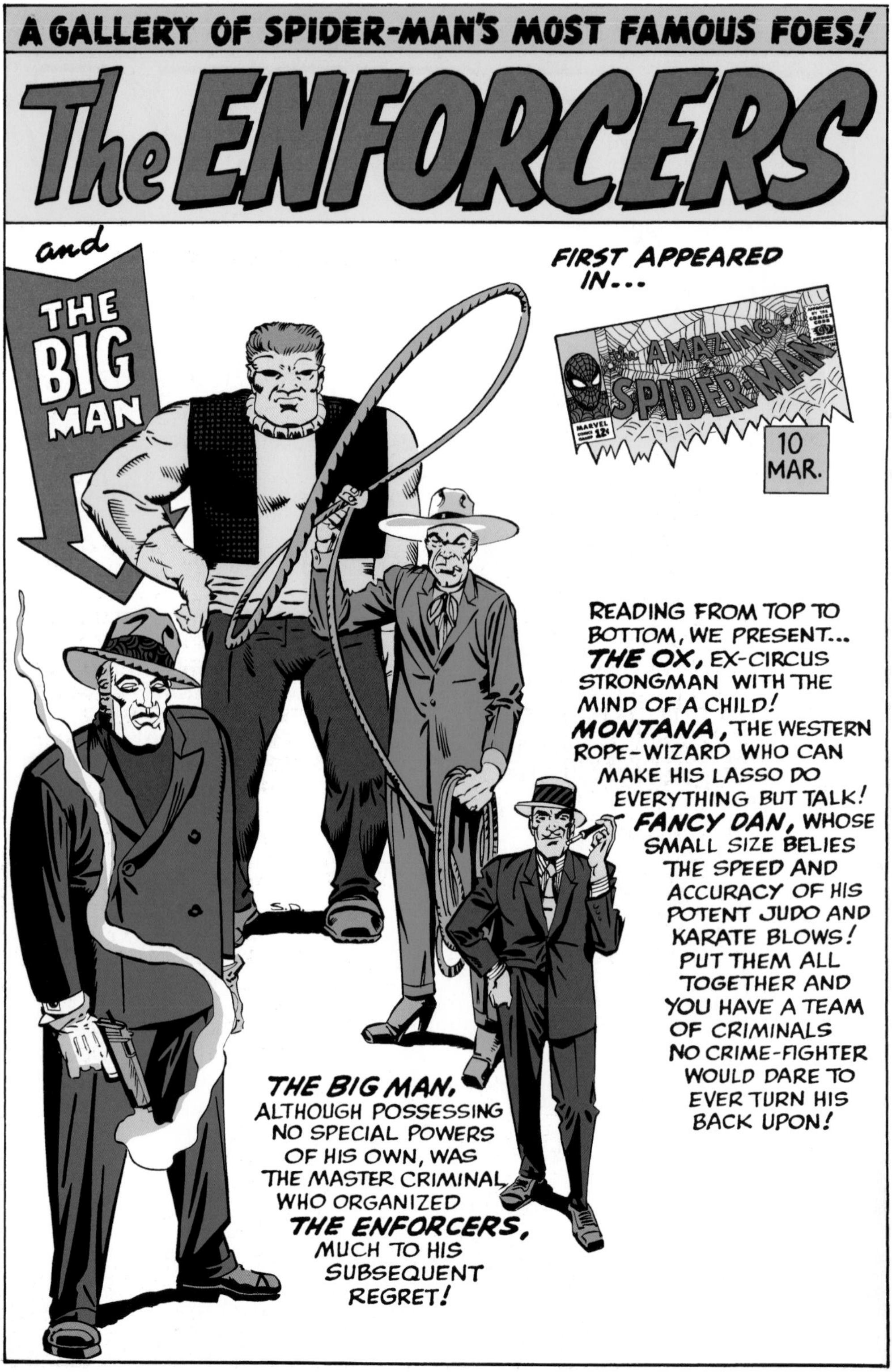
A GALLERY OF SPIDER-MAN'S MOST FAMOUS FOES!
The ENFORCERS
and THE BIG MAN
FIRST APPEARED IN...
THE AMAZING SPIDER-MAN
10 MAR.
READING FROM TOP TO BOTTOM, WE PRESENT... THE OX, EX-CIRCUS STRONGMAN WITH THE MIND OF A CHILD! MONTANA, THE WESTERN ROPE-WIZARD WHO CAN MAKE HIS LASSO DO EVERYTHING BUT TALK! FANCY DAN, WHOSE SMALL SIZE BELIES THE SPEED AND ACCURACY OF HIS POTENT JUDO AND KARATE BLOWS! PUT THEM ALL TOGETHER AND YOU HAVE A TEAM OF CRIMINALS NO CRIME-FIGHTER WOULD DARE TO EVER TURN HIS BACK UPON!
THE BIG MAN, ALTHOUGH POSSESSING NO SPECIAL POWERS OF HIS OWN, WAS THE MASTER CRIMINAL WHO ORGANIZED THE ENFORCERS, MUCH TO HIS SUBSEQUENT REGRET!

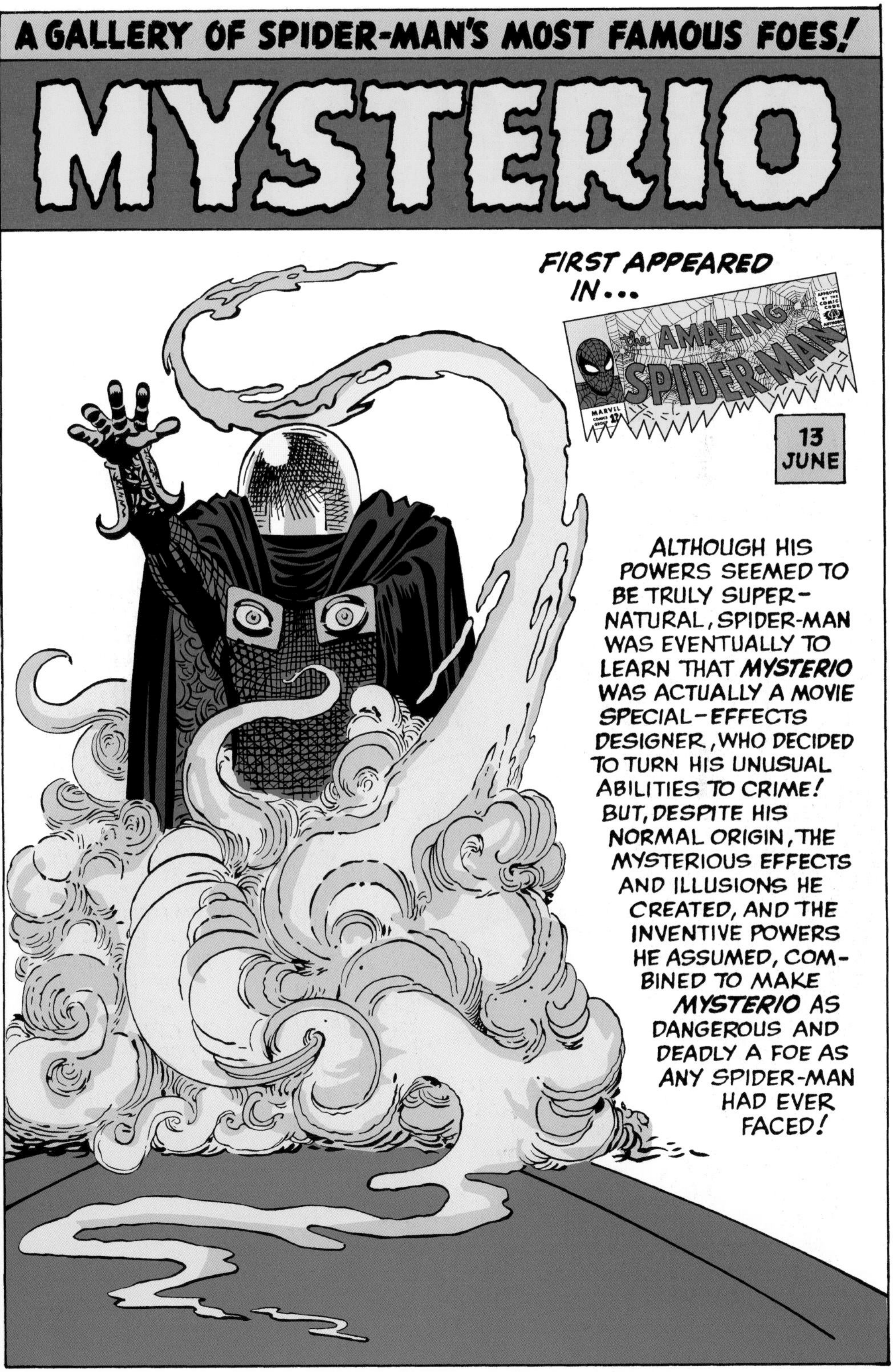

A GALLERY OF SPIDER-MAN'S MOST FAMOUS FOES!
MYSTERIO
FIRST APPEARED IN...
THE AMAZING SPIDER-MAN
13 JUNE
ALTHOUGH HIS POWERS SEEMED TO BE TRULY SUPER-NATURAL, SPIDER-MAN WAS EVENTUALLY TO LEARN THAT MYSTERIO WAS ACTUALLY A MOVIE SPECIAL-EFFECTS DESIGNER, WHO DECIDED TO TURN HIS UNUSUAL ABILITIES TO CRIME! BUT, DESPITE HIS NORMAL ORIGIN, THE MYSTERIOUS EFFECTS AND ILLUSIONS HE CREATED, AND THE INVENTIVE POWERS HE ASSUMED, COMBINED TO MAKE MYSTERIO AS DANGEROUS AND DEADLY A FOE AS ANY SPIDER-MAN HAD EVER FACED!

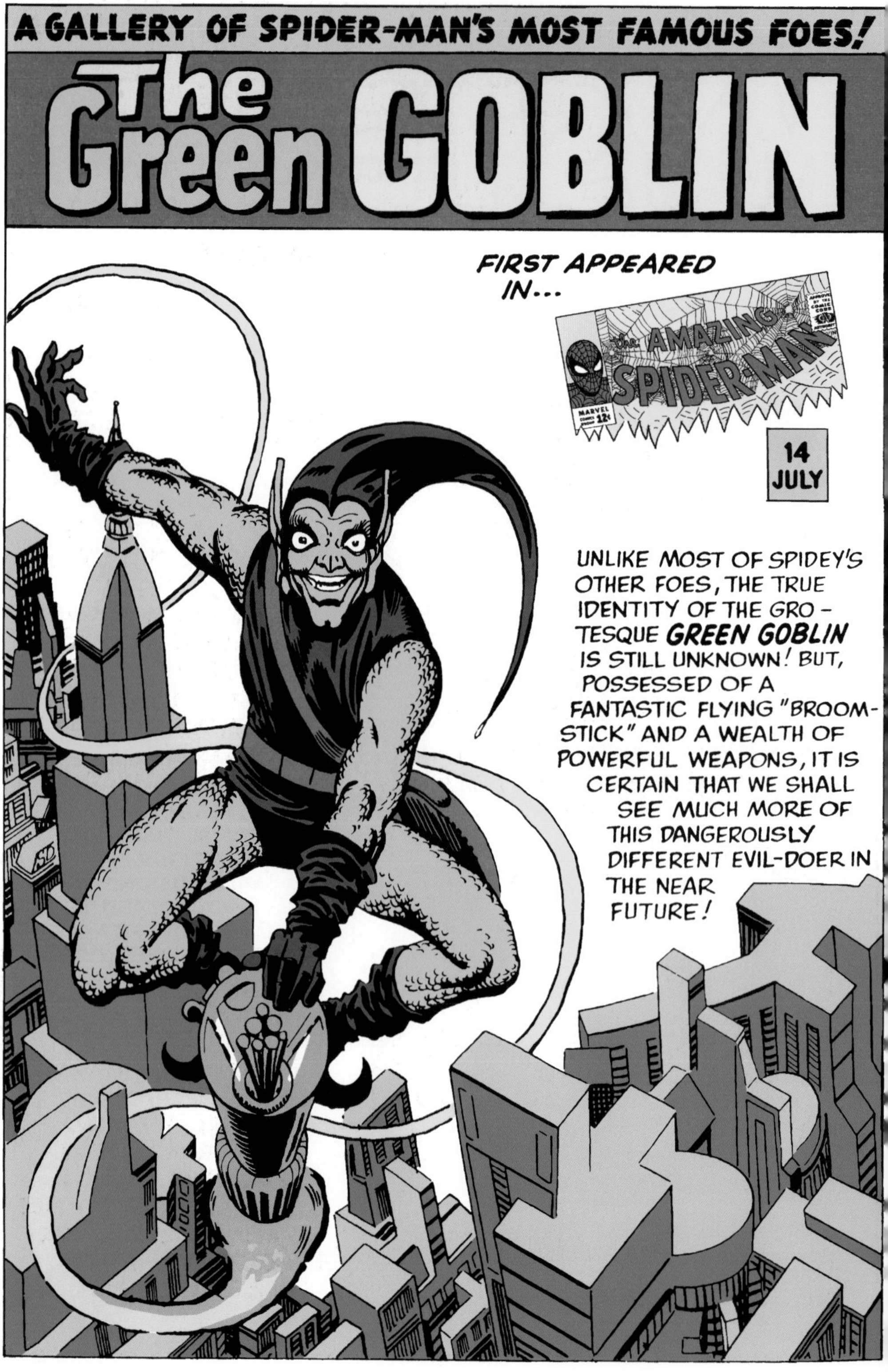
A GALLERY OF SPIDER-MAN'S MOST FAMOUS FOES!
The Green GOBLIN
FIRST APPEARED IN...
The AMAZING SPIDER-MAN
MARVEL COMICS GROUP 12¢
14 JULY
UNLIKE MOST OF SPIDEY'S OTHER FOES, THE TRUE IDENTITY OF THE GRO-TESQUE GREEN GOBLIN IS STILL UNKNOWN! BUT, POSSESSED OF A FANTASTIC FLYING "BROOM-STICK" AND A WEALTH OF POWERFUL WEAPONS, IT IS CERTAIN THAT WE SHALL SEE MUCH MORE OF THIS DANGEROUSLY DIFFERENT EVIL-DOER IN THE NEAR FUTURE!

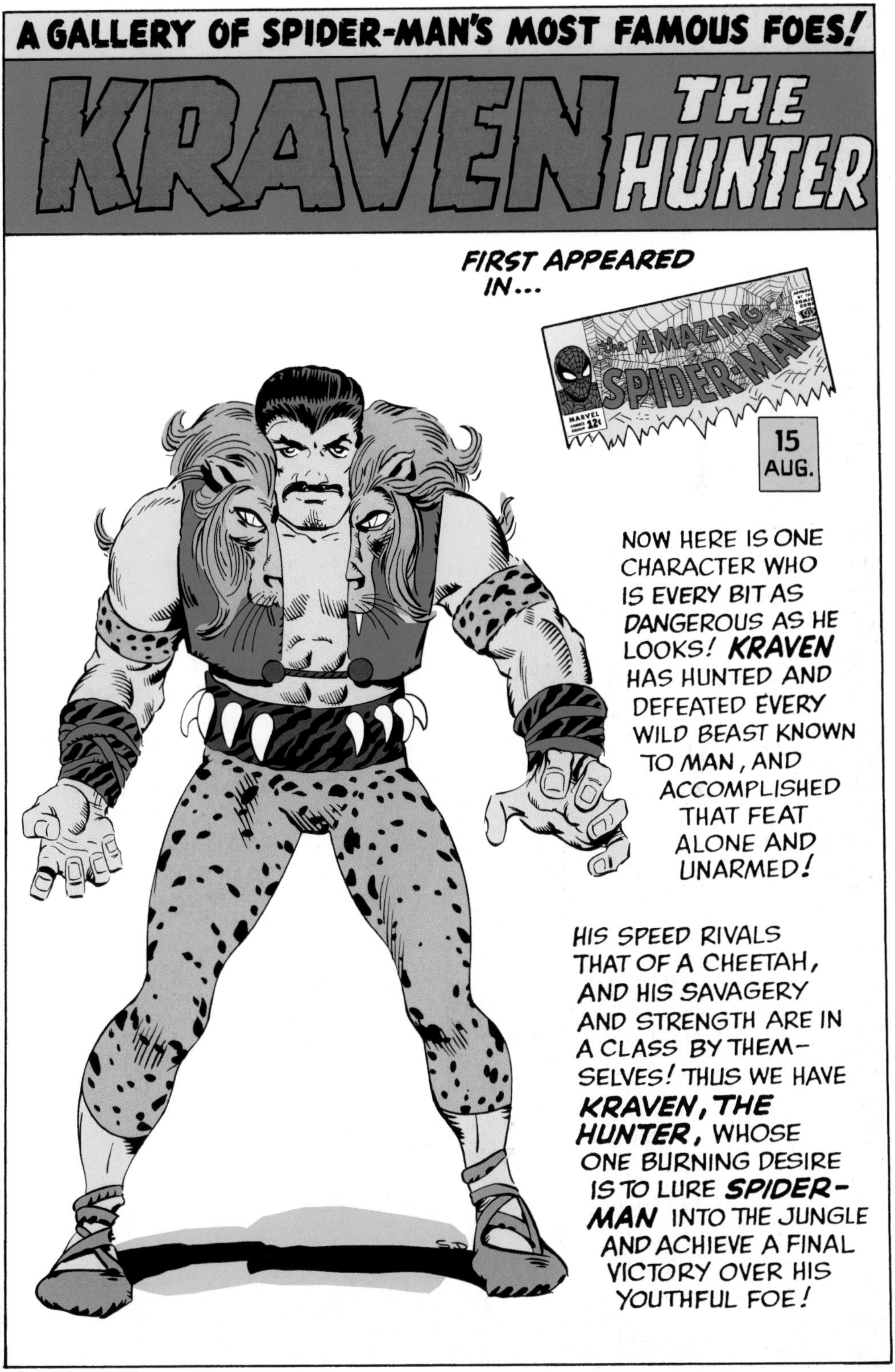
A GALLERY OF SPIDER-MAN'S MOST FAMOUS FOES!
KRAVEN THE HUNTER
FIRST APPEARED IN...
the AMAZING SPIDER-MAN
15 AUG.
NOW HERE IS ONE CHARACTER WHO IS EVERY BIT AS DANGEROUS AS HE LOOKS! KRAVEN HAS HUNTED AND DEFEATED EVERY WILD BEAST KNOWN TO MAN, AND ACCOMPLISHED THAT FEAT ALONE AND UNARMED!
HIS SPEED RIVALS THAT OF A CHEETAH, AND HIS SAVAGERY AND STRENGTH ARE IN A CLASS BY THEM-SELVES! THUS WE HAVE KRAVEN, THE HUNTER, WHOSE ONE BURNING DESIRE IS TO LURE SPIDER-MAN INTO THE JUNGLE AND ACHIEVE A FINAL VICTORY OVER HIS YOUTHFUL FOE!

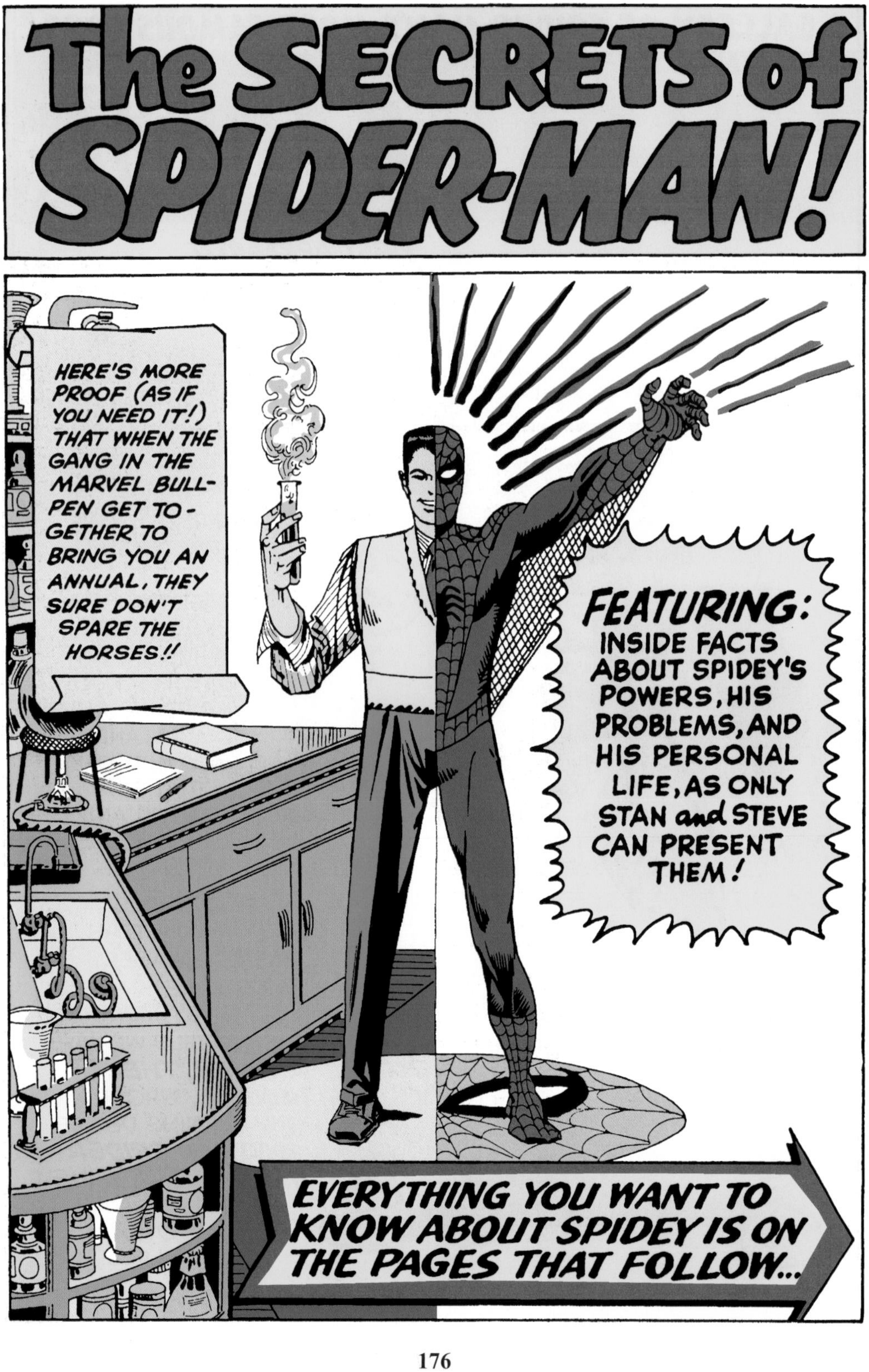
The SECRETS of SPIDER-MAN!
HERE'S MORE PROOF (AS IF YOU NEED IT!) THAT WHEN THE GANG IN THE MARVEL BULL-PEN GET TO-GETHER TO BRING YOU AN ANNUAL, THEY SURE DON'T SPARE THE HORSES!!
FEATURING: INSIDE FACTS ABOUT SPIDEY'S POWERS, HIS PROBLEMS, AND HIS PERSONAL LIFE, AS ONLY STAN and STEVE CAN PRESENT THEM!
EVERYTHING YOU WANT TO KNOW ABOUT SPIDEY IS ON THE PAGES THAT FOLLOW...

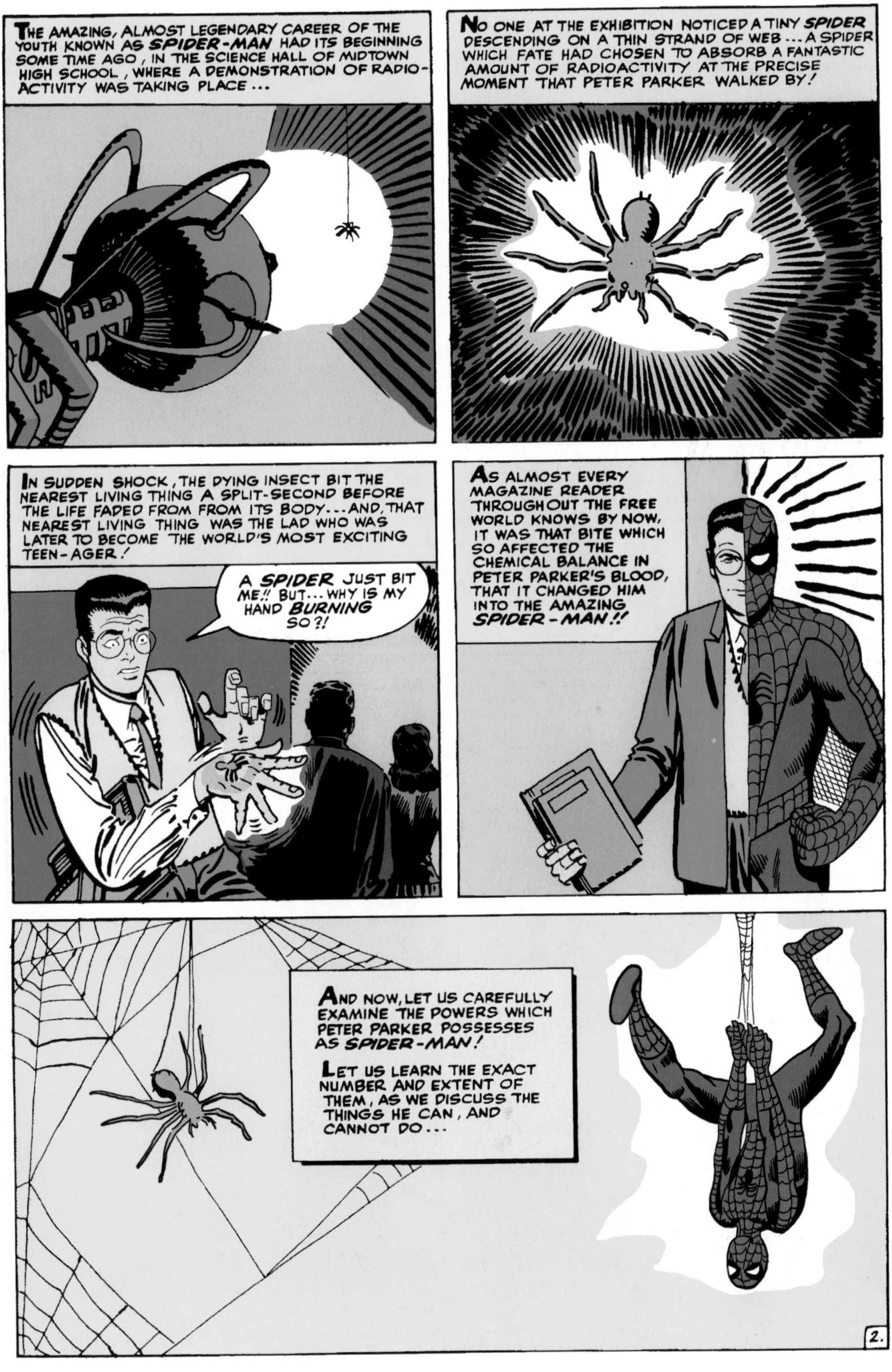
THE AMAZING, ALMOST LEGENDARY CAREER OF THE YOUTH KNOWN AS SPIDER-MAN HAD ITS BEGINNING SOME TIME AGO, IN THE SCIENCE HALL OF MIDTOWN HIGH SCHOOL, WHERE A DEMONSTRATION OF RADIO-ACTIVITY WAS TAKING PLACE...
NO ONE AT THE EXHIBITION NOTICED A TINY SPIDER DESCENDING ON A THIN STRAND OF WEB... A SPIDER WHICH FATE HAD CHOSEN TO ABSORB A FANTASTIC AMOUNT OF RADIOACTIVITY AT THE PRECISE MOMENT THAT PETER PARKER WALKED BY!
IN SUDDEN SHOCK, THE DYING INSECT BIT THE NEAREST LIVING THING A SPLIT-SECOND BEFORE THE LIFE FADED FROM FROM ITS BODY... AND, THAT NEAREST LIVING THING WAS THE LAD WHO WAS LATER TO BECOME THE WORLD'S MOST EXCITING TEEN-AGER!
A SPIDER JUST BIT ME!! BUT... WHY IS MY HAND BURNING SO?!
AS ALMOST EVERY MAGAZINE READER THROUGHOUT THE FREE WORLD KNOWS BY NOW, IT WAS THAT BITE WHICH SO AFFECTED THE CHEMICAL BALANCE IN PETER PARKER'S BLOOD, THAT IT CHANGED HIM INTO THE AMAZING SPIDER-MAN!!
AND NOW, LET US CAREFULLY EXAMINE THE POWERS WHICH PETER PARKER POSSESSES AS SPIDER-MAN!
LET US LEARN THE EXACT NUMBER AND EXTENT OF THEM, AS WE DISCUSS THE THINGS HE CAN, AND CANNOT DO...
2.

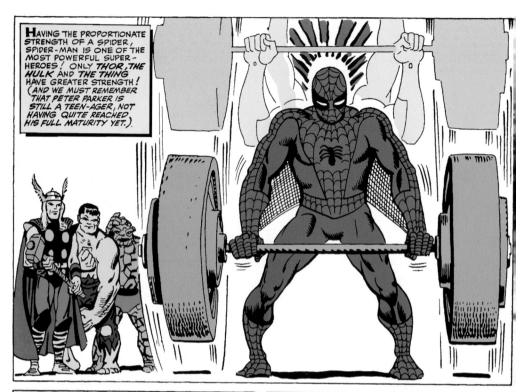

HAVING THE PROPORTIONATE STRENGTH OF A SPIDER, SPIDER-MAN IS ONE OF THE MOST POWERFUL SUPER-HEROES! ONLY *THOR*, *THE HULK* AND *THE THING* HAVE GREATER STRENGTH! (AND WE MUST REMEMBER THAT PETER PARKER IS *STILL A TEEN-AGER*, NOT HAVING QUITE REACHED HIS FULL MATURITY YET.)

ONE OF SPIDER-MAN'S MOST VALUABLE ASSETS IS HIS *CLINGING ABILITY!* LIKE A GIANT HUMAN SPIDER, HIS HANDS AND FEET SUPPORT HIM AGAINST THE PULL OF GRAVITY AS THOUGH THEY HAVE THOUSANDS OF TINY SUCTION CUPS!

NO MATTER HOW SMOOTH A SURFACE MAY BE... NO MATTER HOW HIGH, OR HOW PRECARIOUS IT MAY BE, ANY AREA THAT AN ACTUAL SPIDER CAN CLING TO, CAN ALSO SUPPORT THE AMAZING TEEN-AGE ADVENTURER!

3.

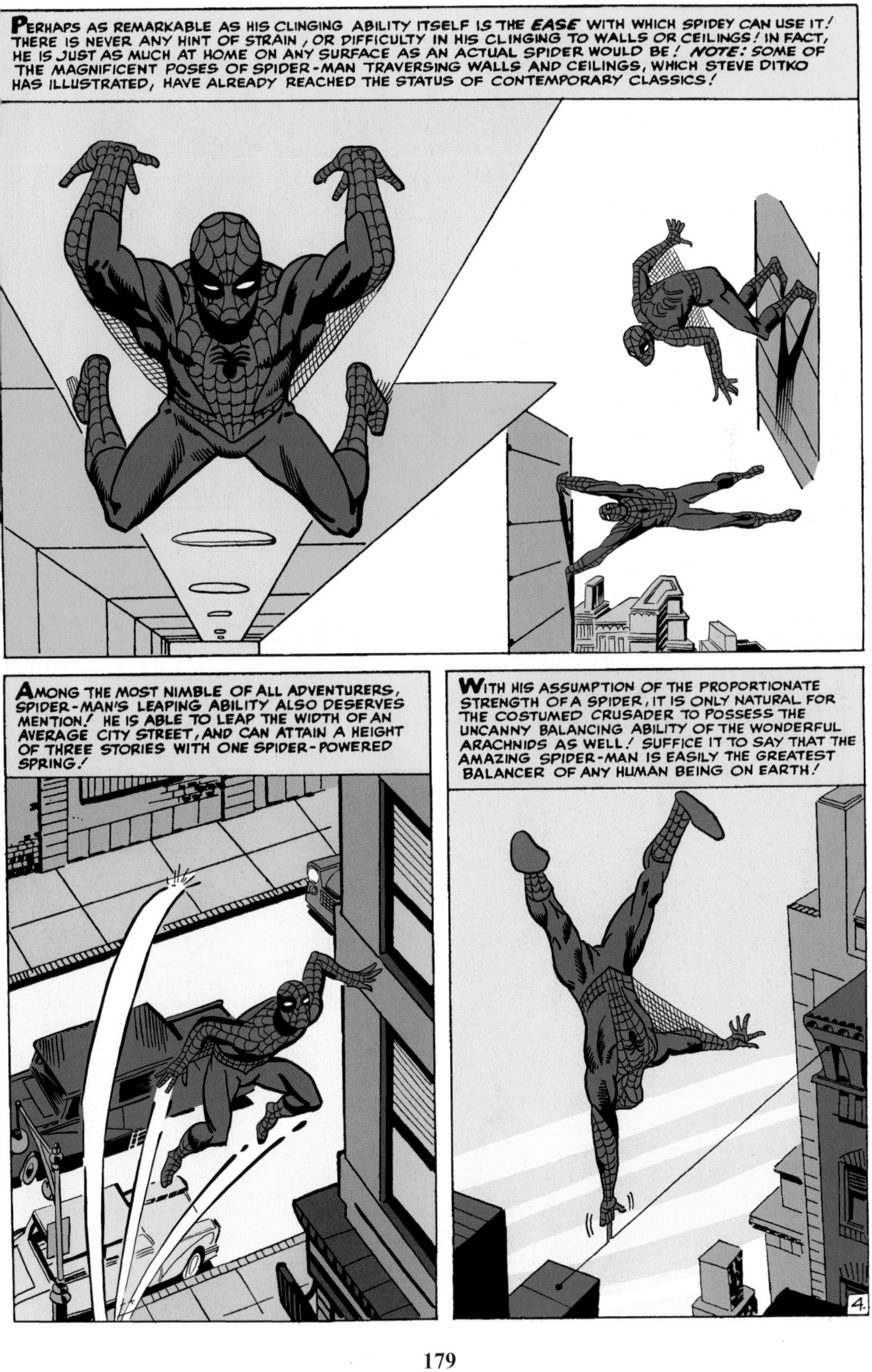
PERHAPS AS REMARKABLE AS HIS CLINGING ABILITY ITSELF IS THE EASE WITH WHICH SPIDEY CAN USE IT! THERE IS NEVER ANY HINT OF STRAIN, OR DIFFICULTY IN HIS CLINGING TO WALLS OR CEILINGS! IN FACT, HE IS JUST AS MUCH AT HOME ON ANY SURFACE AS AN ACTUAL SPIDER WOULD BE! NOTE: SOME OF THE MAGNIFICENT POSES OF SPIDER-MAN TRAVERSING WALLS AND CEILINGS, WHICH STEVE DITKO HAS ILLUSTRATED, HAVE ALREADY REACHED THE STATUS OF CONTEMPORARY CLASSICS!
AMONG THE MOST NIMBLE OF ALL ADVENTURERS, SPIDER-MAN'S LEAPING ABILITY ALSO DESERVES MENTION! HE IS ABLE TO LEAP THE WIDTH OF AN AVERAGE CITY STREET, AND CAN ATTAIN A HEIGHT OF THREE STORIES WITH ONE SPIDER-POWERED SPRING!
WITH HIS ASSUMPTION OF THE PROPORTIONATE STRENGTH OF A SPIDER, IT IS ONLY NATURAL FOR THE COSTUMED CRUSADER TO POSSESS THE UNCANNY BALANCING ABILITY OF THE WONDERFUL ARACHNIDS AS WELL! SUFFICE IT TO SAY THAT THE AMAZING SPIDER-MAN IS EASILY THE GREATEST BALANCER OF ANY HUMAN BEING ON EARTH!
4.

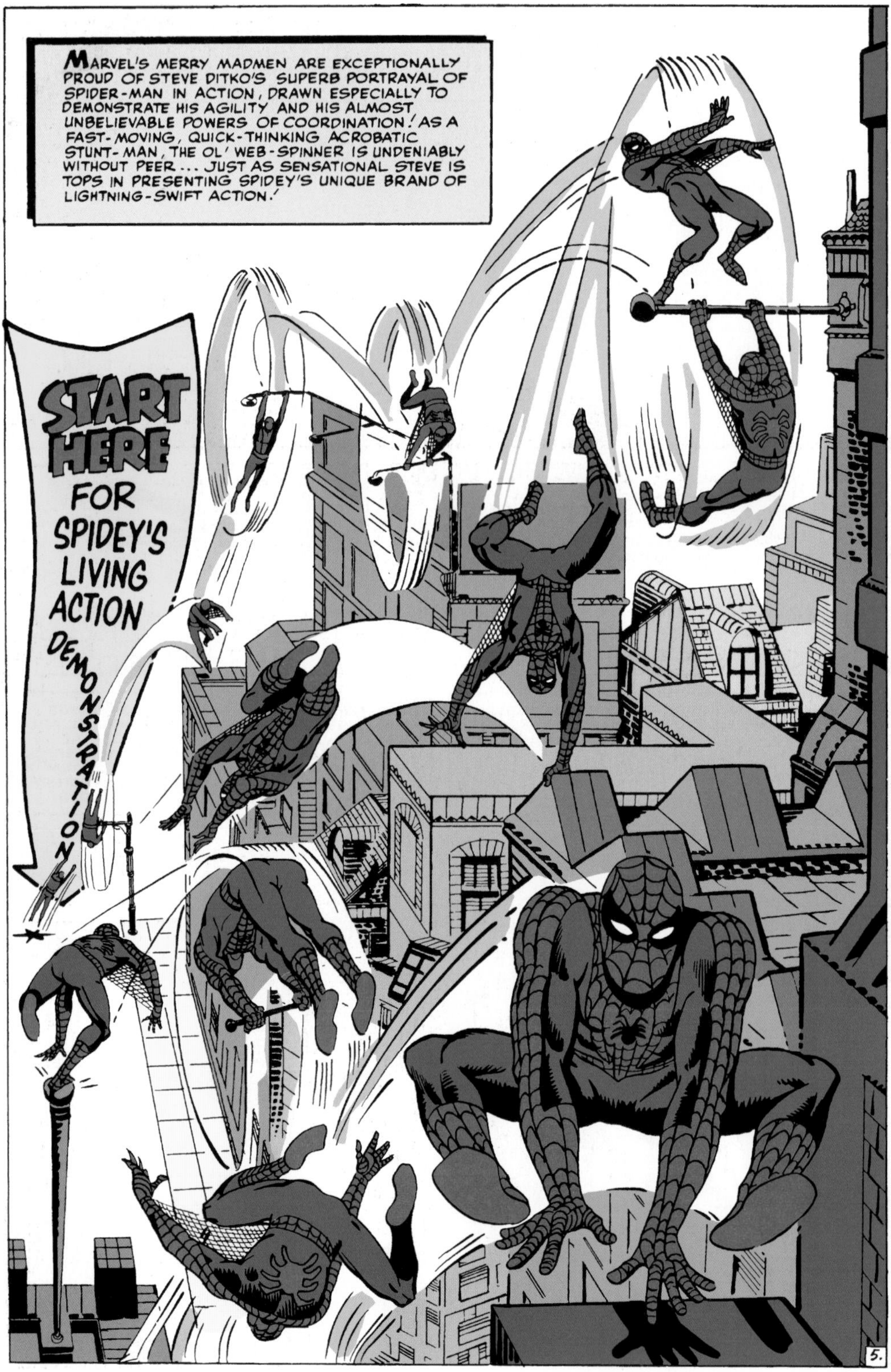
MARVEL'S MERRY MADMEN ARE EXCEPTIONALLY PROUD OF STEVE DITKO'S SUPERB PORTRAYAL OF SPIDER-MAN IN ACTION, DRAWN ESPECIALLY TO DEMONSTRATE HIS AGILITY AND HIS ALMOST UNBELIEVABLE POWERS OF COORDINATION! AS A FAST-MOVING, QUICK-THINKING ACROBATIC STUNT-MAN, THE OL' WEB-SPINNER IS UNDENIABLY WITHOUT PEER... JUST AS SENSATIONAL STEVE IS TOPS IN PRESENTING SPIDEY'S UNIQUE BRAND OF LIGHTNING-SWIFT ACTION!
START HERE FOR SPIDEY'S LIVING ACTION DEMONSTRATION
5.

FORTUNATELY FOR PETER PARKER (AND THE WORLD AT LARGE), THE AMAZING TEEN-AGER IS A BRILLIANT SCIENCE STUDENT! HE HAS DEVOTED LONG HOURS OF STUDY TO LEARNING EVERYTHING HE CAN ABOUT SPIDERS! ALTHOUGH IT IS NOT A MATTER OF PUBLIC KNOWLEDGE, HE IS PROBABLY THE WORLD'S GREATEST AUTHORITY ON THE SUBJECT OF WEBS AND THEIR CREATION...

HIS WEB-MAKING ABILITY IS ONE [OF HIS?] CLOSELY-GUARDED SECRETS! BU[T] [WE CAN TELL] YOU THIS... HE MAKES HIS OWN WEB [UNDER] THE MOST EXACTING CONDITIONS IN [AN EASY?] STORING IT IN SMALL, COMPACT CYLIND[ERS] [LIKE] MINIATURE TOOTHPASTE TUBES!

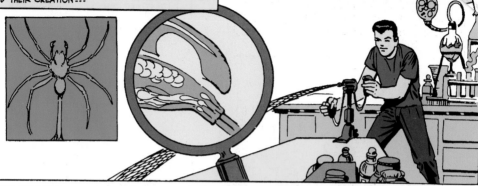

AS ANY SPIDER-MAN READER KNOWS, SPIDEY'S WEB-SHOOTER IS WORN AT HIS WRIST, AND ACTIVATED BY THE SLIGHTEST TOUCH OF HIS FINGER UPON THE SUPER-SENSITIVE ELECTRODE LOCATED ON THE PALM OF HIS HAND!

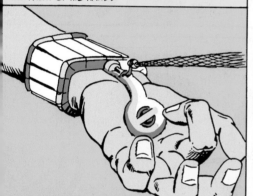

INASMUCH AS HIS WEBBING IS HIS MOST POTENT WEAPON, THE MASKED ADVENTURER ALWAYS CARRIES SPARE WEB-FLUID CAPSULES CLIPPED ONTO HIS INGENIOUSLY DESIGNED UTILITY BELT!

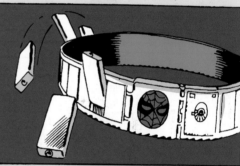

BY ADJUSTING THE NOZZLE OF HIS WEB-SHOOTER IN ONE EASY MOTION, SPIDEY CAN EJECT HIS WEB FLUID IN ANY ONE OF THREE DIFFERENT WAYS...

1. AS A THIN, INCREDIBLY STRONG LINE...

2. AS A FINE, QUICK-SPREADING SPRAY...

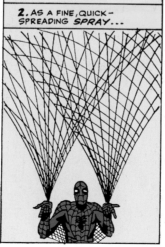

3. OR AS A THICK, TREMENDOUSLY ADHESIVE LIQUID...!

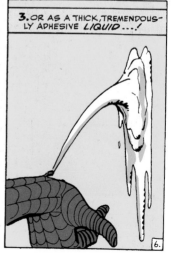

6.

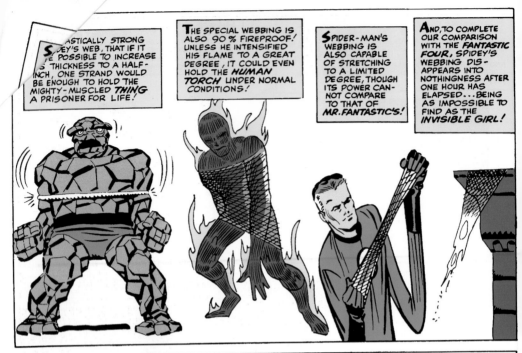

...ASTICALLY STRONG SPIDEY'S WEB, THAT IF IT WE POSSIBLE TO INCREASE ITS THICKNESS TO A HALF-INCH, ONE STRAND WOULD BE ENOUGH TO HOLD THE MIGHTY-MUSCLED *THING* A PRISONER FOR LIFE!

THE SPECIAL WEBBING IS ALSO 90 % FIREPROOF! UNLESS HE INTENSIFIED HIS FLAME TO A GREAT DEGREE, IT COULD EVEN HOLD THE *HUMAN TORCH* UNDER NORMAL CONDITIONS!

SPIDER-MAN'S WEBBING IS ALSO CAPABLE OF STRETCHING TO A LIMITED DEGREE, THOUGH ITS POWER CAN-NOT COMPARE TO THAT OF *MR. FANTASTIC'S!*

AND, TO COMPLETE OUR COMPARISON WITH THE *FANTASTIC FOUR,* SPIDEY'S WEBBING DIS-APPEARS INTO NOTHINGNESS AFTER ONE HOUR HAS ELAPSED...BEING AS IMPOSSIBLE TO FIND AS THE *INVISIBLE GIRL!*

HAVING DEVOTED MANY LONG HOURS OF PRACTICE TO THE OPERATION OF HIS WEB, THE TERRIFIC TEEN-AGER CAN NOW USE IT IN MANY DIFFERENT WAYS....

AS A SHIELD...

A PARACHUTE...

A SAFETY NET...

AS SKIIS...

AS A RAFT...

AS A CLUB...

A BARRIER...

A BALL

OR PLAIN, SIMPLE STICKY GLUE!

7.

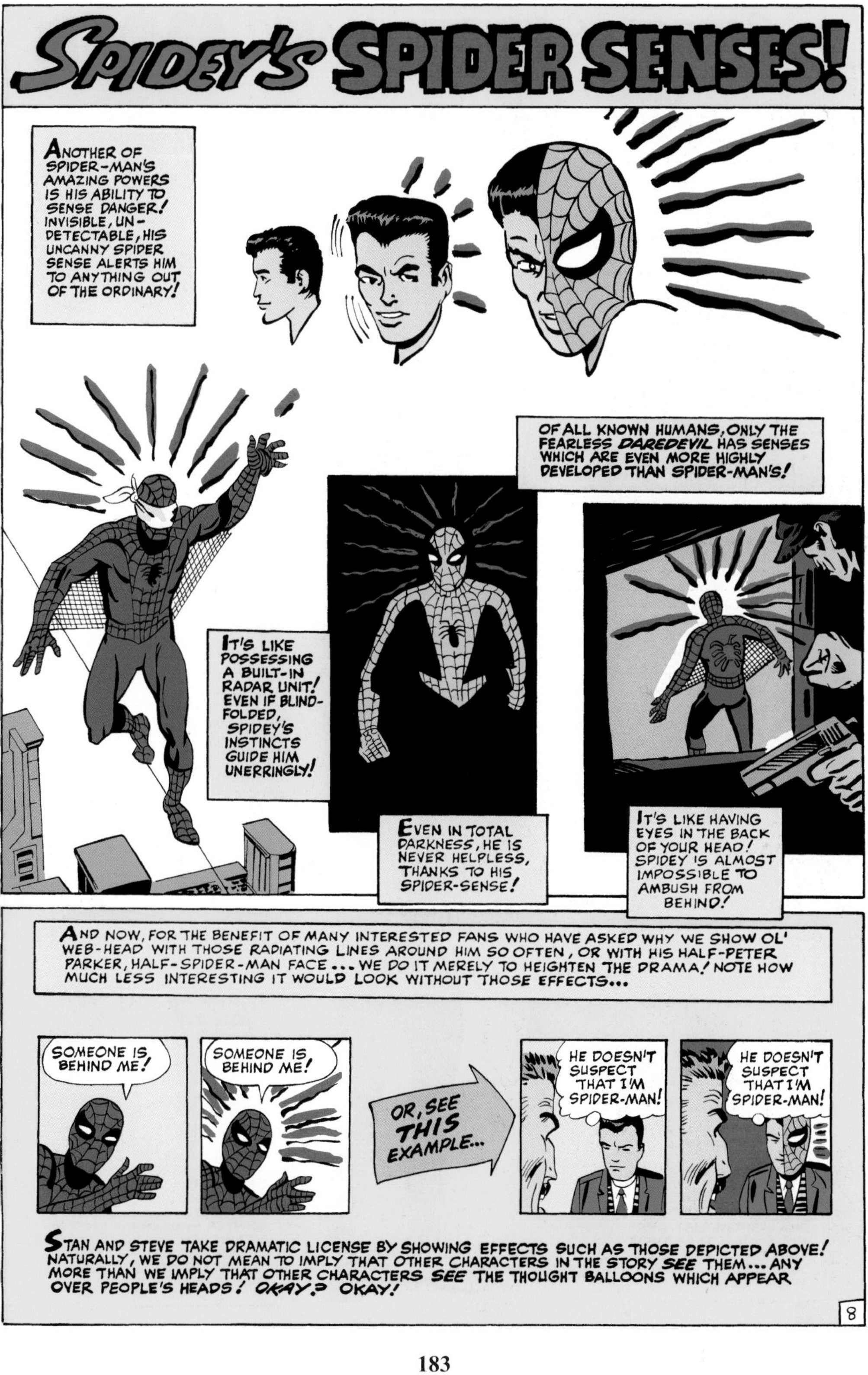
SPIDEY'S SPIDER SENSES!
ANOTHER OF SPIDER-MAN'S AMAZING POWERS IS HIS ABILITY TO SENSE DANGER! INVISIBLE, UN-DETECTABLE, HIS UNCANNY SPIDER SENSE ALERTS HIM TO ANYTHING OUT OF THE ORDINARY!
OF ALL KNOWN HUMANS, ONLY THE FEARLESS DAREDEVIL HAS SENSES WHICH ARE EVEN MORE HIGHLY DEVELOPED THAN SPIDER-MAN'S!
IT'S LIKE POSSESSING A BUILT-IN RADAR UNIT! EVEN IF BLIND-FOLDED, SPIDEY'S INSTINCTS GUIDE HIM UNERRINGLY!
EVEN IN TOTAL DARKNESS, HE IS NEVER HELPLESS, THANKS TO HIS SPIDER-SENSE!
IT'S LIKE HAVING EYES IN THE BACK OF YOUR HEAD! SPIDEY IS ALMOST IMPOSSIBLE TO AMBUSH FROM BEHIND!
AND NOW, FOR THE BENEFIT OF MANY INTERESTED FANS WHO HAVE ASKED WHY WE SHOW OL' WEB-HEAD WITH THOSE RADIATING LINES AROUND HIM SO OFTEN, OR WITH HIS HALF-PETER PARKER, HALF-SPIDER-MAN FACE... WE DO IT MERELY TO HEIGHTEN THE DRAMA! NOTE HOW MUCH LESS INTERESTING IT WOULD LOOK WITHOUT THOSE EFFECTS...
SOMEONE IS BEHIND ME!
SOMEONE IS BEHIND ME!
OR, SEE THIS EXAMPLE...
HE DOESN'T SUSPECT THAT I'M SPIDER-MAN!
HE DOESN'T SUSPECT THAT I'M SPIDER-MAN!
STAN AND STEVE TAKE DRAMATIC LICENSE BY SHOWING EFFECTS SUCH AS THOSE DEPICTED ABOVE! NATURALLY, WE DO NOT MEAN TO IMPLY THAT OTHER CHARACTERS IN THE STORY SEE THEM... ANY MORE THAN WE IMPLY THAT OTHER CHARACTERS SEE THE THOUGHT BALLOONS WHICH APPEAR OVER PEOPLE'S HEADS! OKAY? OKAY!
8

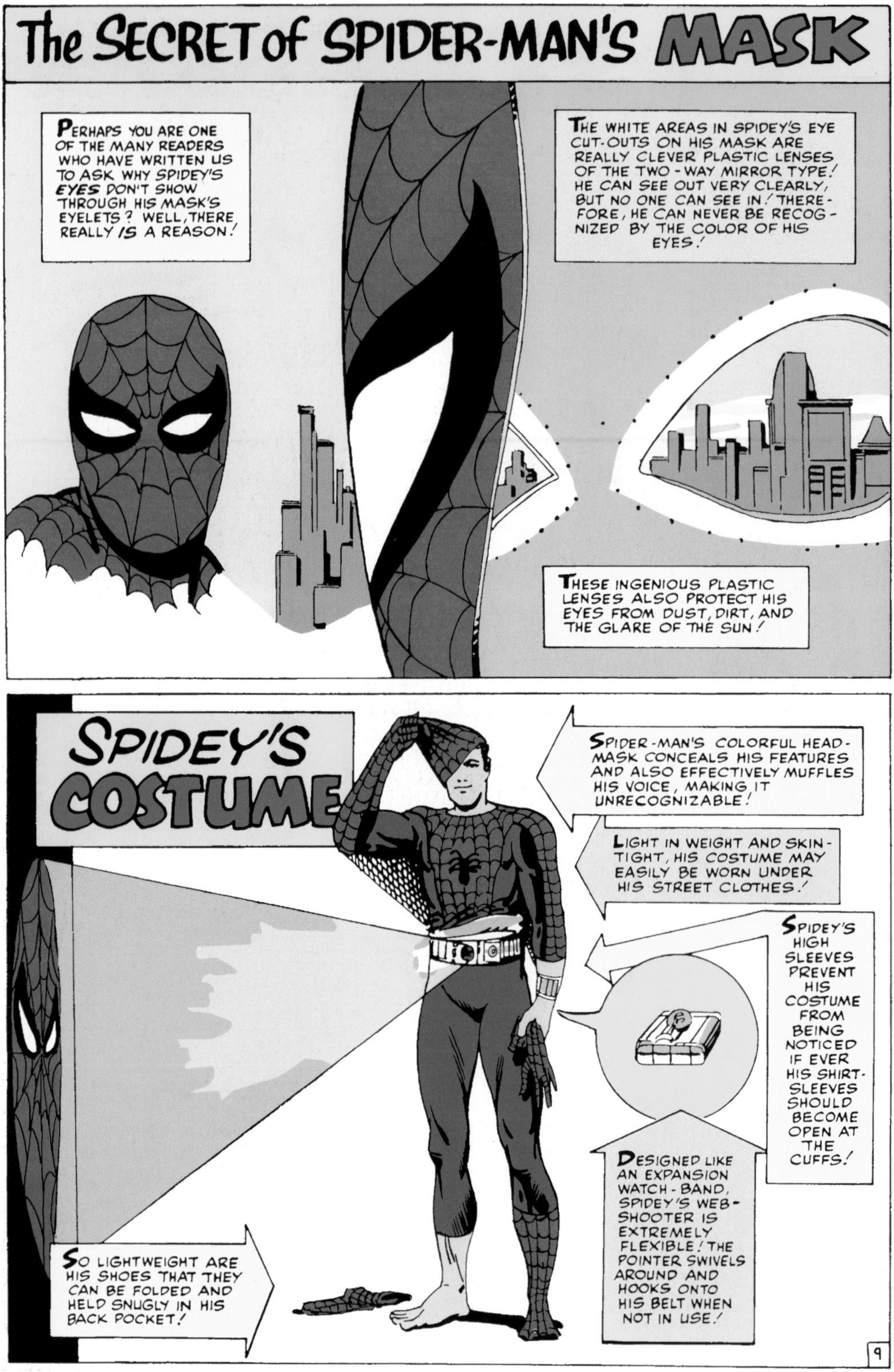

The SECRET of SPIDER-MAN'S MASK

PERHAPS YOU ARE ONE OF THE MANY READERS WHO HAVE WRITTEN US TO ASK WHY SPIDEY'S *EYES* DON'T SHOW THROUGH HIS MASK'S EYELETS? WELL, THERE, REALLY *IS* A REASON!

THE WHITE AREAS IN SPIDEY'S EYE CUT-OUTS ON HIS MASK ARE REALLY CLEVER PLASTIC LENSES OF THE TWO-WAY MIRROR TYPE! HE CAN SEE OUT VERY CLEARLY, BUT NO ONE CAN SEE IN! THERE-FORE, HE CAN NEVER BE RECOG-NIZED BY THE COLOR OF HIS EYES!

THESE INGENIOUS PLASTIC LENSES ALSO PROTECT HIS EYES FROM DUST, DIRT, AND THE GLARE OF THE SUN!

SPIDEY'S COSTUME

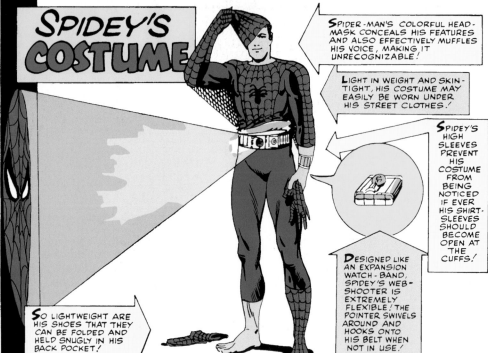

SPIDER-MAN'S COLORFUL HEAD-MASK CONCEALS HIS FEATURES AND ALSO EFFECTIVELY MUFFLES HIS VOICE, MAKING IT UNRECOGNIZABLE!

LIGHT IN WEIGHT AND SKIN-TIGHT, HIS COSTUME MAY EASILY BE WORN UNDER HIS STREET CLOTHES!

SPIDEY'S HIGH SLEEVES PREVENT HIS COSTUME FROM BEING NOTICED IF EVER HIS SHIRT-SLEEVES SHOULD BECOME OPEN AT THE CUFFS!

DESIGNED LIKE AN EXPANSION WATCH-BAND, SPIDEY'S WEB-SHOOTER IS EXTREMELY FLEXIBLE! THE POINTER SWIVELS AROUND AND HOOKS ONTO HIS BELT WHEN NOT IN USE!

SO LIGHTWEIGHT ARE HIS SHOES THAT THEY CAN BE FOLDED AND HELD SNUGLY IN HIS BACK POCKET!

9

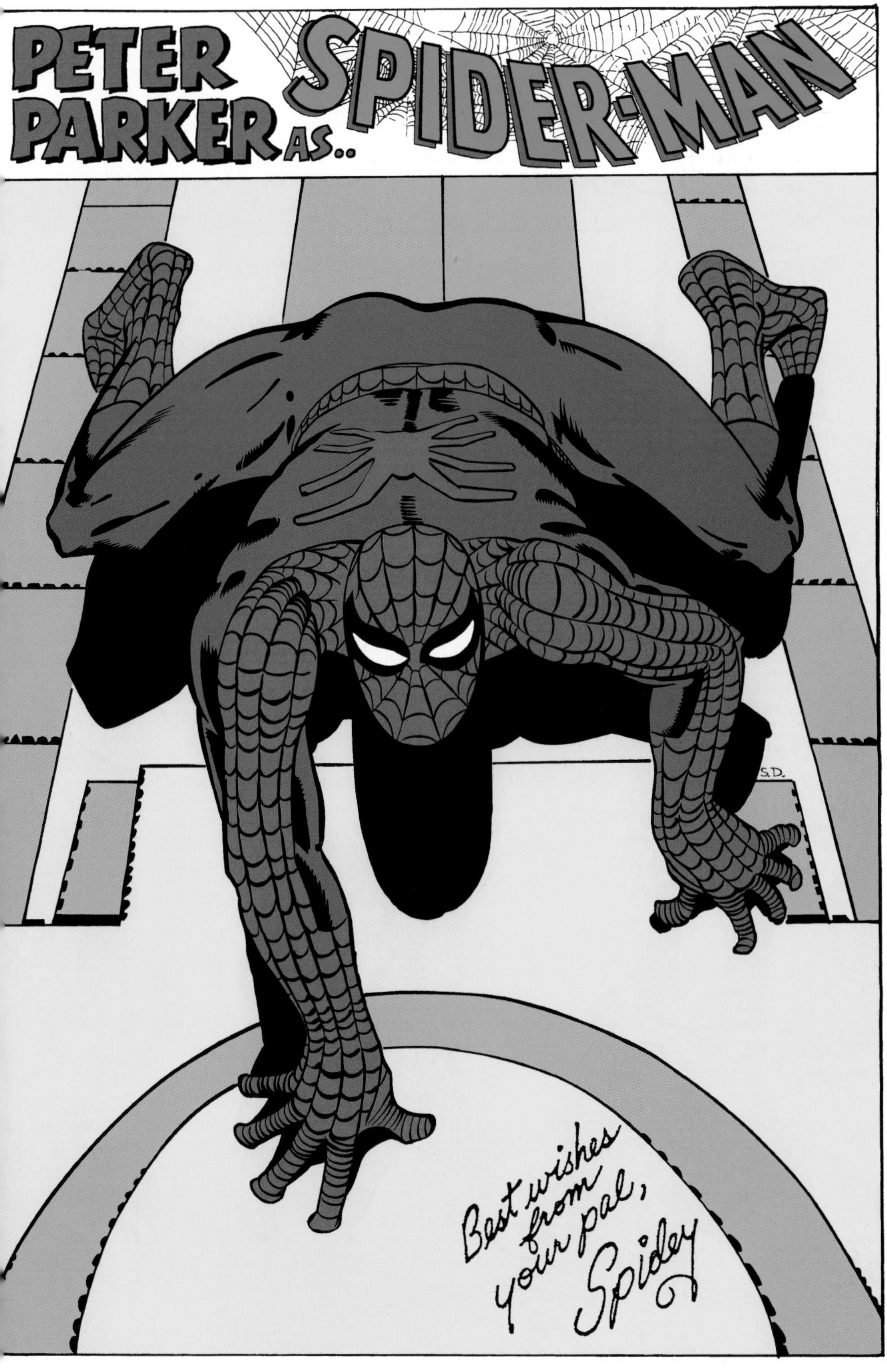
PETER PARKER AS.. SPIDER-MAN
S.D.
Best wishes from your pal, Spidey

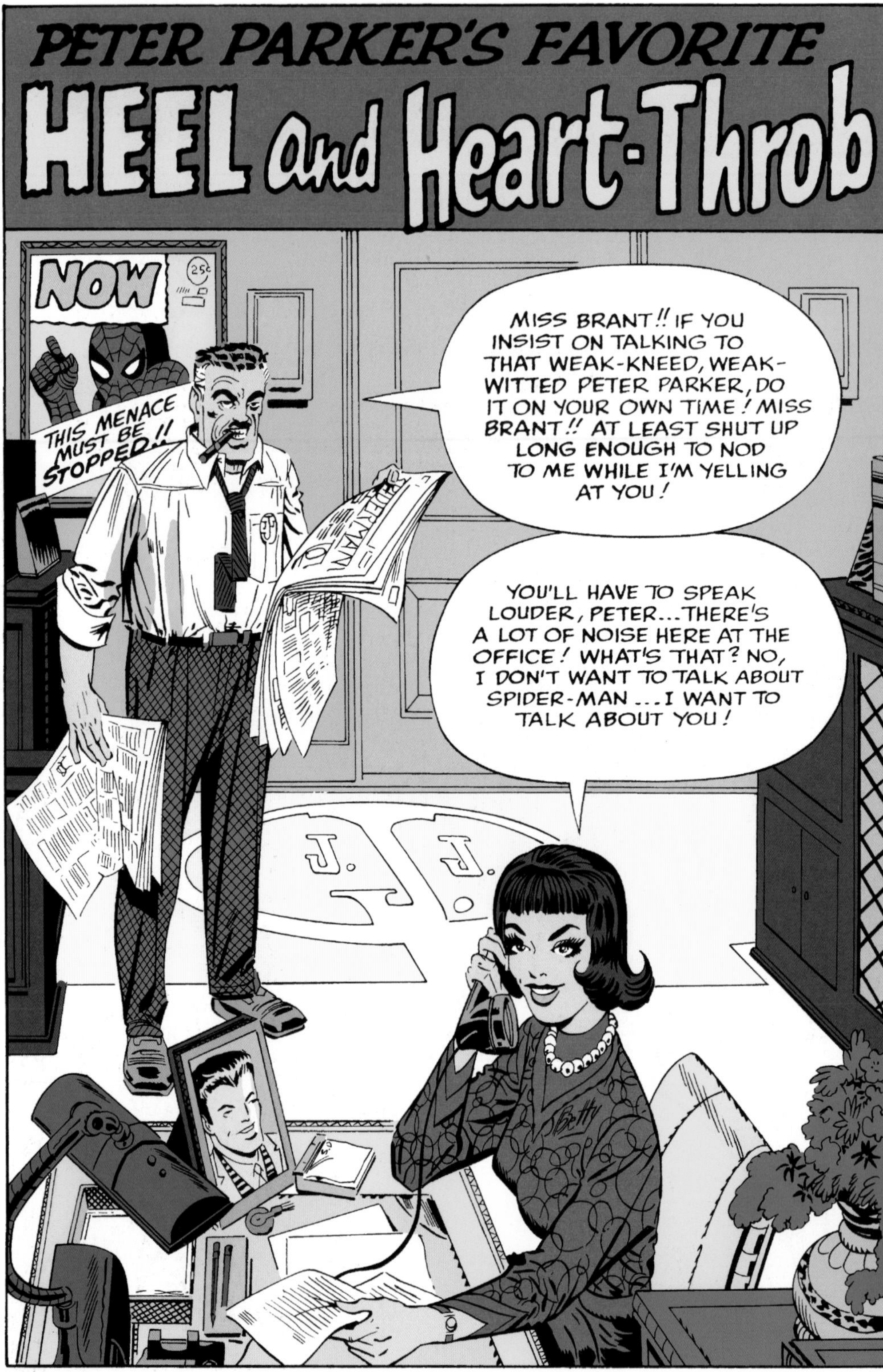
PETER PARKER'S FAVORITE
HEEL and Heart-Throb
NOW
THIS MENACE MUST BE !! STOPPED
MISS BRANT!! IF YOU INSIST ON TALKING TO THAT WEAK-KNEED, WEAK-WITTED PETER PARKER, DO IT ON YOUR OWN TIME! MISS BRANT!! AT LEAST SHUT UP LONG ENOUGH TO NOD TO ME WHILE I'M YELLING AT YOU!
YOU'LL HAVE TO SPEAK LOUDER, PETER... THERE'S A LOT OF NOISE HERE AT THE OFFICE! WHAT'S THAT? NO, I DON'T WANT TO TALK ABOUT SPIDER-MAN ... I WANT TO TALK ABOUT YOU!

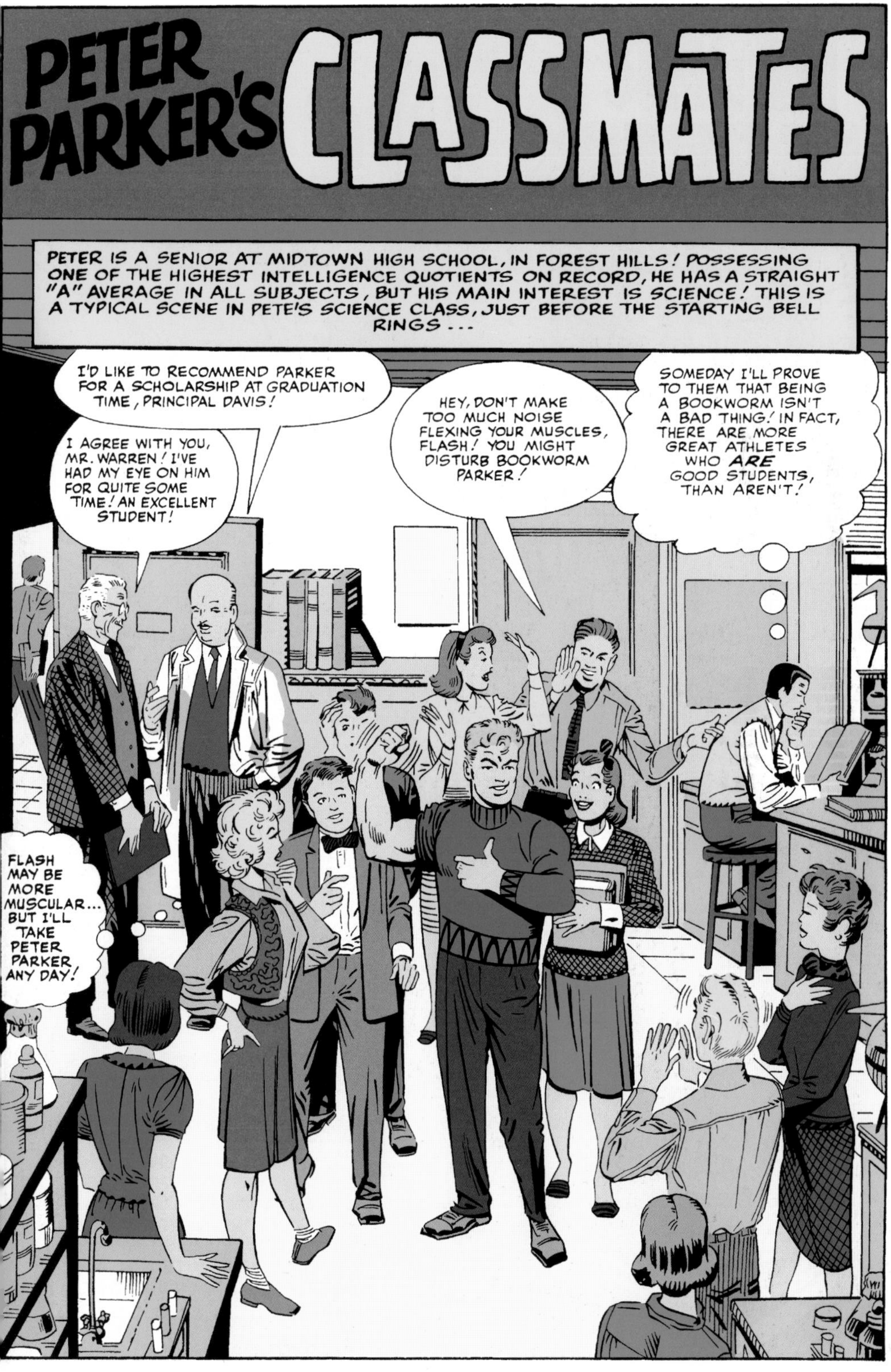
PETER PARKER'S CLASSMATES
PETER IS A SENIOR AT MIDTOWN HIGH SCHOOL, IN FOREST HILLS! POSSESSING ONE OF THE HIGHEST INTELLIGENCE QUOTIENTS ON RECORD, HE HAS A STRAIGHT "A" AVERAGE IN ALL SUBJECTS, BUT HIS MAIN INTEREST IS SCIENCE! THIS IS A TYPICAL SCENE IN PETE'S SCIENCE CLASS, JUST BEFORE THE STARTING BELL RINGS...
I'D LIKE TO RECOMMEND PARKER FOR A SCHOLARSHIP AT GRADUATION TIME, PRINCIPAL DAVIS!
I AGREE WITH YOU, MR. WARREN! I'VE HAD MY EYE ON HIM FOR QUITE SOME TIME! AN EXCELLENT STUDENT!
HEY, DON'T MAKE TOO MUCH NOISE FLEXING YOUR MUSCLES, FLASH! YOU MIGHT DISTURB BOOKWORM PARKER!
SOMEDAY I'LL PROVE TO THEM THAT BEING A BOOKWORM ISN'T A BAD THING! IN FACT, THERE ARE MORE GREAT ATHLETES WHO ARE GOOD STUDENTS, THAN AREN'T!
FLASH MAY BE MORE MUSCULAR... BUT I'LL TAKE PETER PARKER ANY DAY!

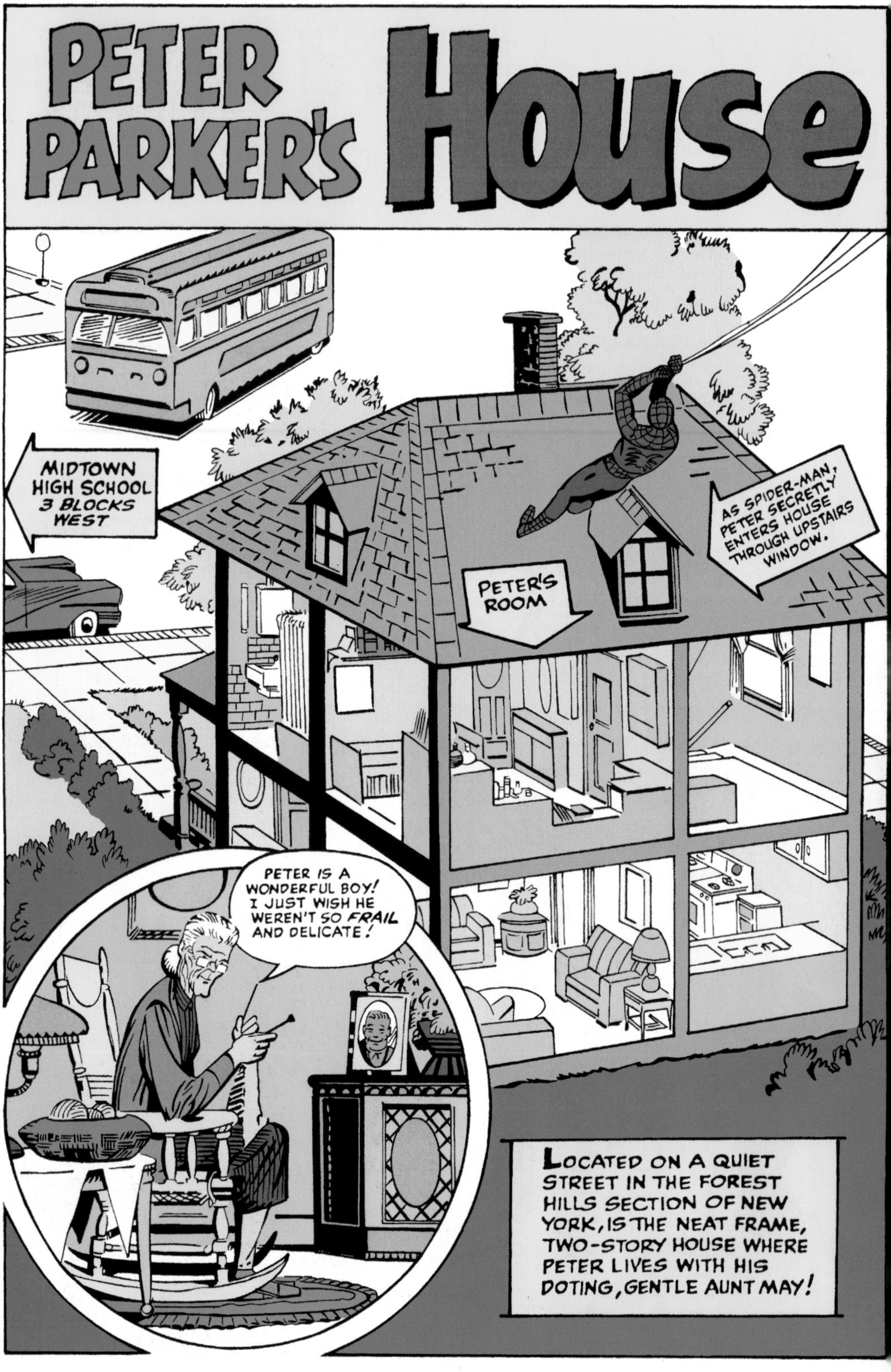
PETER PARKER'S House
MIDTOWN HIGH SCHOOL 3 BLOCKS WEST
PETER'S ROOM
AS SPIDER-MAN, PETER SECRETLY ENTERS HOUSE THROUGH UPSTAIRS WINDOW.
PETER IS A WONDERFUL BOY! I JUST WISH HE WEREN'T SO FRAIL AND DELICATE!
LOCATED ON A QUIET STREET IN THE FOREST HILLS SECTION OF NEW YORK, IS THE NEAT FRAME, TWO-STORY HOUSE WHERE PETER LIVES WITH HIS DOTING, GENTLE AUNT MAY!

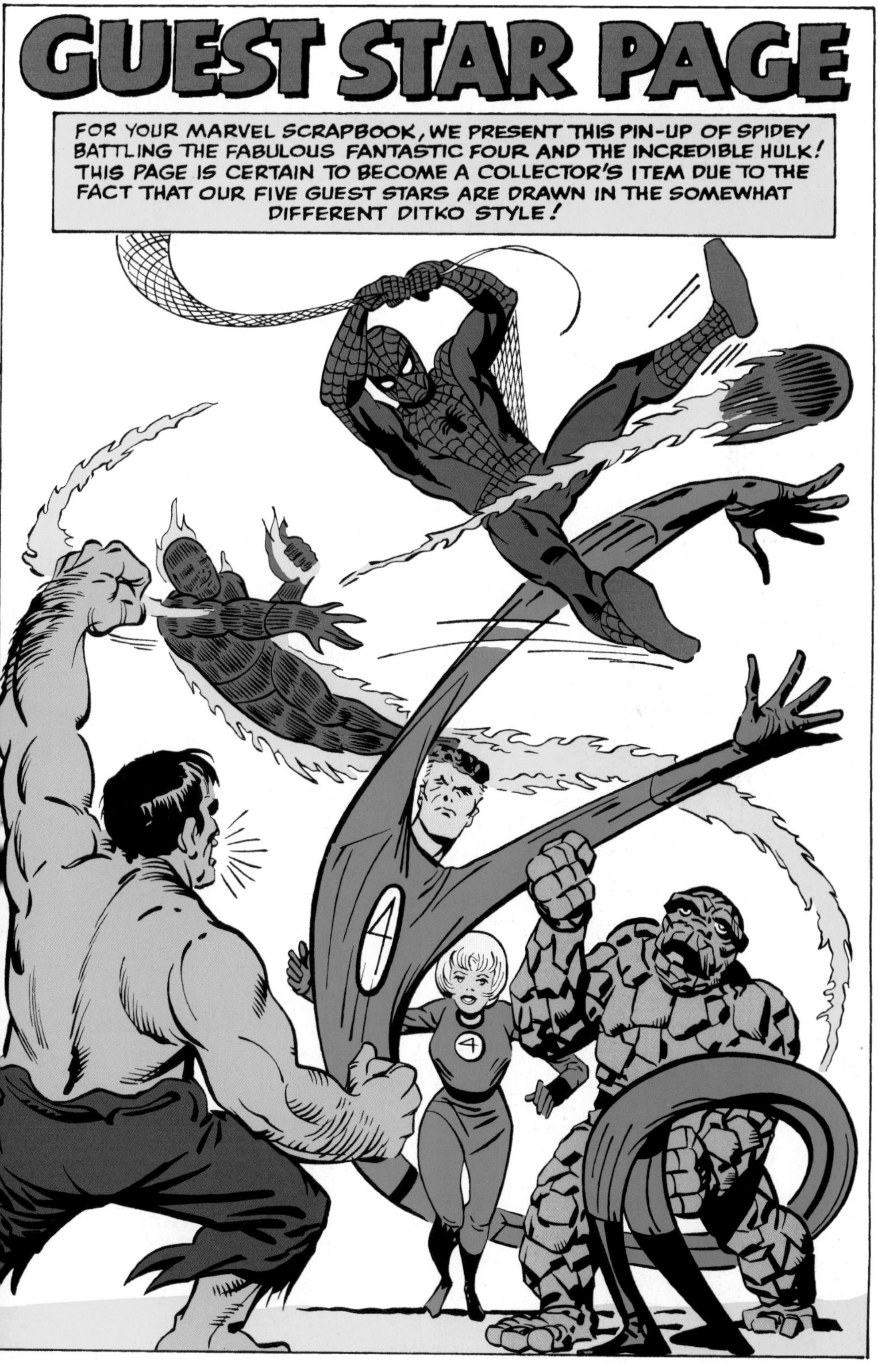
GUEST STAR PAGE
FOR YOUR MARVEL SCRAPBOOK, WE PRESENT THIS PIN-UP OF SPIDEY BATTLING THE FABULOUS FANTASTIC FOUR AND THE INCREDIBLE HULK! THIS PAGE IS CERTAIN TO BECOME A COLLECTOR'S ITEM DUE TO THE FACT THAT OUR FIVE GUEST STARS ARE DRAWN IN THE SOMEWHAT DIFFERENT DITKO STYLE!

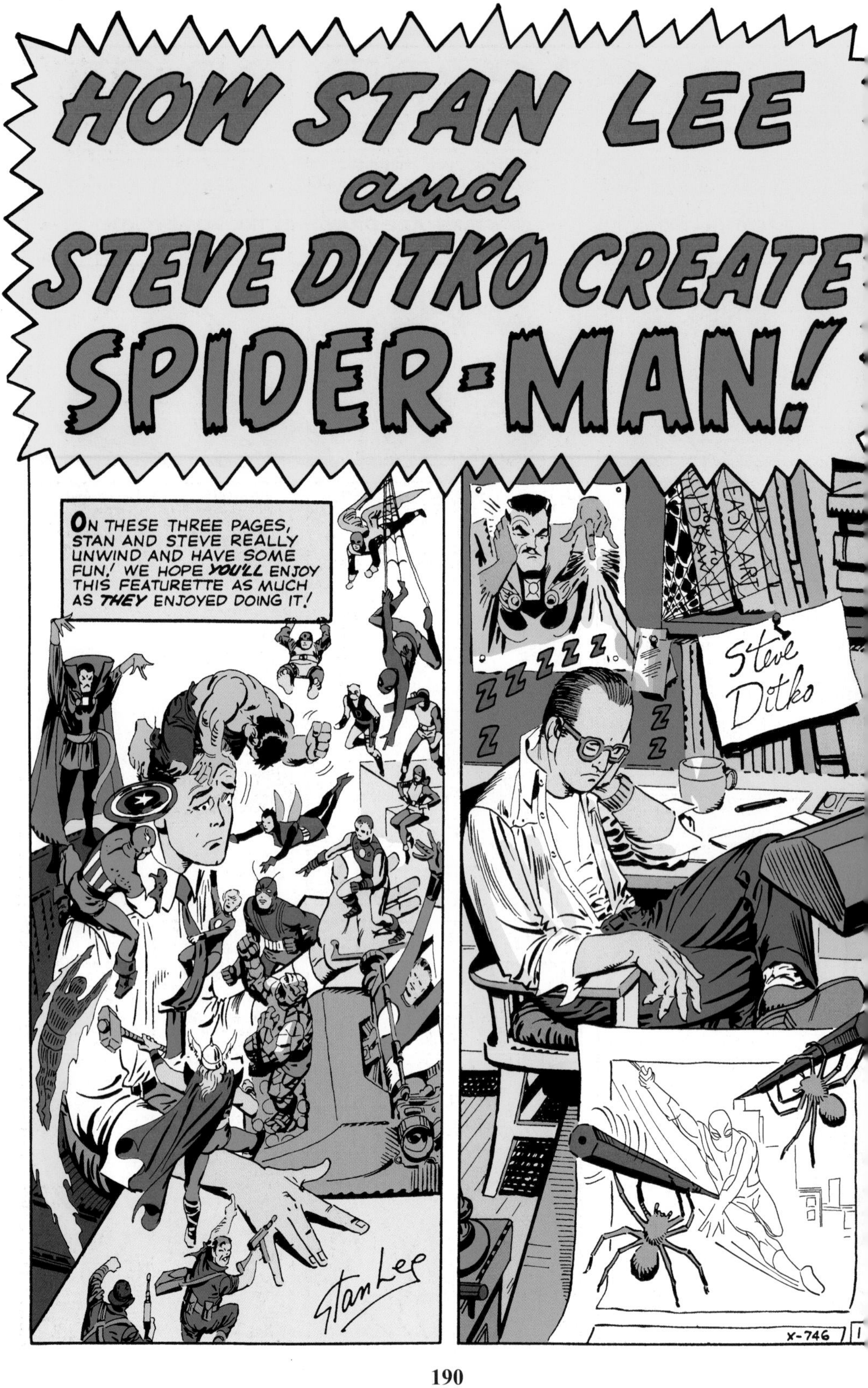
HOW STAN LEE and STEVE DITKO CREATE SPIDER-MAN!
ON THESE THREE PAGES, STAN AND STEVE REALLY UNWIND AND HAVE SOME FUN! WE HOPE YOU'LL ENJOY THIS FEATURETTE AS MUCH AS THEY ENJOYED DOING IT!
Stan Lee
Z Z Z Z Z Z Z Z Z
Steve Ditko
EASY ART
X-746
1

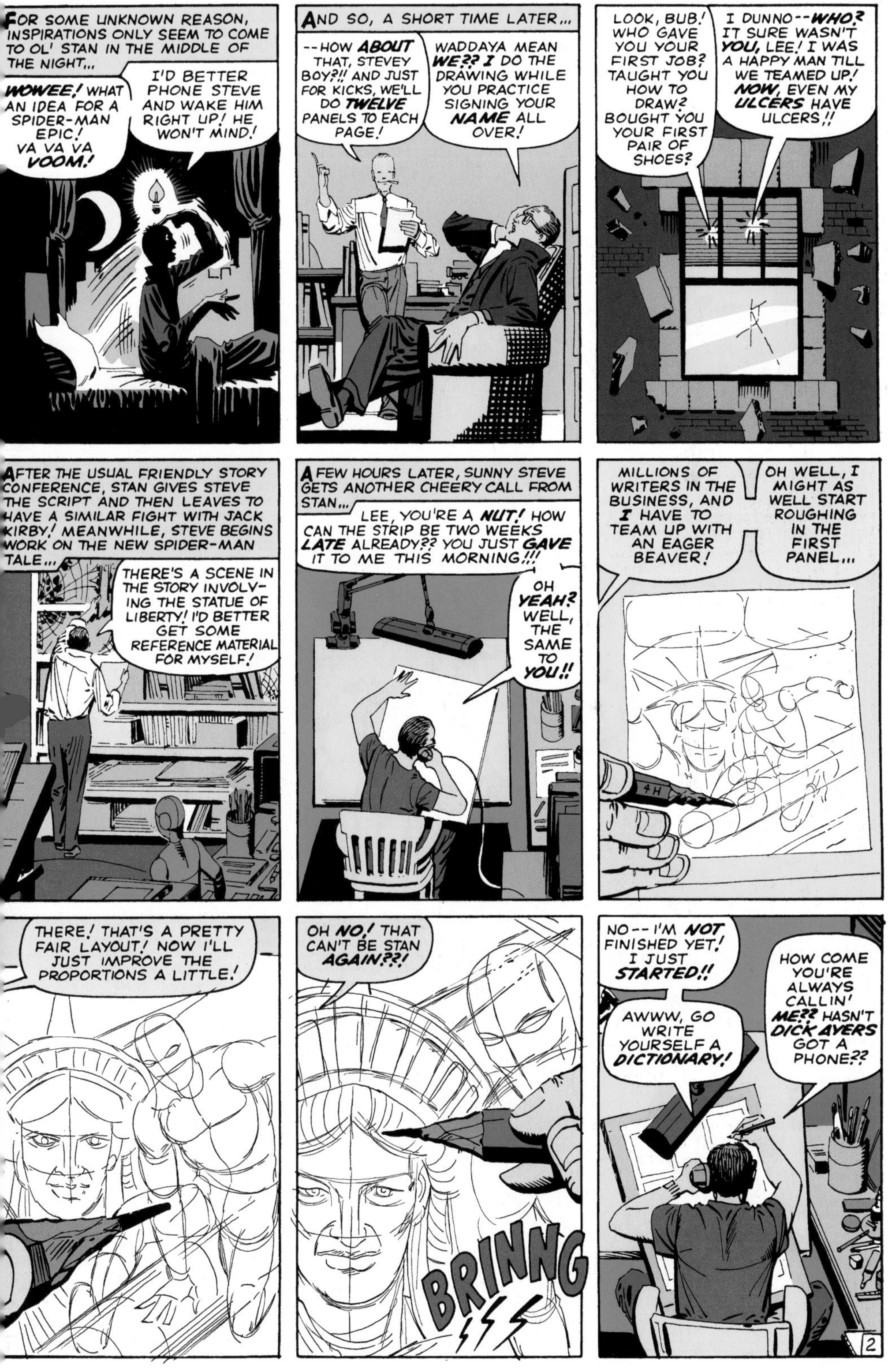
FOR SOME UNKNOWN REASON, INSPIRATIONS ONLY SEEM TO COME TO OL' STAN IN THE MIDDLE OF THE NIGHT...
WOWEE! WHAT AN IDEA FOR A SPIDER-MAN EPIC! VA VA VA VOOM!
I'D BETTER PHONE STEVE AND WAKE HIM RIGHT UP! HE WON'T MIND!
AND SO, A SHORT TIME LATER...
--HOW ABOUT THAT, STEVEY BOY?!! AND JUST FOR KICKS, WE'LL DO TWELVE PANELS TO EACH PAGE!
WADDAYA MEAN WE?? I DO THE DRAWING WHILE YOU PRACTICE SIGNING YOUR NAME ALL OVER!
LOOK, BUB! WHO GAVE YOU YOUR FIRST JOB? TAUGHT YOU HOW TO DRAW? BOUGHT YOU YOUR FIRST PAIR OF SHOES?
I DUNNO--WHO? IT SURE WASN'T YOU, LEE! I WAS A HAPPY MAN TILL WE TEAMED UP! NOW, EVEN MY ULCERS HAVE ULCERS!!
AFTER THE USUAL FRIENDLY STORY CONFERENCE, STAN GIVES STEVE THE SCRIPT AND THEN LEAVES TO HAVE A SIMILAR FIGHT WITH JACK KIRBY! MEANWHILE, STEVE BEGINS WORK ON THE NEW SPIDER-MAN TALE...
THERE'S A SCENE IN THE STORY INVOLVING THE STATUE OF LIBERTY! I'D BETTER GET SOME REFERENCE MATERIAL FOR MYSELF!
A FEW HOURS LATER, SUNNY STEVE GETS ANOTHER CHEERY CALL FROM STAN...
LEE, YOU'RE A NUT! HOW CAN THE STRIP BE TWO WEEKS LATE ALREADY?? YOU JUST GAVE IT TO ME THIS MORNING!!!
OH YEAH? WELL, THE SAME TO YOU!!
MILLIONS OF WRITERS IN THE BUSINESS, AND I HAVE TO TEAM UP WITH AN EAGER BEAVER!
OH WELL, I MIGHT AS WELL START ROUGHING IN THE FIRST PANEL...
4H
THERE! THAT'S A PRETTY FAIR LAYOUT! NOW I'LL JUST IMPROVE THE PROPORTIONS A LITTLE!
OH NO! THAT CAN'T BE STAN AGAIN??!
BRINNG
NO--I'M NOT FINISHED YET! I JUST STARTED!!
AWWW, GO WRITE YOURSELF A DICTIONARY!
HOW COME YOU'RE ALWAYS CALLIN' ME?? HASN'T DICK AYERS GOT A PHONE??
2

FINALLY, THE STORY IS ALL DRAWN IN PENCIL, AND STAN AND STEVE ONCE AGAIN HAVE A CONFERENCE...

PTUI! IT LOOKS LIKE YOU'RE LEARNING TO DRAW WITH YOUR EYES SHUT!

YOU SHOULD TALK AFTER THAT CORNY SCRIPT YOU WROTE!

WADDAYA MEAN "CORNY"?? I COPIED IT FROM ONE OF THE BEST CLASSICS I COULD FIND!

AND SO, THE HOURS SPEED PLEASANTLY BY, AMIDST AN ATMOSPHERE OF CALM UNDERSTANDING AND GENIAL GOOD-FELLOWSHIP...

MY FRIEND SAM CAN WRITE BETTER THAN YOU-- AND HE'S A COCKER SPANIAL!

AH HA!! HE'S PROBABLY THE ONE WHO DOES YOUR INKING FOR YOU!

HOW COME YOU DON'T USE SOME OF THOSE GAGS IN YOUR SCRIPTS??

WHAT FOR? YOU'D ONLY RUIN 'EM WITH YOUR ─UGH─ ARTWORK!

BUT, ALL GOOD THINGS MUST COME TO AN END, AND THE STRIP IS FINALLY SENT TO BE LETTERED! THEN, WHEN STEVE GETS IT BACK...

HELLO, OPERATOR? IF I GET ANY CALLS FROM A GUY NAMED LEE, TELL HIM I'VE BEEN DRAFTED!

NOW MAYBE I'LL GET THIS STRIP INKED IN PEACE!

STAN'S PROBABLY WRITTEN THE AVENGERS AND THE X-MEN BY NOW, AND I'M STILL TIGHTENING UP THE DETAILS HERE WITH A FINE PEN-POINT!

NOW I'LL FILL IN THE HEAVY BLACK AREAS WITH MY BRUSH...

THERE! THAT'S ONE PAGE DONE! NOW TO ERASE THE PENCIL LINES WHICH STILL REMAIN!

OH NO!! I FORGOT TO DRAW SPIDEY'S WEBBING!

IF ALL THE WEB-LINES I'VE DRAWN WERE LAID END TO END, THEY STILL WOULDN'T BE ENOUGH TO FIT AROUND LEE'S SWELLED HEAD!!

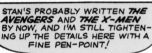

FINALLY, AFTER LONG HARD HOURS OF SLAVING OVER THE DRAWING BOARD, SPARKLING STEVE JOYOUSLY EXCLAIMS...

─WHEW!─ FINISHED AT LAST! I THINK I'LL SLEEP FOR A WHOLE WEEK NOW!

BUT, AT THAT VERY MOMENT, A SHRILL CRY OF UNRESTRAINED EXCITEMENT PIERCES THE SILENT MIDNIGHT AIR...

WOWEE! ANOTHER IDEA! THIS ONE'S BETTER THAN THE LAST!

WON'T STEVERINO BE HAPPY! I'D BETTER CALL HIM RIGHT AWAY AND BREAK THE GOOD NEWS!

THE END

NATURALLY, DEAR FRIENDS, WE'RE ONLY KIDDING! BUT WAIT TILL NEXT "ANNUAL" TIME! WE'LL PROBABLY HAVE SPIDEY TELL HOW HE CREATED STAN AND STEVE!

3

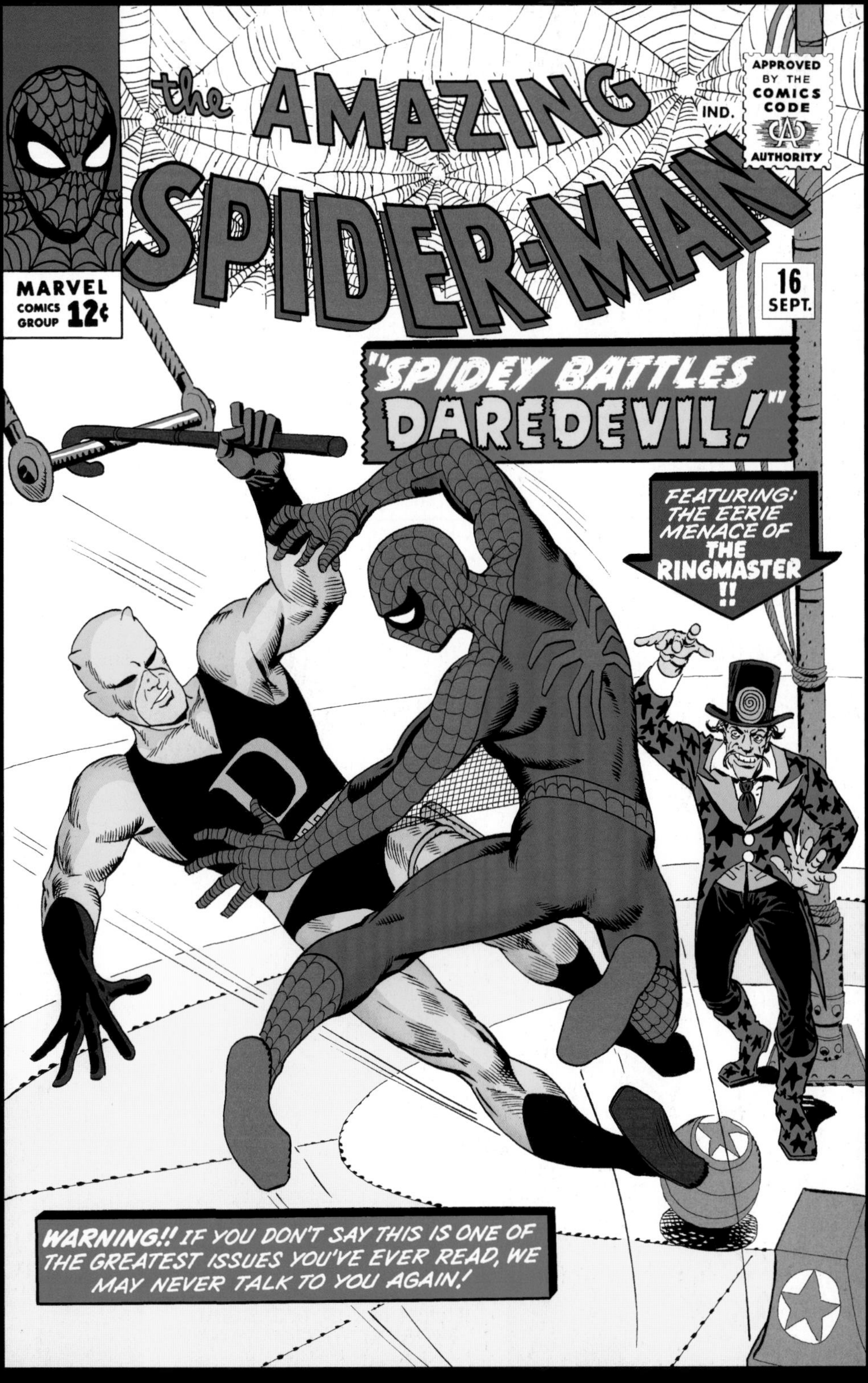

the AMAZING SPIDER-MAN
IND.
APPROVED BY THE COMICS CODE AUTHORITY
MARVEL COMICS GROUP 12¢
16 SEPT.
"SPIDEY BATTLES DAREDEVIL!"
FEATURING: THE EERIE MENACE OF THE RINGMASTER !!
WARNING!! IF YOU DON'T SAY THIS IS ONE OF THE GREATEST ISSUES YOU'VE EVER READ, WE MAY NEVER TALK TO YOU AGAIN!

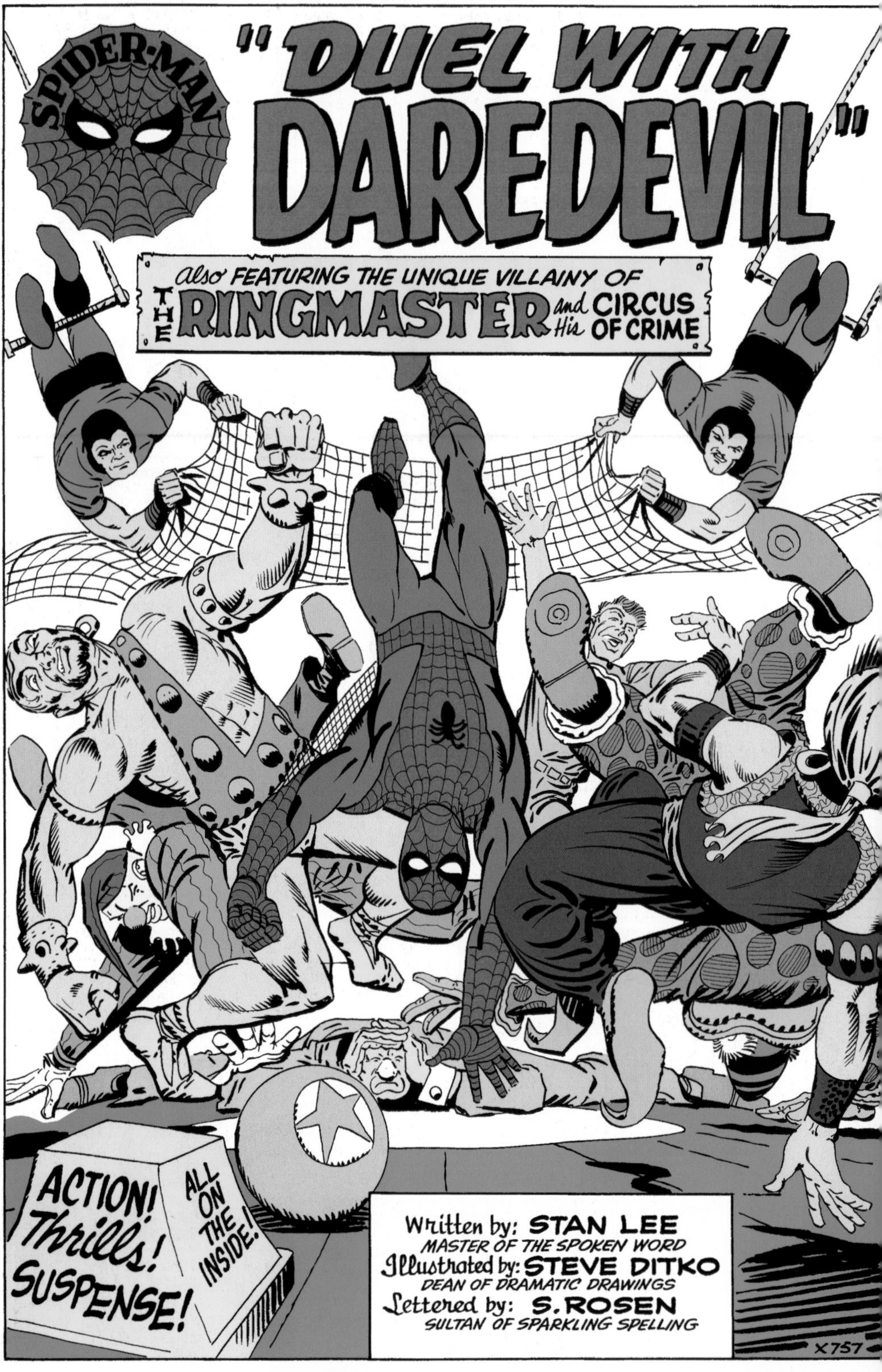
SPIDER-MAN
"DUEL WITH DAREDEVIL"
also FEATURING THE UNIQUE VILLAINY OF THE RINGMASTER and His CIRCUS OF CRIME
ACTION! Thrills! SUSPENSE!
ALL ON THE INSIDE!
Written by: STAN LEE
MASTER OF THE SPOKEN WORD
Illustrated by: STEVE DITKO
DEAN OF DRAMATIC DRAWINGS
Lettered by: S. ROSEN
SULTAN OF SPARKLING SPELLING
X757

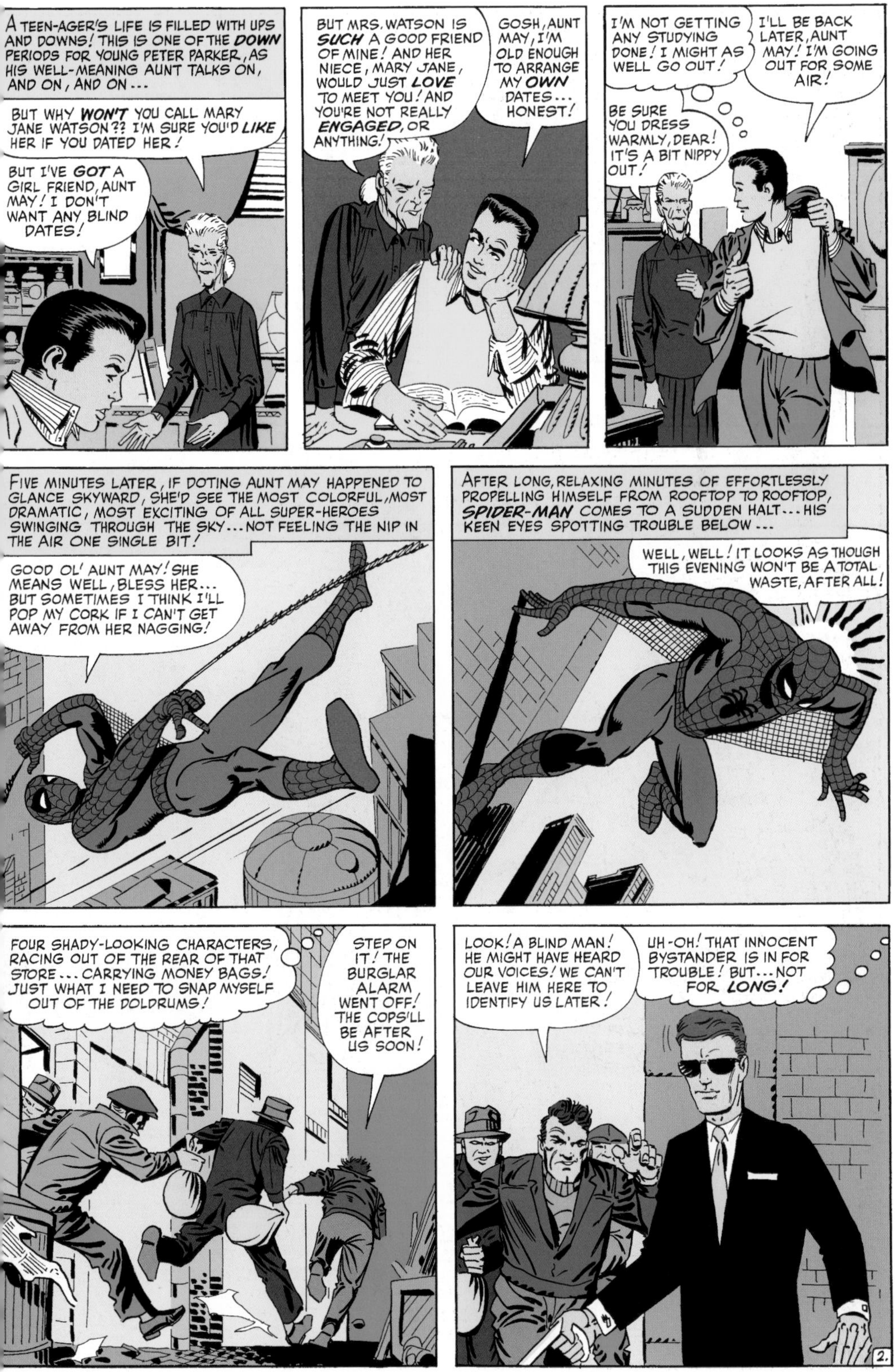
A TEEN-AGER'S LIFE IS FILLED WITH UPS AND DOWNS! THIS IS ONE OF THE DOWN PERIODS FOR YOUNG PETER PARKER, AS HIS WELL-MEANING AUNT TALKS ON, AND ON, AND ON...
BUT WHY WON'T YOU CALL MARY JANE WATSON?? I'M SURE YOU'D LIKE HER IF YOU DATED HER!
BUT I'VE GOT A GIRL FRIEND, AUNT MAY! I DON'T WANT ANY BLIND DATES!
BUT MRS. WATSON IS SUCH A GOOD FRIEND OF MINE! AND HER NIECE, MARY JANE, WOULD JUST LOVE TO MEET YOU! AND YOU'RE NOT REALLY ENGAGED, OR ANYTHING!
GOSH, AUNT MAY, I'M OLD ENOUGH TO ARRANGE MY OWN DATES... HONEST!
I'M NOT GETTING ANY STUDYING DONE! I MIGHT AS WELL GO OUT!
I'LL BE BACK LATER, AUNT MAY! I'M GOING OUT FOR SOME AIR!
BE SURE YOU DRESS WARMLY, DEAR! IT'S A BIT NIPPY OUT!
FIVE MINUTES LATER, IF DOTING AUNT MAY HAPPENED TO GLANCE SKYWARD, SHE'D SEE THE MOST COLORFUL, MOST DRAMATIC, MOST EXCITING OF ALL SUPER-HEROES SWINGING THROUGH THE SKY... NOT FEELING THE NIP IN THE AIR ONE SINGLE BIT!
GOOD OL' AUNT MAY! SHE MEANS WELL, BLESS HER... BUT SOMETIMES I THINK I'LL POP MY CORK IF I CAN'T GET AWAY FROM HER NAGGING!
AFTER LONG, RELAXING MINUTES OF EFFORTLESSLY PROPELLING HIMSELF FROM ROOFTOP TO ROOFTOP, SPIDER-MAN COMES TO A SUDDEN HALT... HIS KEEN EYES SPOTTING TROUBLE BELOW...
WELL, WELL! IT LOOKS AS THOUGH THIS EVENING WON'T BE A TOTAL WASTE, AFTER ALL!
FOUR SHADY-LOOKING CHARACTERS, RACING OUT OF THE REAR OF THAT STORE... CARRYING MONEY BAGS! JUST WHAT I NEED TO SNAP MYSELF OUT OF THE DOLDRUMS!
STEP ON IT! THE BURGLAR ALARM WENT OFF! THE COPS'LL BE AFTER US SOON!
LOOK! A BLIND MAN! HE MIGHT HAVE HEARD OUR VOICES! WE CAN'T LEAVE HIM HERE TO IDENTIFY US LATER!
UH-OH! THAT INNOCENT BYSTANDER IS IN FOR TROUBLE! BUT... NOT FOR LONG!
2.

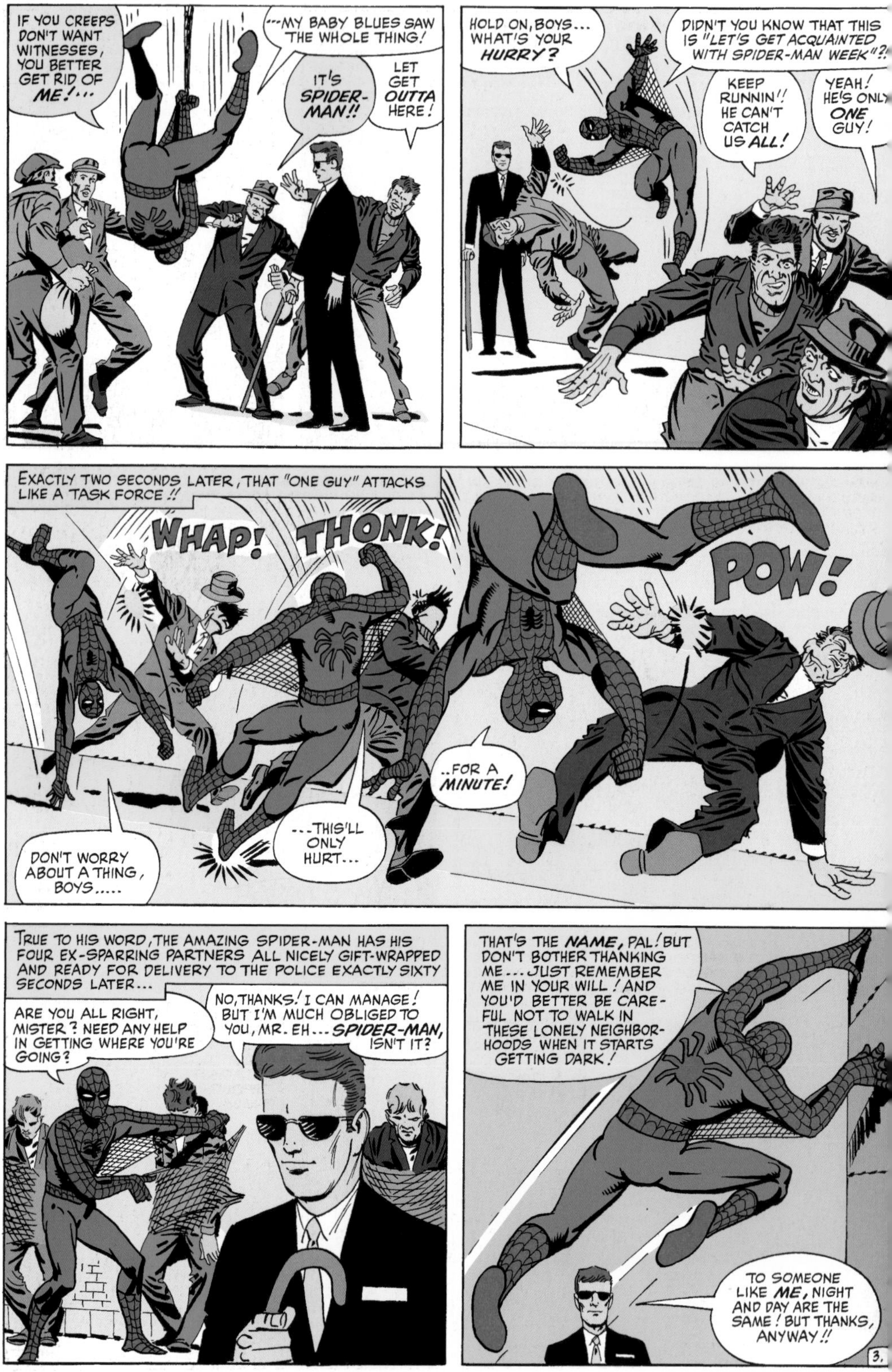

IF YOU CREEPS DON'T WANT WITNESSES, YOU BETTER GET RID OF ME!...
...MY BABY BLUES SAW THE WHOLE THING!
IT'S SPIDER-MAN!!
LET GET OUTTA HERE!
HOLD ON, BOYS... WHAT'S YOUR HURRY?
DIDN'T YOU KNOW THAT THIS IS "LET'S GET ACQUAINTED WITH SPIDER-MAN WEEK"?!
KEEP RUNNIN'! HE CAN'T CATCH US ALL!
YEAH! HE'S ONLY ONE GUY!
EXACTLY TWO SECONDS LATER, THAT "ONE GUY" ATTACKS LIKE A TASK FORCE!!
WHAP!
THONK!
POW!
DON'T WORRY ABOUT A THING, BOYS.....
...THIS'LL ONLY HURT...
..FOR A MINUTE!
TRUE TO HIS WORD, THE AMAZING SPIDER-MAN HAS HIS FOUR EX-SPARRING PARTNERS ALL NICELY GIFT-WRAPPED AND READY FOR DELIVERY TO THE POLICE EXACTLY SIXTY SECONDS LATER...
ARE YOU ALL RIGHT, MISTER? NEED ANY HELP IN GETTING WHERE YOU'RE GOING?
NO, THANKS! I CAN MANAGE! BUT I'M MUCH OBLIGED TO YOU, MR. EH... SPIDER-MAN, ISN'T IT?
THAT'S THE NAME, PAL! BUT DON'T BOTHER THANKING ME... JUST REMEMBER ME IN YOUR WILL! AND YOU'D BETTER BE CAREFUL NOT TO WALK IN THESE LONELY NEIGHBORHOODS WHEN IT STARTS GETTING DARK!
TO SOMEONE LIKE ME, NIGHT AND DAY ARE THE SAME! BUT THANKS, ANYWAY!!
3.

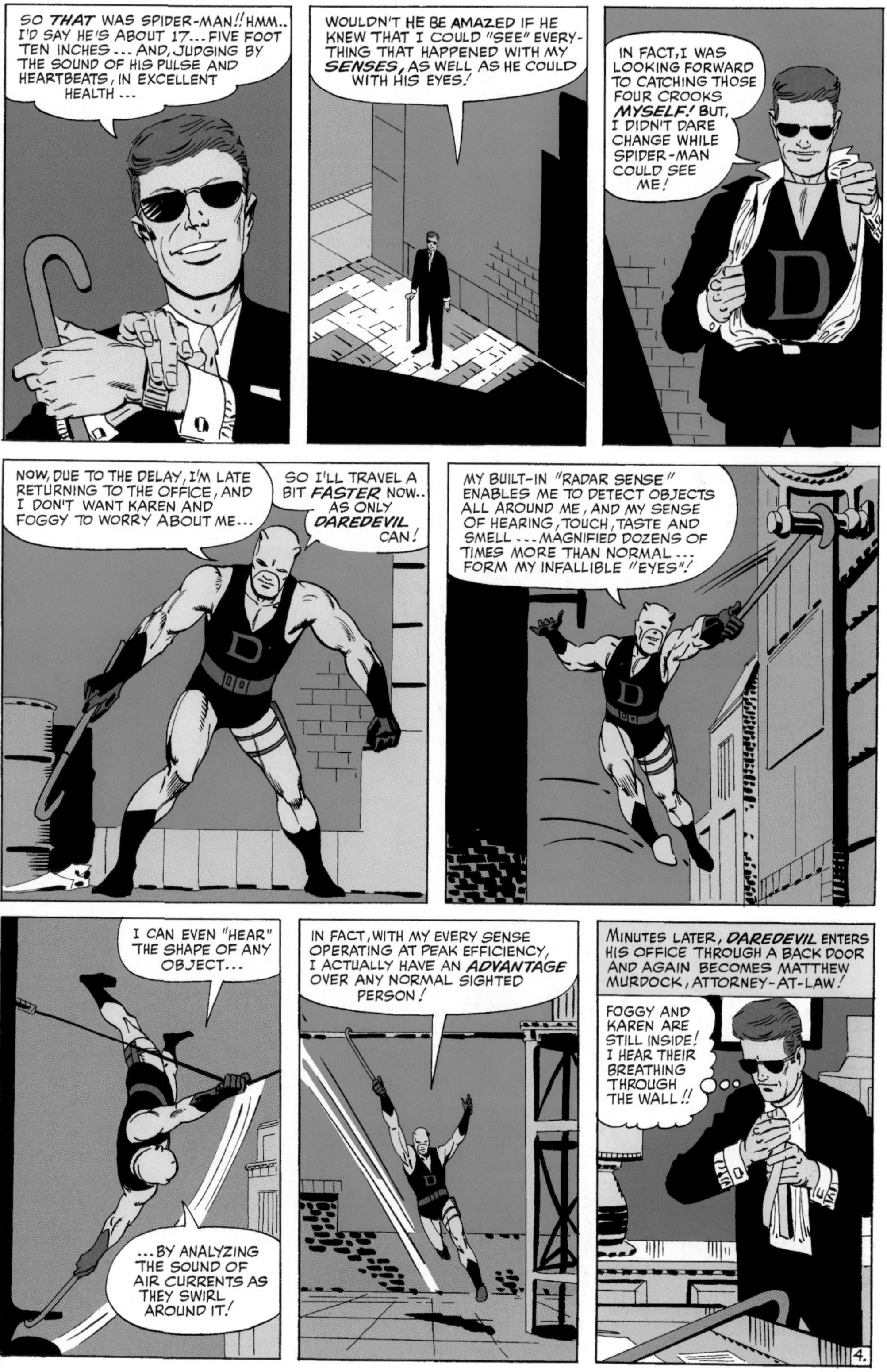
SO THAT WAS SPIDER-MAN!! HMM.. I'D SAY HE'S ABOUT 17... FIVE FOOT TEN INCHES... AND, JUDGING BY THE SOUND OF HIS PULSE AND HEARTBEATS, IN EXCELLENT HEALTH...
WOULDN'T HE BE AMAZED IF HE KNEW THAT I COULD "SEE" EVERYTHING THAT HAPPENED WITH MY SENSES, AS WELL AS HE COULD WITH HIS EYES!
IN FACT, I WAS LOOKING FORWARD TO CATCHING THOSE FOUR CROOKS MYSELF! BUT, I DIDN'T DARE CHANGE WHILE SPIDER-MAN COULD SEE ME!
NOW, DUE TO THE DELAY, I'M LATE RETURNING TO THE OFFICE, AND I DON'T WANT KAREN AND FOGGY TO WORRY ABOUT ME...
SO I'LL TRAVEL A BIT FASTER NOW.. AS ONLY DAREDEVIL CAN!
MY BUILT-IN "RADAR SENSE" ENABLES ME TO DETECT OBJECTS ALL AROUND ME, AND MY SENSE OF HEARING, TOUCH, TASTE AND SMELL... MAGNIFIED DOZENS OF TIMES MORE THAN NORMAL... FORM MY INFALLIBLE "EYES"!
I CAN EVEN "HEAR" THE SHAPE OF ANY OBJECT...
...BY ANALYZING THE SOUND OF AIR CURRENTS AS THEY SWIRL AROUND IT!
IN FACT, WITH MY EVERY SENSE OPERATING AT PEAK EFFICIENCY, I ACTUALLY HAVE AN ADVANTAGE OVER ANY NORMAL SIGHTED PERSON!
MINUTES LATER, DAREDEVIL ENTERS HIS OFFICE THROUGH A BACK DOOR AND AGAIN BECOMES MATTHEW MURDOCK, ATTORNEY-AT-LAW!
FOGGY AND KAREN ARE STILL INSIDE! I HEAR THEIR BREATHING THROUGH THE WALL!!
4.

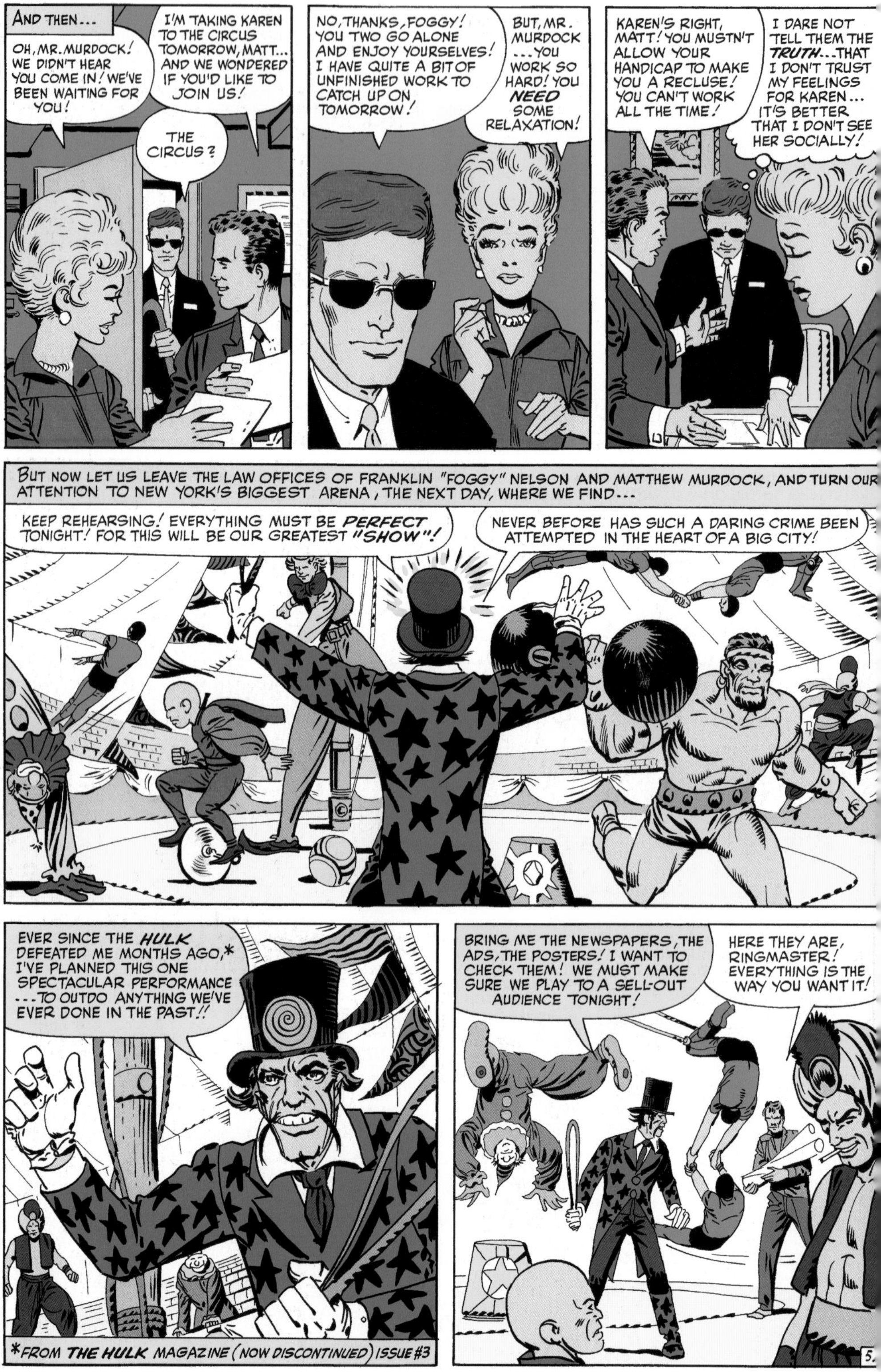
AND THEN...
OH, MR. MURDOCK! WE DIDN'T HEAR YOU COME IN! WE'VE BEEN WAITING FOR YOU!
I'M TAKING KAREN TO THE CIRCUS TOMORROW, MATT... AND WE WONDERED IF YOU'D LIKE TO JOIN US!
THE CIRCUS?
NO, THANKS, FOGGY! YOU TWO GO ALONE AND ENJOY YOURSELVES! I HAVE QUITE A BIT OF UNFINISHED WORK TO CATCH UP ON TOMORROW!
BUT, MR. MURDOCK ...YOU WORK SO HARD! YOU NEED SOME RELAXATION!
KAREN'S RIGHT, MATT! YOU MUSTN'T ALLOW YOUR HANDICAP TO MAKE YOU A RECLUSE! YOU CAN'T WORK ALL THE TIME!
I DARE NOT TELL THEM THE TRUTH...THAT I DON'T TRUST MY FEELINGS FOR KAREN... IT'S BETTER THAT I DON'T SEE HER SOCIALLY!
BUT NOW LET US LEAVE THE LAW OFFICES OF FRANKLIN "FOGGY" NELSON AND MATTHEW MURDOCK, AND TURN OUR ATTENTION TO NEW YORK'S BIGGEST ARENA, THE NEXT DAY, WHERE WE FIND...
KEEP REHEARSING! EVERYTHING MUST BE PERFECT TONIGHT! FOR THIS WILL BE OUR GREATEST "SHOW"!
NEVER BEFORE HAS SUCH A DARING CRIME BEEN ATTEMPTED IN THE HEART OF A BIG CITY!
EVER SINCE THE HULK DEFEATED ME MONTHS AGO,* I'VE PLANNED THIS ONE SPECTACULAR PERFORMANCE ---TO OUTDO ANYTHING WE'VE EVER DONE IN THE PAST!!
*FROM THE HULK MAGAZINE (NOW DISCONTINUED) ISSUE #3
BRING ME THE NEWSPAPERS, THE ADS, THE POSTERS! I WANT TO CHECK THEM! WE MUST MAKE SURE WE PLAY TO A SELL-OUT AUDIENCE TONIGHT!
HERE THEY ARE, RINGMASTER! EVERYTHING IS THE WAY YOU WANT IT!
5.

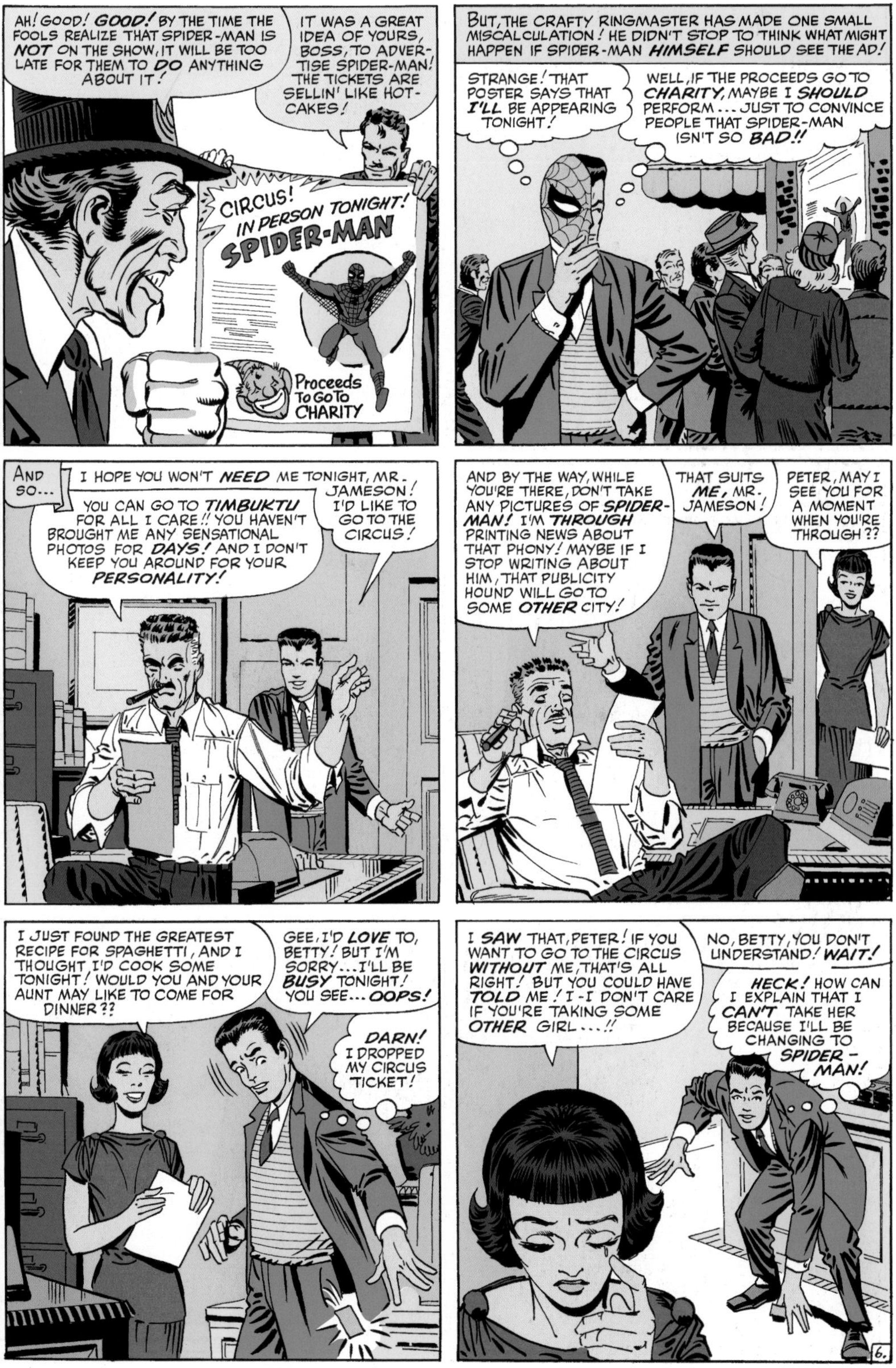

AH! GOOD! GOOD! BY THE TIME THE FOOLS REALIZE THAT SPIDER-MAN IS NOT ON THE SHOW, IT WILL BE TOO LATE FOR THEM TO DO ANYTHING ABOUT IT!
IT WAS A GREAT IDEA OF YOURS, BOSS, TO ADVERTISE SPIDER-MAN! THE TICKETS ARE SELLIN' LIKE HOT-CAKES!
CIRCUS! IN PERSON TONIGHT! SPIDER-MAN
Proceeds To Go To CHARITY
BUT, THE CRAFTY RINGMASTER HAS MADE ONE SMALL MISCALCULATION! HE DIDN'T STOP TO THINK WHAT MIGHT HAPPEN IF SPIDER-MAN HIMSELF SHOULD SEE THE AD!
STRANGE! THAT POSTER SAYS THAT I'LL BE APPEARING TONIGHT!
WELL, IF THE PROCEEDS GO TO CHARITY, MAYBE I SHOULD PERFORM ... JUST TO CONVINCE PEOPLE THAT SPIDER-MAN ISN'T SO BAD!!
AND SO...
I HOPE YOU WON'T NEED ME TONIGHT, MR. JAMESON! I'D LIKE TO GO TO THE CIRCUS!
YOU CAN GO TO TIMBUKTU FOR ALL I CARE!! YOU HAVEN'T BROUGHT ME ANY SENSATIONAL PHOTOS FOR DAYS! AND I DON'T KEEP YOU AROUND FOR YOUR PERSONALITY!
AND BY THE WAY, WHILE YOU'RE THERE, DON'T TAKE ANY PICTURES OF SPIDER-MAN! I'M THROUGH PRINTING NEWS ABOUT THAT PHONY! MAYBE IF I STOP WRITING ABOUT HIM, THAT PUBLICITY HOUND WILL GO TO SOME OTHER CITY!
THAT SUITS ME, MR. JAMESON!
PETER, MAY I SEE YOU FOR A MOMENT WHEN YOU'RE THROUGH??
I JUST FOUND THE GREATEST RECIPE FOR SPAGHETTI, AND I THOUGHT I'D COOK SOME TONIGHT! WOULD YOU AND YOUR AUNT MAY LIKE TO COME FOR DINNER??
GEE, I'D LOVE TO, BETTY! BUT I'M SORRY... I'LL BE BUSY TONIGHT! YOU SEE... OOPS!
DARN! I DROPPED MY CIRCUS TICKET!
I SAW THAT, PETER! IF YOU WANT TO GO TO THE CIRCUS WITHOUT ME, THAT'S ALL RIGHT! BUT YOU COULD HAVE TOLD ME! I-I DON'T CARE IF YOU'RE TAKING SOME OTHER GIRL...!!
NO, BETTY, YOU DON'T UNDERSTAND! WAIT!
HECK! HOW CAN I EXPLAIN THAT I CAN'T TAKE HER BECAUSE I'LL BE CHANGING TO SPIDER-MAN!
6.

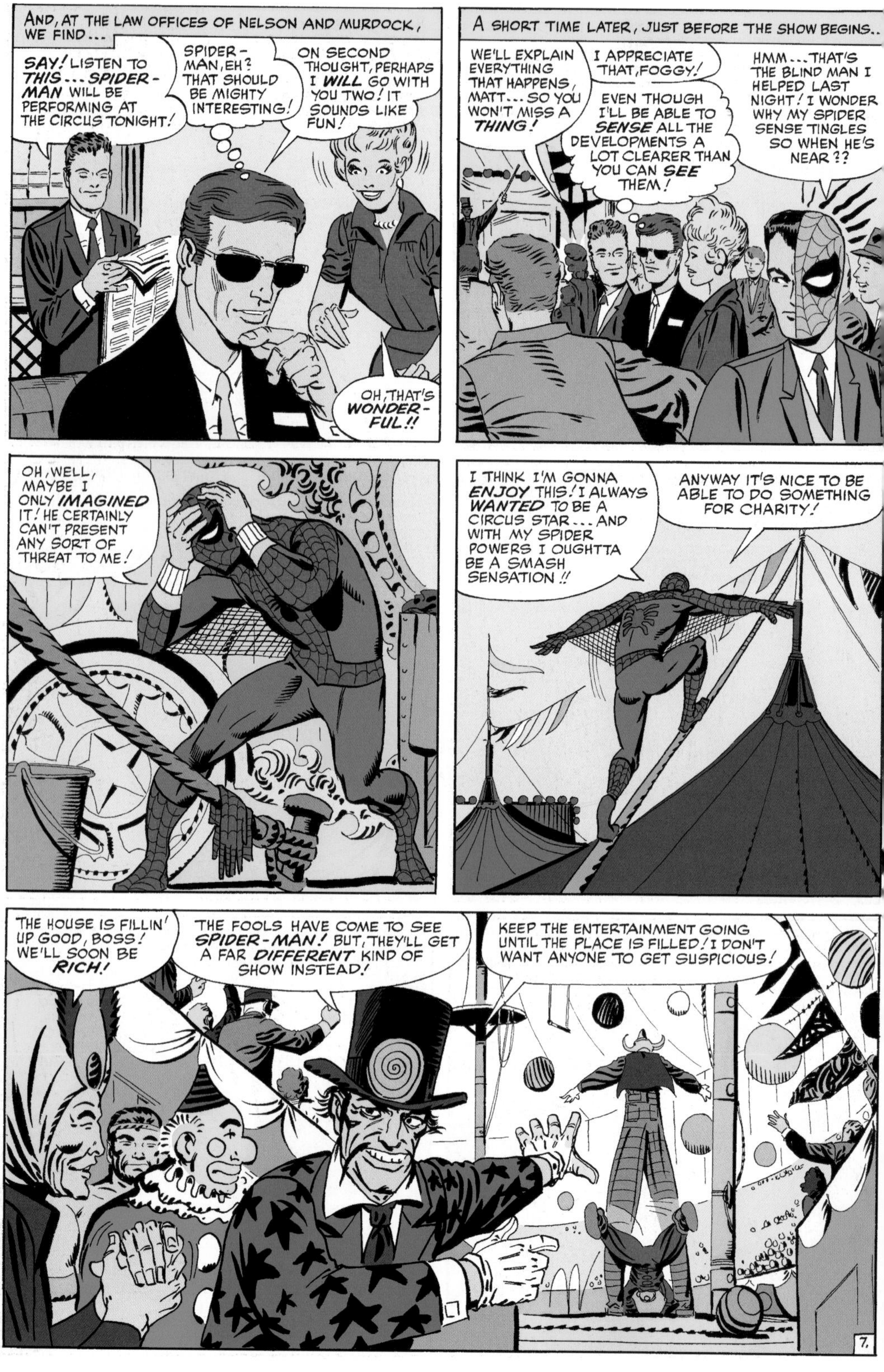

AND, AT THE LAW OFFICES OF NELSON AND MURDOCK, WE FIND...
SAY! LISTEN TO THIS... SPIDER-MAN WILL BE PERFORMING AT THE CIRCUS TONIGHT!
SPIDER-MAN, EH? THAT SHOULD BE MIGHTY INTERESTING!
ON SECOND THOUGHT, PERHAPS I WILL GO WITH YOU TWO! IT SOUNDS LIKE FUN!
OH, THAT'S WONDERFUL!!
A SHORT TIME LATER, JUST BEFORE THE SHOW BEGINS..
WE'LL EXPLAIN EVERYTHING THAT HAPPENS, MATT... SO YOU WON'T MISS A THING!
I APPRECIATE THAT, FOGGY!
EVEN THOUGH I'LL BE ABLE TO SENSE ALL THE DEVELOPMENTS A LOT CLEARER THAN YOU CAN SEE THEM!
HMM... THAT'S THE BLIND MAN I HELPED LAST NIGHT! I WONDER WHY MY SPIDER SENSE TINGLES SO WHEN HE'S NEAR??
OH, WELL, MAYBE I ONLY IMAGINED IT! HE CERTAINLY CAN'T PRESENT ANY SORT OF THREAT TO ME!
I THINK I'M GONNA ENJOY THIS! I ALWAYS WANTED TO BE A CIRCUS STAR... AND WITH MY SPIDER POWERS I OUGHTTA BE A SMASH SENSATION!!
ANYWAY IT'S NICE TO BE ABLE TO DO SOMETHING FOR CHARITY!
THE HOUSE IS FILLIN' UP GOOD, BOSS! WE'LL SOON BE RICH!
THE FOOLS HAVE COME TO SEE SPIDER-MAN! BUT, THEY'LL GET A FAR DIFFERENT KIND OF SHOW INSTEAD!
KEEP THE ENTERTAINMENT GOING UNTIL THE PLACE IS FILLED! I DON'T WANT ANYONE TO GET SUSPICIOUS!
7.

AND, AS THE MINUTES DRAG ON, THE AUDIENCE GROWS MORE AND MORE IMPATIENT...

WE WANT SPIDER-MAN! WE WANT SPIDER-MAN!

SPIDER-MAN IS UP ABOVE THE TENT! I CAN DETECT HIS UNUSUALLY STRONG PULSE-RATE UP THERE!

IF THERE'S ANYTHING YOU WANT US TO DESCRIBE, MATT...JUST SAY SO!

BRING ON SPIDER-MAN! WE WANT SPIDER-MAN!

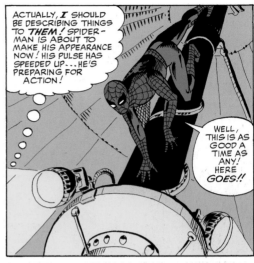

ACTUALLY, I SHOULD BE DESCRIBING THINGS TO THEM! SPIDER-MAN IS ABOUT TO MAKE HIS APPEARANCE NOW! HIS PULSE HAS SPEEDED UP...HE'S PREPARING FOR ACTION!

WELL, THIS IS AS GOOD A TIME AS ANY! HERE GOES!!

I WISH THE RINGMASTER WOULD GIVE US THE SIGNAL! I'M GETTIN' JITTERY! WHAT IF SOMETHIN' GOES WRONG??

LOOK! UP THERE! HE DID SHOW UP! IT'S SPIDER-MAN!!!

YAY, SPIDER-MAN!!

HOWDY, FOLKS!

LISTEN TO 'EM CHEER! I GUESS I'M NOT AS UNPOPULAR AS I USED TO THINK!

JUDGING BY THE DIRECTION OF AIR CURRENTS, SPIDER-MAN IS SLOWLY DESCENDING FROM THE CEILING...AND HE'S UPSIDE-DOWN, BECAUSE HIS HEARTBEAT IS HIGHER THAN THE SOUND OF HIS VOICE!

POOR MATT! HOW CAN HE APPRECIATE ANY OF THIS?!

BOY! IT'S A PLEASURE TO BE ABLE TO DO THIS WITHOUT HAVING SOME DEADLY ENEMY TO WORRY ABOUT AT THE SAME TIME!

YAY, SPIDER-MAN!!

GO! GO! GO! SPIDER-MAN!

MORE! MORE! GIVE US MORE!

ATTABOY, SPIDEY!!!

8.

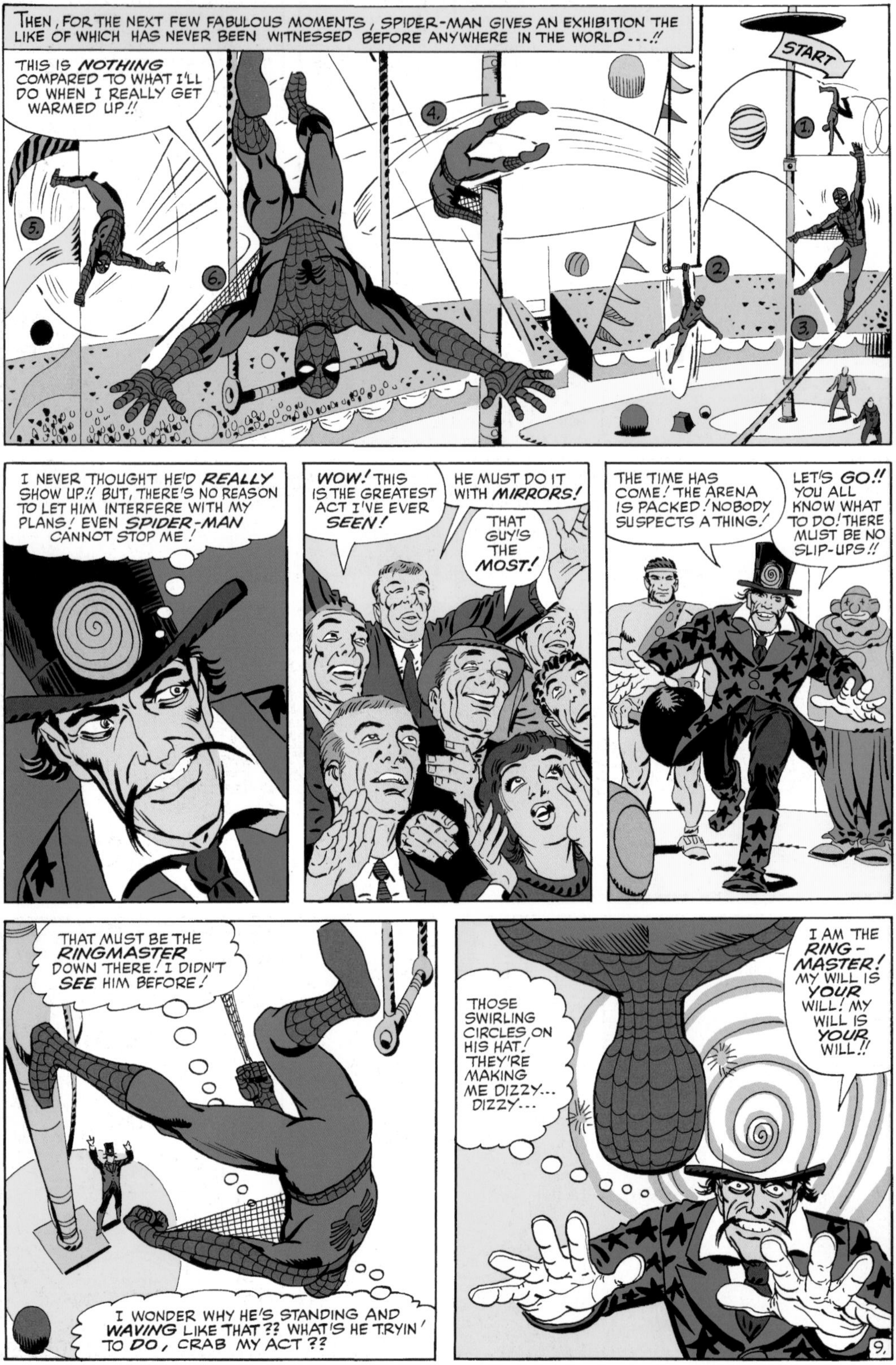
THEN, FOR THE NEXT FEW FABULOUS MOMENTS, SPIDER-MAN GIVES AN EXHIBITION THE LIKE OF WHICH HAS NEVER BEEN WITNESSED BEFORE ANYWHERE IN THE WORLD...!!
THIS IS NOTHING COMPARED TO WHAT I'LL DO WHEN I REALLY GET WARMED UP!!
START
1.
2.
3.
4.
5.
6.
I NEVER THOUGHT HE'D REALLY SHOW UP!! BUT, THERE'S NO REASON TO LET HIM INTERFERE WITH MY PLANS! EVEN SPIDER-MAN CANNOT STOP ME!
WOW! THIS IS THE GREATEST ACT I'VE EVER SEEN!
HE MUST DO IT WITH MIRRORS!
THAT GUY'S THE MOST!
THE TIME HAS COME! THE ARENA IS PACKED! NOBODY SUSPECTS A THING!
LET'S GO!! YOU ALL KNOW WHAT TO DO! THERE MUST BE NO SLIP-UPS!!
THAT MUST BE THE RINGMASTER DOWN THERE! I DIDN'T SEE HIM BEFORE!
I WONDER WHY HE'S STANDING AND WAVING LIKE THAT?? WHAT'S HE TRYIN' TO DO, CRAB MY ACT??
THOSE SWIRLING CIRCLES ON HIS HAT! THEY'RE MAKING ME DIZZY... DIZZY...
I AM THE RING-MASTER! MY WILL IS YOUR WILL! MY WILL IS YOUR WILL!!
9.

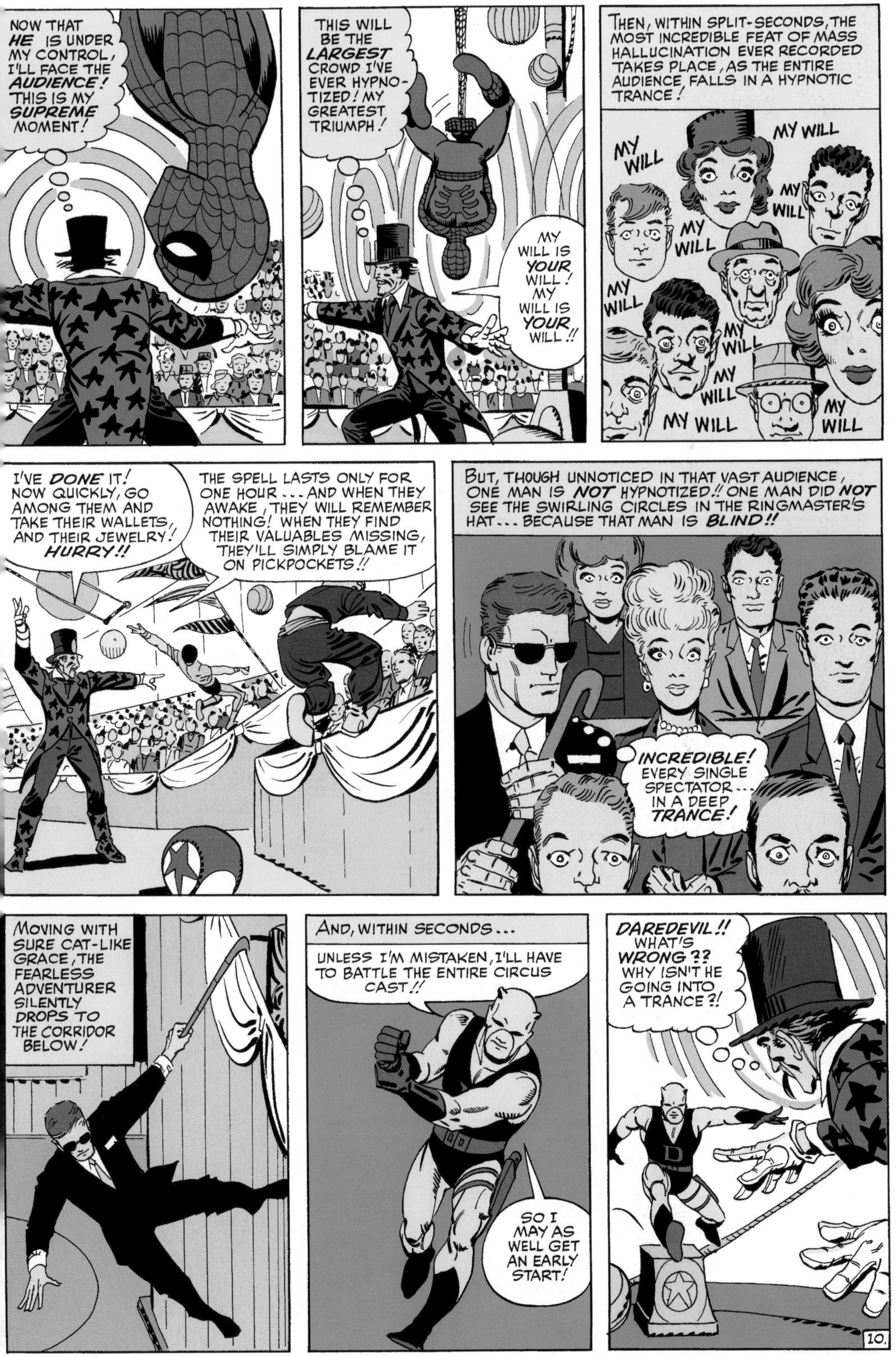
NOW THAT HE IS UNDER MY CONTROL, I'LL FACE THE AUDIENCE! THIS IS MY SUPREME MOMENT!
THIS WILL BE THE LARGEST CROWD I'VE EVER HYPNOTIZED! MY GREATEST TRIUMPH!
MY WILL IS YOUR WILL! MY WILL IS YOUR WILL!!
THEN, WITHIN SPLIT-SECONDS, THE MOST INCREDIBLE FEAT OF MASS HALLUCINATION EVER RECORDED TAKES PLACE, AS THE ENTIRE AUDIENCE FALLS IN A HYPNOTIC TRANCE!
MY WILL
MY WILL
MY WILL
MY WILL
MY WILL
MY WILL
MY WILL
MY WILL
MY WILL
I'VE DONE IT! NOW QUICKLY, GO AMONG THEM AND TAKE THEIR WALLETS, AND THEIR JEWELRY! HURRY!!
THE SPELL LASTS ONLY FOR ONE HOUR... AND WHEN THEY AWAKE, THEY WILL REMEMBER NOTHING! WHEN THEY FIND THEIR VALUABLES MISSING, THEY'LL SIMPLY BLAME IT ON PICKPOCKETS!!
BUT, THOUGH UNNOTICED IN THAT VAST AUDIENCE, ONE MAN IS NOT HYPNOTIZED!! ONE MAN DID NOT SEE THE SWIRLING CIRCLES IN THE RINGMASTER'S HAT... BECAUSE THAT MAN IS BLIND!!
INCREDIBLE! EVERY SINGLE SPECTATOR... IN A DEEP TRANCE!
MOVING WITH SURE CAT-LIKE GRACE, THE FEARLESS ADVENTURER SILENTLY DROPS TO THE CORRIDOR BELOW!
AND, WITHIN SECONDS...
UNLESS I'M MISTAKEN, I'LL HAVE TO BATTLE THE ENTIRE CIRCUS CAST!!
SO I MAY AS WELL GET AN EARLY START!
DAREDEVIL!! WHAT'S WRONG?? WHY ISN'T HE GOING INTO A TRANCE?!
10.

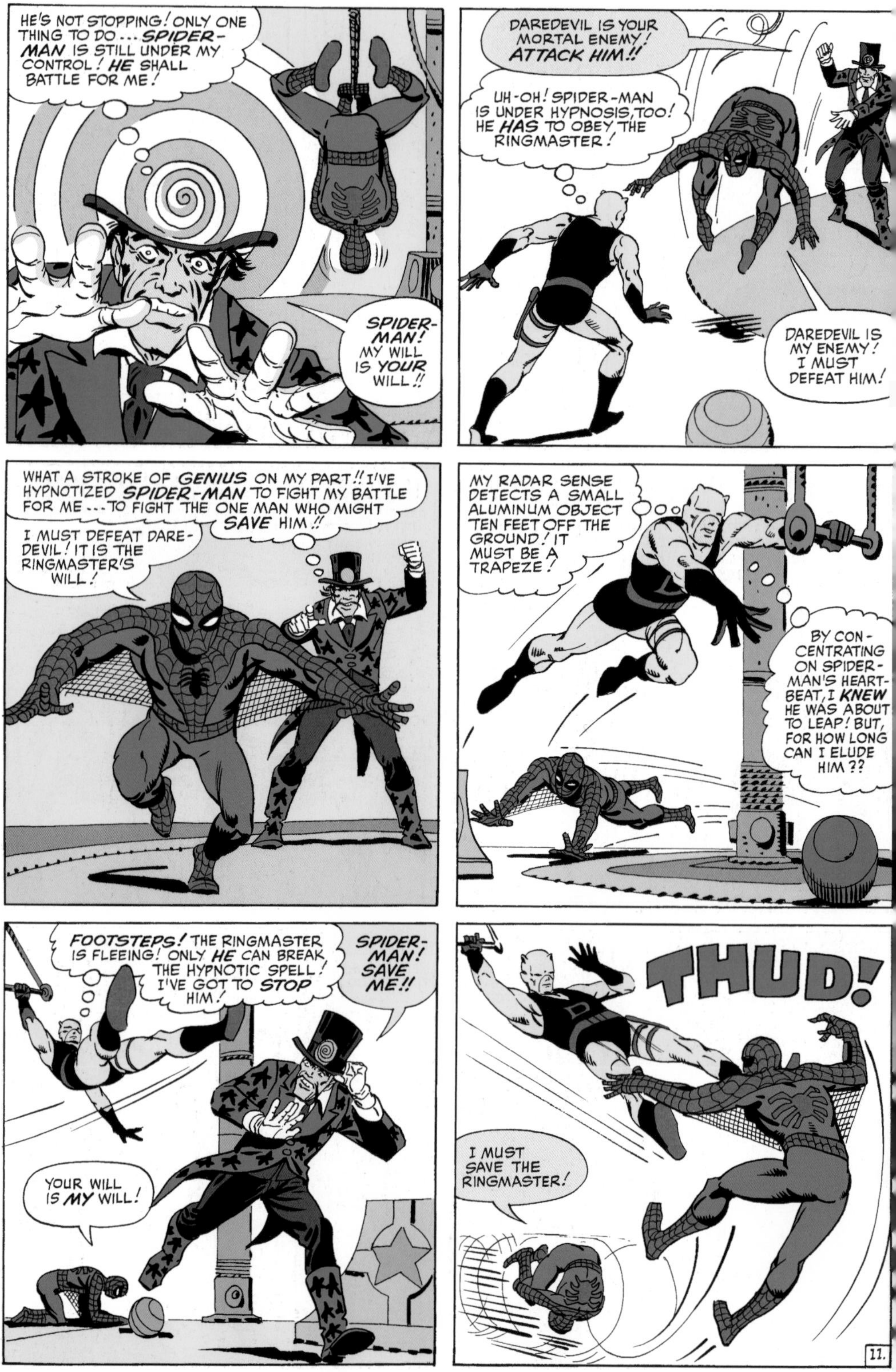
HE'S NOT STOPPING! ONLY ONE THING TO DO... SPIDER-MAN IS STILL UNDER MY CONTROL! HE SHALL BATTLE FOR ME!
SPIDER-MAN! MY WILL IS YOUR WILL!!
DAREDEVIL IS YOUR MORTAL ENEMY! ATTACK HIM!!
UH-OH! SPIDER-MAN IS UNDER HYPNOSIS, TOO! HE HAS TO OBEY THE RINGMASTER!
DAREDEVIL IS MY ENEMY! I MUST DEFEAT HIM!
WHAT A STROKE OF GENIUS ON MY PART!! I'VE HYPNOTIZED SPIDER-MAN TO FIGHT MY BATTLE FOR ME... TO FIGHT THE ONE MAN WHO MIGHT SAVE HIM!!
I MUST DEFEAT DAREDEVIL! IT IS THE RINGMASTER'S WILL!
MY RADAR SENSE DETECTS A SMALL ALUMINUM OBJECT TEN FEET OFF THE GROUND! IT MUST BE A TRAPEZE!
BY CONCENTRATING ON SPIDER-MAN'S HEARTBEAT, I KNEW HE WAS ABOUT TO LEAP! BUT, FOR HOW LONG CAN I ELUDE HIM??
FOOTSTEPS! THE RINGMASTER IS FLEEING! ONLY HE CAN BREAK THE HYPNOTIC SPELL! I'VE GOT TO STOP HIM!
SPIDER-MAN! SAVE ME!!
YOUR WILL IS MY WILL!
THUD!
I MUST SAVE THE RINGMASTER!
11.

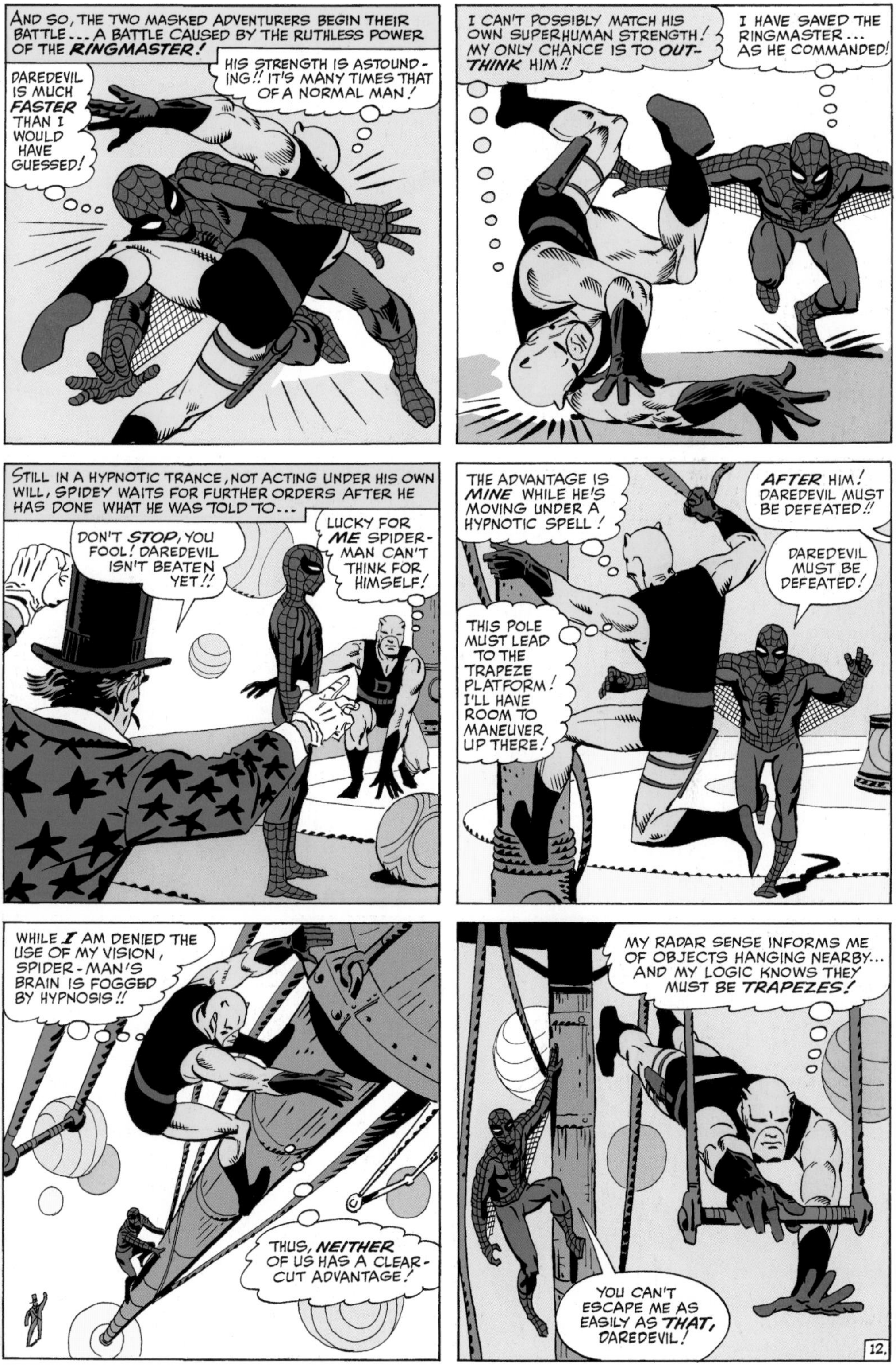

AND SO, THE TWO MASKED ADVENTURERS BEGIN THEIR BATTLE... A BATTLE CAUSED BY THE RUTHLESS POWER OF THE RINGMASTER!
DAREDEVIL IS MUCH FASTER THAN I WOULD HAVE GUESSED!
HIS STRENGTH IS ASTOUNDING!! IT'S MANY TIMES THAT OF A NORMAL MAN!
I CAN'T POSSIBLY MATCH HIS OWN SUPERHUMAN STRENGTH! MY ONLY CHANCE IS TO OUT-THINK HIM!!
I HAVE SAVED THE RINGMASTER... AS HE COMMANDED!
STILL IN A HYPNOTIC TRANCE, NOT ACTING UNDER HIS OWN WILL, SPIDEY WAITS FOR FURTHER ORDERS AFTER HE HAS DONE WHAT HE WAS TOLD TO...
DON'T STOP, YOU FOOL! DAREDEVIL ISN'T BEATEN YET!!
LUCKY FOR ME SPIDER-MAN CAN'T THINK FOR HIMSELF!
THE ADVANTAGE IS MINE WHILE HE'S MOVING UNDER A HYPNOTIC SPELL!
AFTER HIM! DAREDEVIL MUST BE DEFEATED!!
DAREDEVIL MUST BE DEFEATED!
THIS POLE MUST LEAD TO THE TRAPEZE PLATFORM! I'LL HAVE ROOM TO MANEUVER UP THERE!
WHILE I AM DENIED THE USE OF MY VISION, SPIDER-MAN'S BRAIN IS FOGGED BY HYPNOSIS!!
THUS, NEITHER OF US HAS A CLEAR-CUT ADVANTAGE!
MY RADAR SENSE INFORMS ME OF OBJECTS HANGING NEARBY... AND MY LOGIC KNOWS THEY MUST BE TRAPEZES!
YOU CAN'T ESCAPE ME AS EASILY AS THAT, DAREDEVIL!
12.

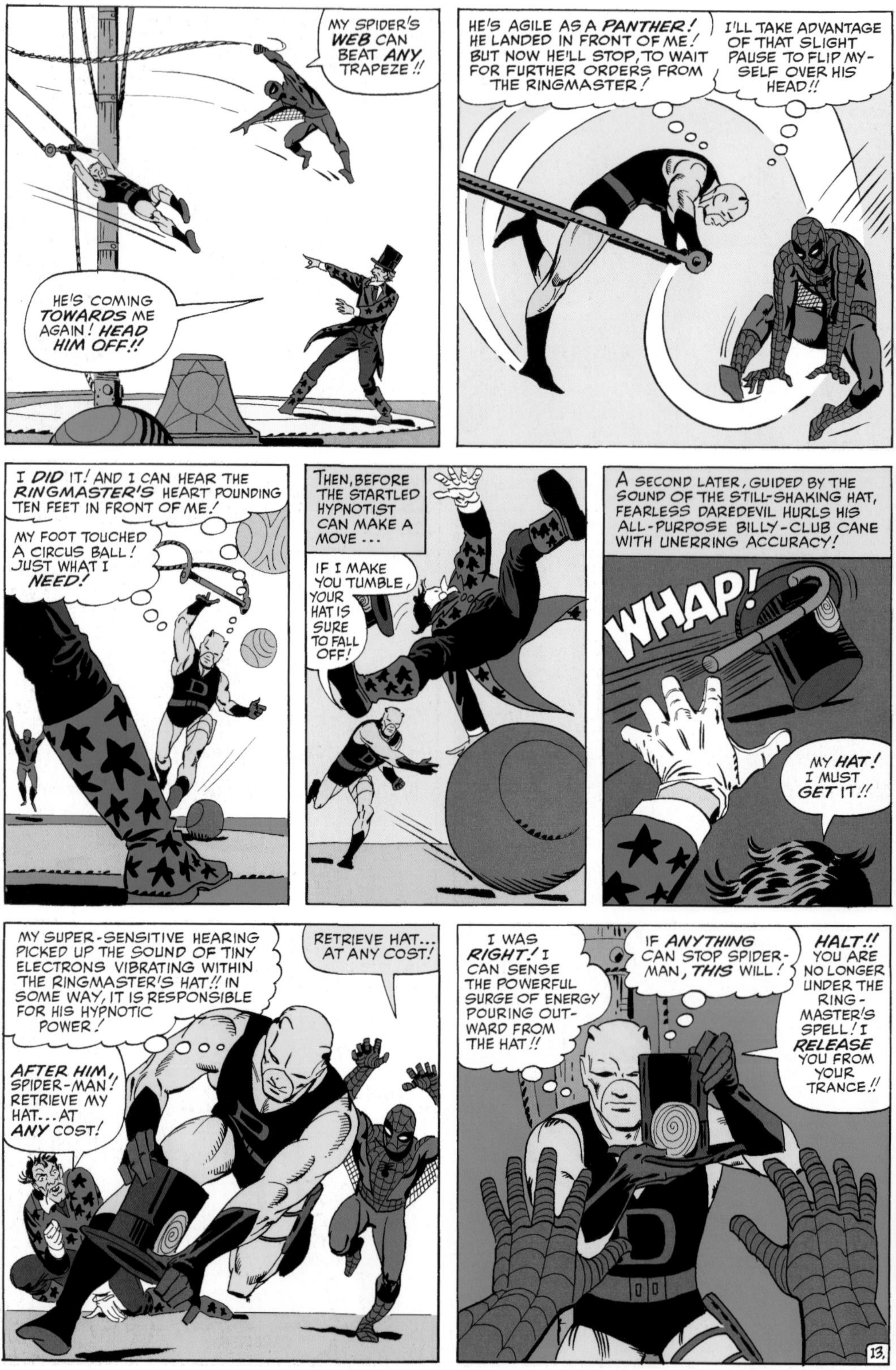
MY SPIDER'S WEB CAN BEAT ANY TRAPEZE!!
HE'S COMING TOWARDS ME AGAIN! HEAD HIM OFF!!
HE'S AGILE AS A PANTHER! HE LANDED IN FRONT OF ME! BUT NOW HE'LL STOP, TO WAIT FOR FURTHER ORDERS FROM THE RINGMASTER!
I'LL TAKE ADVANTAGE OF THAT SLIGHT PAUSE TO FLIP MY-SELF OVER HIS HEAD!!
I DID IT! AND I CAN HEAR THE RINGMASTER'S HEART POUNDING TEN FEET IN FRONT OF ME!
MY FOOT TOUCHED A CIRCUS BALL! JUST WHAT I NEED!
THEN, BEFORE THE STARTLED HYPNOTIST CAN MAKE A MOVE...
IF I MAKE YOU TUMBLE, YOUR HAT IS SURE TO FALL OFF!
A SECOND LATER, GUIDED BY THE SOUND OF THE STILL-SHAKING HAT, FEARLESS DAREDEVIL HURLS HIS ALL-PURPOSE BILLY-CLUB CANE WITH UNERRING ACCURACY!
WHAP!
MY HAT! I MUST GET IT!!
MY SUPER-SENSITIVE HEARING PICKED UP THE SOUND OF TINY ELECTRONS VIBRATING WITHIN THE RINGMASTER'S HAT!! IN SOME WAY, IT IS RESPONSIBLE FOR HIS HYPNOTIC POWER!
RETRIEVE HAT... AT ANY COST!
AFTER HIM, SPIDER-MAN! RETRIEVE MY HAT...AT ANY COST!
I WAS RIGHT! I CAN SENSE THE POWERFUL SURGE OF ENERGY POURING OUT-WARD FROM THE HAT!!
IF ANYTHING CAN STOP SPIDER-MAN, THIS WILL!
HALT!! YOU ARE NO LONGER UNDER THE RING-MASTER'S SPELL! I RELEASE YOU FROM YOUR TRANCE!!
13.

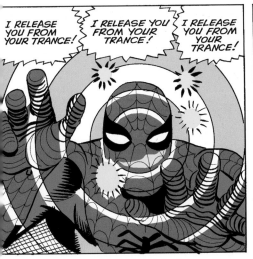

I RELEASE YOU FROM YOUR TRANCE!

I RELEASE YOU FROM YOUR TRANCE!

I RELEASE YOU FROM YOUR TRANCE!

I HEAR HIS PULSE RATE CHANGING! HIS HEART-BEAT HAS BECOME NORMAL! HE'S SNAPPING OUT OF IT!!

MY HEAD...FOG... MISTS SWIRLING ABOUT...BEGINNING TO CLEAR...I CAN *THINK* AGAIN!

ONCE FREE OF THE HYPNOTIC SPELL, THE BRILLIANT BRAIN OF THE MASKED TEEN-AGER GRASPS THE WHOLE SITUATION IN ONE SPLIT SECOND!

MUCH OBLIGED, DAREDEVIL! NO TELLING WHAT *HARM* I MIGHT HAVE CAUSED IF YOU HADN'T BROKEN THE RINGMASTER'S HOLD OVER ME!

CHALK IT UP TO SELF-PRESERVATION ON *MY* PART, FELLA! I'D RATHER HAVE A GENT LIKE YOU *WITH* ME THAN *AGIN'* ME!!

THANKS FOR THE COMPLIMENT, BUT I OWE YOU A FAVOR, AND A SPIDER-MAN NEVER FORGETS!

BETTER SAVE THE HEARTS AND FLOWERS FOR LATER, SPIDEY! I HEAR A MIGHTY ANGRY RING-MASTER GETTING READY TO ATTACK US AGAIN!

WHOOPS! I ALMOST LET THE CAT OUT OF THE BAG ABOUT MY SUPER-HEARING!

DON'T JUST *STAND* THERE, YOU USELESS FOOLS! WE OUTNUMBER THOSE TWO MASKED MEDDLERS! *WE'RE* HIGHLY-TRAINED, ALSO! LET'S *GET* THEM... UNLESS YOU WANT TO DO THE *REST* OF YOUR ACT IN *JAIL!!*

THE RINGMASTER'S *RIGHT!* IT'S ONLY TWO OF THEM AGAINST *ALL* OF US! LET'S GO!!

THE *REST* OF THE AUDIENCE IS STILL HYPNOTIZED! IF WE CAN POLISH OFF SPIDER-MAN AND DAREDEVIL IN TIME, WE'LL *STILL* GET AWAY WITH OUR PLAN!

14.

207

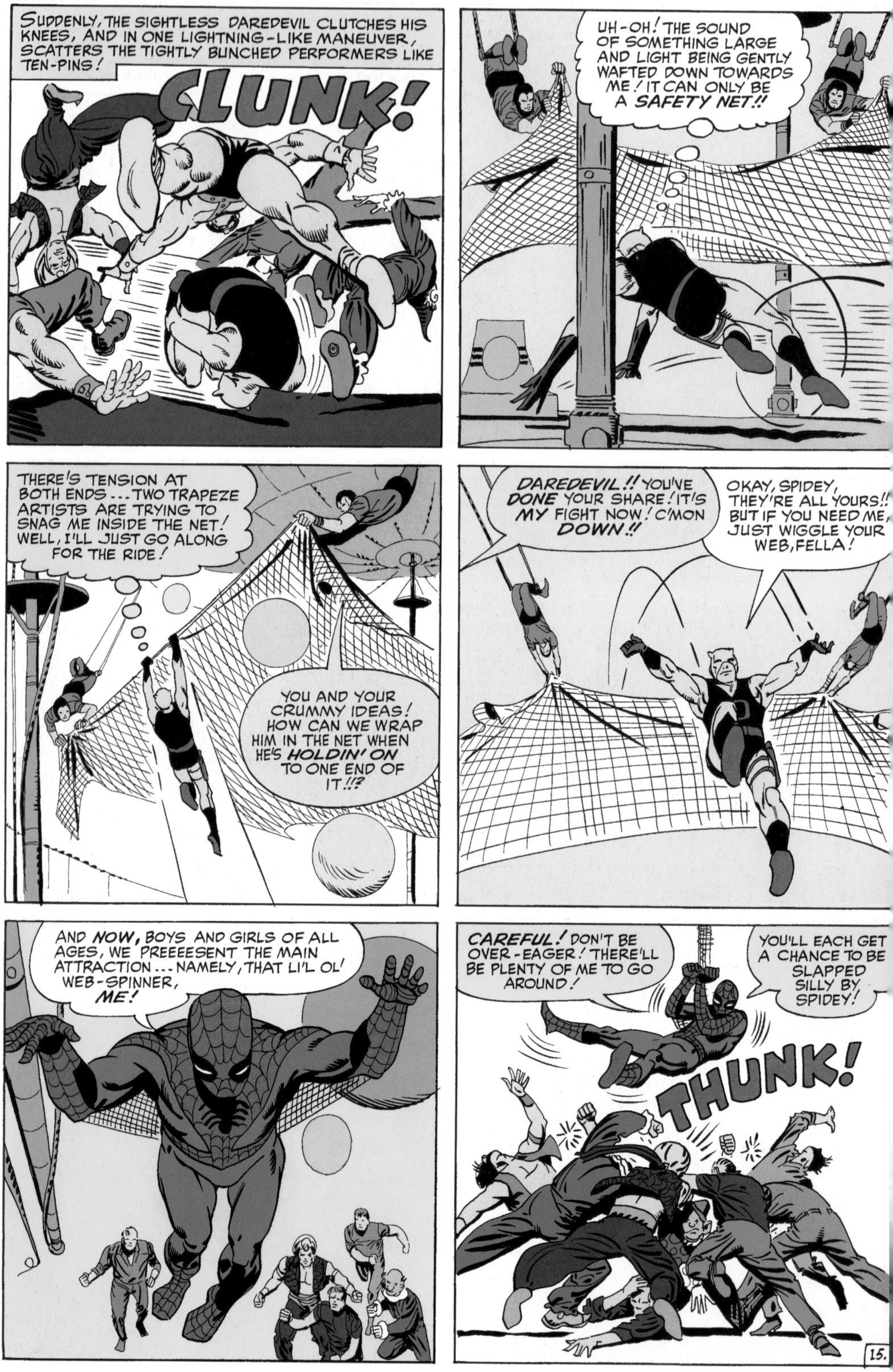
SUDDENLY, THE SIGHTLESS DAREDEVIL CLUTCHES HIS KNEES, AND IN ONE LIGHTNING-LIKE MANEUVER, SCATTERS THE TIGHTLY BUNCHED PERFORMERS LIKE TEN-PINS!
CLUNK!
UH-OH! THE SOUND OF SOMETHING LARGE AND LIGHT BEING GENTLY WAFTED DOWN TOWARDS ME! IT CAN ONLY BE A SAFETY NET!!
THERE'S TENSION AT BOTH ENDS... TWO TRAPEZE ARTISTS ARE TRYING TO SNAG ME INSIDE THE NET! WELL, I'LL JUST GO ALONG FOR THE RIDE!
YOU AND YOUR CRUMMY IDEAS! HOW CAN WE WRAP HIM IN THE NET WHEN HE'S HOLDIN' ON TO ONE END OF IT!!?
DAREDEVIL!! YOU'VE DONE YOUR SHARE! IT'S MY FIGHT NOW! C'MON DOWN!!
OKAY, SPIDEY, THEY'RE ALL YOURS!! BUT IF YOU NEED ME, JUST WIGGLE YOUR WEB, FELLA!
AND NOW, BOYS AND GIRLS OF ALL AGES, WE PREEEESENT THE MAIN ATTRACTION... NAMELY, THAT LI'L OL' WEB-SPINNER, ME!
CAREFUL! DON'T BE OVER-EAGER! THERE'LL BE PLENTY OF ME TO GO AROUND!
YOU'LL EACH GET A CHANCE TO BE SLAPPED SILLY BY SPIDEY!
THUNK!
15.

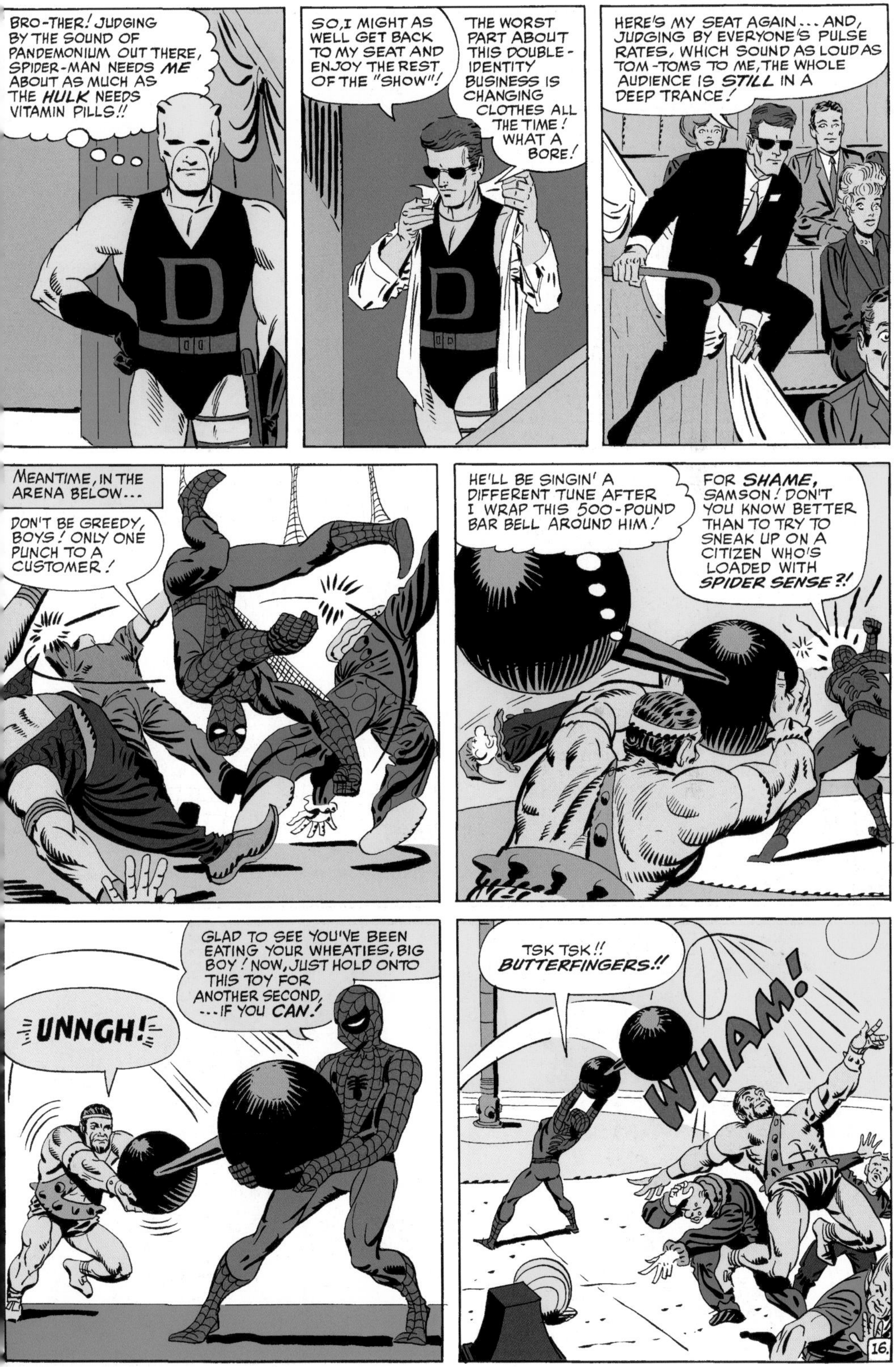
BRO-THER! JUDGING BY THE SOUND OF PANDEMONIUM OUT THERE, SPIDER-MAN NEEDS ME ABOUT AS MUCH AS THE HULK NEEDS VITAMIN PILLS!!
SO, I MIGHT AS WELL GET BACK TO MY SEAT AND ENJOY THE REST OF THE "SHOW"!
THE WORST PART ABOUT THIS DOUBLE-IDENTITY BUSINESS IS CHANGING CLOTHES ALL THE TIME! WHAT A BORE!
HERE'S MY SEAT AGAIN... AND, JUDGING BY EVERYONE'S PULSE RATES, WHICH SOUND AS LOUD AS TOM-TOMS TO ME, THE WHOLE AUDIENCE IS STILL IN A DEEP TRANCE!
MEANTIME, IN THE ARENA BELOW...
DON'T BE GREEDY, BOYS! ONLY ONE PUNCH TO A CUSTOMER!
HE'LL BE SINGIN' A DIFFERENT TUNE AFTER I WRAP THIS 500-POUND BAR BELL AROUND HIM!
FOR SHAME, SAMSON! DON'T YOU KNOW BETTER THAN TO TRY TO SNEAK UP ON A CITIZEN WHO'S LOADED WITH SPIDER SENSE?!
UNNGH!
GLAD TO SEE YOU'VE BEEN EATING YOUR WHEATIES, BIG BOY! NOW, JUST HOLD ONTO THIS TOY FOR ANOTHER SECOND, ...IF YOU CAN!
TSK TSK!! BUTTERFINGERS!!
WHAM!
16.

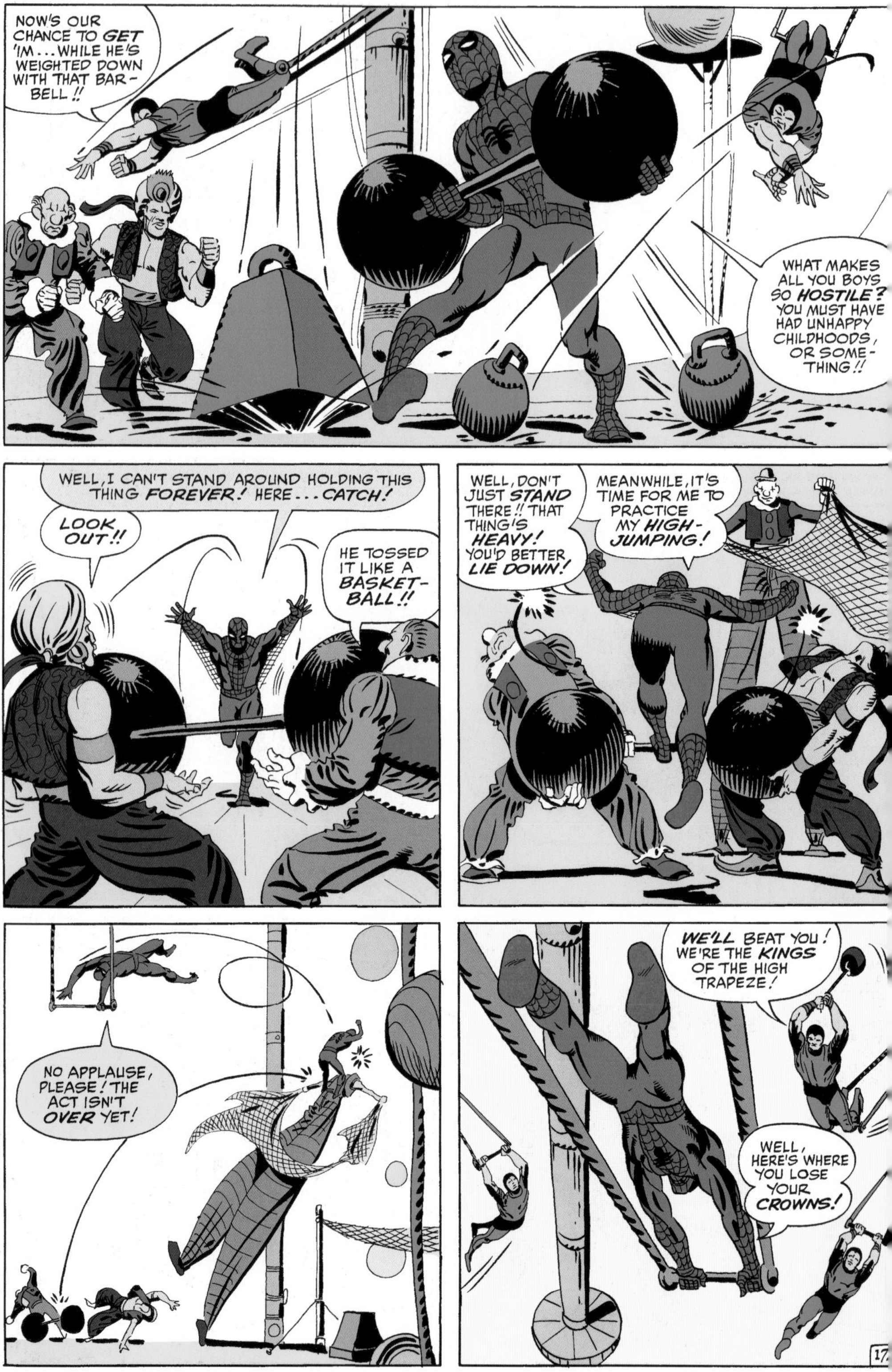
NOW'S OUR CHANCE TO GET 'IM... WHILE HE'S WEIGHTED DOWN WITH THAT BAR-BELL!!
WHAT MAKES ALL YOU BOYS SO HOSTILE? YOU MUST HAVE HAD UNHAPPY CHILDHOODS, OR SOME-THING!!
WELL, I CAN'T STAND AROUND HOLDING THIS THING FOREVER! HERE... CATCH!
LOOK OUT!!
HE TOSSED IT LIKE A BASKET-BALL!!
WELL, DON'T JUST STAND THERE!! THAT THING'S HEAVY! YOU'D BETTER LIE DOWN!
MEANWHILE, IT'S TIME FOR ME TO PRACTICE MY HIGH-JUMPING!
NO APPLAUSE, PLEASE! THE ACT ISN'T OVER YET!
WE'LL BEAT YOU! WE'RE THE KINGS OF THE HIGH TRAPEZE!
WELL, HERE'S WHERE YOU LOSE YOUR CROWNS!
17

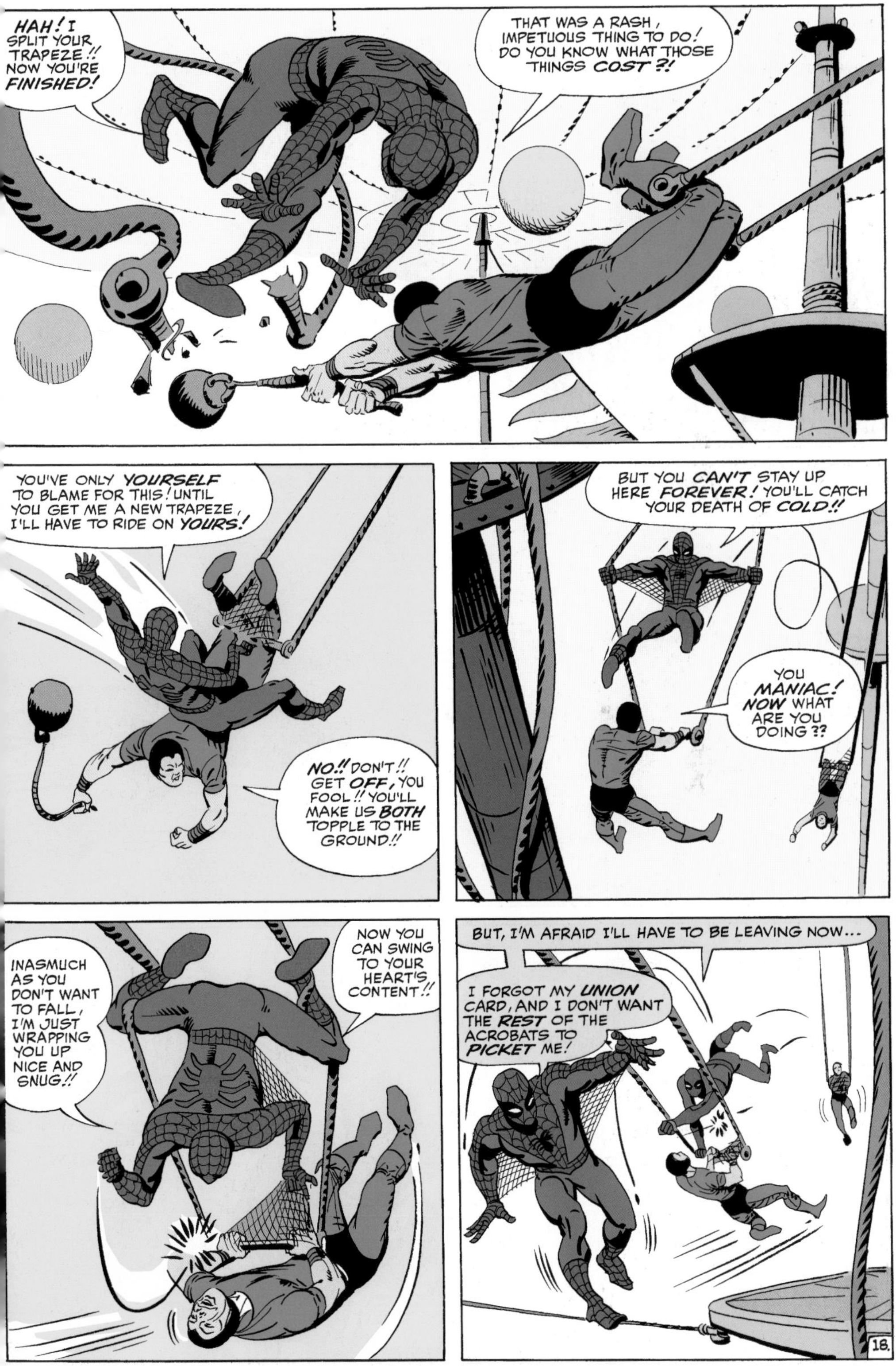
HAH! I SPLIT YOUR TRAPEZE!! NOW YOU'RE FINISHED!
THAT WAS A RASH, IMPETUOUS THING TO DO! DO YOU KNOW WHAT THOSE THINGS COST?!
YOU'VE ONLY YOURSELF TO BLAME FOR THIS! UNTIL YOU GET ME A NEW TRAPEZE, I'LL HAVE TO RIDE ON YOURS!
NO!! DON'T!! GET OFF, YOU FOOL!! YOU'LL MAKE US BOTH TOPPLE TO THE GROUND!!
BUT YOU CAN'T STAY UP HERE FOREVER! YOU'LL CATCH YOUR DEATH OF COLD!!
YOU MANIAC! NOW WHAT ARE YOU DOING??
INASMUCH AS YOU DON'T WANT TO FALL, I'M JUST WRAPPING YOU UP NICE AND SNUG!!
NOW YOU CAN SWING TO YOUR HEART'S CONTENT!!
BUT, I'M AFRAID I'LL HAVE TO BE LEAVING NOW...
I FORGOT MY UNION CARD, AND I DON'T WANT THE REST OF THE ACROBATS TO PICKET ME!
18.

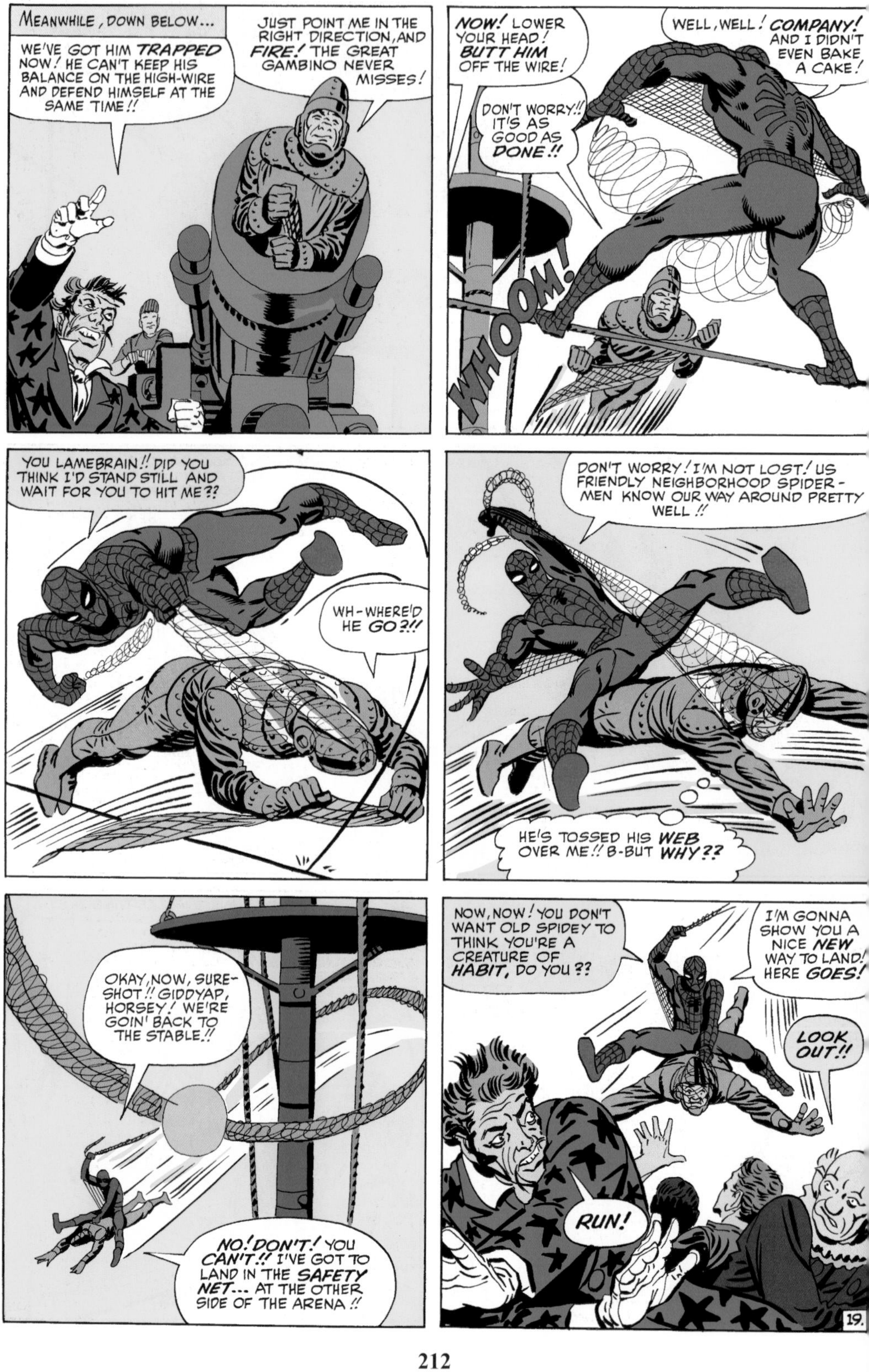
MEANWHILE, DOWN BELOW...
WE'VE GOT HIM TRAPPED NOW! HE CAN'T KEEP HIS BALANCE ON THE HIGH-WIRE AND DEFEND HIMSELF AT THE SAME TIME!!
JUST POINT ME IN THE RIGHT DIRECTION, AND FIRE! THE GREAT GAMBINO NEVER MISSES!
NOW! LOWER YOUR HEAD! BUTT HIM OFF THE WIRE!
DON'T WORRY!! IT'S AS GOOD AS DONE!!
WELL, WELL! COMPANY! AND I DIDN'T EVEN BAKE A CAKE!
WHOOM!
YOU LAMEBRAIN!! DID YOU THINK I'D STAND STILL AND WAIT FOR YOU TO HIT ME??
WH-WHERE'D HE GO?!!
DON'T WORRY! I'M NOT LOST! US FRIENDLY NEIGHBORHOOD SPIDER-MEN KNOW OUR WAY AROUND PRETTY WELL!!
HE'S TOSSED HIS WEB OVER ME!! B-BUT WHY??
OKAY, NOW, SURE-SHOT!! GIDDYAP, HORSEY! WE'RE GOIN' BACK TO THE STABLE!!
NO! DON'T! YOU CAN'T!! I'VE GOT TO LAND IN THE SAFETY NET... AT THE OTHER SIDE OF THE ARENA!!
NOW, NOW! YOU DON'T WANT OLD SPIDEY TO THINK YOU'RE A CREATURE OF HABIT, DO YOU??
I'M GONNA SHOW YOU A NICE NEW WAY TO LAND! HERE GOES!
LOOK OUT!!
RUN!
19.

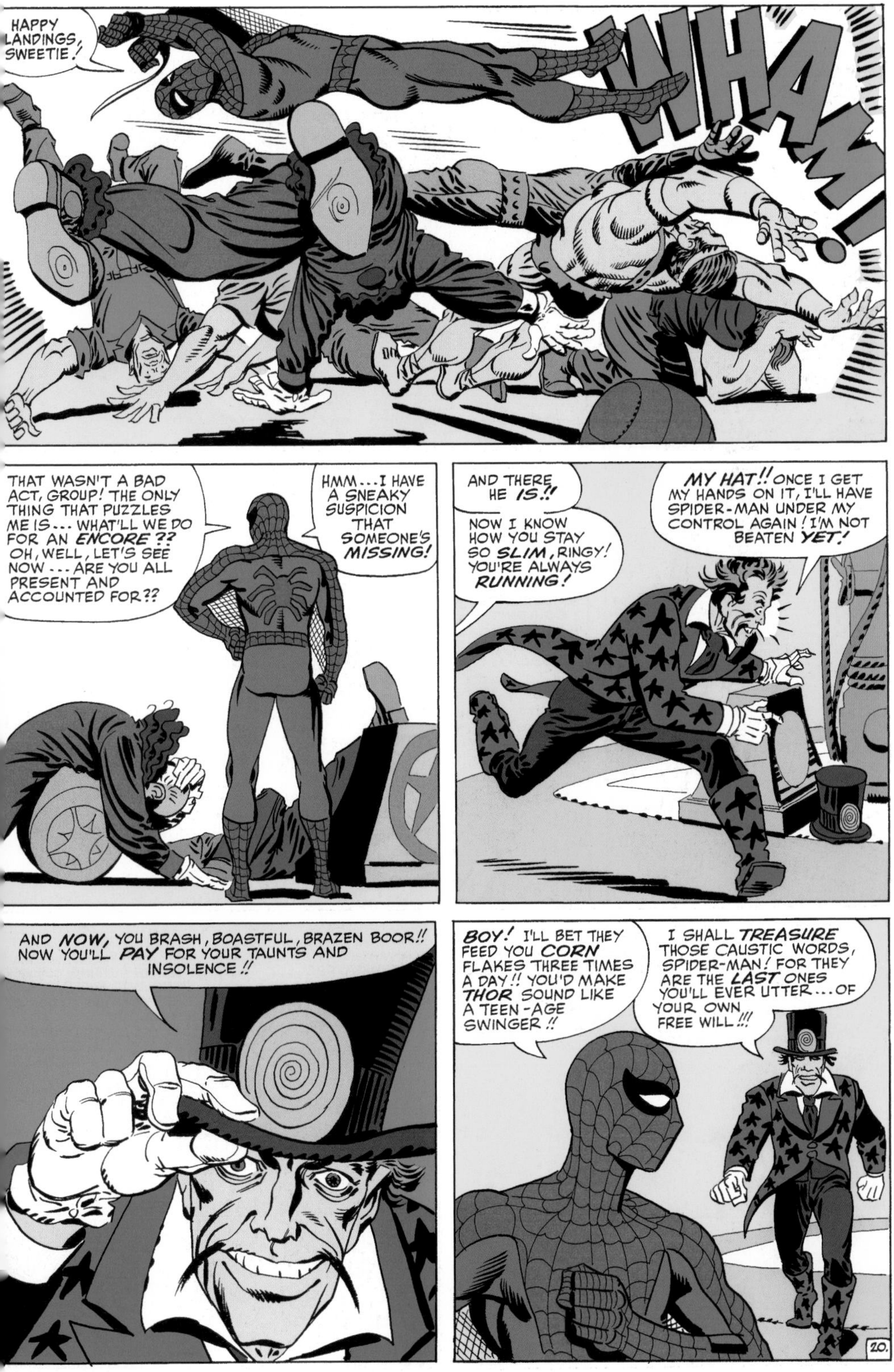

HAPPY LANDINGS, SWEETIE!
WHAM!
THAT WASN'T A BAD ACT, GROUP! THE ONLY THING THAT PUZZLES ME IS... WHAT'LL WE DO FOR AN ENCORE?? OH, WELL, LET'S SEE NOW... ARE YOU ALL PRESENT AND ACCOUNTED FOR??
HMM... I HAVE A SNEAKY SUSPICION THAT SOMEONE'S MISSING!
AND THERE HE IS!!
NOW I KNOW HOW YOU STAY SO SLIM, RINGY! YOU'RE ALWAYS RUNNING!
MY HAT!! ONCE I GET MY HANDS ON IT, I'LL HAVE SPIDER-MAN UNDER MY CONTROL AGAIN! I'M NOT BEATEN YET!
AND NOW, YOU BRASH, BOASTFUL, BRAZEN BOOR!! NOW YOU'LL PAY FOR YOUR TAUNTS AND INSOLENCE!!
BOY! I'LL BET THEY FEED YOU CORN FLAKES THREE TIMES A DAY!! YOU'D MAKE THOR SOUND LIKE A TEEN-AGE SWINGER!!
I SHALL TREASURE THOSE CAUSTIC WORDS, SPIDER-MAN! FOR THEY ARE THE LAST ONES YOU'LL EVER UTTER... OF YOUR OWN FREE WILL!!!
20.

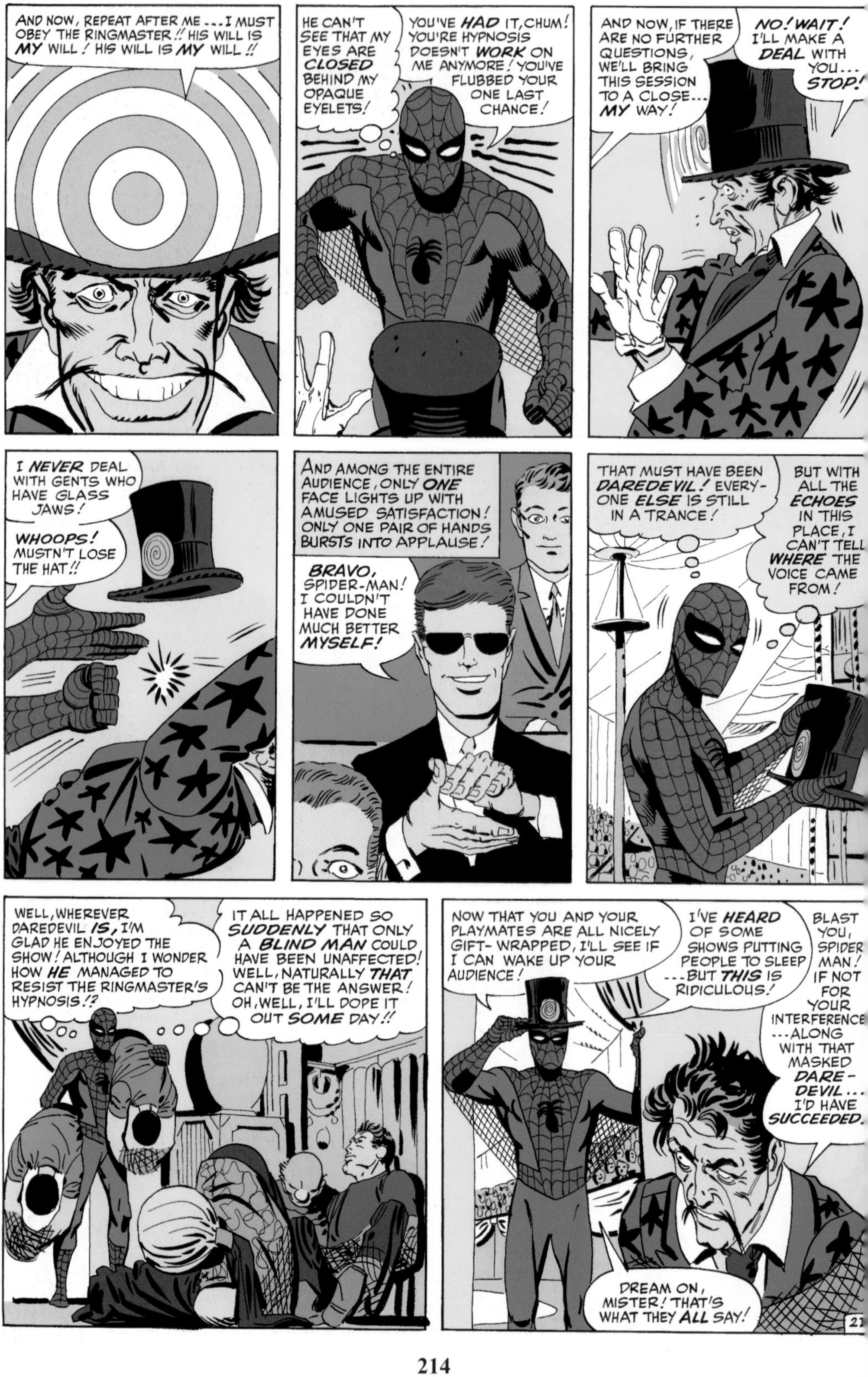
AND NOW, REPEAT AFTER ME ...I MUST OBEY THE RINGMASTER!! HIS WILL IS MY WILL! HIS WILL IS MY WILL!!
HE CAN'T SEE THAT MY EYES ARE CLOSED BEHIND MY OPAQUE EYELETS!
YOU'VE HAD IT, CHUM! YOU'RE HYPNOSIS DOESN'T WORK ON ME ANYMORE! YOU'VE FLUBBED YOUR ONE LAST CHANCE!
AND NOW, IF THERE ARE NO FURTHER QUESTIONS, WE'LL BRING THIS SESSION TO A CLOSE... MY WAY!
NO! WAIT! I'LL MAKE A DEAL WITH YOU... STOP!
I NEVER DEAL WITH GENTS WHO HAVE GLASS JAWS!
WHOOPS! MUSTN'T LOSE THE HAT!!
AND AMONG THE ENTIRE AUDIENCE, ONLY ONE FACE LIGHTS UP WITH AMUSED SATISFACTION! ONLY ONE PAIR OF HANDS BURSTS INTO APPLAUSE!
BRAVO, SPIDER-MAN! I COULDN'T HAVE DONE MUCH BETTER MYSELF!
THAT MUST HAVE BEEN DAREDEVIL! EVERY-ONE ELSE IS STILL IN A TRANCE!
BUT WITH ALL THE ECHOES IN THIS PLACE, I CAN'T TELL WHERE THE VOICE CAME FROM!
WELL, WHEREVER DAREDEVIL IS, I'M GLAD HE ENJOYED THE SHOW! ALTHOUGH I WONDER HOW HE MANAGED TO RESIST THE RINGMASTER'S HYPNOSIS!?
IT ALL HAPPENED SO SUDDENLY THAT ONLY A BLIND MAN COULD HAVE BEEN UNAFFECTED! WELL, NATURALLY THAT CAN'T BE THE ANSWER! OH, WELL, I'LL DOPE IT OUT SOME DAY!!
NOW THAT YOU AND YOUR PLAYMATES ARE ALL NICELY GIFT-WRAPPED, I'LL SEE IF I CAN WAKE UP YOUR AUDIENCE!
I'VE HEARD OF SOME SHOWS PUTTING PEOPLE TO SLEEP ...BUT THIS IS RIDICULOUS!
BLAST YOU, SPIDER MAN! IF NOT FOR YOUR INTERFERENCE ...ALONG WITH THAT MASKED DARE-DEVIL... I'D HAVE SUCCEEDED.
DREAM ON, MISTER! THAT'S WHAT THEY ALL SAY!
21

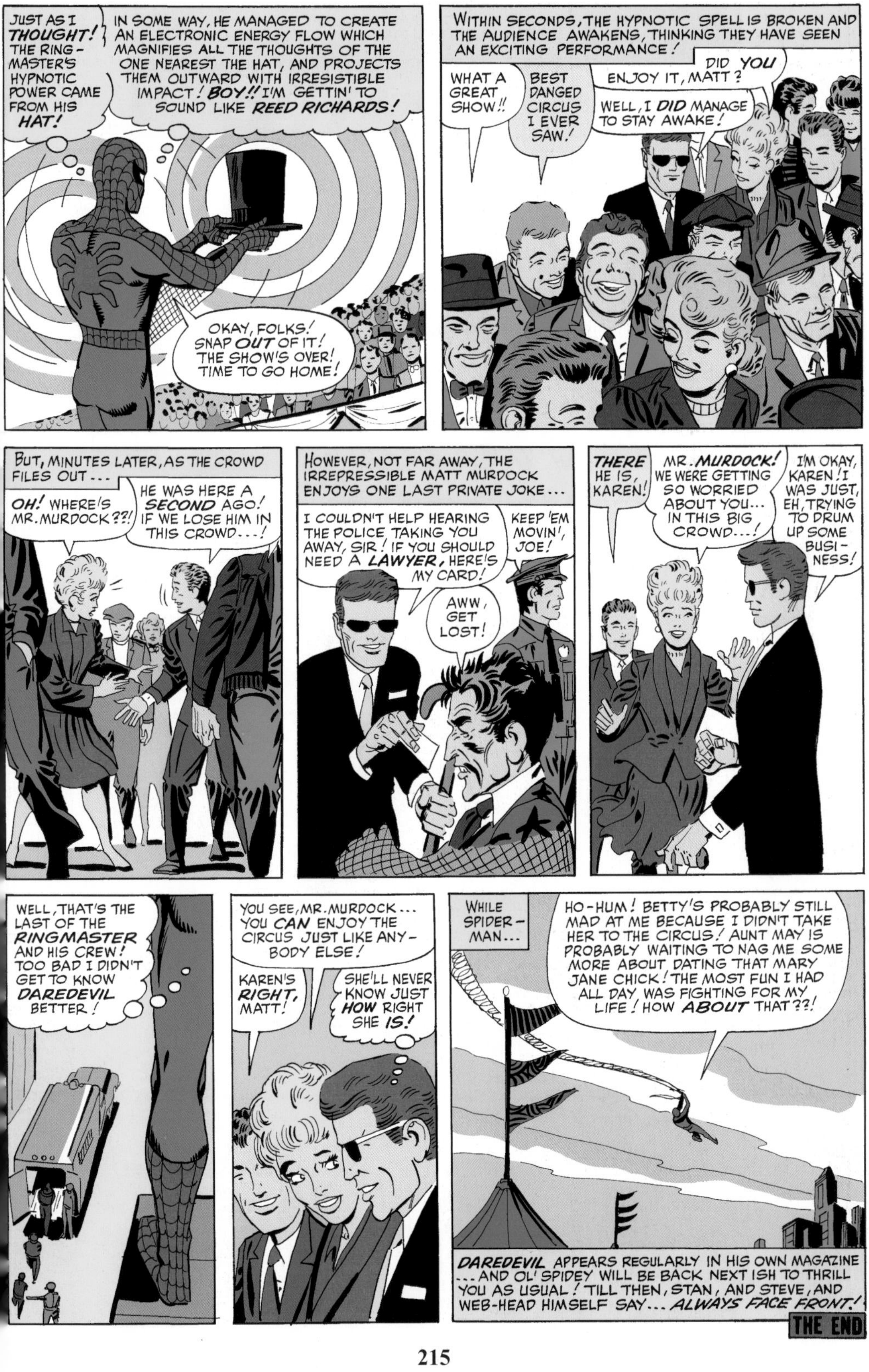
JUST AS I THOUGHT! THE RING-MASTER'S HYPNOTIC POWER CAME FROM HIS HAT!
IN SOME WAY, HE MANAGED TO CREATE AN ELECTRONIC ENERGY FLOW WHICH MAGNIFIES ALL THE THOUGHTS OF THE ONE NEAREST THE HAT, AND PROJECTS THEM OUTWARD WITH IRRESISTIBLE IMPACT! BOY!! I'M GETTIN' TO SOUND LIKE REED RICHARDS!
OKAY, FOLKS! SNAP OUT OF IT! THE SHOW'S OVER! TIME TO GO HOME!
WITHIN SECONDS, THE HYPNOTIC SPELL IS BROKEN AND THE AUDIENCE AWAKENS, THINKING THEY HAVE SEEN AN EXCITING PERFORMANCE!
WHAT A GREAT SHOW!!
BEST DANGED CIRCUS I EVER SAW!
DID YOU ENJOY IT, MATT?
WELL, I DID MANAGE TO STAY AWAKE!
BUT, MINUTES LATER, AS THE CROWD FILES OUT...
OH! WHERE'S MR. MURDOCK??!
HE WAS HERE A SECOND AGO! IF WE LOSE HIM IN THIS CROWD...!
HOWEVER, NOT FAR AWAY, THE IRREPRESSIBLE MATT MURDOCK ENJOYS ONE LAST PRIVATE JOKE...
I COULDN'T HELP HEARING THE POLICE TAKING YOU AWAY, SIR! IF YOU SHOULD NEED A LAWYER, HERE'S MY CARD!
KEEP 'EM MOVIN', JOE!
AWW, GET LOST!
THERE HE IS, KAREN!
MR. MURDOCK! WE WERE GETTING SO WORRIED ABOUT YOU... IN THIS BIG CROWD...!
I'M OKAY, KAREN! I WAS JUST, EH, TRYING TO DRUM UP SOME BUSI-NESS!
WELL, THAT'S THE LAST OF THE RINGMASTER AND HIS CREW! TOO BAD I DIDN'T GET TO KNOW DAREDEVIL BETTER!
YOU SEE, MR. MURDOCK... YOU CAN ENJOY THE CIRCUS JUST LIKE ANY-BODY ELSE!
KAREN'S RIGHT, MATT!
SHE'LL NEVER KNOW JUST HOW RIGHT SHE IS!
WHILE SPIDER-MAN...
HO-HUM! BETTY'S PROBABLY STILL MAD AT ME BECAUSE I DIDN'T TAKE HER TO THE CIRCUS! AUNT MAY IS PROBABLY WAITING TO NAG ME SOME MORE ABOUT DATING THAT MARY JANE CHICK! THE MOST FUN I HAD ALL DAY WAS FIGHTING FOR MY LIFE! HOW ABOUT THAT??!
DAREDEVIL APPEARS REGULARLY IN HIS OWN MAGAZINE ...AND OL' SPIDEY WILL BE BACK NEXT ISH TO THRILL YOU AS USUAL! TILL THEN, STAN, AND STEVE, AND WEB-HEAD HIMSELF SAY... ALWAYS FACE FRONT!
THE END

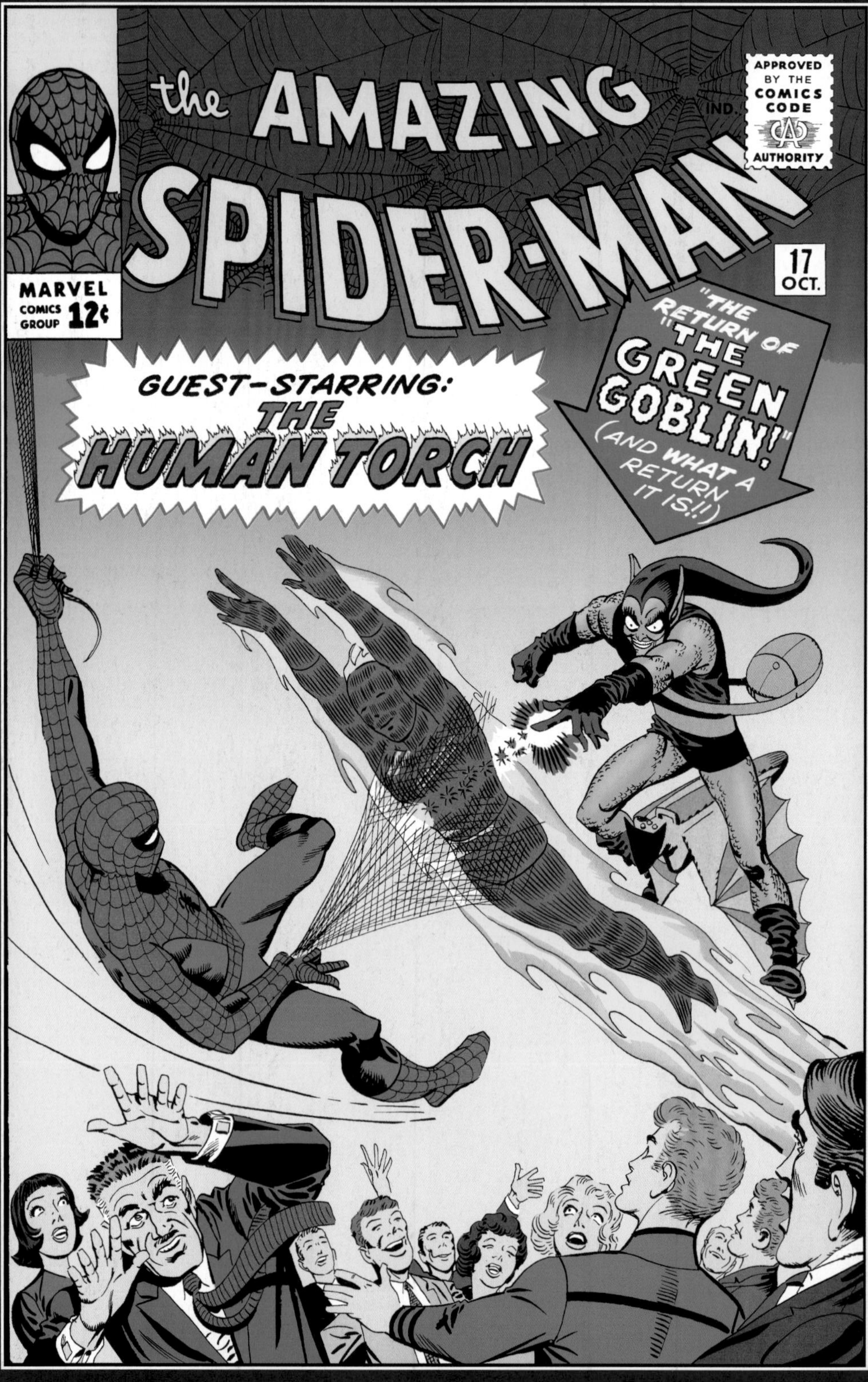
the AMAZING SPIDER-MAN
IND.
APPROVED BY THE COMICS CODE AUTHORITY
17 OCT.
MARVEL COMICS GROUP 12¢
GUEST-STARRING: THE HUMAN TORCH
"THE RETURN OF "THE GREEN GOBLIN!" (AND WHAT A RETURN IT IS!!)

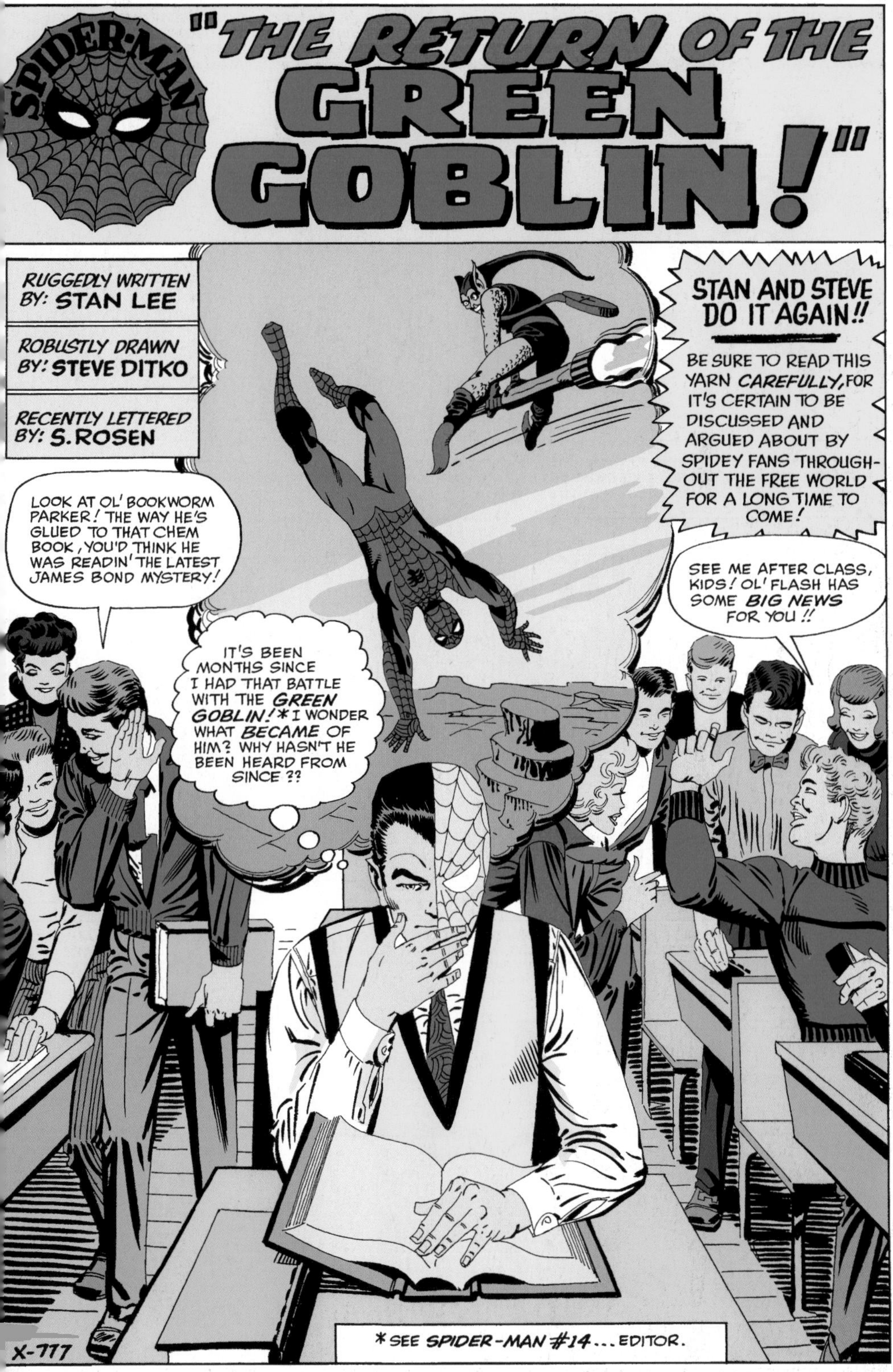

SPIDER-MAN
"THE RETURN OF THE GREEN GOBLIN!"
RUGGEDLY WRITTEN BY: STAN LEE
ROBUSTLY DRAWN BY: STEVE DITKO
RECENTLY LETTERED BY: S. ROSEN
STAN AND STEVE DO IT AGAIN!! BE SURE TO READ THIS YARN CAREFULLY, FOR IT'S CERTAIN TO BE DISCUSSED AND ARGUED ABOUT BY SPIDEY FANS THROUGHOUT THE FREE WORLD FOR A LONG TIME TO COME!
LOOK AT OL' BOOKWORM PARKER! THE WAY HE'S GLUED TO THAT CHEM BOOK, YOU'D THINK HE WAS READIN' THE LATEST JAMES BOND MYSTERY!
SEE ME AFTER CLASS, KIDS! OL' FLASH HAS SOME BIG NEWS FOR YOU!!
IT'S BEEN MONTHS SINCE I HAD THAT BATTLE WITH THE GREEN GOBLIN!* I WONDER WHAT BECAME OF HIM? WHY HASN'T HE BEEN HEARD FROM SINCE??
*SEE SPIDER-MAN #14... EDITOR.
X-777

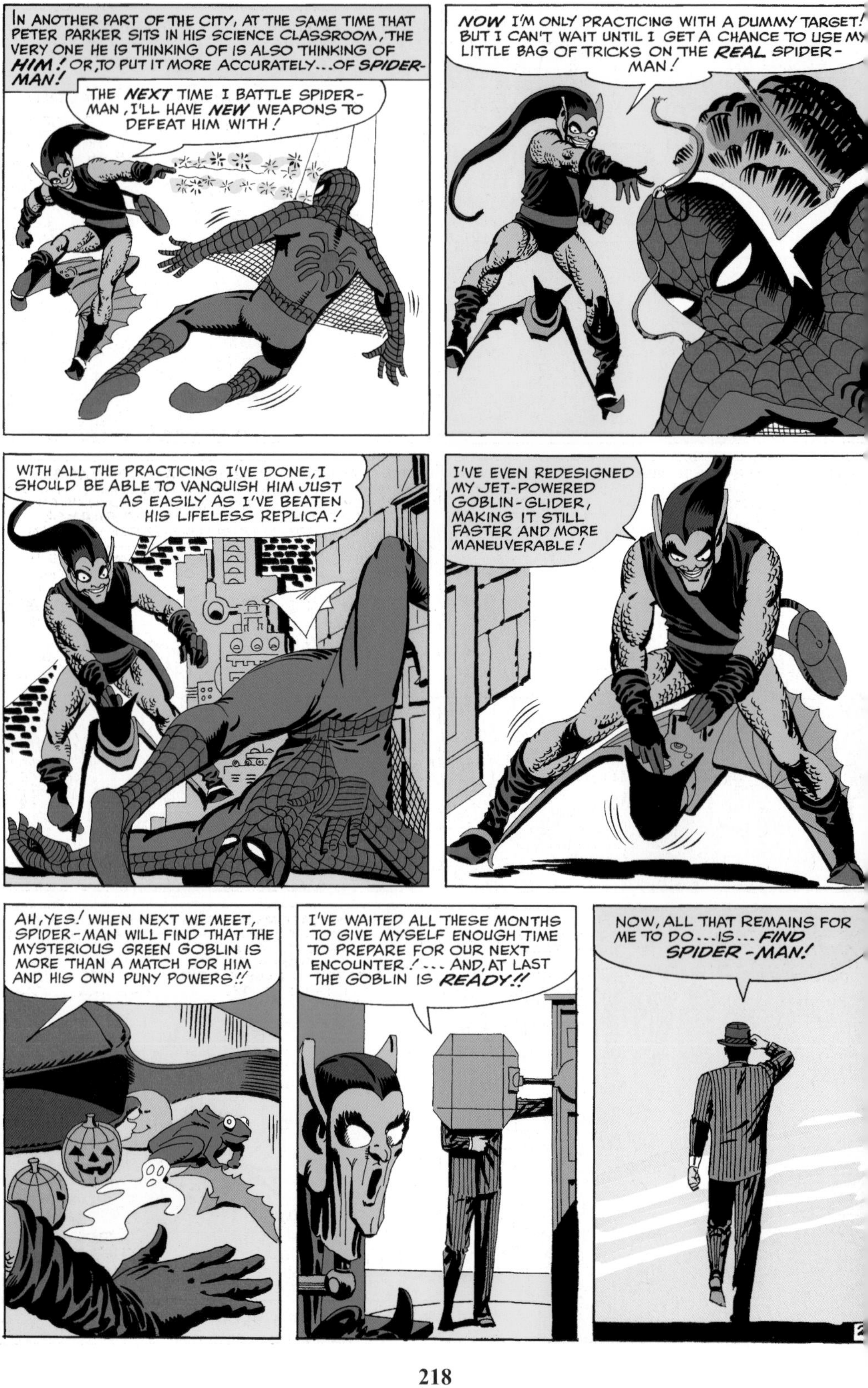

IN ANOTHER PART OF THE CITY, AT THE SAME TIME THAT PETER PARKER SITS IN HIS SCIENCE CLASSROOM, THE VERY ONE HE IS THINKING OF IS ALSO THINKING OF HIM! OR, TO PUT IT MORE ACCURATELY... OF SPIDER-MAN!
THE NEXT TIME I BATTLE SPIDER-MAN, I'LL HAVE NEW WEAPONS TO DEFEAT HIM WITH!
NOW I'M ONLY PRACTICING WITH A DUMMY TARGET! BUT I CAN'T WAIT UNTIL I GET A CHANCE TO USE MY LITTLE BAG OF TRICKS ON THE REAL SPIDER-MAN!
WITH ALL THE PRACTICING I'VE DONE, I SHOULD BE ABLE TO VANQUISH HIM JUST AS EASILY AS I'VE BEATEN HIS LIFELESS REPLICA!
I'VE EVEN REDESIGNED MY JET-POWERED GOBLIN-GLIDER, MAKING IT STILL FASTER AND MORE MANEUVERABLE!
AH, YES! WHEN NEXT WE MEET, SPIDER-MAN WILL FIND THAT THE MYSTERIOUS GREEN GOBLIN IS MORE THAN A MATCH FOR HIM AND HIS OWN PUNY POWERS!!
I'VE WAITED ALL THESE MONTHS TO GIVE MYSELF ENOUGH TIME TO PREPARE FOR OUR NEXT ENCOUNTER! ... AND, AT LAST THE GOBLIN IS READY!!
NOW, ALL THAT REMAINS FOR ME TO DO... IS... FIND SPIDER-MAN!

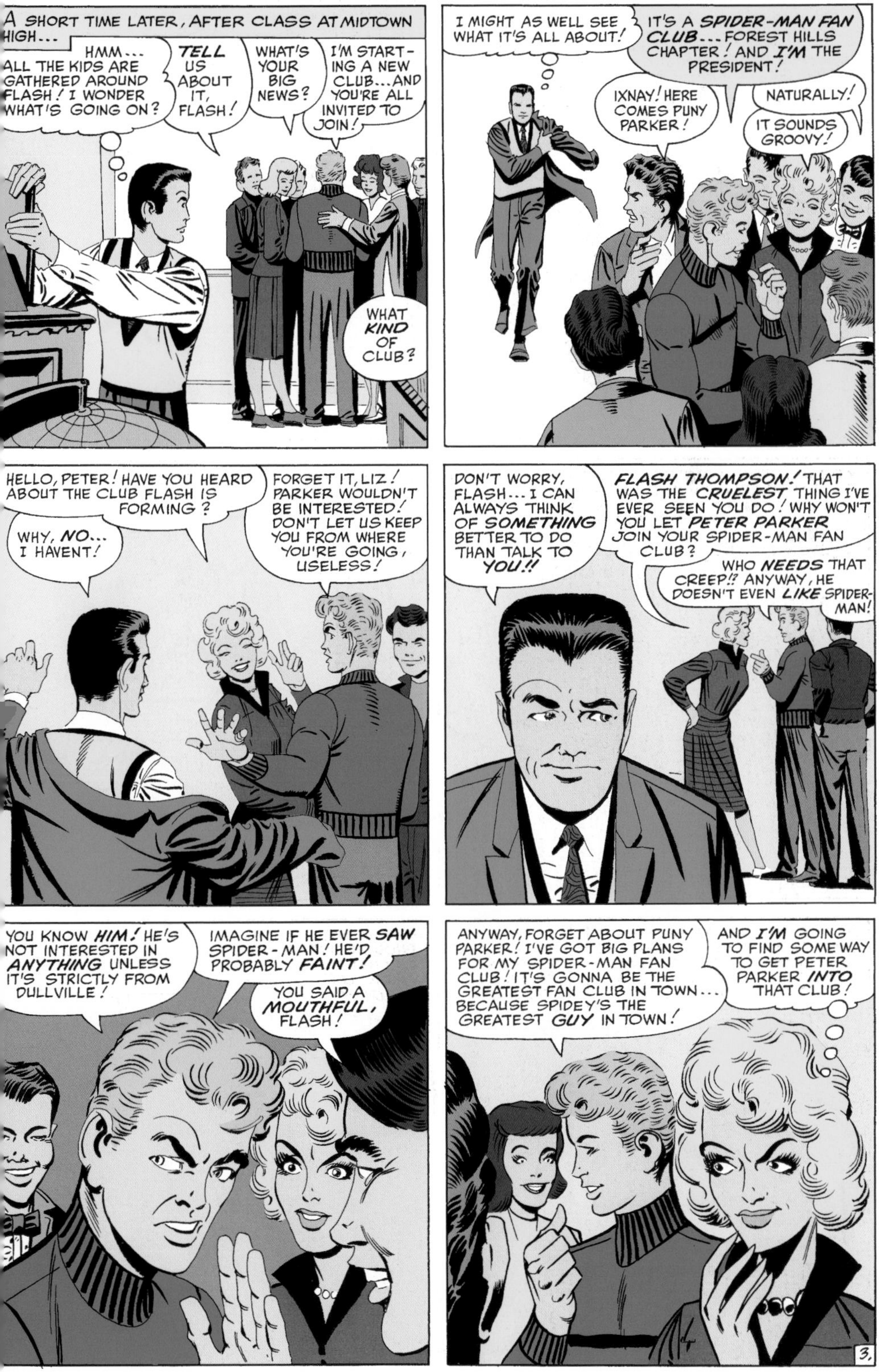
A SHORT TIME LATER, AFTER CLASS AT MIDTOWN HIGH...
HMM... ALL THE KIDS ARE GATHERED AROUND FLASH! I WONDER WHAT'S GOING ON?
TELL US ABOUT IT, FLASH!
WHAT'S YOUR BIG NEWS?
I'M STARTING A NEW CLUB... AND YOU'RE ALL INVITED TO JOIN!
WHAT KIND OF CLUB?
I MIGHT AS WELL SEE WHAT IT'S ALL ABOUT!
IT'S A SPIDER-MAN FAN CLUB... FOREST HILLS CHAPTER! AND I'M THE PRESIDENT!
NATURALLY!
IXNAY! HERE COMES PUNY PARKER!
IT SOUNDS GROOVY!
HELLO, PETER! HAVE YOU HEARD ABOUT THE CLUB FLASH IS FORMING?
WHY, NO... I HAVENT!
FORGET IT, LIZ! PARKER WOULDN'T BE INTERESTED! DON'T LET US KEEP YOU FROM WHERE YOU'RE GOING, USELESS!
DON'T WORRY, FLASH... I CAN ALWAYS THINK OF SOMETHING BETTER TO DO THAN TALK TO YOU!!
FLASH THOMPSON! THAT WAS THE CRUELEST THING I'VE EVER SEEN YOU DO! WHY WON'T YOU LET PETER PARKER JOIN YOUR SPIDER-MAN FAN CLUB?
WHO NEEDS THAT CREEP!? ANYWAY, HE DOESN'T EVEN LIKE SPIDER-MAN!
YOU KNOW HIM! HE'S NOT INTERESTED IN ANYTHING UNLESS IT'S STRICTLY FROM DULLVILLE!
IMAGINE IF HE EVER SAW SPIDER-MAN! HE'D PROBABLY FAINT!
YOU SAID A MOUTHFUL, FLASH!
ANYWAY, FORGET ABOUT PUNY PARKER! I'VE GOT BIG PLANS FOR MY SPIDER-MAN FAN CLUB! IT'S GONNA BE THE GREATEST FAN CLUB IN TOWN... BECAUSE SPIDEY'S THE GREATEST GUY IN TOWN!
AND I'M GOING TO FIND SOME WAY TO GET PETER PARKER INTO THAT CLUB!
3.

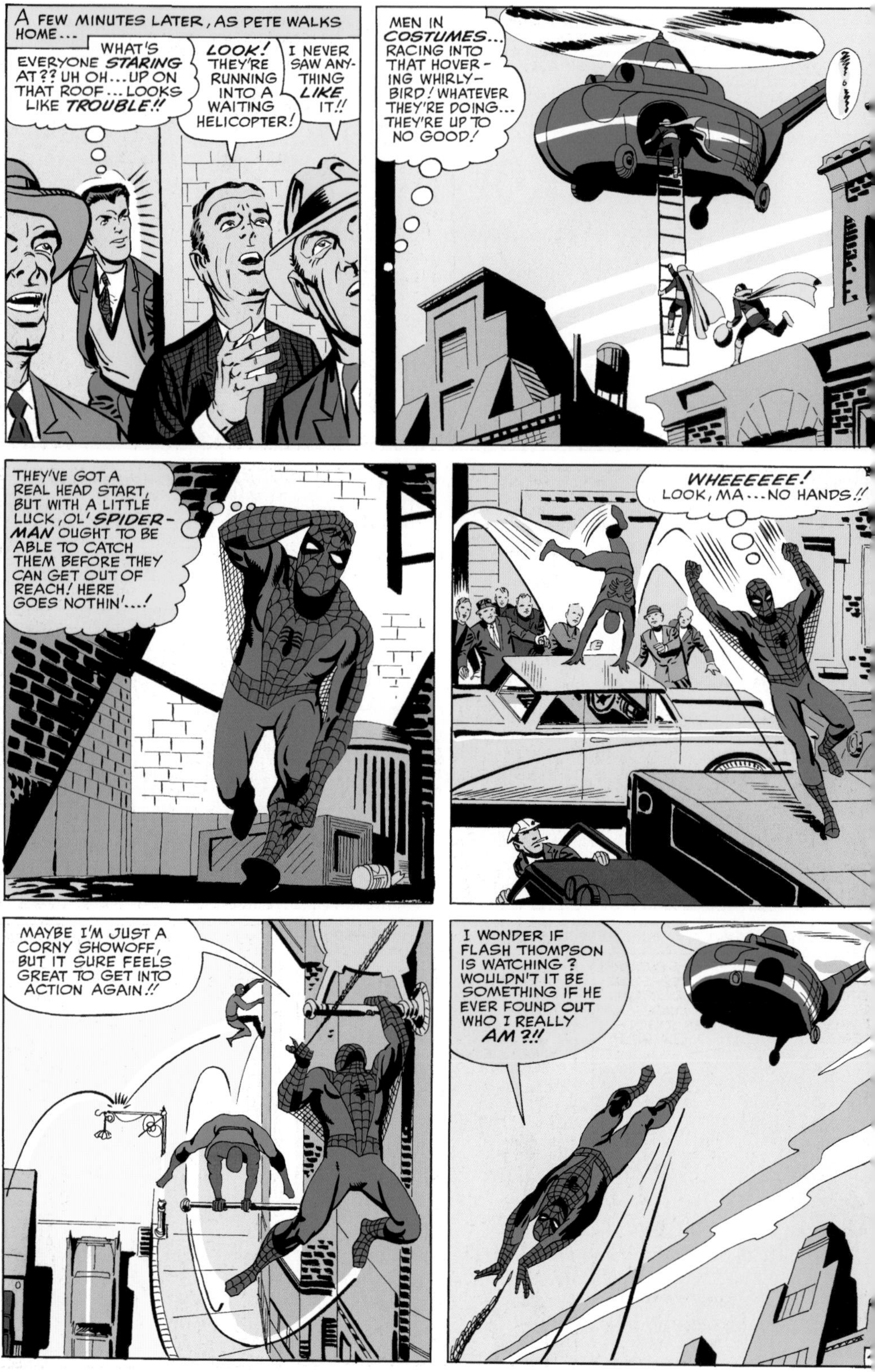
A FEW MINUTES LATER, AS PETE WALKS HOME...
WHAT'S EVERYONE STARING AT?? UH OH... UP ON THAT ROOF... LOOKS LIKE TROUBLE!!
LOOK! THEY'RE RUNNING INTO A WAITING HELICOPTER!
I NEVER SAW ANYTHING LIKE IT!!
MEN IN COSTUMES... RACING INTO THAT HOVERING WHIRLYBIRD! WHATEVER THEY'RE DOING... THEY'RE UP TO NO GOOD!
THEY'VE GOT A REAL HEAD START, BUT WITH A LITTLE LUCK, OL' SPIDER-MAN OUGHT TO BE ABLE TO CATCH THEM BEFORE THEY CAN GET OUT OF REACH! HERE GOES NOTHIN'...!
WHEEEEEE! LOOK, MA... NO HANDS!!
MAYBE I'M JUST A CORNY SHOWOFF, BUT IT SURE FEELS GREAT TO GET INTO ACTION AGAIN!!
I WONDER IF FLASH THOMPSON IS WATCHING? WOULDN'T IT BE SOMETHING IF HE EVER FOUND OUT WHO I REALLY AM?!!

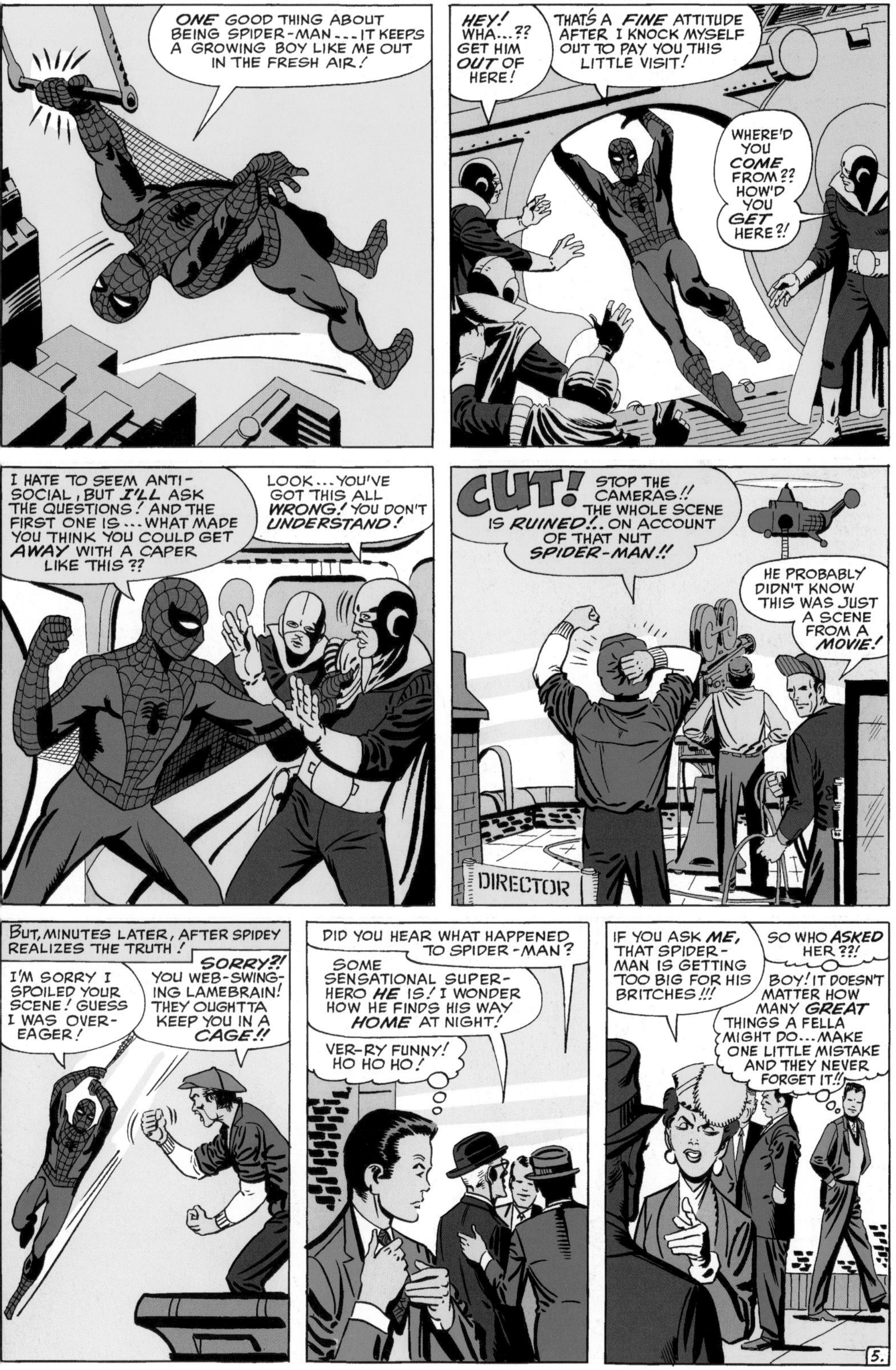
ONE GOOD THING ABOUT BEING SPIDER-MAN... IT KEEPS A GROWING BOY LIKE ME OUT IN THE FRESH AIR!
HEY! WHA...?? GET HIM OUT OF HERE!
THAT'S A FINE ATTITUDE AFTER I KNOCK MYSELF OUT TO PAY YOU THIS LITTLE VISIT!
WHERE'D YOU COME FROM?? HOW'D YOU GET HERE?!
I HATE TO SEEM ANTI-SOCIAL, BUT I'LL ASK THE QUESTIONS! AND THE FIRST ONE IS... WHAT MADE YOU THINK YOU COULD GET AWAY WITH A CAPER LIKE THIS??
LOOK... YOU'VE GOT THIS ALL WRONG! YOU DON'T UNDERSTAND!
CUT! STOP THE CAMERAS!! THE WHOLE SCENE IS RUINED!.. ON ACCOUNT OF THAT NUT SPIDER-MAN!!
HE PROBABLY DIDN'T KNOW THIS WAS JUST A SCENE FROM A MOVIE!
DIRECTOR
BUT, MINUTES LATER, AFTER SPIDEY REALIZES THE TRUTH!
I'M SORRY I SPOILED YOUR SCENE! GUESS I WAS OVER-EAGER!
SORRY?! YOU WEB-SWINGING LAMEBRAIN! THEY OUGHTTA KEEP YOU IN A CAGE!!
DID YOU HEAR WHAT HAPPENED TO SPIDER-MAN?
SOME SENSATIONAL SUPER-HERO HE IS! I WONDER HOW HE FINDS HIS WAY HOME AT NIGHT!
VER-RY FUNNY! HO HO HO!
IF YOU ASK ME, THAT SPIDER-MAN IS GETTING TOO BIG FOR HIS BRITCHES!!!
SO WHO ASKED HER??!
BOY! IT DOESN'T MATTER HOW MANY GREAT THINGS A FELLA MIGHT DO... MAKE ONE LITTLE MISTAKE AND THEY NEVER FORGET IT!!
5.

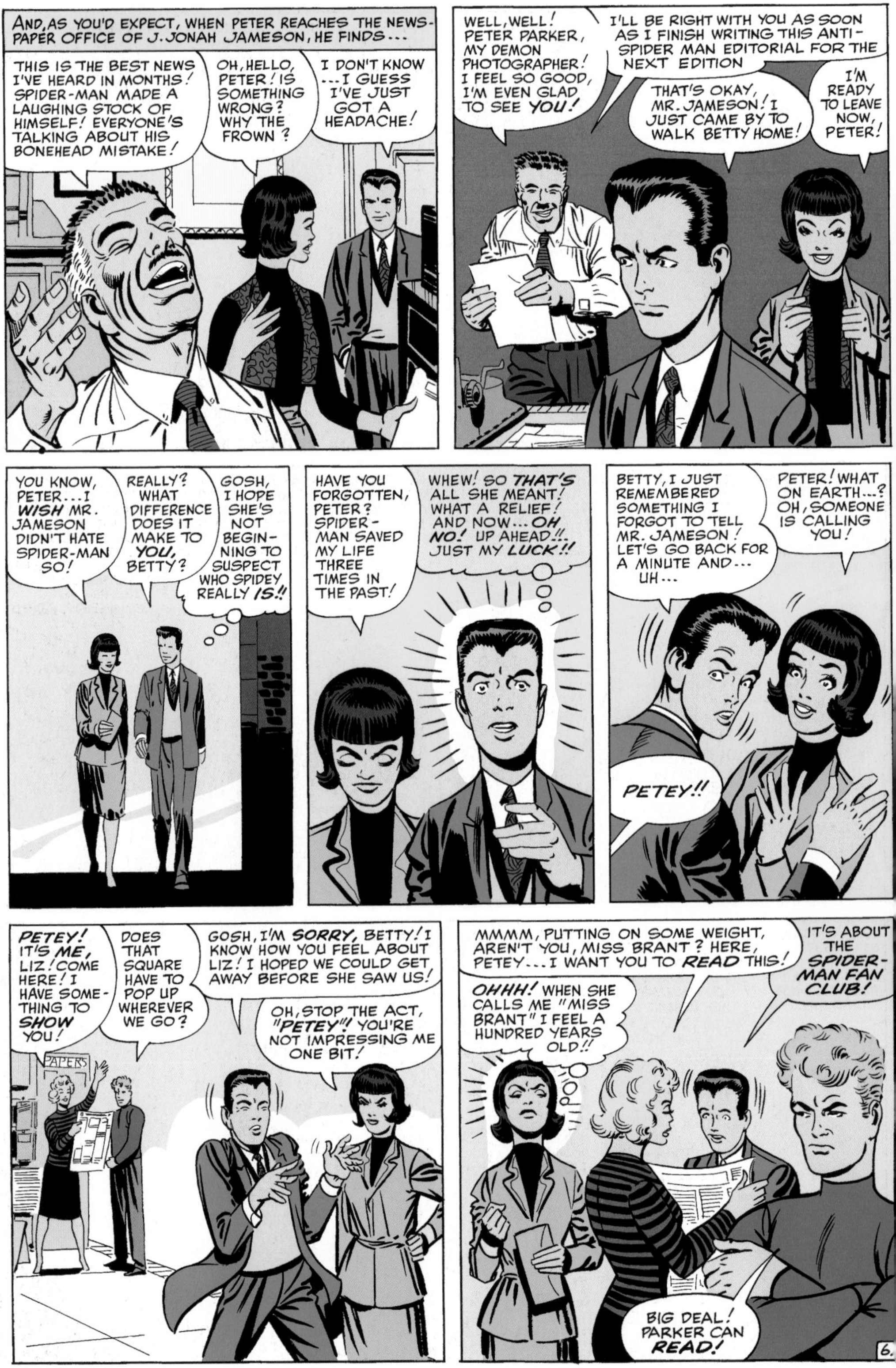
AND, AS YOU'D EXPECT, WHEN PETER REACHES THE NEWSPAPER OFFICE OF J. JONAH JAMESON, HE FINDS...
THIS IS THE BEST NEWS I'VE HEARD IN MONTHS! SPIDER-MAN MADE A LAUGHING STOCK OF HIMSELF! EVERYONE'S TALKING ABOUT HIS BONEHEAD MISTAKE!
OH, HELLO, PETER! IS SOMETHING WRONG? WHY THE FROWN?
I DON'T KNOW ...I GUESS I'VE JUST GOT A HEADACHE!
WELL, WELL! PETER PARKER, MY DEMON PHOTOGRAPHER! I FEEL SO GOOD, I'M EVEN GLAD TO SEE YOU!
I'LL BE RIGHT WITH YOU AS SOON AS I FINISH WRITING THIS ANTI-SPIDER MAN EDITORIAL FOR THE NEXT EDITION
THAT'S OKAY, MR. JAMESON! I JUST CAME BY TO WALK BETTY HOME!
I'M READY TO LEAVE NOW, PETER!
YOU KNOW, PETER... I WISH MR. JAMESON DIDN'T HATE SPIDER-MAN SO!
REALLY? WHAT DIFFERENCE DOES IT MAKE TO YOU, BETTY?
GOSH, I HOPE SHE'S NOT BEGINNING TO SUSPECT WHO SPIDEY REALLY IS!!
HAVE YOU FORGOTTEN, PETER? SPIDER-MAN SAVED MY LIFE THREE TIMES IN THE PAST!
WHEW! SO THAT'S ALL SHE MEANT! WHAT A RELIEF! AND NOW... OH NO! UP AHEAD!! JUST MY LUCK!!
BETTY, I JUST REMEMBERED SOMETHING I FORGOT TO TELL MR. JAMESON! LET'S GO BACK FOR A MINUTE AND... UH...
PETER! WHAT ON EARTH...? OH, SOMEONE IS CALLING YOU!
PETEY!!
PETEY! IT'S ME, LIZ! COME HERE! I HAVE SOMETHING TO SHOW YOU!
DOES THAT SQUARE HAVE TO POP UP WHEREVER WE GO?
GOSH, I'M SORRY, BETTY! I KNOW HOW YOU FEEL ABOUT LIZ! I HOPED WE COULD GET AWAY BEFORE SHE SAW US!
OH, STOP THE ACT, "PETEY"! YOU'RE NOT IMPRESSING ME ONE BIT!
PAPERS
MMMM, PUTTING ON SOME WEIGHT, AREN'T YOU, MISS BRANT? HERE, PETEY... I WANT YOU TO READ THIS!
IT'S ABOUT THE SPIDER-MAN FAN CLUB!
OHHH! WHEN SHE CALLS ME "MISS BRANT" I FEEL A HUNDRED YEARS OLD!!
BIG DEAL! PARKER CAN READ!
6.

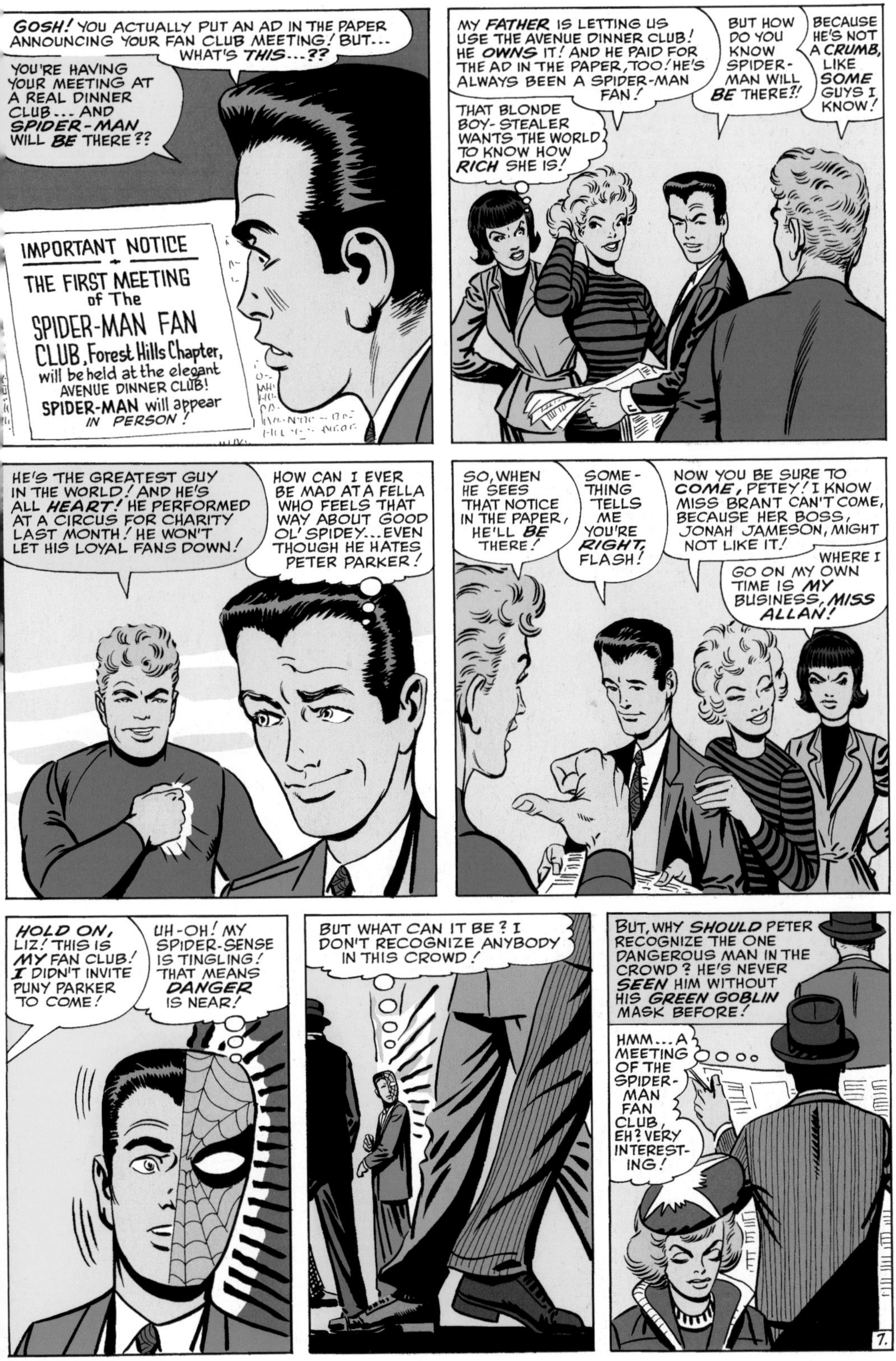
GOSH! YOU ACTUALLY PUT AN AD IN THE PAPER ANNOUNCING YOUR FAN CLUB MEETING! BUT... WHAT'S THIS...??
YOU'RE HAVING YOUR MEETING AT A REAL DINNER CLUB... AND SPIDER-MAN WILL BE THERE??
IMPORTANT NOTICE
THE FIRST MEETING of The SPIDER-MAN FAN CLUB, Forest Hills Chapter, will be held at the elegant AVENUE DINNER CLUB! SPIDER-MAN will appear IN PERSON!
MY FATHER IS LETTING US USE THE AVENUE DINNER CLUB! HE OWNS IT! AND HE PAID FOR THE AD IN THE PAPER, TOO! HE'S ALWAYS BEEN A SPIDER-MAN FAN!
THAT BLONDE BOY-STEALER WANTS THE WORLD TO KNOW HOW RICH SHE IS!
BUT HOW DO YOU KNOW SPIDER-MAN WILL BE THERE?!
BECAUSE HE'S NOT A CRUMB, LIKE SOME GUYS I KNOW!
HE'S THE GREATEST GUY IN THE WORLD! AND HE'S ALL HEART! HE PERFORMED AT A CIRCUS FOR CHARITY LAST MONTH! HE WON'T LET HIS LOYAL FANS DOWN!
HOW CAN I EVER BE MAD AT A FELLA WHO FEELS THAT WAY ABOUT GOOD OL' SPIDEY... EVEN THOUGH HE HATES PETER PARKER!
SO, WHEN HE SEES THAT NOTICE IN THE PAPER, HE'LL BE THERE!
SOMETHING TELLS ME YOU'RE RIGHT, FLASH!
NOW YOU BE SURE TO COME, PETEY! I KNOW MISS BRANT CAN'T COME, BECAUSE HER BOSS, JONAH JAMESON, MIGHT NOT LIKE IT!
WHERE I GO ON MY OWN TIME IS MY BUSINESS, MISS ALLAN!
HOLD ON, LIZ! THIS IS MY FAN CLUB! I DIDN'T INVITE PUNY PARKER TO COME!
UH-OH! MY SPIDER-SENSE IS TINGLING! THAT MEANS DANGER IS NEAR!
BUT WHAT CAN IT BE? I DON'T RECOGNIZE ANYBODY IN THIS CROWD!
BUT, WHY SHOULD PETER RECOGNIZE THE ONE DANGEROUS MAN IN THE CROWD? HE'S NEVER SEEN HIM WITHOUT HIS GREEN GOBLIN MASK BEFORE!
HMM... A MEETING OF THE SPIDER-MAN FAN CLUB, EH? VERY INTERESTING!
7.

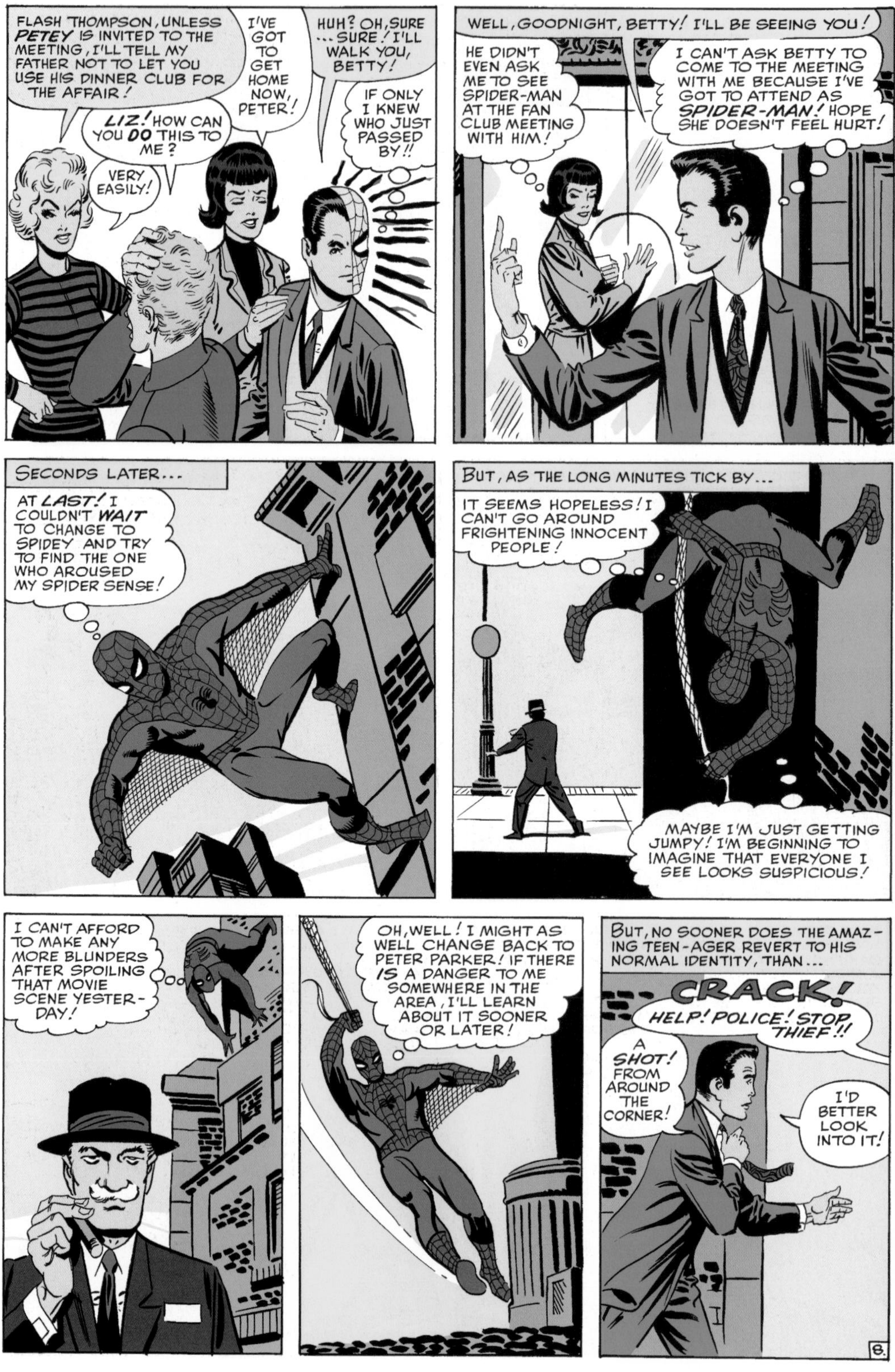

FLASH THOMPSON, UNLESS PETEY IS INVITED TO THE MEETING, I'LL TELL MY FATHER NOT TO LET YOU USE HIS DINNER CLUB FOR THE AFFAIR!
LIZ! HOW CAN YOU DO THIS TO ME?
VERY EASILY!
I'VE GOT TO GET HOME NOW, PETER!
HUH? OH, SURE ... SURE! I'LL WALK YOU, BETTY!
IF ONLY I KNEW WHO JUST PASSED BY!!
WELL, GOODNIGHT, BETTY! I'LL BE SEEING YOU!
HE DIDN'T EVEN ASK ME TO SEE SPIDER-MAN AT THE FAN CLUB MEETING WITH HIM!
I CAN'T ASK BETTY TO COME TO THE MEETING WITH ME BECAUSE I'VE GOT TO ATTEND AS SPIDER-MAN! HOPE SHE DOESN'T FEEL HURT!
SECONDS LATER...
AT LAST! I COULDN'T WAIT TO CHANGE TO SPIDEY AND TRY TO FIND THE ONE WHO AROUSED MY SPIDER SENSE!
BUT, AS THE LONG MINUTES TICK BY...
IT SEEMS HOPELESS! I CAN'T GO AROUND FRIGHTENING INNOCENT PEOPLE!
MAYBE I'M JUST GETTING JUMPY! I'M BEGINNING TO IMAGINE THAT EVERYONE I SEE LOOKS SUSPICIOUS!
I CAN'T AFFORD TO MAKE ANY MORE BLUNDERS AFTER SPOILING THAT MOVIE SCENE YESTER-DAY!
OH, WELL! I MIGHT AS WELL CHANGE BACK TO PETER PARKER! IF THERE IS A DANGER TO ME SOMEWHERE IN THE AREA, I'LL LEARN ABOUT IT SOONER OR LATER!
BUT, NO SOONER DOES THE AMAZ-ING TEEN-AGER REVERT TO HIS NORMAL IDENTITY, THAN...
CRACK!
HELP! POLICE! STOP THIEF!!
A SHOT! FROM AROUND THE CORNER!
I'D BETTER LOOK INTO IT!
8.

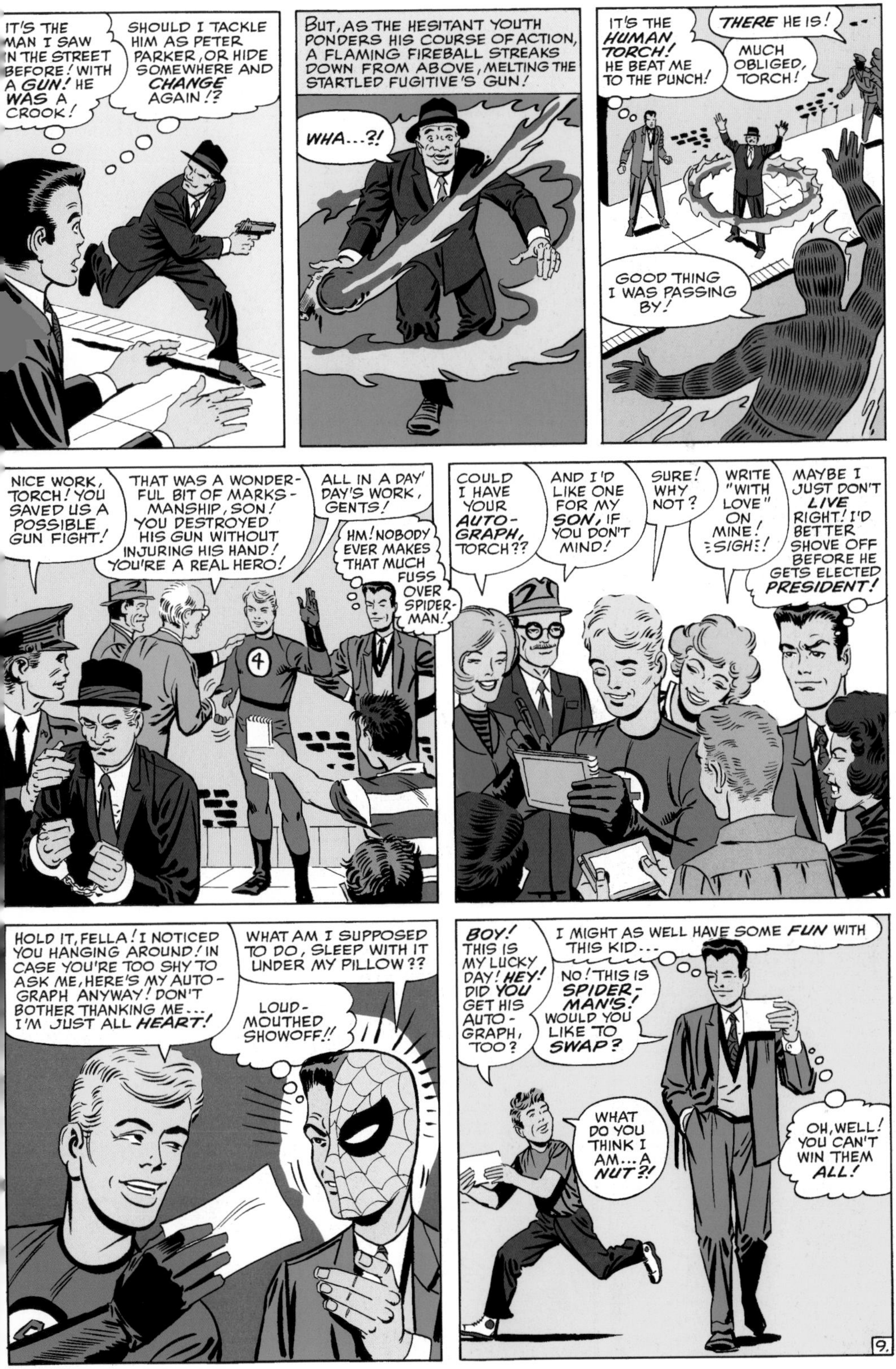
IT'S THE MAN I SAW IN THE STREET BEFORE! WITH A GUN! HE WAS A CROOK!
SHOULD I TACKLE HIM AS PETER PARKER, OR HIDE SOMEWHERE AND CHANGE AGAIN!?
BUT, AS THE HESITANT YOUTH PONDERS HIS COURSE OF ACTION, A FLAMING FIREBALL STREAKS DOWN FROM ABOVE, MELTING THE STARTLED FUGITIVE'S GUN!
WHA...?!
IT'S THE HUMAN TORCH! HE BEAT ME TO THE PUNCH!
THERE HE IS!
MUCH OBLIGED, TORCH!
GOOD THING I WAS PASSING BY!
NICE WORK, TORCH! YOU SAVED US A POSSIBLE GUN FIGHT!
THAT WAS A WONDERFUL BIT OF MARKSMANSHIP, SON! YOU DESTROYED HIS GUN WITHOUT INJURING HIS HAND! YOU'RE A REAL HERO!
ALL IN A DAY' DAY'S WORK, GENTS!
HM! NOBODY EVER MAKES THAT MUCH FUSS OVER SPIDER-MAN!
COULD I HAVE YOUR AUTO-GRAPH, TORCH??
AND I'D LIKE ONE FOR MY SON, IF YOU DON'T MIND!
SURE! WHY NOT?
WRITE "WITH LOVE" ON MINE! SIGH!
MAYBE I JUST DON'T LIVE RIGHT! I'D BETTER SHOVE OFF BEFORE HE GETS ELECTED PRESIDENT!
HOLD IT, FELLA! I NOTICED YOU HANGING AROUND! IN CASE YOU'RE TOO SHY TO ASK ME, HERE'S MY AUTO-GRAPH ANYWAY! DON'T BOTHER THANKING ME... I'M JUST ALL HEART!
WHAT AM I SUPPOSED TO DO, SLEEP WITH IT UNDER MY PILLOW??
LOUD-MOUTHED SHOWOFF!!
BOY! THIS IS MY LUCKY DAY! HEY! DID YOU GET HIS AUTO-GRAPH, TOO?
I MIGHT AS WELL HAVE SOME FUN WITH THIS KID...
NO! THIS IS SPIDER-MAN'S! WOULD YOU LIKE TO SWAP?
WHAT DO YOU THINK I AM... A NUT?!
OH, WELL! YOU CAN'T WIN THEM ALL!
9.

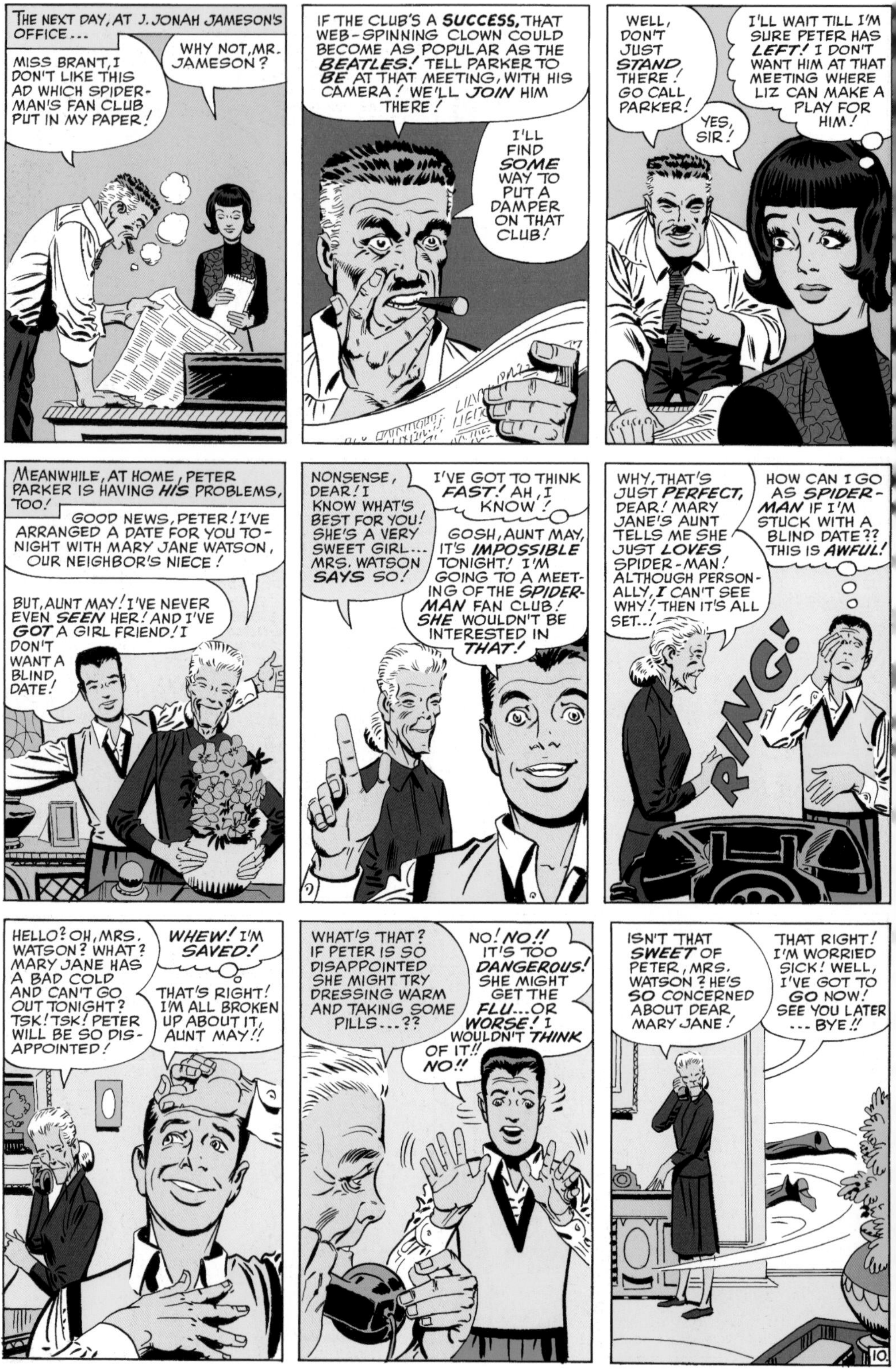
THE NEXT DAY, AT J. JONAH JAMESON'S OFFICE...
MISS BRANT, I DON'T LIKE THIS AD WHICH SPIDER-MAN'S FAN CLUB PUT IN MY PAPER!
WHY NOT, MR. JAMESON?
IF THE CLUB'S A SUCCESS, THAT WEB-SPINNING CLOWN COULD BECOME AS POPULAR AS THE BEATLES! TELL PARKER TO BE AT THAT MEETING, WITH HIS CAMERA! WE'LL JOIN HIM THERE!
I'LL FIND SOME WAY TO PUT A DAMPER ON THAT CLUB!
WELL, DON'T JUST STAND THERE! GO CALL PARKER!
YES, SIR!
I'LL WAIT TILL I'M SURE PETER HAS LEFT! I DON'T WANT HIM AT THAT MEETING WHERE LIZ CAN MAKE A PLAY FOR HIM!
MEANWHILE, AT HOME, PETER PARKER IS HAVING HIS PROBLEMS, TOO!
GOOD NEWS, PETER! I'VE ARRANGED A DATE FOR YOU TONIGHT WITH MARY JANE WATSON, OUR NEIGHBOR'S NIECE!
BUT, AUNT MAY! I'VE NEVER EVEN SEEN HER! AND I'VE GOT A GIRL FRIEND! I DON'T WANT A BLIND DATE!
NONSENSE, DEAR! I KNOW WHAT'S BEST FOR YOU! SHE'S A VERY SWEET GIRL... MRS. WATSON SAYS SO!
I'VE GOT TO THINK FAST! AH, I KNOW!
GOSH, AUNT MAY, IT'S IMPOSSIBLE TONIGHT! I'M GOING TO A MEETING OF THE SPIDER-MAN FAN CLUB! SHE WOULDN'T BE INTERESTED IN THAT!
WHY, THAT'S JUST PERFECT, DEAR! MARY JANE'S AUNT TELLS ME SHE JUST LOVES SPIDER-MAN! ALTHOUGH PERSONALLY, I CAN'T SEE WHY! THEN IT'S ALL SET...!
HOW CAN I GO AS SPIDER-MAN IF I'M STUCK WITH A BLIND DATE?? THIS IS AWFUL!
RING!
HELLO? OH, MRS. WATSON? WHAT? MARY JANE HAS A BAD COLD AND CAN'T GO OUT TONIGHT? TSK! TSK! PETER WILL BE SO DISAPPOINTED!
WHEW! I'M SAVED!
THAT'S RIGHT! I'M ALL BROKEN UP ABOUT IT, AUNT MAY!!
WHAT'S THAT? IF PETER IS SO DISAPPOINTED SHE MIGHT TRY DRESSING WARM AND TAKING SOME PILLS...??
NO! NO!! IT'S TOO DANGEROUS! SHE MIGHT GET THE FLU...OR WORSE! I WOULDN'T THINK OF IT!! NO!!
ISN'T THAT SWEET OF PETER, MRS. WATSON? HE'S SO CONCERNED ABOUT DEAR MARY JANE!
THAT RIGHT! I'M WORRIED SICK! WELL, I'VE GOT TO GO NOW! SEE YOU LATER ...BYE!!
10

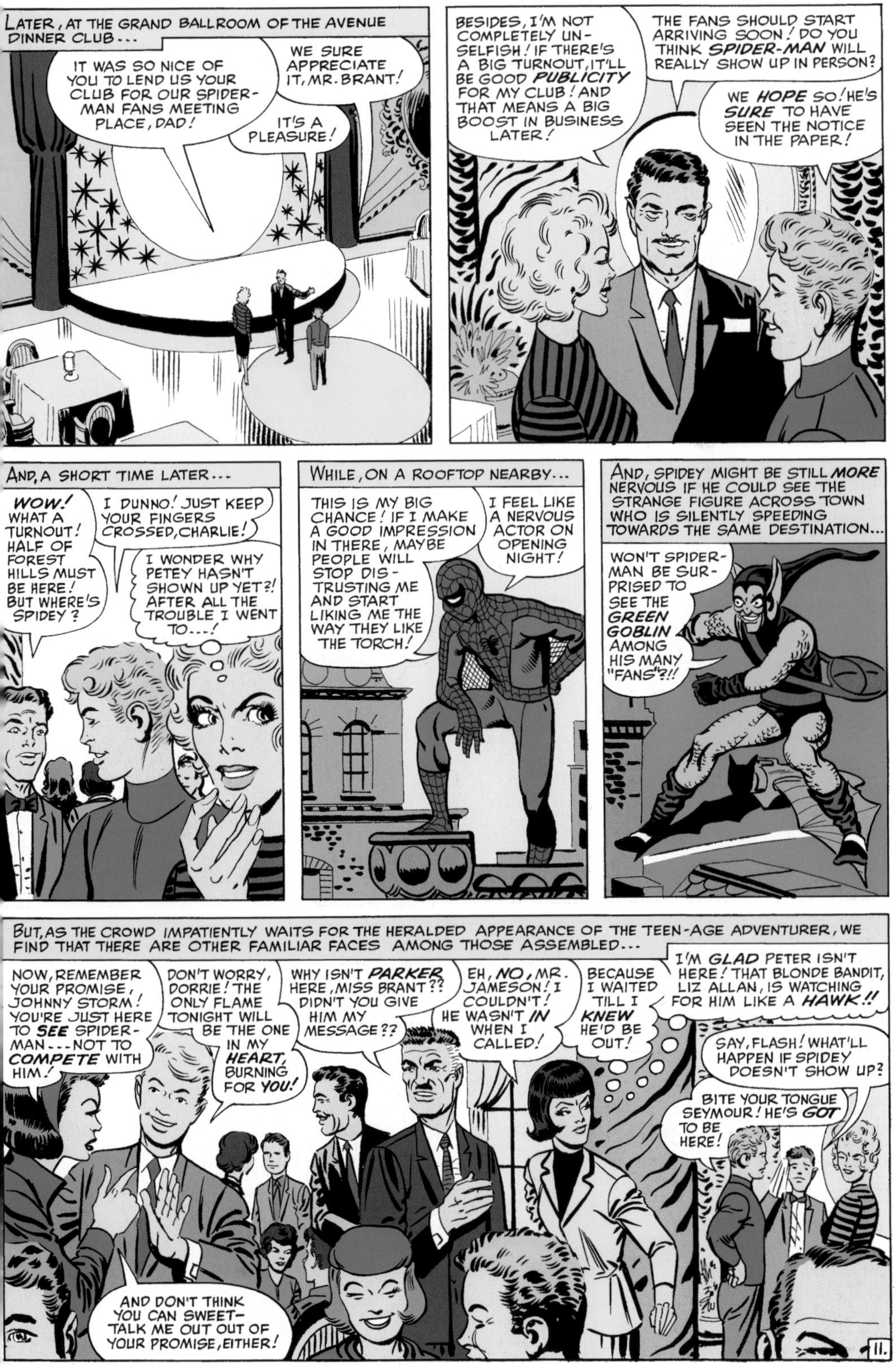

LATER, AT THE GRAND BALLROOM OF THE AVENUE DINNER CLUB...
IT WAS SO NICE OF YOU TO LEND US YOUR CLUB FOR OUR SPIDER-MAN FANS MEETING PLACE, DAD!
WE SURE APPRECIATE IT, MR. BRANT!
IT'S A PLEASURE!
BESIDES, I'M NOT COMPLETELY UN-SELFISH! IF THERE'S A BIG TURNOUT, IT'LL BE GOOD PUBLICITY FOR MY CLUB! AND THAT MEANS A BIG BOOST IN BUSINESS LATER!
THE FANS SHOULD START ARRIVING SOON! DO YOU THINK SPIDER-MAN WILL REALLY SHOW UP IN PERSON?
WE HOPE SO! HE'S SURE TO HAVE SEEN THE NOTICE IN THE PAPER!
AND, A SHORT TIME LATER...
WOW! WHAT A TURNOUT! HALF OF FOREST HILLS MUST BE HERE! BUT WHERE'S SPIDEY?
I DUNNO! JUST KEEP YOUR FINGERS CROSSED, CHARLIE!
I WONDER WHY PETEY HASN'T SHOWN UP YET?! AFTER ALL THE TROUBLE I WENT TO...!
WHILE, ON A ROOFTOP NEARBY...
THIS IS MY BIG CHANCE! IF I MAKE A GOOD IMPRESSION IN THERE, MAYBE PEOPLE WILL STOP DIS-TRUSTING ME AND START LIKING ME THE WAY THEY LIKE THE TORCH!
I FEEL LIKE A NERVOUS ACTOR ON OPENING NIGHT!
AND, SPIDEY MIGHT BE STILL MORE NERVOUS IF HE COULD SEE THE STRANGE FIGURE ACROSS TOWN WHO IS SILENTLY SPEEDING TOWARDS THE SAME DESTINATION...
WON'T SPIDER-MAN BE SUR-PRISED TO SEE THE GREEN GOBLIN AMONG HIS MANY "FANS"?!!
BUT, AS THE CROWD IMPATIENTLY WAITS FOR THE HERALDED APPEARANCE OF THE TEEN-AGE ADVENTURER, WE FIND THAT THERE ARE OTHER FAMILIAR FACES AMONG THOSE ASSEMBLED...
NOW, REMEMBER YOUR PROMISE, JOHNNY STORM! YOU'RE JUST HERE TO SEE SPIDER-MAN---NOT TO COMPETE WITH HIM!
DON'T WORRY, DORRIE! THE ONLY FLAME TONIGHT WILL BE THE ONE IN MY HEART, BURNING FOR YOU!
WHY ISN'T PARKER HERE, MISS BRANT?? DIDN'T YOU GIVE HIM MY MESSAGE??
EH, NO, MR. JAMESON! I COULDN'T! HE WASN'T IN WHEN I CALLED!
BECAUSE I WAITED TILL I KNEW HE'D BE OUT!
I'M GLAD PETER ISN'T HERE! THAT BLONDE BANDIT, LIZ ALLAN, IS WATCHING FOR HIM LIKE A HAWK!!
SAY, FLASH! WHAT'LL HAPPEN IF SPIDEY DOESN'T SHOW UP?
BITE YOUR TONGUE SEYMOUR! HE'S GOT TO BE HERE!
AND DON'T THINK YOU CAN SWEET-TALK ME OUT OUT OF YOUR PROMISE, EITHER!
11.

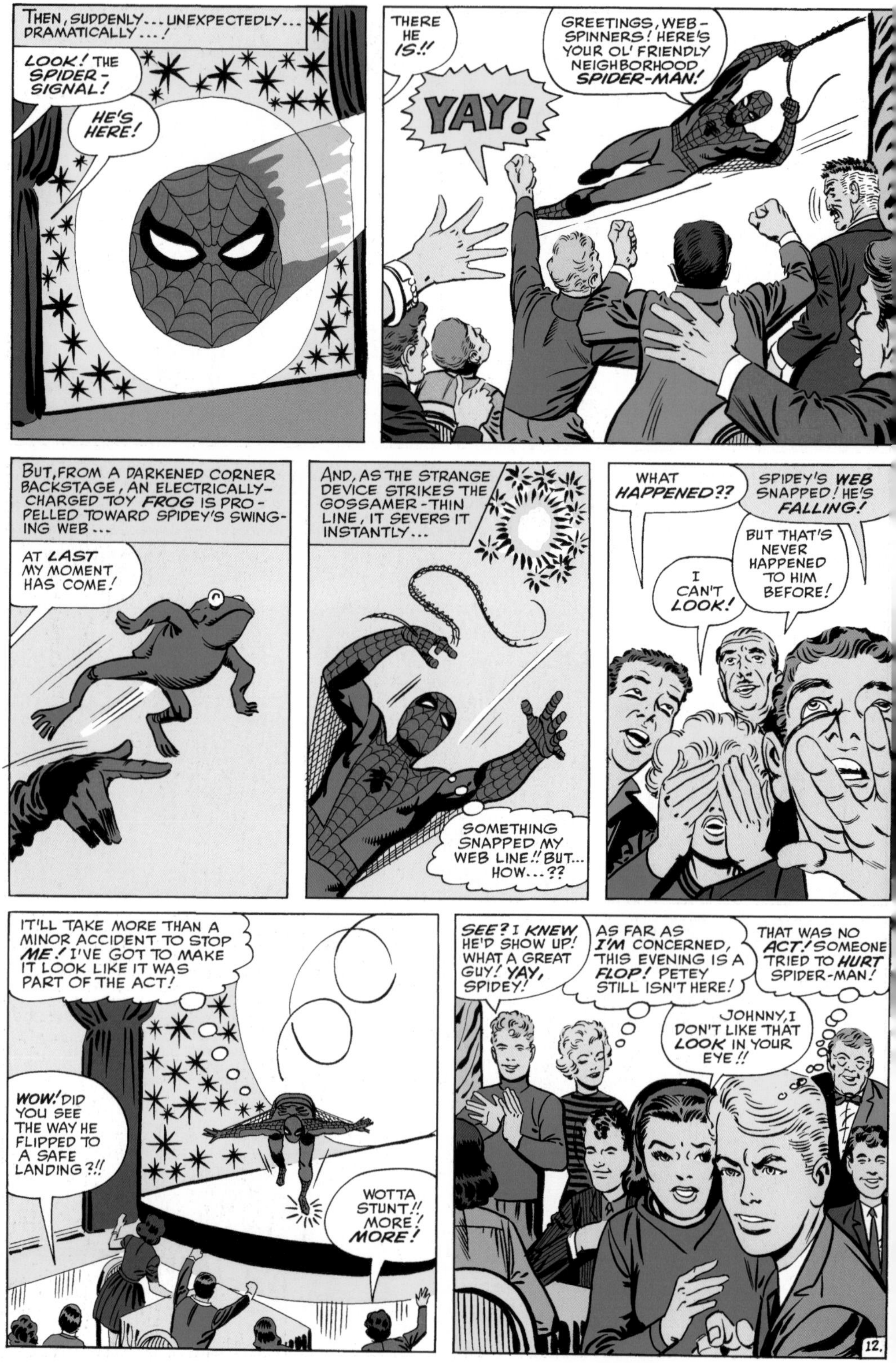
THEN, SUDDENLY... UNEXPECTEDLY... DRAMATICALLY...!
LOOK! THE SPIDER-SIGNAL!
HE'S HERE!
THERE HE IS!!
GREETINGS, WEB-SPINNERS! HERE'S YOUR OL' FRIENDLY NEIGHBORHOOD SPIDER-MAN!
YAY!
BUT, FROM A DARKENED CORNER BACKSTAGE, AN ELECTRICALLY-CHARGED TOY FROG IS PROPELLED TOWARD SPIDEY'S SWINGING WEB...
AT LAST MY MOMENT HAS COME!
AND, AS THE STRANGE DEVICE STRIKES THE GOSSAMER-THIN LINE, IT SEVERS IT INSTANTLY...
SOMETHING SNAPPED MY WEB LINE!! BUT... HOW...??
WHAT HAPPENED??
SPIDEY'S WEB SNAPPED! HE'S FALLING!
BUT THAT'S NEVER HAPPENED TO HIM BEFORE!
I CAN'T LOOK!
IT'LL TAKE MORE THAN A MINOR ACCIDENT TO STOP ME! I'VE GOT TO MAKE IT LOOK LIKE IT WAS PART OF THE ACT!
WOW! DID YOU SEE THE WAY HE FLIPPED TO A SAFE LANDING?!!
WOTTA STUNT!! MORE! MORE!
SEE? I KNEW HE'D SHOW UP! WHAT A GREAT GUY! YAY, SPIDEY!
AS FAR AS I'M CONCERNED, THIS EVENING IS A FLOP! PETEY STILL ISN'T HERE!
THAT WAS NO ACT! SOMEONE TRIED TO HURT SPIDER-MAN!
JOHNNY, I DON'T LIKE THAT LOOK IN YOUR EYE!!
12.

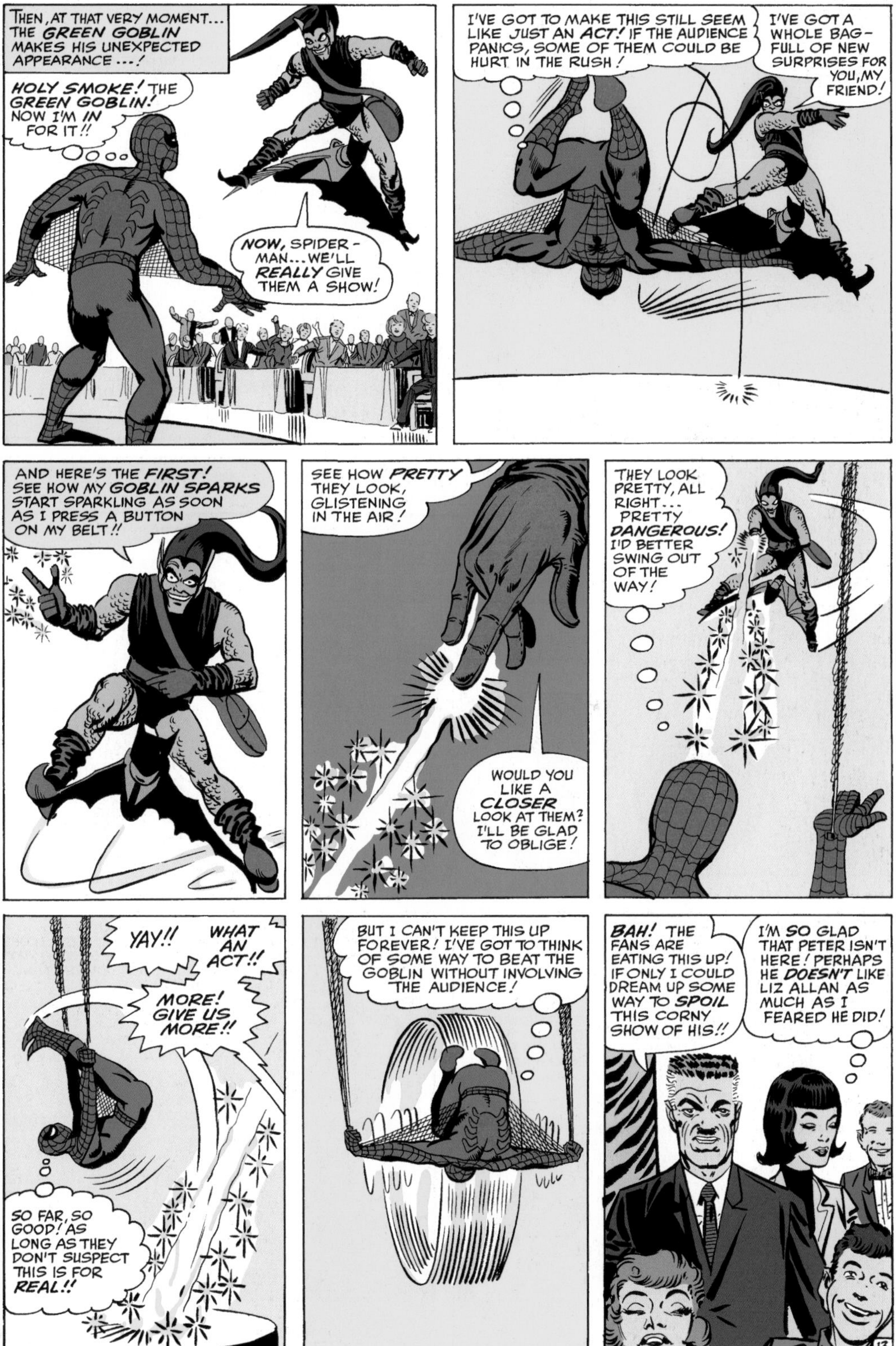
THEN, AT THAT VERY MOMENT... THE GREEN GOBLIN MAKES HIS UNEXPECTED APPEARANCE...!
HOLY SMOKE! THE GREEN GOBLIN! NOW I'M IN FOR IT!!
NOW, SPIDER-MAN... WE'LL REALLY GIVE THEM A SHOW!
I'VE GOT TO MAKE THIS STILL SEEM LIKE JUST AN ACT! IF THE AUDIENCE PANICS, SOME OF THEM COULD BE HURT IN THE RUSH!
I'VE GOT A WHOLE BAG-FULL OF NEW SURPRISES FOR YOU, MY FRIEND!
AND HERE'S THE FIRST! SEE HOW MY GOBLIN SPARKS START SPARKLING AS SOON AS I PRESS A BUTTON ON MY BELT!!
SEE HOW PRETTY THEY LOOK, GLISTENING IN THE AIR!
WOULD YOU LIKE A CLOSER LOOK AT THEM? I'LL BE GLAD TO OBLIGE!
THEY LOOK PRETTY, ALL RIGHT... PRETTY DANGEROUS! I'D BETTER SWING OUT OF THE WAY!
YAY!!
WHAT AN ACT!!
MORE! GIVE US MORE!!
SO FAR, SO GOOD! AS LONG AS THEY DON'T SUSPECT THIS IS FOR REAL!!
BUT I CAN'T KEEP THIS UP FOREVER! I'VE GOT TO THINK OF SOME WAY TO BEAT THE GOBLIN WITHOUT INVOLVING THE AUDIENCE!
BAH! THE FANS ARE EATING THIS UP! IF ONLY I COULD DREAM UP SOME WAY TO SPOIL THIS CORNY SHOW OF HIS!!
I'M SO GLAD THAT PETER ISN'T HERE! PERHAPS HE DOESN'T LIKE LIZ ALLAN AS MUCH AS I FEARED HE DID!
13.

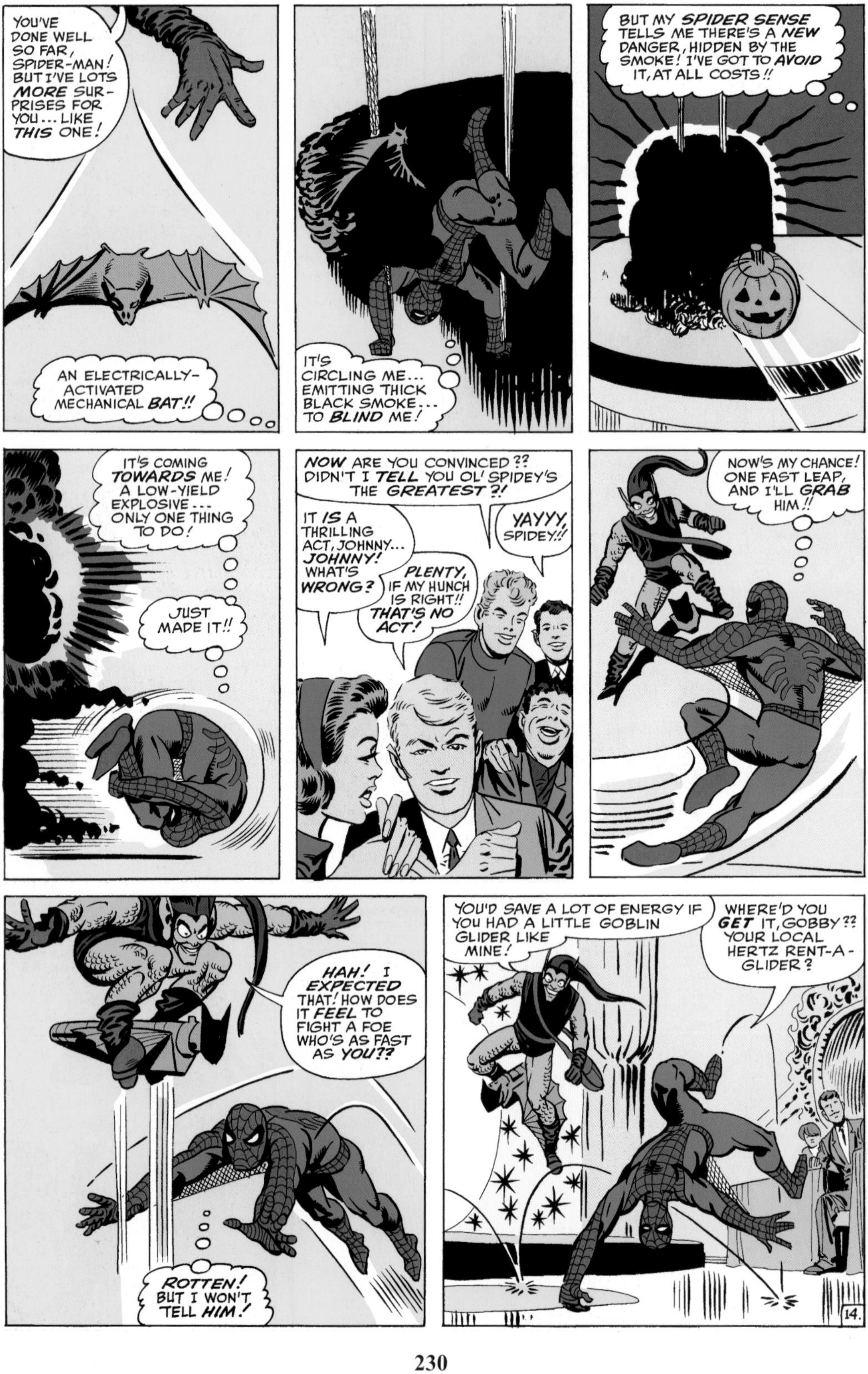
YOU'VE DONE WELL SO FAR, SPIDER-MAN! BUT I'VE LOTS MORE SURPRISES FOR YOU... LIKE THIS ONE!
AN ELECTRICALLY-ACTIVATED MECHANICAL BAT!!
IT'S CIRCLING ME... EMITTING THICK BLACK SMOKE... TO BLIND ME!
BUT MY SPIDER SENSE TELLS ME THERE'S A NEW DANGER, HIDDEN BY THE SMOKE! I'VE GOT TO AVOID IT, AT ALL COSTS!!
IT'S COMING TOWARDS ME! A LOW-YIELD EXPLOSIVE... ONLY ONE THING TO DO!
JUST MADE IT!!
NOW ARE YOU CONVINCED?? DIDN'T I TELL YOU OL' SPIDEY'S THE GREATEST?!
YAYYY, SPIDEY!!
IT IS A THRILLING ACT, JOHNNY... JOHNNY! WHAT'S WRONG?
PLENTY, IF MY HUNCH IS RIGHT!! THAT'S NO ACT!
NOW'S MY CHANCE! ONE FAST LEAP, AND I'LL GRAB HIM!!
HAH! I EXPECTED THAT! HOW DOES IT FEEL TO FIGHT A FOE WHO'S AS FAST AS YOU??
ROTTEN! BUT I WON'T TELL HIM!
YOU'D SAVE A LOT OF ENERGY IF YOU HAD A LITTLE GOBLIN GLIDER LIKE MINE!
WHERE'D YOU GET IT, GOBBY?? YOUR LOCAL HERTZ RENT-A-GLIDER?
14.

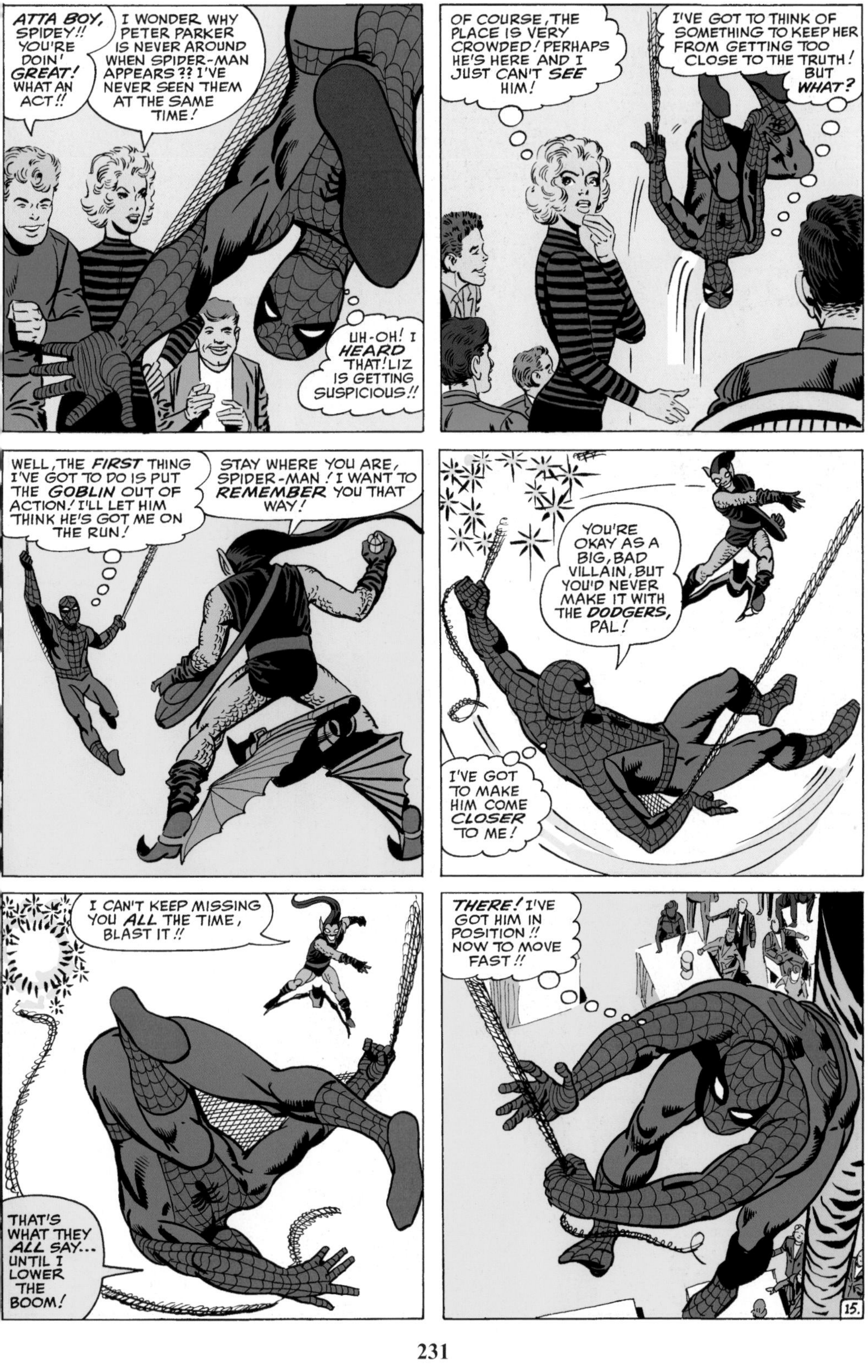
ATTA BOY, SPIDEY!! YOU'RE DOIN' GREAT! WHAT AN ACT!!
I WONDER WHY PETER PARKER IS NEVER AROUND WHEN SPIDER-MAN APPEARS?? I'VE NEVER SEEN THEM AT THE SAME TIME!
UH-OH! I HEARD THAT! LIZ IS GETTING SUSPICIOUS!!
OF COURSE, THE PLACE IS VERY CROWDED! PERHAPS HE'S HERE AND I JUST CAN'T SEE HIM!
I'VE GOT TO THINK OF SOMETHING TO KEEP HER FROM GETTING TOO CLOSE TO THE TRUTH! BUT WHAT?
WELL, THE FIRST THING I'VE GOT TO DO IS PUT THE GOBLIN OUT OF ACTION! I'LL LET HIM THINK HE'S GOT ME ON THE RUN!
STAY WHERE YOU ARE, SPIDER-MAN! I WANT TO REMEMBER YOU THAT WAY!
YOU'RE OKAY AS A BIG, BAD VILLAIN, BUT YOU'D NEVER MAKE IT WITH THE DODGERS, PAL!
I'VE GOT TO MAKE HIM COME CLOSER TO ME!
I CAN'T KEEP MISSING YOU ALL THE TIME, BLAST IT!!
THAT'S WHAT THEY ALL SAY... UNTIL I LOWER THE BOOM!
THERE! I'VE GOT HIM IN POSITION!! NOW TO MOVE FAST!!
15.

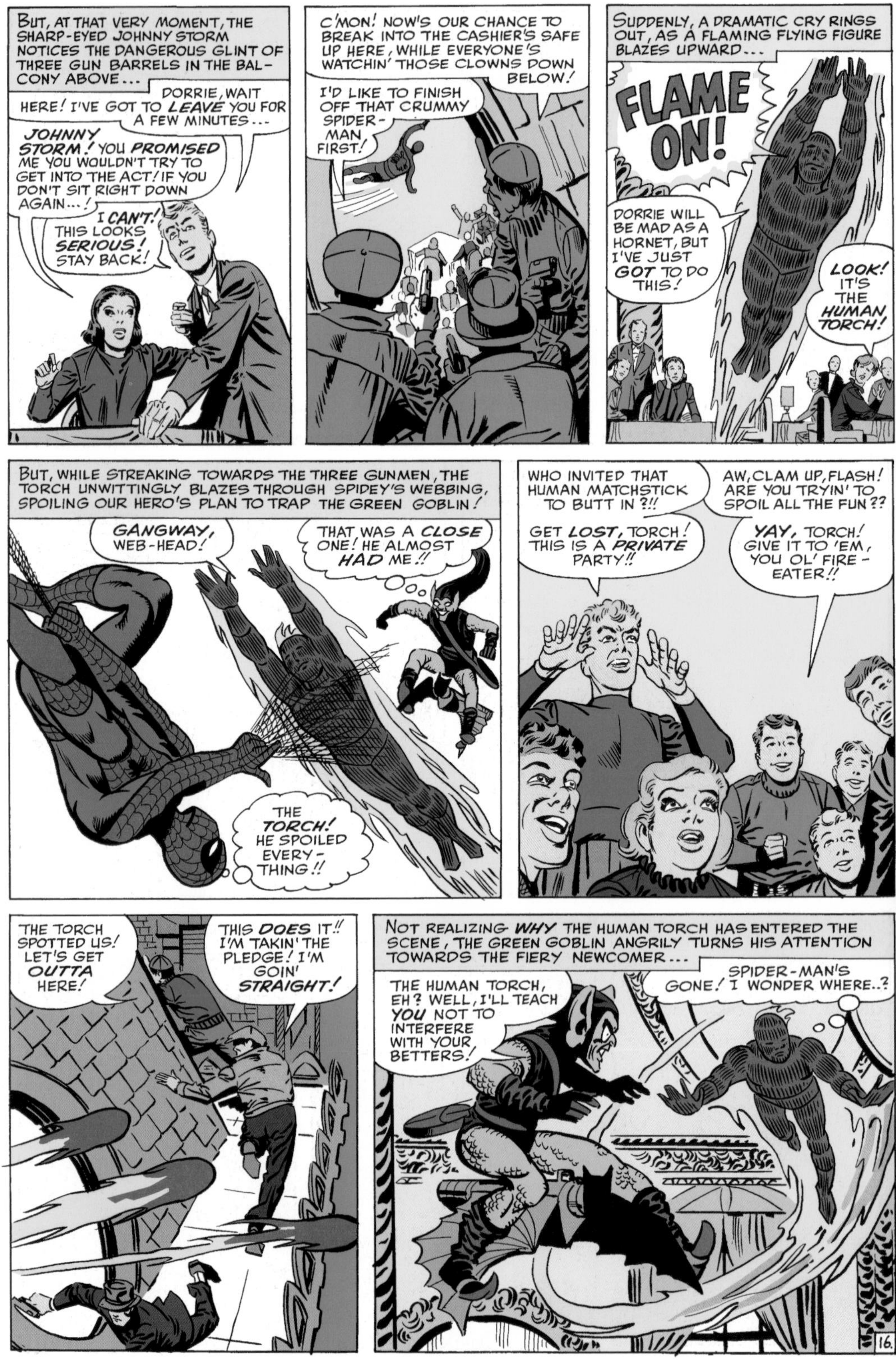
BUT, AT THAT VERY MOMENT, THE SHARP-EYED JOHNNY STORM NOTICES THE DANGEROUS GLINT OF THREE GUN BARRELS IN THE BALCONY ABOVE...
DORRIE, WAIT HERE! I'VE GOT TO LEAVE YOU FOR A FEW MINUTES...
JOHNNY STORM! YOU PROMISED ME YOU WOULDN'T TRY TO GET INTO THE ACT! IF YOU DON'T SIT RIGHT DOWN AGAIN...!
I CAN'T! THIS LOOKS SERIOUS! STAY BACK!
C'MON! NOW'S OUR CHANCE TO BREAK INTO THE CASHIER'S SAFE UP HERE, WHILE EVERYONE'S WATCHIN' THOSE CLOWNS DOWN BELOW!
I'D LIKE TO FINISH OFF THAT CRUMMY SPIDER-MAN FIRST!
SUDDENLY, A DRAMATIC CRY RINGS OUT, AS A FLAMING FLYING FIGURE BLAZES UPWARD...
FLAME ON!
DORRIE WILL BE MAD AS A HORNET, BUT I'VE JUST GOT TO DO THIS!
LOOK! IT'S THE HUMAN TORCH!
BUT, WHILE STREAKING TOWARDS THE THREE GUNMEN, THE TORCH UNWITTINGLY BLAZES THROUGH SPIDEY'S WEBBING, SPOILING OUR HERO'S PLAN TO TRAP THE GREEN GOBLIN!
GANGWAY, WEB-HEAD!
THAT WAS A CLOSE ONE! HE ALMOST HAD ME!!
THE TORCH! HE SPOILED EVERYTHING!!
WHO INVITED THAT HUMAN MATCHSTICK TO BUTT IN?!!
GET LOST, TORCH! THIS IS A PRIVATE PARTY!!
AW, CLAM UP, FLASH! ARE YOU TRYIN' TO SPOIL ALL THE FUN??
YAY, TORCH! GIVE IT TO 'EM, YOU OL' FIRE-EATER!!
THE TORCH SPOTTED US! LET'S GET OUTTA HERE!
THIS DOES IT!! I'M TAKIN' THE PLEDGE! I'M GOIN' STRAIGHT!
NOT REALIZING WHY THE HUMAN TORCH HAS ENTERED THE SCENE, THE GREEN GOBLIN ANGRILY TURNS HIS ATTENTION TOWARDS THE FIERY NEWCOMER...
THE HUMAN TORCH, EH? WELL, I'LL TEACH YOU NOT TO INTERFERE WITH YOUR BETTERS!
SPIDER-MAN'S GONE! I WONDER WHERE..?
16.

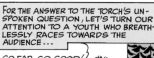

For the answer to the Torch's unspoken question, let's turn our attention to a youth who breathlessly races towards the audience...

So far, so good! Now to put in a brief appearance as Peter Parker!

Hi, Liz! I *thought* I saw you from across the room!

Oh, Petey! Then you *were* here! I'm *so glad!*

First the pesty Torch, and now puny Parker! This place is filling up with a bunch of dead-heads!

Petey, I'm *sure* I can talk Flash into letting you join his *Spider-Man* fan club!

Aw, c'mon, Liz! If we accept *him*, we'll have to accept *anybody!*

Forget it, kids! I may start my *own* club... for the *Green Goblin!*

Echh! That creep is as funny as a second-hand crutch!

You've *such* a cute sense of humor, Petey! But how did your *hair* get so mussed?

It..eh..it's pretty *windy* on the other side of the room!

Now that I've shown myself, I've got to get back to the Goblin, *fast!* But... *yipes!* Look who's here!

Look! Parker *did* come, after all!! But where's his *camera?*

Peter... here with *Liz!* She's running her fingers through his hair!! Oh, *no!*

You look *pale, Petey!* Is anything *wrong?*

Boy! Is *that* the under-statement of the year?!!

Meanwhile, high above everyone's heads, the "show" goes on!

I've got to get rid of the Torch quickly, so I can turn my attention to Spider-Man!

This little "Goblin surprise" ought to do the trick!

Whatever he tossed at me, it formed an air-tight cloud seal, cutting off my air! It'll put my *flame* out!

...Unless I increase my flame to near *nova intensity*... but that might cause a fire in here, injuring innocent people!

He's tossing *more!* I've got to do *something* before I'm completely without oxygen!

17.

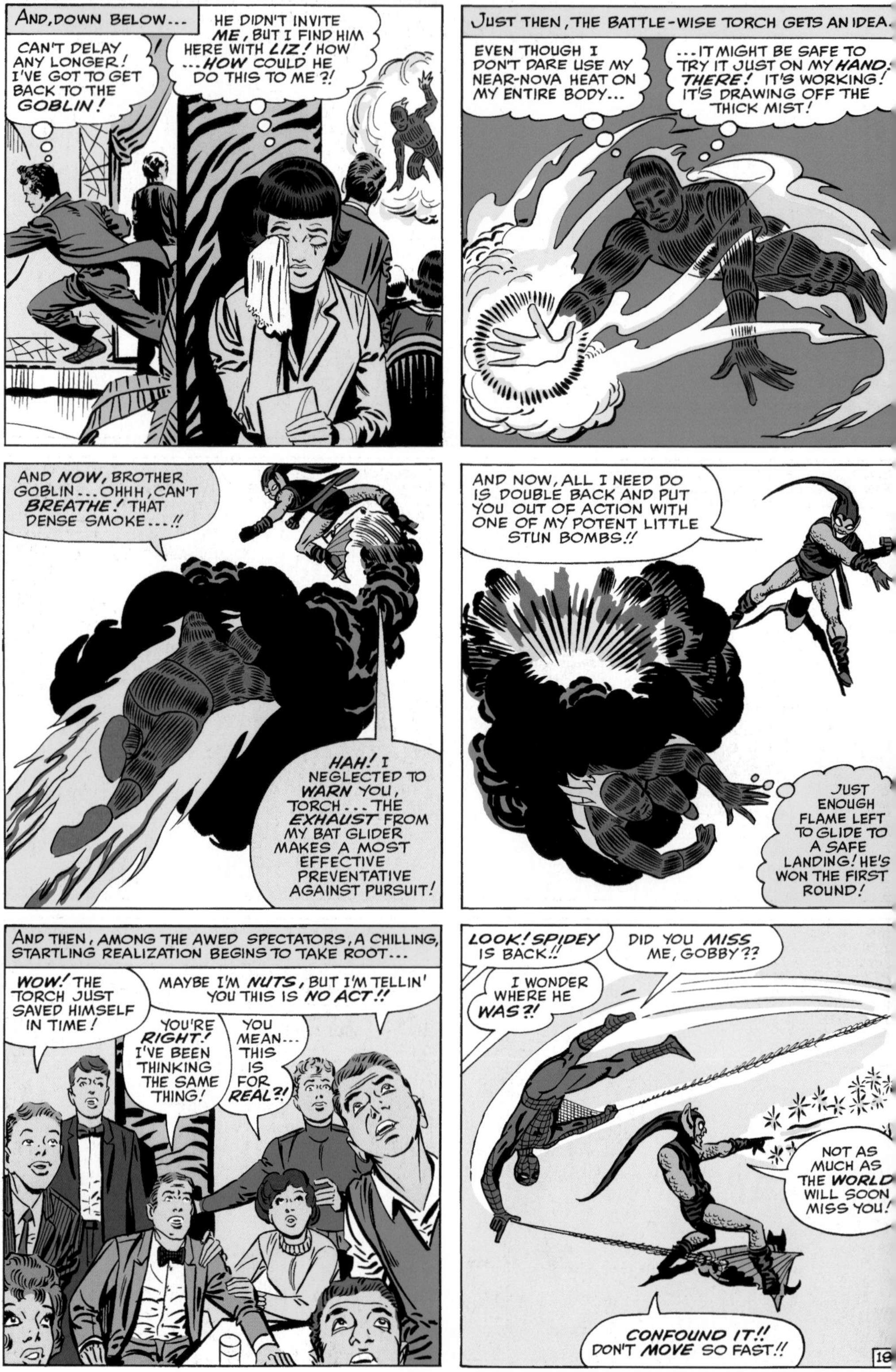
AND, DOWN BELOW...
CAN'T DELAY ANY LONGER! I'VE GOT TO GET BACK TO THE GOBLIN!
HE DIDN'T INVITE ME, BUT I FIND HIM HERE WITH LIZ! HOW ...HOW COULD HE DO THIS TO ME?!
JUST THEN, THE BATTLE-WISE TORCH GETS AN IDEA.
EVEN THOUGH I DON'T DARE USE MY NEAR-NOVA HEAT ON MY ENTIRE BODY...
...IT MIGHT BE SAFE TO TRY IT JUST ON MY HAND; THERE! IT'S WORKING! IT'S DRAWING OFF THE THICK MIST!
AND NOW, BROTHER GOBLIN...OHHH, CAN'T BREATHE! THAT DENSE SMOKE...!!
HAH! I NEGLECTED TO WARN YOU, TORCH... THE EXHAUST FROM MY BAT GLIDER MAKES A MOST EFFECTIVE PREVENTATIVE AGAINST PURSUIT!
AND NOW, ALL I NEED DO IS DOUBLE BACK AND PUT YOU OUT OF ACTION WITH ONE OF MY POTENT LITTLE STUN BOMBS!!
JUST ENOUGH FLAME LEFT TO GLIDE TO A SAFE LANDING! HE'S WON THE FIRST ROUND!
AND THEN, AMONG THE AWED SPECTATORS, A CHILLING, STARTLING REALIZATION BEGINS TO TAKE ROOT...
WOW! THE TORCH JUST SAVED HIMSELF IN TIME!
MAYBE I'M NUTS, BUT I'M TELLIN' YOU THIS IS NO ACT!!
YOU'RE RIGHT! I'VE BEEN THINKING THE SAME THING!
YOU MEAN... THIS IS FOR REAL?!
LOOK! SPIDEY IS BACK!!
I WONDER WHERE HE WAS?!
DID YOU MISS ME, GOBBY??
NOT AS MUCH AS THE WORLD WILL SOON MISS YOU!
CONFOUND IT!! DON'T MOVE SO FAST!!
18

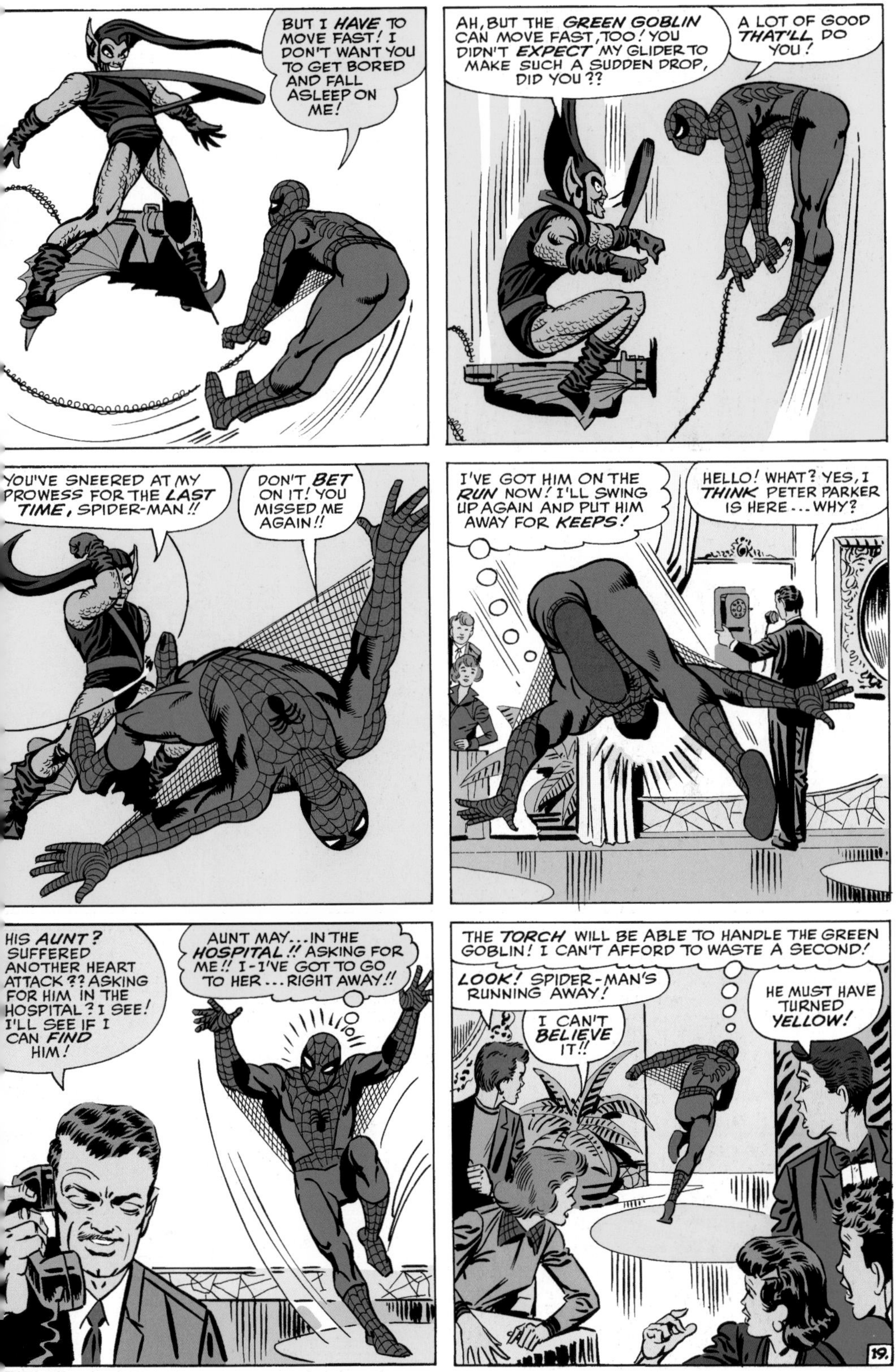
BUT I HAVE TO MOVE FAST! I DON'T WANT YOU TO GET BORED AND FALL ASLEEP ON ME!
AH, BUT THE GREEN GOBLIN CAN MOVE FAST, TOO! YOU DIDN'T EXPECT MY GLIDER TO MAKE SUCH A SUDDEN DROP, DID YOU??
A LOT OF GOOD THAT'LL DO YOU!
YOU'VE SNEERED AT MY PROWESS FOR THE LAST TIME, SPIDER-MAN!!
DON'T BET ON IT! YOU MISSED ME AGAIN!!
I'VE GOT HIM ON THE RUN NOW! I'LL SWING UP AGAIN AND PUT HIM AWAY FOR KEEPS!
HELLO! WHAT? YES, I THINK PETER PARKER IS HERE... WHY?
HIS AUNT? SUFFERED ANOTHER HEART ATTACK?? ASKING FOR HIM IN THE HOSPITAL? I SEE! I'LL SEE IF I CAN FIND HIM!
AUNT MAY... IN THE HOSPITAL!! ASKING FOR ME!! I-I'VE GOT TO GO TO HER... RIGHT AWAY!!
THE TORCH WILL BE ABLE TO HANDLE THE GREEN GOBLIN! I CAN'T AFFORD TO WASTE A SECOND!
LOOK! SPIDER-MAN'S RUNNING AWAY!
I CAN'T BELIEVE IT!!
HE MUST HAVE TURNED YELLOW!
19.

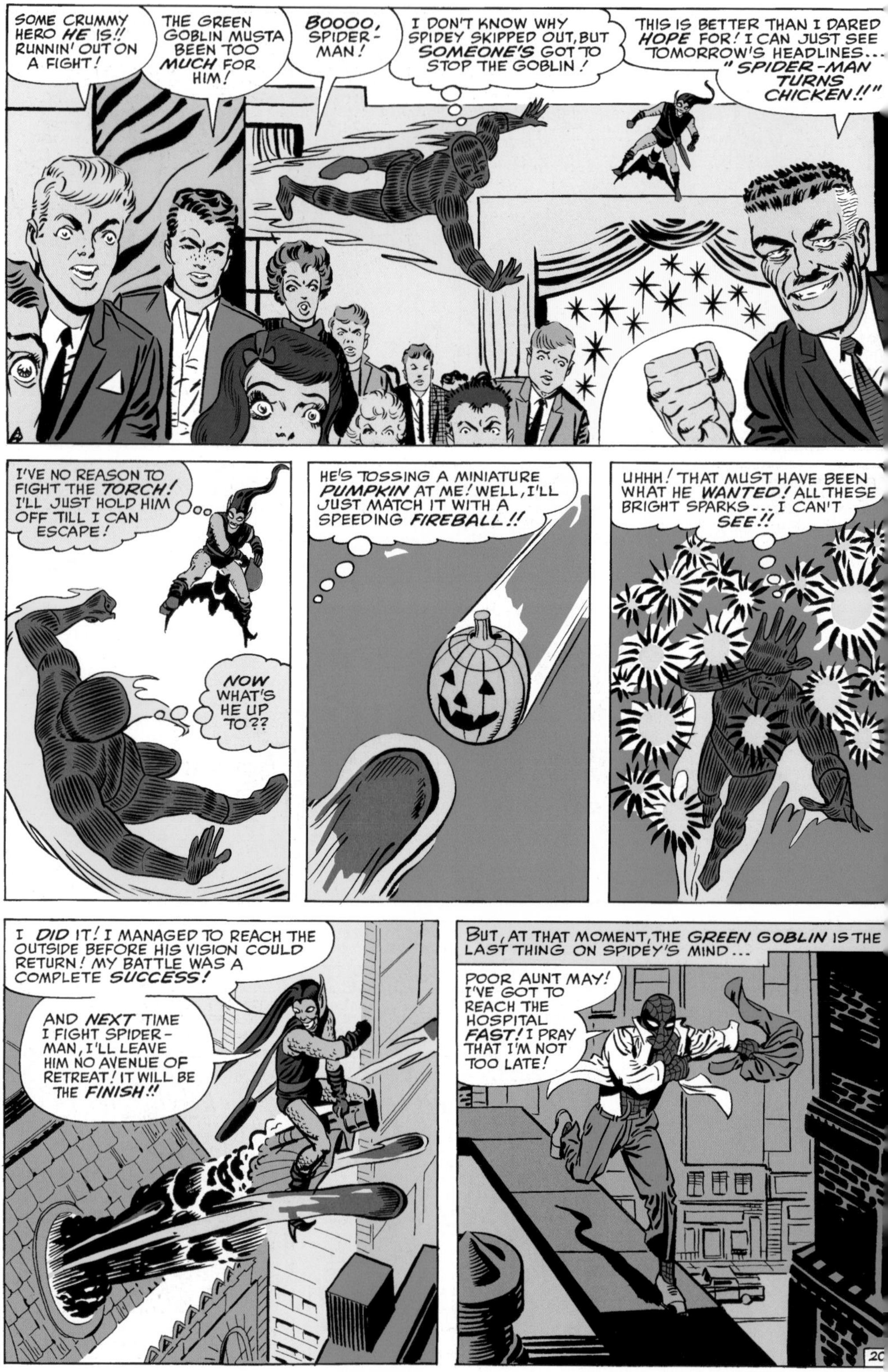
SOME CRUMMY HERO HE IS!! RUNNIN' OUT ON A FIGHT!
THE GREEN GOBLIN MUSTA BEEN TOO MUCH FOR HIM!
BOOOO, SPIDER-MAN!
I DON'T KNOW WHY SPIDEY SKIPPED OUT, BUT SOMEONE'S GOT TO STOP THE GOBLIN!
THIS IS BETTER THAN I DARED HOPE FOR! I CAN JUST SEE TOMORROW'S HEADLINES... "SPIDER-MAN TURNS CHICKEN!!"
I'VE NO REASON TO FIGHT THE TORCH! I'LL JUST HOLD HIM OFF TILL I CAN ESCAPE!
NOW WHAT'S HE UP TO??
HE'S TOSSING A MINIATURE PUMPKIN AT ME! WELL, I'LL JUST MATCH IT WITH A SPEEDING FIREBALL!!
UHHH! THAT MUST HAVE BEEN WHAT HE WANTED! ALL THESE BRIGHT SPARKS... I CAN'T SEE!!
I DID IT! I MANAGED TO REACH THE OUTSIDE BEFORE HIS VISION COULD RETURN! MY BATTLE WAS A COMPLETE SUCCESS!
AND NEXT TIME I FIGHT SPIDER-MAN, I'LL LEAVE HIM NO AVENUE OF RETREAT! IT WILL BE THE FINISH!!
BUT, AT THAT MOMENT, THE GREEN GOBLIN IS THE LAST THING ON SPIDEY'S MIND...
POOR AUNT MAY! I'VE GOT TO REACH THE HOSPITAL FAST! I PRAY THAT I'M NOT TOO LATE!
20

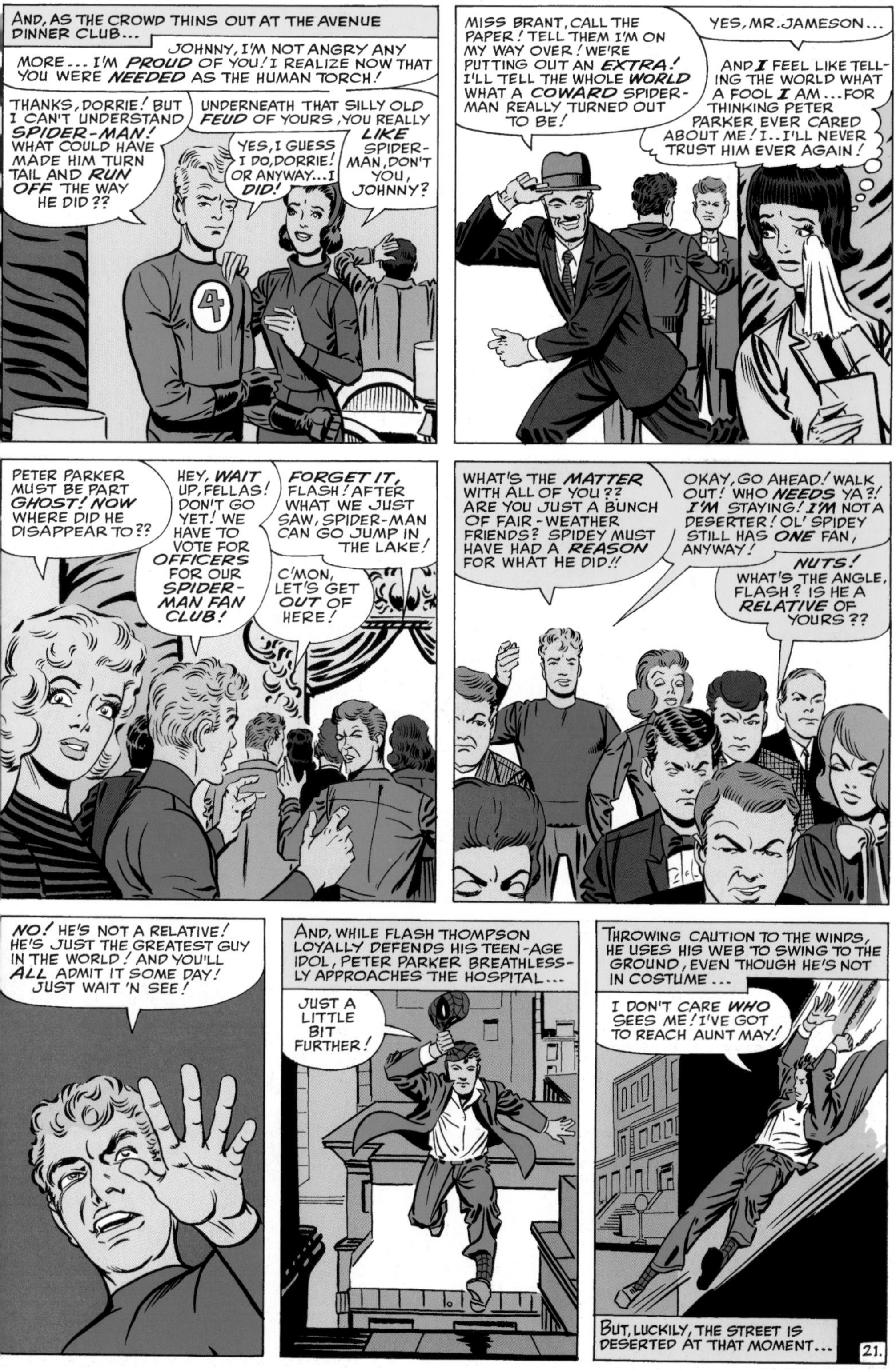
AND, AS THE CROWD THINS OUT AT THE AVENUE DINNER CLUB...
JOHNNY, I'M NOT ANGRY ANY MORE... I'M PROUD OF YOU! I REALIZE NOW THAT YOU WERE NEEDED AS THE HUMAN TORCH!
THANKS, DORRIE! BUT I CAN'T UNDERSTAND SPIDER-MAN! WHAT COULD HAVE MADE HIM TURN TAIL AND RUN OFF THE WAY HE DID??
UNDERNEATH THAT SILLY OLD FEUD OF YOURS, YOU REALLY LIKE SPIDER-MAN, DON'T YOU, JOHNNY?
YES, I GUESS I DO, DORRIE! OR ANYWAY... I DID!
MISS BRANT, CALL THE PAPER! TELL THEM I'M ON MY WAY OVER! WE'RE PUTTING OUT AN EXTRA! I'LL TELL THE WHOLE WORLD WHAT A COWARD SPIDER-MAN REALLY TURNED OUT TO BE!
YES, MR. JAMESON...
AND I FEEL LIKE TELLING THE WORLD WHAT A FOOL I AM... FOR THINKING PETER PARKER EVER CARED ABOUT ME! I.. I'LL NEVER TRUST HIM EVER AGAIN!
PETER PARKER MUST BE PART GHOST! NOW WHERE DID HE DISAPPEAR TO??
HEY, WAIT UP, FELLAS! DON'T GO YET! WE HAVE TO VOTE FOR OFFICERS FOR OUR SPIDER-MAN FAN CLUB!
FORGET IT, FLASH! AFTER WHAT WE JUST SAW, SPIDER-MAN CAN GO JUMP IN THE LAKE!
C'MON, LET'S GET OUT OF HERE!
WHAT'S THE MATTER WITH ALL OF YOU?? ARE YOU JUST A BUNCH OF FAIR-WEATHER FRIENDS? SPIDEY MUST HAVE HAD A REASON FOR WHAT HE DID!!
OKAY, GO AHEAD! WALK OUT! WHO NEEDS YA?! I'M STAYING! I'M NOT A DESERTER! OL' SPIDEY STILL HAS ONE FAN, ANYWAY!
NUTS! WHAT'S THE ANGLE, FLASH? IS HE A RELATIVE OF YOURS??
NO! HE'S NOT A RELATIVE! HE'S JUST THE GREATEST GUY IN THE WORLD! AND YOU'LL ALL ADMIT IT SOME DAY! JUST WAIT 'N SEE!
AND, WHILE FLASH THOMPSON LOYALLY DEFENDS HIS TEEN-AGE IDOL, PETER PARKER BREATHLESSLY APPROACHES THE HOSPITAL...
JUST A LITTLE BIT FURTHER!
THROWING CAUTION TO THE WINDS, HE USES HIS WEB TO SWING TO THE GROUND, EVEN THOUGH HE'S NOT IN COSTUME...
I DON'T CARE WHO SEES ME! I'VE GOT TO REACH AUNT MAY!
BUT, LUCKILY, THE STREET IS DESERTED AT THAT MOMENT...
21.

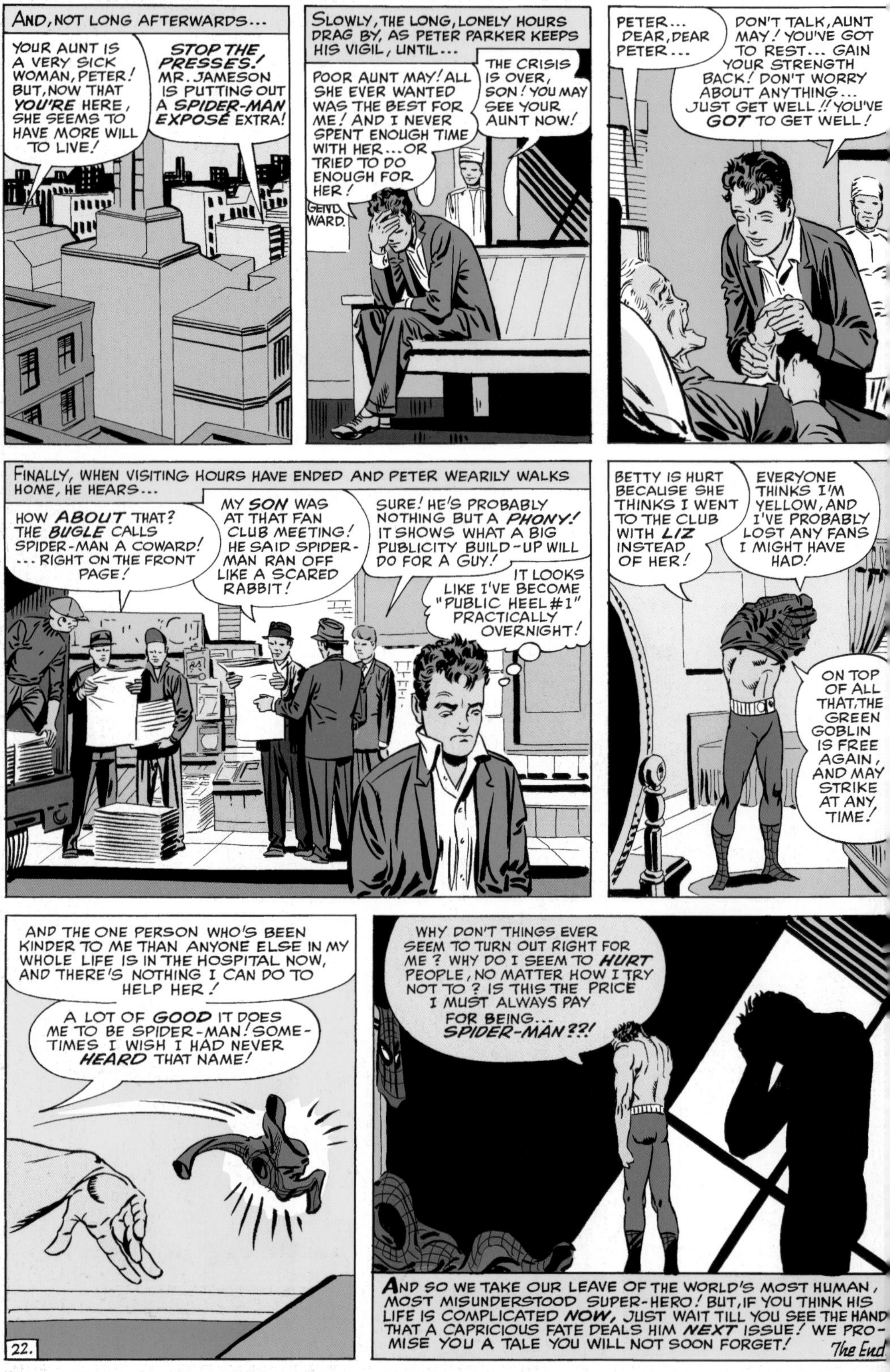
AND, NOT LONG AFTERWARDS...
YOUR AUNT IS A VERY SICK WOMAN, PETER! BUT, NOW THAT YOU'RE HERE, SHE SEEMS TO HAVE MORE WILL TO LIVE!
STOP THE PRESSES! MR. JAMESON IS PUTTING OUT A SPIDER-MAN EXPOSÉ EXTRA!
SLOWLY, THE LONG, LONELY HOURS DRAG BY, AS PETER PARKER KEEPS HIS VIGIL, UNTIL...
POOR AUNT MAY! ALL SHE EVER WANTED WAS THE BEST FOR ME! AND I NEVER SPENT ENOUGH TIME WITH HER...OR TRIED TO DO ENOUGH FOR HER!
THE CRISIS IS OVER, SON! YOU MAY SEE YOUR AUNT NOW!
PETER... DEAR, DEAR PETER...
DON'T TALK, AUNT MAY! YOU'VE GOT TO REST... GAIN YOUR STRENGTH BACK! DON'T WORRY ABOUT ANYTHING... JUST GET WELL!! YOU'VE GOT TO GET WELL!
FINALLY, WHEN VISITING HOURS HAVE ENDED AND PETER WEARILY WALKS HOME, HE HEARS...
HOW ABOUT THAT? THE BUGLE CALLS SPIDER-MAN A COWARD! ...RIGHT ON THE FRONT PAGE!
MY SON WAS AT THAT FAN CLUB MEETING! HE SAID SPIDER-MAN RAN OFF LIKE A SCARED RABBIT!
SURE! HE'S PROBABLY NOTHING BUT A PHONY! IT SHOWS WHAT A BIG PUBLICITY BUILD-UP WILL DO FOR A GUY!
IT LOOKS LIKE I'VE BECOME "PUBLIC HEEL #1" PRACTICALLY OVERNIGHT!
BETTY IS HURT BECAUSE SHE THINKS I WENT TO THE CLUB WITH LIZ INSTEAD OF HER!
EVERYONE THINKS I'M YELLOW, AND I'VE PROBABLY LOST ANY FANS I MIGHT HAVE HAD!
ON TOP OF ALL THAT, THE GREEN GOBLIN IS FREE AGAIN, AND MAY STRIKE AT ANY TIME!
AND THE ONE PERSON WHO'S BEEN KINDER TO ME THAN ANYONE ELSE IN MY WHOLE LIFE IS IN THE HOSPITAL NOW, AND THERE'S NOTHING I CAN DO TO HELP HER!
A LOT OF GOOD IT DOES ME TO BE SPIDER-MAN! SOMETIMES I WISH I HAD NEVER HEARD THAT NAME!
22.
WHY DON'T THINGS EVER SEEM TO TURN OUT RIGHT FOR ME? WHY DO I SEEM TO HURT PEOPLE, NO MATTER HOW I TRY NOT TO? IS THIS THE PRICE I MUST ALWAYS PAY FOR BEING... SPIDER-MAN??!
AND SO WE TAKE OUR LEAVE OF THE WORLD'S MOST HUMAN, MOST MISUNDERSTOOD SUPER-HERO! BUT, IF YOU THINK HIS LIFE IS COMPLICATED NOW, JUST WAIT TILL YOU SEE THE HAND THAT A CAPRICIOUS FATE DEALS HIM NEXT ISSUE! WE PROMISE YOU A TALE YOU WILL NOT SOON FORGET!
The End

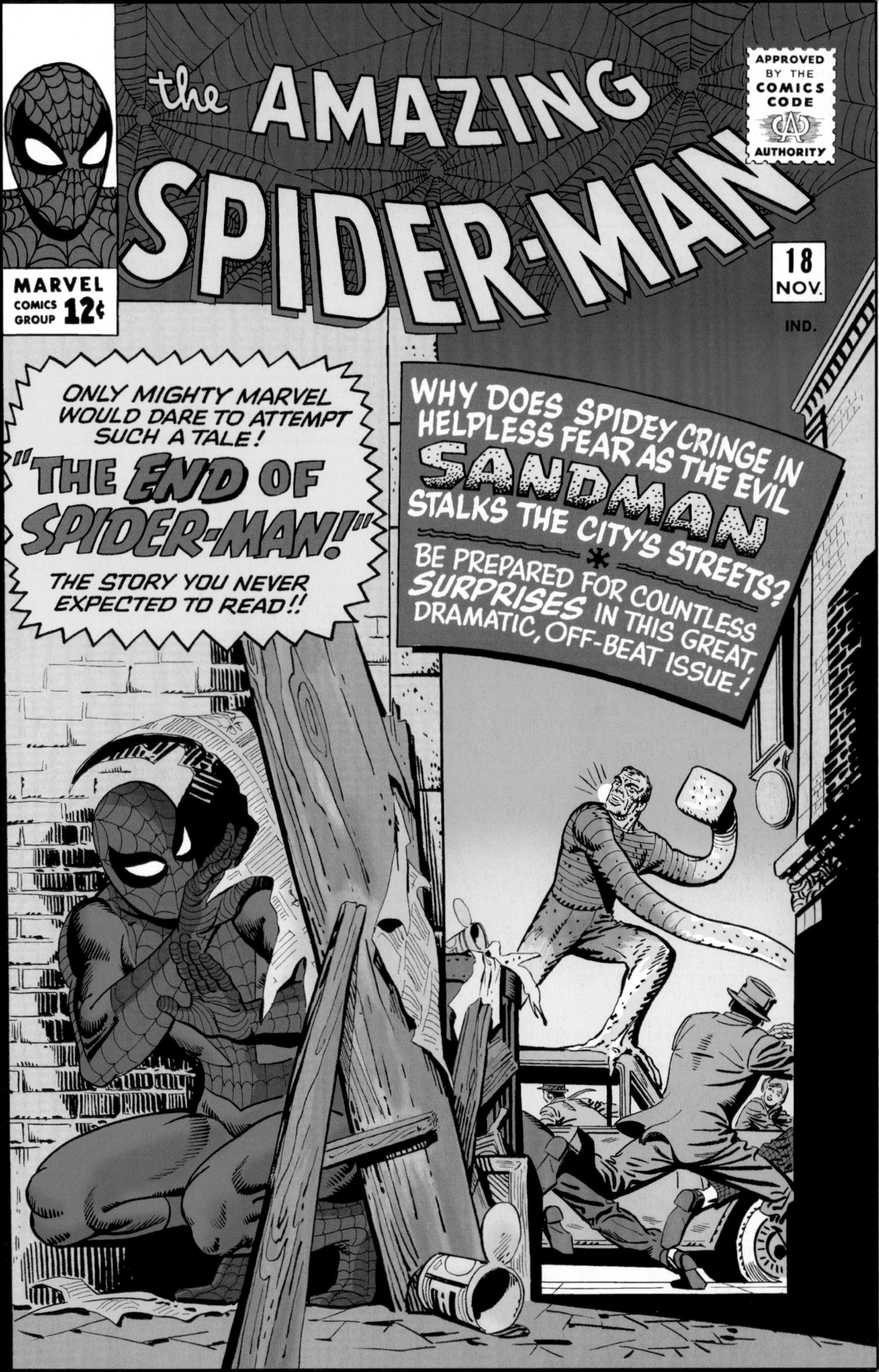
the AMAZING SPIDER-MAN
APPROVED BY THE COMICS CODE AUTHORITY
MARVEL COMICS GROUP 12¢
18 NOV.
IND.
ONLY MIGHTY MARVEL WOULD DARE TO ATTEMPT SUCH A TALE!
"THE END OF SPIDER-MAN!"
THE STORY YOU NEVER EXPECTED TO READ!!
WHY DOES SPIDEY CRINGE IN HELPLESS FEAR AS THE EVIL SANDMAN STALKS THE CITY'S STREETS?
BE PREPARED FOR COUNTLESS SURPRISES IN THIS GREAT, DRAMATIC, OFF-BEAT ISSUE!

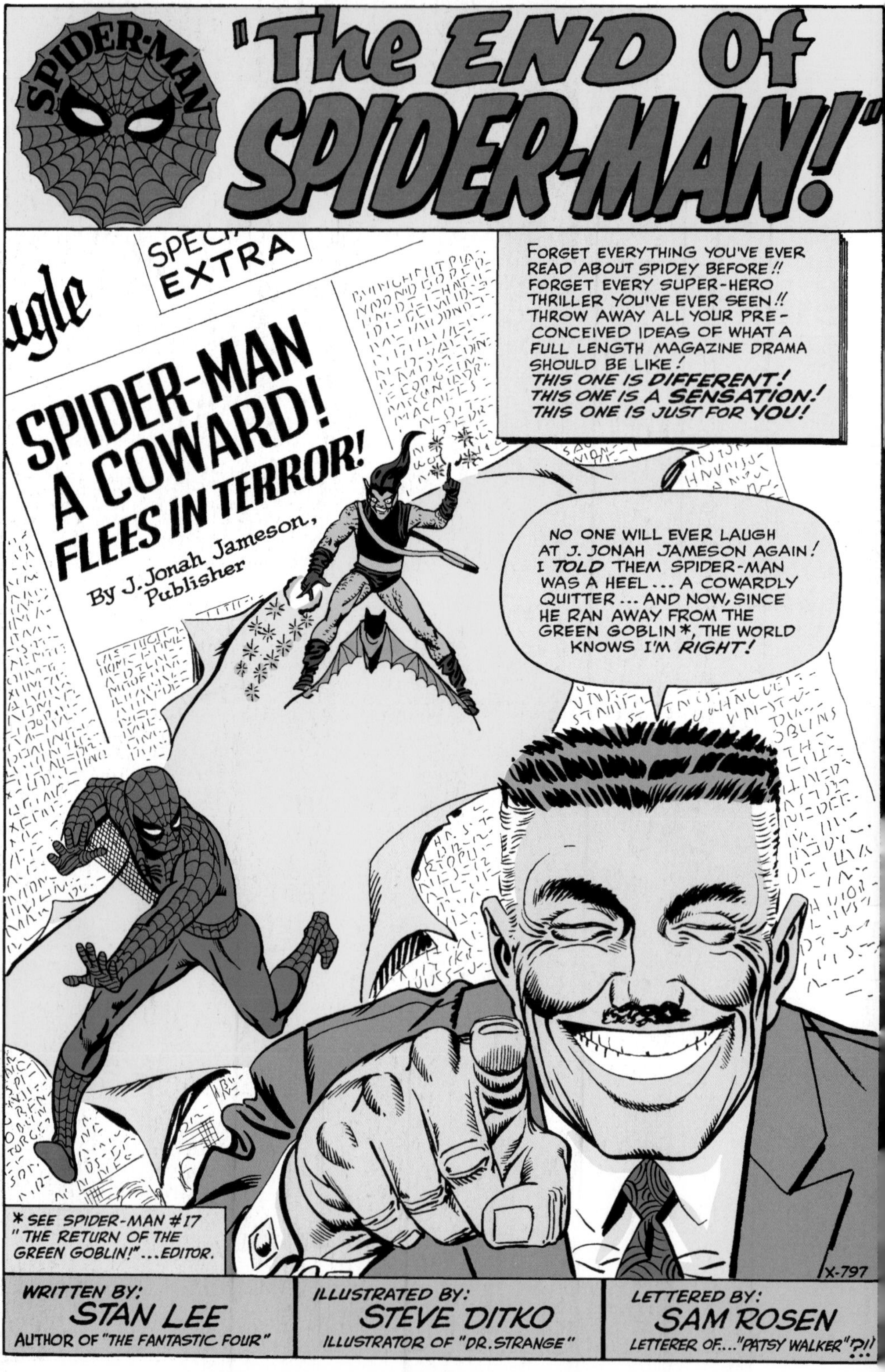

SPIDER-MAN
"The END Of SPIDER-MAN!"
SPECIAL EXTRA
SPIDER-MAN A COWARD! FLEES IN TERROR!
By J. Jonah Jameson, Publisher
FORGET EVERYTHING YOU'VE EVER READ ABOUT SPIDEY BEFORE!! FORGET EVERY SUPER-HERO THRILLER YOU'VE EVER SEEN!! THROW AWAY ALL YOUR PRE-CONCEIVED IDEAS OF WHAT A FULL LENGTH MAGAZINE DRAMA SHOULD BE LIKE! THIS ONE IS DIFFERENT! THIS ONE IS A SENSATION! THIS ONE IS JUST FOR YOU!
NO ONE WILL EVER LAUGH AT J. JONAH JAMESON AGAIN! I TOLD THEM SPIDER-MAN WAS A HEEL... A COWARDLY QUITTER... AND NOW, SINCE HE RAN AWAY FROM THE GREEN GOBLIN*, THE WORLD KNOWS I'M RIGHT!
* SEE SPIDER-MAN #17 "THE RETURN OF THE GREEN GOBLIN!"... EDITOR.
X-797
WRITTEN BY: STAN LEE AUTHOR OF "THE FANTASTIC FOUR"
ILLUSTRATED BY: STEVE DITKO ILLUSTRATOR OF "DR. STRANGE"
LETTERED BY: SAM ROSEN LETTERER OF... "PATSY WALKER"?!!

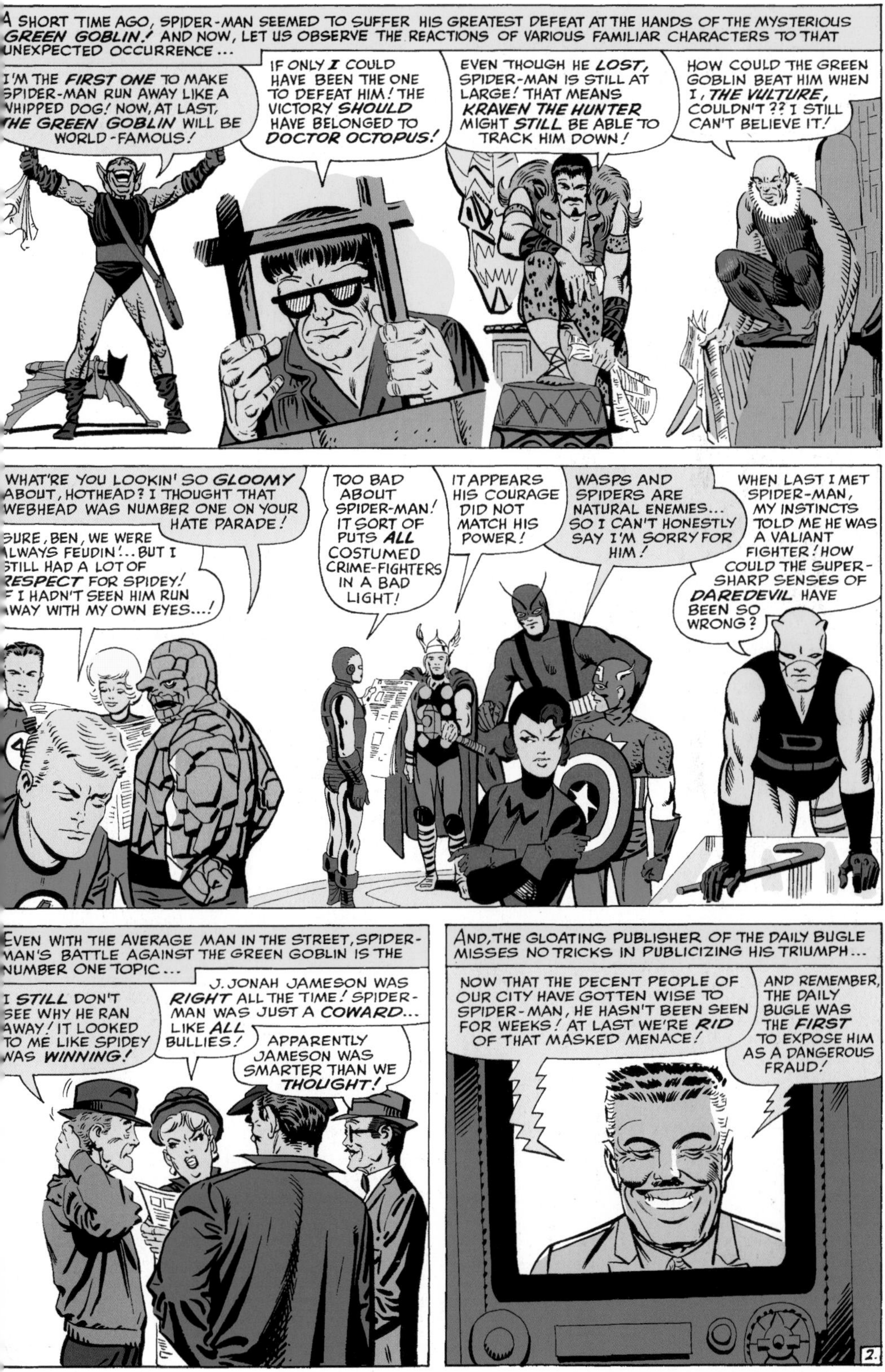

A SHORT TIME AGO, SPIDER-MAN SEEMED TO SUFFER HIS GREATEST DEFEAT AT THE HANDS OF THE MYSTERIOUS GREEN GOBLIN! AND NOW, LET US OBSERVE THE REACTIONS OF VARIOUS FAMILIAR CHARACTERS TO THAT UNEXPECTED OCCURRENCE...
I'M THE FIRST ONE TO MAKE SPIDER-MAN RUN AWAY LIKE A WHIPPED DOG! NOW, AT LAST, THE GREEN GOBLIN WILL BE WORLD-FAMOUS!
IF ONLY I COULD HAVE BEEN THE ONE TO DEFEAT HIM! THE VICTORY SHOULD HAVE BELONGED TO DOCTOR OCTOPUS!
EVEN THOUGH HE LOST, SPIDER-MAN IS STILL AT LARGE! THAT MEANS KRAVEN THE HUNTER MIGHT STILL BE ABLE TO TRACK HIM DOWN!
HOW COULD THE GREEN GOBLIN BEAT HIM WHEN I, THE VULTURE, COULDN'T ?? I STILL CAN'T BELIEVE IT!
WHAT'RE YOU LOOKIN' SO GLOOMY ABOUT, HOTHEAD? I THOUGHT THAT WEBHEAD WAS NUMBER ONE ON YOUR HATE PARADE!
SURE, BEN, WE WERE ALWAYS FEUDIN'!.. BUT I STILL HAD A LOT OF RESPECT FOR SPIDEY! IF I HADN'T SEEN HIM RUN AWAY WITH MY OWN EYES...!
TOO BAD ABOUT SPIDER-MAN! IT SORT OF PUTS ALL COSTUMED CRIME-FIGHTERS IN A BAD LIGHT!
IT APPEARS HIS COURAGE DID NOT MATCH HIS POWER!
WASPS AND SPIDERS ARE NATURAL ENEMIES... SO I CAN'T HONESTLY SAY I'M SORRY FOR HIM!
WHEN LAST I MET SPIDER-MAN, MY INSTINCTS TOLD ME HE WAS A VALIANT FIGHTER! HOW COULD THE SUPER-SHARP SENSES OF DAREDEVIL HAVE BEEN SO WRONG?
EVEN WITH THE AVERAGE MAN IN THE STREET, SPIDER-MAN'S BATTLE AGAINST THE GREEN GOBLIN IS THE NUMBER ONE TOPIC...
I STILL DON'T SEE WHY HE RAN AWAY! IT LOOKED TO ME LIKE SPIDEY WAS WINNING!
J. JONAH JAMESON WAS RIGHT ALL THE TIME! SPIDER-MAN WAS JUST A COWARD... LIKE ALL BULLIES!
APPARENTLY JAMESON WAS SMARTER THAN WE THOUGHT!
AND, THE GLOATING PUBLISHER OF THE DAILY BUGLE MISSES NO TRICKS IN PUBLICIZING HIS TRIUMPH...
NOW THAT THE DECENT PEOPLE OF OUR CITY HAVE GOTTEN WISE TO SPIDER-MAN, HE HASN'T BEEN SEEN FOR WEEKS! AT LAST WE'RE RID OF THAT MASKED MENACE!
AND REMEMBER, THE DAILY BUGLE WAS THE FIRST TO EXPOSE HIM AS A DANGEROUS FRAUD!
2.

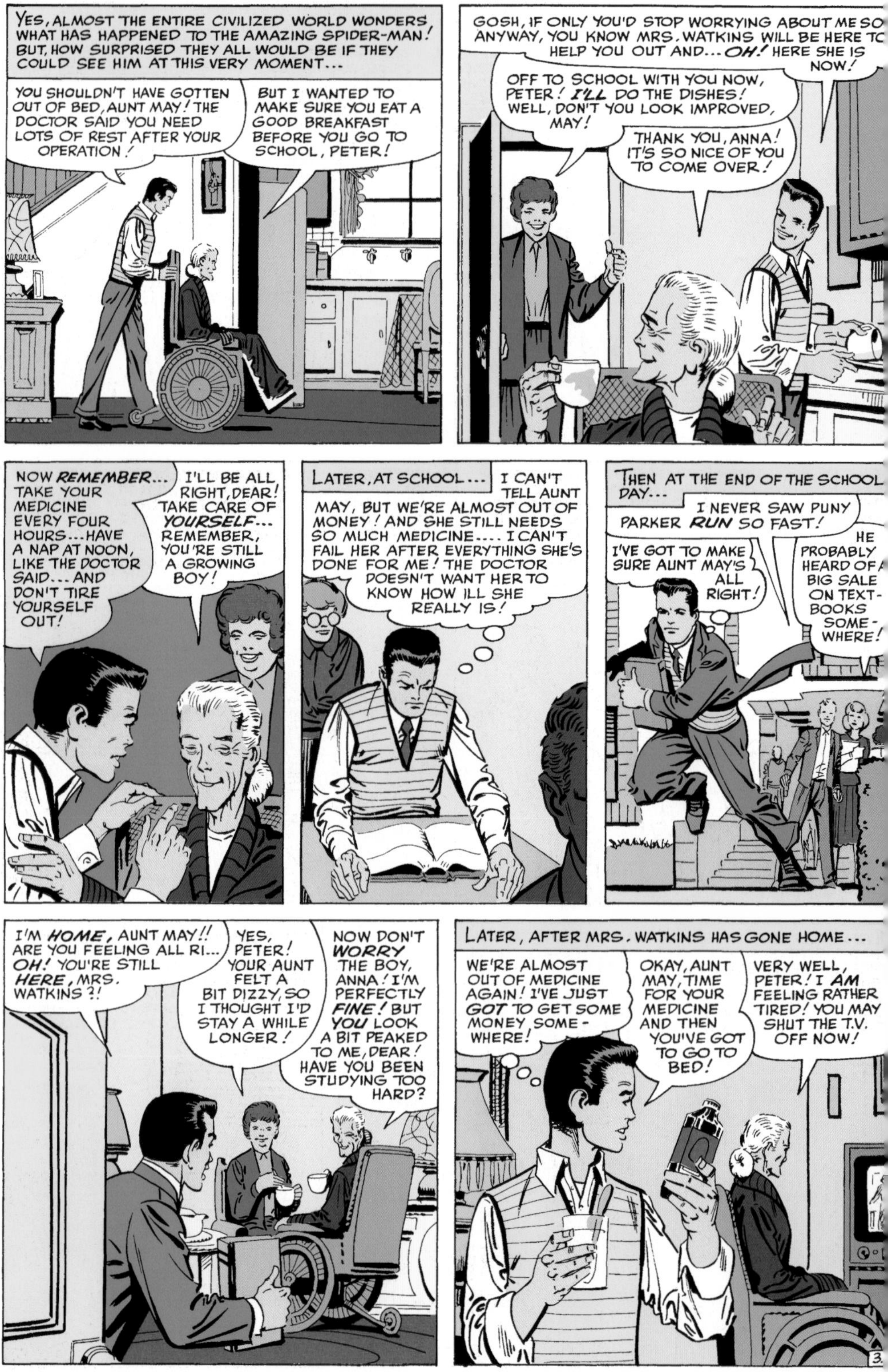
YES, ALMOST THE ENTIRE CIVILIZED WORLD WONDERS WHAT HAS HAPPENED TO THE AMAZING SPIDER-MAN! BUT, HOW SURPRISED THEY ALL WOULD BE IF THEY COULD SEE HIM AT THIS VERY MOMENT...
YOU SHOULDN'T HAVE GOTTEN OUT OF BED, AUNT MAY! THE DOCTOR SAID YOU NEED LOTS OF REST AFTER YOUR OPERATION!
BUT I WANTED TO MAKE SURE YOU EAT A GOOD BREAKFAST BEFORE YOU GO TO SCHOOL, PETER!
GOSH, IF ONLY YOU'D STOP WORRYING ABOUT ME SO! ANYWAY, YOU KNOW MRS. WATKINS WILL BE HERE TO HELP YOU OUT AND... OH! HERE SHE IS NOW!
OFF TO SCHOOL WITH YOU NOW, PETER! I'LL DO THE DISHES! WELL, DON'T YOU LOOK IMPROVED, MAY!
THANK YOU, ANNA! IT'S SO NICE OF YOU TO COME OVER!
NOW REMEMBER... TAKE YOUR MEDICINE EVERY FOUR HOURS... HAVE A NAP AT NOON, LIKE THE DOCTOR SAID... AND DON'T TIRE YOURSELF OUT!
I'LL BE ALL RIGHT, DEAR! TAKE CARE OF YOURSELF... REMEMBER, YOU'RE STILL A GROWING BOY!
LATER, AT SCHOOL...
I CAN'T TELL AUNT MAY, BUT WE'RE ALMOST OUT OF MONEY! AND SHE STILL NEEDS SO MUCH MEDICINE.... I CAN'T FAIL HER AFTER EVERYTHING SHE'S DONE FOR ME! THE DOCTOR DOESN'T WANT HER TO KNOW HOW ILL SHE REALLY IS!
THEN AT THE END OF THE SCHOOL DAY...
I NEVER SAW PUNY PARKER RUN SO FAST!
HE PROBABLY HEARD OF A BIG SALE ON TEXT-BOOKS SOME-WHERE!
I'VE GOT TO MAKE SURE AUNT MAY'S ALL RIGHT!
I'M HOME, AUNT MAY!! ARE YOU FEELING ALL RI... OH! YOU'RE STILL HERE, MRS. WATKINS?!
YES, PETER! YOUR AUNT FELT A BIT DIZZY, SO I THOUGHT I'D STAY A WHILE LONGER!
NOW DON'T WORRY THE BOY, ANNA! I'M PERFECTLY FINE! BUT YOU LOOK A BIT PEAKED TO ME, DEAR! HAVE YOU BEEN STUDYING TOO HARD?
LATER, AFTER MRS. WATKINS HAS GONE HOME...
WE'RE ALMOST OUT OF MEDICINE AGAIN! I'VE JUST GOT TO GET SOME MONEY SOME-WHERE!
OKAY, AUNT MAY, TIME FOR YOUR MEDICINE AND THEN YOU'VE GOT TO GO TO BED!
VERY WELL, PETER! I AM FEELING RATHER TIRED! YOU MAY SHUT THE T.V. OFF NOW!
3

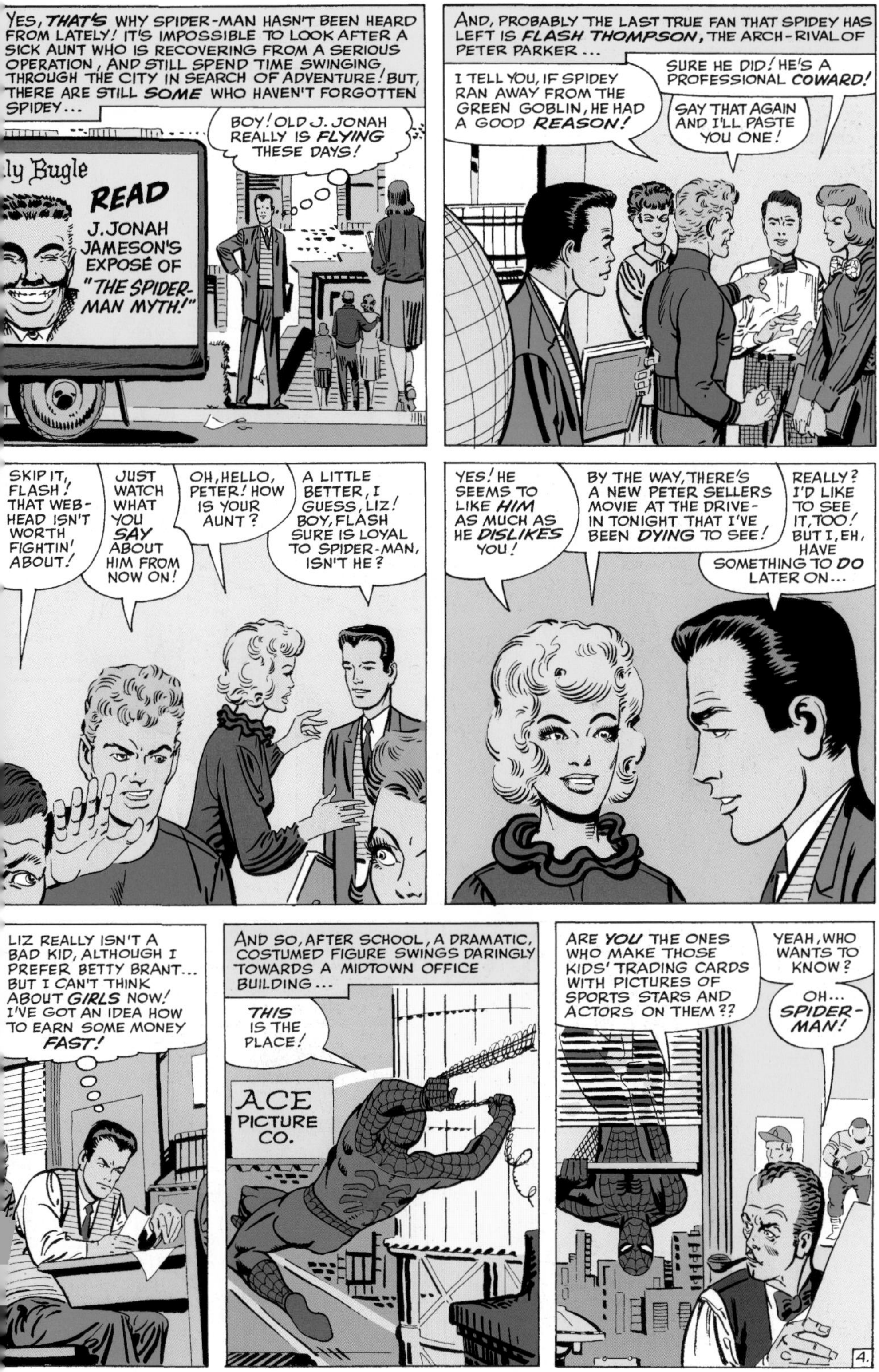
YES, THAT'S WHY SPIDER-MAN HASN'T BEEN HEARD FROM LATELY! IT'S IMPOSSIBLE TO LOOK AFTER A SICK AUNT WHO IS RECOVERING FROM A SERIOUS OPERATION, AND STILL SPEND TIME SWINGING THROUGH THE CITY IN SEARCH OF ADVENTURE! BUT, THERE ARE STILL SOME WHO HAVEN'T FORGOTTEN SPIDEY...
BOY! OLD J. JONAH REALLY IS FLYING THESE DAYS!
ly Bugle
READ J. JONAH JAMESON'S EXPOSÉ OF "THE SPIDER-MAN MYTH!"
AND, PROBABLY THE LAST TRUE FAN THAT SPIDEY HAS LEFT IS FLASH THOMPSON, THE ARCH-RIVAL OF PETER PARKER...
I TELL YOU, IF SPIDEY RAN AWAY FROM THE GREEN GOBLIN, HE HAD A GOOD REASON!
SURE HE DID! HE'S A PROFESSIONAL COWARD!
SAY THAT AGAIN AND I'LL PASTE YOU ONE!
SKIP IT, FLASH! THAT WEB-HEAD ISN'T WORTH FIGHTIN' ABOUT!
JUST WATCH WHAT YOU SAY ABOUT HIM FROM NOW ON!
OH, HELLO, PETER! HOW IS YOUR AUNT?
A LITTLE BETTER, I GUESS, LIZ! BOY, FLASH SURE IS LOYAL TO SPIDER-MAN, ISN'T HE?
YES! HE SEEMS TO LIKE HIM AS MUCH AS HE DISLIKES YOU!
BY THE WAY, THERE'S A NEW PETER SELLERS MOVIE AT THE DRIVE-IN TONIGHT THAT I'VE BEEN DYING TO SEE!
REALLY? I'D LIKE TO SEE IT, TOO! BUT I, EH, HAVE SOMETHING TO DO LATER ON...
LIZ REALLY ISN'T A BAD KID, ALTHOUGH I PREFER BETTY BRANT... BUT I CAN'T THINK ABOUT GIRLS NOW! I'VE GOT AN IDEA HOW TO EARN SOME MONEY FAST!
AND SO, AFTER SCHOOL, A DRAMATIC, COSTUMED FIGURE SWINGS DARINGLY TOWARDS A MIDTOWN OFFICE BUILDING...
THIS IS THE PLACE!
ACE PICTURE CO.
ARE YOU THE ONES WHO MAKE THOSE KIDS' TRADING CARDS WITH PICTURES OF SPORTS STARS AND ACTORS ON THEM??
YEAH, WHO WANTS TO KNOW? OH... SPIDER-MAN!
4.

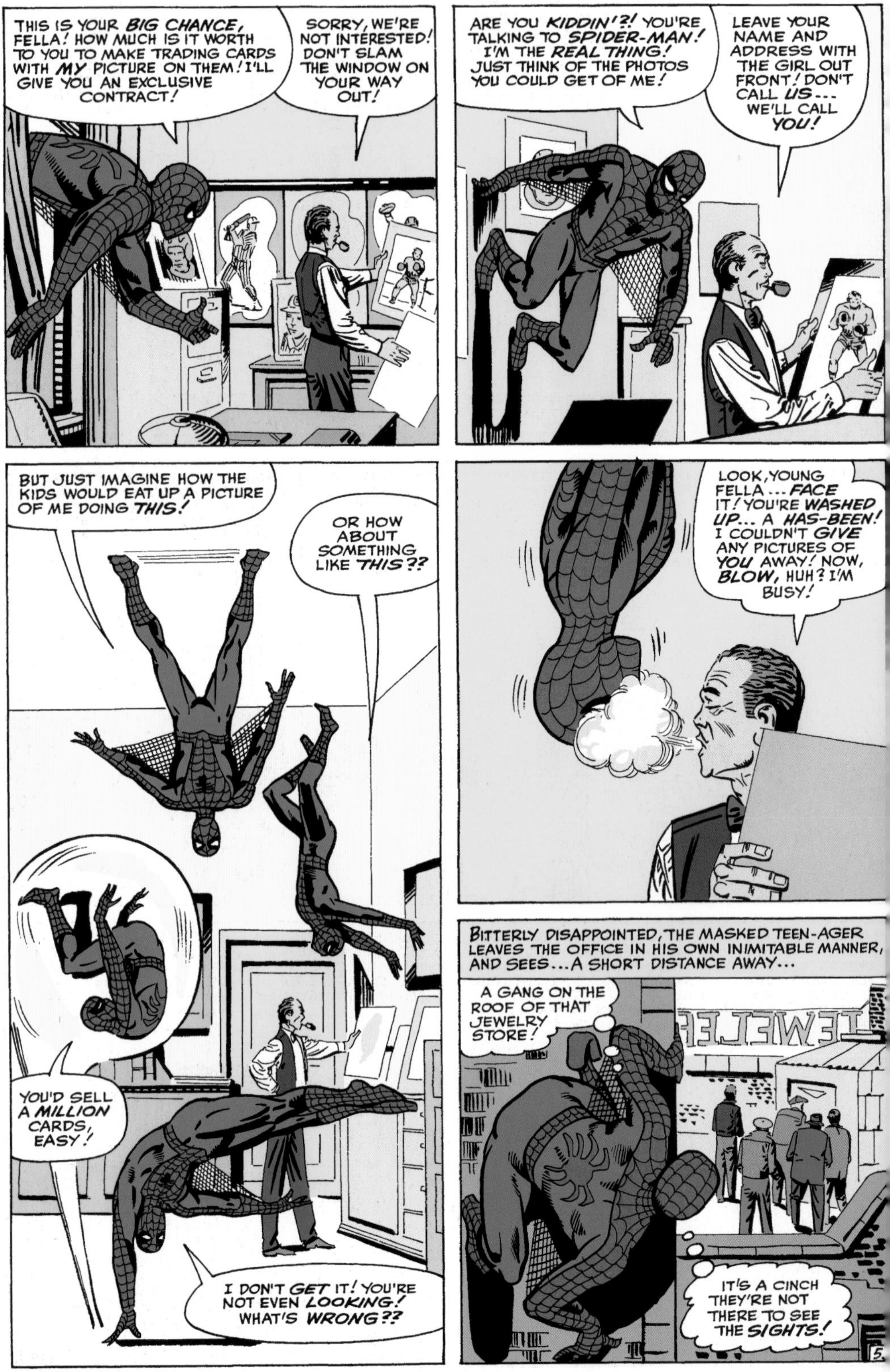
THIS IS YOUR BIG CHANCE, FELLA! HOW MUCH IS IT WORTH TO YOU TO MAKE TRADING CARDS WITH MY PICTURE ON THEM! I'LL GIVE YOU AN EXCLUSIVE CONTRACT!
SORRY, WE'RE NOT INTERESTED! DON'T SLAM THE WINDOW ON YOUR WAY OUT!
ARE YOU KIDDIN'?! YOU'RE TALKING TO SPIDER-MAN! I'M THE REAL THING! JUST THINK OF THE PHOTOS YOU COULD GET OF ME!
LEAVE YOUR NAME AND ADDRESS WITH THE GIRL OUT FRONT! DON'T CALL US... WE'LL CALL YOU!
BUT JUST IMAGINE HOW THE KIDS WOULD EAT UP A PICTURE OF ME DOING THIS!
OR HOW ABOUT SOMETHING LIKE THIS??
YOU'D SELL A MILLION CARDS, EASY!
I DON'T GET IT! YOU'RE NOT EVEN LOOKING! WHAT'S WRONG??
LOOK, YOUNG FELLA... FACE IT! YOU'RE WASHED UP... A HAS-BEEN! I COULDN'T GIVE ANY PICTURES OF YOU AWAY! NOW, BLOW, HUH? I'M BUSY!
BITTERLY DISAPPOINTED, THE MASKED TEEN-AGER LEAVES THE OFFICE IN HIS OWN INIMITABLE MANNER, AND SEES...A SHORT DISTANCE AWAY...
A GANG ON THE ROOF OF THAT JEWELRY STORE!
JEWELE
IT'S A CINCH THEY'RE NOT THERE TO SEE THE SIGHTS!
5

I'LL BREAK UP THAT LITTLE CAPER EASY AS PIE, AND THEN... OH, *NO!* I CAN'T!

I FORGOT! IF ANYTHING HAPPENED TO *ME*, WHO'D LOOK AFTER POOR AUNT MAY *!?*

I JUST CAN'T AFFORD TO TAKE THE CHANCE!

AND THEN, SPIDER-MAN DOES A MOST UNUSUAL THING... HE TURNS AND RUNS *AWAY* FROM THE FURTIVE WOULD-BE JEWEL THIEVES...

THIS MAY NOT BE IN THE BEST SUPER-HERO TRADITION, BUT I HAVEN'T ANY CHOICE!

ANYWAY, I'M GLAD I HAVE SOME *CHANGE* WITH ME!

SECONDS LATER...

HELLO, POLICE? I'D LIKE TO REPORT A CRIME! SOME MEN ARE TRYING TO BREAK INTO A JEWELRY STORE AT THE CORNER OF FORTY-SEVENTH STREET...

AND THEN...

NO, I'D RATHER NOT MENTION MY NAME! I'M JUST A PRIVATE CITIZEN, TRYING TO DO HIS DUTY! THAT'S OKAY... YOU'RE WELCOME!

WELL, IT'S NOT THE WAY THE *HUMAN TORCH* WOULD HAVE HANDLED IT, BUT AT LEAST I'LL BE ABLE TO GET RIGHT HOME AND SEE IF AUNT MAY NEEDS ME NOW!

MINUTES LATER...

DOC! WHAT ARE *YOU* DOING HERE? IS... IS ANYTHING *WRONG*?? WHERE'S AUNT MAY...??

IT'S ALL RIGHT, PETER! I WAS JUST PASSING BY, SO I THOUGHT I'D DROP IN! YOUR AUNT SEEMS TO BE HOLDING HER OWN! BUT *YOU'D* BETTER TRY TO TAKE IT EASY, SON!

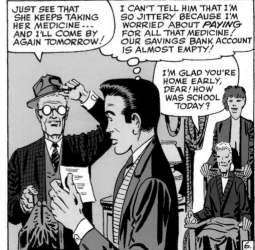

JUST SEE THAT SHE KEEPS TAKING HER MEDICINE... AND I'LL COME BY AGAIN TOMORROW!

I CAN'T TELL HIM THAT I'M SO JITTERY BECAUSE I'M WORRIED ABOUT *PAYING* FOR ALL THAT MEDICINE! OUR SAVINGS BANK ACCOUNT IS ALMOST EMPTY!

I'M GLAD YOU'RE HOME EARLY, DEAR! HOW WAS SCHOOL TODAY?

6.

245

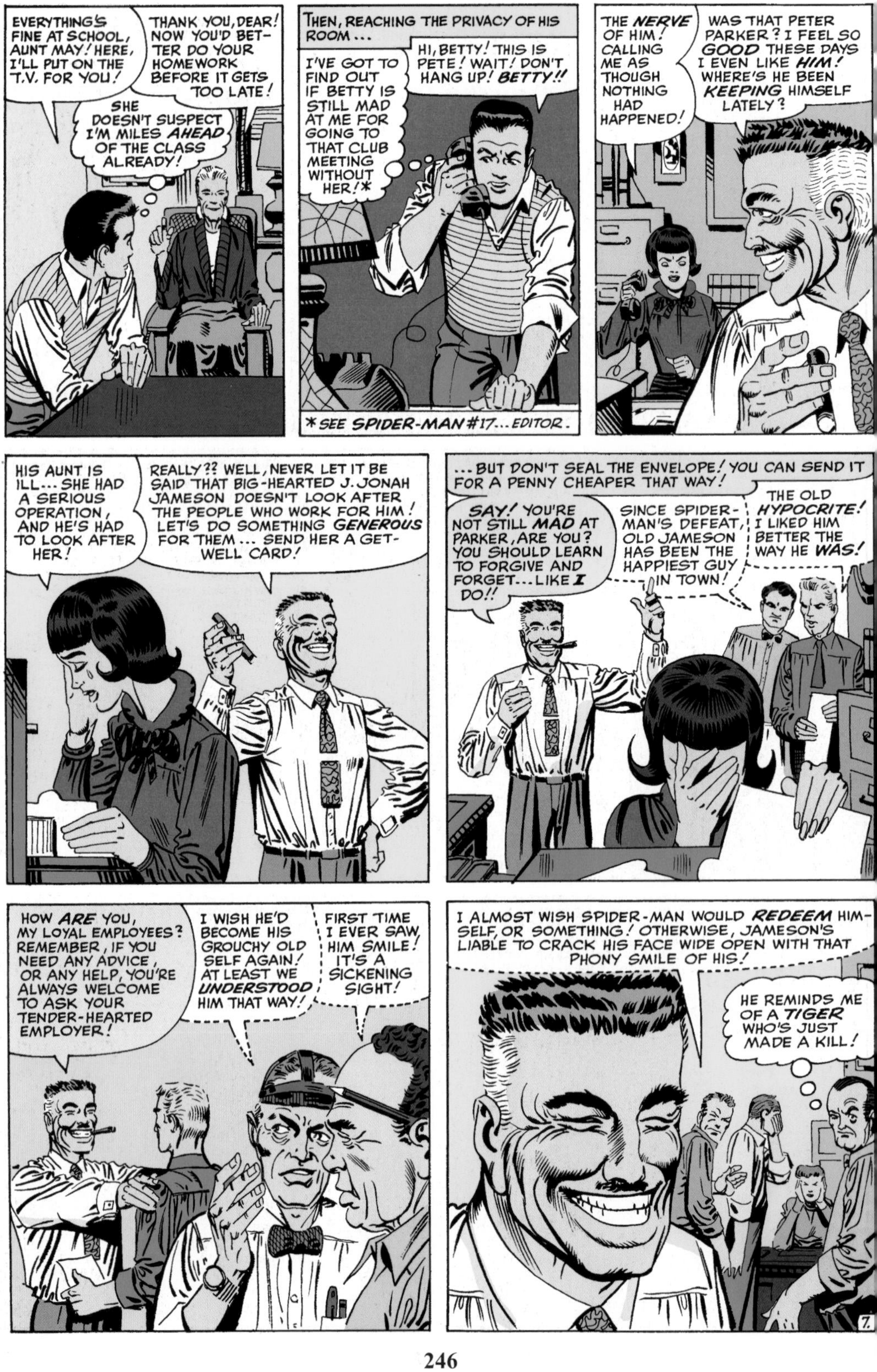
EVERYTHING'S FINE AT SCHOOL, AUNT MAY! HERE, I'LL PUT ON THE T.V. FOR YOU!
THANK YOU, DEAR! NOW YOU'D BETTER DO YOUR HOMEWORK BEFORE IT GETS TOO LATE!
SHE DOESN'T SUSPECT I'M MILES AHEAD OF THE CLASS ALREADY!
THEN, REACHING THE PRIVACY OF HIS ROOM...
I'VE GOT TO FIND OUT IF BETTY IS STILL MAD AT ME FOR GOING TO THAT CLUB MEETING WITHOUT HER!*
HI, BETTY! THIS IS PETE! WAIT! DON'T HANG UP! BETTY!!
*SEE SPIDER-MAN #17... EDITOR.
THE NERVE OF HIM! CALLING ME AS THOUGH NOTHING HAD HAPPENED!
WAS THAT PETER PARKER? I FEEL SO GOOD THESE DAYS I EVEN LIKE HIM! WHERE'S HE BEEN KEEPING HIMSELF LATELY?
HIS AUNT IS ILL... SHE HAD A SERIOUS OPERATION, AND HE'S HAD TO LOOK AFTER HER!
REALLY?? WELL, NEVER LET IT BE SAID THAT BIG-HEARTED J. JONAH JAMESON DOESN'T LOOK AFTER THE PEOPLE WHO WORK FOR HIM! LET'S DO SOMETHING GENEROUS FOR THEM... SEND HER A GET-WELL CARD!
...BUT DON'T SEAL THE ENVELOPE! YOU CAN SEND IT FOR A PENNY CHEAPER THAT WAY!
SAY! YOU'RE NOT STILL MAD AT PARKER, ARE YOU? YOU SHOULD LEARN TO FORGIVE AND FORGET... LIKE I DO!!
SINCE SPIDER-MAN'S DEFEAT, OLD JAMESON HAS BEEN THE HAPPIEST GUY IN TOWN!
THE OLD HYPOCRITE! I LIKED HIM BETTER THE WAY HE WAS!
HOW ARE YOU, MY LOYAL EMPLOYEES? REMEMBER, IF YOU NEED ANY ADVICE, OR ANY HELP, YOU'RE ALWAYS WELCOME TO ASK YOUR TENDER-HEARTED EMPLOYER!
I WISH HE'D BECOME HIS GROUCHY OLD SELF AGAIN! AT LEAST WE UNDERSTOOD HIM THAT WAY!
FIRST TIME I EVER SAW HIM SMILE! IT'S A SICKENING SIGHT!
I ALMOST WISH SPIDER-MAN WOULD REDEEM HIMSELF, OR SOMETHING! OTHERWISE, JAMESON'S LIABLE TO CRACK HIS FACE WIDE OPEN WITH THAT PHONY SMILE OF HIS!
HE REMINDS ME OF A TIGER WHO'S JUST MADE A KILL!
7

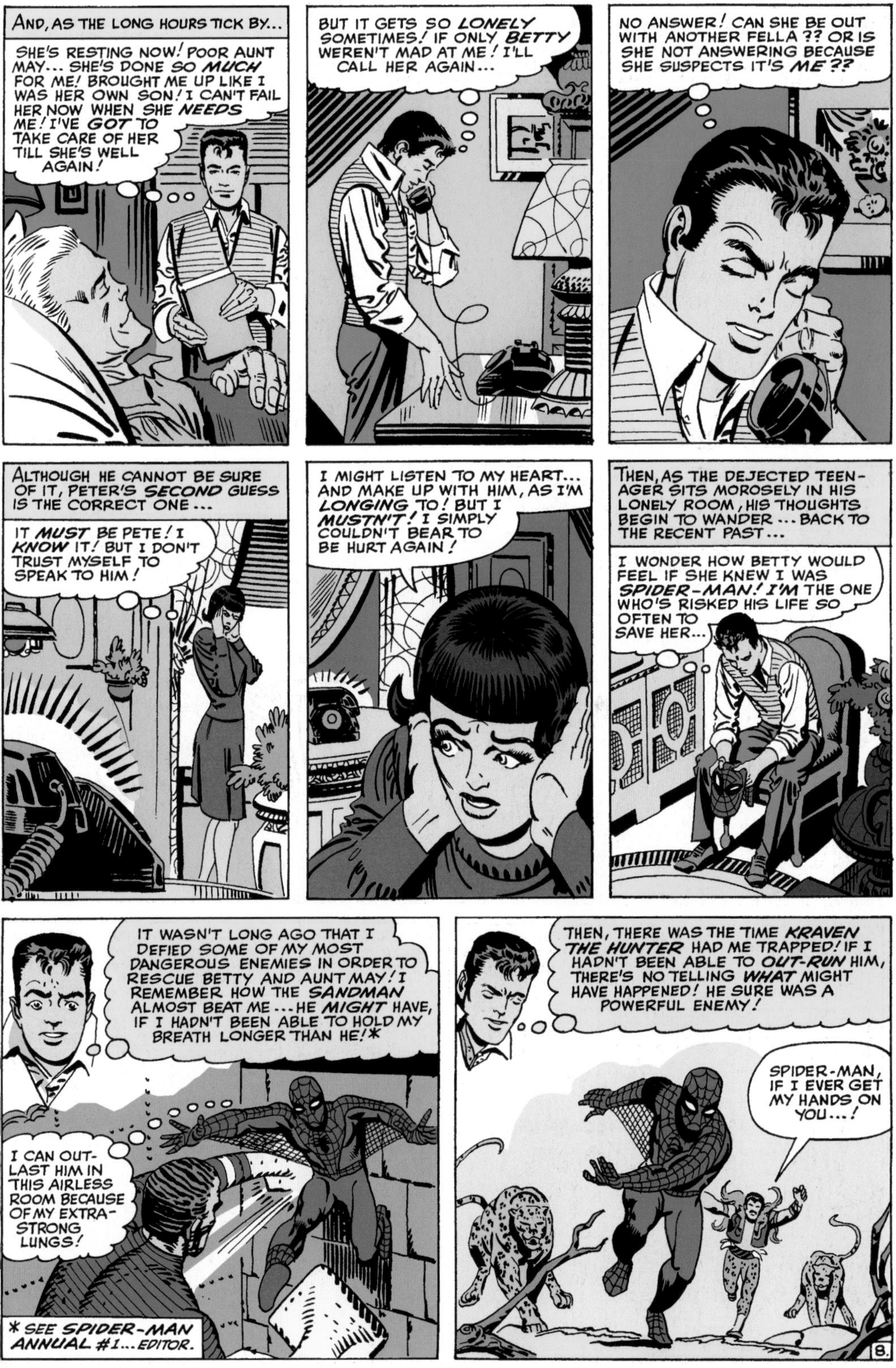

AND, AS THE LONG HOURS TICK BY...
SHE'S RESTING NOW! POOR AUNT MAY... SHE'S DONE SO MUCH FOR ME! BROUGHT ME UP LIKE I WAS HER OWN SON! I CAN'T FAIL HER NOW WHEN SHE NEEDS ME! I'VE GOT TO TAKE CARE OF HER TILL SHE'S WELL AGAIN!
BUT IT GETS SO LONELY SOMETIMES! IF ONLY BETTY WEREN'T MAD AT ME! I'LL CALL HER AGAIN...
NO ANSWER! CAN SHE BE OUT WITH ANOTHER FELLA ?? OR IS SHE NOT ANSWERING BECAUSE SHE SUSPECTS IT'S ME ??
ALTHOUGH HE CANNOT BE SURE OF IT, PETER'S SECOND GUESS IS THE CORRECT ONE...
IT MUST BE PETE! I KNOW IT! BUT I DON'T TRUST MYSELF TO SPEAK TO HIM!
I MIGHT LISTEN TO MY HEART... AND MAKE UP WITH HIM, AS I'M LONGING TO! BUT I MUSTN'T! I SIMPLY COULDN'T BEAR TO BE HURT AGAIN!
THEN, AS THE DEJECTED TEEN-AGER SITS MOROSELY IN HIS LONELY ROOM, HIS THOUGHTS BEGIN TO WANDER... BACK TO THE RECENT PAST...
I WONDER HOW BETTY WOULD FEEL IF SHE KNEW I WAS SPIDER-MAN! I'M THE ONE WHO'S RISKED HIS LIFE SO OFTEN TO SAVE HER...
IT WASN'T LONG AGO THAT I DEFIED SOME OF MY MOST DANGEROUS ENEMIES IN ORDER TO RESCUE BETTY AND AUNT MAY! I REMEMBER HOW THE SANDMAN ALMOST BEAT ME... HE MIGHT HAVE, IF I HADN'T BEEN ABLE TO HOLD MY BREATH LONGER THAN HE!*
I CAN OUT-LAST HIM IN THIS AIRLESS ROOM BECAUSE OF MY EXTRA-STRONG LUNGS!
* SEE SPIDER-MAN ANNUAL #1... EDITOR.
THEN, THERE WAS THE TIME KRAVEN THE HUNTER HAD ME TRAPPED! IF I HADN'T BEEN ABLE TO OUT-RUN HIM, THERE'S NO TELLING WHAT MIGHT HAVE HAPPENED! HE SURE WAS A POWERFUL ENEMY!
SPIDER-MAN, IF I EVER GET MY HANDS ON YOU...!
8.

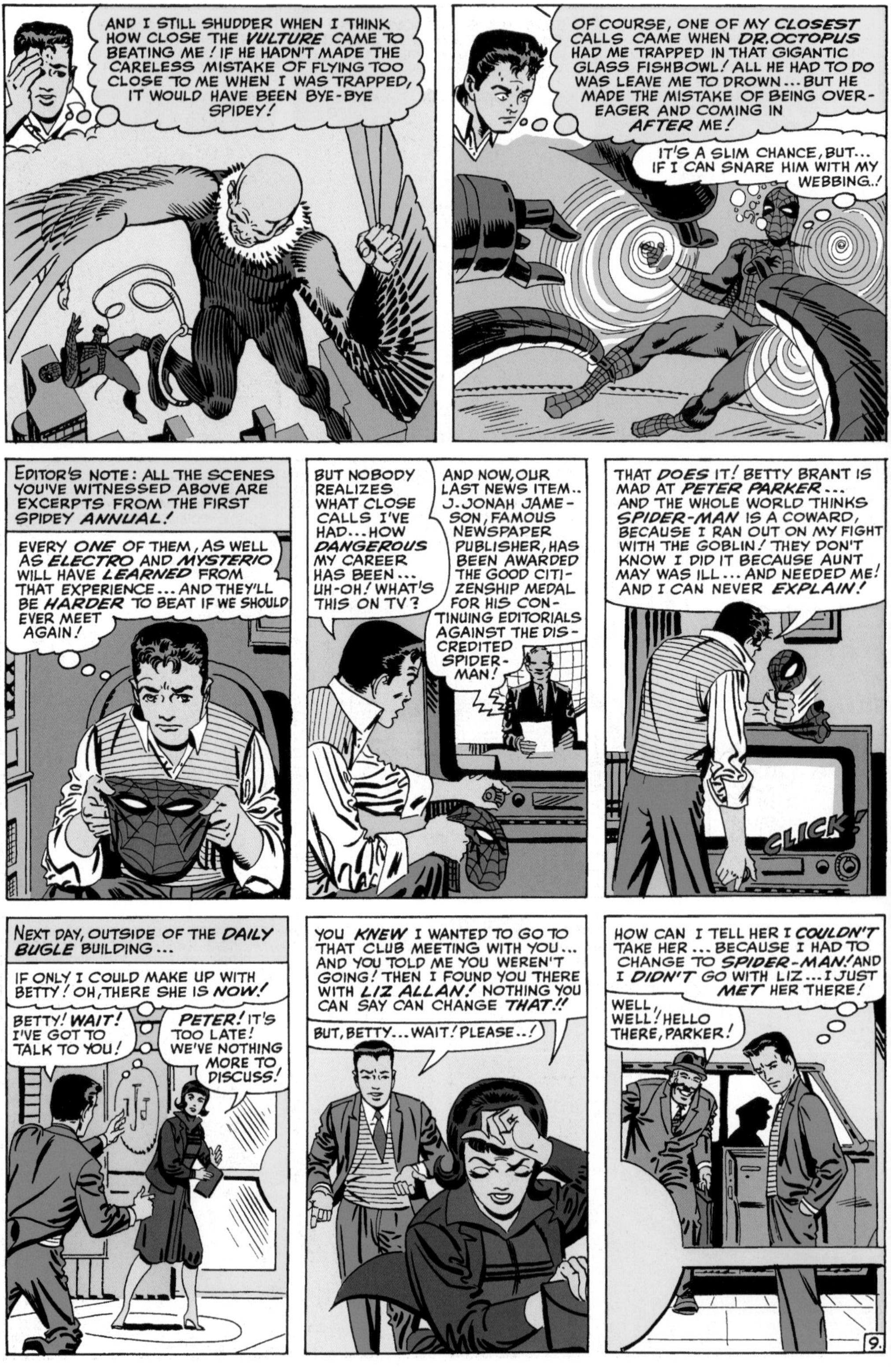
AND I STILL SHUDDER WHEN I THINK HOW CLOSE THE VULTURE CAME TO BEATING ME! IF HE HADN'T MADE THE CARELESS MISTAKE OF FLYING TOO CLOSE TO ME WHEN I WAS TRAPPED, IT WOULD HAVE BEEN BYE-BYE SPIDEY!
OF COURSE, ONE OF MY CLOSEST CALLS CAME WHEN DR. OCTOPUS HAD ME TRAPPED IN THAT GIGANTIC GLASS FISHBOWL! ALL HE HAD TO DO WAS LEAVE ME TO DROWN... BUT HE MADE THE MISTAKE OF BEING OVER-EAGER AND COMING IN AFTER ME!
IT'S A SLIM CHANCE, BUT... IF I CAN SNARE HIM WITH MY WEBBING..!
EDITOR'S NOTE: ALL THE SCENES YOU'VE WITNESSED ABOVE ARE EXCERPTS FROM THE FIRST SPIDEY ANNUAL!
EVERY ONE OF THEM, AS WELL AS ELECTRO AND MYSTERIO WILL HAVE LEARNED FROM THAT EXPERIENCE... AND THEY'LL BE HARDER TO BEAT IF WE SHOULD EVER MEET AGAIN!
BUT NOBODY REALIZES WHAT CLOSE CALLS I'VE HAD... HOW DANGEROUS MY CAREER HAS BEEN... UH-OH! WHAT'S THIS ON TV?
AND NOW, OUR LAST NEWS ITEM.. J. JONAH JAME-SON, FAMOUS NEWSPAPER PUBLISHER, HAS BEEN AWARDED THE GOOD CITI-ZENSHIP MEDAL FOR HIS CON-TINUING EDITORIALS AGAINST THE DIS-CREDITED SPIDER-MAN!
THAT DOES IT! BETTY BRANT IS MAD AT PETER PARKER... AND THE WHOLE WORLD THINKS SPIDER-MAN IS A COWARD, BECAUSE I RAN OUT ON MY FIGHT WITH THE GOBLIN! THEY DON'T KNOW I DID IT BECAUSE AUNT MAY WAS ILL... AND NEEDED ME! AND I CAN NEVER EXPLAIN!
CLICK!
NEXT DAY, OUTSIDE OF THE DAILY BUGLE BUILDING...
IF ONLY I COULD MAKE UP WITH BETTY! OH, THERE SHE IS NOW!
BETTY! WAIT! I'VE GOT TO TALK TO YOU!
PETER! IT'S TOO LATE! WE'VE NOTHING MORE TO DISCUSS!
YOU KNEW I WANTED TO GO TO THAT CLUB MEETING WITH YOU... AND YOU TOLD ME YOU WEREN'T GOING! THEN I FOUND YOU THERE WITH LIZ ALLAN! NOTHING YOU CAN SAY CAN CHANGE THAT!!
BUT, BETTY... WAIT! PLEASE..!
HOW CAN I TELL HER I COULDN'T TAKE HER... BECAUSE I HAD TO CHANGE TO SPIDER-MAN! AND I DIDN'T GO WITH LIZ... I JUST MET HER THERE!
WELL, WELL! HELLO THERE, PARKER!
9.

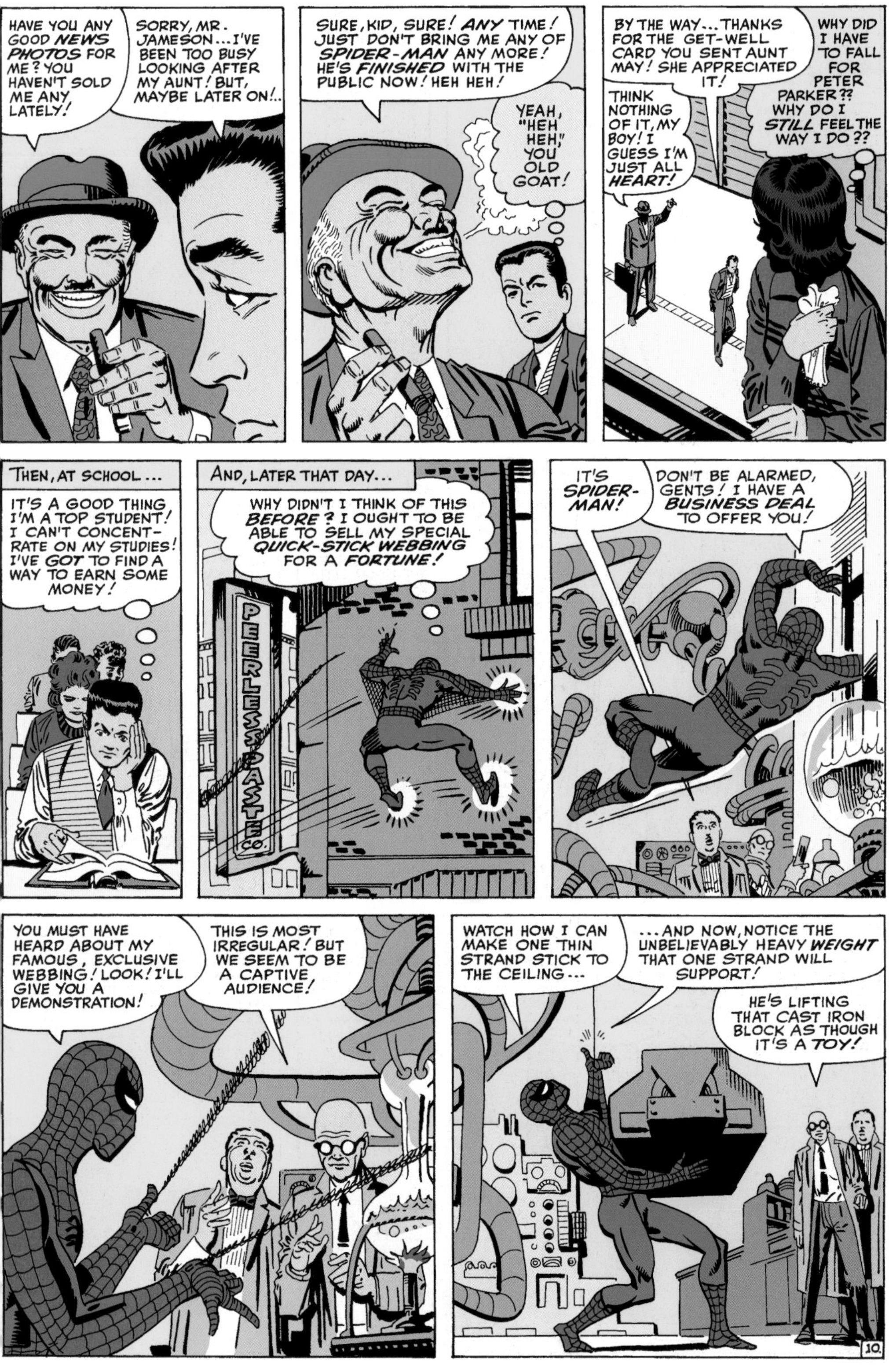
HAVE YOU ANY GOOD NEWS PHOTOS FOR ME? YOU HAVEN'T SOLD ME ANY, LATELY!
SORRY, MR. JAMESON...I'VE BEEN TOO BUSY LOOKING AFTER MY AUNT! BUT, MAYBE LATER ON!..
SURE, KID, SURE! ANY TIME! JUST DON'T BRING ME ANY OF SPIDER-MAN ANY MORE! HE'S FINISHED WITH THE PUBLIC NOW! HEH HEH!
YEAH, "HEH HEH," YOU OLD GOAT!
BY THE WAY...THANKS FOR THE GET-WELL CARD YOU SENT AUNT MAY! SHE APPRECIATED IT!
THINK NOTHING OF IT, MY BOY! I GUESS I'M JUST ALL HEART!
WHY DID I HAVE TO FALL FOR PETER PARKER?? WHY DO I STILL FEEL THE WAY I DO??
THEN, AT SCHOOL...
IT'S A GOOD THING I'M A TOP STUDENT! I CAN'T CONCENTRATE ON MY STUDIES! I'VE GOT TO FIND A WAY TO EARN SOME MONEY!
AND, LATER THAT DAY...
WHY DIDN'T I THINK OF THIS BEFORE? I OUGHT TO BE ABLE TO SELL MY SPECIAL QUICK-STICK WEBBING FOR A FORTUNE!
PEERLESS PASTE CO.
IT'S SPIDER-MAN!
DON'T BE ALARMED, GENTS! I HAVE A BUSINESS DEAL TO OFFER YOU!
YOU MUST HAVE HEARD ABOUT MY FAMOUS, EXCLUSIVE WEBBING! LOOK! I'LL GIVE YOU A DEMONSTRATION!
THIS IS MOST IRREGULAR! BUT WE SEEM TO BE A CAPTIVE AUDIENCE!
WATCH HOW I CAN MAKE ONE THIN STRAND STICK TO THE CEILING...
...AND NOW, NOTICE THE UNBELIEVABLY HEAVY WEIGHT THAT ONE STRAND WILL SUPPORT!
HE'S LIFTING THAT CAST IRON BLOCK AS THOUGH IT'S A TOY!
10.

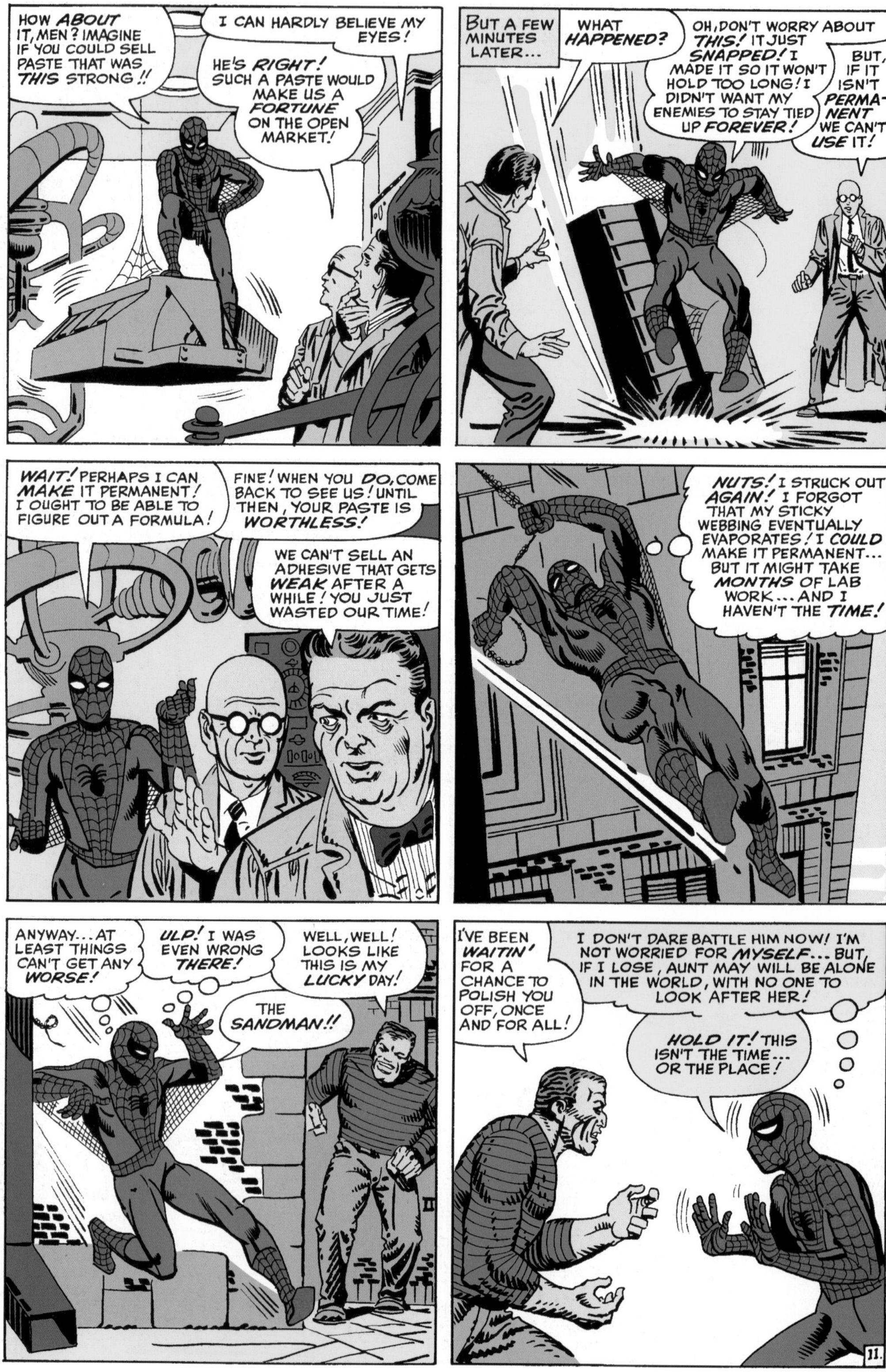
HOW ABOUT IT, MEN? IMAGINE IF YOU COULD SELL PASTE THAT WAS THIS STRONG!!
I CAN HARDLY BELIEVE MY EYES!
HE'S RIGHT! SUCH A PASTE WOULD MAKE US A FORTUNE ON THE OPEN MARKET!
BUT A FEW MINUTES LATER...
WHAT HAPPENED?
OH, DON'T WORRY ABOUT THIS! IT JUST SNAPPED! I MADE IT SO IT WON'T HOLD TOO LONG! I DIDN'T WANT MY ENEMIES TO STAY TIED UP FOREVER!
BUT, IF IT ISN'T PERMANENT WE CAN'T USE IT!
WAIT! PERHAPS I CAN MAKE IT PERMANENT! I OUGHT TO BE ABLE TO FIGURE OUT A FORMULA!
FINE! WHEN YOU DO, COME BACK TO SEE US! UNTIL THEN, YOUR PASTE IS WORTHLESS!
WE CAN'T SELL AN ADHESIVE THAT GETS WEAK AFTER A WHILE! YOU JUST WASTED OUR TIME!
NUTS! I STRUCK OUT AGAIN! I FORGOT THAT MY STICKY WEBBING EVENTUALLY EVAPORATES! I COULD MAKE IT PERMANENT... BUT IT MIGHT TAKE MONTHS OF LAB WORK... AND I HAVEN'T THE TIME!
ANYWAY... AT LEAST THINGS CAN'T GET ANY WORSE!
ULP! I WAS EVEN WRONG THERE!
WELL, WELL! LOOKS LIKE THIS IS MY LUCKY DAY!
THE SANDMAN!!
I'VE BEEN WAITIN' FOR A CHANCE TO POLISH YOU OFF, ONCE AND FOR ALL!
I DON'T DARE BATTLE HIM NOW! I'M NOT WORRIED FOR MYSELF... BUT, IF I LOSE, AUNT MAY WILL BE ALONE IN THE WORLD, WITH NO ONE TO LOOK AFTER HER!
HOLD IT! THIS ISN'T THE TIME... OR THE PLACE!
11.

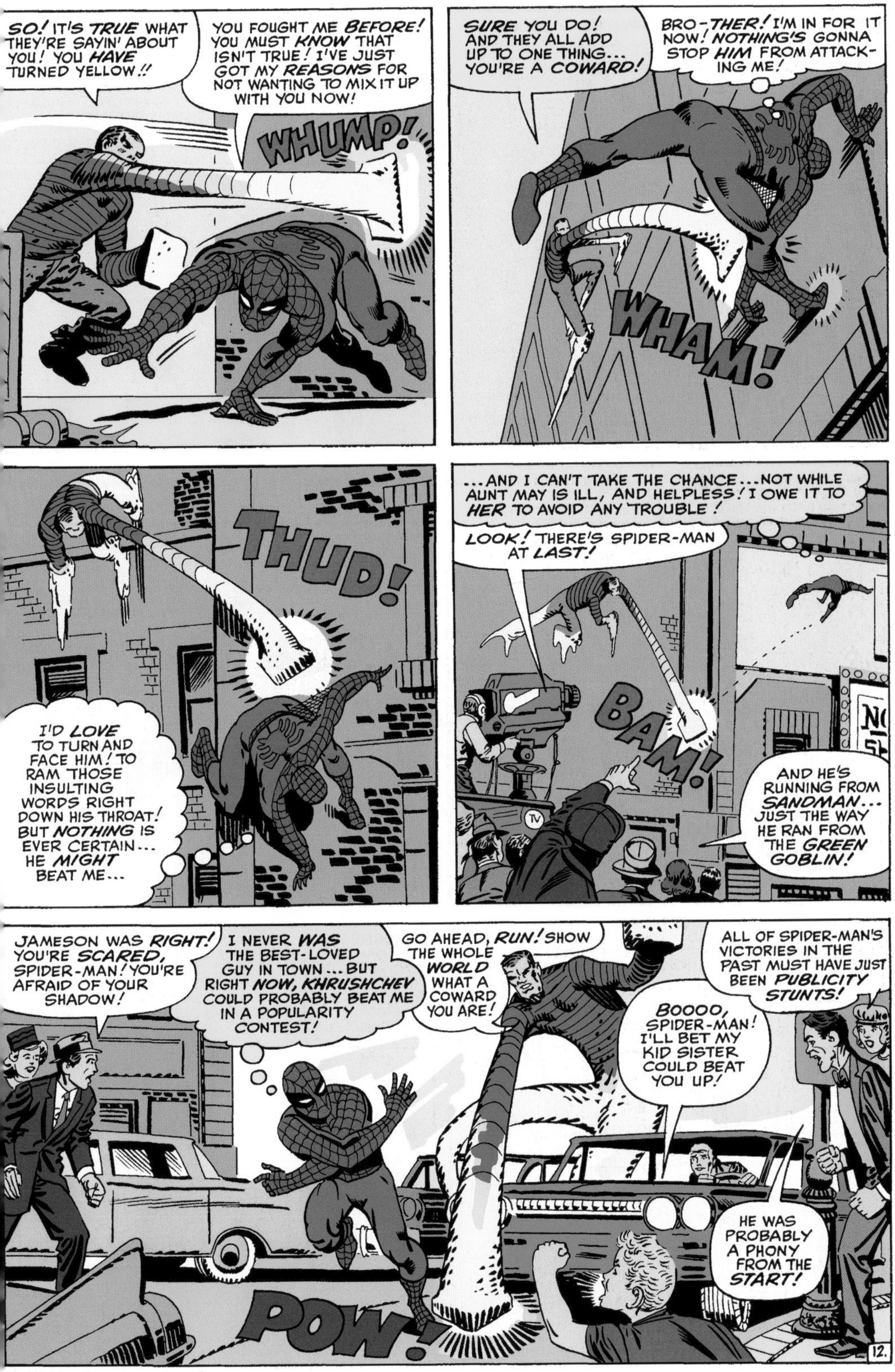
SO! IT'S TRUE WHAT THEY'RE SAYIN' ABOUT YOU! YOU HAVE TURNED YELLOW!!
YOU FOUGHT ME BEFORE! YOU MUST KNOW THAT ISN'T TRUE! I'VE JUST GOT MY REASONS FOR NOT WANTING TO MIX IT UP WITH YOU NOW!
WHUMP!
SURE YOU DO! AND THEY ALL ADD UP TO ONE THING... YOU'RE A COWARD!
BRO-THER! I'M IN FOR IT NOW! NOTHING'S GONNA STOP HIM FROM ATTACKING ME!
WHAM!
THUD!
I'D LOVE TO TURN AND FACE HIM! TO RAM THOSE INSULTING WORDS RIGHT DOWN HIS THROAT! BUT NOTHING IS EVER CERTAIN... HE MIGHT BEAT ME...
...AND I CAN'T TAKE THE CHANCE...NOT WHILE AUNT MAY IS ILL, AND HELPLESS! I OWE IT TO HER TO AVOID ANY TROUBLE!
LOOK! THERE'S SPIDER-MAN AT LAST!
BAM!
TV
AND HE'S RUNNING FROM SANDMAN... JUST THE WAY HE RAN FROM THE GREEN GOBLIN!
JAMESON WAS RIGHT! YOU'RE SCARED, SPIDER-MAN! YOU'RE AFRAID OF YOUR SHADOW!
I NEVER WAS THE BEST-LOVED GUY IN TOWN... BUT RIGHT NOW, KHRUSHCHEV COULD PROBABLY BEAT ME IN A POPULARITY CONTEST!
GO AHEAD, RUN! SHOW THE WHOLE WORLD WHAT A COWARD YOU ARE!
ALL OF SPIDER-MAN'S VICTORIES IN THE PAST MUST HAVE JUST BEEN PUBLICITY STUNTS!
BOOOO, SPIDER-MAN! I'LL BET MY KID SISTER COULD BEAT YOU UP!
HE WAS PROBABLY A PHONY FROM THE START!
POW!
12.

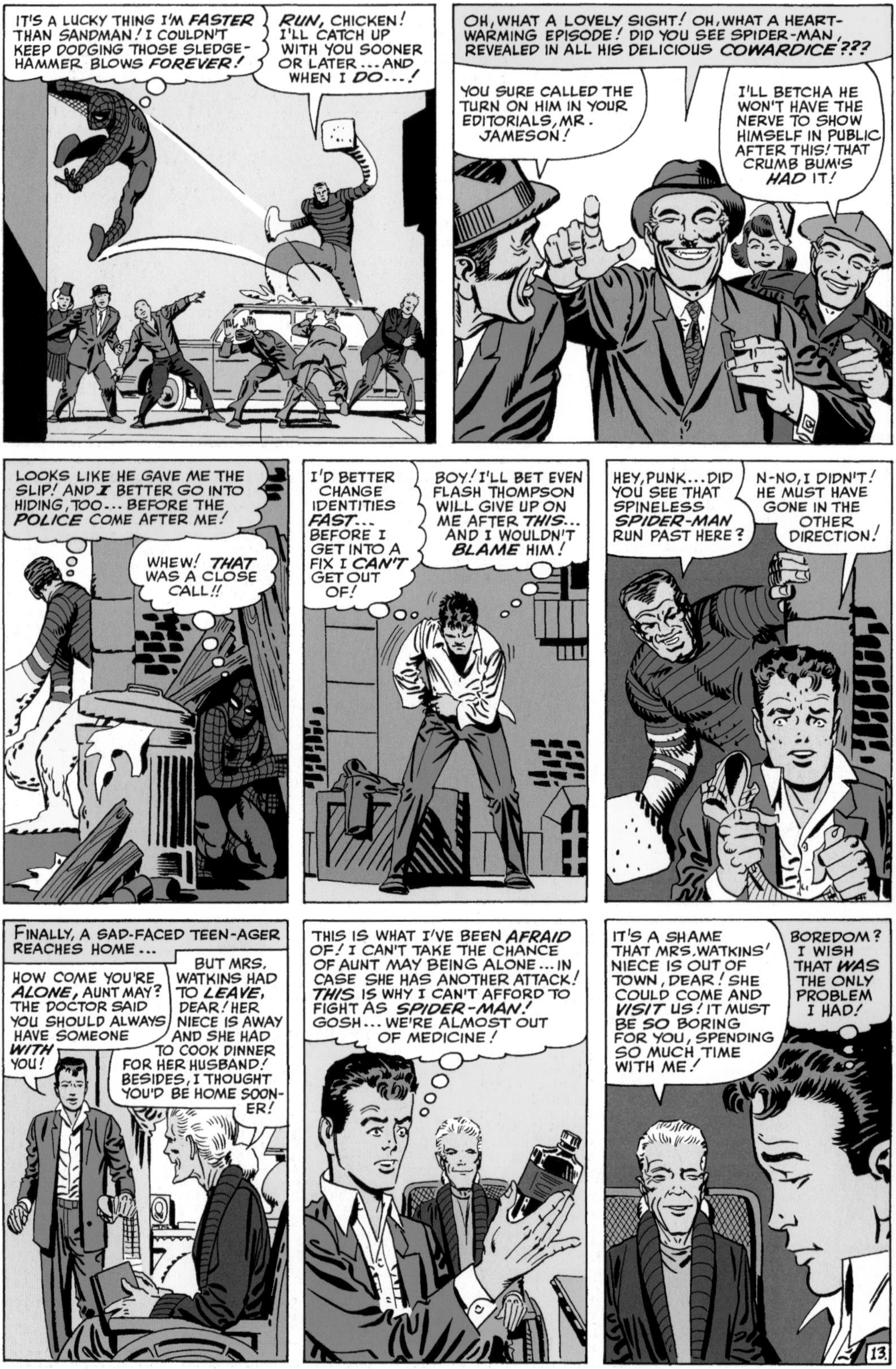

IT'S A LUCKY THING I'M FASTER THAN SANDMAN! I COULDN'T KEEP DODGING THOSE SLEDGE-HAMMER BLOWS FOREVER!
RUN, CHICKEN! I'LL CATCH UP WITH YOU SOONER OR LATER... AND WHEN I DO...!
OH, WHAT A LOVELY SIGHT! OH, WHAT A HEART-WARMING EPISODE! DID YOU SEE SPIDER-MAN, REVEALED IN ALL HIS DELICIOUS COWARDICE???
YOU SURE CALLED THE TURN ON HIM IN YOUR EDITORIALS, MR. JAMESON!
I'LL BETCHA HE WON'T HAVE THE NERVE TO SHOW HIMSELF IN PUBLIC AFTER THIS! THAT CRUMB BUM'S HAD IT!
LOOKS LIKE HE GAVE ME THE SLIP! AND I BETTER GO INTO HIDING, TOO... BEFORE THE POLICE COME AFTER ME!
WHEW! THAT WAS A CLOSE CALL!!
I'D BETTER CHANGE IDENTITIES FAST... BEFORE I GET INTO A FIX I CAN'T GET OUT OF!
BOY! I'LL BET EVEN FLASH THOMPSON WILL GIVE UP ON ME AFTER THIS... AND I WOULDN'T BLAME HIM!
HEY, PUNK... DID YOU SEE THAT SPINELESS SPIDER-MAN RUN PAST HERE?
N-NO, I DIDN'T! HE MUST HAVE GONE IN THE OTHER DIRECTION!
FINALLY, A SAD-FACED TEEN-AGER REACHES HOME...
HOW COME YOU'RE ALONE, AUNT MAY? THE DOCTOR SAID YOU SHOULD ALWAYS HAVE SOMEONE WITH YOU!
BUT MRS. WATKINS HAD TO LEAVE, DEAR! HER NIECE IS AWAY AND SHE HAD TO COOK DINNER FOR HER HUSBAND! BESIDES, I THOUGHT YOU'D BE HOME SOONER!
THIS IS WHAT I'VE BEEN AFRAID OF! I CAN'T TAKE THE CHANCE OF AUNT MAY BEING ALONE... IN CASE SHE HAS ANOTHER ATTACK! THIS IS WHY I CAN'T AFFORD TO FIGHT AS SPIDER-MAN! GOSH... WE'RE ALMOST OUT OF MEDICINE!
IT'S A SHAME THAT MRS. WATKINS' NIECE IS OUT OF TOWN, DEAR! SHE COULD COME AND VISIT US! IT MUST BE SO BORING FOR YOU, SPENDING SO MUCH TIME WITH ME!
BOREDOM? I WISH THAT WAS THE ONLY PROBLEM I HAD!
13.

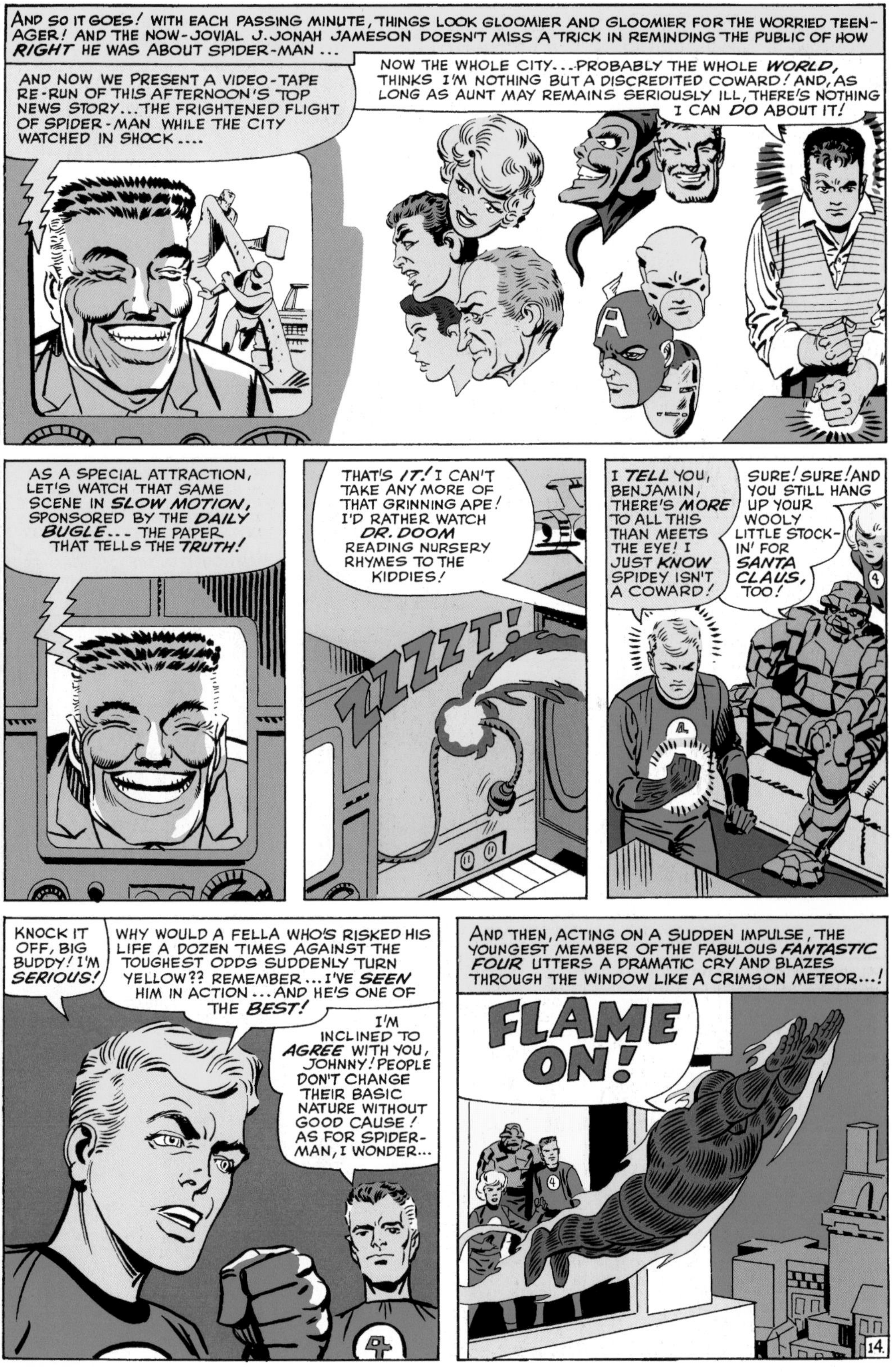
AND SO IT GOES! WITH EACH PASSING MINUTE, THINGS LOOK GLOOMIER AND GLOOMIER FOR THE WORRIED TEEN-AGER! AND THE NOW-JOVIAL J. JONAH JAMESON DOESN'T MISS A TRICK IN REMINDING THE PUBLIC OF HOW RIGHT HE WAS ABOUT SPIDER-MAN ...
AND NOW WE PRESENT A VIDEO-TAPE RE-RUN OF THIS AFTERNOON'S TOP NEWS STORY... THE FRIGHTENED FLIGHT OF SPIDER-MAN WHILE THE CITY WATCHED IN SHOCK....
NOW THE WHOLE CITY...PROBABLY THE WHOLE WORLD, THINKS I'M NOTHING BUT A DISCREDITED COWARD! AND, AS LONG AS AUNT MAY REMAINS SERIOUSLY ILL, THERE'S NOTHING I CAN DO ABOUT IT!
AS A SPECIAL ATTRACTION, LET'S WATCH THAT SAME SCENE IN SLOW MOTION, SPONSORED BY THE DAILY BUGLE... THE PAPER THAT TELLS THE TRUTH!
THAT'S IT! I CAN'T TAKE ANY MORE OF THAT GRINNING APE! I'D RATHER WATCH DR. DOOM READING NURSERY RHYMES TO THE KIDDIES!
ZZZZZT!
I TELL YOU, BENJAMIN, THERE'S MORE TO ALL THIS THAN MEETS THE EYE! I JUST KNOW SPIDEY ISN'T A COWARD!
SURE! SURE! AND YOU STILL HANG UP YOUR WOOLY LITTLE STOCK-IN' FOR SANTA CLAUS, TOO!
KNOCK IT OFF, BIG BUDDY! I'M SERIOUS!
WHY WOULD A FELLA WHO'S RISKED HIS LIFE A DOZEN TIMES AGAINST THE TOUGHEST ODDS SUDDENLY TURN YELLOW?? REMEMBER... I'VE SEEN HIM IN ACTION... AND HE'S ONE OF THE BEST!
I'M INCLINED TO AGREE WITH YOU, JOHNNY! PEOPLE DON'T CHANGE THEIR BASIC NATURE WITHOUT GOOD CAUSE! AS FOR SPIDER-MAN, I WONDER...
AND THEN, ACTING ON A SUDDEN IMPULSE, THE YOUNGEST MEMBER OF THE FABULOUS FANTASTIC FOUR UTTERS A DRAMATIC CRY AND BLAZES THROUGH THE WINDOW LIKE A CRIMSON METEOR...!
FLAME ON!
14.

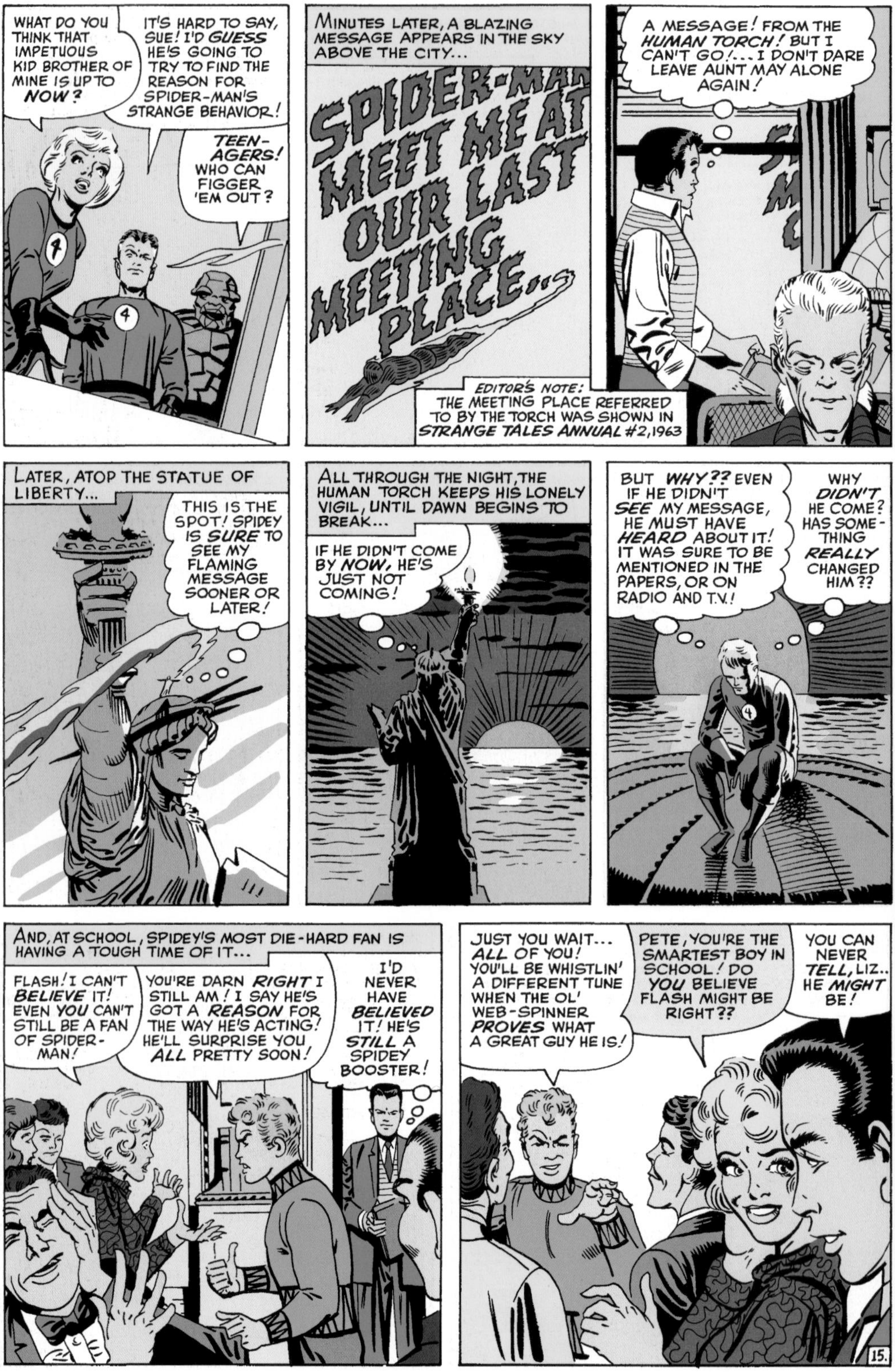

WHAT DO YOU THINK THAT IMPETUOUS KID BROTHER OF MINE IS UP TO NOW?
IT'S HARD TO SAY, SUE! I'D GUESS HE'S GOING TO TRY TO FIND THE REASON FOR SPIDER-MAN'S STRANGE BEHAVIOR!
TEEN-AGERS! WHO CAN FIGGER 'EM OUT?
MINUTES LATER, A BLAZING MESSAGE APPEARS IN THE SKY ABOVE THE CITY...
SPIDER-MAN MEET ME AT OUR LAST MEETING PLACE...
EDITOR'S NOTE: THE MEETING PLACE REFERRED TO BY THE TORCH WAS SHOWN IN STRANGE TALES ANNUAL #2, 1963
A MESSAGE! FROM THE HUMAN TORCH! BUT I CAN'T GO!... I DON'T DARE LEAVE AUNT MAY ALONE AGAIN!
LATER, ATOP THE STATUE OF LIBERTY...
THIS IS THE SPOT! SPIDEY IS SURE TO SEE MY FLAMING MESSAGE SOONER OR LATER!
ALL THROUGH THE NIGHT, THE HUMAN TORCH KEEPS HIS LONELY VIGIL, UNTIL DAWN BEGINS TO BREAK...
IF HE DIDN'T COME BY NOW, HE'S JUST NOT COMING!
BUT WHY?? EVEN IF HE DIDN'T SEE MY MESSAGE, HE MUST HAVE HEARD ABOUT IT! IT WAS SURE TO BE MENTIONED IN THE PAPERS, OR ON RADIO AND T.V.!
WHY DIDN'T HE COME? HAS SOME-THING REALLY CHANGED HIM??
AND, AT SCHOOL, SPIDEY'S MOST DIE-HARD FAN IS HAVING A TOUGH TIME OF IT...
FLASH! I CAN'T BELIEVE IT! EVEN YOU CAN'T STILL BE A FAN OF SPIDER-MAN!
YOU'RE DARN RIGHT I STILL AM! I SAY HE'S GOT A REASON FOR THE WAY HE'S ACTING! HE'LL SURPRISE YOU ALL PRETTY SOON!
I'D NEVER HAVE BELIEVED IT! HE'S STILL A SPIDEY BOOSTER!
JUST YOU WAIT... ALL OF YOU! YOU'LL BE WHISTLIN' A DIFFERENT TUNE WHEN THE OL' WEB-SPINNER PROVES WHAT A GREAT GUY HE IS!
PETE, YOU'RE THE SMARTEST BOY IN SCHOOL! DO YOU BELIEVE FLASH MIGHT BE RIGHT??
YOU CAN NEVER TELL, LIZ.. HE MIGHT BE!
15.

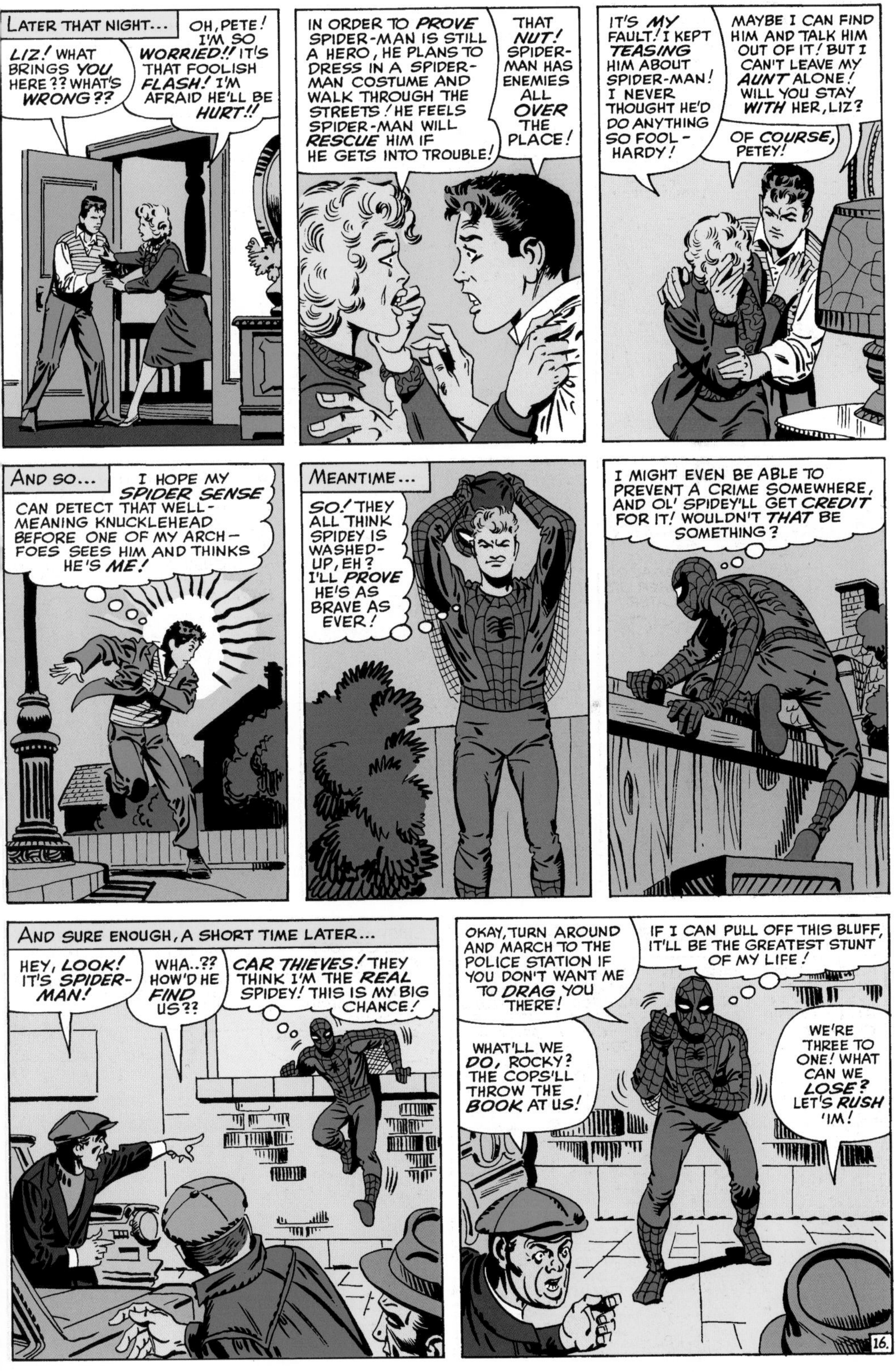
LATER THAT NIGHT...
LIZ! WHAT BRINGS YOU HERE?? WHAT'S WRONG??
OH, PETE! I'M SO WORRIED!! IT'S THAT FOOLISH FLASH! I'M AFRAID HE'LL BE HURT!!
IN ORDER TO PROVE SPIDER-MAN IS STILL A HERO, HE PLANS TO DRESS IN A SPIDER-MAN COSTUME AND WALK THROUGH THE STREETS! HE FEELS SPIDER-MAN WILL RESCUE HIM IF HE GETS INTO TROUBLE!
THAT NUT! SPIDER-MAN HAS ENEMIES ALL OVER THE PLACE!
IT'S MY FAULT! I KEPT TEASING HIM ABOUT SPIDER-MAN! I NEVER THOUGHT HE'D DO ANYTHING SO FOOL-HARDY!
MAYBE I CAN FIND HIM AND TALK HIM OUT OF IT! BUT I CAN'T LEAVE MY AUNT ALONE! WILL YOU STAY WITH HER, LIZ?
OF COURSE, PETEY!
AND SO...
I HOPE MY SPIDER SENSE CAN DETECT THAT WELL-MEANING KNUCKLEHEAD BEFORE ONE OF MY ARCH-FOES SEES HIM AND THINKS HE'S ME!
MEANTIME...
SO! THEY ALL THINK SPIDEY IS WASHED-UP, EH? I'LL PROVE HE'S AS BRAVE AS EVER!
I MIGHT EVEN BE ABLE TO PREVENT A CRIME SOMEWHERE, AND OL' SPIDEY'LL GET CREDIT FOR IT! WOULDN'T THAT BE SOMETHING?
AND SURE ENOUGH, A SHORT TIME LATER...
HEY, LOOK! IT'S SPIDER-MAN!
WHA..?? HOW'D HE FIND US??
CAR THIEVES! THEY THINK I'M THE REAL SPIDEY! THIS IS MY BIG CHANCE!
OKAY, TURN AROUND AND MARCH TO THE POLICE STATION IF YOU DON'T WANT ME TO DRAG YOU THERE!
IF I CAN PULL OFF THIS BLUFF, IT'LL BE THE GREATEST STUNT OF MY LIFE!
WHAT'LL WE DO, ROCKY? THE COPS'LL THROW THE BOOK AT US!
WE'RE THREE TO ONE! WHAT CAN WE LOSE? LET'S RUSH 'IM!
16.

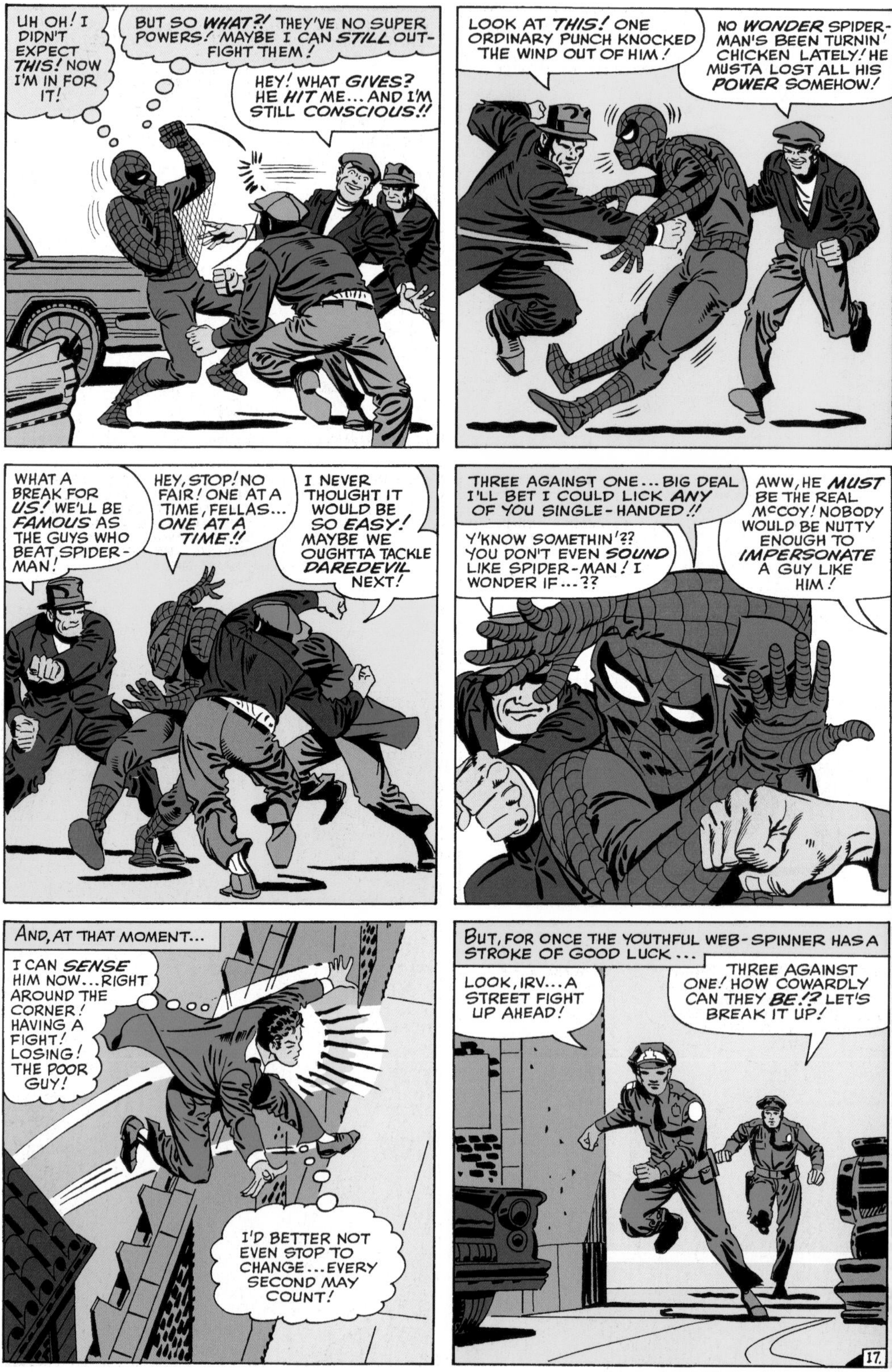
UH OH! I DIDN'T EXPECT THIS! NOW I'M IN FOR IT!
BUT SO WHAT?! THEY'VE NO SUPER POWERS! MAYBE I CAN STILL OUT-FIGHT THEM!
HEY! WHAT GIVES? HE HIT ME... AND I'M STILL CONSCIOUS!!
LOOK AT THIS! ONE ORDINARY PUNCH KNOCKED THE WIND OUT OF HIM!
NO WONDER SPIDER-MAN'S BEEN TURNIN' CHICKEN LATELY! HE MUSTA LOST ALL HIS POWER SOMEHOW!
WHAT A BREAK FOR US! WE'LL BE FAMOUS AS THE GUYS WHO BEAT SPIDER-MAN!
HEY, STOP! NO FAIR! ONE AT A TIME, FELLAS... ONE AT A TIME!!
I NEVER THOUGHT IT WOULD BE SO EASY! MAYBE WE OUGHTTA TACKLE DAREDEVIL NEXT!
THREE AGAINST ONE... BIG DEAL I'LL BET I COULD LICK ANY OF YOU SINGLE-HANDED!!
Y'KNOW SOMETHIN'?? YOU DON'T EVEN SOUND LIKE SPIDER-MAN! I WONDER IF...??
AWW, HE MUST BE THE REAL McCOY! NOBODY WOULD BE NUTTY ENOUGH TO IMPERSONATE A GUY LIKE HIM!
AND, AT THAT MOMENT...
I CAN SENSE HIM NOW... RIGHT AROUND THE CORNER! HAVING A FIGHT! LOSING! THE POOR GUY!
I'D BETTER NOT EVEN STOP TO CHANGE... EVERY SECOND MAY COUNT!
BUT, FOR ONCE THE YOUTHFUL WEB-SPINNER HAS A STROKE OF GOOD LUCK...
LOOK, IRV... A STREET FIGHT UP AHEAD!
THREE AGAINST ONE! HOW COWARDLY CAN THEY BE!? LET'S BREAK IT UP!
17.

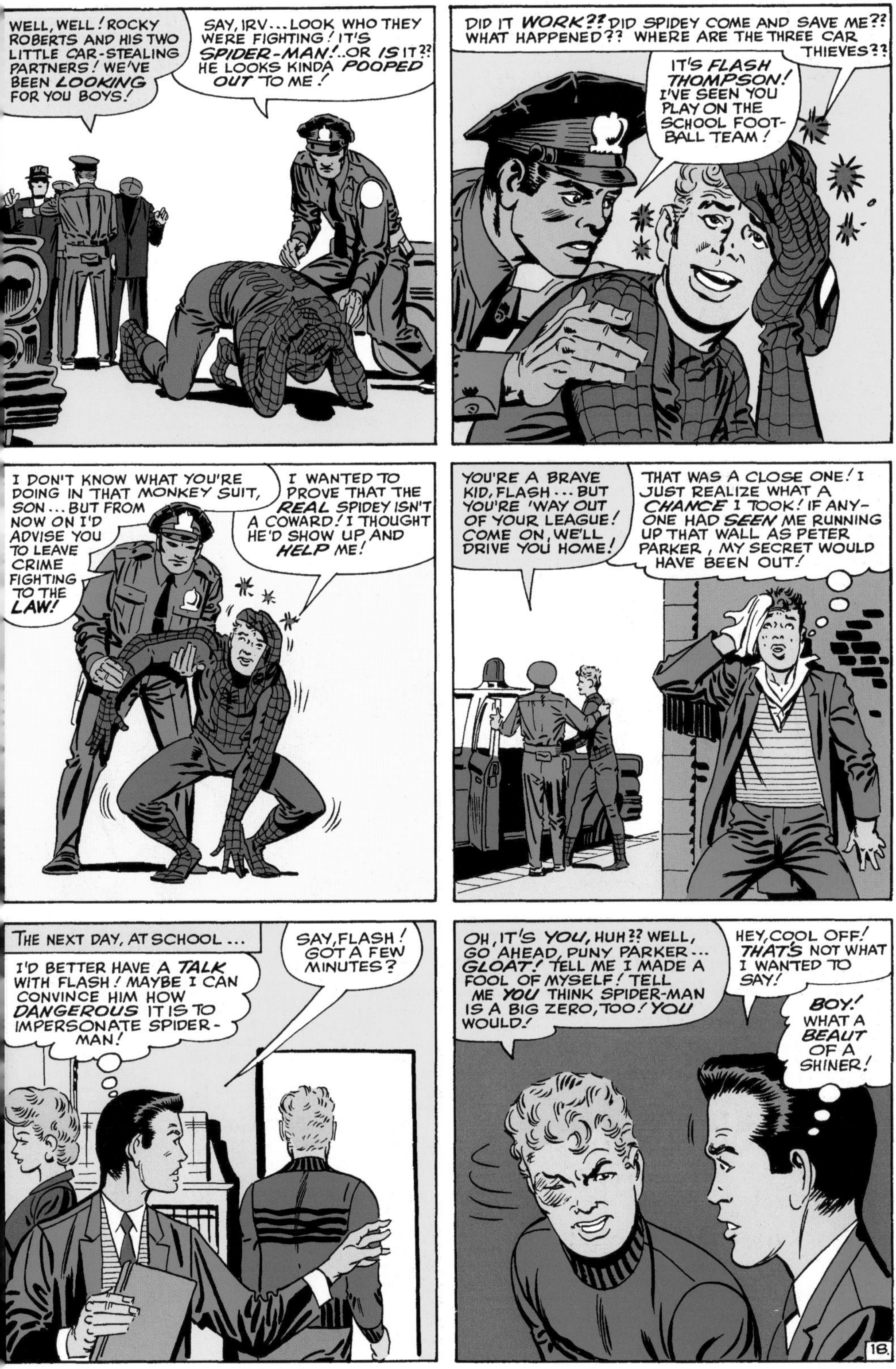

WELL, WELL! ROCKY ROBERTS AND HIS TWO LITTLE CAR-STEALING PARTNERS! WE'VE BEEN LOOKING FOR YOU BOYS!
SAY, IRV... LOOK WHO THEY WERE FIGHTING! IT'S SPIDER-MAN!..OR IS IT?? HE LOOKS KINDA POOPED OUT TO ME!
DID IT WORK?? DID SPIDEY COME AND SAVE ME?? WHAT HAPPENED?? WHERE ARE THE THREE CAR THIEVES??
IT'S FLASH THOMPSON! I'VE SEEN YOU PLAY ON THE SCHOOL FOOT-BALL TEAM!
I DON'T KNOW WHAT YOU'RE DOING IN THAT MONKEY SUIT, SON... BUT FROM NOW ON I'D ADVISE YOU TO LEAVE CRIME FIGHTING TO THE LAW!
I WANTED TO PROVE THAT THE REAL SPIDEY ISN'T A COWARD! I THOUGHT HE'D SHOW UP AND HELP ME!
YOU'RE A BRAVE KID, FLASH... BUT YOU'RE 'WAY OUT OF YOUR LEAGUE! COME ON, WE'LL DRIVE YOU HOME!
THAT WAS A CLOSE ONE! I JUST REALIZE WHAT A CHANCE I TOOK! IF ANY-ONE HAD SEEN ME RUNNING UP THAT WALL AS PETER PARKER, MY SECRET WOULD HAVE BEEN OUT!
THE NEXT DAY, AT SCHOOL...
I'D BETTER HAVE A TALK WITH FLASH! MAYBE I CAN CONVINCE HIM HOW DANGEROUS IT IS TO IMPERSONATE SPIDER-MAN!
SAY, FLASH! GOT A FEW MINUTES?
OH, IT'S YOU, HUH?? WELL, GO AHEAD, PUNY PARKER... GLOAT! TELL ME I MADE A FOOL OF MYSELF! TELL ME YOU THINK SPIDER-MAN IS A BIG ZERO, TOO! YOU WOULD!
HEY, COOL OFF! THAT'S NOT WHAT I WANTED TO SAY!
BOY! WHAT A BEAUT OF A SHINER!
18.

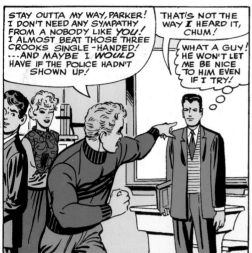

STAY OUTTA MY WAY, PARKER! I DON'T NEED ANY SYMPATHY FROM A NOBODY LIKE *YOU!* I ALMOST BEAT THOSE THREE CROOKS SINGLE-HANDED! ---AND MAYBE I *WOULD* HAVE IF THE POLICE HADN'T SHOWN UP!

THAT'S NOT THE WAY *I* HEARD IT, CHUM!

WHAT A GUY! HE WON'T LET ME BE NICE TO HIM EVEN IF I TRY!

BETTER STAY AWAY FROM FLASH FOR A WHILE, PETEY! HE'S SENSITIVE ABOUT WHAT HAPPENED! HE'S EVEN MAD AT *ME*, BECAUSE I TOLD *YOU* ABOUT IT!

DON'T WORRY ABOUT *ME*, LIZ! STAYING AWAY FROM FLASH IS THE EASIEST THING I CAN DO! I'VE HAD A LOT OF *PRACTICE!*

THINGS ARE GETTING *WORSE!* AUNT MAY WILL NEED MORE MEDICINE BY TOMORROW AND I'M STILL *BROKE!* NOBODY BUT FLASH HAS ANY USE FOR SPIDER-MAN ANY MORE! AND TO TOP IT OFF, BETTY BRANT WON'T GIVE ME A TUMBLE! WHERE DO I GO FROM *HERE?*

ARE *YOU* THE WISE-GUY WHO SAID THAT EVEN PUNY PARKER COULD LICK SPIDER-MAN? *WELL?? ARE* YOU?

N-NO, FLASH! I NEVER SAID IT! *HONEST!*

POOR FLASH! HE HASN'T BEEN RIGHT ABOUT *ANYTHING* IN YEARS!! HOW I'D LIKE TO TELL HIM THAT...*HEY!*

THERE'S BETTY...WITH ANOTHER BOY!! LOOK HOW SHE'S HOLDING HIS ARM! AND HOW *HAPPY* THEY SEEM!!

DID YOU LIKE THE MOVIE, BETTY?

OH, YES! I JUST COULDN'T STOP LAUGHING!

IT'S STILL EARLY! HOW ABOUT A SODA BEFORE I TAKE YOU HOME?

THAT'S THE BEST OFFER I'VE HAD IN WEEKS, KIND SIR!

FACE IT, BOY! YOU'VE LOST HER! HOW DID THIS ALL *HAPPEN?* EVERYTHING SEEMS TO BE TUMBLING DOWN AROUND MY EARS!

ALL MY PROBLEMS...ALL MY TOUGH BREAKS..ARE DUE TO BEING *SPIDER-MAN!!* IF I WERE JUST AN ORDINARY JOE, BETTY WOULD STILL BE MY GIRL, AND ALL THE OTHER WORRIES I'VE GOT WOULD JUST MELT AWAY!

19.

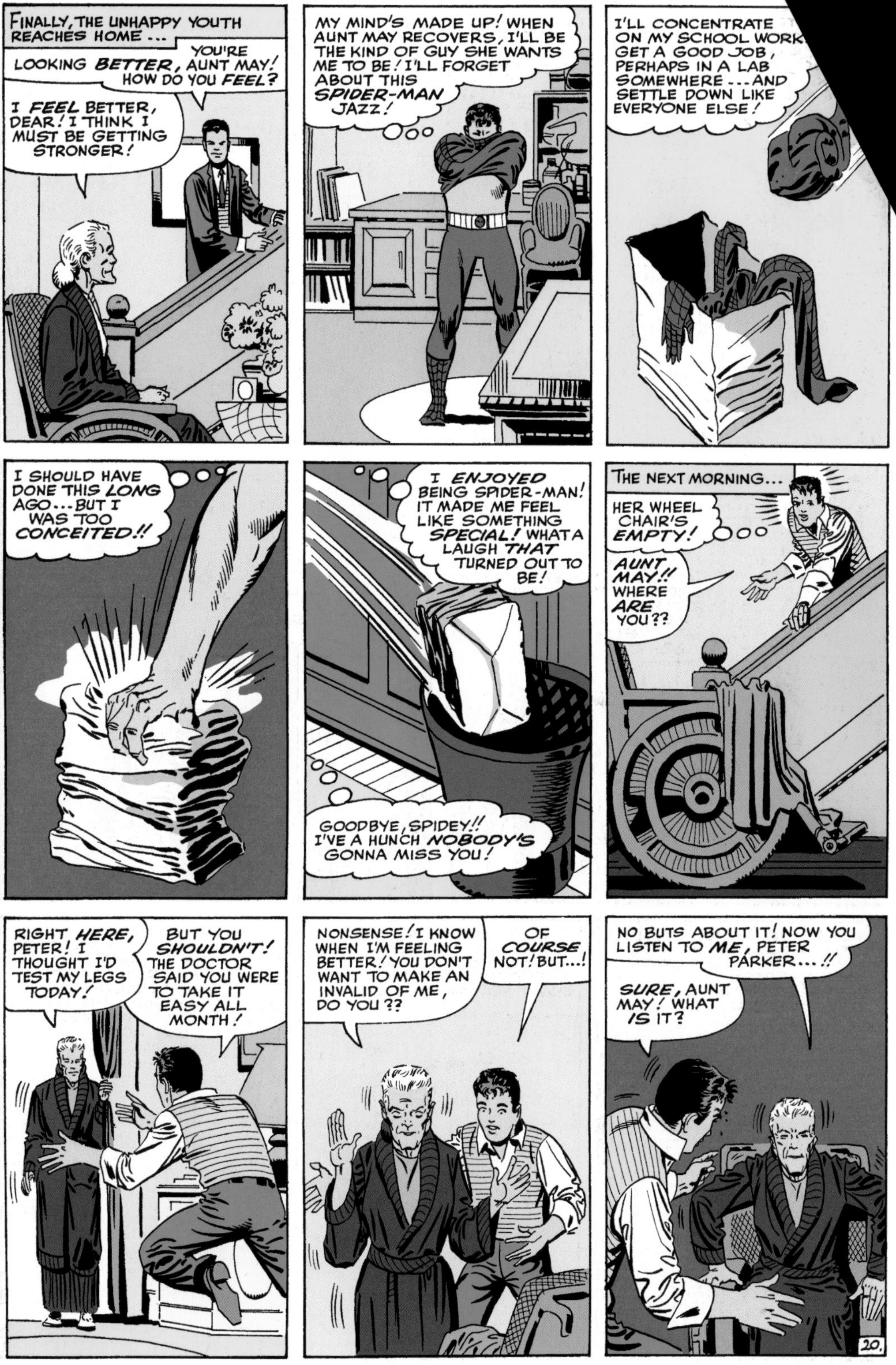
FINALLY, THE UNHAPPY YOUTH REACHES HOME ...
YOU'RE LOOKING BETTER, AUNT MAY! HOW DO YOU FEEL?
I FEEL BETTER, DEAR! I THINK I MUST BE GETTING STRONGER!
MY MIND'S MADE UP! WHEN AUNT MAY RECOVERS, I'LL BE THE KIND OF GUY SHE WANTS ME TO BE! I'LL FORGET ABOUT THIS SPIDER-MAN JAZZ!
I'LL CONCENTRATE ON MY SCHOOL WORK, GET A GOOD JOB, PERHAPS IN A LAB SOMEWHERE ... AND SETTLE DOWN LIKE EVERYONE ELSE!
I SHOULD HAVE DONE THIS LONG AGO ... BUT I WAS TOO CONCEITED!!
I ENJOYED BEING SPIDER-MAN! IT MADE ME FEEL LIKE SOMETHING SPECIAL! WHAT A LAUGH THAT TURNED OUT TO BE!
GOODBYE, SPIDEY!! I'VE A HUNCH NOBODY'S GONNA MISS YOU!
THE NEXT MORNING...
HER WHEEL CHAIR'S EMPTY!
AUNT MAY!! WHERE ARE YOU??
RIGHT HERE, PETER! I THOUGHT I'D TEST MY LEGS TODAY!
BUT YOU SHOULDN'T! THE DOCTOR SAID YOU WERE TO TAKE IT EASY ALL MONTH!
NONSENSE! I KNOW WHEN I'M FEELING BETTER! YOU DON'T WANT TO MAKE AN INVALID OF ME, DO YOU??
OF COURSE NOT! BUT...!
NO BUTS ABOUT IT! NOW YOU LISTEN TO ME, PETER PARKER ... !!
SURE, AUNT MAY! WHAT IS IT?
20.

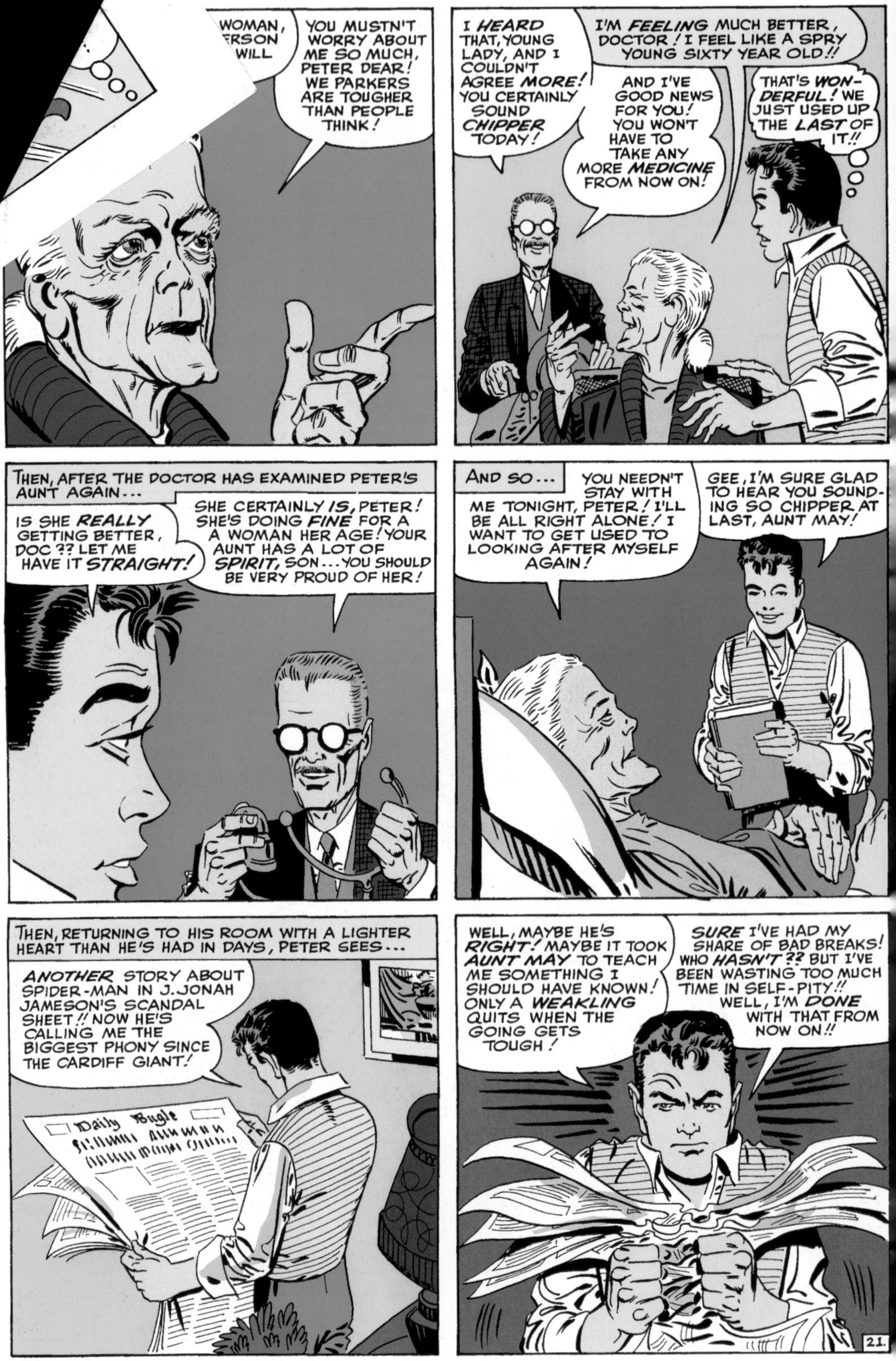

YOU MUSTN'T WORRY ABOUT ME SO MUCH, PETER DEAR! WE PARKERS ARE TOUGHER THAN PEOPLE THINK!
I'M FEELING MUCH BETTER, DOCTOR! I FEEL LIKE A SPRY YOUNG SIXTY YEAR OLD!!
I HEARD THAT, YOUNG LADY, AND I COULDN'T AGREE MORE! YOU CERTAINLY SOUND CHIPPER TODAY!
AND I'VE GOOD NEWS FOR YOU! YOU WON'T HAVE TO TAKE ANY MORE MEDICINE FROM NOW ON!
THAT'S WON-DERFUL! WE JUST USED UP THE LAST OF IT!!
THEN, AFTER THE DOCTOR HAS EXAMINED PETER'S AUNT AGAIN...
IS SHE REALLY GETTING BETTER, DOC?? LET ME HAVE IT STRAIGHT!
SHE CERTAINLY IS, PETER! SHE'S DOING FINE FOR A WOMAN HER AGE! YOUR AUNT HAS A LOT OF SPIRIT, SON... YOU SHOULD BE VERY PROUD OF HER!
AND SO...
YOU NEEDN'T STAY WITH ME TONIGHT, PETER! I'LL BE ALL RIGHT ALONE! I WANT TO GET USED TO LOOKING AFTER MYSELF AGAIN!
GEE, I'M SURE GLAD TO HEAR YOU SOUNDING SO CHIPPER AT LAST, AUNT MAY!
THEN, RETURNING TO HIS ROOM WITH A LIGHTER HEART THAN HE'S HAD IN DAYS, PETER SEES...
ANOTHER STORY ABOUT SPIDER-MAN IN J. JONAH JAMESON'S SCANDAL SHEET!! NOW HE'S CALLING ME THE BIGGEST PHONY SINCE THE CARDIFF GIANT!
Daily Bugle
WELL, MAYBE HE'S RIGHT! MAYBE IT TOOK AUNT MAY TO TEACH ME SOMETHING I SHOULD HAVE KNOWN! ONLY A WEAKLING QUITS WHEN THE GOING GETS TOUGH!
SURE I'VE HAD MY SHARE OF BAD BREAKS! WHO HASN'T?? BUT I'VE BEEN WASTING TOO MUCH TIME IN SELF-PITY!! WELL, I'M DONE WITH THAT FROM NOW ON!!
21.

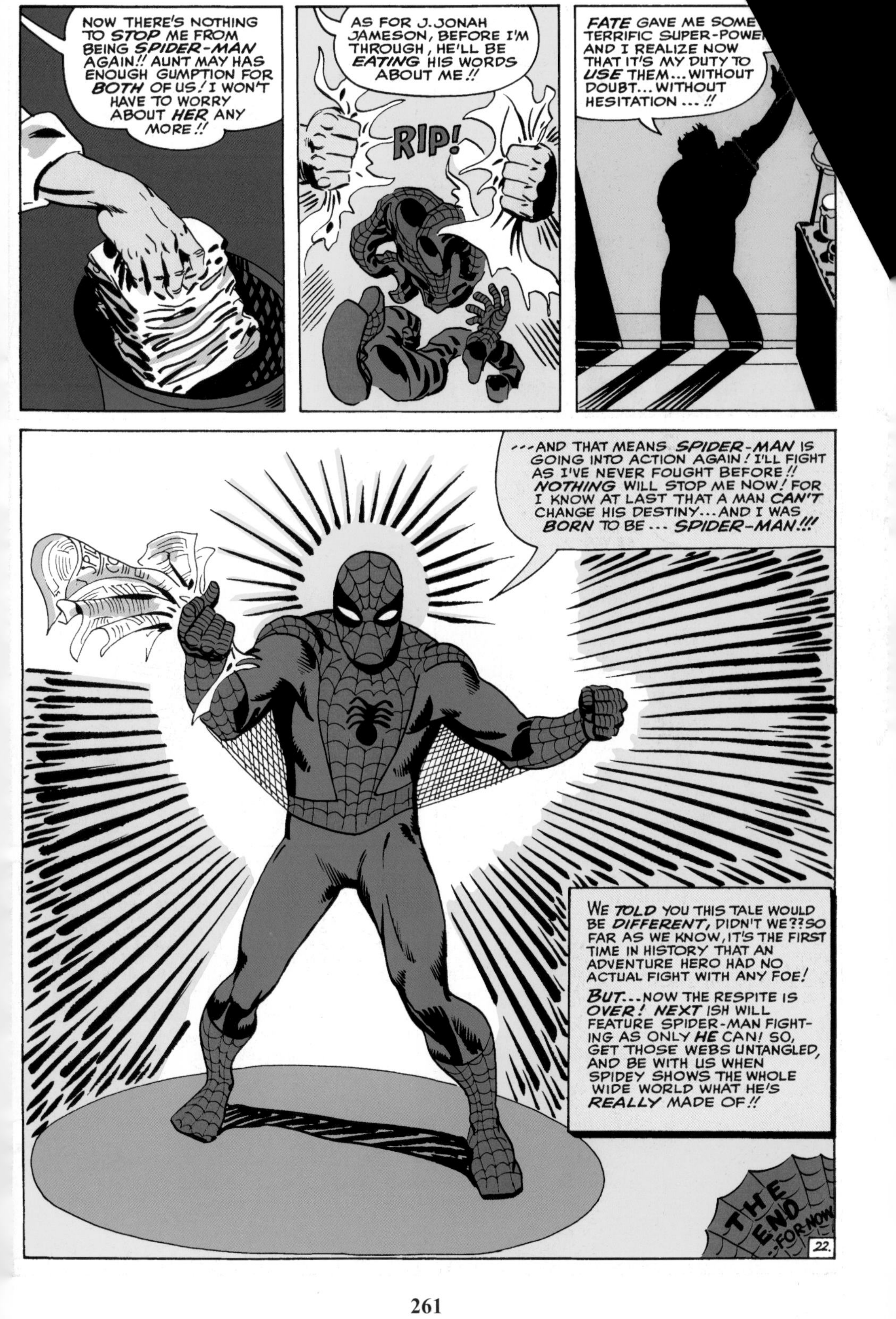

NOW THERE'S NOTHING TO STOP ME FROM BEING SPIDER-MAN AGAIN!! AUNT MAY HAS ENOUGH GUMPTION FOR BOTH OF US! I WON'T HAVE TO WORRY ABOUT HER ANY MORE!!
AS FOR J. JONAH JAMESON, BEFORE I'M THROUGH, HE'LL BE EATING HIS WORDS ABOUT ME!!
RIP!
FATE GAVE ME SOME
TERRIFIC SUPER-POWE
AND I REALIZE NOW THAT IT'S MY DUTY TO USE THEM... WITHOUT DOUBT... WITHOUT HESITATION ...!!
...AND THAT MEANS SPIDER-MAN IS GOING INTO ACTION AGAIN! I'LL FIGHT AS I'VE NEVER FOUGHT BEFORE!! NOTHING WILL STOP ME NOW! FOR I KNOW AT LAST THAT A MAN CAN'T CHANGE HIS DESTINY... AND I WAS BORN TO BE ... SPIDER-MAN!!!
WE TOLD YOU THIS TALE WOULD BE DIFFERENT, DIDN'T WE?? SO FAR AS WE KNOW, IT'S THE FIRST TIME IN HISTORY THAT AN ADVENTURE HERO HAD NO ACTUAL FIGHT WITH ANY FOE!
BUT... NOW THE RESPITE IS OVER! NEXT ISH WILL FEATURE SPIDER-MAN FIGHTING AS ONLY HE CAN! SO, GET THOSE WEBS UNTANGLED, AND BE WITH US WHEN SPIDEY SHOWS THE WHOLE WIDE WORLD WHAT HE'S REALLY MADE OF!!
THE END ...FOR NOW
22.

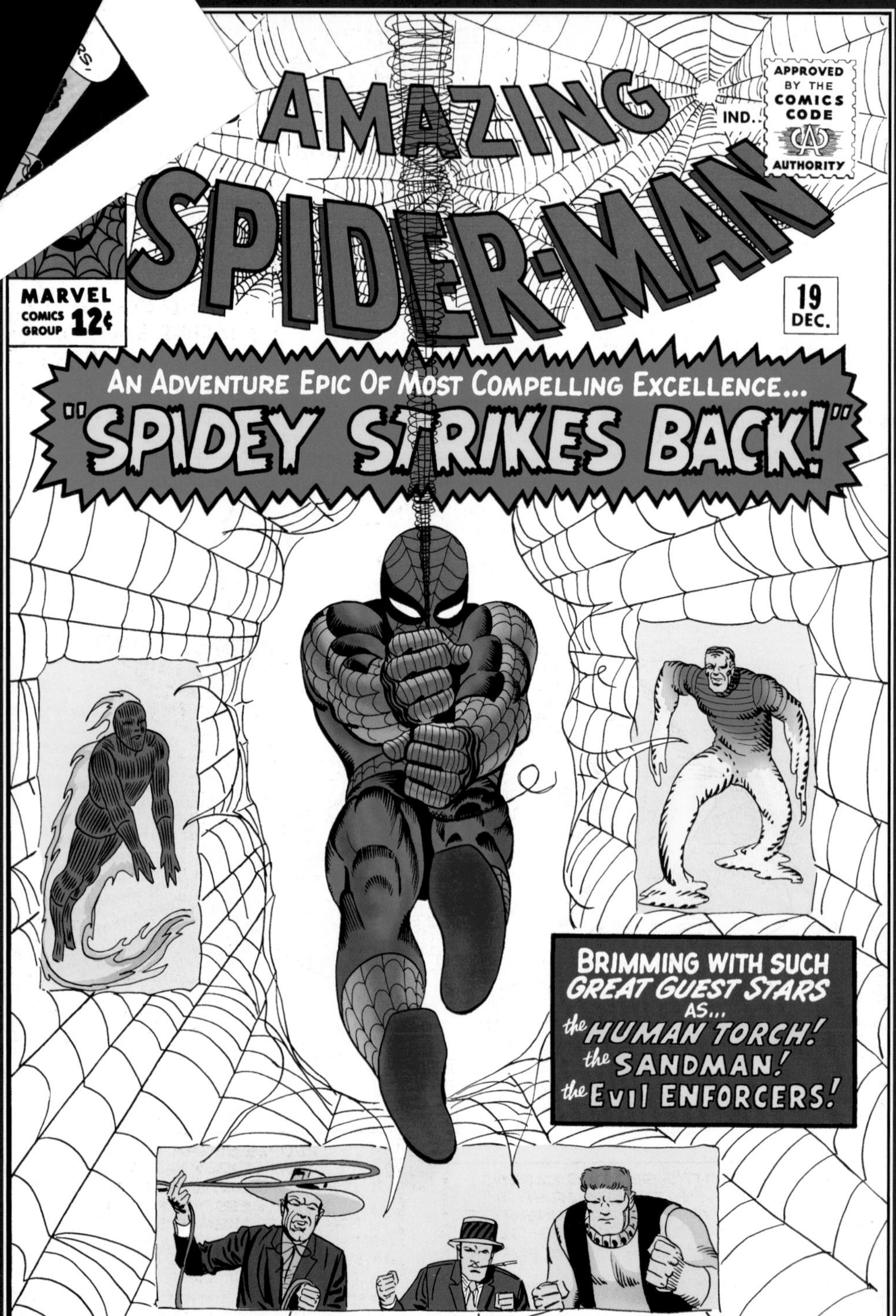
AMAZING SPIDER-MAN
IND.
APPROVED BY THE COMICS CODE AUTHORITY
MARVEL COMICS GROUP 12¢
19 DEC.
AN ADVENTURE EPIC OF MOST COMPELLING EXCELLENCE...
"SPIDEY STRIKES BACK!"
BRIMMING WITH SUCH GREAT GUEST STARS AS...
the HUMAN TORCH!
the SANDMAN!
the EVIL ENFORCERS!

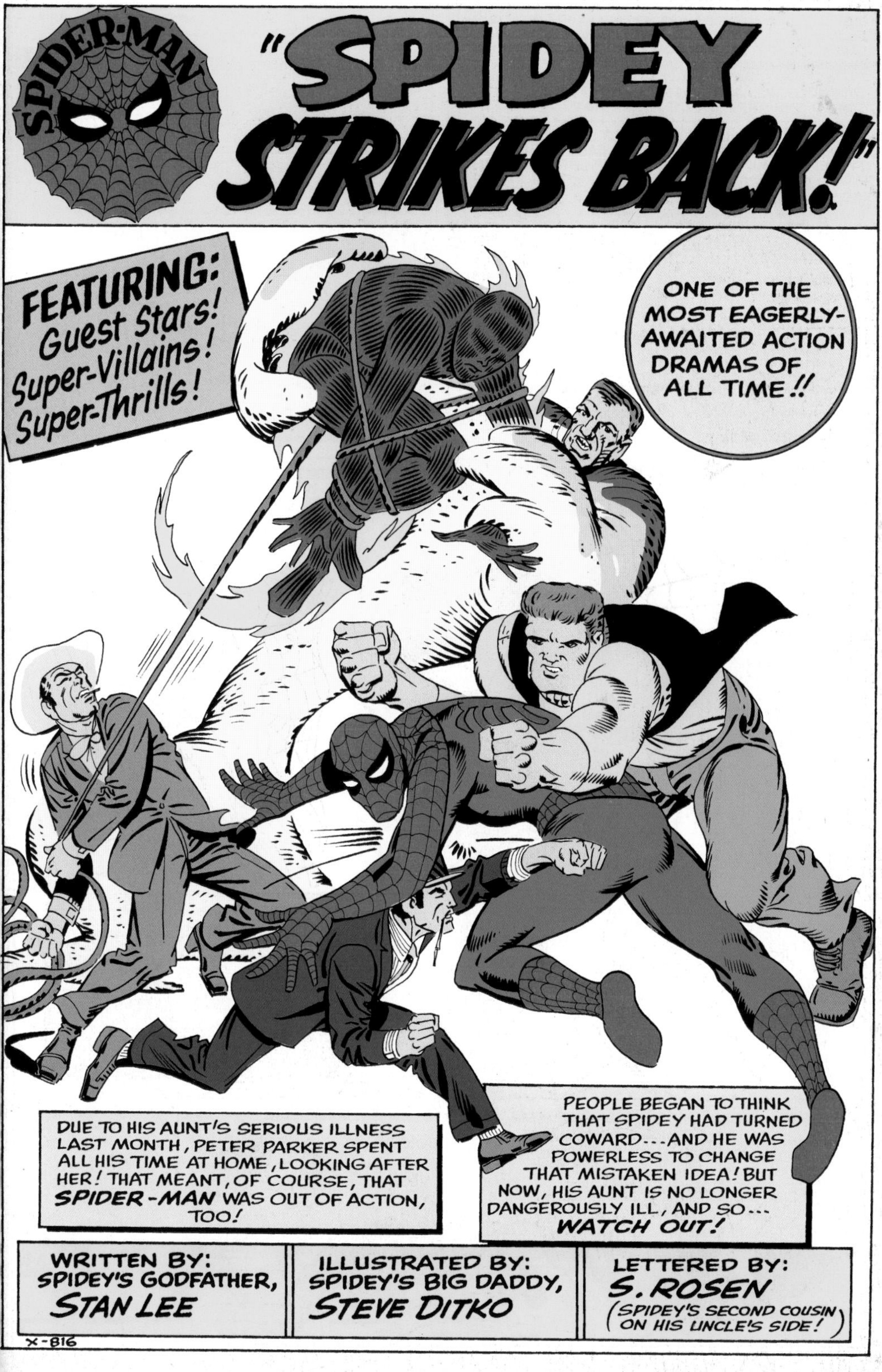
SPIDER-MAN
"SPIDEY STRIKES BACK!"
FEATURING: Guest Stars! Super-Villains! Super-Thrills!
ONE OF THE MOST EAGERLY-AWAITED ACTION DRAMAS OF ALL TIME!!
DUE TO HIS AUNT'S SERIOUS ILLNESS LAST MONTH, PETER PARKER SPENT ALL HIS TIME AT HOME, LOOKING AFTER HER! THAT MEANT, OF COURSE, THAT SPIDER-MAN WAS OUT OF ACTION, TOO!
PEOPLE BEGAN TO THINK THAT SPIDEY HAD TURNED COWARD... AND HE WAS POWERLESS TO CHANGE THAT MISTAKEN IDEA! BUT NOW, HIS AUNT IS NO LONGER DANGEROUSLY ILL, AND SO... WATCH OUT!
WRITTEN BY: SPIDEY'S GODFATHER, STAN LEE
ILLUSTRATED BY: SPIDEY'S BIG DADDY, STEVE DITKO
LETTERED BY: S. ROSEN (SPIDEY'S SECOND COUSIN ON HIS UNCLE'S SIDE!)
X-816

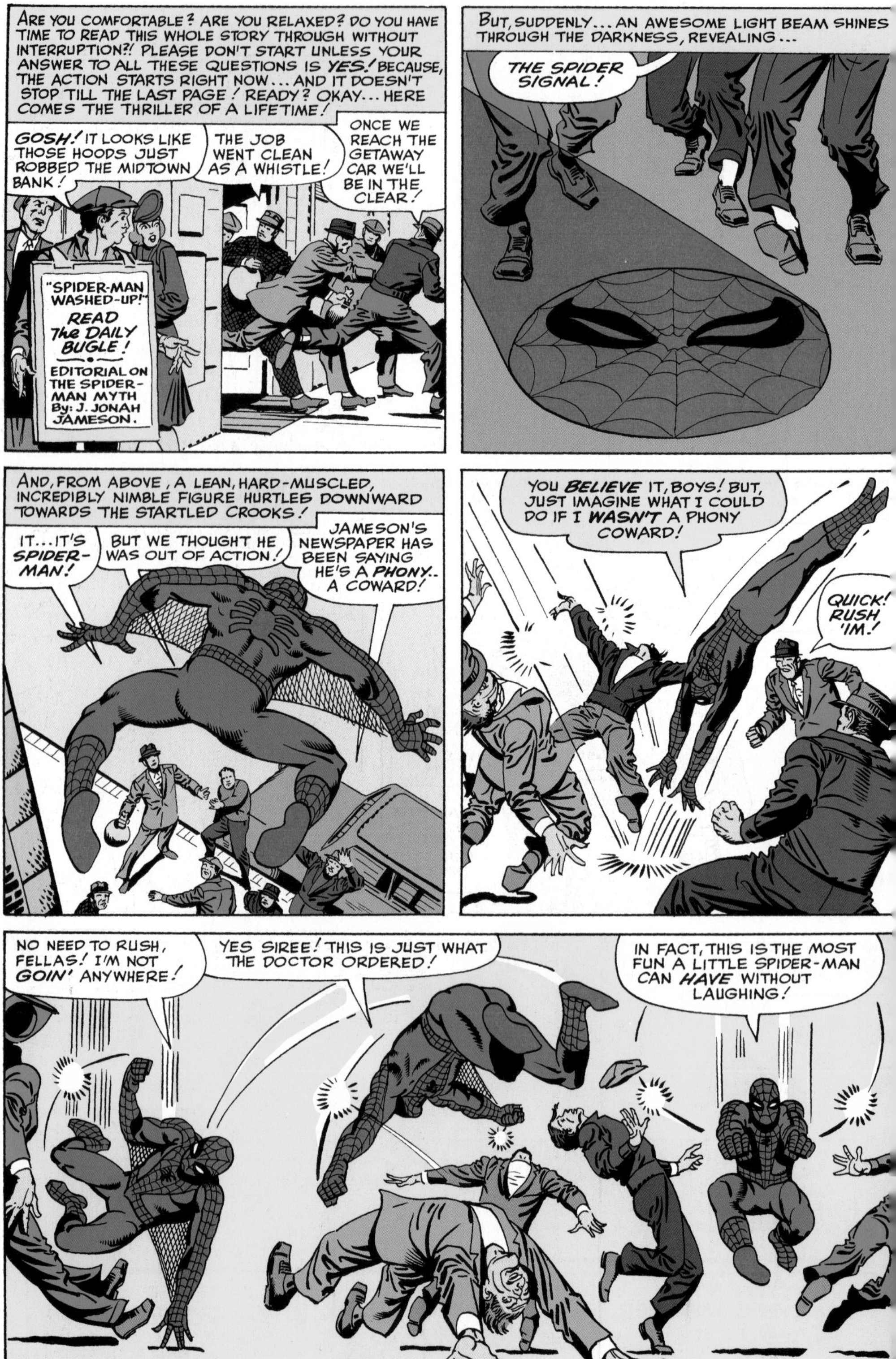

ARE YOU COMFORTABLE? ARE YOU RELAXED? DO YOU HAVE TIME TO READ THIS WHOLE STORY THROUGH WITHOUT INTERRUPTION?! PLEASE DON'T START UNLESS YOUR ANSWER TO ALL THESE QUESTIONS IS YES! BECAUSE, THE ACTION STARTS RIGHT NOW... AND IT DOESN'T STOP TILL THE LAST PAGE! READY? OKAY... HERE COMES THE THRILLER OF A LIFETIME!
GOSH! IT LOOKS LIKE THOSE HOODS JUST ROBBED THE MIDTOWN BANK!
THE JOB WENT CLEAN AS A WHISTLE!
ONCE WE REACH THE GETAWAY CAR WE'LL BE IN THE CLEAR!
"SPIDER-MAN WASHED-UP!" READ The DAILY BUGLE! EDITORIAL ON THE SPIDER-MAN MYTH By: J. JONAH JAMESON.
BUT, SUDDENLY... AN AWESOME LIGHT BEAM SHINES THROUGH THE DARKNESS, REVEALING...
THE SPIDER SIGNAL!
AND, FROM ABOVE, A LEAN, HARD-MUSCLED, INCREDIBLY NIMBLE FIGURE HURTLES DOWNWARD TOWARDS THE STARTLED CROOKS!
IT... IT'S SPIDER-MAN!
BUT WE THOUGHT HE WAS OUT OF ACTION!
JAMESON'S NEWSPAPER HAS BEEN SAYING HE'S A PHONY.. A COWARD!
YOU BELIEVE IT, BOYS! BUT, JUST IMAGINE WHAT I COULD DO IF I WASN'T A PHONY COWARD!
QUICK! RUSH 'IM!
NO NEED TO RUSH, FELLAS! I'M NOT GOIN' ANYWHERE!
YES SIREE! THIS IS JUST WHAT THE DOCTOR ORDERED!
IN FACT, THIS IS THE MOST FUN A LITTLE SPIDER-MAN CAN HAVE WITHOUT LAUGHING!
2.

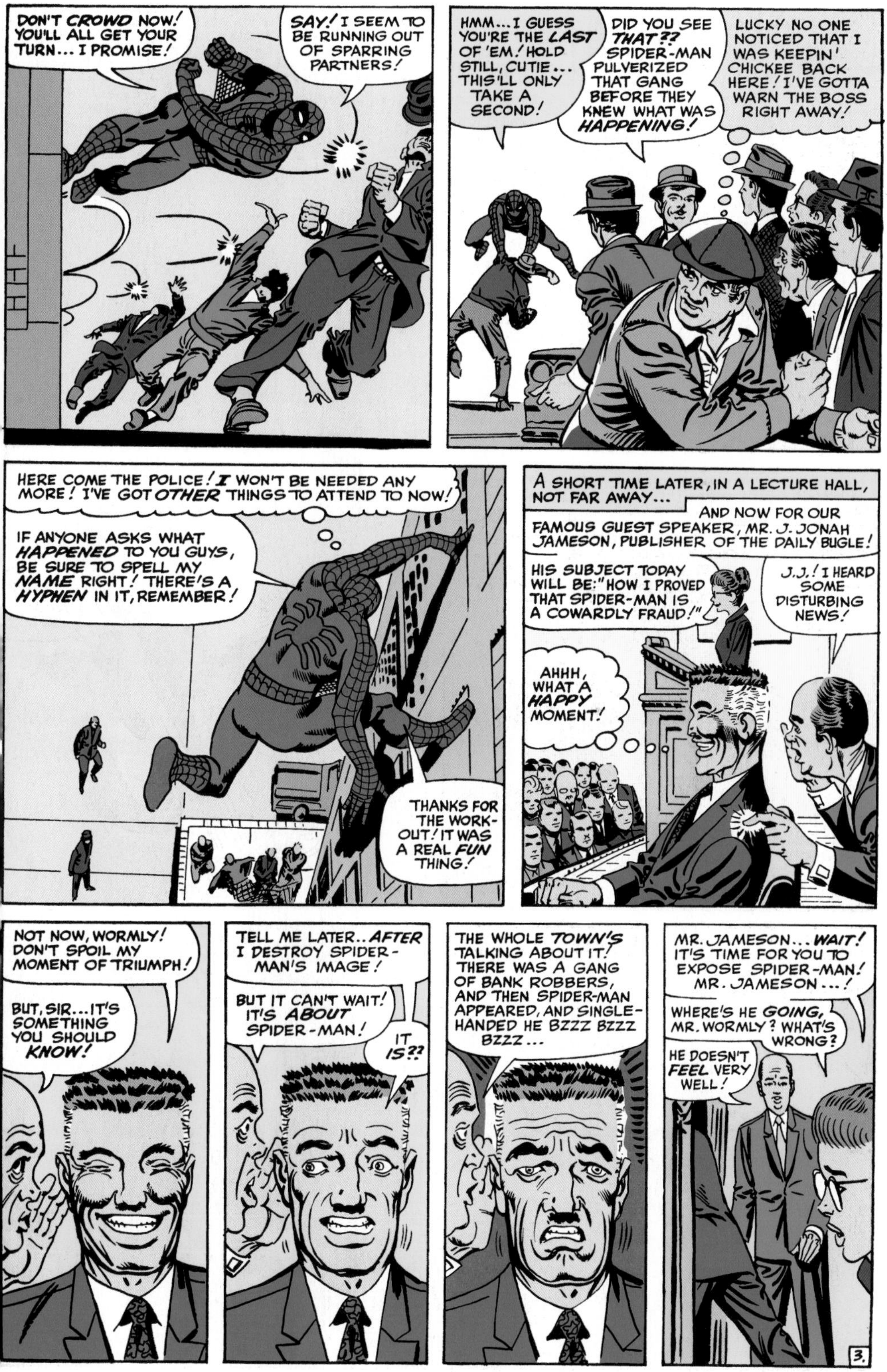
DON'T CROWD NOW! YOU'LL ALL GET YOUR TURN... I PROMISE!
SAY! I SEEM TO BE RUNNING OUT OF SPARRING PARTNERS!
HMM... I GUESS YOU'RE THE LAST OF 'EM! HOLD STILL, CUTIE... THIS'LL ONLY TAKE A SECOND!
DID YOU SEE THAT?? SPIDER-MAN PULVERIZED THAT GANG BEFORE THEY KNEW WHAT WAS HAPPENING!
LUCKY NO ONE NOTICED THAT I WAS KEEPIN' CHICKEE BACK HERE! I'VE GOTTA WARN THE BOSS RIGHT AWAY!
HERE COME THE POLICE! I WON'T BE NEEDED ANY MORE! I'VE GOT OTHER THINGS TO ATTEND TO NOW!
IF ANYONE ASKS WHAT HAPPENED TO YOU GUYS, BE SURE TO SPELL MY NAME RIGHT! THERE'S A HYPHEN IN IT, REMEMBER!
THANKS FOR THE WORK-OUT! IT WAS A REAL FUN THING!
A SHORT TIME LATER, IN A LECTURE HALL, NOT FAR AWAY...
AND NOW FOR OUR FAMOUS GUEST SPEAKER, MR. J. JONAH JAMESON, PUBLISHER OF THE DAILY BUGLE!
HIS SUBJECT TODAY WILL BE: "HOW I PROVED THAT SPIDER-MAN IS A COWARDLY FRAUD!"
J.J.! I HEARD SOME DISTURBING NEWS!
AHHH, WHAT A HAPPY MOMENT!
NOT NOW, WORMLY! DON'T SPOIL MY MOMENT OF TRIUMPH!
BUT, SIR... IT'S SOMETHING YOU SHOULD KNOW!
TELL ME LATER.. AFTER I DESTROY SPIDER-MAN'S IMAGE!
BUT IT CAN'T WAIT! IT'S ABOUT SPIDER-MAN!
IT IS??
THE WHOLE TOWN'S TALKING ABOUT IT! THERE WAS A GANG OF BANK ROBBERS, AND THEN SPIDER-MAN APPEARED, AND SINGLE-HANDED HE BZZZ BZZZ BZZZ...
MR. JAMESON... WAIT! IT'S TIME FOR YOU TO EXPOSE SPIDER-MAN! MR. JAMESON...!
WHERE'S HE GOING, MR. WORMLY? WHAT'S WRONG?
HE DOESN'T FEEL VERY WELL!
3.

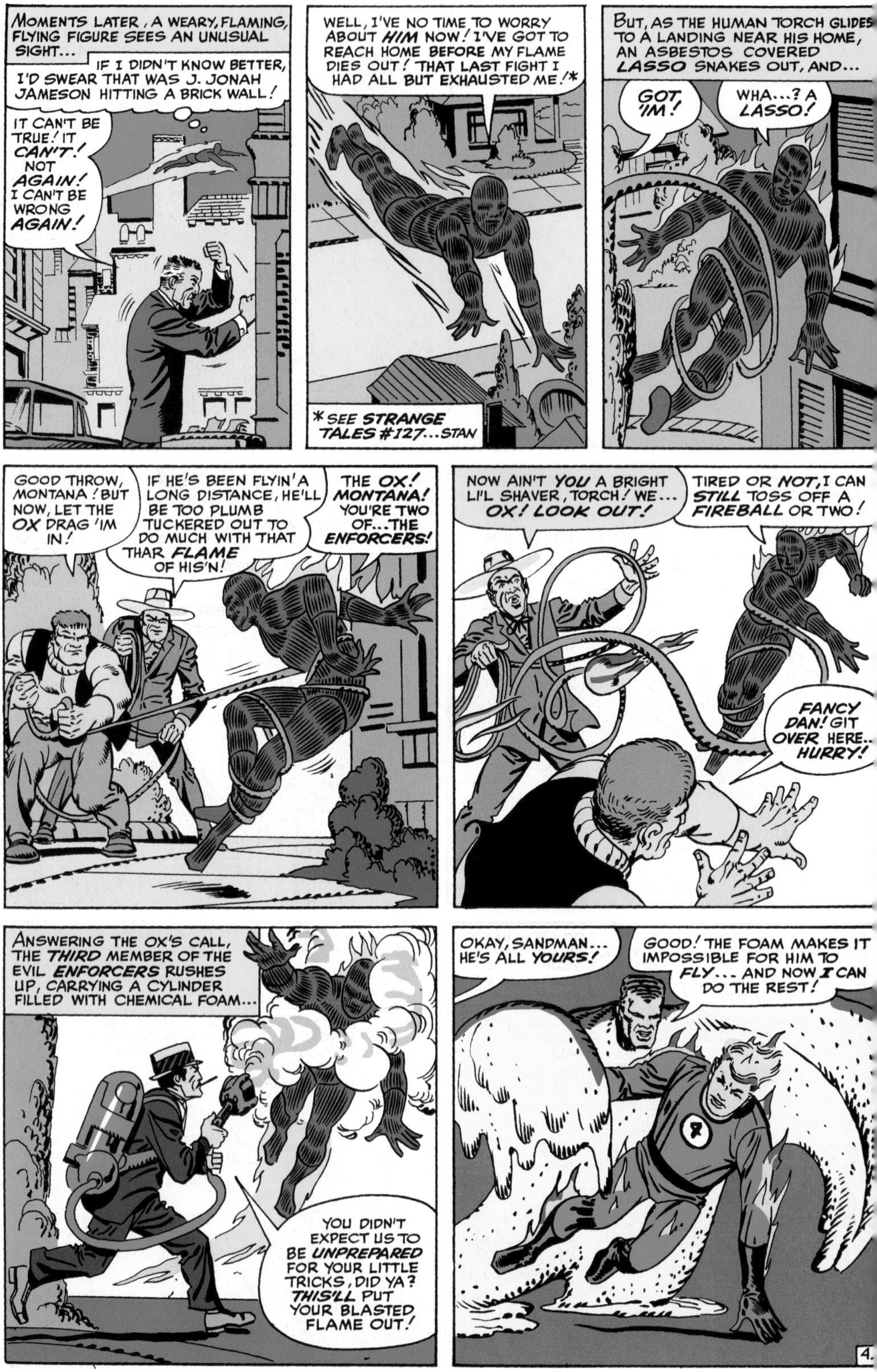
MOMENTS LATER, A WEARY, FLAMING, FLYING FIGURE SEES AN UNUSUAL SIGHT...
IF I DIDN'T KNOW BETTER, I'D SWEAR THAT WAS J. JONAH JAMESON HITTING A BRICK WALL!
IT CAN'T BE TRUE! IT CAN'T! NOT AGAIN! I CAN'T BE WRONG AGAIN!
WELL, I'VE NO TIME TO WORRY ABOUT HIM NOW! I'VE GOT TO REACH HOME BEFORE MY FLAME DIES OUT! THAT LAST FIGHT I HAD ALL BUT EXHAUSTED ME!*
*SEE STRANGE TALES #127...STAN
BUT, AS THE HUMAN TORCH GLIDES TO A LANDING NEAR HIS HOME, AN ASBESTOS COVERED LASSO SNAKES OUT, AND...
GOT 'IM!
WHA...? A LASSO!
GOOD THROW, MONTANA! BUT NOW, LET THE OX DRAG 'IM IN!
IF HE'S BEEN FLYIN' A LONG DISTANCE, HE'LL BE TOO PLUMB TUCKERED OUT TO DO MUCH WITH THAT THAR FLAME OF HIS'N!
THE OX! MONTANA! YOU'RE TWO OF...THE ENFORCERS!
NOW AIN'T YOU A BRIGHT LI'L SHAVER, TORCH! WE... OX! LOOK OUT!
TIRED OR NOT, I CAN STILL TOSS OFF A FIREBALL OR TWO!
FANCY DAN! GIT OVER HERE.. HURRY!
ANSWERING THE OX'S CALL, THE THIRD MEMBER OF THE EVIL ENFORCERS RUSHES UP, CARRYING A CYLINDER FILLED WITH CHEMICAL FOAM...
YOU DIDN'T EXPECT US TO BE UNPREPARED FOR YOUR LITTLE TRICKS, DID YA? THIS'LL PUT YOUR BLASTED FLAME OUT!
OKAY, SANDMAN... HE'S ALL YOURS!
GOOD! THE FOAM MAKES IT IMPOSSIBLE FOR HIM TO FLY... AND NOW I CAN DO THE REST!
4

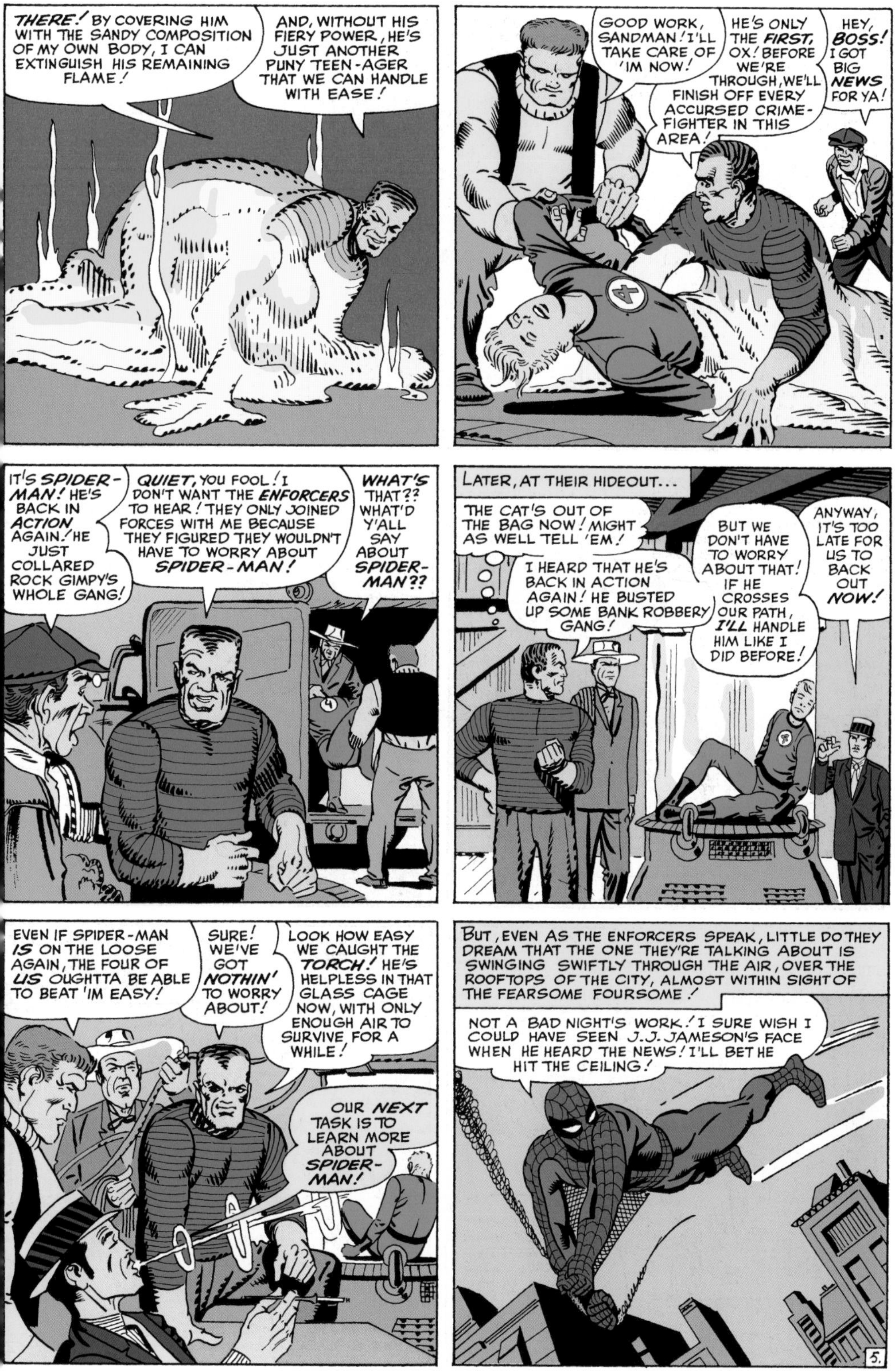
THERE! BY COVERING HIM WITH THE SANDY COMPOSITION OF MY OWN BODY, I CAN EXTINGUISH HIS REMAINING FLAME!
AND, WITHOUT HIS FIERY POWER, HE'S JUST ANOTHER PUNY TEEN-AGER THAT WE CAN HANDLE WITH EASE!
GOOD WORK, SANDMAN! I'LL TAKE CARE OF 'IM NOW!
HE'S ONLY THE FIRST, OX! BEFORE WE'RE THROUGH, WE'LL FINISH OFF EVERY ACCURSED CRIME-FIGHTER IN THIS AREA!
HEY, BOSS! I GOT BIG NEWS FOR YA!
IT'S SPIDER-MAN! HE'S BACK IN ACTION AGAIN! HE JUST COLLARED ROCK GIMPY'S WHOLE GANG!
QUIET, YOU FOOL! I DON'T WANT THE ENFORCERS TO HEAR! THEY ONLY JOINED FORCES WITH ME BECAUSE THEY FIGURED THEY WOULDN'T HAVE TO WORRY ABOUT SPIDER-MAN!
WHAT'S THAT?? WHAT'D Y'ALL SAY ABOUT SPIDER-MAN??
LATER, AT THEIR HIDEOUT...
THE CAT'S OUT OF THE BAG NOW! MIGHT AS WELL TELL 'EM!
I HEARD THAT HE'S BACK IN ACTION AGAIN! HE BUSTED UP SOME BANK ROBBERY GANG!
BUT WE DON'T HAVE TO WORRY ABOUT THAT! IF HE CROSSES OUR PATH, I'LL HANDLE HIM LIKE I DID BEFORE!
ANYWAY, IT'S TOO LATE FOR US TO BACK OUT NOW!
EVEN IF SPIDER-MAN IS ON THE LOOSE AGAIN, THE FOUR OF US OUGHTTA BE ABLE TO BEAT 'IM EASY!
SURE! WE'VE GOT NOTHIN' TO WORRY ABOUT!
LOOK HOW EASY WE CAUGHT THE TORCH! HE'S HELPLESS IN THAT GLASS CAGE NOW, WITH ONLY ENOUGH AIR TO SURVIVE FOR A WHILE!
OUR NEXT TASK IS TO LEARN MORE ABOUT SPIDER-MAN!
BUT, EVEN AS THE ENFORCERS SPEAK, LITTLE DO THEY DREAM THAT THE ONE THEY'RE TALKING ABOUT IS SWINGING SWIFTLY THROUGH THE AIR, OVER THE ROOFTOPS OF THE CITY, ALMOST WITHIN SIGHT OF THE FEARSOME FOURSOME!
NOT A BAD NIGHT'S WORK! I SURE WISH I COULD HAVE SEEN J.J. JAMESON'S FACE WHEN HE HEARD THE NEWS! I'LL BET HE HIT THE CEILING!
5.

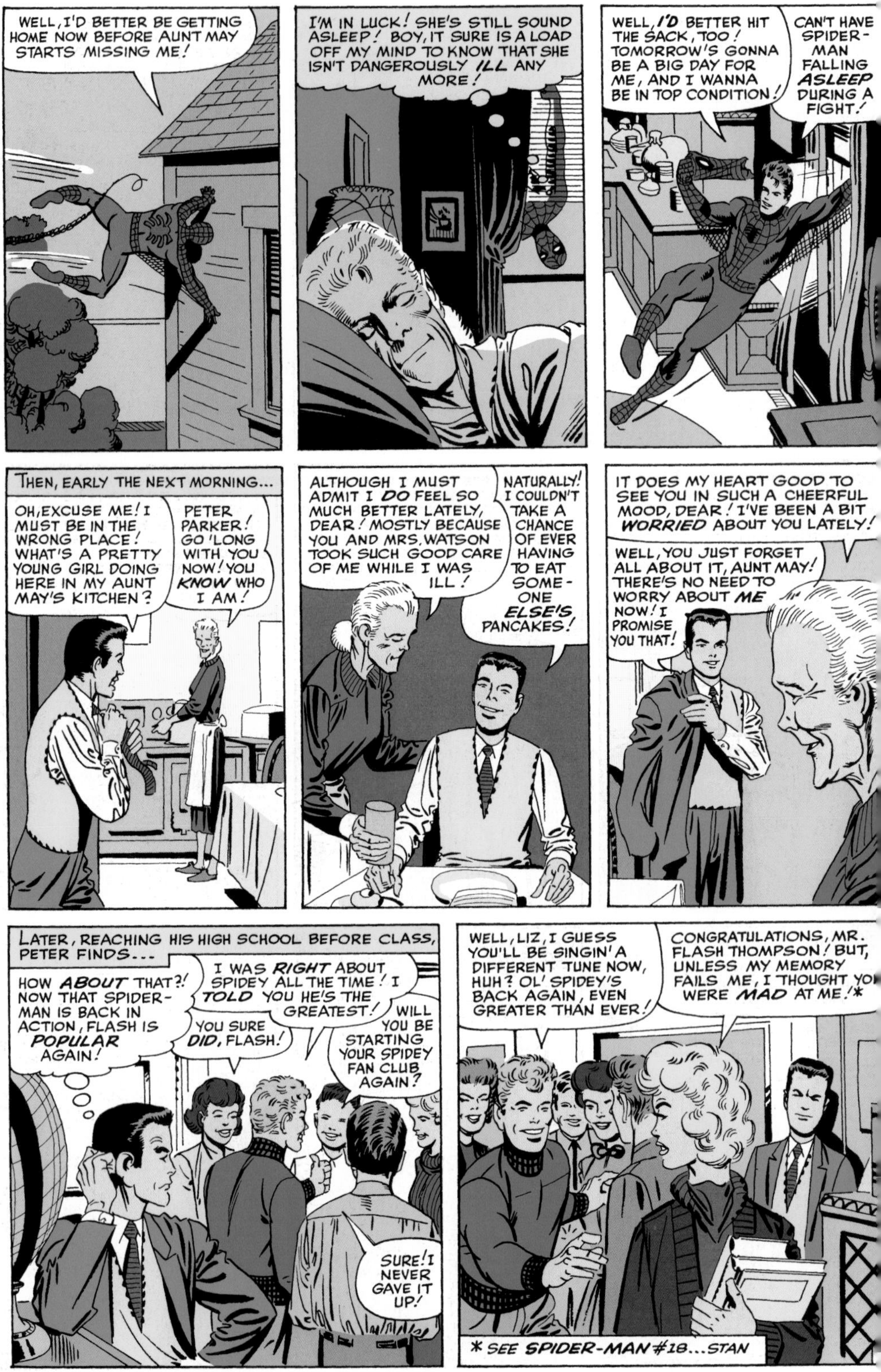
WELL, I'D BETTER BE GETTING HOME NOW BEFORE AUNT MAY STARTS MISSING ME!
I'M IN LUCK! SHE'S STILL SOUND ASLEEP! BOY, IT SURE IS A LOAD OFF MY MIND TO KNOW THAT SHE ISN'T DANGEROUSLY ILL ANY MORE!
WELL, I'D BETTER HIT THE SACK, TOO! TOMORROW'S GONNA BE A BIG DAY FOR ME, AND I WANNA BE IN TOP CONDITION!
CAN'T HAVE SPIDER-MAN FALLING ASLEEP DURING A FIGHT!
THEN, EARLY THE NEXT MORNING...
OH, EXCUSE ME! I MUST BE IN THE WRONG PLACE! WHAT'S A PRETTY YOUNG GIRL DOING HERE IN MY AUNT MAY'S KITCHEN?
PETER PARKER! GO 'LONG WITH YOU NOW! YOU KNOW WHO I AM!
ALTHOUGH I MUST ADMIT I DO FEEL SO MUCH BETTER LATELY, DEAR! MOSTLY BECAUSE YOU AND MRS. WATSON TOOK SUCH GOOD CARE OF ME WHILE I WAS ILL!
NATURALLY! I COULDN'T TAKE A CHANCE OF EVER HAVING TO EAT SOMEONE ELSE'S PANCAKES!
IT DOES MY HEART GOOD TO SEE YOU IN SUCH A CHEERFUL MOOD, DEAR! I'VE BEEN A BIT WORRIED ABOUT YOU LATELY!
WELL, YOU JUST FORGET ALL ABOUT IT, AUNT MAY! THERE'S NO NEED TO WORRY ABOUT ME NOW! I PROMISE YOU THAT!
LATER, REACHING HIS HIGH SCHOOL BEFORE CLASS, PETER FINDS...
HOW ABOUT THAT?! NOW THAT SPIDER-MAN IS BACK IN ACTION, FLASH IS POPULAR AGAIN!
I WAS RIGHT ABOUT SPIDEY ALL THE TIME! I TOLD YOU HE'S THE GREATEST!
YOU SURE DID, FLASH!
WILL YOU BE STARTING YOUR SPIDEY FAN CLUB AGAIN?
SURE! I NEVER GAVE IT UP!
WELL, LIZ, I GUESS YOU'LL BE SINGIN' A DIFFERENT TUNE NOW, HUH? OL' SPIDEY'S BACK AGAIN, EVEN GREATER THAN EVER!
CONGRATULATIONS, MR. FLASH THOMPSON! BUT, UNLESS MY MEMORY FAILS ME, I THOUGHT YO WERE MAD AT ME!*
* SEE SPIDER-MAN #18...STAN

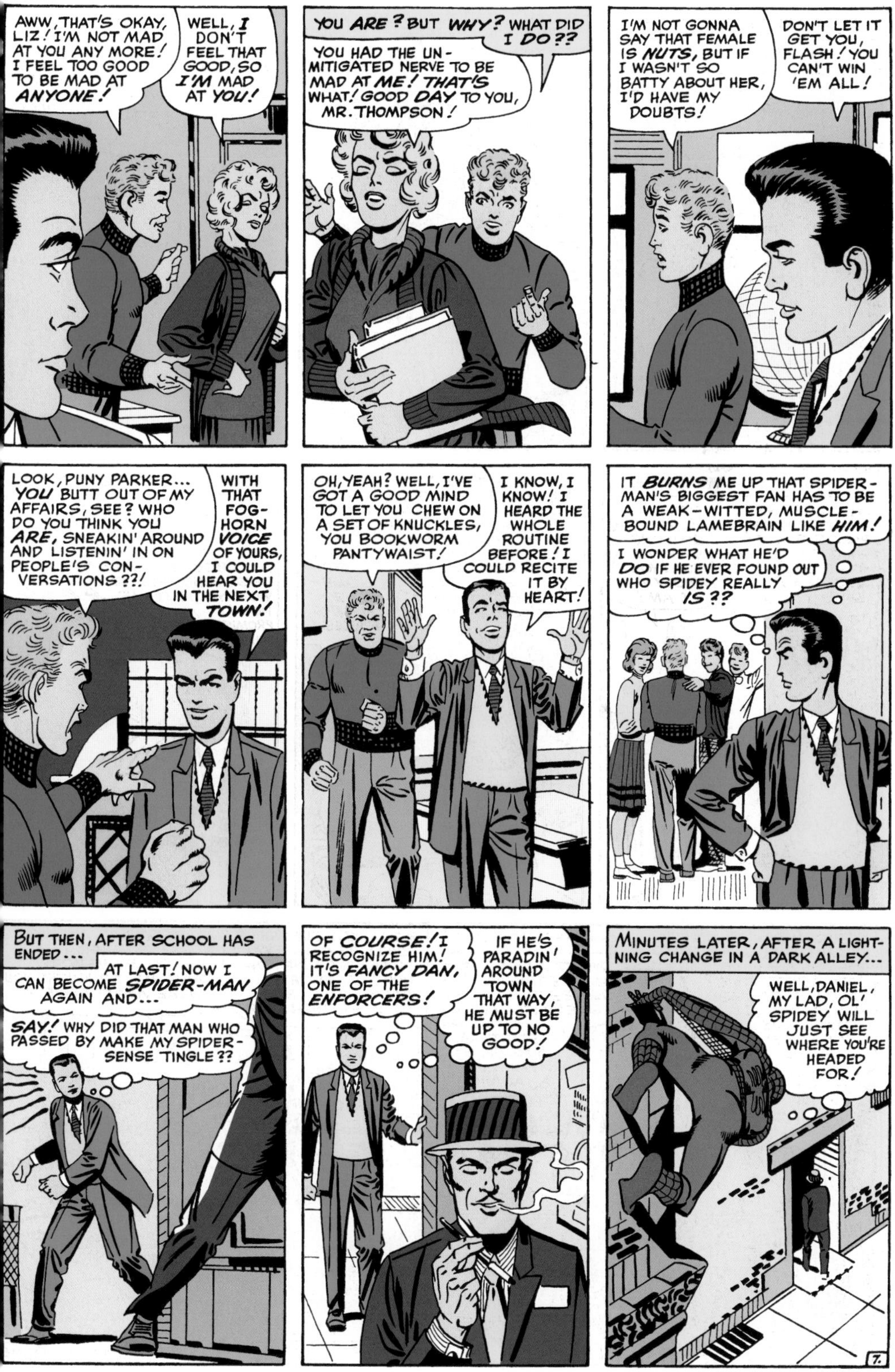
AWW, THAT'S OKAY, LIZ! I'M NOT MAD AT YOU ANY MORE! I FEEL TOO GOOD TO BE MAD AT ANYONE!
WELL, I DON'T FEEL THAT GOOD, SO I'M MAD AT YOU!
YOU ARE? BUT WHY? WHAT DID I DO??
YOU HAD THE UN-MITIGATED NERVE TO BE MAD AT ME! THAT'S WHAT! GOOD DAY TO YOU, MR. THOMPSON!
I'M NOT GONNA SAY THAT FEMALE IS NUTS, BUT IF I WASN'T SO BATTY ABOUT HER, I'D HAVE MY DOUBTS!
DON'T LET IT GET YOU, FLASH! YOU CAN'T WIN 'EM ALL!
LOOK, PUNY PARKER... YOU BUTT OUT OF MY AFFAIRS, SEE? WHO DO YOU THINK YOU ARE, SNEAKIN' AROUND AND LISTENIN' IN ON PEOPLE'S CON-VERSATIONS??!
WITH THAT FOG-HORN VOICE OF YOURS, I COULD HEAR YOU IN THE NEXT TOWN!
OH, YEAH? WELL, I'VE GOT A GOOD MIND TO LET YOU CHEW ON A SET OF KNUCKLES, YOU BOOKWORM PANTYWAIST!
I KNOW, I KNOW! I HEARD THE WHOLE ROUTINE BEFORE! I COULD RECITE IT BY HEART!
IT BURNS ME UP THAT SPIDER-MAN'S BIGGEST FAN HAS TO BE A WEAK-WITTED, MUSCLE-BOUND LAMEBRAIN LIKE HIM!
I WONDER WHAT HE'D DO IF HE EVER FOUND OUT WHO SPIDEY REALLY IS??
BUT THEN, AFTER SCHOOL HAS ENDED...
AT LAST! NOW I CAN BECOME SPIDER-MAN AGAIN AND...
SAY! WHY DID THAT MAN WHO PASSED BY MAKE MY SPIDER-SENSE TINGLE??
OF COURSE! I RECOGNIZE HIM! IT'S FANCY DAN, ONE OF THE ENFORCERS!
IF HE'S PARADIN' AROUND TOWN THAT WAY, HE MUST BE UP TO NO GOOD!
MINUTES LATER, AFTER A LIGHT-NING CHANGE IN A DARK ALLEY...
WELL, DANIEL, MY LAD, OL' SPIDEY WILL JUST SEE WHERE YOU'RE HEADED FOR!
7.

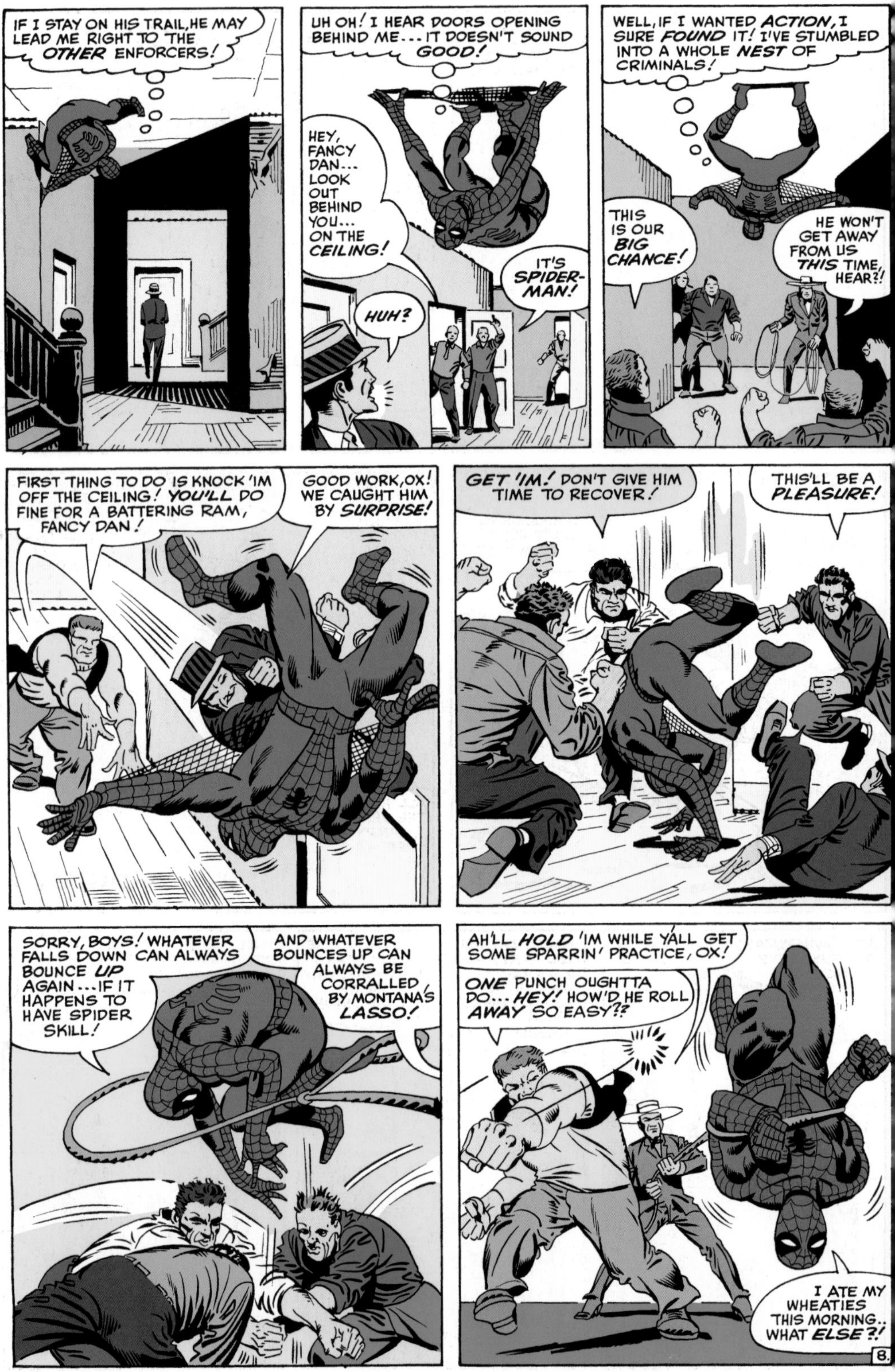
IF I STAY ON HIS TRAIL, HE MAY LEAD ME RIGHT TO THE OTHER ENFORCERS!
UH OH! I HEAR DOORS OPENING BEHIND ME... IT DOESN'T SOUND GOOD!
HEY, FANCY DAN... LOOK OUT BEHIND YOU... ON THE CEILING!
HUH?
IT'S SPIDER-MAN!
WELL, IF I WANTED ACTION, I SURE FOUND IT! I'VE STUMBLED INTO A WHOLE NEST OF CRIMINALS!
THIS IS OUR BIG CHANCE!
HE WON'T GET AWAY FROM US THIS TIME, HEAR?!
FIRST THING TO DO IS KNOCK 'IM OFF THE CEILING! YOU'LL DO FINE FOR A BATTERING RAM, FANCY DAN!
GOOD WORK, OX! WE CAUGHT HIM BY SURPRISE!
GET 'IM! DON'T GIVE HIM TIME TO RECOVER!
THIS'LL BE A PLEASURE!
SORRY, BOYS! WHATEVER FALLS DOWN CAN ALWAYS BOUNCE UP AGAIN... IF IT HAPPENS TO HAVE SPIDER SKILL!
AND WHATEVER BOUNCES UP CAN ALWAYS BE CORRALLED, BY MONTANA'S LASSO!
AH'LL HOLD 'IM WHILE Y'ALL GET SOME SPARRIN' PRACTICE, OX!
ONE PUNCH OUGHTTA DO... HEY! HOW'D HE ROLL AWAY SO EASY??
I ATE MY WHEATIES THIS MORNING.. WHAT ELSE?!
8.

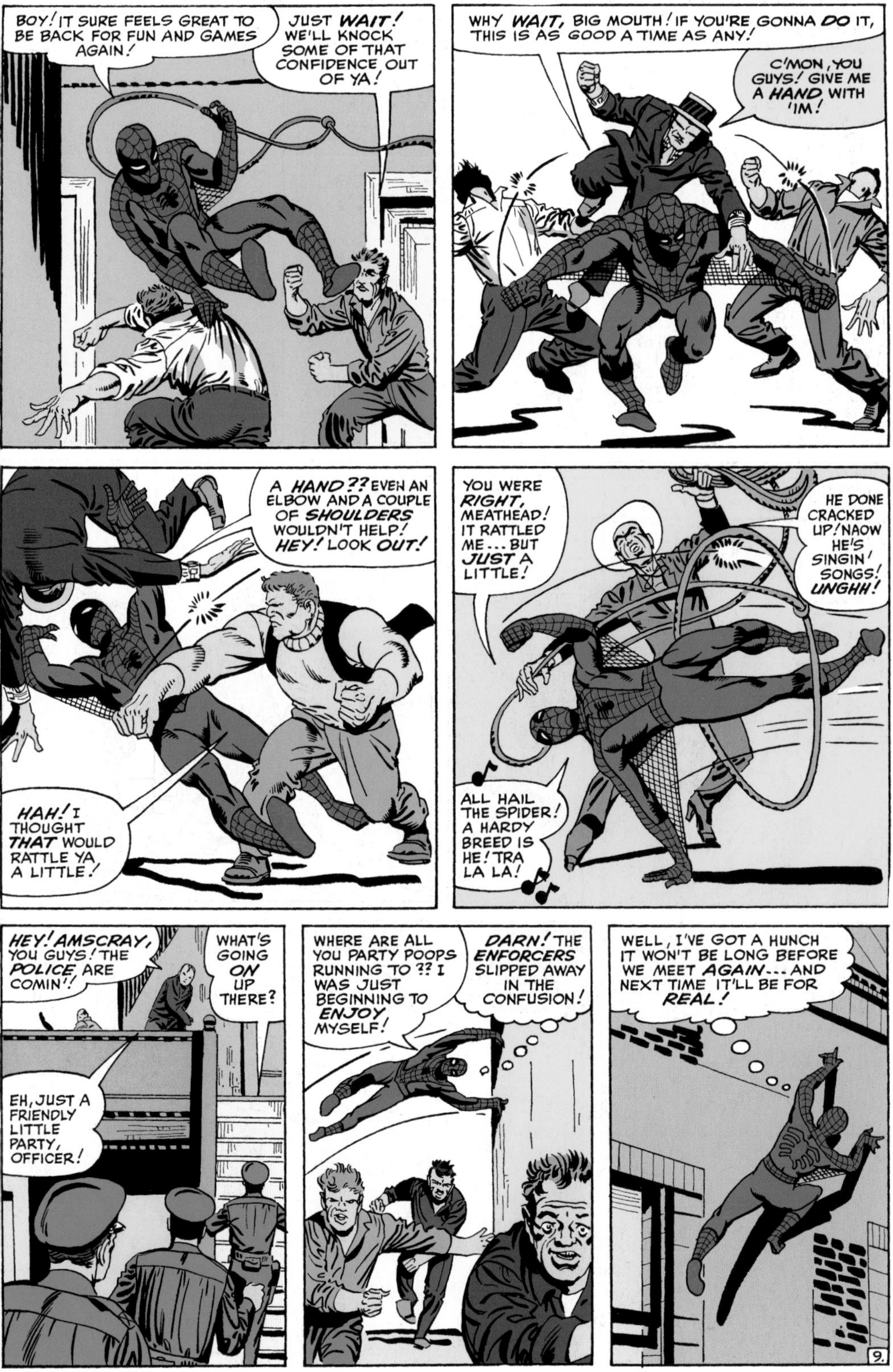

BOY! IT SURE FEELS GREAT TO BE BACK FOR FUN AND GAMES AGAIN!
JUST WAIT! WE'LL KNOCK SOME OF THAT CONFIDENCE OUT OF YA!
WHY WAIT, BIG MOUTH! IF YOU'RE GONNA DO IT, THIS IS AS GOOD A TIME AS ANY!
C'MON, YOU GUYS! GIVE ME A HAND WITH 'IM!
A HAND?? EVEN AN ELBOW AND A COUPLE OF SHOULDERS WOULDN'T HELP! HEY! LOOK OUT!
HAH! I THOUGHT THAT WOULD RATTLE YA A LITTLE!
YOU WERE RIGHT, MEATHEAD! IT RATTLED ME... BUT JUST A LITTLE!
HE DONE CRACKED UP! NAOW HE'S SINGIN' SONGS! UNGHH!
ALL HAIL THE SPIDER! A HARDY BREED IS HE! TRA LA LA!
HEY! AMSCRAY, YOU GUYS! THE POLICE ARE COMIN'!
WHAT'S GOING ON UP THERE?
EH, JUST A FRIENDLY LITTLE PARTY, OFFICER!
WHERE ARE ALL YOU PARTY POOPS RUNNING TO?? I WAS JUST BEGINNING TO ENJOY MYSELF!
DARN! THE ENFORCERS SLIPPED AWAY IN THE CONFUSION!
WELL, I'VE GOT A HUNCH IT WON'T BE LONG BEFORE WE MEET AGAIN... AND NEXT TIME IT'LL BE FOR REAL!
9.

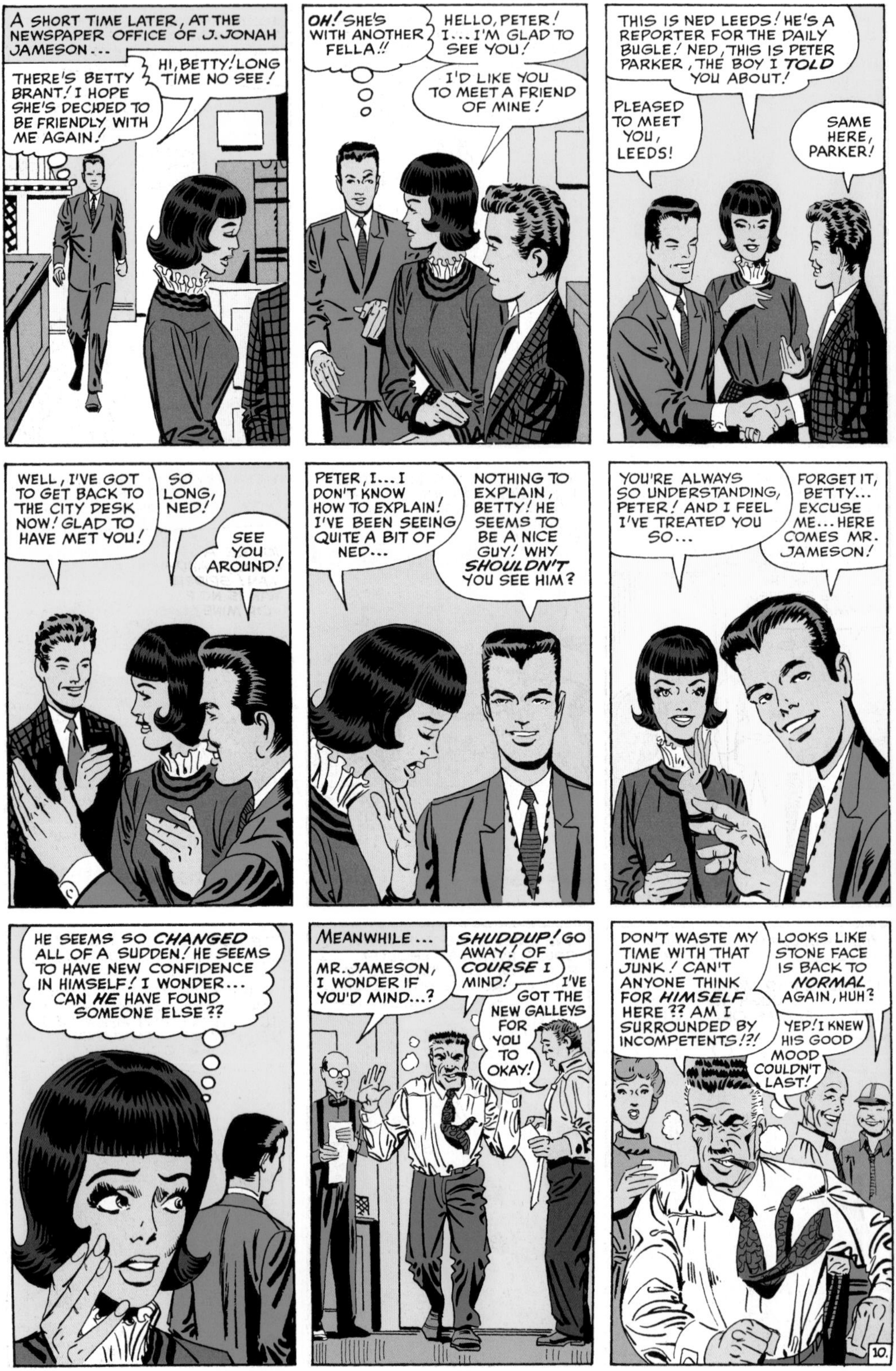

A SHORT TIME LATER, AT THE NEWSPAPER OFFICE OF J. JONAH JAMESON...
THERE'S BETTY BRANT! I HOPE SHE'S DECIDED TO BE FRIENDLY WITH ME AGAIN!
HI, BETTY! LONG TIME NO SEE!
OH! SHE'S WITH ANOTHER FELLA!!
HELLO, PETER! I... I'M GLAD TO SEE YOU!
I'D LIKE YOU TO MEET A FRIEND OF MINE!
THIS IS NED LEEDS! HE'S A REPORTER FOR THE DAILY BUGLE! NED, THIS IS PETER PARKER, THE BOY I TOLD YOU ABOUT!
PLEASED TO MEET YOU, LEEDS!
SAME HERE, PARKER!
WELL, I'VE GOT TO GET BACK TO THE CITY DESK NOW! GLAD TO HAVE MET YOU!
SO LONG, NED!
SEE YOU AROUND!
PETER, I... I DON'T KNOW HOW TO EXPLAIN! I'VE BEEN SEEING QUITE A BIT OF NED...
NOTHING TO EXPLAIN, BETTY! HE SEEMS TO BE A NICE GUY! WHY SHOULDN'T YOU SEE HIM?
YOU'RE ALWAYS SO UNDERSTANDING, PETER! AND I FEEL I'VE TREATED YOU SO...
FORGET IT, BETTY... EXCUSE ME... HERE COMES MR. JAMESON!
HE SEEMS SO CHANGED ALL OF A SUDDEN! HE SEEMS TO HAVE NEW CONFIDENCE IN HIMSELF! I WONDER... CAN HE HAVE FOUND SOMEONE ELSE??
MEANWHILE...
MR. JAMESON, I WONDER IF YOU'D MIND...?
SHUDDUP! GO AWAY! OF COURSE I MIND!
I'VE GOT THE NEW GALLEYS FOR YOU TO OKAY!
DON'T WASTE MY TIME WITH THAT JUNK! CAN'T ANYONE THINK FOR HIMSELF HERE?? AM I SURROUNDED BY INCOMPETENTS!?!
LOOKS LIKE STONE FACE IS BACK TO NORMAL AGAIN, HUH?
YEP! I KNEW HIS GOOD MOOD COULDN'T LAST!
10.

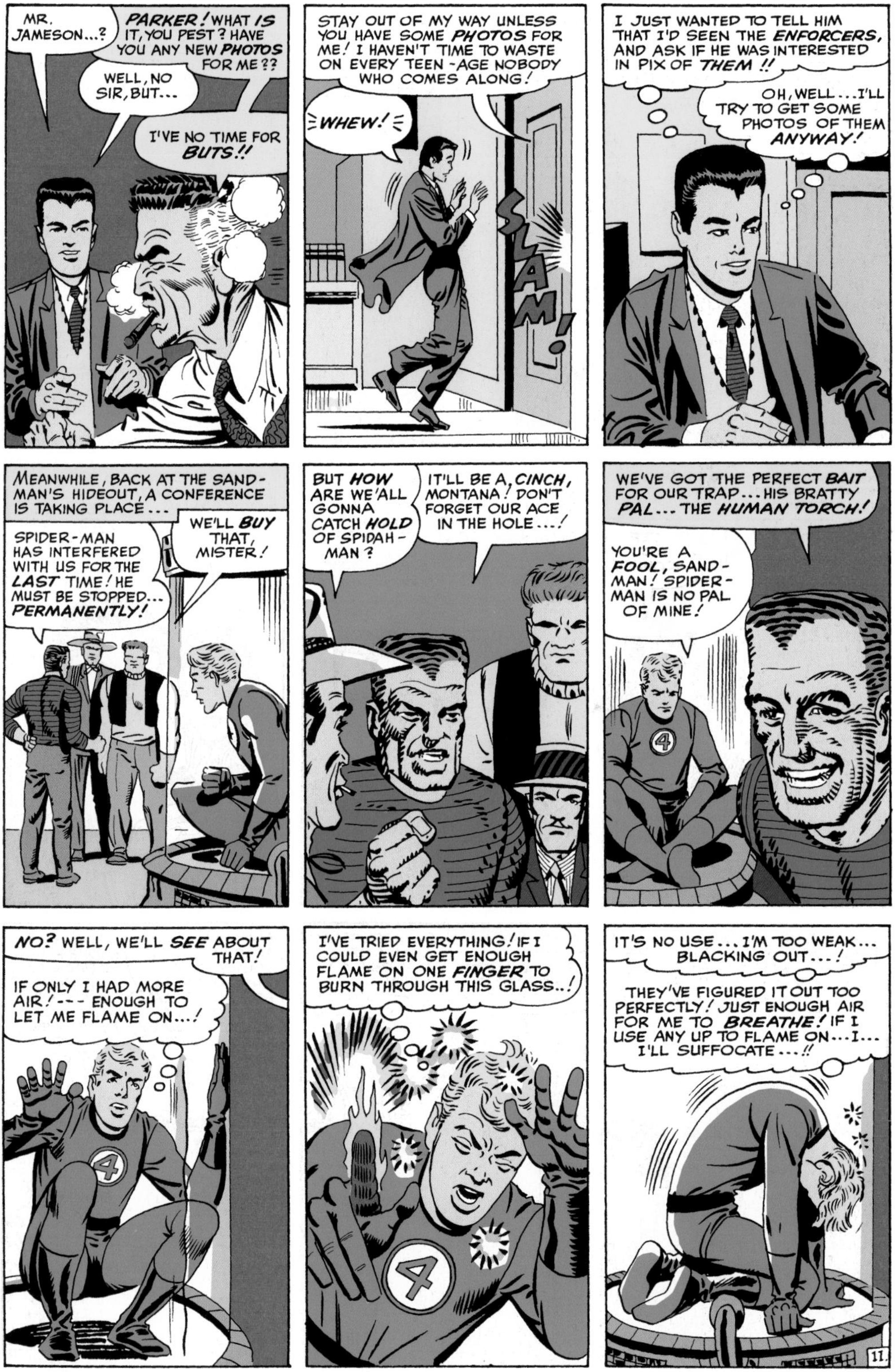
MR. JAMESON...?
PARKER! WHAT IS IT, YOU PEST? HAVE YOU ANY NEW PHOTOS FOR ME??
WELL, NO SIR, BUT...
I'VE NO TIME FOR BUTS!!
STAY OUT OF MY WAY UNLESS YOU HAVE SOME PHOTOS FOR ME! I HAVEN'T TIME TO WASTE ON EVERY TEEN-AGE NOBODY WHO COMES ALONG!
WHEW!
SLAM!
I JUST WANTED TO TELL HIM THAT I'D SEEN THE ENFORCERS, AND ASK IF HE WAS INTERESTED IN PIX OF THEM!!
OH, WELL...I'LL TRY TO GET SOME PHOTOS OF THEM ANYWAY!
MEANWHILE, BACK AT THE SAND-MAN'S HIDEOUT, A CONFERENCE IS TAKING PLACE...
SPIDER-MAN HAS INTERFERED WITH US FOR THE LAST TIME! HE MUST BE STOPPED... PERMANENTLY!
WE'LL BUY THAT, MISTER!
BUT HOW ARE WE'ALL GONNA CATCH HOLD OF SPIDAH-MAN?
IT'LL BE A CINCH, MONTANA! DON'T FORGET OUR ACE IN THE HOLE...!
WE'VE GOT THE PERFECT BAIT FOR OUR TRAP... HIS BRATTY PAL... THE HUMAN TORCH!
YOU'RE A FOOL, SAND-MAN! SPIDER-MAN IS NO PAL OF MINE!
NO? WELL, WE'LL SEE ABOUT THAT!
IF ONLY I HAD MORE AIR!--- ENOUGH TO LET ME FLAME ON...!
I'VE TRIED EVERYTHING! IF I COULD EVEN GET ENOUGH FLAME ON ONE FINGER TO BURN THROUGH THIS GLASS..!
IT'S NO USE... I'M TOO WEAK... BLACKING OUT...!
THEY'VE FIGURED IT OUT TOO PERFECTLY! JUST ENOUGH AIR FOR ME TO BREATHE! IF I USE ANY UP TO FLAME ON...I... I'LL SUFFOCATE...!!
11.

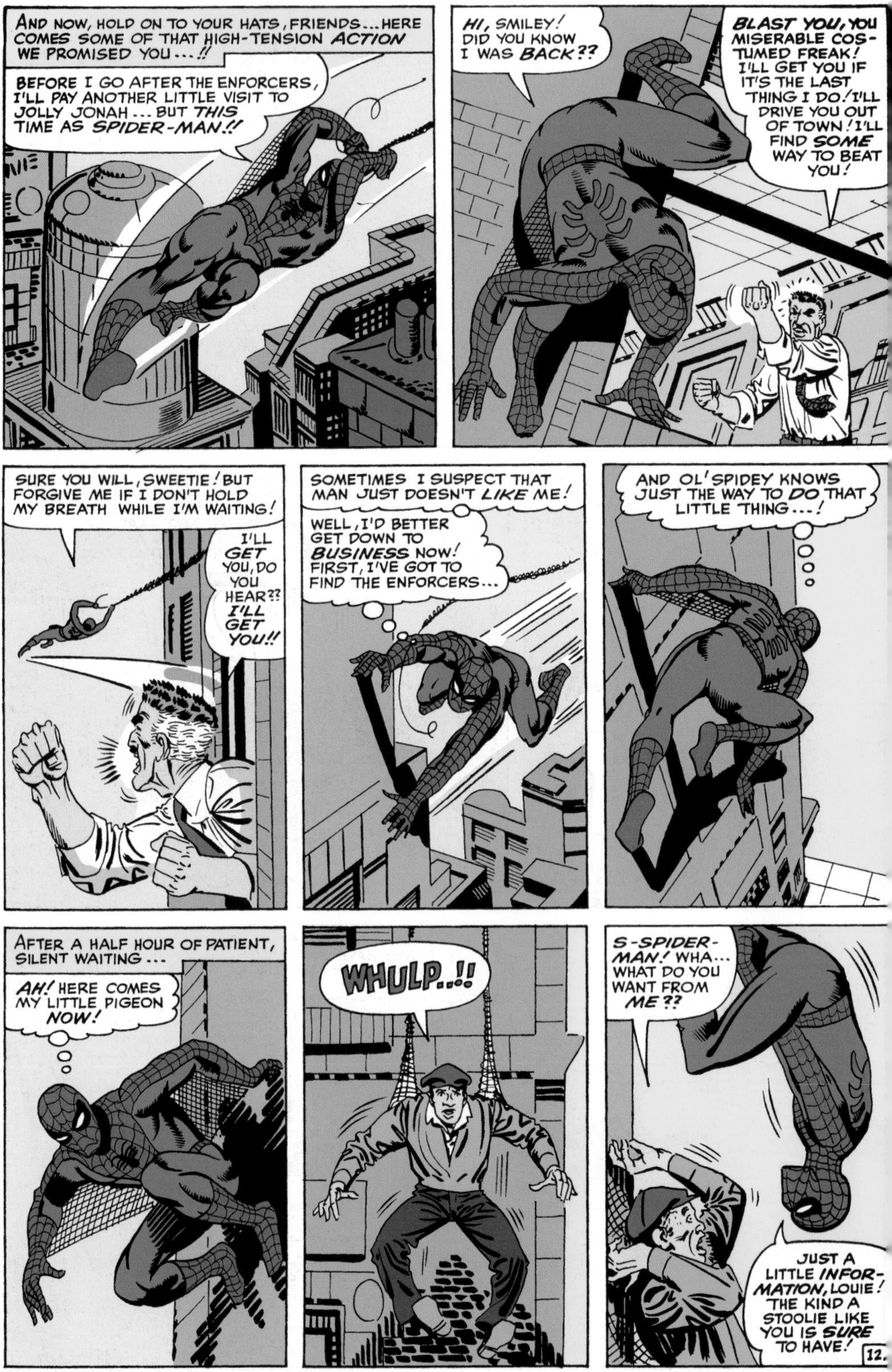
AND NOW, HOLD ON TO YOUR HATS, FRIENDS... HERE COMES SOME OF THAT HIGH-TENSION ACTION WE PROMISED YOU...!!
BEFORE I GO AFTER THE ENFORCERS, I'LL PAY ANOTHER LITTLE VISIT TO JOLLY JONAH... BUT THIS TIME AS SPIDER-MAN!!
HI, SMILEY! DID YOU KNOW I WAS BACK??
BLAST YOU, YOU MISERABLE COS-TUMED FREAK! I'LL GET YOU IF IT'S THE LAST THING I DO! I'LL DRIVE YOU OUT OF TOWN! I'LL FIND SOME WAY TO BEAT YOU!
SURE YOU WILL, SWEETIE! BUT FORGIVE ME IF I DON'T HOLD MY BREATH WHILE I'M WAITING!
I'LL GET YOU, DO YOU HEAR?? I'LL GET YOU!!
SOMETIMES I SUSPECT THAT MAN JUST DOESN'T LIKE ME!
WELL, I'D BETTER GET DOWN TO BUSINESS NOW! FIRST, I'VE GOT TO FIND THE ENFORCERS...
AND OL' SPIDEY KNOWS JUST THE WAY TO DO THAT LITTLE THING...!
AFTER A HALF HOUR OF PATIENT, SILENT WAITING...
AH! HERE COMES MY LITTLE PIGEON NOW!
WHULP..!!
S-SPIDER-MAN! WHA... WHAT DO YOU WANT FROM ME??
JUST A LITTLE INFOR-MATION, LOUIE! THE KIND A STOOLIE LIKE YOU IS SURE TO HAVE!
12

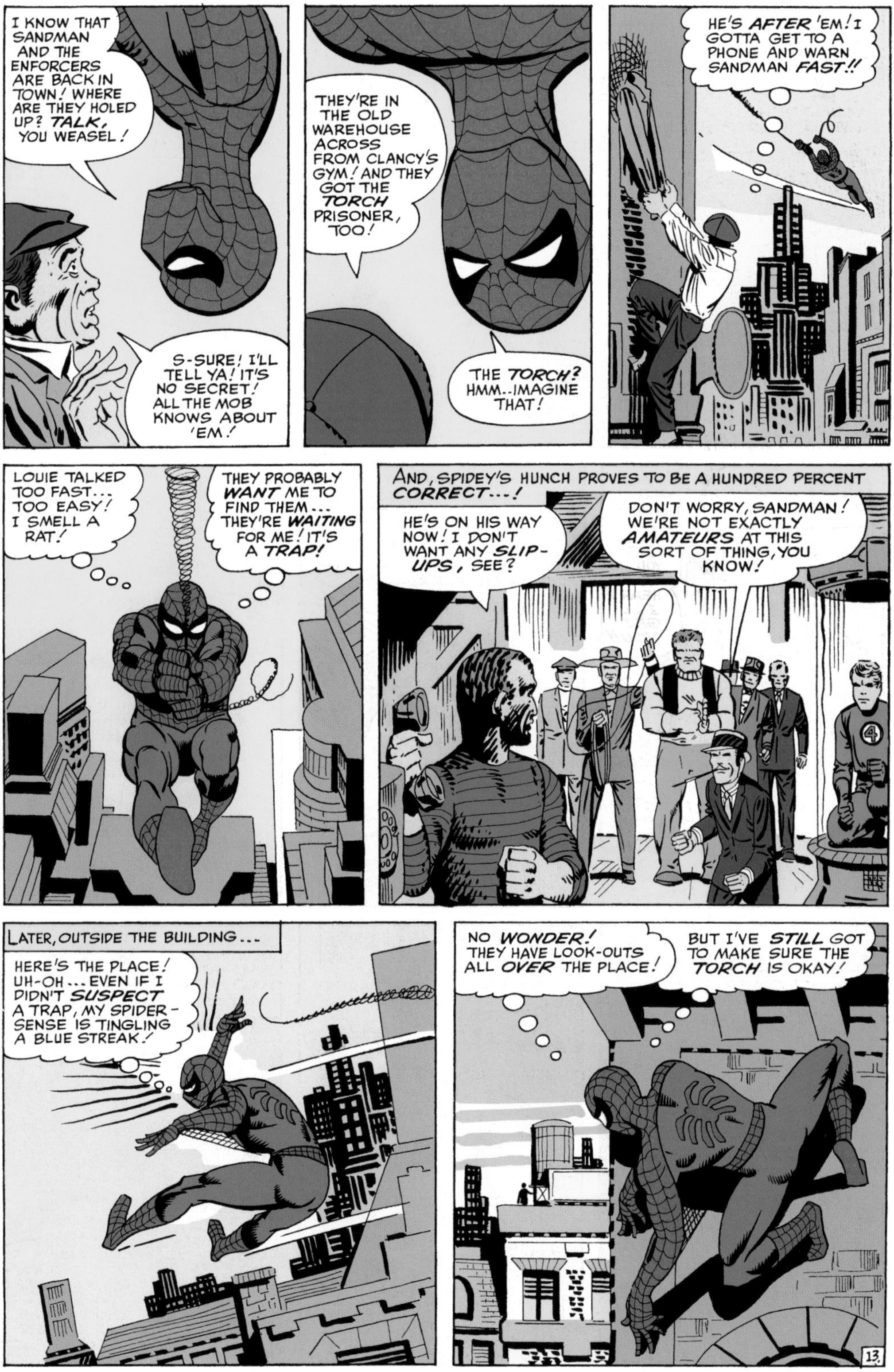
I KNOW THAT SANDMAN AND THE ENFORCERS ARE BACK IN TOWN! WHERE ARE THEY HOLED UP? TALK, YOU WEASEL!
S-SURE! I'LL TELL YA! IT'S NO SECRET! ALL THE MOB KNOWS ABOUT 'EM!
THEY'RE IN THE OLD WAREHOUSE ACROSS FROM CLANCY'S GYM! AND THEY GOT THE TORCH PRISONER, TOO!
THE TORCH? HMM..IMAGINE THAT!
HE'S AFTER 'EM! I GOTTA GET TO A PHONE AND WARN SANDMAN FAST!!
LOUIE TALKED TOO FAST... TOO EASY! I SMELL A RAT!
THEY PROBABLY WANT ME TO FIND THEM... THEY'RE WAITING FOR ME! IT'S A TRAP!
AND, SPIDEY'S HUNCH PROVES TO BE A HUNDRED PERCENT CORRECT...!
HE'S ON HIS WAY NOW! I DON'T WANT ANY SLIP-UPS, SEE?
DON'T WORRY, SANDMAN! WE'RE NOT EXACTLY AMATEURS AT THIS SORT OF THING, YOU KNOW!
LATER, OUTSIDE THE BUILDING...
HERE'S THE PLACE! UH-OH... EVEN IF I DIDN'T SUSPECT A TRAP, MY SPIDER-SENSE IS TINGLING A BLUE STREAK!
NO WONDER! THEY HAVE LOOK-OUTS ALL OVER THE PLACE!
BUT I'VE STILL GOT TO MAKE SURE THE TORCH IS OKAY!
13

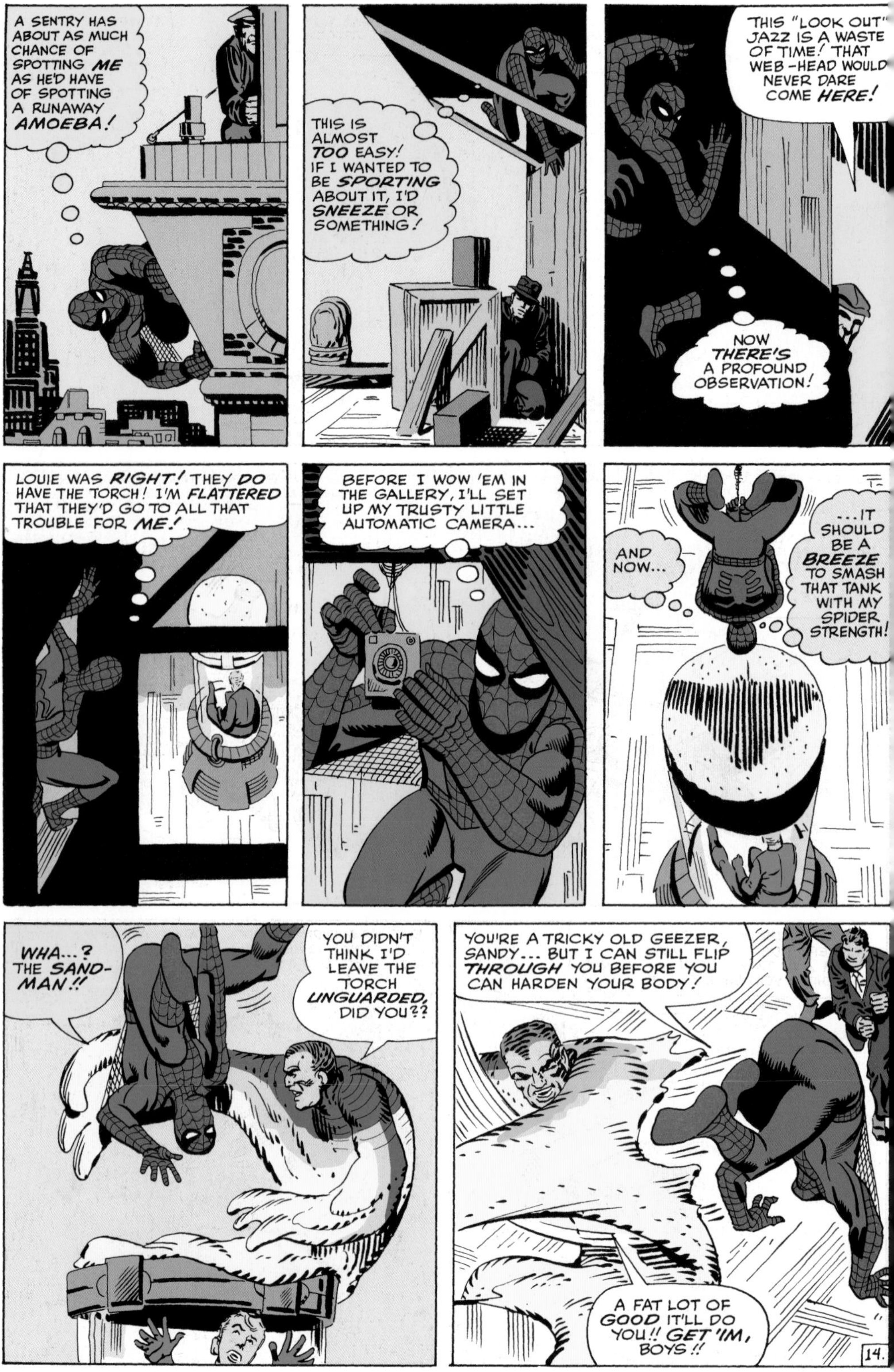
A SENTRY HAS ABOUT AS MUCH CHANCE OF SPOTTING ME AS HE'D HAVE OF SPOTTING A RUNAWAY AMOEBA!
THIS IS ALMOST TOO EASY! IF I WANTED TO BE SPORTING ABOUT IT, I'D SNEEZE OR SOMETHING!
THIS "LOOK OUT" JAZZ IS A WASTE OF TIME! THAT WEB-HEAD WOULD NEVER DARE COME HERE!
NOW THERE'S A PROFOUND OBSERVATION!
LOUIE WAS RIGHT! THEY DO HAVE THE TORCH! I'M FLATTERED THAT THEY'D GO TO ALL THAT TROUBLE FOR ME!
BEFORE I WOW 'EM IN THE GALLERY, I'LL SET UP MY TRUSTY LITTLE AUTOMATIC CAMERA...
AND NOW...
...IT SHOULD BE A BREEZE TO SMASH THAT TANK WITH MY SPIDER STRENGTH!
WHA...? THE SAND-MAN!!
YOU DIDN'T THINK I'D LEAVE THE TORCH UNGUARDED, DID YOU??
YOU'RE A TRICKY OLD GEEZER, SANDY... BUT I CAN STILL FLIP THROUGH YOU BEFORE YOU CAN HARDEN YOUR BODY!
A FAT LOT OF GOOD IT'LL DO YOU!! GET 'IM, BOYS!!
14.

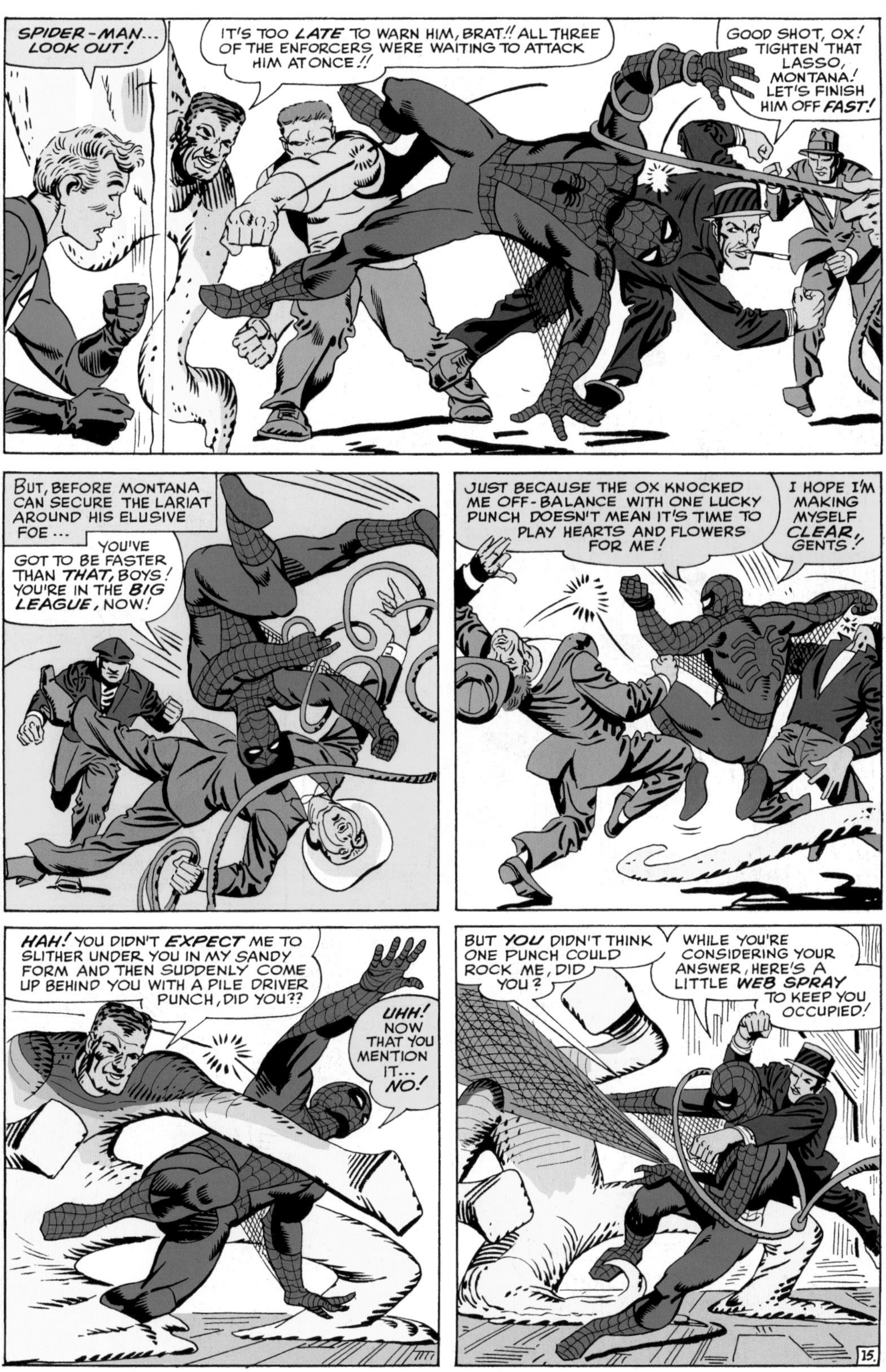
SPIDER-MAN... LOOK OUT!
IT'S TOO LATE TO WARN HIM, BRAT!! ALL THREE OF THE ENFORCERS WERE WAITING TO ATTACK HIM AT ONCE!!
GOOD SHOT, OX! TIGHTEN THAT LASSO, MONTANA! LET'S FINISH HIM OFF FAST!
BUT, BEFORE MONTANA CAN SECURE THE LARIAT AROUND HIS ELUSIVE FOE...
YOU'VE GOT TO BE FASTER THAN THAT, BOYS! YOU'RE IN THE BIG LEAGUE, NOW!
JUST BECAUSE THE OX KNOCKED ME OFF-BALANCE WITH ONE LUCKY PUNCH DOESN'T MEAN IT'S TIME TO PLAY HEARTS AND FLOWERS FOR ME!
I HOPE I'M MAKING MYSELF CLEAR, GENTS!
HAH! YOU DIDN'T EXPECT ME TO SLITHER UNDER YOU IN MY SANDY FORM AND THEN SUDDENLY COME UP BEHIND YOU WITH A PILE DRIVER PUNCH, DID YOU??
UHH! NOW THAT YOU MENTION IT... NO!
BUT YOU DIDN'T THINK ONE PUNCH COULD ROCK ME, DID YOU?
WHILE YOU'RE CONSIDERING YOUR ANSWER, HERE'S A LITTLE WEB SPRAY TO KEEP YOU OCCUPIED!
15

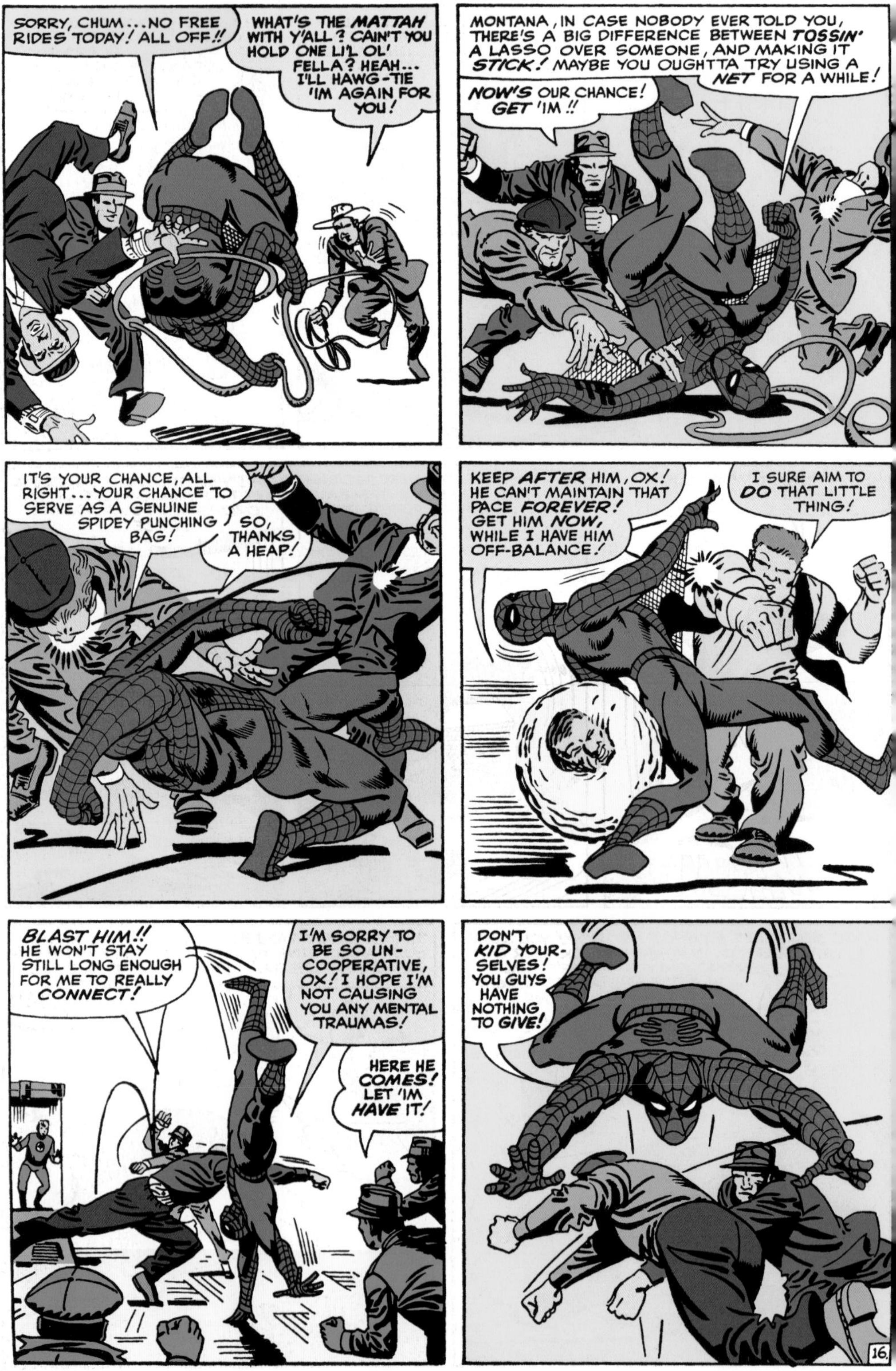

SORRY, CHUM... NO FREE RIDES TODAY! ALL OFF!!
WHAT'S THE MATTAH WITH Y'ALL? CAIN'T YOU HOLD ONE LI'L OL' FELLA? HEAH... I'LL HAWG-TIE 'IM AGAIN FOR YOU!
MONTANA, IN CASE NOBODY EVER TOLD YOU, THERE'S A BIG DIFFERENCE BETWEEN TOSSIN' A LASSO OVER SOMEONE, AND MAKING IT STICK! MAYBE YOU OUGHTTA TRY USING A NET FOR A WHILE!
NOW'S OUR CHANCE! GET 'IM!!
IT'S YOUR CHANCE, ALL RIGHT... YOUR CHANCE TO SERVE AS A GENUINE SPIDEY PUNCHING BAG!
SO, THANKS A HEAP!
KEEP AFTER HIM, OX! HE CAN'T MAINTAIN THAT PACE FOREVER! GET HIM NOW, WHILE I HAVE HIM OFF-BALANCE!
I SURE AIM TO DO THAT LITTLE THING!
BLAST HIM!! HE WON'T STAY STILL LONG ENOUGH FOR ME TO REALLY CONNECT!
I'M SORRY TO BE SO UN-COOPERATIVE, OX! I HOPE I'M NOT CAUSING YOU ANY MENTAL TRAUMAS!
HERE HE COMES! LET 'IM HAVE IT!
DON'T KID YOUR-SELVES! YOU GUYS HAVE NOTHING TO GIVE!
16

AND, AS FOR *YOU*, OX, I'M GETTING A LITTLE *TIRED* OF YOU TAKING SWIPES AT ME!

SO, I FIGURE IT'S TIME FOR ME TO GET *MY* LICKS IN NOW!

ALTHOUGH THERE *IS* ONE THING I'M GRATEFUL TO YOU FOR...

USUALLY I HAVE TO PULL MY PUNCHES WITH OTHER GUYS... BUT WITH *YOU*, I CAN REALLY LET MYSELF *GO!*...AHHH, THAT WAS LIKE A *SYMPHONY!!*

SANDMAN*!!* DON'T YOU *EVER* GIVE UP??

WHUMP!

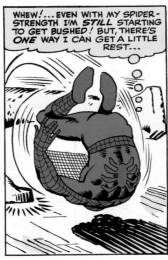

WHEW*!*...EVEN WITH MY SPIDER-STRENGTH I'M *STILL* STARTING TO GET BUSHED*!* BUT, THERE'S *ONE* WAY I CAN GET A LITTLE REST...

IF I TIME THIS JUST RIGHT, I'LL HIT THAT GLASS CAGE OF THE TORCH'S WITH JUST ENOUGH FORCE...

...TO *SHATTER* IT... LIKE *THIS!!*

BOY! YOU SURE TOOK YOUR OWN SWEET TIME ABOUT *FREEING* ME*!!*

THAT'S *GRATITUDE* FOR YOU! SOME GUYS ARE *NEVER* SATISFIED!

I WAS BEGINNING TO THINK YOU WANTED TO HOG THE WHOLE FIGHT FOR *YOUR-SELF!*

17.

279

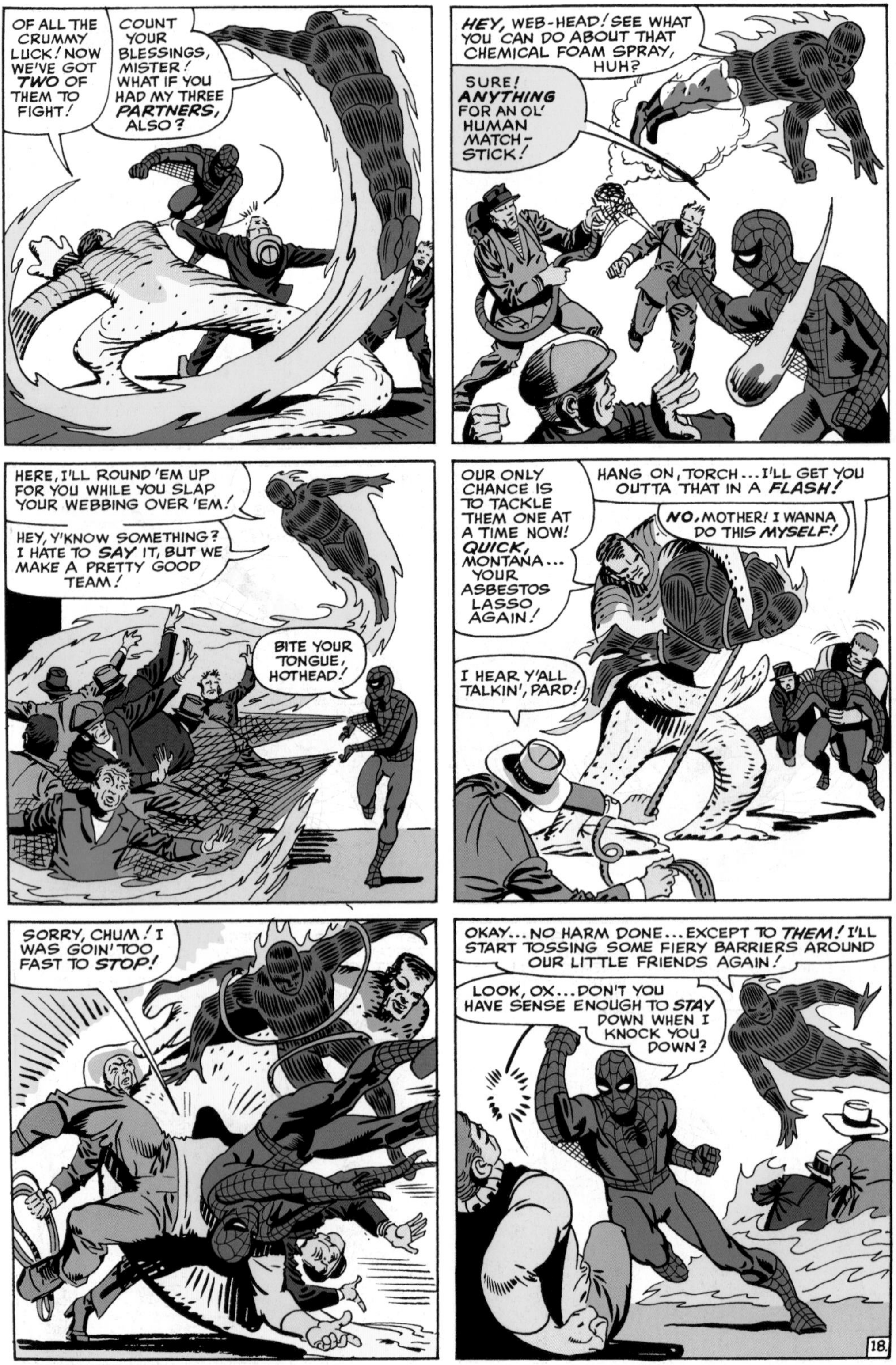
OF ALL THE CRUMMY LUCK! NOW WE'VE GOT TWO OF THEM TO FIGHT!
COUNT YOUR BLESSINGS, MISTER! WHAT IF YOU HAD MY THREE PARTNERS, ALSO?
HEY, WEB-HEAD! SEE WHAT YOU CAN DO ABOUT THAT CHEMICAL FOAM SPRAY, HUH?
SURE! ANYTHING FOR AN OL' HUMAN MATCH-STICK!
HERE, I'LL ROUND 'EM UP FOR YOU WHILE YOU SLAP YOUR WEBBING OVER 'EM!
HEY, Y'KNOW SOMETHING? I HATE TO SAY IT, BUT WE MAKE A PRETTY GOOD TEAM!
BITE YOUR TONGUE, HOTHEAD!
OUR ONLY CHANCE IS TO TACKLE THEM ONE AT A TIME NOW! QUICK, MONTANA... YOUR ASBESTOS LASSO AGAIN!
HANG ON, TORCH... I'LL GET YOU OUTTA THAT IN A FLASH!
NO, MOTHER! I WANNA DO THIS MYSELF!
I HEAR Y'ALL TALKIN', PARD!
SORRY, CHUM! I WAS GOIN' TOO FAST TO STOP!
OKAY... NO HARM DONE... EXCEPT TO THEM! I'LL START TOSSING SOME FIERY BARRIERS AROUND OUR LITTLE FRIENDS AGAIN!
LOOK, OX... DON'T YOU HAVE SENSE ENOUGH TO STAY DOWN WHEN I KNOCK YOU DOWN?
18.

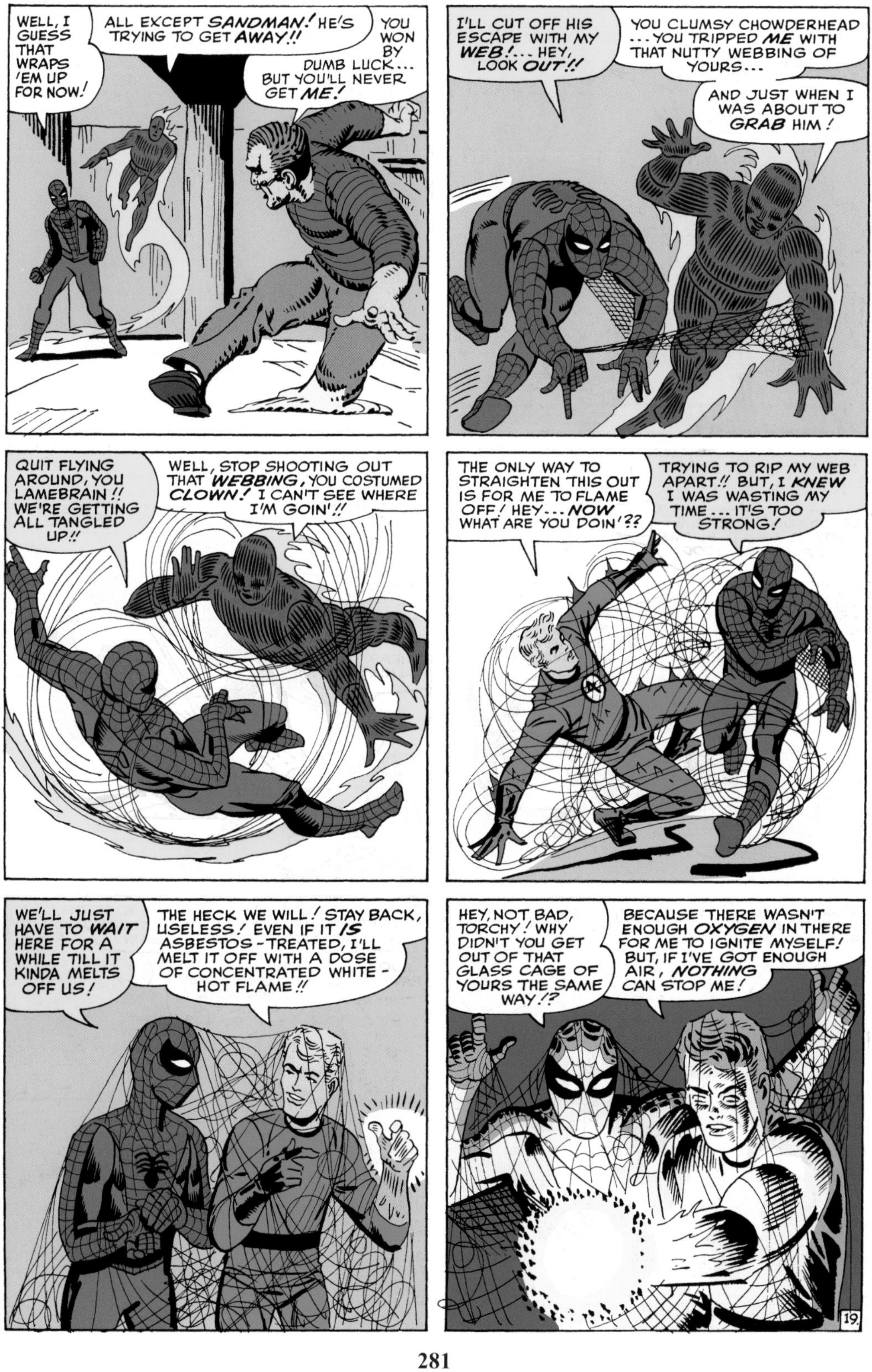
WELL, I GUESS THAT WRAPS 'EM UP FOR NOW!
ALL EXCEPT SANDMAN! HE'S TRYING TO GET AWAY!!
YOU WON BY DUMB LUCK... BUT YOU'LL NEVER GET ME!
I'LL CUT OFF HIS ESCAPE WITH MY WEB!... HEY, LOOK OUT!!
YOU CLUMSY CHOWDERHEAD ... YOU TRIPPED ME WITH THAT NUTTY WEBBING OF YOURS...
AND JUST WHEN I WAS ABOUT TO GRAB HIM!
QUIT FLYING AROUND, YOU LAMEBRAIN!! WE'RE GETTING ALL TANGLED UP!!
WELL, STOP SHOOTING OUT THAT WEBBING, YOU COSTUMED CLOWN! I CAN'T SEE WHERE I'M GOIN'!!
THE ONLY WAY TO STRAIGHTEN THIS OUT IS FOR ME TO FLAME OFF! HEY... NOW WHAT ARE YOU DOIN'??
TRYING TO RIP MY WEB APART!! BUT, I KNEW I WAS WASTING MY TIME... IT'S TOO STRONG!
WE'LL JUST HAVE TO WAIT HERE FOR A WHILE TILL IT KINDA MELTS OFF US!
THE HECK WE WILL! STAY BACK, USELESS! EVEN IF IT IS ASBESTOS-TREATED, I'LL MELT IT OFF WITH A DOSE OF CONCENTRATED WHITE-HOT FLAME!!
HEY, NOT BAD, TORCHY! WHY DIDN'T YOU GET OUT OF THAT GLASS CAGE OF YOURS THE SAME WAY!?
BECAUSE THERE WASN'T ENOUGH OXYGEN IN THERE FOR ME TO IGNITE MYSELF! BUT, IF I'VE GOT ENOUGH AIR, NOTHING CAN STOP ME!
19.

AND, IT LOOKS LIKE NOTHING STOPPED SANDMAN, EITHER! HE SEEMS TO HAVE GOTTEN AWAY!

NUTS! HE'S THE ONE I WAS MOST ANXIOUS TO GET... AFTER THE HARD TIME HE GAVE ME LAST MONTH!

YEAH, I REMEMBER THAT! EVERYONE THOUGHT YOU'D TURNED CHICKEN! WHAT MADE YOU RUN OUT ON THAT FIGHT WITH THE GREEN GOBLIN, ANYWAY?

ANYONE EVER TELL YOU THAT YOU ASK TOO MANY QUESTIONS, FELLA??

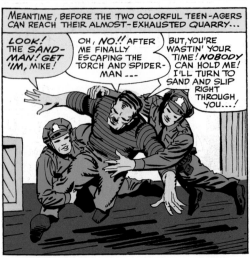

MEANTIME, BEFORE THE TWO COLORFUL TEEN-AGERS CAN REACH THEIR ALMOST-EXHAUSTED QUARRY...

LOOK! THE SANDMAN! GET 'IM, MIKE!

OH, NO!! AFTER ME FINALLY ESCAPING THE TORCH AND SPIDER-MAN ---

BUT, YOU'RE WASTIN' YOUR TIME! NOBODY CAN HOLD ME! I'LL TURN TO SAND AND SLIP RIGHT THROUGH YOU...!

NOT THIS TIME, MISTER! WE'LL HANG ONTO YOU EVEN IF WE HAVE TO SCOOP YOU UP WITH A PAIL AND SHOVEL!!

IT'S NO USE! I'M TOO TIRED! CAN'T MAKE THE EFFORT... TOO MUCH OF A STRAIN... MIGHT AS WELL SURRENDER!

WE'VE GOT HIM! HE CAN'T GET AWAY!

ALL RIGHT, YOU WIN! I'LL GO BACK TO JAIL PEACEFULLY! ANYTHING IS BETTER THAN HAVING TO FACE SPIDER-MAN AND THAT FLAMING FREAK AGAIN!

SPIDER-MAN? THEN THE REPORTS MUST BE TRUE! HE IS BACK IN ACTION, FIGHTING CRIME ONCE MORE!

AND MORE POWER TO HIM, AS FAR AS I'M CONCERNED!

WELL, IT LOOKS AS THOUGH THE POLICE HAVE THINGS WELL IN HAND! NOTHING MORE FOR US TO DO!

THERE'S STILL ONE THING... THE THING YOU ALWAYS TRY TO GET ALL THE CREDIT, WHILE I TAKE A POWDER! SO LONG, JUNIOR!

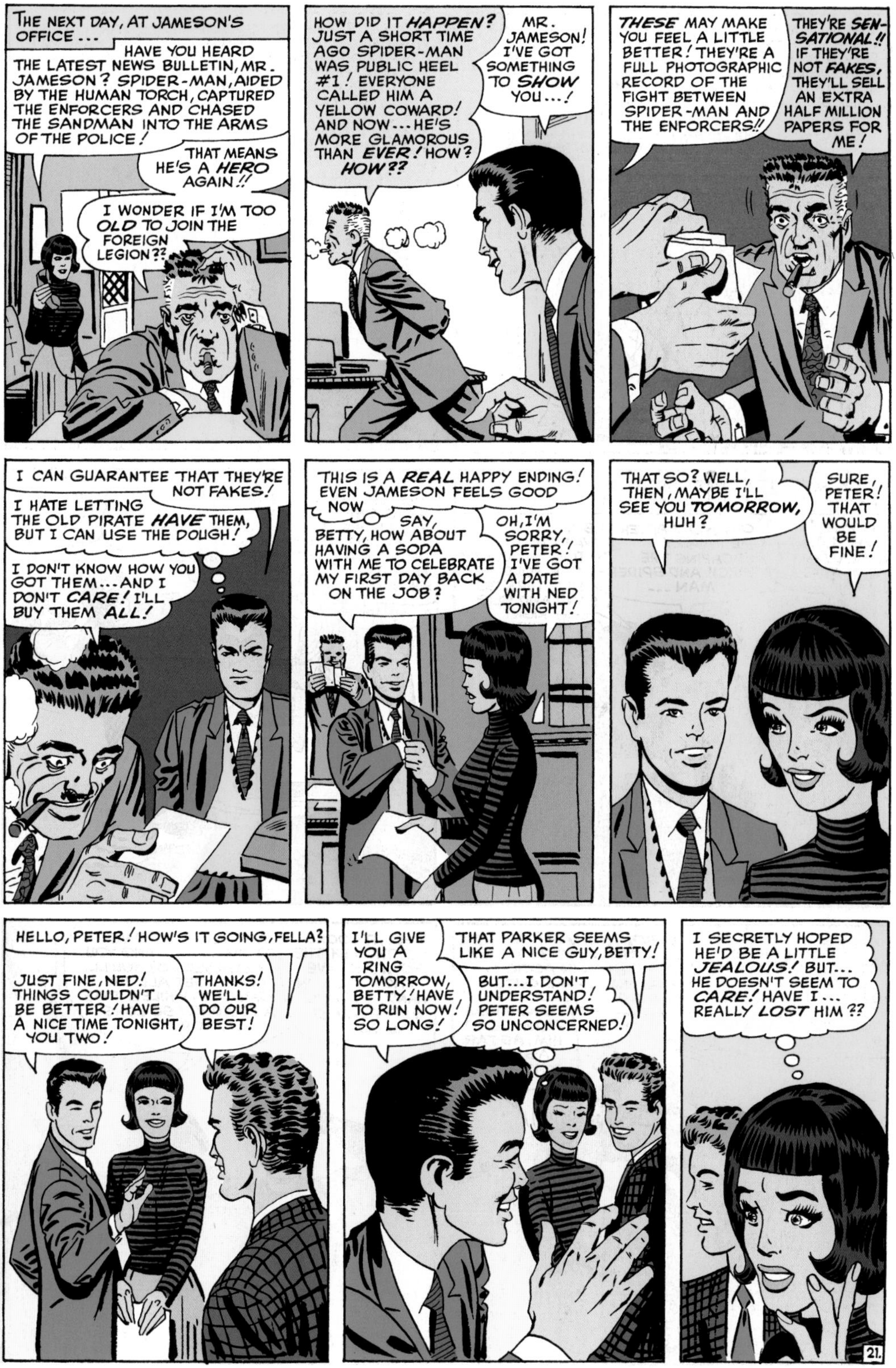
THE NEXT DAY, AT JAMESON'S OFFICE...
HAVE YOU HEARD THE LATEST NEWS BULLETIN, MR. JAMESON? SPIDER-MAN, AIDED BY THE HUMAN TORCH, CAPTURED THE ENFORCERS AND CHASED THE SANDMAN INTO THE ARMS OF THE POLICE!
THAT MEANS HE'S A HERO AGAIN!!
I WONDER IF I'M TOO OLD TO JOIN THE FOREIGN LEGION??
HOW DID IT HAPPEN? JUST A SHORT TIME AGO SPIDER-MAN WAS PUBLIC HEEL #1! EVERYONE CALLED HIM A YELLOW COWARD! AND NOW... HE'S MORE GLAMOROUS THAN EVER! HOW? HOW??
MR. JAMESON! I'VE GOT SOMETHING TO SHOW YOU...!
THESE MAY MAKE YOU FEEL A LITTLE BETTER! THEY'RE A FULL PHOTOGRAPHIC RECORD OF THE FIGHT BETWEEN SPIDER-MAN AND THE ENFORCERS!!
THEY'RE SENSATIONAL!! IF THEY'RE NOT FAKES, THEY'LL SELL AN EXTRA HALF MILLION PAPERS FOR ME!
I CAN GUARANTEE THAT THEY'RE NOT FAKES!
I HATE LETTING THE OLD PIRATE HAVE THEM, BUT I CAN USE THE DOUGH!
I DON'T KNOW HOW YOU GOT THEM... AND I DON'T CARE! I'LL BUY THEM ALL!
THIS IS A REAL HAPPY ENDING! EVEN JAMESON FEELS GOOD NOW
SAY, BETTY, HOW ABOUT HAVING A SODA WITH ME TO CELEBRATE MY FIRST DAY BACK ON THE JOB?
OH, I'M SORRY, PETER! I'VE GOT A DATE WITH NED TONIGHT!
THAT SO? WELL, THEN, MAYBE I'LL SEE YOU TOMORROW, HUH?
SURE, PETER! THAT WOULD BE FINE!
HELLO, PETER! HOW'S IT GOING, FELLA?
JUST FINE, NED! THINGS COULDN'T BE BETTER! HAVE A NICE TIME TONIGHT, YOU TWO!
THANKS! WE'LL DO OUR BEST!
I'LL GIVE YOU A RING TOMORROW, BETTY! HAVE TO RUN NOW! SO LONG!
THAT PARKER SEEMS LIKE A NICE GUY, BETTY!
BUT... I DON'T UNDERSTAND! PETER SEEMS SO UNCONCERNED!
I SECRETLY HOPED HE'D BE A LITTLE JEALOUS! BUT... HE DOESN'T SEEM TO CARE! HAVE I... REALLY LOST HIM??
21.

LATER, AS THE NEXT EDITION GOES ON SALE...

JONAH JAMESON DID IT AGAIN! AN EXCLUSIVE SET OF PHOTOS SHOWING SPIDER-MAN IN ACTION!

BUT, JUST THE OTHER DAY HE WAS CALLING SPIDEY A FRAUD!

DON'T YOU UNDERSTAND PUBLICITY? HE JUST DID IT TO GET PEOPLE INTERESTED! THEN HE PULLS OFF A STUNT LIKE THIS! I'LL BET THEY'RE BOTH IN CAHOOTS!

I WOULDN'T BE AT ALL SURPRISED!

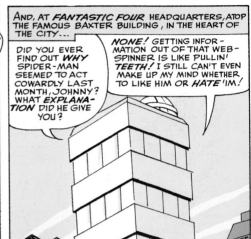

AND, AT FANTASTIC FOUR HEADQUARTERS, ATOP THE FAMOUS BAXTER BUILDING, IN THE HEART OF THE CITY...

DID YOU EVER FIND OUT WHY SPIDER-MAN SEEMED TO ACT COWARDLY LAST MONTH, JOHNNY? WHAT EXPLANATION DID HE GIVE YOU?

NONE! GETTING INFORMATION OUT OF THAT WEB-SPINNER IS LIKE PULLIN' TEETH! I STILL CAN'T EVEN MAKE UP MY MIND WHETHER TO LIKE HIM OR HATE 'IM!

WHILE, OUTSIDE MIDTOWN HIGH SCHOOL, AT 3:00 P.M....

SO LONG, PETEY!

SEE YOU TOMORROW, LIZ!

"PETEY"! HE'S THE ONE!

SLOWLY, AT A SAFE DISTANCE, THE SILENT STRANGER FOLLOWS THE UNSUSPECTING TEEN-AGER...

IT'S GREAT TO HAVE THINGS BACK TO NORMAL AGAIN! I HAVEN'T A WORRY IN THE WORLD NOW!

HMM! HE TURNED OUT THE LIGHTS SOME TIME AGO! I GUESS IT'S SAFE TO PHONE AND CHECK IN NOW!

ALL RIGHT! NOW GET BACK TO YOUR POST UNTIL YOU'RE RELIEVED! I WANT HIM UNDER SURVEILLANCE EVERY MINUTE!

I'VE GOT TO KNOW FOR CERTAIN! AND THEN... WHEN I'M SURE... I'LL ACT!

WHAT'S THIS?? IT SEEMS THAT A NEW AND DIFFERENT MENACE IS ABOUT TO ENTER THE LIFE OF PETER PARKER! BE PREPARED FOR THE UNEXPECTED, AS SURPRISE FOLLOWS SURPRISE IN OUR NEXT SHOCK-FILLED ISSUE OF THE MAGAZINE THAT HAS BECOME ONE OF AMERICA'S FAVORITE READING HABITS...THE AMAZING SPIDER-MAN!

22.

This production photostat of *The Amazing Spider-Man* #11 cover shows Steve Ditko's original depiction of Doctor Octopus without glasses and with a thinner face.

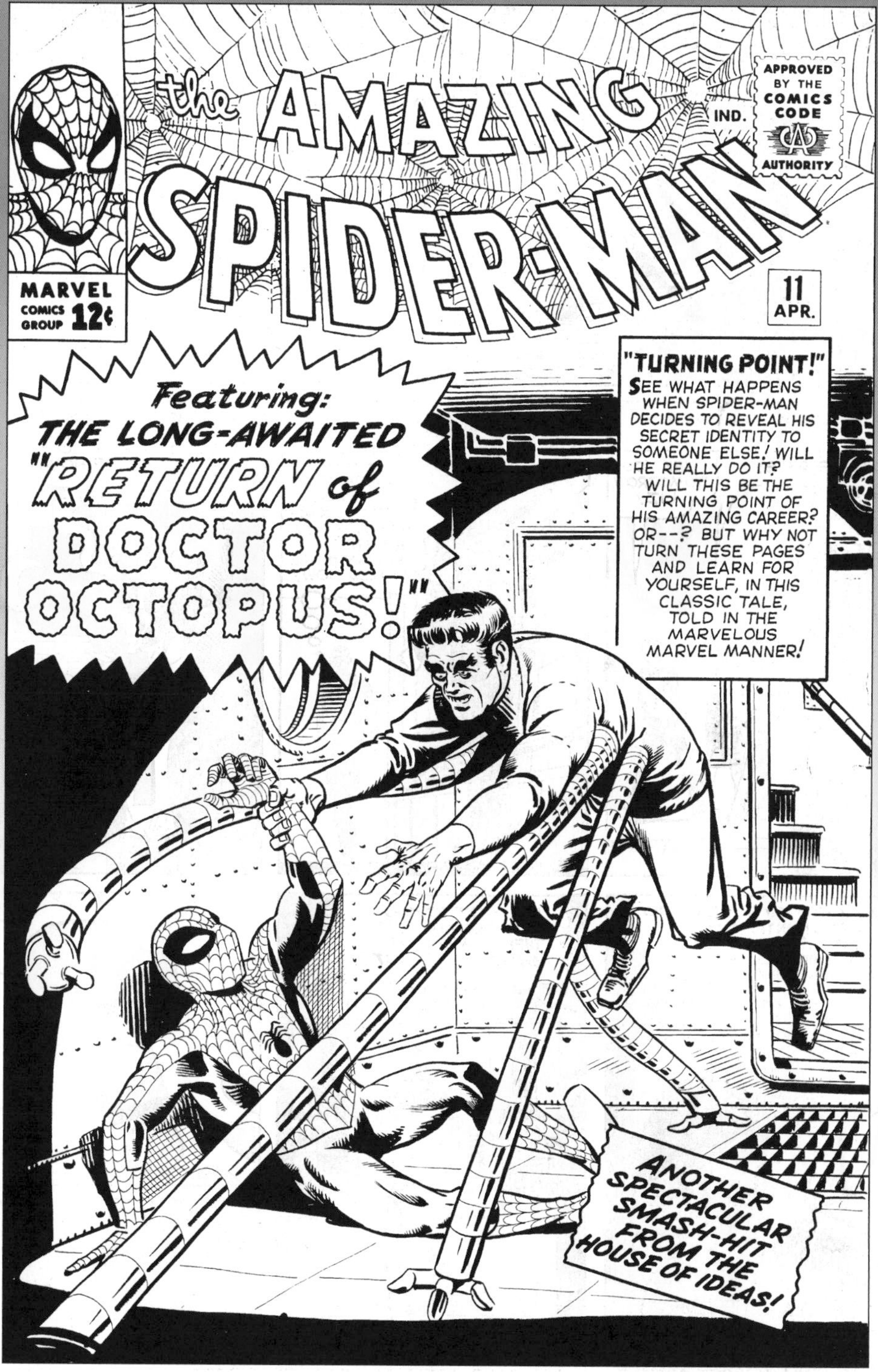
the AMAZING SPIDER-MAN
APPROVED BY THE COMICS CODE AUTHORITY
IND.
MARVEL COMICS GROUP 12¢
11 APR.
Featuring: THE LONG-AWAITED "RETURN of DOCTOR OCTOPUS!"
"TURNING POINT!" SEE WHAT HAPPENS WHEN SPIDER-MAN DECIDES TO REVEAL HIS SECRET IDENTITY TO SOMEONE ELSE! WILL HE REALLY DO IT? WILL THIS BE THE TURNING POINT OF HIS AMAZING CAREER? OR--? BUT WHY NOT TURN THESE PAGES AND LEARN FOR YOURSELF, IN THIS CLASSIC TALE, TOLD IN THE MARVELOUS MARVEL MANNER!
ANOTHER SPECTACULAR SMASH-HIT FROM THE HOUSE OF IDEAS!

The Amazing Spider-Man **#12 page 1 original art**
by Steve Ditko

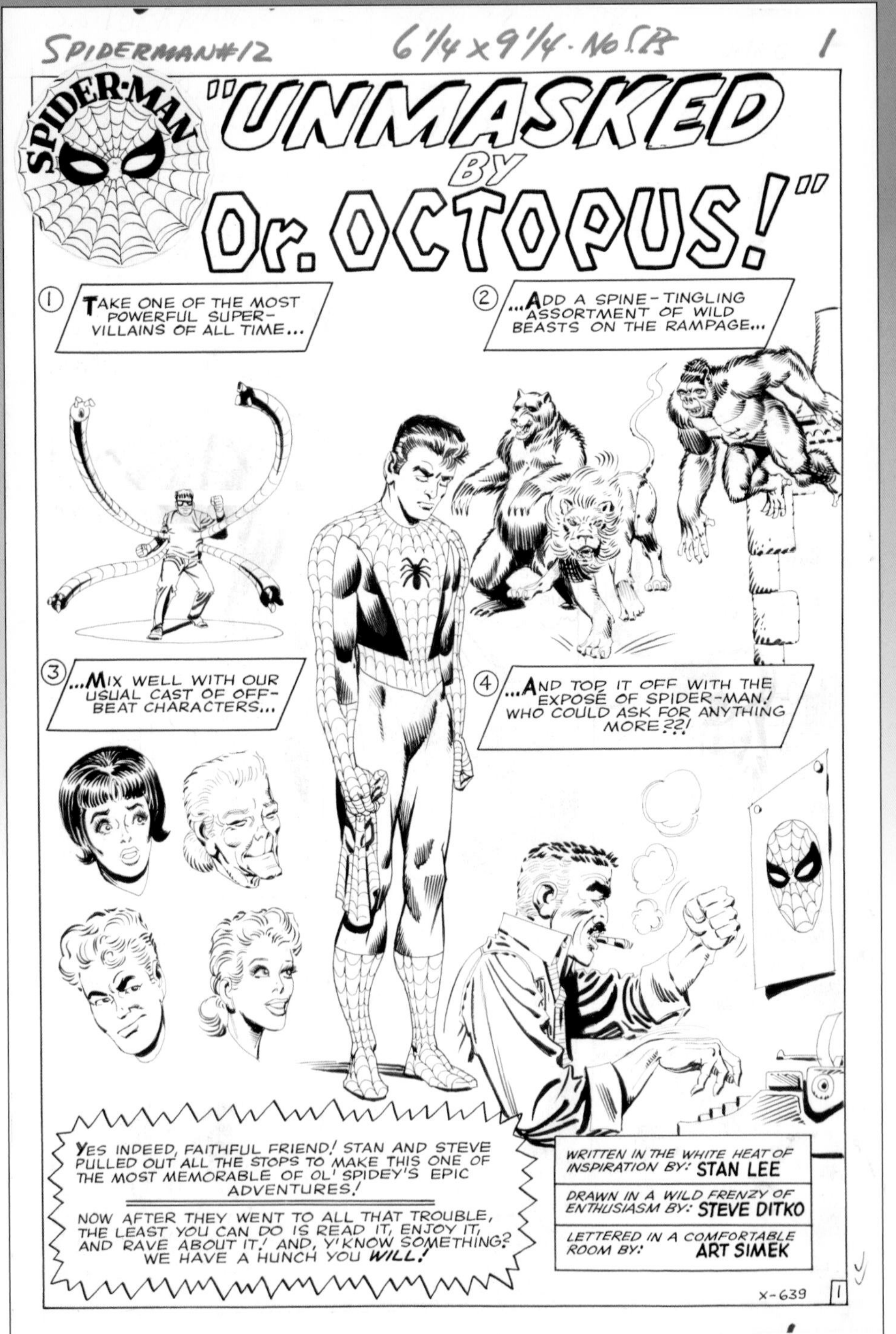
SPIDERMAN#12
6 1/4 x 9 1/4 · No S.B
1
SPIDER-MAN
"UNMASKED BY Dr. OCTOPUS!"
1 TAKE ONE OF THE MOST POWERFUL SUPER-VILLAINS OF ALL TIME...
2 ...ADD A SPINE-TINGLING ASSORTMENT OF WILD BEASTS ON THE RAMPAGE...
3 ...MIX WELL WITH OUR USUAL CAST OF OFF-BEAT CHARACTERS...
4 ...AND TOP IT OFF WITH THE EXPOSÉ OF SPIDER-MAN! WHO COULD ASK FOR ANYTHING MORE??!
YES INDEED, FAITHFUL FRIEND! STAN AND STEVE PULLED OUT ALL THE STOPS TO MAKE THIS ONE OF THE MOST MEMORABLE OF OL' SPIDEY'S EPIC ADVENTURES!
NOW AFTER THEY WENT TO ALL THAT TROUBLE, THE LEAST YOU CAN DO IS READ IT, ENJOY IT, AND RAVE ABOUT IT! AND, Y'KNOW SOMETHING? WE HAVE A HUNCH YOU WILL!
WRITTEN IN THE WHITE HEAT OF INSPIRATION BY: STAN LEE
DRAWN IN A WILD FRENZY OF ENTHUSIASM BY: STEVE DITKO
LETTERED IN A COMFORTABLE ROOM BY: ART SIMEK
X-639
1

Courtesy HeritageAuctions.com

The Amazing Spider-Man #12 page 17 original art
by Steve Ditko

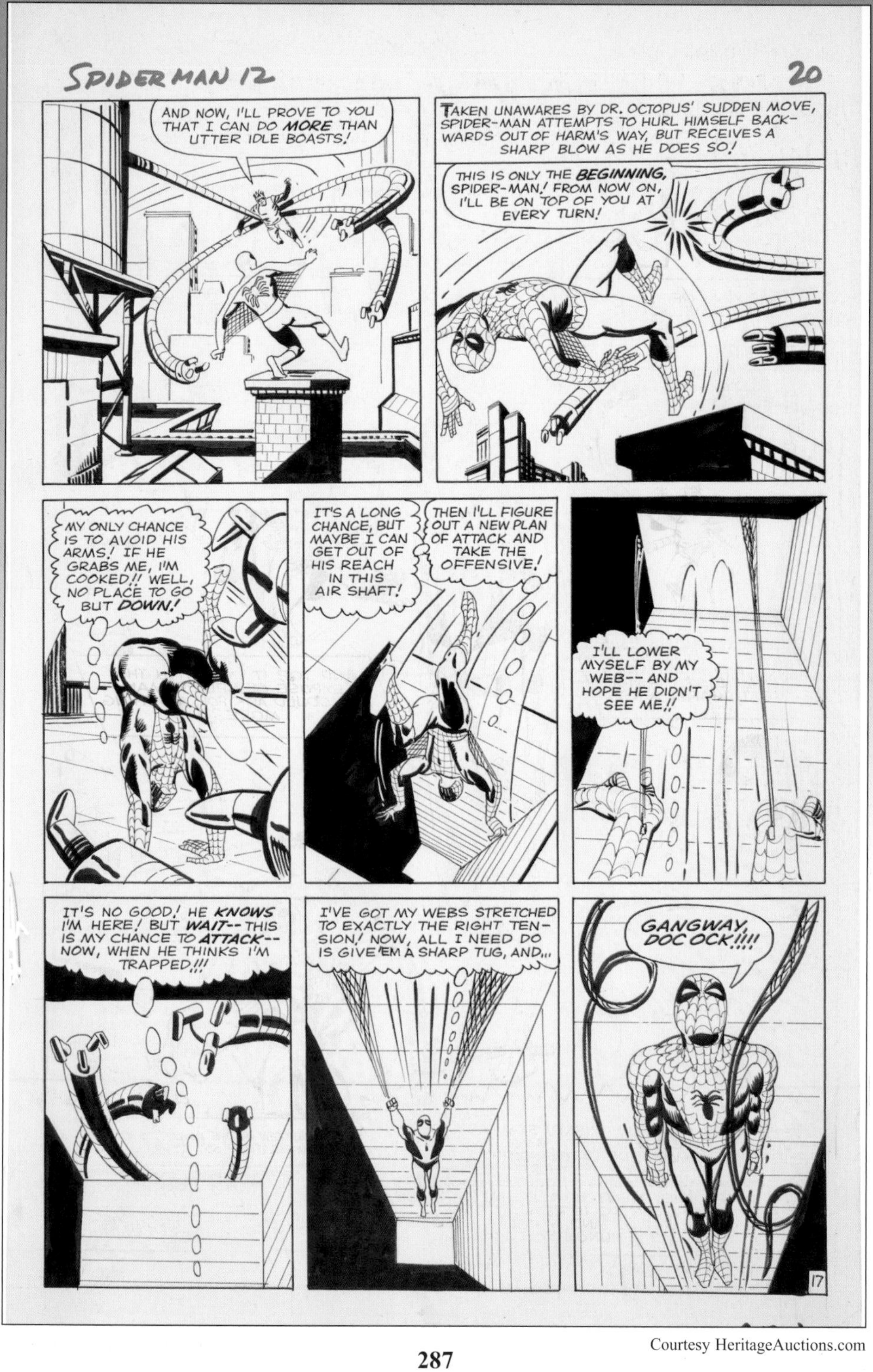
SPIDERMAN 12
20
AND NOW, I'LL PROVE TO YOU THAT I CAN DO MORE THAN UTTER IDLE BOASTS!
TAKEN UNAWARES BY DR. OCTOPUS' SUDDEN MOVE, SPIDER-MAN ATTEMPTS TO HURL HIMSELF BACKWARDS OUT OF HARM'S WAY, BUT RECEIVES A SHARP BLOW AS HE DOES SO!
THIS IS ONLY THE BEGINNING, SPIDER-MAN! FROM NOW ON, I'LL BE ON TOP OF YOU AT EVERY TURN!
MY ONLY CHANCE IS TO AVOID HIS ARMS! IF HE GRABS ME, I'M COOKED!! WELL, NO PLACE TO GO BUT DOWN!
IT'S A LONG CHANCE, BUT MAYBE I CAN GET OUT OF HIS REACH IN THIS AIR SHAFT!
THEN I'LL FIGURE OUT A NEW PLAN OF ATTACK AND TAKE THE OFFENSIVE!
I'LL LOWER MYSELF BY MY WEB-- AND HOPE HE DIDN'T SEE ME!!
IT'S NO GOOD! HE KNOWS I'M HERE! BUT WAIT-- THIS IS MY CHANCE TO ATTACK-- NOW, WHEN HE THINKS I'M TRAPPED!!!
I'VE GOT MY WEBS STRETCHED TO EXACTLY THE RIGHT TENSION! NOW, ALL I NEED DO IS GIVE 'EM A SHARP TUG, AND...
GANGWAY, DOC OCK!!!!
17

Courtesy HeritageAuctions.com

***The Amazing Spider-Man* #18 page 22 original art**
by Steve Ditko

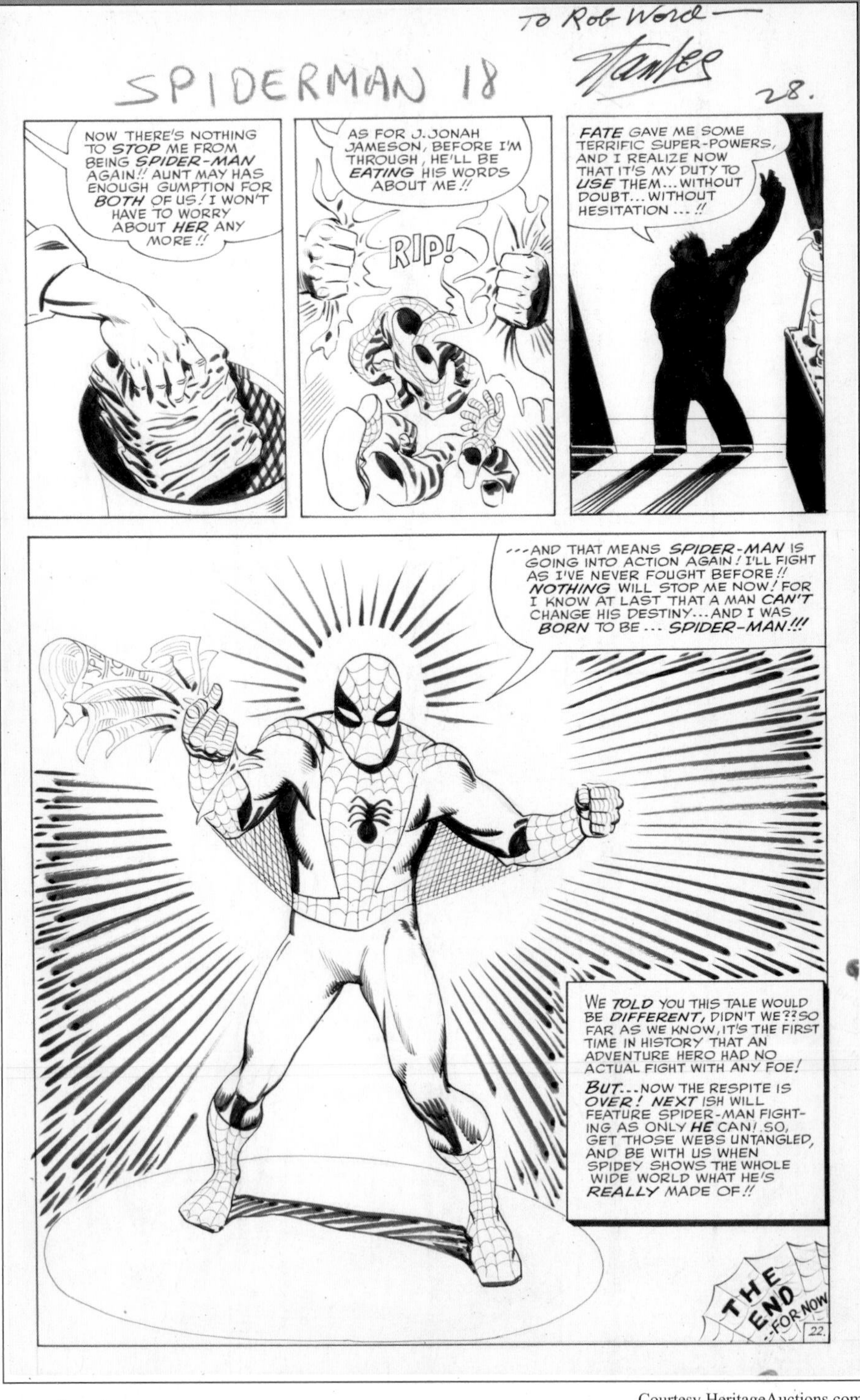
To Rob Word —
SPIDERMAN 18
28.
NOW THERE'S NOTHING TO STOP ME FROM BEING SPIDER-MAN AGAIN!! AUNT MAY HAS ENOUGH GUMPTION FOR BOTH OF US! I WON'T HAVE TO WORRY ABOUT HER ANY MORE!!
AS FOR J. JONAH JAMESON, BEFORE I'M THROUGH, HE'LL BE EATING HIS WORDS ABOUT ME!!
RIP!
FATE GAVE ME SOME TERRIFIC SUPER-POWERS, AND I REALIZE NOW THAT IT'S MY DUTY TO USE THEM... WITHOUT DOUBT... WITHOUT HESITATION...!!
...AND THAT MEANS SPIDER-MAN IS GOING INTO ACTION AGAIN! I'LL FIGHT AS I'VE NEVER FOUGHT BEFORE!! NOTHING WILL STOP ME NOW! FOR I KNOW AT LAST THAT A MAN CAN'T CHANGE HIS DESTINY... AND I WAS BORN TO BE... SPIDER-MAN!!!
WE TOLD YOU THIS TALE WOULD BE DIFFERENT, DIDN'T WE?? SO FAR AS WE KNOW, IT'S THE FIRST TIME IN HISTORY THAT AN ADVENTURE HERO HAD NO ACTUAL FIGHT WITH ANY FOE!
BUT... NOW THE RESPITE IS OVER! NEXT ISH WILL FEATURE SPIDER-MAN FIGHTING AS ONLY HE CAN! SO, GET THOSE WEBS UNTANGLED, AND BE WITH US WHEN SPIDEY SHOWS THE WHOLE WIDE WORLD WHAT HE'S REALLY MADE OF!!
THE END ...FOR NOW
22.

Courtesy HeritageAuctions.com